HELLBOUND

HELLBOUND

KATIE JAROS

Text copyright © 2016 by Katie Jaros

Print ISBN: 978-0-9968176-2-2
E-book ISBN: 978-0-9968176-3-9

Published by Bonne Chance Books

For my children.

PROLOGUE
NEW YORK CITY— SEPTEMBER, 1975

HELL IS A waiting room.

All waiting rooms have several things in common: bad lighting, out-of-date reading material, and loads of impatient people who are usually about to go through something unpleasant, like a driver's education test or a medical examination. This place embodied all of that—and worse.

"Number 26!" a gorgeous girl in a tight gold macramé dress calls from behind the counter, her cocoa-colored skin glowing under the fluorescent lights. A woman in a headscarf sitting across the way with her five children crowding 'round looks anxiously at her ticket, hope shinning in her eyes, before sitting back and shaking her head forlornly. I sigh and scuff my loafers against the hard linoleum; looking down, I realize that I didn't return them with the rest of my uniform. I shrug to myself. They owed me that and more.

"Number 26!" the girl yells again, tapping her pen irritably against the partition window. A long wall painted vomit green separates us from them, the dream-makers and truth-sayers. Everyone's future on this side of the wall lies in their hands.

"Sir, are you number 26?" the girl asks a man standing at the bank of payphones opposite the desk. He shakes his head, pulls a cigarette from his bellbottom jeans' pocket, and goes back to shouting into the phone in a language that no one else in the room understands. I slouch down in my chair, my arms crossed over my chest.

"Long day," a screechy voice murmurs next to me.

I turn and see an old woman hunched over a sandwich, her silver hair pulled into a tight bun at the nape of her neck. She wears a faded red cardigan buttoned up to her chin. She nods at me and takes a bite of her food.

"Yeah. At least you had the good sense to bring lunch. I should've grabbed something before I walked in." I chuckle, fondly remembering the rows of hotdog carts waiting on the other side of the double doors.

She tuts. "Where I come from, you learn to always be prepared—especially when it comes to food." She pulls the uneaten half of her sandwich away from the foil in her lap. "Sometimes the only thing between you and death is a sandwich." Her tongue twists in a Slavic manner over her Ls and Rs. "We also learn that it's useful to make friends. You hungry?"

She gives me a gummy smile, offering up a handful of turkey and mayonnaise. I shake my hand kindly. "Thank you, but I'll be all right. They should be calling me soon." I look down at my ticket and back at the girl behind the window, now reorganizing a stack of files.

The old woman lets out a grunt. "You think just because they call your number, you're in and out, hello, goodbye?" She smirks. "No, no, boy. Once you get back there, that's when the real adventure begins." She chews thoughtfully for a moment, watching me out of the corner of her eye.

"Where you from? English?" She taps my knee.

I clear my throat and sit up. "Ireland, actually." I smile,

my best attempt at being rakish. "First time in the States." I nod excitedly.

She shakes her head. "It shows." She purses her lips. "Let me give you a bit of advice…"

"Number 27!" the girl calls from the door on the wall, staring down at a clipboard.

I get to my feet, turning back to the woman. "That's me," I say with a grin, grabbing my beige canvas jacket from the back of my chair. "Best not to keep them waiting." I scramble into the arms and zip it midway up the clean, light-blue button down that I'm wearing underneath. "How do I look?"

The woman sighs. "Like a lamb walking into a lion's den." She shakes her head and shoves the rest of the sandwich into her mouth. "Get your head out of the clouds, boy. Before it gets chopped off by an airplane propeller." She shifts heavily in her chair.

"Is that an old Russian proverb?" I joke, bending down to pick up the brown, crinkled shopping bag that holds all of my worldly possessions.

She glares at me, her mouth drawn into a grim line. "I'm Czech," she mutters. "Good luck."

"Thanks." I smile widely, then rush over to the girl who is still waiting by the door, my ticket in hand.

"That's me, I'm number 27. Here, I have it…" I breathe, pressing the ticket into her palm.

She raises a stylishly shaped eyebrow and seems to bite the inside of her cheek, holding back a laugh. "Okay, Number 27," she giggles, holding open the door. "Let's go." The door clicks closed behind us.

"Mr. Burman is just finishing up with another case, so he should be in shortly." Her hips sway from side to side as she guides me into a small office, tall stacks of files surrounding the desk. She gestures to a chair that's wedged between a storage cabinet and a pile of cardboard boxes, 'Altair 8800' printed in thick black ink on the side. Atop a cluttered desk sit the contents of that box: a new computer with a whole mess of wires coming off of the back like it's on life support.

The girl smiles and scratches her ear. "Sorry about the mess. Mr. Burman is very busy, and housekeeping is at the bottom of his list." She clears her throat. "Can I get you a cigarette or something to drink? Water? Coffee?" She leans coyly against the doorframe, her dark eyes scanning me.

I sit down, placing my bag under the chair. "Water would be great, thanks." I fidget with my jacket zipper, my knees jittery.

The girl nods and grins. "Sure. Don't be nervous. Mr. Burman is the best agent we have here. Whatever your situation, Mr. Burman has seen it all." She drums the door with her nails. "I'll be right back with that water." She disappears down the hall.

I take a breath and glance at the contents of the desk. Beyond the sea of papers and computer parts, there's a gold nameplate labeled *Jay Burman: Employee of the Year, 1962*. There are a couple of small, framed black-and-white photos of a large black man shaking hands with several severe-looking white men in suits— American politicians, by my guess. Next to the photos, half hidden under a greasy fast food wrapper, is an old baseball, its skin browning. I lean over and pick it up, seeing that it's signed by Don Newcombe...whoever that is. I hear heavy footsteps coming down the hall.

"Sorry to keep you waiting. Just had a rough case with a Dominican family that took nearly all morning." The large black man from the pictures comes through the door, several files in hand. He's older now than he was in the photographs, a touch of gray at his temples and a pair of large glasses perched on the end of his nose. He grins when he looks up and sees me holding the baseball. I quickly put it back on the desk.

"That's all right, you can look at it. You like baseball, Mr...?" He scrunches his mouth and flips through the envelopes in his arms.

I stand and shake my head. "Murphy, Alden Murphy. And I don't think you'll have a file for me yet. This is my first time here," I ramble.

He nods and moves behind his desk, maneuvering carefully so as not to knock over the papers on the floor. He sits down heavily in his chair, smoothing out his rumpled suit jacket as he does so. He spins and faces the computer.

"Okay, Mr. Murphy. Mr. Murphy who likes baseball…" He punches a couple of keys with his index fingers and furrows his brow, letting out a long sigh. "What is your original country of origin?" he asks, not looking up from the screen.

"Um, Ireland, s-sir," I stutter.

He nods and clucks his tongue. "Should have guessed from the accent. Hang on, we're still getting used to the new system…" He taps one button repeatedly, getting more forceful with every hit. "Goddammit… Excuse me." He glances at me, shaking his head. "We just started switching over all the files. I swear—this thing is gonna put me in an early grave. REGINA!" he yells out into the hall. A moment later, the girl in the gold dress returns and saunters over to the desk, a glass of water in her hand.

"Here you go," she purrs, handing me the water. She then sits on the edge of the desk, her long legs pressing into mine. She's so close that I can smell her perfume: lilac. I cross my legs to hide my erection.

"What's up, Mr. Burman?" She leans back over the desk, peering at the screen.

He sighs and rubs tiredly at the bridge of his nose. "I need to access the U.K. files, but it's stuck on Central America. I keep pressing the E.S.C. key," he grits out, baring his teeth.

Regina smiles and picks up the keyboard. "You can say 'Escape,' Mr. Burman. But that's not the command you need anyway." She deftly hits a few buttons, and the box makes an uplifting robotic sound.

Mr. Burman leans forward, nodding. "All right, all right.

Thank you, Regina!" He looks over at me and grins sheepishly. "This is how I know I'm getting too old for this." He pushes his glasses up his nose and takes the keyboard back. Regina hops off the desk and gives me a wink.

"I'm taking Computer Science at City College. Expecting a promotion over here any day now," she says with a laugh.

Mr. Burman shakes his head. "You and me both…" He squints at the computer. I cautiously sip my water.

"Is there anything else you need, Mr. Burman?" Regina asks.

He nods, not looking away from the screen. "Yeah…the Mankowitz files on the floor there need to get put away. They're coming back on Monday to finish up their paperwork. Can you file those now, so we'll at least have a chance of finding them next week?" He purses his lips, lost in thought.

"Sure, Mr. Burman." She picks up a few files from the rug and opens up one of the storage cabinets, occasionally glancing over at me as she does her work. I give her a tight smile and turn back to the computer, staring at Mr. Burman apprehensively.

After a moment, he looks up at me. "Are you sure you went through processing in Ireland?"

I furrow my brow. "Processing?" I repeat.

Mr. Burman nods. "Yeah— when you filed for your visa to come here. You would have needed to go through processing in either the Dublin or Cork offices before you left. Unless you maybe did it in London… Did you go through London?" He taps at the keyboard, shaking his head. "I would expect this from maybe South America or Russia, but the U.K. usually has their act together and mails their applicants to us as soon as they're filed." He scratches his head. "Takes a couple of weeks. Maybe your paperwork is still on its way. When did you say you filed?"

I shake my head, dumbfounded.

"Lemme see your passport and visa." He motions with his hand.

I lick my lips hesitantly. "Well, here is my passport…" I reply, reaching into my jacket. I place the little green notebook with the Irish flag stamped across the front on top of the desk. "But...I, um...I didn't know I needed a visa. They just told me I needed to come here."

Regina looks over as Mr. Burman stops typing. "Who's 'they'?" he asks suspiciously.

"K-Kenny...and Mark from...dining services," I stammer. I gulp, spit catching in my throat.

He stares at me over his glasses. "So...you didn't go through Processing," he states wearily.

I shake my head. "No, I...I guess not. The guys on the boat said I only needed a passport to work." I can feel my palms starting to sweat. I wipe them on my slacks.

"What boat?" Mr. Burman demands. Regina quietly closes the file drawer.

I clear my throat. "The—the boat I worked on. The QE2?" My knees bob uncontrollably. "I um, work...I *worked* in the Engine Room. But I don't...anymore." I look down at my lap.

Mr. Burman sighs and sits back in his chair. "I see. Were you recently...let go...from this position?" he asks carefully.

I shake my head. "No—nothing like that! This was our first time...well, *my* first time docking in New York. We were given a couple of hours leave to see the city, and I just, um, decided to... stay." My eyes darting nervously around the room.

Mr. Burman closes his eyes and blows out his cheeks.

"I'm sorry." I sit forward in my seat. "Am...am I in trouble?"

Mr. Burman cocks his head to the side. "That all depends on your definition of 'trouble'..." He pops his tongue into his cheek and keeps his eyes trained on the screen.

I shake my head and chuckle uncomfortably. "I don't understand. Everyone I talked to said I just needed to go through immigration in New York, and I would be fine." I pause and cough. "I'm fine, right?"

Mr. Burman holds up his hands. "Let's get the facts established before we get hysterical," he sighs. "You arrived in New York...?" He looks at me tiredly.

"Last night," I fill in.

"Yeah, last night." His voice is low and gravely. "Got a good look at Lady Liberty beckoning majestically in the harbor, bright lights, big city...maybe took in a show?" He raises his eyebrows.

I shake my head. "A couple of the engineers and I went out for Chinese in Greenwich Village..." I mutter, looking down at the floor.

He laughs. "They *do* make good Chinese down there. I get it. Anyway..." He shifts in his chair. "After taking in some of the tourist attractions and a couple of A-MAZING egg rolls, instead of heading back to port with your fellow travelers, you decided to stay on land and pursue U.S. citizenship... Am I getting this straight?" He looks at me.

I nod. He cranes his head back. "No premeditation, no paperwork, just pure passion?" he asks with a squint.

I smile. "Um, yeah. I guess so..."

He groans. "You know that's illegal, right? You just entered this country *illegally*." He crosses his arms in front of his chest and sits back like a frustrated bear, pondering a particularly nasty patch of honeycomb.

I put my head in my hands, my whole body starting to shake. "That's why I came here," I mumble. "The guys on the ship said that immigrants went through Ellis Island, and then they could stay here. I...I went there this morning...but it was all boarded up..."

"That's because it closed in 1954! Holy mackerel!" Mr. Burman crows.

Regina busies herself with papers, keeping her eyes down.

"Okay, so, you took the ferry over to Ellis and realized that there was nothing there but a bunch of bums and junkies, and then what? You came all the way up here to Harlem from Port Authority?" Mr. Burman continues with a laugh.

I nod. "Walked, yes," I grumble.

Mr. Burman whoops. "Unbelievable! Wow, son, you are either incredibly stupid or incredibly honest." He shakes his head and grins.

I grimace. "Guess that remains to be seen," I say, slumping down in my chair. My hands tremble, and I close my eyes.

Mr. Burman sits back and nods. "Guess so. You know, most people in your situation would have just walked away, disappeared into the city, started new lives, new families—probably never encountering any trouble until they needed heart surgery or a bail out from jail. But you came here to talk to me. That's admirable." He smiles, bright white teeth glinting.

I look frantically back and forth between him and Regina, who suddenly seems to have forgotten that I'm in the room. She looks everywhere but in my direction. I grip the arms of my chair. "Please," I whisper, "please don't send me back."

Mr. Burman sits in silence, rubbing his forehead. "So when does your ship leave?" he asks after a while, straightening some papers in front of him.

I feel my stomach sink into my shoes. "I think it already left, sir," I mumble.

He nods. "Of course it did." He clears his throat and taps the stack of papers neatly against his desktop. "Well, I'm not going to let my hard-earned tax dollars go to sending you back, so I guess we'll have to figure this out." He looks at me. "Unless you *want* to go home?" he asks, his brows raised.

I shake my head. "No, sir, Mr. Burman. No...I don't," I sigh. "I don't ever want to go back there." I stare at him earnestly.

Mr. Burman lets out a small chuckle. "A young, good-looking kid like you—must be girl trouble." He snickers over his papers.

I scoff. "No, I've never been with a..." I glance over at Regina, whose fingers have stopped flicking through the files. I clear my throat and blush profusely. "I've never had a girlfriend before," I mutter.

Regina turns to gawk at me, her eyes wide. "Seriously? How is that possible?" Red creeps up over my collar, my face burning like a matchhead. She purses her lips coquettishly.

"Thank you, Regina. I think I've got it covered from here," Mr. Burman interjects with a sigh. Regina shuts the file drawer and slips out of the office, closing the door behind her. Mr. Burman turns to me and rolls his eyes.

"You gotta watch out for the women here, Mr. Murphy. They're a new breed—liberated, you dig?"

I sit up straight. "Yes, sir." I nod, looking down at my lap again.

He sighs and looks at his computer screen. "Okay, we're just going to let this machine hang out and do its thing…" He slides the keyboard under the monitor and opens a file drawer next to his knee, taking out a long piece of carbon print paper.

"It's more reliable the old-fashioned way, anyway." He grabs a sharpened pencil from a coffee mug next to a very heavy-looking black telephone and wets the lead with the tip of his tongue. "Plus, a little extra red tape will buy us some time." He unbuttons his shirt sleeve and rolls his cuff, revealing a shiny gold watch face, the brown leather band starting to crack.

I smile. "That's a nice watch, sir," I comment, thinking a little flattery couldn't hurt the situation.

Mr. Burman looks down at his wrist casually. "Thanks. Gift from everyone here at my retirement party six years ago." He snickers and looks up at me through his foggy lenses. "All right, full name: Alden Murphy, yeah?"

I nod. "Yes, sir."

He writes my name on the top line. "Al-den. Interesting name, kind of like Aladdin…from *Arabian Nights*?" He chuckles to himself. "Guess that makes me your magic genie," he adds with a grin. "Okay, birthdate?"

"15 March, 1955," I answer.

He juts out his chin as he writes. "Dangerous birthday.

Explains a lot." He pushes his glasses up his nose. "Reason for leaving Country of Origin?" He stares at me placidly.

I bite my tongue. I'm guessing 'escaping a dismal existence' isn't going to look too good on paper. "Um, work," I say with a cough.

He nods. "Popular answer. Okay, Mr. Murphy, here's how this is going to work. I think this goes without saying, but given my role in your current predicament, I feel the need to express it."

He settles into his chair and glares at me over his glasses. "This is not a vacation. You are not here to drink, do drugs, gamble, or chase fast American tail." He takes a breath. "You are here for a fresh start to your young life, a second chance. The American Dream *is* possible, if you are willing to work for it."

I put my shoulders back. "I am giving you one week to find work and a place to live," he continues. "So that puts us at…" He brushes away the debris in front of him and looks at his desktop calendar. "I'm taking off that Friday, so let's call it next Monday, October 4th. On the fourth, you will return here and regale me with your new job and living situation…at…" He glances up at the wall clock. "…2 p.m." He scratches his forehead. "No, let's make that noon. Show up on time, and I'll buy you lunch." He clears his throat and stares at me sharply. "So, what do you say, Mr. Murphy? Do we have a deal?" He holds out his right hand.

I grin, jumping out of my chair. "Yes, of course, Mr. Burman!" I grab his hand and shake it wildly, my heart beating madly out of my chest. "Thank you! Thank you so much!" I bend down and pick up my bag. "Can…can I go now?" I want to get out of here before he comes to his senses and throws me into a detention center.

Mr. Burman nods. "It's a free country—but hang on a second." He sits back, scratching his temple. "Is that all you have on you?" He points at my grocery bag.

I nod and sit back down on the edge of the chair. "Just a couple of things from the ship." I rifle through it, pulling out

the contents to show him. "Toothbrush, razor, pair of socks…"
I reach down to the bottom of the bag and pull out a white envelope, then count its contents. "Fifty…no, forty…forty dollars
cash in furlough." I fumble with the bills. "Sorry, still getting used
to American money." I wipe nervously at my brow.

Mr. Burman lets out a heavy sigh and reaches into his back
pocket. "That's all they paid you on that ship? That's not going to
get you very far around here." He snorts.

I shake my head. "Well, they also covered room and board,
and you know—gave me the priceless chance to see the world." I
look down at the money, my jaw tightening.

Mr. Burman nods. "Yeah, yeah, I got it. I was a Navy man
myself." He pulls out his wallet and counts out his cash.

"I've got $60 on me right now, and I want you to take it." He
pushes the money across the desk.

I shake my head. "Thank you for everything, Mr. Burman,
really—but I can't take your money." I purse my lips, painfully
pushing it back with the tips of my fingers.

Mr. Burman sighs and pushes it toward me again. "Yes, you
can. Believe me, you're going to need it. And I'm going to do
you one better." He grabs a notepad and scribbles down a name
and address.

"I have an old friend I knew back in Korea that now runs a
kitchen in Midtown. Pretty fancy place." He rips off the note and
hands it to me along with the cash. "He always needs more guys to
wash dishes, bus tables, whatever. Go see him, and I bet he can set
you up with a job. You said you worked in dining services, right?"

I shake my head. "No, that was Kenny and Mark—"

He clears his throat and glares, holding out the paper. I shut
my mouth and take it. He nods. "It won't pay much," he continues, "but it's honest work. Tell him Jay sent you."

I stare down at the note in my hand, my eyes wide. "Wow,
thank you, Mr. Burman. I don't know what to say." I grin. I read

the name: Eddie Robbins. "I didn't know 'Robbins' was a Korean last name," I chuckle.

He looks at me, his expression pained. "The Korean *War*, son! You're going to need to brush up on your American history if you're planning on staying!"

I nod vigorously, my eyes wide. He shakes his head. "And stop looking so surprised every time a black man does something nice for you. This is New York...we are everywhere. There's a lot of *everybody* everywhere, here." He checks the clock again. "All right, Mr. Murphy, get outta here. Go get your dream." He smiles and picks up the baseball from his desk.

"Yes, sir, Mr. Burman!" I reply, getting back to my feet. I reach for the knob and turn back. "Thank you again, sir," I murmur. "I won't let you down."

"Mm-mm." He nods. "Noon on Monday. Do not make me come looking for you, Mr. Murphy." He glares at me over his glasses, tossing the ball back and forth.

I smile tightly. "Of course. Noon on Monday." I step out into the hall and run into Regina. She winks again as she walks into the office.

"Good luck, 27," she hums.

I grin and head down the corridor. "What do you think, Mr. Burman?" I hear Regina ask as I leave.

"I think one of two things," he replies. "Either this city eats him alive, or he eats all of us. Only time will tell."

CHAPTER 1
LOS ANGELES—PRESENT DAY

"DANIEL, IF YOU don't stop squirming around, you're going to lose an ear. Christa, don't distract him!" Mary Carmen shakes her head, the long dark braid draped over one of her shoulders shimmering in the vanity lights, a pair of scissors clasped dangerously in her right hand. Daniel sits on a footstool in front of her, his shaggy, wet blond hair hanging down in front of his brown eyes. He smiles and bites his lip as he reaches out and playfully grabs my ankle. I squeal, almost falling from my perch on the bathroom sink.

"Quit it!" I screech with a laugh. "I'm trying to watch history in the making."

Daniel shakes his head. "Nah-nah-nah-nah—no. Don't listen to her, Mary Carmen. Just a trim, just a trim." He steadies himself on the stool, then explains seriously, "Like Robert Plant circa Zeppelin 2."

Mary Carmen sighs. "You know very well I have no idea who that is." She glances over at me. "Christa, hand me the spritzy thing."

I reach down and toss her the water bottle. She steps back and sprays the top of his head. "I swear, you have the kinkiest hair, boy! The minute I look away, it starts to curl up again," she murmurs, her Latina accent thick as the gentle snipping of the scissors resumes.

"What can I say—it's part of my charm. The ladies are swooning over my gorgeous, flowing locks. I have to fight to keep them off." Daniel grins at me.

I roll my eyes. "Yeah, maybe back when long hair on guys was actually cool," I counter with a smirk.

He snorts. "Wait a couple more years, Christa—it's coming back around. You'll see." He tickles my knee.

I pull away quickly and look in the mirror, blushing at his touch as I tuck a strand of long brown hair behind my ear. I know Mary Carmen goes into red-alert mode any time we make contact; she's been watching me like a hawk ever since I moved in last month.

Not that I necessarily mind my new roommate—but it's not like I was given much of a choice in the matter. With Mom still in rehab and me finishing out my senior year at Sacred Heart, it was generally considered to be socially unacceptable for me to be living on my own just yet. Last month, my life had been forever changed after my ex-boyfriend Riley drunkenly crashed his car into an underpass wall—with me and one of my best friends, Tom, along for the ride. This had led to my very rude awakening to the Divine world of Angels and Demons. It was my Guardian, Daniel, who saved my life, pulling me from the burning wreckage. Tom wasn't so lucky; he died in the hospital two weeks later. Riley must have totally flipped out, because he disappeared shortly thereafter. Can't say I blame him—there seems to be a lot of that going around lately.

My throat tightens at the thought as I force a smile and stare back at my Rock 'n' Roll Angel as he and Mary Carmen laugh together in the mirror, Mary Carmen wielding the scissors maniacally while she pretends to be a crazed barber. I still miss Tom every day, his absence a harsh reminder of everything that went down: learning about how the Universe *really* works, Daniel saving my life again when he took a stabbing from a crazed Demon-Pet I had affectionately nicknamed "Zompocalypse." Witnessing Daniel's bloody injuries heal right before my eyes had sent me Haloing, my soul bared to the world, and he'd been forced to reveal that I was the Catalyst; which is not nearly as cool as it sounds.

I'm still totally Human, with zero super powers and 100% doomsday prophecy. Pretty lame, when you have Guardians—who can lift, like, 30 times their body weight and go all Supernova— and Demons who can control and manipulate people with just a few simple words. All I got was this lousy blue tinge to my skin— making me a moving target to anyone with the Sight.

"How's it looking?" Daniel shoots me a crooked half grin that makes my stomach melt.

I grin and nod approvingly. "Good. You wanted it all business in the front, party in the back, right?" I tease, waving a finger at his head. When he swats my bare leg, my butterflies go nuts.

My Haloing had set off a cataclysmic chain of events that included my mother being kidnapped by a psychopathic Demon named Alden, a three-day stint in an alternate dimension called the Warehouse with said psychopath, and a fieldtrip to Level 3—a.k.a., Hell—accompanied by a bratty Amalgam redhead named Trevor. It was there that I found Daniel beaten and bloody and chained to a wall; he'd been captured while once again try-ing to help me. It was my turn to save him at that point, and I almost died in the process. If it hadn't been for my Demon captor sharing his blood with me, I would have been toast. I shiver at the memory of Alden's coal black hair and clear blue eyes fading away in his skull as I saw his Demon face for the first time. Not only did his blood bring me back from the brink, it also gave me the ability to *see* all of the insanity that everyone had been talking about, including my own Catalyst-blue glow.

I peek at my reflection in the mirror and sigh, straightening the pink tank top I try to wear whenever Daniel's around, since it's one of the few articles of clothing that makes me look like I've got any boobs to speak of. All in all, it had been a rough November, and I'm secretly relieved to have a couple of Angels on my side as I move forward, trying to make sense of my role in this unfamiliar, crazy world.

"Just sit straight!" Mary Carmen laughs, batting at Daniel's shoulder.

"All right, all right," he snickers back, going perfectly still.

Mary Carmen crinkles her lip as she carefully pulls a few curls between her fingers and measures them out, snipping them even. After a minute or two of this, she stops cutting and taps him on the shoulder. "Hey, don't forget to get the boxes out of the garage before you go. You promised me you'd bring in all the Christmas stuff, like, last week." She fluffs her fingers through his hair, looking for uneven spots, her set of silver bangles jangling down her arm. Satisfied, she reaches into the vanity drawer.

"Oh, I am on it," Daniel answers with a nod. "Year-old candy canes, tangled up lights, an opportunity to dress up like Santa Claus?" He puffs out his cheeks to make himself look fatter. "Tell me, Christa, have you been naughty or nice this year?"

I roll my eyes rather than replying. "Hold that thought," he adds with a grin.

"It doesn't count unless you're sitting on my lap."

I pick up my toothbrush off the counter and chuck it at his head. He watches it fall to the floor and lets out a yowl. "Hey! Don't throw my stuff on the floor!"

"Relax, it's mine," I scoff.

He shakes his head. "*I'm* the red one!" he yells, picking up the toothbrush and pulling away from Mary Carmen.

"What?" I yip. "Are you serious? I'm the red!"

"Um, I'm always red." He makes a face.

I let out a huff and wrinkle my nose. "*I* live here. Gross, Daniel! Have you been using my toothbrush this whole time?"

"I thought you were green." He smiles. "You strike me as a green toothbrush kind of girl."

I throw my hands in the air. "What does that even mean?"

"It means I'm gonna shave you both bald if you don't stop messing around!" Mary Carmen interjects, holding up an electric shaver in menace.

Daniel stares at me, his mouth wide. "I'll do it if you do it," he offers in a hushed voice.

I arch a brow. "Really? You'd give up the love and adoration of all the ladies in the world just to see me with a shaved head?"

"In a heartbeat," he answers gleefully.

I clear my throat and lean forward to brush his bangs out his face, considering. It really would be a shame to see all that beautiful hair on the floor. I sit back and shake my head. "No, no way." I look down at my lap.

His golden-brown eyes dance as he claps his hands. "Ha! I knew you were chicken." He jerks his head back and forth.

"What are you—twelve?" I hiss in reply.

"A 12-year old with a very hairy neck—hold still!" Mary Carmen angles Daniel's head forward and turns on the razor, a dull buzzing filling the room.

As she takes a few inexpert swipes at his collar, I take the opportunity of their mutual distraction to watch them. They are both illuminated in gold against the pink bathroom tile, Mary Carmen's bright red streak gleaming against her right cheekbone and adding a certain badass element to her beauty. It's the mark of a Seraphim, someone who has seen the face of God. Unlike Daniel and the other Guardians, Mary Carmen is one of the rare souls on Earth who has actually been to Heaven.

Badass or not, though, she's still all over me about keeping my room clean.

"Done," she sings, turning off the razor and putting it back in the drawer. "You're pretty as the first time I saw you." She dusts off his shirt with the back of her hand, then starts to head out of the bathroom. "I'm gonna go get started in the kitchen. Christa, you're on pots and pans."

I hop off the counter. "Okay, be right there."

I bend down to help Daniel sweep the clippings off the floor. He smiles at me, our knees touching as we brush the hair into the trash. "Seems like you two are getting along better," he offers quietly, picking up the last few strands with his fingers. "Like a pair of happy house cats."

"I wouldn't go that far," I grumble, shaking my head. "She went off on me pretty hard last week when I was late coming home from Jodie's." I run a hand through my hair. "The minute I walked through the door, she starts yelling about how she didn't know where I was, even though I've been going to Jodie's since I was like…I don't know…seven." I let out an irritated sigh. "How I could have been picked up by anybody and she wouldn't have been able to stop it, I don't know… But I guess she called my phone, like, fifty times." I stand and wipe my hands on my shorts. "We got into this huge fight. It was…bad."

Daniel leans against the sink. "Hot-tempered—she's always been like that. I've learned to just let it roll over me." He shrugs and chuckles. "She blows up, and then she's over it in five minutes. Try not to let it get to you."

I purse my lips. "That might work for you. You screw up, and she yells about how you'll never learn—then you give her your movie-star grin and she melts, and it's all cookies and milkshakes from there. If I screw up, it's long lectures over loads of laundry, very LOUD lectures." I shake my head. "The thing is, I had my phone on me the whole time, and I knew she was trying to track me down—but I didn't pick up." I look down at the floor. "I just wanted to be in my own space for a little while…just be myself again." I scratch the back of my neck. "Whatever. It's fine."

He puts his hands in the pockets of his jeans. "I get it. I think you've earned the right to be a little frustrated—it's not like your world didn't get completely turned upside down less than a month ago. All things considered, I think you're doing fairly well." He nudges me with his shoulder.

I scrunch my nose. "Yeah… I guess I can appreciate the extra security detail, particularly when there is a whole army of Demons out there waiting for me."

Daniel sniffs. "There is that."

I turn and face him. "But I have to be able to get out of here, Daniel. Like—not *move out*, but at least go out for coffee, see my friends." I cross my arms in front of me. "I swear to God, if I'm stuck at home one more Friday night listening to old Enrique Iglesias CDs…" I grimace and bug out my eyes.

Daniel laughs. "I thought she was into Julio."

I look at him smugly. "She is an equal-opportunity Iglesias lover. Seriously, promise me you'll talk to her." I lean in, smelling his familiar cinnamon scent. It fills me with both comfort and nostalgia, as if we've been together for years.

His eyebrows rise. "I will. I'll do it right now."

"Thank you." Closing the distance between us, I ruffle my hand through his hair, which is now almost dry. I smile up at him. "Looks good, for real. She did a nice job."

He grins and tugs gently at my own hair, pulling me close to him. "You think so? Maybe I should try something different next time. I'm thinking about growing a beard, maybe some sweet chops." He holds up my hair under his chin to illustrate his point.

I giggle and slap his chest, but he pulls me closer still. His muscles are tight under his shirt, his arms now wrapped around my waist. I feel my whole body come alive at the contact, the proximity.

I allow myself to linger for a moment before pushing away, hard as it is. "You'd be even more of a hipster than you are now," I joke, using humor to deflect…everything.

Ever since our conversation at the Pier, the lines between Daniel and I have only become more blurred. There are some pretty strict rules about how Guardians are supposed to interact with Humans—no kissing, no syrupy confessions, and definitely no…anything else. Unfortunately, none of that has changed how

I feel about Daniel; the only difference is that we don't talk about it anymore, the big pink elephant in the room any time we come near each other.

Right now, though, Daniel lets out a guffaw and steps away from me, making a face. "Ouch! That hurts, Christa." He grabs his side in mock anguish.

"Christa, these pans aren't going to clean themselves!" Mary Carmen hails from the kitchen before I can think of a reply. I sigh, then pat Daniel on the elbow and slouch my way into the hall.

"Duty calls," I order. "Come on."

In the kitchen, I see Mary Carmen standing by the dishwasher, loading the salad bowls from dinner. She gestures to where the sink is piled high with dirty pots and pans. "I got them soaking for you—should be ready to go," she says cheerfully, wiping her hands on a towel and clicking the dishwasher shut with one hip. I take my place by the sink and start scrubbing.

"Hey, did you feed Daphne today?" Mary Carmen asks, motioning over to the fish tank on the counter where my grumpy angelfish swims laps through a sunken pirate ship. I can thank Alden for the fish and Daniel for the corny tank decor.

"Yeah." I nod. "Just before dinner." I arch my brows at Daniel. "Her appetite's picked up. I think she likes her new space."

"Who wouldn't? That's the Rolls Royce of fish gear, right there." He smirks, plopping himself down on a bar stool. "Lucky I found it at the garage sale last week."

I glare at him out of the corner of my eye. "You're not going to help?" I mutter, running the water.

"I cooked!" he protests, spinning in circles on his stool.

I roll my eyes. "Yeah, no kidding... Who else uses every pot in the kitchen when they make dinner?" I hold up a giant frying pan covered in grease.

Mary Carmen sighs. "Thank you for the wonderful meal, Daniel. It was delicious," she interjects diplomatically.

Daniel grins. "The pleasure is all mine, cooking for two

beautiful girls." He leans back on his stool. "Especially after your recent Thanksgiving debacle, I thought it would be a good idea to take the reins in the kitchen."

Mary Carmen looks up at him, aghast. "It wasn't that bad!" she shouts.

Daniel snickers. "That bird was still gobbling, M.C.—ice cold!"

She throws her towel at him, her expression turning disgusted. "Why do they put that plastic baggie up in there anyway? Extra bird guts—who uses that stuff?"

I shake my head at their bickering, my eyes focusing on the row of cactus plants blooming on the windowsill in front of me. "People use it for gravy, I guess," I answer, adding more soap to the water.

"Revolting!" Mary Carmen declares, waving her hand dismissively. "Those are the parts we throw away in Guatemala." She points at Daniel as he gives her a look. "It's a mistake anyone could have made, thank you very much!"

He shakes his head. "Not a trained professional."

"You work at a Chinese takeout; let's not get carried away," I snigger, accidentally splashing dishwater on my tank top.

He spins on his stool to face me again. "Hey! I've got moves you two have never seen—kitchen moves, chef moves…" He grins. "Which is why I'm proposing that I make Christmas dinner!" he states grandly.

Mary Carmen nods in appreciation. "Wow… To what do we owe this great honor?" she teases.

Scoffing, Daniel takes a little bow in his chair. "Consider it my gift to you—the gift of cooked meat." He drums his palms on the counter. "Surf and turf, ladies! I'm thinking some choice filet mignon, maybe lobster tails, a little haricot verts almondine…"

"Ooh la la," I offer with a grin.

"Are you planning on robbing a bank next week?" Mary Carmen wonders, balking at him.

Daniel spins around in a circle again. "Well, at least we'll have some melt-in-your-mouth garlic mashed potatoes. That, you can count on." He stops spinning and clears his throat, glancing at me. "So, speaking of Christmas, Mary Carmen... I was thinking about taking Christa out for a little shopping this evening." He raises his eyebrows politely. I turn off the tap and stand very still.

Mary Carmen stares at him, resting her hands on the counter. "I don't know if that's such a good idea, Daniel," she murmurs.

I scrunch my brow and kick the baseboard angrily with my toe, letting out a silent cry as it starts to throb. "Oh come on!" Daniel cajoles. "If you don't let us go out alone, there isn't going to be anything under the tree for you come Christmas morning." He folds his hands in front of him. "That would be very disappointing."

Mary Carmen shakes her head. "What *would* be disappointing, really, is if you were attacked by Demons while out there and didn't have back up. I don't care about presents, Daniel! I care about Christa's safety!" She clucks her tongue. "And you should, too!"

When Daniel just slaps his thighs and sits back, annoyed, I shout, "What about Christa's sanity?!" splashing water all over the floor. They both jerk to the side and look at me, but I've heard enough. "I'm going crazy, being on lockdown 24/7!" Trying to calm my voice, I let out a sigh. "I know you're just looking out for me, Mary Carmen, and I am grateful, really I am—but I need a little freedom too."

Mary Carmen's gaze is starting to soften. "Please," I continue. "I'm not asking to go out alone; Daniel can protect me, and it would just be for an hour or two."

I bite my lip nervously as Daniel cocks his head back toward Mary Carmen, silently echoing my plea. She lets out a heavy sigh. "All right, fine."

I squeal and jump excitedly, high-fiving Daniel. "Just for an hour!" Mary Carmen adds. "And I don't want you guys walking past Melrose. There is plenty of good shopping in this neighbor-hood. You don't need to go far."

I rush over and hug her. "Thank you, Mary Carmen! We're going to get you something awesome…"

She looks at my grin and pats my back. "Yeah, okay. Just be home by 11." She picks up a purple sponge and starts to clean off the stove top. "Daniel, I mean it. And don't let her out of your sight!"

I start to rush around the counter. Mary Carmen interrupts me by pointing at the sink. "Um, excuse me, chica… Yes, you can go out—*after* you finish your chores."

Right, I should have expected that. Scurrying back, I grab the scrub brush again. "Tight ship," Daniel jokes.

I give him a look, then drop the brush into the soapy water. "Oh my gosh—I almost forgot!" I turn back to Mary Carmen. "Um, Mary Carmen?" I ask quietly.

"Mmm?" Her eyes are still trained on a particularly nasty stain on the pilot light.

I take a deep breath. "So, tomorrow night is the midseason finale for *Vampires Suck*—you know, my favorite TV show ever?" I begin.

"I may have noticed it a few times on the DVR in the last few weeks, yes," she drawls. "What is your question?"

"Well, they're lost at sea on an abandoned cruise liner and have almost run out of blood. It's going to be *insane*," I sing-song, scrubbing hurriedly at a cookie sheet. "Anyway, I was hoping it might be okay if Jodie comes over and watches it with me—maybe spends the night?" Jodie's dictator parents don't allow her to watch *Vampires Suck!*, so she usually covertly catches it a few days later here—but we absolutely have to watch this one live before social media spoils it.

Mary Carmen sighs. "I don't know, Christa. Don't you think you could use some quiet time? I know you have your history final coming up next week. Do you feel prepared?"

I turn off the water. "I studied all last night! You saw… Daniel quizzed me for like—four hours!" In my room, with the door wide open, of course. Mary Carmen must have walked by 'looking for her reading glasses' about twenty times.

"It's my best subject," Daniel adds, puffing out his chest. "I consider myself a piece of Living History, a valuable asset to any student."

"'Living' is a bit generous," Mary Carmen grunts.

Daniel furrows his brow. "I think she's pretty solid." He spins toward me. "Quick, think fast—list the three main branches of the United States government!"

I sigh. "Executive, Judicial, Legislative," I recite.

"And in alphabetical order, no less!" Daniel responds proudly with a grin.

Mary Carmen clicks her teeth. "Fine, fine! Jodie can sleep over tomorrow night! But you have a very busy weekend, Christa: Sober Students, and then we're going to visit your mother. I don't want to have to drive three hours each way with a grumpy, exhausted teenager, okay?"

I draw in a sharp breath. I can suck it up for a few hours and put on a happy face for the drive down to Del Mar when the conclusion to Catalina and Mario's torrid love affair is on the line. I nod happily.

"Anything else you two want?" Mary Carmen barks. "Maybe a new Mercedes or the Hollywood sign?"

"Can I sleep over too?" Daniel asks puckishly.

Mary Carmen rushes at him and shoos him off the stool. "NO BOYS ALLOWED! Not while Christa is staying here!" she yells, swatting him on the arm.

"You said it yourself—I'm already dead! What's the harm?" he crows, deflecting her punches.

"*Especially* the dead ones! Now, you two better get out of here before I change my mind!"

Daniel jumps over the counter and swoops me up onto his

shoulder, carrying me back to my room to get changed Tarzan and Jane style. I shriek ecstatically and smack his back.

"DANIEL!" Mary Carmen bellows. "You better stay on the other side of that door, if you know what's good for you! And be home by 11!"

*

"What do you think about this for her?" I pull a short, red floral print dress off the rack and hold it up to myself.

Daniel leans against a changing room mirror and scratches his chin. "Doesn't she have something like that? I could have sworn I've seen her in a dress just like that before." He tucks his hands into his jacket pockets.

I pucker my lips and nod. "She *does* wear a lot of red, but I go through her closet on a daily basis, and I can assure you, she doesn't have this. I would have totally borrowed it already." I hang it back on the rack and move toward the jewelry counter. "This shop is so cute. I can't believe it's only two blocks from the house."

"Yeah, really eclectic," Daniel mumbles, running his hand along a set of paintings resting against the wall.

I walk behind a shelf full of kitschy rain boots and let out a whoop. "Holy cow—no way!" I yell, gesturing to Daniel. "Check this out!"

It's an old military motorcycle, jet black with a shiny chrome engine and oversized headlight. The seat drops down low, like something out of *Easy Rider*. I straddle it and grip the handlebars, pretending to rev it up. I look at Daniel and grin. "Now, this is what *I* want for Christmas…" I purr.

Daniel laughs. "*That* is completely unsurprising. You even know how to ride a motorcycle?" he asks, sitting behind me on the seat.

I run my fingers over the cool metal. "Don't poke holes in my fantasy, Daniel." I demur.

He grins and stands. "You know, I used to have a bike just like that."

I cock my head to the side. "Really? I took you for more of an old Studebaker guy," I tease.

He quirks his eyebrows. "You calling me Fozzie Bear?" he asks, appalled.

I grin. "Moving right along..." I continue the tune by humming.

He scrunches his nose. "For the record, I would totally be Gonzo."

"Oh really?" I giggle, easing back into the leather.

Daniel snorts. "Um, yeah. Cruising around on my sweet hog, picking up all the chicks..." He snaps his fingers like he's one of the T-Birds.

I furrow my brow, letting a small smile creep across my face. "Wasn't Gonzo a plumber? He had that truck with the weird faucet coming off it."

He narrows his eyes. "Your knowledge of the Muppets is both disturbing and alluring." Shaking his head, he starts to walk off to another part of the store. "Unless you're planning on throwing Mary Carmen on the back of that bike, you better keep looking," he calls back to me.

I nod and get off the motorcycle, moving to the front of the store where the jewelry is located. I glance down into the one of the cases, a pair of sapphire earrings catching my eye. The girl behind the counter smiles and comes over to me. "Can I help with something?" she asks warmly.

I nod at the earrings. "Yeah, can I take a look at the blue ones right there?" I point.

She pulls them out of the case. "These would look amazing with your coloring," she gushes. "It would be a contest between your eyes and the jewels!"

Little does she know. "Oh," I correct, "they're not for me. I'm looking for my friend." I hold the earrings in the palm of my hand, the sapphires sparkling merrily up at me in their elaborate settings. "These *are* beautiful, but they might be a little too flashy for her; she has really…modest taste," I hand them back to the girl and move down the counter.

"Oooh, that's pretty!" I point down at a large polished amethyst pendant that's carved into the shape of a teardrop. I can already see it perched within Mary Carmen's abundant cleavage. "Oh my God, it's stunning," I murmur, beckoning Daniel over. "Yeah, I think that's the one."

He sidles over to me and nods. "Nice," he says nonchalantly, glancing over to the back wall of the store.

I sigh. "Please contain yourself, Daniel," I deadpan. "I know it's not the meat counter at Lindy and Grundy's, but you could at least attempt to be helpful." I turn back to the girl and shake my head. "I'll take a look at that one, please."

She grins and places it on the counter. "This is a new find that one of our collectors brought in last week. The setting is from 1923, fully handcrafted detailing. We haven't been able to date the stone, but we believe it was cut some time in the late part of the 19th century." She traces the gem respectfully with her fingers. "Truly a gorgeous vintage piece."

"It's perfect for her." I nod, turning to Daniel again. "What do you think?"

He smiles, his eyes still trained on the back of the room. "Mary Carmen's pretty vintage; I bet she'll love it."

I roll my eyes. The clerk laughs, tucking her short brown hair behind her ears. "It's also February's birthstone," she continues. "Do you know when your friend's birthday is?"

I let out a breath. "No, I don't." I glance at Daniel. "When's Mary Carmen's birthday?"

He looks away from the back wall and stares down at me, his eyes unfocused. "You know, I never thought to ask her. Huh." He scratches his head and shrugs. "Yeah, I don't know." He switches back to the wall again.

I slap him on the arm. "Oh my God, what is so interesting back there?" I ask irritably.

He shakes his head. "Sorry." He turns to the girl. "Are those old records back there? In the boxes?"

She nods. "Yes. The owner brought those in from an estate sale earlier today. None of them are priced yet, but you are welcome to look through them. Bring any up to me that you're interested in, and I can hold them for you until the owner comes back and can appraise them." She rests her hands on the counter.

Daniel nods. "I *have* been looking all over for Black Sabbath's unreleased B-Sides. I think I might see Ozzy peeking through over there." He smiles at me before nodding at the clerk. "Thanks, I'll just be a minute." He pets my hand as he leaves.

I sigh. "Like a kid in a candy store," I explain to the girl. I look down at the pendant, trying to see if there is a price tag. It's unlabeled. "And how much is this one?" I ask.

The clerk looks down at a notebook next to the register. "It's $75."

I bite my lip and pick up the jewel. "Hmm, a little bit more than I wanted to spend. I don't know..." I wrinkle my forehead, turning the pendant in my hand. Mary Carmen, being the total Angel that she is, is covering all my room and board stuff. I know Mom offered to chip in with rent, but Mary Carmen vehemently refused to take her money—saying something about the mortgage having been paid off for years and utilities being pretty much free because of fault lines under the house... I sort of zoned out after that part. And I *did* have my savings account that I'd been using for odds and ends. It's enough to carry me through the rest of the school year if I'm careful, and Mary Carmen has been nothing but kind and generous to me; she deserves a nice present...

"Oh, you should go for it, splurge a little. Christmas only comes once a year," a woman's voice chimes melodically from behind me.

I drop the pendant on the counter and spin around. Two

large gaping holes greet me where eyes should be, accompanied by a violent pair of horns and a perfect smile. "Mandisa," I breathe. I glance quickly at the clerk behind the counter, who is beaming kindly as she takes in Mandisa's long white wool coat and designer handbag. Fortunately, she can't see what I see.

"So wonderful to see you, Christa! It's been a while," the Demon purrs through her teeth, patting my shoulder.

I flinch away, flashbacks of the Warehouse clouding my mind. My whole body shivers. "What are you doing here?" I mutter, cringing away from her horrifying visage.

"Same as you, of course! Catching up on a little Christmas shopping. What is it—only eight days left?" Mandisa readjusts her purse on her arm and looks down at the pendant on the counter-top. "Hmm… It really *is* lovely, Christa. A gift for your mother?" She raises her eyebrows pleasantly.

"Don't talk about my mother," I snap, the hackles on the back of my neck going up.

The clerk clears her throat. "Is there something I can help you with, ma'am?" she asks Mandisa sweetly.

Mandisa stands back and shakes her head. "Oh, no thank you. I—"

"—was just leaving," Daniel interrupts, stepping between Mandisa and I. "Weren't you, Mandisa?" He smiles tightly, placing a stack of vinyl records on the counter.

The Demon's eyes narrow for a moment, before she breaks into a large grin. "Daniel! What a charming surprise! You're looking well." Her lips purse. "Considering."

Daniel laughs. "Ah well, I was a bit preoccupied last time I visited, what with the giant stakes tacking me to the wall."

Mandisa glances coyly over at the clerk, who stares at Daniel with a bewildered expression on her face. "Metaphorically, of course," he assures the girl, coughing under his breath.

Mandisa lets out a light chuckle. I seethe at the sound of her laugh.

Daniel turns back to her. "Kind of slumming it right now, aren't you, Mandisa? I didn't know you shopped in places that didn't have a 90210 stamped after the address." He sniffs, looking her over. "Wouldn't want to get your new coat dirty, playing down in the mud with the rest of us."

The Demon smiles and takes a small step back. "Oh, but then I would be missing out on all the surprising treasures a quaint shop like this offers; you never know what you're going to find." She looks down into the jewelry case. "Ah! Like that delightful little gem right there. May I look at that one, please?" The clerk nods and opens the case. "Yes, the green one," Mandisa affirms, pointing.

The girl brings the item to the counter. "Exquisite," Mandisa croons. "Is this an old-fashioned hatpin?" She picks up the object, twirling it in her hand. I shift behind Daniel.

"Yes, ma'am," the girl answers. "Dating back to 1910. The setting is sterling grade silver topped with Colombian emeralds. One of our rarest pieces in the shop," she adds proudly.

Mandisa nods. "I can see that." She tests the pin on her fingertip. "Ooh! And sharp!" she exclaims with a little jump. She smiles at the clerk and sets the hatpin back on the counter.

I exhale, not realizing 'til now that I've been holding my breath. Likewise, I feel Daniel ease back next to me.

Mandisa grins over at us, tilting her head. "You both look so tense! Holiday fatigue getting to you?"

Daniel juts out his chin. "What are you doing here, Mandisa?" he mutters.

She clears her throat and straightens her coat. "I have something I want to discuss with Christa. But first, I want to make sure I have your full attention." She turns back to the clerk and gestures to the hatpin. "Thank you so much for showing me that." She grins. "Now, take a nap."

Mandisa gives a dismissive wave, and the girl's chin droops down to her chest, her eyes closed and her body relaxed. I gasp as Daniel pounces at the Demon. "What do you think you're doing?" he snarls, inches from her face.

Mandisa startles dramatically, feigning surprise. "Do be careful, please! I would hate it if dear…" She pauses and glances over at the shopgirl's nametag. "…Mellie had an accident!" Her gaze darts mischievously down to the hatpin on the counter. "Pick it up, my dove," she croons.

Daniel and I watch in horror as Mellie's now zombie-like arm flops onto the case and grasps the hatpin, aiming the point at the soft spot behind her own jaw, her face slack and unaware.

"Don't you dare," Daniel hisses, his stance coiled and ready. "The Law—"

Mandisa turns her wicked grin on us. "—says nothing about Humans killing themselves," she interrupts smartly. "It's open season there, darling."

I can see Daniel's mind working through his rage. His face contorts, furious. "You dirty piece of—"

"Please," I murmur, taking a small step forward. Daniel stops as Mandisa turns her focus to me, a smile still teasing her lips. I suck in a breath. "Please don't hurt her. You have my attention. I'm listening." I rest my hand on top of Daniel's.

Mandisa gives a satisfied tut and jerks her head in Mellie's direction, the girl's jelly arm dropping to her side as the hatpin clatters noisily on the floor. "Such a sweet girl!" Mandisa trills, nodding to me. I bristle at the use of my father's nickname as she spins back to Daniel, chuckling. "Manners *are* what separate us from beasts. Watch out, Daniel—she's going to put you out of a job."

"Tell us what you want, then get out," he fumes, gripping my hand tightly. I can tell I'm the only thing keeping him from ripping off Mandisa's face right now.

Since the Demon is probably aware of this, she sighs and stops baiting us, instead going into her handbag and pulling out a cheerful red envelope. She sets it on the counter in front of me.

I stare at it, baffled. "What is this?" I ask.

Mandisa smiles. "Open it and find out, silly goose!" she giggles with an excited squeal.

I cautiously pick up the envelope and tear it open, a shower of sparkly gold and red confetti pouring out onto the jewelry case. Seeing that, Mandisa rolls her eyes. "Sorry, the girls in admin try to outdo themselves every year. It's the card that really matters." She gestures for me to hurry up.

I hastily pull out a piece of white cardstock embossed in merry red and gold ink:

> *Join Us for the Feast of King Herod!*
>
> *Friday, December 24th at Trinity Lounge on Sunset*
>
> *Light Refreshments and Open Bar until Closing*
>
> *Wear your finest Masquerade Dress: Masks will be provided at the door.*
>
> *The Passion Begins at 9:30.*

"Oh, you have got to be kidding me!" Daniel jeers, reading over my shoulder. This is seriously a thing?" He lets out a snort.

I shake my head and look up at Mandisa again, scrunching my forehead. "What is the 'Feast of King Herod'? I thought only saints have feast days."

Mandisa nods and begins to speak, but Daniel cuts her off. "That's true, Christa—but like they do with everything else, our friends downstairs have twisted that notion to fit some messed-up party theme." He glares at the Demon.

She sighs. "It is a dedication to our heritage! Commemorating a great moment in Human and Demon cooperation."

Daniel huffs. "More like commemorating the slaughter of thousands of Human children," he snaps.

As my eyes widen, Mandisa shakes her head. "The Feast of

King Herod is a tradition that's been celebrated for generations. It harkens back to the night when King Herod found out about the birth of Jesus and ordered the removal of all children under two in the city of Bethlehem." She pauses to make sure we're both following. "He called upon Hell, who sent a party of Demons to aid in the search. They helped Herod's soldiers countless times that night—"

"You mean helped murder countless babies," Daniel seethes, his eyes on fire. "Don't try to sugarcoat it."

Mandisa laughs gaily. "Really, Daniel—you can be so melodramatic sometimes!" She rolls her neck and turns to me. "It has been part of our history for as long as any of us can remember, and it always promises to be an amazing night—something we could all use after the year we've had."

As Daniel and I balk at her, she shakes her head and gives a light laugh. "Oh, don't give yourselves too much credit! There have just been some rumblings...down below..." She straightens her back. "But there's always the threat of mutiny on any ship, of course! Nothing that hasn't already been handled, nipped in the bud."

She smiles winningly as I look back at Daniel, confused, still processing the event behind the feast night. "Why didn't Heaven do anything, with Herod and the babies? Weren't there Guardians back then too?"

Daniel nods slowly. "There were. But before it all began, Herod made a sacrifice that allowed the Demons to walk amongst the Humans in their full glamour. No horns, no gaping eye sockets." He jerks his chin at Mandisa. "They looked completely normal, so Heaven never saw them coming."

Mandisa beams. "And per Feast Day rules, we will again be in Full Glamour on Christmas Eve. From dusk 'til dawn—the one night of the year it's allowed." She looks down at me, her gnarled tree root horns protruding from the top of her forehead. "So in case that was a reason for you not to come, I can assure you, you will not see a single horn or cloven hoof."

I look down at the floor. "Oh, even without your ugly face on, we'd still see you a mile away," Daniel grits out, his voice dripping with contempt. "The big hole where your soul should be sells you out."

Mandisa grabs her chest and feigns being stabbed in the heart. "Ouch! That cuts me, Daniel, right to the core." She holds a wrist to her forehead. "Ah, why doesn't he like me? I'm just going to go home, curl into a little ball and cry and cry and cry." Her voice changes. "Oh wait, none of this has anything to do with you, Golden Boy." She grins and holds her hand up to her ear. "I think I hear the cries of a bag of puppies being thrown into the river. Why don't you just flitter off and go rescue them? Christa's the only one I care about." She hones in on me. "What do you think? Are you in?"

I shake my head and push the invitation away, feeling sick to my stomach. "This is beyond jacked up," I mutter.

Mandisa groans and sets the card back in front of me. "Listen, the day is just an excuse to throw a party. You haven't even let me get to the best part!" She reaches into her coat pocket and pulls out her phone, tapping the screen and holding it up to me. It's a list of names. "Do you know who these people are?"

Begrudgingly, I read down the list. I don't recognize any of them. "No," I answer. Daniel looks over the list and shakes his head as well.

"Of course you don't," Mandisa breathes. "I'm guessing Heaven has made no attempt to help you on your quest as Catalyst. They are famous for their lack of information."

Daniel scoffs and looks at Mellie, who is still completely unconscious.

"These wonderful people I have listed here," Mandisa continues, "have made it their life's work to know anything and everything about the Catalyst." She puts her phone back into her coat.

"Even before you were born, Christa, these fine men and women with their big brains and big glasses have been traveling the world, searching for every artifact, reading every prophecy, and questioning anybody who might have information about you and why you are here." She smiles widely. "And I am happy to report that they will be in attendance on Christmas Eve! I would love to make an introduction." She arches an eyebrow. "Truly, this is an opportunity not to miss."

My breath catches in my lungs. I *have* been growing more and more frustrated lately with not knowing anything about my sudden blueness. Other than the little piece of the prophecy that Mary Carmen was able to report, I'm still totally in the dark. If what Mandisa says is true, these people could really help me. I bite my lip and run a hand through my hair, picking up the invitation.

I can feel Daniel watching me as he steps forward. "Flash the shiny-shiny all you want, Mandisa—we're not coming," he sneers.

I turn and look at him slowly, lowering the invite down to my hip. Mandisa shakes her head. "Let her speak for herself, Daniel!" she scolds. "While you may not appreciate our tactics or business model, you cannot deny that we have a passion for the truth." She lays her hands on the counter. "We are just as curious as you are about what happens next. Don't you want to know why you were chosen?" she implores me, her lips pressed into a tight line.

I look at her for a moment; staring into the abyss behind her empty eyes. I shudder and glance down at the floor.

"There's your answer," Daniel replies calmly.

Mandisa sighs. "I can assure you that you would be perfectly safe." She looks between the two of us. "*Both* of you, if you choose to accept. Come on, why don't we shake on it?" She holds out her hand, grinning from ear to ear.

I glare at her and take a step back, knowing not to make anything close to resembling a deal with a Demon. I can tell Daniel is thinking the same as he straightens angrily.

Mandisa sighs again, rolling her eyes at us. "Harming you,

Christa, goes against all of our own interests." She glances at Daniel. "And I'm sure we can make an exception for your plus one."

Daniel crosses his arms. "Yeah, maybe *you* can say that, Mandisa, but I'm sure there are other guests at that party who won't feel the same way," he chortles.

Mandisa gives a small smile. "If you are referring to Alden, you can relax. He won't be there."

I watch Daniel visibly tense up. Mandisa sees it, too. "Yes, he's away on holiday overseas through the New Year. He really needed a break after that nasty business last month," she purrs. "I thought it went without saying that whatever happened between the three of you then was completely personal. The rest of us aren't as…" She searches for the right word. "…involved?" She chuckles.

Daniel's eyes narrow. "Unbelievable," he mutters.

Shaking her head, the Demon turns back to me. "Well, I've delivered my message. I hope you will consider our invitation." She taps the counter and buttons her coat. "I do hope you can put the past behind you and think of the future, Christa. This meeting could be a really good thing for you." She glares at Daniel. "Try to think about it, without any third party interruption."

She starts to sashay toward the front door. I look down at my hands where they're trembling in front of me, still holding the card.

"Again, I wouldn't hold your breath: we already have plans," Daniel calls out to Mandisa's retreating back. He puts his hand on my shoulder and gives it a little shake. "Right?"

I look up into his eyes and nod quickly. "Right," I whisper.

Mandisa snickers. "Well, I'll still hold your place on the list. I hope you change your mind." She opens the door, a set of jingle bells clanking against the glass.

Daniel's eyes dart to her, and he clears his throat. "Um, forgetting something?" he barks, gesturing to where Mellie is still frozen in place and starting to snore.

Mandisa exhales. "Oh, what the Hell—it's Christmas. There's no vacancy in the Green Room, anyway." She gives a wave of her hand, and Mellie's head snaps back, her eyes blinking awake.

Daniel lets out an audible sigh of relief as Mandisa finally leaves, her mouth twisting as the door slams behind her. As if on cue, we both turn to Mellie, whose gaze is unfocused and glazed. She clears her throat and shakes her head, her pupils returning to normal size, before rubbing her neck and looking at us. "Wow, sorry. Just checked out for a second there." She lets out an embarrassed laugh.

I smile uncomfortably. "Are you...okay?" I ask.

Mellie looks at me oddly. "Of course. Have you made a decision?"

I startle, shoving the invitation into my jeans. "I'm sorry?"

She smiles cheerfully at me. "About the pendant. Did you want it just boxed or gift wrapped?"

*

Standing back in front of Mary Carmen's door and letting the small shopping bag with the necklace dangle by my knee, I finally break the silence. "That was unreal."

Daniel nods, his eyes wary. "It was bound to happen sooner or later, us running into one of them," he says, looking out at the street. "I'm just glad you're okay."

"I'm glad *Mellie's* okay." I stare at him, dumbfounded. "Was she really asleep that whole time? She has no idea?"

"Yep." Daniel's face is pinched. "Demons have some pretty wicked tricks up their sleeves." He looks down at the porch. "It's a pretty dangerous time to be Human."

"Guess so," I agree. "Did...did you think she was going to kill her?"

He sighs. "They're not supposed to. It goes against the Law... but they've found ways to work around that, like with tonight or having their Human Pets do the dirty work." He reaches up and grips one of my shoulders. "They thrive on being unpredictable. I think Mellie got lucky tonight."

I bow my head and shudder, remembering a moment from my three days with Alden—how he had held his finger over mine at the Underpass, the gun cold and resilient in my hand. I close my eyes, trying to will the terrifying image of Pete, a veteran, a war hero, reeling backwards away from my mind. Am I just as bad as one of their Pets, a pawn in their game?

Daniel squeezes my shoulder again. "Hey, you okay?" he asks.

I force myself to nod. "Yeah, fine." I glance over at the blue door. "Are you coming in?" I step back and lean against the wall.

Daniel gives me a small smile. "Probably shouldn't. You know how she gets after curfew." He reaches over and tucks a loose lock of hair behind my ear. I shift against the wall, butterflies fluttering lightly in my stomach. "It's also probably in your best interest if I don't," he continues, pulling away. "If you ever want to leave the house again, that is."

I groan. "Yeah, she'd probably give you the third degree pretty bad, and then there would be ash all over the floor when you try to cover up what happened." I sigh. "And I can promise you that my punishment would include sweeping it all up."

I reach behind me and put my hands in my back pocket, feeling the invitation there, waiting for me. I bite my lip.

"What?" Daniel furrows his brow, trying to read me.

I shake my head. "Nothing." I look down. "Just…the whole Catalyst thing. Do you really think there are people out there who know about me?" I shrug. "Or…about what I am, anyway?"

Daniel's eyes widen. "You can't seriously be thinking about going to that party! They're probably going to have people in cages being fed scraps of baby seal meat or something!" He shakes his head. "It's going to be a nightmare."

I nod and cross my arms. "I know, I know—you're totally right." I grip myself tightly. "It would just be really nice to know what's going on—why I am…" I gesture with my blue hands. "…this way."

Daniel gazes at me and exhales. "We *will* find out, I promise—but we're going to do it the right way. I'm on it, Mary Carmen's on it… You're not alone, Christa." He leans in and pulls me into a hug.

I close my eyes and breath in his smell, all of my muscles sinking into him. I reach around his waist and squeeze tightly. "They can find me whenever they want, can't they?" I mumble into his chest. "This isn't going to stop."

I feel him sigh. "Not any time soon." He pats my back. "Go get some rest, and I'll see you tomorrow," he says into my hair.

I nod and turn the doorknob behind me, stepping away. "Yeah," I murmur. "Tomorrow."

CHAPTER 2
NEW YORK CITY— SEPTEMBER, 1975

THE DOORS TO Chez Monique are painted a bright blue, reminiscent of the domes and archways from some far-away Greek island, offsetting the red brick that makes up the rest of the establishment. I stop on the sidewalk and take in how the small building is wedged between a pair of new high-rise apartment complexes, letting out a heavy sigh. I hope I did a good enough job washing off the stink this morning in the bus depot men's room; that dried out bar of soap didn't give me a lot to work with. I quickly sniff myself and zip up my jacket, trying to look presentable.

A crowd of people come up from the subway stop just behind me and hustle past, bumping into my shoulder and knocking me off to the side like a dying salmon being pushed out of the way to make room for its more eager comrades. I suppose New York isn't the type of place to sit around and think about what you're doing; you just do it.

I nod and straighten my sleeves. "No time like the present," I mutter, pushing open the doors. "Sink or swim, I guess."

The restaurant lights are still off, but the sun filters in through the front windows, sending warm beams of light across the dark wood that makes up the bar and floors. The outside of the building was deceiving: while this isn't a very wide space, it goes all the way back to the next block and is crammed full of tables covered in fine white linen cloths. The main focus is clearly the large crystal chandelier that dips down from the ceiling, the rest of the room spiraling around it as if it was a large, glowing star. I stare at it dreamily, but startle at the sound of someone clearing their throat.

I look over and find a man with black, slicked-back hair and a matching mustache standing behind a maître-d podium. His shirtsleeves are rolled and his eyebrows are arched as he scrawls something at the desk. I stand up straight as he finishes what he's writing before glancing up at me haughtily.

"I'm sorry, we do not open until 4—unless you'd care to make a reservation for another time…" he murmurs in a thick French accent.

I shake my head. "Um, no, *I'm* sorry," I mumble. "I'm actually here to see Eddie Robbins…Mister Eddie Robbins." I shuffle nervously.

He narrows his eyes. "I see," he clucks, drumming his fingers against the podium. "Well then, you should have used the back service entrance." He sighs impatiently. "No matter. I can take you to him; this way."

He motions with his hand and walks out from the stand, his shiny shoes clacking noisily on the floor. I trot behind him, gripping my paper bag in my hands. We walk past the tables and chandelier all the way to a door marked *Cuisine* in peeling gold paint. The Frenchman holds it open and ushers me inside.

It's a good-sized kitchen, similar to the one we had on the ship—but instead of polished chrome, the ovens here are blackened with age, a thick film of grease covering the vents and fans. I hear a radio playing some rock-and-roll blues song in the back. "Chef!" the Frenchman calls out irritably. "Someone to see you!"

"What?!" a voice shouts from the back. "What did you say, Pascal?"

The Frenchman rolls his eyes. "Someone...to...SEE...YOU!" he over-enunciates.

A freezer door slams. "Hey—turn that racket down!" the same voice shouts. The radio goes to half-volume.

A bald, wiry black man steps out from behind a rack filled with spices and pots and pans. He's wearing striped pants and a white chef's coat, the front smeared with what looks like tomato sauce...or blood. He's holding a large side of frozen meat, which he promptly tosses onto the metal counter in front of him.

He glares at Pascal, mouth mashed thin. I can't tell if he's angry or if that's just his face. "Who's here to see me?" he demands, wiping his hands on a dishtowel.

Pascal sighs. "Dis per-sonne!" he sneers, gesturing to me. "He came in asking for you."

I try to smile winningly. The black man's eyebrows draw down. "I've never seen this kid in my whole life!" He shakes his head and looks back at the meat, patting it with his hand. "Now, if you'll excuse me, I've got to get this baby butchered before service tonight, so that is your cue to respectfully get the fuck out!"

He reaches over to a knife block and pulls out a very large blade. Pascal sighs and starts to pull me by the arm. I look between them frantically and dig my heels into the floor. "No, no—wait, uh, Mr. Robbins!" I shove my hand into my pocket and take out the note from Burman. "I was sent here by Jay...Mr. Jay Burman!" I cry, holding out the paper.

The man's head shoots up, and he puts out his palm. "Hang on a second!" he exclaims, setting the knife down. "Lemme see that."

I quickly give him the note, and he holds it up to his face, squinting through the bottom of his glasses. "Yep, that *is* ol' J.J.'s handwriting." He frowns, setting it on the counter, then nods at Pascal. "It's okay, Frenchie. Leave him back here."

After Pascal clenches his jaw and huffs out of the kitchen,

Robbins sighs and crosses his arms. "So." He leans against the counter and gives me the onceover. "Did Mr. Jay Burman propose what I am supposed to do with you?" he asks with a blink.

I swallow and take a breath. "He, um," I stammer, "he thought maybe you might have work for me—extra…kitchen stuff…to do." The back of my neck breaks out in a cold sweat.

Robbins snorts and stands up. "Kitchen *stuff*, huh?" He turns the side of beef towards him. "Yeah…we've got a lotta that around here." He picks up the knife, the handle in one hand, the tip of the blade pressed into the palm of the other. I inhale, waiting for the point to break skin. "What's your prior experience?" He juts out his chin at me.

I look down and scratch my ear. "I used to work on a ship," I say into my chest. "Long trips across the Atlantic."

He puts his tongue in his cheek thoughtfully. "Mmm-hmm." He twists the knife nice and slow in his palm. "I meant cooking experience."

I draw in a sharp breath. "I can make poached eggs…and toast," I offer. "I also can grill a pretty mean sardine…" I stuff my hands in my pockets in embarrassment.

He tosses the knife next to the meat and holds up his hand. "Okay, okay." He rubs his forehead. "So, you can't cook, you don't look like you can lift much." He exhales. "And I'm detecting an accent. What is that—Australian?"

I shake my head. "No. Irish, sir," I reply quietly.

He scrunches his mouth. "Are you even legal to work in this country?"

I catch myself making a face. "Mr. Burman and I are working on that," I say with a wince.

The man lets out a boisterous laugh. "I bet you are!" He picks up the knife and starts in on the meat. "You know, I haven't seen that old bastard in almost fifteen years, and then he goes and pulls this." He slices deftly through the bones. "Oh, he's sent me workers in the past, usually browner than you, certainly more useful than you." He purses his lips. "Although I gotta say, you *are* exotic! Ireland—wow! Like *Brigadoon* and "Somewhere over the Rainbow" and all that shit?" He glances up at me excitedly, pitching bone fragments off to the side.

I smile tightly. "That's right," I joke. "Leprechauns and fair folk going 'round with their pots of gold." I keep my voice rich. "Just like in the stories."

He nods and cracks the rib cage open effortlessly, making his very ghoulish work seem almost majestic. I watch wide-eyed.

"Never been to Ireland, or to Europe at all, really," he comments, pulling the slabs apart. "Always wanted to go. I'm sure J.J. mentioned we were in Korea together, so we saw a bit of Asia—goddamn shithole." He shakes his head. "Freeze your balls off in winter, hot as hell in summer. Makes the Bronx in July feel like the North Pole. Pretty girls though…very nice." He sighs and looks up at me again, considering. "To J.J.'s credit, he's never sent me any lemons," he hems.

I hold the side of my leg, trying to stop it from shaking. I'm rewarded when the man finally nods. "All right, Irish. I've got something you can do." He motions with his hand as he steps back behind the rack.

I follow hastily. We walk around to a row of wide, deep sinks pressed against the wall where a tall, tan, blond guy in a t-shirt and jeans is peeling carrots and potatoes, jamming to the radio next to him on the counter. A guitar solo goes off, and he thrusts his arm in the air and swings his hips in time with the music, his eyes closed.

Robbins rolls his eyes. "Jesus Christ… Hey, Kirschbaum!" he barks, making the guy jump out of his skin and drop his knife in the sink. "What did I tell you about that radio, boy?"

The guy turns and grins. "Come on, Chef! That's Ronnie Wood from Kilburn!" he replies with the slightest hint of a New York accent. He picks up his knife and gestures at the radio. "With Keith Richards and Rod Stewart!"

Robbins shakes his head. "Where on my face does it look like

I give a damn?" He points to the radio. "You better switch over to 770; there's a Series game starting in 10 minutes."

The guy pitches the potato he was working on into the sink with a thud. "No way, Chef! I came in early just for this!" He takes a step forward. "Alison Steele is playing the whole set, no commercials. Do you have any idea how rare these tracks are?"

Robbins puts his hands on his hips, his face grave. "You change the station before I come over and rip that box out the wall and beat your sauerkraut-lovin' ass with it!" he thunders. "My kitchen, my radio!"

The guy hangs his head and slumps over to the radio, glaring sullenly at Robbins as he clicks over to AM. Robbins jerks his chin at him. "Don't give me that look, boy—I'm not your daddy." He sniffs. "A cat like you ain't got no daddy, the way you run wild all over this town… You're lucky you're *not* one of mine: I'd tan your backside." He sniffs. "And those carrots and potatoes better be perfectly julienned; if I see one, ONE, out of order, I'm gonna make you start all over."

I see the kid hiding a smile as he starts peeling again. "Yes, Chef," he snickers.

Robbins sighs and looks back at me, gesturing to the sink. "Get familiar, Irish. See that stack?" He points to a tower of dirty pots and dishes caked with old food and grease. I nod. "I've got three more just like it next bay over. Start scrubbing." I step over to the sink, set down my bag, and pick up a brush.

I turn to him. "Thank you, Mr. Robbins. I really appreciate—"

"It's Chef," he interrupts. "As long as you're here, you call me Chef." He jerks his head at the guy, who is just finishing off his last couple carrots. "Don't let this one fill your head with daydreams and all that tune in, drop out crap." He points at the guy. "I lived free love, okay?! While you were still in diapers, toddling under your mama's skirt!" He shifts back to me. "Just keep your head down, do your job, and we'll get along fine, you dig?"

I nod fervently. "Yes, Chef." Satisfied, he growls and leaves to go back to his butchering.

Setting my jaw, I get to work. I scrub frantically at the soup pot in my hand, running scalding water over my knuckles. I keep at it even as my skin starts to redden and pucker, I'm so relieved to have work.

The guy next to me clears his throat and turns the cold water tap on. "You know, it works just the same, hot or cold—just use a little Borax." He nods back at the racks. "You don't need to go burning your hands off."

I shake my head. "Just trying to do what Chef said—keep my head down, do my job." I set the clean soup pot off to the side.

He sighs. "I get it, he's pretty scary. But I promise you, his bark is worse than his bite." He picks up the pot I just cleaned and throws his carrots and potatoes in.

I look at him irritably for a minute before shaking my head and picking up the next pan. "I don't care what his bark or bite is like; he gave me work when he didn't have to, and for that I am forever grateful." I train my eyes back on the sink.

He nods, moving the pot over to a prep station. "So, Irish, huh? That's pretty close to England…" He grins. "You ever been to London?"

I nod. "Couple times. The ship I used to work on docked there when we were between jobs. They'd usually send us home on leave then, so I'd travel north to Liverpool to get the ferry over to Dublin…"

"Liverpool? Like the Beatles?" he interrupts excitedly.

I shrug. "Yeah, I guess." I drip some Palmolive onto my brush.

He shakes his head. "That is so cool… Man, the farthest out of the city I've ever been is Lancaster to visit some of my grandparents' friends." He begins to swiftly cut the carrots and potatoes into long, elegant strips. "But the UK…that's where all the best bands come from." He glances over at me.

I arch my eyebrows. "I wouldn't know. I'm not really into rock and roll or whatever." I rinse the pan in my hand.

He lets out a little scoff and smiles. "Ah well, then you're missing out! Don't worry—even if you weren't into it before, New York gets all the best acts. We're the litmus test for anything and everything that rocks." He cranes his neck back toward me.

I scoop up a handful of dirty silverware. "Again, I'm just here to work, not have fun." I look down at the sink.

His smile fades and he stares at his knife. "Sure, I get it." He clears his throat, going back to his vegetables. We work in silence for a bit, the game having started on the radio. My hands chap from the harsh soap, but I keep washing.

Once he's finished cutting, the guy steps back over to the sink and cleans out the old peelings from earlier. "Make a little room for you," he mumbles, dumping the rubbish in a tin behind him. I nod and move part of the stack into the now empty sink, soaking them in hot water.

He leans against the wall and watches me, his arms crossed over his white t-shirt. "So you're from Dublin then?" he asks. "You said you would take a ferry there?"

I shake my head. "I'm actually from a small town called Caherconlish, just outside of Limerick." I turn off the water.

"Try saying that five times fast!" he laughs.

I tilt my head. "It's mostly farms and stuff—nothing like here. The one pub in town closes by 9, and if you're not in church every Sunday, people start to talk." I shake my head. "Everyone knows everybody else's dirty laundry." Even the laundry you wish you could throw away and burn.

"That doesn't sound so bad...nice place to call home."

I grimace. If you *could* call it that.

He gets off the wall and hops up onto one of the counters. "Chef didn't say your name... I think you'll quickly discover he has a way with nicknames, racial slurs being his obvious favorite." He chuckles, leaning back. "It's how you know you're one of us. I'm sure he's got a couple colorful ones coming up for you. But unless you want me to keep calling you Irish…"

"It's Alden," I reply, glancing back at him.

He grins and holds out his hand. "I'm Daniel, but everyone around here calls me Danny or Danny Boy."

"Like the song," I state, staring at his open hand.

He nods, still keeping his arm out. "Yeah, that's right!" He smiles awkwardly and glances at his fingers.

I clear my throat and shake his hand quickly. "Nice to meet you," I murmur, going back to scrubbing.

He snickers. "Likewise. Although, I have to say, you're different than I pictured someone from Ireland being—much more…stoic."

I take a pot from the sink. "And you're German? Kirschbaum?" I ask.

His eyes narrow as he pops off the counter. "I'm American. That's just my last name." He diverts his attention to the back door as a pair of Hispanic men enter the kitchen. "Hey, Pedro, Juan Julio! *¿Qué pasa? ¿Cómo estás?*"

He walks over and gives them each a high five and starts conversing in rapid Spanish. I stay where I am, my eyes cast down at the sink full of dirty water as they move about the kitchen putting on chef coats and getting set up for dinner service. Daniel clears the rest of the vegetables and moves them to Pedro's station, where he starts sautéing them in butter and spices. Juan Julio slips around the supply rack and returns with a tray full of beautifully trimmed steak filets, a result of Chef's earlier handiwork. They move together like a well-oiled machine, all the while chattering in broken Spanish. Neither of the new guys introduce themselves or even ask about me, which is fine. I'm happy to keep to myself.

"…*Así que esta chica preciosa, con enormes aldabas anda en … como…como el tamaño de mi cabeza…*my head, right?" Daniel laughs, holding his hands out in front of his chest like he's cradling a pair of watermelons. Pedro whistles and whacks him on the arm. "She comes marching back here like the Queen of England…*y te* *juro por Dios, creo que su blusa va a pop derecha abierta; No sé dónde mirar! Y todo lo que puedo decir es…* 'We can't make any substitutions on the Cobb Salad—it's premade.' *Estaba tan enojado!*"

At that, all three of them lose it. I roll my eyes and pull the drain, setting the last of the stack in the sink.

Finally, Daniel shushes them and steps over to the grill. "And then we made it in the walk-in." He grins wickedly, picking up a pair of tongs. Pedro and Juan Julio both howl and slap him on the back like he just won the World Cup. Daniel takes a bow before turning the filets.

"All right ladies, sorry to shut down the sewing circle!" Chef comes around the corner, holding a pencil and pad of paper. Daniel and the others stop what they're doing and stand at attention. I take that as a cue to stop washing and step next to them, flanking Daniel's right side.

Chef looks at me and nods, scratching the back of his neck. "Looks like we're going to be understaffed for service. I just got a call from Baxter; he's stuck on Long Island waiting for a train… There was some sort of accident on the tracks a couple hours ago— thinks he might able to make it by the time the theater crowd starts making their way in." He sighs and looks up at us. "And Dennis is still in Maine visiting his mother, so everyone's gonna have to haul a little extra ass tonight."

Daniel glances over at Pedro and Juan Julio and grins. "We got it locked down, Chef—could do this menu in our sleep!" He bumps Pedro with his shoulder, who crosses his arms confidently.

Chef exhales and puts his pencil behind his ear. "Yeah, don't be so sure of that. We will be having a special guest joining us for Tasting this evening. Madame is coming in, and you know how there are always changes after she visits."

He barely gets his words out before being met with a chorus of groans. Pedro rests his forehead on Daniel's arm as Juan Julio shakes his head at the floor. "Who's Madame?" I whisper to Daniel.

"Monique," he mumbles out of the side of his mouth. "She owns the place."

"HEY!" Chef shouts, everyone standing up straight. "I want clean jackets and OUTSTANDING manners in the dining room while she's here!" He glares right at Daniel. "You know I'm talking to you." Chef clenches his jaw as Daniel rolls his eyes. "I want that MESS—" He points to Daniel's wild blond hair. "—under a do-rag, you hear?"

Daniel gives a phony salute. "And your mouth shut!" Chef adds, grinding his teeth. "I will not have a repeat of last time—"

"It was a compliment! I told her I liked her dress!" Daniel exclaims with injured innocence.

Pedro and Juan Julio both chuckle, but Chef hisses angrily. "We all know what you were getting at—nearly gave Francois a heart attack. I will have you know he wanted to fire you on the spot! You're lucky turnover is so high around here."

Daniel snorts. "All right, all right." He glances down at his shoes. "You won't hear a peep outta me, cross my heart." He looks up again and grins, drawing an X on his chest.

Chef shakes his head and glances down at his notepad. "Juan, I'm gonna have you filling in for Baxter as my Sous, so then I want Pedro on your station with first and lasts and Danny pulling double duty on grill and veg." Chef smirks up at Daniel. "Since you've got this so 'locked down.'"

Daniel grimaces. Chef motions to me. "Irish, you're gonna take a break from dish detail and help this poor chump on grill." He nods at Daniel.

Daniel scoffs and puts his hands on his hips. "Can he even cook?"

I feel my face redden as Chef glares at him. "You think I'd let him hang with my crew if he couldn't?!" he bellows. "You're always going on about how you want more responsibility around here, and now I'm throwing some your way; show me what you got!"

Daniel purses his lips and stares at the wall. Shaking his head,

Chef looks out at us over his glasses. "Now, unless there are any *real* questions, get to work! Tasting in thirty." He spins and stalks back to the front.

When he's gone, Daniel turns to me and sighs. "Well, you heard the man: let's do it." He looks at my tan coat, now splattered with dirty dish water, then steps into the pantry and pulls out a clean white chef's coat. "You're gonna need this, unless that one holds some sort of sentimental value."

I cringe and grab the jacket. Daniel turns toward the grill as I hastily change, putting more meat on the fire. Once I'm ready, I push up my sleeves and sidle up next to him.

He clears his throat and gestures at the steaks. "Okay, so what we're going for are those nice crisscrossed grill marks, like on that one." He points to a filet on the back of the griddle. "It's all about the timing and flipping them at just the right moment before we throw them in the oven to finish—that one looks ready." He nods and hands me the tongs, motioning to a steak right in front of me. "You try." I bite my lip and grab the meat with the tongs, turning it over. A row of perfect black scorch marks crackle up at me. I grin and look at Daniel.

He smiles and nods. "Great. Now you want a matching set on the other side." He picks up a wet washcloth and starts cleaning the other half of the grill, hot steam billowing up in his face. "We'll make one of each dish for the Tasting, but when service starts tonight, it's gonna get really busy. If you're cool with it, I'll put you on steaks so I can keep an eye on the quail."

I nod. "I'm cool," I reply, reaching over to flip another filet. "Or…fine with the plan, that is." I blush.

Daniel laughs and slaps me on the back. "You're cool, Irish—and you just turned your first piece of meat." He arches a brow. "Now all you need is to sleep with one of the waitresses, and you're in."

*

"She's here. All right, everyone line up!" Chef yells, holding open the kitchen door. We all drop what we're doing as a row of servers in black enter from the dining room. I recognize Pascal from earlier and try to catch his eye, but he keeps his gaze focused in front of him. Without even looking at us, they pick up the plates for the tasting and quickly walk back out, Chef closing the door behind them. He motions to us, his eyes bugging out of his head. "Let's move it, *gentlemen!*"

We hustle over to him, Daniel haphazardly tying a red bandana over his head. Chef gives him a look and sighs. "Stand behind your plates and only speak to say what the dish is or if Madame or Francois asks you a question." He nods to me. "There is no other reason on this green earth that you should have to butt in!" He glares at Daniel, who shrugs. "Are we cool?"

We all nod. Chef clenches his jaw and opens the door. "Okay, nice and easy." He leads the way out, his troops marching single file behind him. I inhale sharply as I take in the dining room. It's undergone a Cinderella-like transformation since I showed up this afternoon: silver and crystal glitter from the tables, the chandelier lights throwing little rainbows across the walls. It's magnificent.

I only realize that I've stopped walking when Daniel gives me a shove between my shoulder blades from behind. "Put your tongue back in your mouth, Irish," he grunts. "It's not frickin' Cyndi Wood up there."

I clear my throat and quickly follow Chef to the bar where our plates have been set. He ushers us over to the side, opposite the row of servers from earlier. I take a look at them: there are seven altogether, three of them girls dressed in tasteful black dresses. I glance over at the two on the end, both blonde and whispering to one another. They see me looking and burst into a fit of giggles. I grimace as I feel my face reddening.

Chef coughs and nods to the tall, graying man standing at the host podium. Like the male servers, he is also wearing a black tuxedo, looking more like he should be ordering a martini at the bar instead of waiting tables—shaken, not stirred. He finishes writing something and then drops the pen back onto the desk, flexing his hand. He nods back at Chef and motions to Pascal. "*Nous sommes prêts…s'il vous plaît apporter son.*"

Pascal whisks himself out of line and goes through a door behind the bar to what I guess is some sort of office. The older man steps out from behind the stand and smiles kindly. "We are ready to begin," he says. "Madame will be joining us momentarily; I would ask now that if you have any questions or concerns, you save them for after the Tasting and address them to me privately." His voice is low and affected, French his obvious native tongue despite the switch to English. He glances back at the book on his desk. "We have a full house tonight, complementing one of the best Septembers we've had on record." He bows his head. "I believe that this can be fully attributed to your menu choices, Chef. Quite revolutionary."

Chef stands up straight and folds his hands in front of him, the rest of us doing the same. "Thank you, Francois. That means a lot," he replies, keeping his eyes trained on the floor.

Francois nods and walks over to the bar, making sure the plates are perfectly straight. I watch the waiters communicate with one another via a raised eyebrow or pursed lip, a natural sense of disgust shared amongst their ranks. I wonder if that level of revulsion is a job requirement. I feel Daniel shift nervously next to me.

The silence is broken as the office door bangs open, accompanied by a loud, cantankerous laugh. "*Vous êtes une telle carte! Puis-je vous ramener à la maison avec moi?*"

Pascal comes around the corner, escorting a woman who I can only assume is Madame Monique by the arm. I can see instantly why she'd be an easy target for Daniel's wry sense of humor, since she looks like a relic from a time long forgotten. She seems to be about 150 years old, which would excuse the floor-length white satin evening gown she's squeezed herself into, the matching head wrap, and the ratty fox fur coat with the head still attached at the shoulder. The entire getup makes her more suitable for a journey on the Trans-Siberian Railway than for running a New York restaurant in the late summer heat of 1975.

She grins out at us with a smear of red lipstick on her teeth and pats Pascal lovingly on the arm. "*Merci, ma cadeau...* You are so good to me." She steps forward and claps her hands together. "*Alors!* What a MARRRVELOUS assemblage we have tonight!" She looks at us wildly, her thick pancake foundation cracking around the edges. "Such youth you all have—how lucky I am to have so many beautiful children working in my restaurant!"

She totters over to the line of waiters and almost falls into them, one of them surging forward hastily to steady her. Cradled in his arms, she reaches up and strokes his chin. "Ah...skin like warm milk," she purrs into his chest. "You remind me of a boy I used to know, back in Toulouse." She shakes her head and furrows her brow, mumbling, "Henri, maybe...or Max," to the floor.

Daniel clears his throat. I turn and watch him working very hard to keep from laughing. The waiter stares at Francois wide-eyed while Madame appears to be lost in memory. Francois nods and walks quietly over to her.

"We are so glad you could join us, Madame." He places his hand on her shoulder, dangerously close to the taxidermied fox's teeth. "Chef has prepared a wonderful sampling of tonight's menu for you, right over here." He guides her toward the plates.

Madame nods and grips Francois's wrist. "*Oui*...very good." They take baby steps to the bar, and he helps hoist her up onto one of the stools. "That *is* why I came here tonight," she snorts, jerking her head back to us. "To make sure everything is...how you say... up to snuff?" She giggles.

Francois nods and motions toward the plates. "I'm sure you will find that everything is just so, Madame." He folds his hands behind his back. "We are very fortunate to have Chef Robbins with us."

Her eyes lazily wander over to our line. "Are you sure it was wise to hire the, um," she stage whispers as she pulls a plate towards her, "*le negre?*"

Both Francois and Chef sigh at the same time. "Madame, Chef has been with us for almost eleven years now, remember?" Francois replies softly. "We have never had any complaints, and he is *very* talented." He glances to Chef apologetically.

Madame adjusts herself on the stool and picks up a knife and fork. "Well, maybe just for a trial run." She cuts into the meat on the plate and shovels it into her mouth, brown gravy running down her chin. "What is this that I am eating?" she mumbles in a slovenly fashion.

Chef shoots Daniel a look. Daniel coughs and steps forward. "That's the braised quail with wild mushrooms," he states, keeping his head down. "A mix of trompettes, chanterelles, and cremini, sent direct from a farm in central Massachusetts." He glances over at Chef, who nods encouragingly. "It's accompanied by a side of potato mash and assorted seasonal vegetables: zucchini, baby carrots, corn..." He smiles tightly. "Hope you enjoy." He nods and steps back into line.

Madame chews thoughtfully. "It's okay," she says after a moment. "Needs salt."

Daniel does a double take and opens his mouth. "You're crazy! That'll kill the whole dish!"

He's drowned out by Chef breaking into a fit of heavy coughing, his eyes dark. As Daniel huffs and crosses his arms, Madame looks over at them and arches a brow. "Are you well, Chef? Can't have you spreading disease to all of our loyal patrons coming in this evening." She moves on to the next plate.

Chef clears his throat. "Of course, Madame. I assure you, I am perfectly fine." He glares at Daniel as she takes a bite of the filet.

"Mmm...*absolutment*." She picks at her teeth with her tongue and looks back at the spread. "Filet, quail, pork, salmon..." She purses her lips. "And so many vegetables! Am I not giving you enough for rations, Francois? Must we eat like peasants?!" When he shakes his head, she hunches in her seat. "What I am not seeing is something rich, something *decadent*." Her words roll off her tongue. "What about a nice duck? Or lobster?"

Chef shakes his head. "Both of those come into season around the holidays, Madame." He glances at Francois, who nods for him to continue. "We're trying something they've been doing out in California for the last couple years: keeping a strong focus on eating seasonally and farm-fresh." He puts his hands in his jacket pockets. "We've done really well with some of the local growers from New Jersey and upstate…"

Madame clucks irritably. "What is this of *California*?" she sneers, flicking her hand at him. "Why we would ever want to imitate a bunch of lewd movie stars is beyond me." She laughs and looks around. "This is New York, the center of the Universe! We already give them the most beautiful staff—now let's give them the most beautiful food, okay? Change it." She glares at Chef, challenging, her lip curled.

He sighs and nods. "Of course, Madame," he murmurs.

Her face cracks into a large smile. "Wonderful!" She hops off the stool and claps. "Now, inspection time, and then I must be off."

She takes Francois's arm, and they slowly walk down the line of servers. She nods at all the boys, but stops when she gets to the petite brunette girl, standing in the middle of the line.

"Ah, is this Muriel?" She beams, grabbing the girl's cheek. The girl smiles nervously, her dark, inky eyes darting up to Francois. He looks back at her and tilts his head. Madame presses her nose to hers.

"I remember you in your pram, little one—a baby angel dressed in silk and lace." She pats Muriel's cheek and steps back. "You've grown into quite the young lady, worthy of your *nationalite*." She nods approvingly.

"Merci, Madame," Muriel answers in the same French accent.

Francois squeezes her arm as they move down the line. They stop when they get to the two blonde girls. Madame frowns. "Aren't you a ragtag bunch," she grumbles. The girls shift in their spots.

"Pull down your dress. Get that hair out of your face." Madame points with a bony finger, turning away. The blondes quickly correct themselves. "Cheap American girls… Class, the one thing they cannot teach."

Madame sighs, letting Francois lead her over to our line. She sucks her teeth as she nods at Chef, stopping to squint in front of Daniel. "I remember you…from last time."

Daniel straightens up, staring over the top of her cap. Madame shakes her head, confused, then looks at me. "You're new," she mumbles, holding onto Francois for support.

I look her right in the eye and nod. "Yes, Madame. I am."

She grins, running her fingers down the side of my face. "And very pretty…*tres joli*…" she murmurs, coming closer. I can smell sherry on her breath; it makes me nauseous. "Those eyes—like the sea…" Her hand wavers over my chest, like she's afraid to touch me. "But what is this? Why do you wear this uniform?" She leers down at the chef's coat.

I look over at Chef, not knowing what to say. "He's a new hire, Madame. Just started working earlier today," he answers.

She stares deep into my eyes. "But my darling, sweet boy," she breathes, "a beauty like you shouldn't be kept in the kitchen." She jerks her head towards the waiters. "You should be out where everyone can see you and admire you…" She cups my chin with her palm.

I blush and glance back at Chef. He coughs. "We're severely understaffed this evening, Madame. I could really use his help back in the kitchen—"

She snaps her fingers, cutting him off. "Ah, I see." She spins on her heels and points at the two blonde girls. "You two—get outta here. You're fired!" she screeches.

One of the girls lets out a little squeak of surprise, and they look frantically toward Francois. He hangs his head. Madame snaps her fingers again. "I mean it! Leave—NOW!"

One of them bursts into tears as the other wraps her arms

around her, and they scurry out the front door. Everyone stares at Madame, all the air sucked from the room.

Oblivious, she grins at Chef. "Now it would appear that *I* am severely understaffed, Chef," she simpers.

As he crosses his arms and stares at the floor, she puts her hands on my shoulders. "You don't really want to be stuck in that dirty old sweatbox, do you, my love?" she asks, arching an eyebrow at me.

I shake my head and glance at Daniel and Chef, neither of them looking back. "I'm just here to work, Madame, wherever you need me," I try to answer diplomatically.

She chuckles. "I need that gorgeous face in my dining room!" She pulls me across the room to the line of servers. "What is your name, pet?" She squeezes my arm.

"Alden, Madame."

She scrunches her shoulders. "Oooh, I just love it! You remind me of all those handsome English boys from the magazines!" She beams up at me. "You are English, right? I can hear it in your voice."

I clear my throat. "Irish, actually, Madame. Near Limerick."

She shakes her head and turns me toward her. "Oh no, that won't do. The Irish are notoriously filthy people, constantly whelping like dogs…" She giggles and looks at Francois, who rubs the bridge of his nose tiredly. "All of them—so poor with the body lice!" She smacks Francois on the arm. "*Droite? Les poux de corps?*" He shakes his head. "No, you should be from England., like Princess Margaret and…Cary Grant!" Her eyes crinkle as she chucks me on the chin.

I cringe. "I guess I could…try," I mumble.

She nods. "Oui. I think it will really add something…special. The English are always so polite, royal. An air of sophistication, *non?*"

I grimace; clearly, she hasn't met many Englishmen. Undeterred, Madame pats my back. "Ah, *c'est fantastique!*" she croons, guiding me over at a snail's pace to the line of waiters. All except Muriel wear the same fake smile, thinly veiling their utter contempt.

Madame beams at them. "Pascal, *me cher*," she calls, handing me over like a mouse to a pack of hungry cats. "Be a darling and help our newest addition find something to wear for tonight, will you?"

Pascal bows dramatically and takes me roughly by the arm. Madame doesn't notice. "Of course, Madame. Right this way, monsieur," he grits out through his teeth.

As he hauls me back toward the bar door, I spin around and see Madame blowing a kiss as Chef scratches the back of his head and Daniel and the rest of the crew shuffle their feet, looking all around pissed.

"Move it, dog shit; we've got ten minutes 'til doors open," Pascal hisses in my ear. "Madame might think you're something special, but your good luck ends there." He shoves open the door.

I take a shaky breath. Sink or swim.

CHAPTER 3
LOS ANGELES—PRESENT DAY

"*H*EY, CHRISTA! OVER here!"

I startle as I spy Daniel waving by the big oak tree, waiting at our regular spot. I was expecting Mary Carmen today, as Daniel usually does a shift at the Chinese take-out on Friday afternoons. I smile and return his wave, adjusting my backpack as he springs off of the tree and jogs over to me, dressed in his standard blue jeans, leather jacket, and Stones t-shirt. I chuckle to myself as a group of Junior girls on their way to the parking lot to stop watch him run, their tongues lolling out of their mouths. He doesn't even notice, his eyes trained on me.

"I was starting to wonder what was taking so long…" He takes my heavy bag and slings it over his shoulder.

I shake my head as we begin our walk to the bus stop. "I thought you had to work today. I was looking for Mary Carmen's car—"

"I quit!" he chirps.

I stop and balk at him. He grins. "It's fine! Just with everything going on, I thought it would be better to not be so busy, focus on my top priority."

"Which would be me?" I raise an eyebrow. "Glad to know I still rank over egg foo young."

"It was a tight race—but yeah." He laughs, putting his hand on my back as we walk again. "How was school?"

I blush—it always feels a little dirty when he asks me that question. Like he's robbing the cradle or something. But I know for him, there's no subtext there. "Good," I answer. "I had to talk to Sister Margarite after class…uh, my Brit Lit—"

"—British Literature, 4th period," Daniel fills in quickly. "I know… Was it about your term paper?"

I roll my eyes. "Yes! Jeez—what's the point of me telling you about my day if you already know everything?" I clench my fist around a handful of my skirt, keeping it in place as a chilly gust of wind follows us down the sidewalk.

Daniel grins. "Sorry, go ahead." He makes a dramatic gesture to portray giving me the floor.

I sigh. "I had to pick a different topic. Yeats was already taken, so I'm going with Wordsworth now." We arrive at the bus stop, and I lean against the bench, crossing my arms.

Daniel wrinkles his forehead. "Wasn't Yeats Irish anyway? How does he count for Brit Lit?"

I leer at him appreciatively as he purses his lips and shuffles closer to my side. "Very impressive! Yes, he was…and it doesn't matter. He's in the right vicinity—the UK." I shake my head. "Jenny Martinez picked him. How did you know that? Are you a secret poetry fan?"

Daniel shrugs and taps his temple. "Just popped into my brain. One of those weird odds and ends from way back when…" He gives me a smile and winks. "Or I'm just a genius. Deal with it."

"Yeah, okay!" I laugh and nudge his sneaker with the toe of my boot—any excuse to touch him. "What did your genius mind get up to this afternoon while I was slugging away in the sugar mines?" I wonder, acknowledging Johnny P. and a couple of the other football players as they join us at the stop and hang out a few feet away.

Daniel watches them for a minute, his eyes narrowing,

before he turns back to me. "You know, same old, same old—perimeter checks before lunch, picked up that book we need for Science Club..."

At that, I grin. "Thank you!" Daniel has been helping me get ready for my first project since I returned to Science Club last month. My very public, judged presentation is next week, and the mere thought of it is giving me stomach lobsters.

Daniel quirks a smile at me and continues. "...hung out with Mr. Trundi in the teacher's lounge for a bit, then made my way over to the fieldhouse while you were out playing lacrosse in gym." He flashes his eyebrows. "Nice knee socks, by the way."

After I shove into him playfully, he puts his hands into his pockets and stares out at the street, James Dean all over again. "Then I just messed around with some of the equipment, did some weights..."

Johnny P. whistles over at us to get our attention and points to Daniel. "Yo, homes! I saw you during 6th!" He gets his friends to look over at us and crows, "Dude, this guy benched like 280... It was sick! You believe that? Skinny motherfucker like that!"

The football players all grumble in approval, standing up a little straighter. I shake my head. "Show off," I whisper. Daniel smirks.

"You coming to Jones's tonight, Christa?" Johnny P. calls over again. "His parents went to France or some shit for Christmas, and he's got the beach house all to himself... Should be pretty dope." He nods at Daniel. "You could bring your friend. All of Varsity's gonna be there, and some of the girls from JV..."

Daniel's eyes light up, and he looks back at me. "A party? Is—is that what he's talking about? I think we just got invited to a real-life party!"

I scoff and shake my head. A few months ago, I wouldn't have missed a rager at Jones's for the world—first in line at the keg, last to leave sometime around 4 a.m. Now, though, I don't miss those days at all. "We have other plans, remember?" I murmur, snuggling into my Guardian. "Involving a cute Vietnamese girl?" I make sure the guys hear that last part loud and clear.

They look at Daniel like he's the man as he nods, remembering how Jodie's coming over for *Vampires Suck!* "Right! That's gonna be awesome!" He holds a hand up to the boys earnestly. "Raincheck, guys! We've got a thing tonight."

I turn away, chuckling under my breath. "Yeah, dawg, do what you gotta do!" Johnny P. replies, all macho. Since the bus chooses that moment to pull around the corner, our conversation's effectively over. The football guys gather up their stuff.

I sigh, my good mood fleeing as I think about another evening stuck at home with nothing to do until Jodie arrives. Noting my expression, Daniel frowns as the others step toward the curb. "What's wrong? How come you've got your Gloomy Onion face on?"

I can't help but smile when he calls me that, a stupid nickname from the one time I tried to make dinner for us and was struggling through chopping the onions. That came to a stop right then and there, and Daniel quickly took over. Now, I stare at the ground, scuffing my boot on the sidewalk. "I'm just sick of the house right now," I finally explain. "I mean, tonight's going to be fun...but I wish..." I exhale and slowly join the bus line. "I just hate that there are all these strict rules in place: 'brush your teeth, do your homework, come straight home from school.'" I shrug, putting my hands in my coat. "You know...that's tough for me! That kind of—I dunno consistency." I motion at Johnny P.'s back. "I couldn't go to that party even if I wanted to. Mary Carmen would blow a gasket."

Daniel grins, stepping behind me. "Can't be tamed, Christa Nichols..." He puts on his goofy movie-preview guy voice. "Asskicking her way to a theater near you—THIS SUMMER!"

I bite my lip and rock backwards into him, throwing him off balance for a minute. "Shut up! You know what I mean."

My eyes widen in surprise when he tugs me out of line, back

to the bus stop. I startle as the bus pulls away without us. "What's this?" I wonder, twirling my hair.

Daniel crinkles his nose. "Let's mix it up! Life's too short to be bummed out." He gives my cheek a quick swipe with his finger. "*I* should know!"

I shake my head. "What about Mary Carmen? She's gonna freak out when I'm not home..."

"*I'm* your Guardian, not Mary Carmen," he tuts, taking me by the arm. We start to walk across the street toward a Starbucks. "Besides, you have study hours today with Trundi, right?"

"No, he goes home early on Fridays—" When he jams his elbow into my ribs, a lightbulb goes off. "Oh...right, a little lying by omission. I see."

Daniel grins as we hop the curb. "'Lying' is such a strong word...but I've just assessed this situation and am making an executive call: you are in serious need of some fun and caffeine!" He bows, holding open the door.

I close my eyes, inhaling the warm coffee smell coming from the shop, and waggle my eyebrows mischievously. "I dunno—that hot chocolate with the peppermint shavings looks pretty risky! Danger danger!" I joke.

He guides me up to the register with a hand on the small of my back. "Don't worry—I'll be your taste tester." He scratches his chin. "Although, I don't know if a poison would register on me. One of the downsides of being superhuman."

"Oh, stop! I'll just go with an Americano...to be on the safe side." I snicker and take his hand.

Daniel squeezes my fingers back casually, then holds up two fingers to the barista. The barista smiles in reply and ducks over to the machines, little bells and whistles tinkling merrily as he gets our drinks together. Quick as a flash, he's back with two cups of coffee in hand.

"Thanks." Daniel reaches into his pocket and pulls out a couple of dollar bills. He shakes his head as I reach for my own wallet. "Put your money away."

I huff. "Daniel—I can pay! You're unemployed now. You don't always have to be so nice to me—"

"Occupational hazard." He grins, popping his change into the tip jar, then hands me one of the steaming cups.

Spotting an empty couch by the main doors, we plop down next to each other, smiling as we sip our coffee. "Awesome…" I exhale, glancing out the front window. I can see school from here. Everyone's cleared out, replaced by landscapers cleaning out the last fall leaves from the few deciduous trees that line campus. "Beats the couch at Mary Carmen's," I muse, adding, "The semblance of freedom is nice, too." I cozy up to Daniel, careful not to spill my drink.

Daniel scoffs. "You make it sound like we've got you locked away in some deep dark dungeon, never to see the light of day again!" He shakes his head. "We still do fun stuff… We all went to that farm up north to get the turkey for Thanksgiving…"

"Yeah—totally my idea of a good time: getting up close and personal with our dinner!" I chortle, taking a draw off my cup. Mary Carmen was in tears the whole time at the idea of slaughtering a live bird as Daniel went around and introduced himself to each prisoner in the muddy pen before selecting the largest gobbler they had. I just laughed from the sidelines while Benny Woo chainsmoked from his yellow truck in the parking lot. Actually, the more I think about it…it *was* pretty fun.

"I told her not to put that thing in the freezer when we got back," Daniel grumbles, staring out at the road. "Just keep it the garage, it'll stay cold enough…but she never listens. Complaining about mice the whole way back from Pasadena…"

The mention of Pasadena snaps another memory into my head—one that I would rather forget. Pete was from Pasadena. He said he used to work at his uncle's auto shop there, after he returned from the war and was trying to get his life back on track. I wonder if Daniel knew that about his friend when we were there, walking down the quaint small town sidewalks, checking out the early Christmas decorations, admiring the beautiful Santa Anita Raceway. He's never talked about Pete…not since I told him what happened at the underpass with Alden. Daniel's face had crumbled for only a second before he was onto the next crisis at hand. I look up at him now, his jaw relaxed, his eyes cheerful. Maybe *I* need to talk about it—even if he can't.

I clear my throat. "That *was* a fun day," I murmur, trying to figure out how to bring the dead lieutenant up delicately. "Really cute town. Must have been a nice place to grow up…you know… for Pete." I hold my breath as the corner of Daniel's eye twitches.

"Yeah," he whispers, keeping his gaze focused out the window. "He used to talk about it all the time, before…that is, back when we first met." He nods and sips his coffee quietly.

I squirm, wanting to ask more questions, but knowing that it might be risky. I wait until he takes another drink before my curiosity gets the best of me. "Like…what would he say?" I try to keep the exasperation out of my voice. "When you first met?" Getting Daniel to talk about his past is worse than trying to herd cats.

Case in point: he sighs and pulls back, setting his cup down on an end table next to the couch. He shrugs and looks away. "You know, just that everyone was friendly, the girls were all pretty California blondes, the food was fantastic…" His mouth twitches into that half-smile I love. "And the mountains…how they were similar to the ones where we were—no snow, just brown, rolling hills. Said he would look out at the horizon and pretend he was home. Said I could do the same…"

"You were in the war together?" I ask quietly. I use Pete's assumed age and figure it was probably something in the middle east, maybe Afghanistan. I have a hard time picturing Daniel in full-out military gear, a machine gun strapped to his chest, but I wonder if that's where he…

Daniel answers my question with a chuckle before I get a chance to ask. "*I* wasn't in any war—already dead, remember?" I nod and snuggle into the couch. "But I have spent some time overseas, trying to rack up Angel points… Warzones are usually pretty good places to do that." He sighs and shakes his head. "He was a good kid, Pete, really honest…" His face pinches and he leans back, massaging his neck.

"You never talk about him," I reply, my tone low.

Daniel blows out his cheeks and smiles grimly. "It's not exactly a happy subject! Just another one I found too late…" His smile becomes a grimace. "I should've…I dunno, I should've kept better tabs after we got back. I knew it was going to be hard for him—" He suddenly stops, furrowing his brow like he's remembering something.

"What? What is it?" I sit up, setting my coffee cup down and watching him.

Daniel shakes his head. "Oh…nothing. I, um…I was having him hold onto something for me…" He scratches his cheek, lost in thought. "A Guardian thing—this pocket knife the Archangel gave me…" He sniffs and looks at me. "We're supposed to give it to one of our charges for safekeeping, to ensure that we keep serving in the Mortal Realm until we Ascend… Funny." I can see him bite the tip of his tongue in thought. "I'd forgotten all about it until now."

"Is it important?" I ask, staring at him intently.

He shrugs. "I guess… I mean, it's from an Archangel, right?" He shakes his head with a little laugh. "I've just been so preoccupied with everything that's been going on with us…yeah." He puckers his lips. "Should probably go by Pete's old haunts and try to track it down." He sits back calmly.

"Um…yeah!" I exclaim, batting him on the arm. "It sounds like a big deal!" I wrack my own brain, trying to remember everything from that night with Alden at the underpass—but it all goes fuzzy after I feel the kickback of the gun, Pete's chest exploding before my very eyes. I shudder.

Daniel sees my reaction and wraps his arm around my shoulder. "Hey, it's okay! It's not like it's started raining stars or anything, right?" My Guardian grins, waving his other hand. "Everything's cool... I'm sure it's hanging in one of his old coats or something at his parents' place. I'll try to head up that way again in the next couple days."

I nod, taking a deep breath and letting his touch comfort me as the coffee warms me up inside. I smile and flash my eyebrows. "Mmm, road trip back to Pasadena—maybe find a gaggle of geese to befriend and then cook them up for Christmas..."

Daniel snickers under his breath. "I dunno, I really had my heart set on steak."

I smirk. "Then we're gonna need a bigger boat."

This makes him laugh out loud, and I snuggle into the crook of his arm, very pleased with myself. We sit quietly like that for a moment, watching the cars go by. I catch a glimpse of a red Porsche convertible, a couple of the JV girls that Johnny P. mentioned cruising by with the top down, laughing and flipping their long, blonde hair—which just seems dumb in December. They're like something out of a gum commercial. I bet they're off to get ready for the Beach House tonight, deciding between the shredded Hollister tank and the Roxy sweatshirt, wondering which one says 'I go to the beach all the time'? I roll my eyes. It's all so fake—just another reason not to go.

They speed off, and I turn to Daniel, whose attention is focused on the barista making some incredibly complicated beverage. I tap the frayed denim over his knee. "I'm sorry we can't go to that party tonight." I check myself. "Well, *I'm* not sorry—I'm super excited about Jodie and *Vampires Suck!*" In fact, I'd stayed up into the wee hours of the morning re-watching the previous episodes last night so I'd be ready for anything. "But you seemed kind of jazzed at the idea..." I pause, trying to read his expression.

He breaks into a grin and scratches his chin. "Aww, you know I'm game for whatever!" He rests his head against mine. "I'm excited about Jodie, too...and getting a real taste of the full sleepover experience!"

We both chuckle. "If Mary Carmen doesn't throw you out before the pillow fight," I reply demurely.

Daniel shifts, puckering his lips. "Don't wanna miss that!" He smiles and shrugs. "No—I don't feel like I'm missing out on anything. Being with you beats hanging out on Skid Row, *any* day of the week!"

"That's one for the Christmas card," I joke.

He snickers again, patting my leg as he finishes off his coffee. "Seriously…I don't need to go to any parties, hang out with a bunch of jocks… You're not here to entertain me, Christa. In fact, it's probably safer that we stay home—"

I grimace, smacking him lightly on the belly. "DON'T jinx it! Now a bunch of Demons are going to blow up the living room before we finish the show. Thanks a lot!"

Daniel lets out an exasperated sigh. "You know what I mean! I don't know if I'm crazy about you hanging out with those guys, anyway." He shakes his head and looks at his lap. "If I recall, they haven't always been very nice to you…"

I cringe, remembering that Daniel's had a front-row seat to my past, present, and future. He always tries to be polite about what he saw while I was Haloing, but awkward moments like this are sometimes hard to avoid…especially when it comes to my less-than-spotless record with certain members of the Sacred Heart sports teams.

"Yeah, I know…" I blush, pulling my knees up to my chest. "It's not a big deal, Daniel. That stuff's in the past. We've all grown up a lot. I'm different, they're different…"

He snorts. "I'm not judging *you*, Christa—you're good." He stops and chooses his words carefully. "But anyone who treats you poorly…or *has* treated you like that—" His eyes grow stormy. "Well…it's going to take more than a couple compliments and a Friday night invite for *me* to forgive and forget, okay?"

I bite the inside of my cheek, liking this protective side of him. "Okay."

He nods and exhales, settling back into the couch.

"What were you like—in high school?" I ask with a smile, rubbing his arm. "I mean…obviously you *went* to high school, right?"

"Yes, I went to high school," Daniel says with a snort, his mood lightening again.

I perk up, about to go nuclear with questions. "So, what was your story?" I bob my head in excitement. "Were you a jock, a nerd, total burn out? Come on! Give me something!"

He laughs at my attempt to sound like Judd Nelson, then sighs and rubs his forehead. "What do you think I was?"

I furrow my brow, considering. "Definitely not a nerd…" Seeing his expression, I shrug. "What? You're smart, Daniel, but not that smart…"

"*You're* a nerd!" he chortles, his expression playful. "Really smart… You don't think I could hang with your crowd? Come on! I know stuff!"

"I'm not a nerd—Jodie's a nerd," I reply matter-of-factly. And I love that about her. "No…I'm a total burn out." He blows a raspberry as I nod diplomatically. "And yes, you know *some* stuff… like how many albums Grand Funk Railroad put out and how to cook a five-course dinner." I laugh. "Which is stuff I know nothing about! So that's great! But *not* calculus, Daniel, or advanced biochemistry…"

He sniffs, feigning being put out. "Whatever. You've said all you need to say—I get the drift."

I wrinkle my nose, getting back to the topic at hand. "Maybe a jock—you are really athletic…"

He grunts in appreciation. I sigh, trying to figure out this riddle. "But you're also really sweet and funny. I just don't know…"

Daniel blushes and arches a brow. "I'm an enigma. What can I say?"

I gasp, my eyes growing wide. "Oh my God—YES!" He stares at me as I grin, smacking his chest. "You're totally a theater kid! Ahhh!" I bounce on the couch excitedly.

He shakes his head, his eyes narrowed. "What does that even mean?"

I squeal with glee. "Like—you did shows and stuff—performed on stage…singing and dancing!" He lets out a scoff as I practically jump on his lap, going all serious. "Did you play Conrad Birdie in *Bye, Bye Birdie*? I can totally see it!"

"What—no!" He guffaws, giving me a gentle shove. "No, I was not some musical theater person—"

"Then what?" I grin, taking his hand. "What were you like?"

He huffs, biting his lip as he looks away. The small smile teasing his face fades, and he blinks, shaking his head. "Why does it even matter what I was?"

I sit on my haunches, perplexed. He clears his throat and grins. "I'm here now with you, and that's all that's important."

He rolls his eyes at himself as he starts coughing. It's not a horrible spell, but enough for both of us to know he's lying. I sigh, pulling away. "It's fine, Daniel. I know you don't like to talk about that stuff—your past." I frown, staring out the window.

"It's not that…" he whispers, shaking his head as he clears up our empty cups.

I hold up my hand. "Don't worry about it. You don't have to explain anything." I sigh. "Let's not stress… It's been a nice afternoon." Normal. Charmingly commonplace for the Catalyst and her Guardian. I look up at him to see if he knows what I mean, my face wary.

"Right." He nods, gesturing with our mugs. "I'm gonna take these back."

"Fine." I give him a weak smile as he walks over to the counter. When he can't see me anymore, I exhale and glance back out the window.

The horizon is starting to purple behind the school. It's going to be dark soon… And I'm sure Mary Carmen is home, angrily pacing across the front garden, her heels getting stuck in the soil. I can see her murderous expression in my head—her red Seraphim mark all scrunched up, Halo burning auburn gold… I smile smugly.

I almost fall off the couch as I watch a similar shade of gold streak by the front window. Getting up hastily and tripping over my backpack, I press up close to the glass to get a better look, my hands sweating. She came looking for me. Shit. I'm never leaving the house again.

My eyes dart left to right, but I don't see Mary Carmen. I crane my neck to check the door, waiting for her to come barreling through any second…but all I see are a happy older couple walking in arm-in-arm, a stylish pink shawl tied around the woman's shoulders. I exhale—false alarm. But…if it wasn't Mary Carmen, what… or *who*…the Hell was that?

"Christa—wait! Where are you going?" I hear Daniel call behind me as I rush out the front entrance, the glass doors swooshing shut in my wake. I squint and shade my eyes, swinging my backpack over my shoulder as I search up and down the street for the mysterious glowing phantom.

"HEY!" Daniel bolts out of the Starbucks and joins me on the sidewalk, slightly out of breath. "You can't just go running out like that—gave me a heart attack—"

"I saw something!" I exclaim, waving at the road. I check again, to no avail… Whoever or *whatever* I saw is long gone. I sigh forlornly and drag a hand through my hair.

"A Demon?" Daniel asks urgently, straightening up and coming up to my side.

"No, I don't think so…" I shake my head and stare at him. "I think…I think it was another Guardian."

Daniel relaxes, but crinkles his brow thoughtfully. "Another Guardian? Really?"

I nod, crossing my arms. "I thought it was Mary Carmen tracking me down at first, but it wasn't." I blink at him. "There *are* other Guardians around, right? It's not that far off-base…"

Daniel shrugs. "Sure…Ellis is down in Long Beach, said she'd come up for Christmas—and there are others around." He puts his hands in his jacket pockets. "I mean…as a general rule, we try to keep pretty spread out so as to avoid stepping on each other's toes, M.C. and I kind of being the exception to that rule. But if another Guardian was here, they would have come in to say hi, stopped at the shop…" He motions to the doors. "Are you sure what you saw was a Guardian? Maybe it was the sunset catching your eye funny."

"No—it wasn't that! I…I don't know!" I shout, exasperated. I bite my lip. "I know I don't have a ton of experience with all this, but I can assure you, it wasn't the light playing tricks on me." I grit my teeth and lean irritably against the building.

Daniel sighs and steps closer to me. "Okay, okay, I believe you. We'll get to the bottom of this, all right?" Eying me warily, he reaches over and strokes the top of my hand with his index finger.

The small gesture disarms me. I take a breath and nod. "Okay." I look down at my wrist and check the old watch that the Agent gave me back in the Warehouse. I'd taken to wearing it every day when I found it wedged between a few boxes of clothes that Daniel brought over for me from the apartment. The time had changed over automatically to standard Pacific, further illustrating that I wasn't the only thing here surrounded by unanswered questions.

What *is* abundantly clear, though, is that we are very late. I sigh. "We have to get back, or Mary Carmen really will come and find me—and it won't be pretty." I glower at Daniel as I check my phone.

He grins. "Yeah…and the last thing we want is for you to get grounded and miss our big night—ohmyGodVAMPIRES-SUCK!!!!" he warbles like a total ham, making me laugh.

"You are so weird. Are you sure you weren't a performer back in the day? With a voice like that…just like Donny Osmond in *Joseph and the Amazing Technicolor Dreamcoat*—a dead ringer!"

I snicker as he gives me a look and holds out his hand. I take it, and we start walking.

The unnerving feeling that we're being watched follows me all the way back to the bus stop.

*

"Oh my God, Dwight Carroll is seriously, like…the hottest human being on the planet," Jodie mumbles, shoving a handful of popcorn into her mouth.

I nod. "Yeah, there should totally be a law against cheekbones like that," I reply, not taking my eyes off the TV. I pick up a bag of Gummy Bears.

"I wasn't talking about his face…" Jodie chuckles, her eyes flashing behind her glasses as she tucks her perfect, straight black hair back over one shoulder.

I grin and nudge her with my shoulder, leaning back against the coffee table. "Take it easy, J…so scandalous!"

On the couch, Daniel huffs. "That's the kind of guy you girls are into?" he scoffs. "He's so, I don't know…generic."

I turn and make a face at him. "Jealous?"

Daniel snorts. "Yeah, right." He picks at a hole in his jeans. "I have way better hair than that guy."

I roll my eyes and face the TV. Jodie passes me the popcorn.

"We can't hold 'em, Cap—the water's just too strong! The ship's going down!"

Daniel sighs. "You know they pretty much stole the entire plot of *Titanic* for this, right?" He sniggers. "Like that guy is obviously supposed to be Leo—"

"SHHH!" Jodie and I both spin around and shush him violently. "Quiet in the cheap seats!" I add with a smile. "You promised you wouldn't talk." I pitch a handful of Gummy Bears at him.

He scrunches his nose as a green one hits him right in the middle of his forehead. "How can you expect me to sit idly by while the youth of America rots in front of horrible storylines!" he demands petulantly, motioning at the screen. "We could at least be watching something good, like *Master Chef* or old reruns of *Happy Days*."

I shake my head. "That *would* be your favorite show." I turn my attention back to the TV.

Jodie offers me the oversized box of movie Milk Duds. "I think this is it," she murmurs, her gaze glued.

"Yeah, totally." We both edge a little closer.

"*I love you, Catalina… 'til the day I draw my last, dying breath… or…you know what I mean…whatever it is we vampires do.*"

Jodie and I grab each other and squeal. "AHH! Oh my God, he said it! He FINALLY said it!" Jodie shrieks, her knees bobbing up and down like a butterfly.

"I can't believe that just happened!" I cry as the screen fades to black.

"You have got to be kidding me!" Daniel groans, watching the credits roll. "That's it? *That's* what we sat through fifty minutes of bad fight scenes and cable access commercials for?! I feel totally gipped!" He sits up and tosses a throw pillow onto the floor.

I stand and stretch, my pajama top riding up and exposing my navel. "You said you wanted to hang out and see what all the fuss was about! Nobody *made* you watch it." I step over and pick up the pillow, thrusting it into his stomach as I plop down next to him. Jodie sits up and turns off the TV.

"I think he just stuck around for the snacks." Jodie smiles, clearing the popcorn and candy from the new sleeping bags that Mary Carmen bought today.

I glance at Daniel haughtily. "Or to see cute girls in their PJs." I tackle him back down on the couch.

He lets out a grunt as I smoosh into him and holds up his hands. "The jig is up! You got me, Officer… If I come quietly, will you put a good word in for me down at the station?" He laughs as he adjusts my ponytail and wraps his arms around me.

I smile and glance up at Jodie. She looks back and gives me a small grin as she folds an old checkered blanket. I lay my head on Daniel's chest, feeling the soft thump of his heart against my ear. My eyes flutter shut as he starts to dust his fingers across my back.

"That's nice…" I murmur, breathing into his t-shirt. He lets out a low chuckle, but doesn't stop.

I hear Jodie clear her throat. "So…do you guys want me to leave, or stay and take pictures?" She giggles awkwardly.

My eyes pop open and I blush. "Sorry, J…totally lame." I sit up and cough, taking one last glance back at Daniel, his gold halo burning brightly. Jodie stares at us, having no idea that an immortal being similar to the ones we just watched on TV is lounging three feet away from her on the sofa. And I fully intend to keep it that way.

I clear my throat and smile at her. "So, what do you want to do now?"

"My vote's for pillow fight," Daniel interjects, his Cheshire Cat grin in place. I give him a look and get up. "Or truth or dare… Rock stars always pick 'dare.'"

Jodie stifles a laugh. I cross my arms. "I was thinking it might be time for makeovers. I just got a new eyeshadow in the most adorable shade of violet… Would look amazing on you." I grin at Daniel, then back at Jodie mischievously.

She smiles at him. "I *am* a whiz with a fan brush. We'd have you ready for prom in no time."

He sits up and scratches the side of his neck. "It's not one of my usual fantasies, but I can roll with it." He shrugs, sitting back on the couch and rests his arms behind his head. "You two *will* still be dressed just like that?" Jodie and I burst out laughing as Jodie's bag buzzes by the door.

"Oh crap, I forgot to let my mom know I got here." She trots over and pulls out a sparkly silver phone.

I let out a little gasp as she starts typing a text. "Holy cow, J… Is that an Ion?" I step over and take the phone away from her once she's done messaging.

She shrugs and perches on the arm of the paisley easy chair. "It was Francine's. She just got a new one from the 'rents, since she's on track for straight As again this semester." She clucks her tongue.

I glance at her as I start thumbing through the phone's menu options. "*You're* on track for straight As this semester." I pout sexily as I take a selfie, saving it to my contact info.

Jodie sighs. "Yes, but it's *Brown*, Christa. She's bringing Ivy League gold back to the homestead. You know what that means to them." She stares down at her lap. "I haven't heard back from any of the schools out East that I applied to. Everyone's starting to get... antsy." She lets out a heavy sigh. "I dunno...maybe they'll be a little more generous with the praise if I get early acceptance to Stanford. It all depends on how my genome presentation goes next week at Science Club." She looks up and smiles. "You feeling ready? How's your project going?"

I shrug. "I feel pretty good about it. Didn't have a ton of time to prepare, but I've had an extra set of hands to help, so that's been nice." I grin over at Daniel.

He wrinkles his nose smugly. "I *do* take excellent notes with beautiful penmanship. We're totally going to send that Liu kid home cryin'."

I roll my eyes. "We'll see... You're just mad about what he said about your Stones shirt."

Daniel crosses his arms and scowls as Jodie looks between the two of us. "What did he say?" she asks, confused.

Daniel shakes his head. "Don't even repeat it!" he barks. "Sacrilege."

I snigger. "He called the Rolling Stones a bunch of crusty old guys who haven't rocked since 1968," I stage whisper.

Jodie giggles as Daniel lets out an explosive exhale. "That kid has no idea what he's talking about!" he yells. "He had an Of Monsters & Men sticker on his pencil case. I mean...are you kidding me? They're *barely* a notch away from folk music! Somebody get the tambourine..."

I ignore him and turn back to Jodie. "Anyway, *you're* totally going to take first. Those scouts will be tripping over themselves to get to you, no doubt."

Jodie sighs wearily. "I really hope you're right. It would make the last couple of months worth it. This is my first night off in weeks. I'm so tired." She rests her head on my knee, and I lean in to give her a hug.

"Which is why we need to do it right. What kind of music do you have on this thing?" I scrunch my lip and click her playlist. "Oh my God, J. You have a ridiculous amount of Sheryl Crow and Tracy Chapman—what are you, like, perimenopausal?"

She flushes and grabs the phone back, holding it protectively to her chest. "You know I like singer/songwriters!" She wrinkles her nose. "Just tell me what you want and I'll find it for you."

I stand in front of the TV and break into the tootsie roll. "Something we can dance to! You know…get turned up!" I sway my hips around in circles like I've got a hula hoop around my waist, my shorts just covering my butt. I smile as I catch Daniel staring before he quickly looks away.

Jodie rolls her eyes at me. "All right, all right, I've got something for that." She scrunches her face confidently and lays the phone on the coffee table. Dirty hip hop blasts out of the tiny speakers.

I thrust my arms into the air, victorious. "Oh my God, shut up!" I crow. "Flashbacks to freshman Sadie Hawkins, anyone?"

Jodie grins and dances up next to me. "When Andy Monroe told everyone he spiked the punch, but really didn't, and everyone still freaked out like they were totally wasted!" she guffaws, grinding her flannel jammied backside against me. I encircle her in my arms and laugh, nodding at Daniel.

"Don't just sit there with that goofy look on your face—you said you wanted the full sleepover experience! Come on, dance party!" I call.

He blushes and puts his hands on his knees. "Not exactly what I had in mind…but I'm never one to turn down an invitation from a couple of pretty girls." He gets up and does a twirl.

Jodie laughs as he moves behind me and puts his hands on my waist; I can feel how warm he is through the cotton of my shorts.

My own skin starts to tingle as we move to the music, the feel of his body behind me intoxicating—his height, his smell, the soft hairs on his arm… I take a deep breath and shake my head. All of it is too much. I need to stop before I do something I regret.

"Okay—tickle fight!" I ram my fingers between Jodie's ribs and send her shrieking to the other side of the room. I step away from Daniel and turn to smile at him, beads of sweat prickling across my chest.

"Oh my God, Christa—you know I hate when you do that!" Jodie squeals as she jumps on the couch. "I told you that's what my cousin Hien used to do whenever we went over to their house, and he wouldn't stop. The ribs are the worst!" she pants, holding her side.

I put my hands up placatingly. "Okay, okay, I'm sorry—truce, all right?" I crawl over to her and nestle next to the couch, my hands still in front of me.

She watches me warily, then breaks into a huge grin. "You are such a liar," she slurs into the cushions. I grin and go for her stomach again.

Jodie screams and starts tickling me too, aiming for my armpits. "Ahh! You remembered!" I screech, trying to get away. Jodie grabs my arm and rolls on top of me, pinning me to the floor. I gasp and snuffle for air, laughing and choking at the same time. Before I can stop it, a huge, glorious wheeze/snort escapes my lips. Jodie's mouth goes wide, and she gets off of me, laughing hysterically. I do it again, louder this time, grabbing my mouth with embarrassment as my eyes water.

"*What is that?*" Daniel breathes from the other side of the coffee table. Jodie looks up at him, her arms wrapped around her middle, gulping for air.

"It's her horse laugh!" she howls, trying to catch her breath. "Once she gets going, she can't stop!" She doubles over and helps me up. I make my way over to the easy chair and fall into it, making the ridiculous noise again.

"I can't believe you went for my pits—that is so...cold-blooded!" I hiccup, wiping my tears.

Jodie flops on the couch, still giggling. "Oh man, I missed that laugh..." she warbles, winding down.

Daniel shakes his head, grinning at me. "Me, too!"

I stop hiccupping just as Mary Carmen walks into the living room, dressed in her long, white nightgown and reading glasses. "What is going on in here? Sounds like someone shot a baboon in the throat..." She looks over at Daniel, who's still standing in front of the TV. "Show's over?"

I nod and quickly turn off the song. "It just finished a few minutes ago," I answer.

She puts her hands on her hips. "Good... Seems like you enjoyed it." She looks back at Daniel and arches a brow. "You're here late."

He puts his hands in his pockets and glances at the floor. "Yeah, well...I wanted to see what these two were always obsessing about." He motions to the TV, smirking at me. "Still a mystery."

I scrunch my nose, pretending to be mad. Mary Carmen's mouth twitches. "Well, it's getting pretty late, and I'm sure the girls are starting to feel tired..." She smiles tightly at Jodie and I, both of us still catching our breath.

"Thanks for letting me stay over, Mary Carmen—and for all the snacks," Jodie interjects super politely. "My mom never lets me eat stuff like this." She reaches out and motions to the bag of Gummy Bears.

Mary Carmen's eyes widen. "It's okay that you had them, yes?" She looks over at me nervously. "Christa didn't say you had any dietary restrictions..."

I sigh. "It's fine, Mary Carmen... She's just saying you're the cool mom."

Daniel tenses in the corner, and I see Mary Carmen soften and rock back onto her heels. "Oh," she replies quietly, rubbing her shoulder. We all watch her for a moment as she stares down at the floor. She clears her throat and nods. "Well, I'm glad you like them…and are having fun." She smiles, her voice thick. "You're welcome any time, Jodie. It's a real treat to have you here." Clearing her throat, she juts out her chin at Daniel. "But *you* really should get going."

He nods and grabs his hat from the couch. "Yeah, gotta beat that 11 o'clock rush," he snickers, pulling his cap around his ears. He starts to step toward the door.

I let out a little noise and perch up on my heels. "Wait," I call, not ready for him to go. Mary Carmen looks at me. "We were just talking about watching a movie or something," I fib as I bite my lip and look at her sweetly. "Maybe he could stay 'til it's over and then go home?"

Daniel grins as Mary Carmen sighs and shakes her head. "It just so happens that I thought you might say that." She winks and steps over to the bookshelf by the TV, pulling out a large cardboard box. She sets it on the coffee table, and we all peek inside.

"What—where did you get these?" I chuckle, pulling out a handful of old VHS tapes. "Can we even play them?"

Mary Carmen had been beaming at me, but her face falls slightly at this. "Of course we can! I have a player right here." She leans down and pats an ancient VCR wrapped in dust under the TV stand. "It may not get much use, but it still works…"

Daniel lets out a hoot and stands up. "Jackpot. I know what we're watching!" He holds up a tattered movie box. "*Hellraiser 3,* return of Pinhead…" He raises an eyebrow at Mary Carmen. "How do you even have this?"

She shakes her head and takes the box away from him. "I got them for the girls! Raymond in Pediatrics let me borrow them. They used to do a teen movie night in the ward—these were just sitting in a closet…" She looks down at the cover. "NO! This looks awful! " she cries, tossing it back to him. "Pick something nice!"

He laughs and sets it down on the table, riffling through the box. "I don't know, M.C.—Pinhead's gonna seem pretty tame compared to the rest of the stuff in here." He holds up a copy of *Silence of the Lambs*, and Jodie and I lose it. "Those kids were sick *and* twisted."

Mary Carmen flushes and shakes her head. She tears the movie out of his hands and shoves it back into the box. "All right, just forget it!" She slams the lid shut. "It was just supposed to be something nice for tonight, and I didn't get a chance to look through it to make sure…" She trails off, frowning.

Jodie and I stop laughing as she starts to cart the box out of the room. "Come on, Mary Carmen, don't go!" I call, reaching out and putting my hand on her arm. "It *is* nice; we're having a great time." Seeing Jodie nod in agreement, I add, "You got us all this food, bought new sleeping bags, let us use your house… That's really cool. Thank you."

Mary Carmen pauses and puts the box down. "It's just not every night that we have company…like *Jodie*," she murmurs intently, her red streak glaring back at me. I nod and lower my hand. "I wanted it to be, special for you." She shrugs.

Daniel moves over and picks up the box. "And it *is* special—Christa's special night." He smiles, taking the movies over to the couch. "Lemme take another gander at these."

Mary Carmen sighs and looks at me. "You're sure everything has been all right?" she asks under her breath. Her eyes dart over to Jodie, who has sat back down on the chair and is playing with her phone. "You know—normal?"

I chuckle. "Yes—very normal. And probably one of the best sleepovers I've ever had." I give her bare arm a gentle swipe with my finger. "My mom never went all out like you did."

She smiles and tilts her head. "I thought the movie candy was a nice touch. It was on sale at Rite Aid…"

We look over as Daniel clears his throat. "Okay, I think I've found the solution to our problem." He holds up a beat-up copy of *My Best Friend's Wedding*. "Found this little delinquent hanging out at the bottom of the box."

Mary Carmen smiles and takes the faded pink case. "And it's not scary or gory?" She looks up at him apprehensively.

He draws in a sharp breath. "Only if you count the horror of forced romantic chemistry and average movie reviews," he replies, his face molded into a terrified scream. "It's just too horrible! Look away! Look away!"

Mary Carmen grins and bats his knee. "Okay, put it on. Christa and Jodie have their sleeping bags on the floor, so I want *you* on the couch where I can keep an eye on you, mister."

She settles into her chair, and Jodie and I cuddle up in our sleeping bags as Daniel brings the VCR to life. "Strictly PG, Mary Carmen…like always," he mutters.

"I liked it!" Mary Carmen proclaims as the movie comes to an end. Jodie and I turn to her, both of us snugly cocooned in our sleeping bags. "I even liked the one with the teeth—"

"Julia Roberts," I quickly fill in. Jodie grins at me.

Mary Carmen nods. "Yes…I didn't care for her much in the beginning—such a selfish woman. But she became more agreeable as it went on… What do you think?" She blinks at us.

"I think 'agreeable' is one of the best adjectives ever used to describe Julia Roberts," I chuckle. "Let's check in with the peanut gallery: Daniel, did you find her 'agreeable'?"

I poke my nose over the coffee table. "Daniel?"

Mary Carmen presses her finger to her lips and gets out of her chair. "He's asleep," she whispers, stepping over to him. I wriggle out of my sleeping bag and join her. Sure enough, he's totally out, his mouth hanging slightly open with his arm draped over his face. I smile as he breathes out a quiet snore.

Mary Carmen shakes her head. "The only time he's innocent." She takes the checkered blanket from the end of the couch and drapes it over him, tucking it under his chin.

I raise my eyebrows at her. "You're going to let him stay?" I murmur.

She shrugs. "I don't think he'll get into any trouble." She looks at me over her glasses. "Besides, if I put him out now, he'd just go and lay down in the front garden, like he's done every night since you first came here."

My lips part, and I let out a little puff of air. She sighs and rubs my arm. "He's worried about you, that's all." She glances back at Daniel. "Wants to make sure you're safe."

"Safe from what?" Jodie asks from the floor. She looks up at us curiously.

I stare, wide eyed, as Mary Carmen clears her throat. "Oh, this and that." She puts her fist to her mouth and swallows a cough. "Christa's just been through so much these last few weeks, with her mother checking into rehab, moving out of her apartment..." She looks like she's about to gag, swallowing back all the stuff about Heaven, Hell, and Catalysts. "Lots of changes." She pats her chest and grimaces.

Jodie tilts her head. "I guess that makes sense." She grins up at me. "Or maybe he's just trying to get a little closer to a certain Ms. Nichols and her short shorts." She stretches over the coffee table and slaps the back of my leg playfully.

Mary Carmen glares at me. "He's just looking out for me," I say, recovering quickly. "You all have been. I don't know if I've had a chance to say thank you for everything... It really means a lot to have you on my team." I look down at the rug. "I don't think I could get through this without you." Truth.

I see Jodie's eyes crinkle as Mary Carmen takes my hands. "We're not going anywhere," she replies softly. She gives me a squeeze and lets go as I smile. "Anywhere except bed," she amends, letting out a large yawn. "I'm ready to turn in. You should do the same." She clambers to her feet and steps into the hall, then points back at Daniel. "I trust you girls will behave yourselves and let sleeping dogs lie."

I grin at him before shuffling back over to my sleeping bag. "Jodie packed a permanent marker in her with her stuff; I figured we'd draw on him a little before we call it a night." Jodie giggles, so I add, "Nothing too gross—maybe a hairy mustache or cat whiskers."

Mary Carmen rolls her eyes. "He'd probably like that, the odd bird." She taps the wall tiredly with her palm. "'Night."

"'Night," we chorus. I listen as her feet pad down the hall and wait for her door to close.

When it does, I turn and grin at Jodie. "Now we can get to the good stuff," I giggle, plopping back down on my sleeping bag.

Jodie gives a little laugh that turns into yawn. "If by 'good stuff,' you mean talking trash about everyone we know until we both fall asleep…then yeah, I'm totally in." She sighs and nestles into her pillow.

I snuggle up next to her. "That sounds about right, although I don't know how much good I'll be on the trash-talking front. I'm still feeling disconnected from everyone after what happened." I catch myself and clear my throat. "After I was suspended."

Jodie nods. "It's been pretty much same old, same old… The jocks are still the jocks, the nerds are still the nerds, Marcus Brady is still Marcus Brady." She rolls her eyes. "You've been back a couple weeks—you must have made at least one or two casual observations about our charming classmates."

I chuckle and scratch my ear. "I've mostly been trying to make up for the piss-poor job I've done the last—I dunno, three semesters." I cringe.

Jodie quirks her eyebrows. "I can tell. You've been going to study hours almost every day for the last month. Is it helping?"

I nod. "Mr. Trundi's been awesome. Along with the regular bio stuff, he's been tutoring me in math and English—he does a really sweet Shakespearian accent!"

Jodie laughs. "We'll find out if it's done any good once grades come out," I add with a sigh. "It's something to do, and I have to admit—I kind of like hanging out with him." And his classroom also happens to be a completely Demon-free zone, which doesn't hurt.

Jodie smiles. "Not exactly the juicy tidbits I was hoping for, but I'm glad to hear you're doing better." She lifts her arm and grabs the Gummy Bears from the coffee table.

I sit up and crinkle my nose. "I do have *some* insider information… Brit Cornell came storming into study hours last Wednesday, screaming at Trundi about how he has no right to give her a C- for the semester. She's been in emotional distress, and Schaffer has given all of the varsity athletes leniency." I scoff and twiddle with my sleeping bag zipper. "So full of shit."

Jodie's lips twist as she chews on a Gummy Bear. "They've all been a little on edge since Riley disappeared," she replies thoughtfully, looking down at the bag of candy. "Like they're all worried that they're going to be next."

I blow out my lips. "Whatever; he probably got pissed at his parents over something dumb and decided to drive his crap car down to Tijuana and get laid and wasted for Christmas. It's so typical Riley: he'll be back after New Year's, tan and bragging about all the raunchy sex he had." I snort. "He'll probably get crabs."

Jodie winces and smacks me lightly with her pillow. "Gross! I don't know, Christa… Don't you think it's a little weird that *no one* has heard from him?" She sits up and looks at me. "Not his family, or Coach Cryer, or anyone else from the team?"

I prop myself up with my elbow. "It's not like he can call his best friend anymore. I know if it were me, that'd be my first phone call." I stare at her sadly.

She wraps her arms around her knees. "Guess that's as good a reason as any to completely lose it and go off the grid for a while," she murmurs, tossing the candy back onto the table. "After what happened with Tom."

I exhale and suck my teeth, instantly clamming up. Jodie watches me, her eyes soft. "How are *you* doing with all that?" she whispers. "Have you talked to anyone around here about him?

Maybe Mary Carmen? She seems like someone who could handle it."

I frown. "She's been...great, surprisingly." Jodie grins at my admission, so I shrug. "I know, I know—I complain about her 24/7—but it's cool she lets me stay here, and she's been super helpful with my mom..."

"You're seeing her tomorrow, right?" Jodie asks.

I nod. "Yeah, that'll be a laugh riot: an hour of Julie Nichols baring her soul and sobbing on some ocean-view balcony... I could hardly understand her two weeks ago when I last went down."

Jodie furrows her brow. "But you need to talk about the accident and Tom. If not with your mom or Mary Carmen..."

I sigh. "There's not much to say. It was a bad accident, and he didn't make it. I did, and now I have to make the best of my second chance and not waste it." *Second chances...* I shiver, thinking about Alden as I lay on the floor of Level 3 at the Warehouse, unable to move after witnessing Daniel Alter. Who knows if I would have made it if Alden hadn't helped me...and he's *still* helping me with Mom's rehab bill. I bite my tongue bitterly. Even on the other side of the world, he's found a way to insert himself into my life.

Jodie watches me and sighs. "I know I'm not a doctor...yet." She chuckles quietly. "But that sounds a lot like survivor's guilt... If you're looking for a *Grey's Anatomy* diagnosis." She tilts her head. "You need to talk about it, Christa—what happened, how you're feeling. These kind of emotions can really mess with you."

I snicker and draw my knees to my chest. "Yeah, compounded with the massive amount of rage I'm still feeling about my dad, I'm just a ticking time bomb," I joke. Jodie opens her mouth to say something, but I hold my hand up. "I'm fine, J...really. You just said a few minutes ago that you were glad to hear I was doing better. Can we leave it at that?" First priority goes to figuring out what my role in the coming apocalypse is; after that, I can sort out my own issues. My mind flashes across the house to my bed, where the red and gold invitation from Mandisa sits crushed between my mattresses. Daniel may have RSVP-ed with a big fat NO, but part of me is still conflicted about attending. While I never want to go back to the Dark Side or even see another Demon again, I can't quiet the little voice in my head that keeps whispering, *'What if?'*

I look at down at my sleeping bag and smile tightly. Jodie narrows her eyes and glances back at Daniel. "Well, I just hope you're talking to *someone*, even if it's not me," she sniffs. "What's going on with you and him anyway? You guys were all over each other tonight." She arches a brow.

I laugh out loud and then cover my mouth quickly, not wanting to wake Daniel. "Nuh-uh! We were not 'all over each other.'" I snort. "We were just messing around, having a good time. That's all." I glance at him out of the corner of my eye.

Jodie notices and shakes her head. "Okay, that might work on someone who hasn't known you since before the time of braces and Tampax." She smirks at me through her glasses. "But you can't fool me, Christa. I know you've got it bad for this guy. And he so obviously has it bad for you, too… It's, like, completely hurting."

I sigh and take my ponytail out. "It's not like that, Jodie." *It can't be.* I look away sullenly, running my hand through my hair.

She tosses her head back and gnashes her teeth. "You've been saying that this whole time! I don't get it!" When I slap her knee, she lowers her voice. "If he were any other guy, you would have hooked up with him and been over it by now. What—does he only date blondes or something stupid like that?"

I give her a look. "No, just…" I sigh, exasperated. "It's just different with him. I can't explain it." I watch his chest rise and fall peacefully.

Jodie's eyes follow mine. "That seems to be a major theme tonight," she replies, her tone chilly. I reach out and touch her elbow, but she leans away and shakes her head. "No, it's fine… Have your secrets. I just think your new life and the people in it are very interesting."

"You have no idea," I grumble.

She tilts her head at Daniel and nods at his dirty Converse sneakers hanging off the other end of the couch. "Should we take his shoes off or something? Make him more comfortable?"

I snort and shake my head. "You don't want to be anywhere near West Hollywood when those things come off! Totally lethal." Standing up, I cross over to the floor lamp in the corner right next to Daniel's head. Reaching down, I gently shift his arm to his side and sweep his hair out of his face.

He seems to be lost in dreaming, his eyelashes fluttering ever-so-slightly. "Mary Carmen was right," I murmur. "He does look innocent."

Jodie sighs. "Completely obsessed. Why you're fighting it is beyond me," she grumbles, turning over in her sleeping bag. "You gonna get the light?"

I look up and nod. "Yeah." I switch off the lamp, Daniel now bathed in blue from the moonlight coming through the front window, which mingles with the soft glow from his Halo. I've started to notice that his light changes depending on his mood: bright gold when he's happy, almost a dull copper when he's angry or frustrated. Right now, he's in sleep mode, shining pale yellow. I look down at my own hands, wondering if I do the same thing. At any rate, we both make pretty good nightlights.

I sigh and move back over to Jodie. "I'm really glad you're here, J," I whisper as I get back into my sleeping bag.

I hear her smile in the dark. "Like you said, I'm on your team. Always have been, always will be." She reaches over and tugs my hair. "Even if you're in massive denial."

I roll my eyes and go to sleep.

CHAPTER 4
NEW YORK CITY—
SEPTEMBER, 1975

I EMERGE FROM the back office dressed in the black tuxedo Pascal gave me, the disgusted sneer on his face as he tossed it over the desk chair still burned in my brain. I believe his exact words as he stalked out of the room were, "We'll be watching, rat fetus." Such colorful use of the language, for a non-native speaker. As if I wasn't rattled enough on my own without the entire front-of-house staff waiting for me to fail.

I scrunch my shoulders uncomfortably, the starch in my shirt a little too strong, the jacket arms a little too short. As far as uniforms go, though, I've had worse. I step over to the long wooden bar and start in on my bowtie, fumbling with the knot as I try to secure it without a mirror.

Muriel, the French girl from earlier, stands behind the counter, restocking the lemon twists and maraschino cherries. She looks up at me with her dark eyes and watches me struggle. "Here," she sighs after a minute, motioning for me to come closer. "Let me help you." I nod at her gratefully and lean over the bar, her slender fingers folding the bow in a matter of seconds. She gives the ends a tight jerk and pats my shoulder. "Ready for battle," she murmurs, going back to her work.

I reach up and feel the knot at my throat, acknowledging her precision. "Thank you." I smile as she moves onto polishing the glassware, her hands working quickly with a dishrag. "Where did you learn to tie such a good knot? You spend some time at sea?"

She smiles briefly at my joke, not looking up from the cloth. "Hardly. I help my father get ready for work; he has bad arthritis." She nods over at the host's stand. "Francois."

I follow her gaze, remembering their familiarity during the tasting. "Yes... It seemed like you've both known Madame a very long time." I try to keep my tone neutral.

She looks back at me, a wine glass in hand, considering. "Our family knew hers back in France. My father worked at her restaurant in Toulouse, and when she opened this place here in New York, she asked him to come over and manage it. So here we are." She sets the glass aside and purses her lips. "She seemed very taken with you."

I feel my cheeks redden. "Well, to be fair, she seemed very taken with just about anybody in the room of the male persuasion." Again, Muriel lets a tight smile sneak through. I keep a straight face; any sort of positive reaction from this girl is a victory.

"She wasn't always like she is now, or so Papa tells me." Muriel looks up thoughtfully for a moment, before clearing her throat and spinning around to the back wall filled with bottles of hard liquor. "Sorry... It's really none of my business." Even when she's abrupt, the romance in her voice betrays her, marks her as impossibly French. She begins to meticulously check and turn out all the labels.

I lean against one of the bar stools. "You don't have to worry about me saying...anything to anyone," I scoff. "I don't know anyone to tell."

She looks at me out of the corner of her eye. "She's had a hard life, that's all. People here don't understand that." She straightens a bottle of Remy Martin and glances over her shoulder, her dark brown hair cascading down her back like Audrey Hepburn in *Gigi*. "How long have you been in the states? Your accent is still quite strong."

I exhale and grin at her stupidly. "Just arrived a few days ago, actually. I, um…I used to work on a cruise liner that did trips across the Atlantic. Decided it was time for a change." I bite my lower lip coyly, leaving out the part concerning my current immigration woes. "Why? Am I really that obvious?"

She doesn't answer. "Do you feel ready for service tonight?" she asks instead. "We usually have a pretty good crowd on Saturdays." She juts out her chin, her tone back to no-nonsense.

I straighten up and nod. "Yes, yes." I try to sound confident, but probably come off as foolhardy. "I mean…how hard can it be? Walk about, take the orders, tell the kitchen, bring the food out." I shrug, giving the bar a rap with my knuckles before running my finger along the rim of one of the wineglasses. "Simple."

Muriel winces and reaches for her dishrag again. "Just…um… try to come up with a system for yourself… Hit each table in succession—drinks, appetizers, main course, dessert. Keep checking in, and don't leave anyone out." I blush as she hastily polishes where my finger touched the glass. "The worst thing you can do as a waiter is disappear. Customers hate that." She sighs, scrunching her nose. "But don't be *too* present; you don't want to make them uncomfortable." She looks up at me and grimaces. "Just…be there the right amount."

I nod, my nerves creeping back again as I try to remember everything she just said in perfect detail. "System, drinks, check in, don't disappear, lurking's bad." I exhale, sinking down onto a stool. Muriel gives me an honest-to-God smile, one of her front canines slightly overlapping the tooth next to it. It's charming.

She looks past me and her smile is gone in a flash, replaced with an emotion I don't recognize as she ducks down and busies herself behind the bar. I turn and see Daniel walking over to us, his chef's jacket splattered in new gravy stains, his expression grim. "Hey." He sidles up next to me and rests his forearms on the bar, giving me a onceover before looking away to hide his eye roll. "Nice suit."

My face grows hot again, and I scratch the back of my neck. "Look," I mutter, "I had no idea this was going to happen…"

He waves me off coolly, still refusing to look in my direction. "Don't worry about it. You gotta do what's right for you, I get it." He straightens up as he breaks into a large grin, knocking 'Shave and a Haircut' against the bar. "Hey, Muriel!" he calls playfully.

She bounces back up, out of breath. "Daniel," she murmurs, tucking her hair behind her ears. I notice her fingers tremble as she reaches down to smooth her skirt. "Did…did you need something?" She stares at him intently.

He sighs and blows out his cheeks. "Chef needs the Rolodex… Has to call around to everyone and their mother to see if he can find two hundred lobsters for tonight." He looks at me irritably. "He's pretty pissed about what happened at Tasting."

I keep my eyes trained on the floor. "That's understandable," Muriel puts in, stepping over to the telephone. "Madame was not very kind to him." She pulls the Rolodex from the lower shelf and sets it on the bar.

Daniel snorts, flipping through the cards. "No, she was not." He arches a brow as he pulls one from the deck. "But Chef's tough. He's mad as hell right now, but he can take the heat. You know who *I* feel bad for right now? Trish and Amanda." He glances over at me. "The girls you got fired."

I balk at him, aghast. "Daniel!" Muriel exclaims. "That wasn't Alden's fault…"

I glower at the back wall, embarrassed that this beautiful girl feels the need to fight my battles for me. Daniel holds up his hands. "Sure, sure. I'm just saying that everyone had a good thing going, and all of that got blown to smithereens in a matter of minutes because Madame's got a crush." He shakes his head and lets out a low whistle. "Love makes you do crazy things." He holds up the Rolodex. "Thanks, Muriel. Good luck tonight, Irish—or should I say, pip pip, cheerio?"

As he walks back across the dining room, salutes, and opens the kitchen door with a swift kick, I clench my jaw so hard that I swear I can hear my teeth start to crack.

"Bye," Muriel sighs, her gaze lingering on his backside.

My scowl forgotten, I turn and gawk between her and the kitchen door. Noticing me staring, her eyes widen. "What?" she cries, tossing the dish towel at me.

I catch it and chuckle. "Nothing." I quirk my eyebrows. "That was…informative."

Muriel blushes. "Aren't you supposed to be practicing your English accent for tonight?! Surely you have something better to do than harass me!"

I laugh as she comes around the bar and shoos me off my stool. "Okay, okay!" I crow as she pokes me in the ribs, pushing me back towards the office. "Such a taskmaster!"

She glares at me sternly. "That's right. If you thought Chef was bad…" She stops and puts on a phony American accent. "Well, you ain't seen nothin' yet!"

*

"Jesus!" I curse under my breath as I slam a tray of on-the-rocks glasses down on the bar, my forehead dripping with sweat. I find a space in the crowd and squeeze next to a couple waiting for a table as they laugh and swing glasses of champagne around. Murmuring an apology, I catch Muriel's eye.

She looks up at me and arches a brow, holding her hand steady as she pours a finger of scotch that's probably worth more than my entire life. With a smile, she slides the glass in front of another patron and turns to me.

A flicker of concern crosses her face. "You look terrible," she mutters, grabbing a fresh towel from under the bar. "Here, clean yourself up."

I take the towel and run it across my forehead, letting out a little pant. "I have been running, literally *running*, for the last three hours," I breathe, tugging at my collar. "And this suit is murder!"

She tilts her head knowingly. "Just wait 'til the shows get out around 10; it's a marathon until close." She looks up and nods at a man across the bar who is tapping the side of his pint glass. "Are you using your system?"

I nod, then shake my head, sighing. "Yes... no."

Muriel stifles a giggle, moving back to the other side of the bar and stopping to light a customer's cigarette before grabbing the empty pint glass. "You're doing fine, really!" she calls as she refills the man's beer at the tap. "Just remember—'present, but not too present.'" She jerks her chin towards the dining room.

I grimace and step away from the bar. "Should've never left the kitchen..." I pace quickly back to my section, a sea of grumpy faces trying to catch my eye.

"Waiter, I had a question about the carrot soup..." an old lady who has something green stuck in her teeth at table 3 whines, trying to grab my jacket.

I glance at her and shake her off, still moving. "One minute, Madame..." I exhale and nod, muttering to myself. "System, system."

I step over to table 1 by the window: a single older man in what I can only guess is a very expensive suit, the lapels ironed perfectly and not a stitch out of line, his silvering blonde hair slicked back in an elegant widow's peak. He's been my easiest customer all night, content to spend the last hour or so drinking brandy, always very polite. I blink and compose myself. "Have you decided on dinner, sir?" I ask, smooth as silk—but scrambling inside to remember to keep my phony accent in place.

He looks up at me and nods, the corners of his blue eyes

crinkling. "I have. Think I'm going to try the quail tonight." He hands his menu back to me. "Is it any good?"

I picture Daniel swearing over the ovens. "Delicious, sir. Fantastic fall flavors. The mushrooms are from a farm in central Massachusetts," I reply brightly.

He nods, pleased with his choice. "Pretty country up there. Very good." He motions to his empty brandy glass. "I'll also have another Remy, if you don't mind." He says this without any hint of sarcasm, but I hurry to pick up the glass just the same.

"Of course, sir. I'll have that right back to you. Thank you." I give a short nod and hustle back to the bar, not saying anything to Muriel, just setting the glass down in front of her. When she nods, I march back to the kitchen, making sure the door closes firmly behind me before I call out to Chef. "Quail for table 1!" I shout loud and clear, not wanting to get reprimanded again for mumbling.

Chef looks up from the bright red lobster tail he's garnishing and nods. "Danny Boy! Fire another bird!" he yells over his shoulder. Pots and pans bang together, accompanied by a string of words you wouldn't hear in church. Juan Julio and Pedro glance at each other and chuckle, their hands never leaving their knives.

Chef nods back at me. "Order up on 4 when you come back," he grunts. "Right?" he calls to Daniel. "You got that filet ready?"

The sound of a heavy frying pan clattering against the floor echoes from the back. Chef furrows his brow. "What's goin' down, Danny? You sound like my Mama cookin' right now."

"Lucy's on fire again—I'm just trying—goddammit!" Daniel exclaims.

Chef sighs tiredly. "Pedro, get some wet towels and go help him—and turn on the fans! I do not want us to get backed up, gentleman! We're doing really well tonight..." He stops and jerks his jaw at me. "Get goin', Irish! We're good!"

I startle and rush out the door, dashing back to Muriel. Grabbing table 1's drink, I slow to a confident walk as I present it to him. "Here you are, sir," I purr. "And your dinner should be out shortly." I smile, remembering to elongate my vowels and not chew my Rs as I set his glass on the table.

The man's mouth twitches as he picks up the brandy. "Thank you." He gives me a light toast before turning his attention to the window, watching the city stroll by. I nod and spin back to the restaurant.

"Waiter, I really needed to ask you about the carrot soup..." the lady at table 3 snivels.

I hold up a finger calmly. "Yes, Madame—quite shortly..." System. I spin around to Table 2. A party of three that looks like a family just arrived and is still getting seated. Perfect timing. I step over and help an older woman who is wearing a floral-print polyester dress with her chair, gently pulling out the back for her.

She smiles and lets out a surprised little coo. "Oh! Thank you!" she exclaims, her hand fluttering to her neck. "That's so nice of you." And I know she means it.

"Of course, Madame." I smile, carefully laying her napkin across her lap. I glance up at the bald man across from her in a faded brown suit—her husband, I assume. His bushy mustache twitches with approval. He takes his own chair and starts looking over the menu. I step over to the pretty girl in a green silk dress and hold out her chair for her. She blushes behind a pair of black glasses—a popular style maybe fifteen years ago—and sits down, her thick curly red hair brushing my fingers as she settles against the seatback. My hand instantly feels like it's on fire, along with the rest of me. I take my time pushing her in.

"Thank you," she murmurs shyly, looking down at her menu. I watch her for a minute, taking in her smooth ivory skin and bright emerald eyes that match her dress. She looks like a fairytale princess. I can feel my palms starting to sweat as I glance down at the rest of her, her soft curves swelling over her neckline. She looks up and sees me staring and sinks down behind her menu, a fresh blush infusing her cheeks.

I clear my throat and take a step toward the man with the mustache, training my gaze on the table. "Good evening." It's my turn to blush as my voice cracks. I grimace as the girl bites her lip, hiding a smile. I cough and try again. "Good evening, and welcome to Chez Monique," I begin to recite the speech that Pascal begrudgingly taught me back in the office. "Are we celebrating tonight, and can I get you started with a cocktail?"

"Oh, yes!" the older woman chimes in, smiling happily. She reaches across the table and pats the pretty girl's bare arm. "We are definitely celebrating tonight! Tell him, Derald."

Derald, her husband, grins up at me as if he's about to burst with pride. "Tomorrow's my Jilly's first day at Columbia." He straightens his thick glasses and nods at the girl. "Freshman year, studio art. She's been drawing her whole life, before she could even talk! I always knew all that doodling in class would pay off."

The girl grows redder and redder by the second. "Okay, Dad..." She grimaces. "He doesn't want to hear all this."

Oh yes, I do. "You're an artist...Jilly?" I ask.

She looks at me for the first time tonight, with those vivid eyes, her skin flushed. "It's, um...it's actually Jillian," she whispers, shooting her dad a look. "And yeah—sort of." She shrugs. "I like to draw faces...uh, portraits, I guess." She smiles bashfully and tucks her hair back. "Just something I do."

Her dad beams. "She's so modest! She's a great student, too—best in her class!" He looks up at me, his tone grave. "They don't let just *anybody* into Columbia... It's an Ivy League school!"

I shake my head, confused. "He's not from here, Daddy," Jillian mumbles down at her lap. "He doesn't know what that means."

Derald nods at me knowingly, giving me a familiar tap on the elbow. "Don't worry about it. I didn't know much about it myself either when Jilly first told me she wanted to go there. Nobody *I* know ever went to *college*. Well..." He rests his hand on top of his wife's. "Alice here went to beauty school. That's how we met! She was filling in at the barber and gave me a cut and a shave!" His wife blushes and smiles. "And it was the closest one I've ever had," he teases, pretending to slice his neck with his finger.

"Dad…" Jillian rubs the bridge of her nose. "He just asked if we wanted drinks, not for our whole life story."

"Jillian, please." Derald holds out his hand. "He's interested. You're interested, right?"

He glances up at me, and I nod fervently.

"You know," Derald continues, "when Alice and I were coming up, everybody just hung around the neighborhood doing the same as the old man… I've been working in heating and cooling systems for the last 25 years!"

His wife nods in agreement. Derald pauses and grins at Jillian. "But times change! And for the better!" He offers his hand to Jillian. She rolls her eyes, but takes it, giving him a light squeeze. "My little girl's gonna make something of herself… She's going to be a big deal, you wait!" He stops and looks away. "Smarter than her old man, that's for sure," he croaks, his voice full of emotion.

Jillian tsks and leans into her father, smiling. "Hey, Daddy, you're gonna get me going…"

Derald turns back to her and grins. "Aw, you're right! We're here to celebrate!" He wipes his eyes and picks up his menu, looking at me. "I think some champagne is in order. Can you make a recommendation?"

I clear my throat and lean in, remembering what Muriel was serving at the bar. "The Bollinger is very nice…" I run my finger down the menu. "And of course there is Dom and Lanson, people like those…but I suppose the best would be the Moet." I point at the top of the list.

Derald's eyes go wide, and he coughs, his hand nervously reaching down to check his wallet in his trouser pocket. He grimaces and looks at the ladies. "The Bollinger sounds perfect." He smiles awkwardly. "Let's do three glasses."

I nod and step back. "Very good, sir. I'll have those right

out for you." I glance back at Jillian and see her eyes flicker away quickly, like maybe she was watching me, too. Hope wells in my stomach as I walk back to the bar.

Muriel smiles at me as I go around to the wine cellar, a converted storage closet that used to house horse-grooming tack when the building was first built as a hitch and drink establishment. There's still a lucky horseshoe nailed to the doorframe, but the walls are now lined with wine cubbies, storing well over 600 bottles. I start searching for the Bollinger and hear someone walk in behind me.

"Move it, dog shit," a familiar voice sneers. I sigh and turn to see Pascal, his face contorted in what I now believe is just his normal expression. "You're in my way."

I bite my tongue and step aside, making room in front of the champagne.

"Looks like you found your people out there," Pascal sniggers, his hand tracing up the wall. "The cheap family in the cheap clothes." He arches a brow. "Although maybe the redhead wouldn't be so bad if she lost that dress…"

My eyes narrow. "Shut your mouth, Pascal," I snap. "You don't know what you're talking about."

He lets out a cruel laugh. "Right. They'll probably order the special, skip dessert, and shortchange you on the tip," he sing-songs, reaching up to the top shelf. "Tough break for you." He starts to pull down a bottle of Moet.

"Actually, I need that." I hastily reach up and grab the Moet from him. "They're celebrating a special occasion."

Pascal balks. "That's a '64 Moet, turd!" he hisses. "There's no way they can afford that bottle!"

I shrug complacently. "What are you, their banker? Now *move*." He glares as I shove past him. "You're in *my* way."

I return to the table a moment later, three champagne flutes in one hand, the Moet in the other. I set the glasses down and present the bottle grandly.

"A gift from Madame when she heard about your special night!" I lie with a flourish.

All three of them look up, surprised. Derald turns the label towards him and lets out a whistle. "I dunno, this looks..." He eyes the bottle warily, shaking his head. "...like too much."

I peek at Jillian, whose mouth is drawn into a thin line. I feel my insides twist in knots. "Really, sir...it's on the house," I proclaim.

Derald still doesn't look convinced, but Alice gives a shrug and rests her hand on top of his. "It *is* Jilly's special night," she murmurs. "She's gonna be gone in the morning... Why not make it one to remember?" Alice looks up at me humbly. "And he did say it's a gift. It would be impolite to refuse..." She gives Derald a small smile.

He looks over at her and sighs. "All right." He waves at me and breaks into a grin. "Open 'er up!"

I nod, relieved, and wrap a napkin around the cork, watching Jillian out of the corner of my eye as I work it open, practically melting as she jumps and giggles when it goes *pop*. I force my hand to stop shaking as I pour and hand them each a glassful of bubbles, letting my fingers linger as I give Jillian hers. She glances up at me, her sweet pink lips breaking into a smile.

I step back as Derald holds his up to the chandelier. "To Jilly," he toasts, "my little girl... May the road rise up to meet you, may the wind be always at your back. We love you."

They're words that I've heard many times before, but never with this sense of nostalgia. I hold my breath as they all raise a glass and take a sip. "I'll, um...I'll give you a chance to look over the menu," I murmur, nodding as I turn away from the table. I see Jillian look up from her glass, her gaze following me.

I take a deep breath as I head back to the kitchen, picking up dinners for both table 4 and table 1. After dropping off 4, I carefully take the quail over to the man by the window. "Waiter…" the old lady at 3 breathes, begging for my attention. I smile kindly as I walk past.

I set the plate down in front of the gentleman at table 1 and take a step back. "The braised quail, sir," I present. "With an assortment of wild mushrooms and summer vegetables."

He looks down at his food and nods. "Very nice." He smiles, inhaling deeply. "Give my compliments to the boys in the back, will you?"

I nod and watch as he picks up his knife and fork. "Did you need anything else, sir?" I ask.

He takes his time cutting into the meat and savors his first bite. "No, I think I'm good." He closes his eyes and moans, satisfied. "Yes…very nice." He blots his mouth with his napkin and look up at me. "That was also a very nice bottle of champagne you brought those folks." He nods over to Jillian and her parents.

I blink, time stopping. "Yes…it was." I eye him cautiously.

He picks up his fork again, spearing a baby carrot. "Have you figured out how you're going to pay for it yet?" He doesn't look up as he pops the carrot into his mouth.

I don't answer, stunned. He takes another bite of the quail and looks up at me. "I know Madame doesn't give anything away 'on the house.'" He smiles. "And I also have it on personal authority that she spends every Saturday down at Elaine's holding court, so she's not even here to be such a generous host." He stares at me, his blue eyes not so jolly anymore.

I let out a heavy sigh. "I *will* pay for it…once I get my first paycheck," I reply. And it's the truth—while I hadn't really spent a whole lot of time planning out my large gesture, I did fully intend to pay back the restaurant once I had a little extra cash in my pocket. And I was definitely counting on the grace of no one noticing that the bottle was missing, least of all another customer. Although, now that I stop and think it through, Pascal *did* see me take it and will probably be checking the books personally tonight. My stomach sinks into my shoes as I exhale, the giant chandelier starting to spin.

The man watches as my face turns green. "It's gonna take more than a couple weeks to pay *that* off," he chuckles, mashing a bit of mushroom with his knife. "But you must of had a really good reason for making the switch…" His eyes drift over to Jillian, laughing at something her father said.

I follow his gaze before looking down at the floor. "Please… please don't say anything," I mutter. "I promise I will pay back every penny."

The man puts down his knife and looks at me. "I'll do you one better." He picks up his brandy. "Put it on my tab."

I jerk my head back and stare at him. "Sir," I rasp, my tone low. "I…I can't let you do that…"

He waves me off as he takes a sip of brandy. "It's Callaghan. John Callaghan. What do they call you?" he asks with a grin.

"Alden Murphy, sir." I sigh and shift uncomfortably, already feeling in debt after Mr. Burman. Owing one American is enough. "I don't like to borrow money…"

He leans forward conspiratorially. "I'm not loaning any to you. We were all young once, Mr. Murphy." He sighs and sits back. "And we all get old, if we're lucky. Please." He smiles sadly. "Offer me the same kindness that you did for yourself a while ago and let me do a good deed. It would be the perfect end to this perfect day for you to allow me to pay for that very expensive bottle of Moet."

I find myself chuckling along with him as I glance between him and Jillian. I exhale. "All right, yes. Thank you."

He grins, toasting me with his brandy. "My pleasure. Just make sure you get that girl's number." His eyes dance across to the other tables. He stops and points with his glass. "But first, I think you've got your hands full with her… Looks like some sort of allergic reaction."

I turn and see who he's pointing to, my eyes going wide. The old lady at table 3 is grasping her throat like she's choking, spittle-covered wheezes escaping her mouth.

"Christ!" I hiss, springing into action. "Goddamn carrot soup!"

*

"That was lovely," Alice breathes, settling into her chair. Jillian nods as she pokes a spoon around the edges of her lemon meringue pie. I furrow my brow and step over to clear her plate. She hasn't eaten much of anything tonight...not that I'm watching.

"Was everything all right with your dinner this evening, Miss?" I whisper in her ear. I desperately want to say her name, but I remember my place this time.

I hear her breath catch. "Yes, fine," she replies with a tight smile. "Thank you."

I pick up the dessert and stare down at the table, hiding my frown. Ever since the champagne, she's been increasingly more reserved, stopping mid-sentence whenever I come to the table, silent except for when she told me what she wanted to eat or offered a polite thank you. I sigh and glance back at table 1; Mr. Callaghan is gone for the evening, but won't he be disappointed to hear about the outcome of all this...my moment quickly slipping away, becoming just another missed opportunity.

Jillian's parents burst into a fit of giggles and hold hands. I stop and watch them laughing together. At least someone's enjoying themselves.

"Just the check," Derald calls as they settle down. "Thank you again for such a wonderful night." They both grin up at me.

I put on a smile and nod. "Of course, sir, right away..." I can practically hear my heart shattering into a million pieces.

I clear away the rest of the plates and reach to pick up one of the champagne flutes. Instead, though, my hand knocks clumsily into it and sends a spray of cold champagne all over Jillian.

"Oh—oh my God…" I sputter as she gasps and raises her hands in alarm.

The rest of the table reacts quickly. "Jillian, your dress!" her mother cries, searching around for a napkin. "Quick, Derald! Before it stains…" Derald hastily tosses her his napkin, and she leans in to blot Jillian's lap.

"Please, please…everyone, stop!" Jillian exclaims, her cheeks burning red. "I'm fine…really! Just…" She clenches her jaw and stares down at the table. "I just need a chance to clean up."

I nod and set down my armload of dirty dishes as she picks up her purse from the floor. "The ladies' room is right this way. I can show you…" I motion towards the front.

She grimaces and pushes back from the table, careful to avoid touching me as she stands. She glumly follows as I lead the way to the toilets. "I am so sorry," I say with a cringe, craning my neck back to check on her. "I feel like a prize idiot knocking that drink into you. Is there anything I can do—?"

"No, no—I'm fine, *really*." She bites her lip like she's trying to hold back from crying. "It's not like this night could get any worse." We stop in front of the ladies' room door.

I stare at her, concerned. "What do you mean? This is supposed to be your big night." I shake my head. "Did I do…was something…wrong?" That's it, it's over. She saw right through me and thinks I'm a total fool. Classic.

She scoffs, a single, crystalline tear rolling down her cheek. "Of course not—you're…*perfect!*" she exclaims, flustered. "No… Just between my father trying to be something he's not and the horrid scene Mother just threw over my dress…and me, barely able to even *speak* to you." She blushes again, lowering her voice to a mumble. "What you must think of us—we're just…the most ridiculous people." She grasps her purse in front of her, tears spilling from her eyes in earnest now.

I fight the urge to pull her into my arms, tucking my hands under my elbows to avoid temptation. "Jillian," I breathe, leaning in closer. I can smell her scent from here, sweet and cloying like honey. "I don't think that at all! I think...I think you're lovely." I flush at my honesty.

She stares up at me, her eyes glistening. "Please, just stop being so nice," she begs, choking back a sob. "You don't have to pretend anymore." She shakes her head and pushes open the restroom door.

"Jillian—wait!" I slam my hand against the frosted window, holding it open as she rushes inside. Another woman comes round the corner and gives a little squeal. I hastily step back, looking up across the way to see Muriel glaring at me from behind the bar, mouthing '*What are you doing?!*' I must look like a complete scoundrel, loitering by the ladies' room.

I sigh and slink back to the kitchen, silently cursing rule one of my system—no lurking. With a final defeated glance back at table 2, I let the door swish closed behind me.

The guys are already sitting around out in the alley, toasting each other with smokes and freshly cracked beers for a service well done. I hang back in the doorway, feeling like I'm invading some sort of fraternal order, but the desire to avoid my own designated turf wins. Muriel kindly agreed to deliver the rest of my checks, promising she'd make sure I got all my tips. I puff out my cheeks and look at where Chef is perched on an empty milk crate, taking a long drag off his cigarette.

He motions to Daniel, leaning on the opposite wall. "I gotta give it to you, Danny Boy, you really pulled it together tonight," he remarks smoothly. "I thought you'd have a nervous breakdown or something, having to deal with all that meat, but you proved me wrong." He glares up at him. "And you know that doesn't happen often."

Daniel grins and pops off the brick, cigarette in hand, strutting to the middle of the alley. I can't help but scoff: he looks like a dragon with smoke curling around his hair—a dragon who is quite pleased with himself.

"I told you I was ready, Chef!" he exclaims, letting his cigarette hang off his lip. "Throw whatever at me...I'm like a ninja, ready to pounce!" Juan Julio and Pedro start laughing as he jumps up with both feet, his long, lanky legs catching underneath his chef's coat. He stumbles and starts laughing with everyone else.

Chef rolls his eyes. "We'll see if you feel so enthusiastic tomorrow morning," he chides. "You know you have market duty."

Daniel sighs and nods. "Yeah yeah, like you'd let me forget." He stops and looks up at me. "How'd it go on the outside, Irish? Rub some elbows with the rich and famous?"

I look down at the pavement. "Not so much," I mutter. "It was kind of a nightmare."

Daniel arches a brow, content with my answer. "Well, have a beer, forget about it!" He motions to Juan Julio, who tosses him a bottle. He steps over and removes the cap, handing it to me. "Take some time to lick your wounds before it starts all over again tomorrow."

Surprised by his peace offering, I nod and lift the bottle to my chin, not wanting to reveal in front of everyone that I don't drink. "Sure, yeah...thanks." I press the beer to my closed mouth, not letting a drop pass my lips. Daniel nods and meanders back over to Chef. Once his back is turned, I tilt my bottle behind me, letting it run off into the alley.

"All right, boys...Juan and Pedro are on cleanup, and I am going home to Song-Yi." Chef gets to his feet and stretches. "Gonna eat *my* dinner and try to forget about all you fools for a while." He pitches what's left of his smoke to the ground and stubs it out with his shoe. "Good fight and good night." He nods and starts walking down the alleyway.

Daniel unbuttons his chef's jacket and wads it up, tossing it to Juan Julio. "I'm takin' off, too... Got a thing with a Puerto Rican girl tonight." He leers at the guys, who nod knowingly,

Pedro sniggering behind his beer. Daniel jerks his chin at me. "You good, Irish?"

I shrug, not sure what he's implying. Something tells me he's not asking for a third wheel on his date. "Yeah, really good," I lie.

He blinks and then breaks into a grin, moving down the alley. "Well then...*good!* We're all good." He gives a wave and disappears around the corner.

I exhale and watch Juan Julio and Pedro get up to toss their beers, not saying anything as they step past me into the kitchen. I slowly follow and watch them attack the piles of dirty dishes and filthy stovetops, the kitchen quickly returning to its earlier state of aged cleanliness.

I hover by the back door as they scrub away, clearing my throat loudly. "Goodnight!" I shout, holding my hand up. Juan Julio glances at me and nods, bowing his head back down to his work. I wait for both of them to be looking away before I dart into the dark produce closet.

Holding my breath, I sneak between sacks of rutabagas and onions, finding a hidden corner by a large bag of dried chickpeas. I listen to the muted sounds of fast-paced Spanish and clinking glassware. Finally, I hear them put on their coats and open the backdoor, shutting the lights off behind them. Exhaling deeply, I finally rest my head back on the wall, the soft thrum of the ventilation fans running behind my ears. I give the bag of beans next to me a soft punch, creating a makeshift pillow.

"Beats the toilets at Port Authority..." I murmur, settling in. I'm still wearing my tux from earlier, so I wrap the jacket tightly around myself, feeling suddenly colder as my muscles relax and exhaustion sets in. The last thing I see before being taken over by sleep is Jillian, her bright red hair flashing behind my closed eyes.

CHAPTER 5

LOS ANGELES—PRESENT DAY

"ALL RIGHT, EVERYONE! I think that's where we're gonna wrap up for today." Mary Carmen claps her hands and stands, the rest of us following by climbing off our floor pillows. "Seth, can you please collect the packets and hand out those little bags I put on the back table? There's one there for you, too."

Seth nods and dashes over to the back table with the type of enthusiasm that is usually reserved for competitive cheerleading. Grabbing six little red and green gift bags, he scurries around the circle to hand them out one at a time.

Out of breath, he finally takes my packet and hands me a bag. "Happy Holidays, Christa," he effuses. "Hope it's a magical one!" He smiles with his crooked teeth.

I nod and gesture with the bag. "Thanks, Seth. You too."

He practically squeals as he steps over to Livie and presents her with her gift. She turns and grins at me, shaking the bag. "What do you think it is?"

I look at the gift and consider. "Too small for a chainsaw; I'm gonna go with dead batteries or dismembered baby doll parts."

Livie laughs. "You are so weird." Michela scoffs from my

other side, rolling her heavily made-up eyes and crossing her arms sullenly.

I shake my head. "That was just for you, Wednesday Addams! Come on, where's your Christmas spirit?" I bat her lightly on the arm.

She clenches her jaw. "Whatever. The best part about Christmas is that I don't have to see you losers for a whole two weeks. Best. Gift. Ever." She smooths her midnight black extensions over her shoulders.

I shrug and look back at Livie. "Easy to please. I wish everyone on my list was as simple to shop for." I arch a brow. "What are your plans for break? Going anywhere?"

Live shakes her head. "We *were* planning on going back to my grandma's in Gatlinburg, but it looks like my Dad's gonna have to work... So we're stayin' put." The corners of her mouth curl. "Which I am totally okay with, cuz that means I get to spend more time with Brennan." She purses her lips and looks at me coquettishly.

I grin and lean toward her. "That is the second time I've heard you mention this guy. Is it getting serious?"

Livie scrunches her shoulders. "We only just met a few weeks ago—but yeah, I guess so..." She clears her throat, her cheeks tight from smiling. "I mean, don't get the wrong idea! It's all still *very* tame." She presses up to my shoulder and murmurs in my ear. "He's a total gentleman...not that I want him to be—SO FINE!" When I chuckle, she adds, "We just had our first kiss a few nights ago, and oh my God, Christa—I swear I saw stars!" She grips my wrist excitedly. "I dunno—I feel like this could be something really special, you know? I don't want to rush anything...but right now, I feel like we're both just stuck in limbo, waiting for something to happen. You know what I mean?" She runs a hand through her blonde hair.

I nod and look down at the floor. I do know what she means—all too well. "Yeah, I get that." I smile weakly. "I'm really happy for you, Livie. Sounds like you've found a good one. You deserve it."

She squeezes my hand one more time, but Mary Carmen calls us to attention before either of us can add anything more. "Well, don't just stand there," the Seraphim laughs, motioning to our gift bags. "Open them!"

We all start to unwrap our presents. I pull out a tightly bound wad of green tissue paper.

"I know some of you might not celebrate the coming holiday—" Mary Carmen looks on as Jackson tugs at the tape around his gift. "—but I just wanted you to have a little something to remember our group by, especially with such a long break coming up!"

Jackson frowns, having freed his present from the paper. "It's a bell," he states plainly, holding it up in front of his face. I finish unwrapping mine and do the same, looping the ornament string around my finger. Indeed, it is a small, silver bell. When I flick my nail against it, it chimes brightly, my nose distorted in its polished reflection.

Mary Carmen smiles. "Yes! You can hang it on your tree or in your car...wherever you might need a little reminder of your friends back here." She glances at me warmly.

"Wait—I get it! Just like in *Miracle on 34th Street*..." Livie beams. "At the end where the little girl says—wait, how does it go?"

Michela sighs. "Oh my God, get your Christmas movies straight," she sneers. "It's from *It's a Wonderful Life,* and the line is—" She wrinkles her nose. "'Teacher says every time a bell rings, an Angel gets his wings.' Don't you know anything?" She shakes her head.

I smirk at Mary Carmen. *Really?* I mouth. She shrugs and smiles, a little blush creeping across her cheeks. "Anyway, I hope you like them and that you all have a safe and wonderful break spending time with your friends and family," she exclaims, holding out her arms. "We'll see you in two weeks! You are dismissed."

Livie smiles and pulls me into a hug. "Merry Christmas, Christa! Maybe I'll see you over break?" She pulls back and looks at me hopefully.

I grin. "Sure. We could do coffee or something." I arch my eyebrows. "You could bring Brennan."

Livie bites her tongue. "*You* could bring that cute boy that brings you to class all the time...Daniel, right?" She squats and picks up her coat from the floor. "The one you met the night of your crash?"

I nod. "Yeah, that's Daniel. And I'm sure he'd like that." Any excuse to hang out with my Human friends.

Livie shrugs into her coat, pleased. "Awesome! You got my number?" I nod. "Good—it's a date then...a double date." She grins.

I grimace. "Yep, you got it." I see Mary Carmen motioning to me from across the room. "That's my cue—merry Christmas, Livie."

She bumps me with her shoulder as she turns toward the door. "Merry Christmas, Christa... Don't do anything I wouldn't do," she drawls.

I give her a wave, swinging my leather jacket over my shoulder. "You got it."

Spinning around, I come face to face with Unabomber, his blue sweatshirt hood pulled tight over his head. "Oh, sorry... didn't see you there." I attempt to step past him, but he tries to do the same thing at the same time and awkwardly steps in front of me again. He glares down at the floor, his blue eyes panicked.

Quickly wiping the exasperated expression off my face, I take hold of his shoulders. "Okay, just stay there," I say, shifting over to his left and moving past him. "There we go."

He looks up at me, his stare so intense that for a minute, I wonder if he…never mind. "Merry Christmas, Christa," he mumbles, pulling his hood down further.

I startle—it's strange to hear him say my name. "Merry Christmas…Bryan," I manage. I shake my head as he trips to the door, almost running into the wall.

Mary Carmen is just finishing packing things up with Seth. "You ready to go?" she asks, looking up at me as she sets our reading packets inside a large red tote. "I think if we just grab something to eat on the road, we'll beat traffic. You okay with that?"

I shrug, pulling on my jacket. "Sure…it's going to take forever, no matter how we do it." I've been dreading this trip down to Del Mar extra all through class, since this is the first time Daniel hasn't accompanied us. He was out bright and early this morning saying he had 'things to do'…whatever that means. It'll just be me, Mary Carmen, and the open road today.

Mary Carmen sighs and chucks me on the arm. "Hey, don't look so sour! I'll give you full control of the radio." She grins. "Maybe you'll get lucky and find a station that isn't playing Christmas music right now."

I roll my eyes. "That's overly optimistic, even for you, Mary Carmen," I reply dejectedly. "Let's just get this over with."

She chuckles. "Such holiday cheer! Try not to oversell it… You're putting the candy stripers down the hall to shame." She winks, leading me out the door.

*

The Transitions Healing and Recovery Center sits atop a quiet cliff overlooking the ocean, its smooth, white stucco walls making it look more like a seashell jutting out of the sand than a place where addicts come to dry out. That's probably intentional, given the messy business going on inside. I get out of the car and slam my door, Mary Carmen following suite.

"Do you want your coat? You might get cold…" she calls from across the car's roof.

I look out at the water. "I dunno… Should be fine."

She sighs and reaches back inside, pulling my jacket out and tossing it to me. "You'll be happy you have it!" she exclaims when I roll my eyes, locking the doors. I tuck the jacket under my arm and start moving toward the front entrance.

"Hey," Mary Carmen murmurs, patting my shoulder. "What's going on? You were quiet the whole way down."

I shrug. "It's just…weird, seeing *her*…here." I jerk my chin at the building.

Mary Carmen follows my gaze. "Christa, I can assure you, this is one of the best facilities in the country—she's being well taken care of—"

I shake my head. "No, I know that. Every time we come, the people are super nice, and it *is* beautiful." I sigh. "I just never know what I'm supposed to say—or if I'm even allowed to touch her, hug her…"

Mary Carmen stops me with a hand on my the elbow. "Of course you can touch her. She's your mother." She watches me kindly. "She is so happy to see you any time you come. There's no right way for you to be or anything you need to say. Just be yourself—her daughter." She nods. "And she *is* getting better. Whenever I talk to her, she's stronger." She tugs me forward, and we slowly meander toward the doors. "Let her speak to you; all you have to do is listen and be open." She rings the front buzzer.

"Easier said than done," I mumble. "I wish Daniel was here."

Mary Carmen sighs again as a pleasant voice comes on over the intercom. "How can I help you?"

Mary Carmen pushes the reply button. "We're here to visit a patient, Julie Nichols? This is her daughter, Christa Nichols, and Mary Carmen."

"Ah! Mary Carmen!" the voice answers cheerfully. "Come on in!" The main lock clicks, and we go inside.

We stop at the front desk where Debbie, the usual attendant, is waiting to greet us. She smiles at us from behind her computer, a happy Rudolph blinking up from her red sweater. "Hi, guys! Good to see you again!" She grins, her plump cheeks bright. I nod, trying not to stare at the flashing nose on her matronly chest. "Hope the traffic wasn't too rough…"

Mary Carmen shakes her head. "No, it was fine… We made good time." She looks over at me. I shrug and look hesitantly down the hall.

"Your mom should be ready for you," Debbie says, holding out a candy tray. "Butterscotch?" She sets it in front of Mary Carmen.

"Oh, no thank you." Mary Carmen puts her hand on my back. "You okay?"

I nod. "Sure." I smile back at Debbie. "I'll take one, thanks." She grins as I take a candy and tuck it into my coat pocket.

"I just love your dress, Mary Carmen! You always look like such a star when you come in here—you show those celebrities upstairs how it's done!" Debbie crinkles her nose.

Mary Carmen blushes. "Oh, I just threw it on for workshop today. I like your sweater…" She clears some phlegm from her throat.

Debbie beams. "Thanks! The nurses got it for me. I think they said it would work for one of those, whatdya call 'em…ugly sweater parties?" She snorts. "I said— 'What are you talkin' about? It's adorable!' Practically worn it every day since." She laughs, glancing over at me. "You can go on through, hon."

I nod and walk down the hall.

Someone, I can guess who, has taken the liberty of fully decking out the front reception room in floor-to-ceiling Christmas decorations, the minimalist seascape design and beige tile now looking like an elf vomited glitter all over it. The large bay windows and couches are still the same, and I see my mother sitting in an overstuffed chair by the window, watching the waves through the glass. I cough.

She turns and looks at me. "Christa, hi…" she breathes,

standing up quickly. I glance at her and nod, gripping my jacket in my hands. Mary Carmen was right: she does seem stronger, her red hair more vibrant and color returning to her cheeks. She wears a clean pair of soft gray sweatpants and a chunky white cable-knit sweater. It's the best I've seen her look in years.

"Hi, Mom," I reply quietly.

She tugs at the sides of her sweater. "You look pretty," she murmurs, taking a few steps closer, pointing to my shirt. "Seasonal."

I look down and remember that I wore an evergreen long-sleeve t-shirt today. I cross my arms. "Happy accident," I mutter.

She nods and scratches the back of her neck. We stare at each other awkwardly for what feels like an eternity before she opens her mouth. "I'm happy you—"

She stops as Mary Carmen walks briskly into the hall, her heels clacking noisily.

"Good to see you, Julie. Merry Christmas!" she interrupts.

Mom grimaces. "You too, Mary Carmen. Thanks for coming." She takes a breath and leans against one of the couches.

Mary Carmen turns to me, realization crossing her face. I shrug. "It's fine," I whisper.

Mary Carmen clears her throat and smiles, motioning around the room. "I love all the decorations!" she exclaims.

Mom nods, not taking her eyes off of me. "They went a little over the top, but it's nice." She wets her lips. "Did you guys get to eat? I think there are some leftover sandwiches from lunch, if you're hungry…"

I shake my head. "We ate in the car," I answer dully.

As Mom looks down at the floor, Mary Carmen furrows her brow. "How about I give you two some time to catch up?" she says a little too boisterously. "Debbie had some paperwork she needed me to go over." I glare at her as she squeezes my shoulder before walking back to the main desk.

When we're alone again, Mom wrings her hands. "I think the balcony is free; everyone else is in Group right now." She gestures to the set of French doors at the other end of the room. "If that was okay last time…"

I sigh and nod. "Works for me."

As I follow Mom, I notice that she's shuffling across the floor in a pair of snuggly white slippers. They're something she would have totally worn around the house before, but I know they're required here, as the patients aren't allowed shoelaces, cords, wire, sharp implements, or anything else that they could use to hurt themselves or others. I cringe as she holds open the door.

We walk out to the balcony. "Kind of cool today, brisk…" Mom wraps her arms around herself and motions to two chairs by the ledge. "Those good?"

I nod and move over to one, shrugging into my coat as I sit. I'm not going to dwell too much on the fact that Mary Carmen was right about the weather.

Mom exhales and sits down across from me. "Your other friend didn't come today—Daniel." She gives a small smile.

I raise my eyebrows. "Yeah, he had stuff to do—errands, I guess." I squint up at her. "I'm sure he'll come down for the next one."

She nods. "I'm glad you have such a good support system while I'm…here." She clears her throat. "I wouldn't be able to do all this if I thought you weren't okay back home." She looks up at me. "You *are* okay, right?"

I shrug. "Sure, never better. Though Mary Carmen's pretty strict, which is…different. Chores, curfew, all that good stuff—but she buys groceries and doesn't forget to pay the power bill, so there's a silver lining." I bite my tongue when my tone comes out harsher than I intended.

I watch Mom's face collapse, before she quickly collects herself again. "I…I can't begin to express how grateful I am…" She grimaces as her voice cracks. "…how grateful I am to Mary Carmen. How she got me in here—I still don't know how any of this is possible…who's paying for all this…"

I tense, the wind whipping hair in my face. "Miracles do happen." I cross my arms. "I'm sure there's some old rich guy out there who gets his jollies doing nice things for poor people...philanthropy, or whatever." Or a deranged Demon who's only goal in life is to have complete control over me. Kind of the same thing, I guess.

Mom shrugs, an attempt at being lighthearted. "Yeah, maybe." She sighs. "You know, she calls me every day at 2 o'clock."

I raise my eyebrows, surprised. Mom nods. "Mary Carmen. She tells me how you are, how school's going, your friends." She stares at her lap. "She's a godsend."

Tears well behind my eyelids as I swallow back a bitter laugh. "Funny choice of words," I murmur. "Probably just wanna keep that between you and me; it might go to her head."

She chuckles and shakes her head. "I doubt it." Nervously, she reaches over and tucks my hair behind my ear. My breath catches in my throat.

"I can't get over how great you look. So grown up." She smiles.

I wrinkle my nose. "You saw me like, two weeks ago. How different could I be?" I look down at my hands.

She sits back in her seat. "Feels longer here," she murmurs, pressing her fingers between her knees. "I know it might be hard to believe, but it's—" She twists her mouth. "It's...difficult to be away from you, for me."

I flush and look out at the waves, the water and the sky awash in the same shade of gray. "Didn't seem that hard before," I mutter.

"What?" she whispers, leaning in.

I sigh and shake my head. "Nothing. How is...everything going?" I ask distantly.

She takes a breath and tilts her chin, resting her elbows on the chair arms. "Better. The shakes in the morning have stopped, and I don't want the stuff anymore—like, physically." She tightens her knuckles. "Dr. Herschel said that once I got over that hurdle, recovery would take a real turn for the positive."

I stare at her. "Has it?"

She smiles and sighs. "Yeah, I think so. I'm not going to lie: there are still a lot of bad days, but I'm starting to get a couple of...*okay* ones in there, too." She pulls her hair over her shoulder and begins to braid, an old habit.

I squint out at the ocean. "So that means you'll be coming home soon," I state, trying to keep any bias out of my voice.

Mom takes a breath. "I don't know." She lets her hands flutter back to her lap. "I'm just starting to make a breakthrough in my sessions; there's a lot to cover, from before..." She fades off, her eyes searching my face. "Tell me what you're thinking, Christa. Do you want me to come home?"

I exhale and stand, facing the water. "How can you ask me that?" I lean against the railing to avoid her gaze.

She coughs and pulls her knees to her chest. "There's just so much that we haven't talked about, with what happened..."

I roll my eyes. "You were kidnapped by a madman, we found you and took you to the hospital; that's it," I bark into the wind, trying to sound convincing. "He's been dealt with, and you're safe and getting better... That's all you have to worry about."

She grabs the back of her neck. "That's not even what I was..." She breathes loudly and stretches back out. "Yes, that night was horrible, and I don't even remember all of it—just...bits and pieces that flash in and out." She bites her lip and looks up at me. "But I do remember that he was *nice*, when he first came to the apartment—and he told me he could make everything better... for *you*." Her hands shake. "And I don't know if I was just too drunk or high to make sense of it. But—" She bows her head. "I *believed* him. I did, Christa." She reaches up and wipes under her lower eyelid with the heel of her hand. "And I'm ashamed to say it, but I thought everything would be okay after that. All the awful mistakes I'd made, how I'd royally screwed up both our lives." She shrugs. "I thought that would all be gone, that I'd make this one sacrifice and you'd be all right—great, even. Have the life you were always supposed to have." She scowls. "I could finally do something a…real mother would have done."

I hold my breath as she looks down at the floor, whispering, "Stupid," to herself.

Softening, I take a step toward her. "Hey, Mom…" I stop when I get about half a foot away from her, not ready to go any closer. "Come on, don't talk like that. You can't…blame yourself for what happened with…*him*." I know better than anyone how manipulative Alden can be. "He got you when you were fragile and said some stuff that he knew you wanted to hear. It could happen to anyone."

She looks up at me, the pale skin around her bright blue eyes blotchy. She's beautiful. "It wouldn't happen to you," she rasps.

I snort and jerk my chin. "Yeah, don't be so sure about that." I turn back toward the view and bite the inside of my cheek. "I have my moments of weakness, just like everybody else."

She shakes her head. "No…you're strong, always have been." She smiles. "And you don't get that from me."

I feel my back go rigid. "Can't we just…talk about what we want from Christmas and if I'm ready for Finals?" I clench my jaw. "Do we really need to go there?"

Mom blinks and sits up straight. "What would you like for Christmas, Christa?" she whispers.

I slam my hand against the cold metal railing. "Don't—don't do that! I know that voice!" I tug at my hair, spinning back to her. "You know what I really want? Some fucking peace and quiet. Think you can manage that?"

I look over at Mom, expecting her to go off on me for talking back—but she just watches me, her eyes sad. I sigh. "I'm sorry…I shouldn't yell at you. It's not right." I hang my head and rub the bridge of my nose.

She slowly tucks her hair back. "It's okay," she replies after a minute. "I know you have a lot of…anger…about what happened."

I scoff. "Would everyone *please* stop talking about my anger issues? You all make it sound like I'm stomping around kicking puppies and going off on old people. I'm fine." I cross my arms irritably.

Mom pauses, searching for the right words. "I only bring it up because of what I've learned here," she murmurs. "Anger is a gateway emotion… It's the one that usually precedes everything else."

I laugh. "So it's like the marijuana of feelings?" I roll my eyes. "Yeah, okay."

"It's a cover up for sadness, shame, fear, grief." She looks at me intently. "The big stuff we don't want to deal with."

I nod. "So what? You want me to say that I hate what you did to him? What you did to all of us?" I white-knuckle the railing. "Yeah, you wrecked our family—like, tore it apart—and that makes me *angry*." The words taste like poison in my mouth. "And what I really want to know is, was it worth it? Whatever you had with that guy?" I glare at her.

Her face tightens. "Not for a second," she rasps. "I regret it every day. It's a choice that has haunted me."

I shake my head. "Good, you *should* feel horrible." I open my mouth to say more, but the words don't come.

Mom clears her throat. "But a big part of my work here is separating what I am responsible for and what is completely out of my control." She takes a deep breath. "I didn't kill Daddy, Christa. My actions didn't bring his plane down. I'm not going to blame myself for that anymore." My throat wells up and I scrunch my face, knowing more about *that* truth than I'd like to…again, thanks to Alden.

"He would have never been on that plane if it wasn't for you!" I cry, whirling around. "If you had never cheated on him, he would have been home, with me…with you!" I wave my arms wildly. "And you just threw it all away, and for what? A little attention? Some sex?"

She winces and shakes her head. "Like I've said a million times—or *tried* to say," she stammers, "it was a *mistake*. I'm not perfect, Christa."

"Yeah, no kidding," I spit.

She closes her eyes and nods. "I was lonely," she mutters. "Your dad was traveling all the time, and I was left behind raising a child by myself in that huge house." She bites her lip. "There was so much you didn't see. You couldn't—you were so young…"

I dig my nails into my palms. "Don't you dare make excuses to me!" I sneer. "Boohoo: you had to be a single parent part-time and live in a beautiful house while someone else paid your bills. Cry me a river." I jerk my chin. "People do it every day with far less. Get some perspective."

She exhales and puts her face in her hands. "You're right," she mumbles behind her knuckles. "What I did was selfish and irresponsible." She looks up at me. "But I didn't kill him, Christa. I know that now. I will say it again and again…as many times as it takes. I. Didn't. Kill. Him." She sits back.

I grimace, about to truly lose it. "You took away his home and made him feel like he had to go! He would've never—never gone." My hand trembles as I scratch my temple. "You hurt him so bad." I turn to her, hot tears streaking down my face. "You…you hurt *me* so bad."

Mom's face crumbles. "Christa…" She gets up and crosses over to me, pulling me into a hug. I mash my face into her shoulder, ugly sobs coming out of my mouth.

"I'm sorry. I'm so sorry." She rocks me softly, petting my hair. I close my eyes and breathe in her scent: sweet pea and vanilla shampoo, the same stuff she's used for as long as I can remember. I push away hastily and wipe my eyes.

She grabs my arm. "Please, don't…" she begs.

I brush her off and walk toward the doors. "I have to go," I mutter over my shoulder. "Mary Carmen's waiting."

She holds onto the chair back. "Christa—" she calls.

I shake my head. "Merry Christmas. I'll come by in the new year." I wrench open the doors and run out.

*

"Do you want any more of these?" Mary Carmen holds up the container of onion rings from earlier, keeping her other hand firmly on the wheel. "I know we ate pretty early."

I shake my head and stare out the window. "No, I'm fine." I watch the mountains roll past us on the horizon, now shrouded in darkness.

Mary Carmen glances around quickly and finds the paper bag from dinner, shoving the food inside. "Pretty short visit today," she murmurs, looking back at the road. "We could've stayed longer—"

"She was tired," I interrupt. "I guess her sessions have been pretty intense lately…lots to work on." I tuck my hair behind my ears.

Mary Carmen watches me from the driver's seat. "Sure, okay. As long as you feel like you got to spend some time with her." She puts on her blinker to change lanes. "Did she mention what time she wanted us to come down on Friday?"

I sniff. "For what?" I mutter.

Mary Carmen huffs and pats my knee. "For Christmas, silly! I figured we'd visit in the morning, see her before dinner."

I cross my arms. "No—we don't need to do that." I clench my jaw. "She has her own stuff going on down there, and I know Daniel has a big thing planned for us—don't want to miss that."

Mary Carmen frowns. "I'm sure we could make it back in time. Traffic should be pretty light—"

"I said *no*, Mary Carmen," I answer curtly.

She stops talking and sits back in her seat. I sigh. We drive in silence.

"Let's just see what's going on here," I mumble after a little while, reaching for the radio dial, the nighttime dashboard lights

twinkling back at me. I grimace as an EDM version of *Rockin'
Around the Christmas Tree* blasts inside the car. "God, haven't we
suffered enough?" I grumble, changing the station. The next five
stations are all playing the same loud, raucous holiday songs, so I
finally settle on Bing Crosby's *White Christmas*.

"Probably the best you're gonna get," Mary Carmen agrees
with a chuckle.

I roll my eyes. "I can't wait 'til this stupid holiday is over. Just
get past it and move on." I slouch in my chair.

"I didn't take you for a Scrooge, Christa!" Mary Carmen tuts.
"Anti-Valentine's Day, maybe." She smiles at me. "But aside from
an Indie-dislike of the music—" I snort, surprised that she knows
what the word "indie" means. "—you seemed like you were really
enjoying yourself up until now." She glances back at the road.
"Did everything go all right in there today?"

I rub the back of my neck. "No, not really." I exhale, not
having the energy to lie right now. "The whole thing was pretty
rough. Just…lots of stuff from the past, old wounds…" I stare at
myself in the side mirror. "I really don't want to go into it."

Mary Carmen nods, her chin turned toward me. "I respect
that. It's your business." She clears her throat nervously. "Did
she…ask about Alden? Or any of us?"

I shake my head. "She doesn't know anything. Anything that
seemed weird or out of the ordinary, she's chalking up to her
being drunk and stoned." I arch a brow. "I figured that's how we
wanted it."

Mary Carmen sighs. "I suppose that *is* best for now. Being
bombarded with…everything… might really throw her recovery
at this point." She looks over at me. "You okay with that?"

I wrinkle my forehead. "I don't want any of them to know," I
whisper. While it's hard keeping secrets—especially from Jodie—I
can't help thinking about the couple of Smudged Humans I've met
and how totally jacked up they both were. Hell, I'm not exactly

the picture of mental stability either. I sigh. "Maybe someday I'll tell them, but…not now. The less they know, the better."

Mary Carmen nods. "Okay." She smiles tightly.

I shake my head and look out the window. "I just want to get home and not think about this day anymore," I explain, running my hands along my seatbelt. I see Mary Carmen's face soften. "I mean…" I blush. "Back to your house."

She raises her eyebrows. "You can call it 'home,'" she corrects quietly. "It *is* your home."

I press my jaw against my shoulder. "K," I cough. "I, um… still have to finish shopping for you guys." I look over at her. "Anything special you want for Christmas?" I have the necklace already for her, but I'm just wondering.

Mary Carmen raises her eyebrows. "Hmm…I'll have to think about that." She grins. "I don't get asked that question often."

I pucker my mouth in thought. "I'm stuck on Daniel… What *do* you get for your Guardian?"

Mary Carmen laughs. "I'm sure he'd be very happy with anything you get for him." She tilts her cheek. "A stack of old records should do the trick… Even if he already has them, he'll love that you thought of him."

My mind flashes back to the store we went to a few nights ago before we were confronted by Mandisa. "When's your birthday, Mary Carmen?" I wonder, turning to her in my chair.

She opens her mouth to answer, then stops. "I don't remember," she breathes after a moment. She gives me a small smile and shrugs.

My shoulders sag as I look at her. "You…don't remember?" I repeat, confused. "You don't seem all that upset by this."

Mary Carmen chuckles. "Just part of how it all works, being an Angel. As we go along serving God in our new…existence, I guess you could call it, we forget or lose the memories of our lives before." She nods warmly. "It's a trade-off."

I look down at my lap. "So…you don't have any memories of

your life before this? Nothing?" I shake my head. "But you know you're from Guatemala, and you speak Spanish…"

She nods. "Yes, but I am also a Seraphim. We're allowed to retain a little more." She sighs. "But depending on how long I'm here, that could all be gone, too. It's just how it goes." She stares out at the highway. "The memory loss is far more devastating for Guardians, being that they spend so much time in the Mortal Realm."

A pit drops in my stomach. "Daniel…he doesn't remember his old life?" I can feel my heart aching for him already.

Mary Carmen scrunches her mouth. "That is something you'll have to ask him. I'm sure he still has some bits and pieces." She checks her speedometer. "It's not something that happens over-night, like amnesia. It's more gradual; it takes years. You have a chance to get used to it, to let go." She glances over at me, her eyes severe. "We are not supposed to be *here*. You have to remember his true purpose, Christa: he's atoning."

I look away, my cheeks burning. "I know that," I mumble.

Mary Carmen sighs. "In the end, you don't miss them—the memories. You're looking forward to what is to come, and your heart is full with God's love. When you have reached that, you are ready to Ascend."

I shudder. "I just can't imagine…forgetting everyone I loved, ever cared about. That would be horrible."

Mary Carmen tilts her head. "Well, some things, you can't forget." Her eyes crinkle as she looks over and reads one of the road signs. She reaches down and picks up her phone from the cup holder, checking something on the screen. Turning on her blinker, she gets into the exit lane.

I furrow my brow: we're getting off in Encinitas, still about an hour from home. "This isn't us. Where are we going?"

"There is a stop I need to make," Mary Carmen explains, her hands tightening on the wheel. "It shouldn't take long. Is that okay?"

I shrug and settle into my seat. "Sure… I have to say, I'm curious." I smirk. "It's not every day I get to see *the* Mary Carmen veer off the straight and narrow. Should be interesting."

Mary Carmen gives me a look. "Don't get too excited, it's just a quick detour—five minutes." She takes a deep breath and stares forward at the road. "Just five minutes."

We drive about a mile off the highway, away from the little downtown and civic center, the street lights abandoning us a few blocks along as we pass clusters of dilapidated housing projects. Mary Carmen pulls up next to a building on the right and heads into an empty parking lot, turning off the car. I shift uncomfortably, taking in the smashed windows and boarded-up doors.

I whistle. "So, I know I'm not one to judge sketchy apartment buildings…but what are we doing here, Mary Carmen? This place is mad questionable."

She sighs and unbuckles her seat belt. "There is someone I need to see here; like I said, it shouldn't take long." She looks out her window. "I'd say you could wait in the car, but I think you should come with me, just in case."

I snicker. "Um, I wouldn't wait in the car even if you paid me to. The buddy system is now in full effect." I follow as Mary Carmen opens her door.

She nods distantly and steps over to the entryway. "Okay, yes…stay close." She pushes the front security door, which swings wildly on its hinges before falling off of its frame altogether. Mary Carmen's eyes go wide as she rest the door against the outside wall.

I cover a laugh with my hand. "I feel safer already," I joke, immediately wincing at myself. That sounded just like Daniel. I check myself and follow Mary Carmen as we enter the main foyer and stop at the bottom of the stairs.

A single dirty bulb flickers a few floors up, throwing a wash of brown light down on us. Mary Carmen squints and looks at her phone. "We're looking for apartment 3C," she mutters, glancing upward.

I follow her gaze. "Okay… Do you think these are safe to walk up—holy shit!" I let out a super girlie squeal as something skitters across my boots. Mary Carmen spins around as I gape at the floor and see a flesh-colored tail eking out from a crack in the plaster. Rats. I hate rats.

"Okay, time to move!" I cringe, pushing into her backside. She nods and heads up the stairs.

We quickly make our way to the third floor and stop in front of the apartment marked 3C. I can hear Spanish rap playing on the other side of the door. Mary Carmen glances at me and grins. "Here goes nothing," she murmurs excitedly. Her hand shakes as she makes a fist and taps on the door.

No one answers. She looks over at me, her face lined with concern. "Do you think they're okay in there? Should…should we go in—if they need help?"

I shake my head. "Um, no, Mary Carmen—we're not going to blast in there SWAT team style." I roll my eyes and motion at the door. "They probably just didn't hear you with that crappy music on in the background. Here—"

I ball up my fist and slam it against the door a few times, making the whole wall vibrate. I give the baseboard a swift kick with my boot just for good measure. "HEY! You in there! Answer the door!" I bellow.

A minute later, the music gets turned down, and we hear footsteps on the other side. "*Quién es?*" a male voice calls out.

Mary Carmen exhales and smiles. "*Abre la puerta, por favor. Tenemos que hablar con usted,*" she replies.

The door opens to young Hispanic guy, maybe 25, wearing a flannel shirt buttoned all the way to the top. His head is shaved. I'm sure when he puts on a suit, he thinks he looks just like Pitbull.

His scowl turns into a grin when he sees Mary Carmen. "*Buenos noches. Tu hablas anglese?*" she asks.

Pitbull shrugs and crosses his arms. "For a pretty honey like you, sure." He purses his lips, glancing over at me and arching a brow. "Two pretty honeys. Must be my lucky day."

I roll my eyes and put my hands on my hips. Mary Carmen takes a breath. "I'm looking for a Miguel Alvarez. Does he live here?"

He smiles and leans against the doorframe. "That all depends on who wants to know. What's your name, *bonita*?"

Mary Carmen hesitates. I clear my throat. "Her name's Sofia. And I'm…Brit." I fill in. Mary Carmen looks at me gratefully.

"*Sofia*…sounds hot." Pitbull sucks his teeth, his hand dangerously close to his crotch. I sneer and shake my head as he checks out Mary Carmen, his eyes stopping on her boobs. "Why are you looking for Miguel? You two lady cops?" he asks after he's seen his fill.

Mary Carmen shifts; I can hear her nylons rubbing together. "No, we're not with the police," she answers. "It is just very important that I get to speak with him."

He nods. "Must be pretty important for you to come all the way down to Encinitas." He eyes her hungrily. "You're not from around here—I'm sure I would have seen *you* before. Mmm!" He grunts and bites his knuckle. "The things I could do to you…"

"Gross," I mutter, crossing my arms.

"Please," Mary Carmen breathes, her whole body trembling. "Is there a Miguel Alvarez who lives here?" She cranes her neck to get a better look inside the apartment.

Pitbull shifts in the doorway. "You're looking at him, baby. The one and only," he scoffs, lifting his chin defiantly.

Mary Carmen's face falls. "You are him?" she repeats quietly.

He laughs. "Yeah. You got a hearing problem, sweetheart? That's all right… We don't gotta talk." He wets his lips and looks down at her thighs. "All you need to do is hike that skirt up a little…" His hand creeps to lift the hem of her dress.

I swat him away before he can touch her. "HEY! Don't even think about it!" I bark, eying him up and down.

His mouth twists angrily. "What are you, her pimp?" he hisses. "Whatever—you're probably just jealous, being so skinny and mean." He sniffs.

I shake my head. "Asshole," I grumble under my breath.

"And you're positive there is no one else here by that name?" Mary Carmen interjects, looking like she's about to cry.

Pitbull snorts. "Honey, you're hot as fuck, but unless you come in and make it worth my while, I'm not gonna sit around repeating myself all night to a couple of hos! There is no one else by that name—period!" He juts out his chin. "Now, you gonna come in and suck my dick, or what?"

Mary Carmen lets out a little gasp as I get up in his face. "Don't you dare talk to her like that. I don't care how tough you think you are—you watch your mouth." I grit my teeth, our noses almost brushing. Part of me wants to waver, but I hold my ground. "Now apologize and mean it," I growl.

"If you think I'm gonna take that from some tight-ass *guera*, you got a another thing comin'." He clucks his tongue. "You're lucky you caught me at home… You should see what we do to little girls like you down on the street." His lip curls.

Now it's my turn to laugh. "Wow, I'm shaking in my boots! Big bad Human gangbanger—really scary!" I hold up my hands mockingly. "You're seriously misguided. You wouldn't know what a real bad guy looks like if he came and punched you in the face!"

His cheeks redden as Mary Carmen pulls me by the arm. "Come on, Christa, let's just go…" she murmurs, her voice sounding like it's a million miles away.

Pitbull leans out of his doorway as we hustle back down the stairs. "Yeah, take your *loca* friend and don't come back!" he shouts. "And I thought you said your name was Brit!"

Mary Carmen hauls me hard by the arm, my feet tripping over the steps. "Hey—slow down!" I grumble as we rush back to the parking lot. Mary Carmen wrenches open my car door and throws me inside. "Seriously, Mary Carmen, what is your damage?"

She gets in on the driver's side and locks the car. "What were you thinking up there?" she exhales, running her hands raggedly through her hair.

I shake my head and glare at her. "Me? Mary Carmen—he was trying to touch you! He wanted to—"

She holds up her hand. "None of that matters! This body is no longer my own!" she yells, staring at me. "What you said—"

I scoff. "What? When I called him an asshole? Whatever. He totally was—"

"No!" she shouts. "When you called him *Human*! Did you even think at all before that fell out of your mouth?!"

My eyes widen. "What—no..." I stammer, looking out the windshield. "Why is that a big deal..."

She sighs and thumps her head back on the seat rest. "You can't say stuff like that, Christa! Do you understand that it puts us all in jeopardy?" She shakily jams her keys into the ignition. "Rule number one: stay hidden from the Mortals! And calling any of them 'Human' is incredibly suspicious. You should know better by now!" She spins the wheel and careens out of the lot.

I sigh and quickly put on my seatbelt. "I'm sorry; it was an accident—just slipped out," I mumble.

"And what are you doing, talking like that anyway?! You sounded like a Demon- brazen, superior."

I glare at her as she speeds back to the highway. "That...that is completely unfair!" I sputter. "I was trying to protect you!"

"I don't *need* your protection, Christa—you need mine!" she shouts, jerking her face in my direction. I slouch in my seat. "Lest we forget, you *are* still Human! Mortal, breakable! Who are you to separate yourself from them?" She shakes her head.

I clench my jaw and glare down at my palms, glowing blue against the dark car interior. "Doesn't feel that way," I grumble, tucking my hands between my legs. "I don't know what I am anymore."

Mary Carmen sighs and merges onto the main road. "I'm sorry, okay?" She glances at me. "I know you're still adjusting, and that takes time. I didn't mean to get angry. I sometimes forget how much you've been through, what you're still going through." She taps my knee. "And I appreciate you sticking up for me." She pauses and takes a breath. "I can count all of the people who've ever done that on one hand, you included." She raises her eyebrows. "So are we good?"

"Whatever, don't worry about it." I look down at my lap. "So…why did we go see that guy tonight? Miguel Alvarez?" The name *Miguel* sounds familiar.

Mary Carmen exhales. "Chasing ghosts in the dark," she replies, propping her head up with one hand on the armrest. "He wasn't the one. Too young."

I look at her quizzically. "What do you mean, 'too young'?" I repeat.

She shakes her head. "It's not important." She instantly starts coughing.

I roll my eyes and open up the glove compartment, searching for a tissue. "You're a terrible liar. Here, before you hurt yourself." I hand her a travel pack of Kleenex.

She catches her breath and holds a tissue up to her lips, wiping away a small ring of ash. "Maybe if you didn't ask such probing questions," she rasps, adding the tissue to the fast food bag, "I wouldn't be going to pieces every three seconds."

She inhales, her lungs crackling like she's about to lose the battle with pneumonia. I wince; I hate that sound. The same thing happens to Daniel any time we start talking about things he doesn't want to discuss—i.e., anything to do with our relationship.

I sigh. "Hey, let's just enjoy the ride, okay?" I pat her shoulder tentatively. "We're almost home… I'll even relinquish my hold on the radio."

Mary Carmen nods and crinkles her nose. "Do you think we might get lucky and find *Silver Bells*? That's my favorite."

I smirk and arch a brow, reaching over to turn on the stereo. "I think the odds are very much in your favor," I answer, turning up the volume on *Feliz Navidad*. "If we can't find it out here, we can try again when we get a little closer to town and the stations change over."

She smiles slightly. "Second chances."

I flinch. "Yeah, something like that." I turn and stare out the window at dark shadows twisting and morphing in the night.

A while later, we pull into the driveway and Mary Carmen turns off the car. I take off my seatbelt and reach over to open my door. "Christa, wait." She places her hand on top of mine.

I turn back to her. "What's up?" I ask.

Mary Carmen takes a breath. "I would really…um…" She smiles awkwardly. "I would really appreciate it if you didn't say anything to Daniel about our little…side trip."

I stare at her. "Why does it matter if he knows?"

She looks down at her lap. "It doesn't… I just don't want him to know I'm looking…again." She grimaces. "Especially right now, with everything that's going on… He might, I don't know—" She lowers her voice to a whisper. "—think I'm being selfish."

I let out a little laugh. "Okay. I am definitely not an expert on any of this stuff, but I think this is what the psych community calls 'projection.'" She glances at me as I lightly slap her thigh. "You're crazy, Mary Carmen! There is no way anyone could ever call *you* selfish." I shake my head. "Least of all Daniel; he loves you." I blush, catching myself using the words *love* and *Daniel* in the same sentence. "Uh…you know what I mean."

She nods, her gaze intent. "Just please don't say anything to him about it, okay?"

I nod and run a hand through my hair. "Sure, my lips are sealed. I don't know what I'd tell him anyway, as you haven't given me a whole lot to work on." I glare back at her.

She sighs. "I promise I'll tell you everything—everything I can remember." She smiles warily. "Another time. I'm exhausted, and I know you are, too."

I nod and open my door. "Yeah, PJs and bed sound really good right now." I follow as she walks around the front of the car and up to the front porch, pulling out her keys. "Maybe some hot chocolate, too."

Mary Carmen nods appreciatively. "I can get on that if you find the marshmallows." She grins, grabbing the doorknob to put her key in the lock.

The door pops open. She looks back at me, her jaw set. "Did I forget to lock up this morning?" she asks quietly.

I shake my head. "I don't think so…"

Mary Carmen's eyes narrow, and she pushes open the door. I lean in, expecting the worst.

We both let out a little gasp as warm light fills the entryway. "Wow…" I breathe, stepping inside. The front hall has been transformed into a magical winter wonderland. We're greeted by a beautiful display of tinsel and gold sparkle candles on the front table, with evergreen wrapped in little twinkly lights trimming the mirror and archways and framing the living room. It seems like it's ready for a holiday catalog photoshoot.

Behind me, Mary Carmen beams. "Amazing." she murmurs.

My eyes are drawn to a bright little Christmas tree in the far corner of the living room; Daniel stands beside it, hanging a final ornament. He spins around and sees me, breaking into a large grin. "You're here! Finally!" He bounds over and holds out his arms. "What do you think?"

I shake my head in disbelief. "It's perfect," I whisper, walking over to the tree. I reach up and touch one of the ornaments, a fragile-looking snowflake.

Mary Carmen smiles and pats Daniel warmly on the back. "You've outdone yourself again!"

He grins, his teeth glinting in the candlelight. "I was starting to wonder where you were," he answers, leaning against the couch. "Seemed like it took longer than usual."

I look back at Mary Carmen. "Mmm…" she murmurs, picking up a pair of aged looking porcelain elves. "Were these in the garage?"

Daniel nods. "Yeah… We haven't put them out the last couple years, so I thought it might be nice to let them get some air." He scratches the back of his head. "I also needed some more stuff for around the house—had to spread the wealth around."

Mary Carmen arches an eyebrow. "Interesting. Am I going to find a creepy old stuffed Santa propped up on my mirror, watching me sleep tonight?" She chuckles as Daniel gives her a look. "I'm kidding, *mi amor*. You did a wonderful job; thank you." She leans over and gives him a small hug. "I'm beat. Gonna turn in. Raincheck on that hot cocoa?" she calls to me.

I nod, still enamored with the tree. "Sure. See you in the morning." I give her a quick smile as she disappears down the hall.

Daniel watches me from the couch. "Do you like it, Christa?" he asks softly.

I turn and look at him. "It's…" I take a breath. "Stunning. The whole thing—" I motion around the room. "I can't believe you did this all by yourself."

Daniel smiles and stands up, crossing over behind me. "Christmas has always been a special day for me. I don't know why." He reaches over my shoulder and straightens one of the ornaments. "I mean, sure, the presents are great, fantastic eats… but there's something else that I can't quite put my finger on." He puts his hand on my arm and gently turns me to face him. "I guess

I just wanted to share a little piece of that with you. Especially if it's our—" He stops himself.

"What?" I whisper, staring deeply into his dark eyes, tiny flecks of gold glittering back at me.

He frowns for a second, but replaces it quickly with his easy grin and a shrug. "Our *first* Christmas together!" He grips my arm. "That's something you don't get a repeat on, and I want it to be great." He pulls me in for a friendly hug.

I feel my knees start to go weak and break away before I fall over. God, why does my body have to give me away every time? Stupid endorphins. "Well, it's been a long time since I've had a Christmas like this," I sigh, stepping over to the fireplace. "Mom and I didn't even get a tree last year." I stop and gasp, staring at the mantle.

"I hope it's okay," Daniel breathes, taking a few tentative steps toward me. "One of my errands today may have involved a little breaking and entering at your storage unit…"

I reach out and graze the tight yarn with my fingertips. "You found my stocking," I whisper, staring at the faded reindeer under my hand-stitched name.

Daniel nods. "I thought you might want something from home."

My throat tightens as I gingerly take it off the hook. "My Nana made this for me when I was a baby." I hold it to my chest. "She could do anything with a needle and thread: knit, embroider…" I blink, my eyes going glassy. "I—I haven't seen this since before my Dad died."

Daniel looks at me intently. "Thank you," I tell him, hanging the stocking back up gently.

He smiles. "Sure. Merry Christmas." He brushes my hand with his, a little static traveling up my arm.

We both react, me flushing as Daniel spins away hurriedly, clearing his throat. "So, um…I'm sorry I don't have any presents for you yet." He motions to the empty space under the tree. "But I promise I'll get my act together before the big day."

I chuckle and shake my head. "*This* is enough." I nod at the decorations. "My mom used to say that there was always a moment, usually a couple days before the actual holiday, that everything would just...I don't know, *click*—and it suddenly feels like Christmas, for real." I bite my lip and grin. "This is it."

Daniel crosses his arms, satisfied. "Who's making Christmas dreams come true? This guy." He points to his own chest. "Better than the fat man himself."

I laugh and smack him on the arm. "Okay, someone's a little full of themselves..." Scoffing, I start to mosey back to the front hall.

Daniel follows. "I think I deserve a little credit after checking strings of lights all day." He quirks his eyebrows. "You should see what I've got planned for the front yard."

"I'm sure it's spectacular." Catching sight of something out of the corner of my eye, I look up. I didn't notice it when I came in, but hanging from the archway is a small bundle of mistletoe, its delicate white flowers blooming down on us.

I look back at Daniel and moisten my lips. "Seriously?" I breathe, gesturing up at it.

He shrugs. "Tradition, right? Wouldn't be Christmas without it." I hear his breath quicken, his eyes seeming to smolder.

We stare at each other, each waiting for the other to do something. A minute passes, both of us frozen in place.

"Well," I finally exhale, running my hands through my hair. "I should...go to bed. It's been a long day."

Daniel nods, stepping back. "Yeah...of course. I should get going, too." He coughs.

I turn and smile shyly to myself, remembering what Mary Carmen said about him camping out in the garden. I look back and watch him walk to the front door and open it. "I should be by early tomorrow to finish the lights," he adds over his shoulder.

"Okay. Goodnight," I whisper.

He smiles and shuts the door quietly behind himself.

I close my eyes and practically float down the hall to my room. The lights are still off inside, but something glows softly from my dresser. I move in to get a closer look and see that it's a baby Christmas tree lit up like the one in Charlie Brown, with tiny white sparkle lights. Magical.

"Daniel…" I smile and lean in. Instead of ornaments, he's hung cut-out pictures of all of us from Thanksgiving, Mary Carmen in her apron smiling over her green bean casserole, Jodie with a mouthful of pumpkin pie, and one of Daniel himself, shaking his head over the frozen raw turkey. At the top of the tree is one of the two of us together, cuddled up on the couch after dinner, sleeping off our respective food comas. I don't know who took it, probably Jodie—but my cheek is snuggled into Daniel's chest, his head lolled back in his usual way, mouth hanging open (of course).

I pull the picture up to my nose. Our glows are nothing but a faint afterthought, looking like no more than a trick of the flash—which I remember happening from the first time I took a photo of Daniel. This is what it would look like if we were a normal couple, happy, carefree, content. I reach into my pocket and pull out Mary Carmen's bell from Sober Students, hooking it on the top of the tree with a little chime, trading it out for the photo. I sigh and perch on the end of my bed.

"Better than the fat man himself," I murmur, laying back against the pillows. I fall asleep curled around the only known picture of us together.

CHAPTER 6
NEW YORK CITY—
SEPTEMBER, 1975

"HEY, IRISH—WAKE UP!"

My eyes bolt open as someone gives my foot a light kick. Looking up, I see Daniel standing over me in the closet doorway, silhouetted by the bright kitchen behind him. Daylight pours in through the smudgy window over the ovens. I sit up quickly and rub my face.

"Did you sleep here?" he asks speculatively, glancing between my rumpled tux and the bags of vegetables on the floor. He sets the clipboard he was holding down on the counter.

I blink and get to my feet. "Are you going to tell Chef?" I ask, my voice hoarse with sleep.

Daniel scoffs and leans against the doorframe. "Um…sure—if I wanted him to have a coronary before his morning coffee." His eyes crinkle. "Do you not have somewhere to stay?"

I bristle and search around for my brown paper bag. I find it by a basket of apples and pick it up, hastily checking the contents inside. Money, toothpaste, razor, passport. "What's it to you?" I ask with a grimace, tucking the bag under my arm as I move past him into the kitchen. I look at the clock above the dining room door: it's 6:30 a.m.

"What are you doing here so early anyway?" I wonder with a scowl. I'd figured he'd still be curled around some gorgeous brown-skinned girl instead of hanging around here.

He motions to his clipboard. "I'm just getting back from making the market order. Chef likes to sleep in on Sundays." He crosses his arms and stares at me. "You didn't answer my question. Where are you staying?"

I blush and look towards the backdoor. "Nowhere, okay?!" I shake my head, my tone clipped. "I thought I could sneak out before anyone came in... I'm sorry—it won't happen again." Especially if Daniel decides to rat me out. I cringe and start to leave.

"Hey!" Daniel yells, blocking my way. "Don't walk away— we're talkin' here!"

I stare at him sullenly. He sighs and runs a hand through his hair. "You should've said something...to me, to Chef." He glances back at the closet. "There's no reason you should have to spend the night on a bag of rice flour. All right?!" He looks at me wildly.

"I've had worse." I shrug defiantly. "I said I was sorry, and I won't do it again—now let me through."

I try to shove past him, but he put his hands on my arms and holds me in place. "Hey, I get it," he snaps. "I don't know shit about your life or where you're coming from. You're obviously one tough bastard with a major chip on your shoulder—I can't argue with that." He breaks into a grin. "But you're using a bunch of carrots for a pillow. Come on, man!" He laughs and puts his hands on his hips. "What do you have to prove?"

I glower and push past him. "It's not about proving anything," I grit out. "I'm just doing what I have to do to get by." I storm over to the exit and get my hand on the door.

"That's what I'm trying to say to you!" Daniel calls, exasperated. "You don't have to do it all on your own. You're...you're one of us now, and we help our own, all right?" He stops and scratches his temple.

I let go of the door, his words giving me pause. I've never been one of anything…*belonged* to anyone before, and not from a lack of want on my part.

Daniel watches me and nods. "Now, I'm not going to say anything to Chef…"

I sigh, relieved. Daniel glares at me and continues. "If you wanna keep sneaking in like a dog coming outta the rain, that's your business. But," he holds up a finger, "I would strongly suggest that you are gone by 5 every morning, just to be safe. Chef does all the shopping during the week, and he's the first face the vendors see, bright and early. And then he comes here when he's done."

I nod, making a mental note to try to set an alarm, somehow.

"Or…" Daniel smiles his whitest, shiniest smile. I feel my stance soften, not entirely immune to his charm. I've already seen what it does to Chef and the rest of the crew; no wonder Muriel can barely stand up straight around him.

"Or what?" I roll my eyes as the pause goes on, instinctually wary again.

He tilts his head. "You could come stay at my place 'til you figure out what you're gonna do next." He leans against the counter.

My breath catches in my throat; that was the last thing I was expecting. He was quick to forgive and forget the business from last night, but this is something else altogether.

"You don't mean that." I shake my head, putting my hands in my pockets. "You don't want a…a grumpy Irishman for a roommate." Surely that would cramp his style.

Daniel laughs out loud. "Oh, I already *have* a roommate—and I promise, he is *waaay* grumpier than you!" He snorts. "No, you're gonna be like the RKO Christmas Special compared to him."

He composes himself and looks at me. I stare back at him, gobsmacked. "So what do you say? Feel like stayin' in an actual house tonight, or are you worried the rutabagas might miss you?" He smirks back toward the storage closet.

I sigh heavily and cross my arms. The thought of a real bed and a hot shower are very, very tempting. After a moment of deliberation, my pride loses the battle and I nod, looking less pleased than I probably should.

Daniel doesn't seem to notice my expression, though, and slaps me heartily on the back. "Yeah! Good pick...good pick, Irish! That was the right choice!" He walks over to the backdoor and holds it open. "Come on, let's get outta here. I'll show you to your new digs."

He ushers me into the alley, which is illuminated by the bright September sun. Parked next to the stairs is a shiny black motorcycle, similar to the ones you'd see in an old war movie. I give Daniel a look. "Is that *your* bike?" I ask, slightly awestruck.

He grins and pulls the keys from his pocket. "Her name's Wendy, after this girl I knew from Yonkers..." He sighs and looks up at the sky, lost in memory. "You never forget your first, right?" He laughs and bats me on the arm.

I blush and walk down to the motorcycle, smoothing the leather seat with my palm. I can see my reflection in the dark chrome, like it's just been polished. He obviously takes really good care of this bike. "It's beautiful," I murmur, stepping back.

He nods proudly and comes down the stairs. "Are we..." I motion to the seat. "Is this how we're getting...back?" I cough nervously.

Daniel grins. "This your first time on a bike, Irish?" He raises an eyebrow, sauntering over.

I roll my eyes. "No, I've been on one before..." I scratch my neck. "Just not while it was moving."

Daniel eyes me gleefully as he swings out a leg and straddles Wendy. "Well, hop on, sweetheart!" He pats the seat behind him.

I grimace and climb up gingerly, trying to keep a safe space between us. Daniel tuts at me. "*That's* not going to work... Come on, don't be shy, Irish!" He takes my hands and places them on his sides before putting the key in the ignition. "Wouldn't want you to wipe out on your first time out!"

I find myself gripping tight as he revs the engine to life, glancing over his shoulder. "There you go, listen to that purr! Don't worry—I'll be gentle!" he calls with a whoop as we speed out of the alley.

*

We dip through the Midtown tunnel, or at least I think that's what Daniel yells back at me over the traffic as we clip away from Manhattan's skyscrapers and into a different part of town. To be honest, I keep my eyes closed most of the way, clenching onto the back of Daniel's shirt for dear life as we zip between taxi cabs and delivery trucks, the crowded roads doing nothing to hold us back. As we pass through a bunch of small ethnic neighborhoods, Daniel slows down, and I can finally brave a look around. We're surrounded by brightly colored shops and cafes that are accentuated by different regional cooking smells—Greek, Dominican, Middle Eastern. The world is still waking up, and I watch a Hispanic grocer taking his time setting out his wares, lovingly placing a mango atop the pile as we zoom by.

We turn a corner and continue our world tour, passing a Polish bakery. My mouth waters as I inhale the aroma of fresh bread. Even from the street, I can feel the heat of the ovens inside.

About a block away from Little Poland, Daniel turns again onto a narrow, tree-lined street. The storefronts are less flamboyant here, more reserved. He slows the bike to a dull roar, the tires treading easily down the quiet street. I squint and read the signs, all of them in English, but with what looks like German subtext below. There is a music shop that boasts the fastest, most precise piano tuning in town, a watch and shoe repair next door. Daniel pulls into a tight driveway on the other side of the watch shop and turns off the bike.

He looks back at me and grins, swinging his feet onto the drive. "You made it! Still in one piece?"

I nod and follow his lead, not looking nearly as cool. "Yeah… it wasn't so bad. Where are we?"

"Welcome to Queens!" Daniel waves, ushering me out to the sidewalk. "Home of the Mets, Louis Armstrong, and the best pierogi you're gonna find this side of Warsaw." He jerks his head towards the white house on our left. "Come on. We're over here."

I nod and follow him around to the house's front. It's a small, traditional three-flat building in need of a fresh coat of paint, but still nice. Someone has taken the time to plant daisies and geraniums in the flower boxes outside, their bright little heads bobbing in the late summer breeze. I draw my eyebrows down; this is not the unruly bachelor pad that I expected.

When Daniel hops up the front steps and unlocks the door, I follow cautiously. "This is great!" I exclaim, glancing over at the front window. I catch a flicker of movement through the yellowing lace curtains and quickly turn my attention back to Daniel, lowering my voice. "Are you sure it's okay that I'm here?"

Daniel smiles and pushes open the door. "Of course it is! We got plenty of room…"

I clutch my bag and follow him into the front hall, careful to wipe my shoes on the welcome mat before going any further. "*Oppa…du wach?*" Daniel calls as he tosses his keys onto a small table by the door.

I hear the light clink of silverware coming from somewhere inside. "*Ja, in der Küche,*" a rough voice replies.

"*Nun stellen Sie sicher, vorzeigbar sind, haben wir Unternehmen.*" Daniel chuckles, turning back to me. "He's having breakfast. Come on, I'm sure there's coffee."

"Oppa…is that 'grandfather'? German, right?" I ask as I shut the front door quietly behind us, surprised at his fluency in yet another language.

Daniel nods. "Yeah…the grumpy roommate I promised." He sniggers. "Kitchen's this way."

I nod and follow him further in.

The walls and ceiling are trimmed in soft dark wood that matches the floor and the open staircase that goes up to the second story. You can tell that the house has always been a family home, never broken into smaller apartments. We step into the living room, and I can't help but gasp: there are wall-to-wall books crammed on shelves and covering tabletops and chairs. I'm sure there's some sort of organizational system happening, but one that I could never fully grasp. Next to the window sits a beautiful upright piano, its accompanying bench the only book-free spot in the room. I exhale and look around nervously. While it's definitely what one would call a middle-class house, it's all much grander than I ever anticipated. I feel my stomach twist in knots.

Daniel's about to step into the kitchen when I stop and tap him on the shoulder. "I'm sorry… I think I misunderstood you when I came here." I grimace. "I'm just gonna go. I'll find somewhere else to stay…"

Daniel frowns. "What's the matter? What happened?" He looks at me, confused.

I blow out my cheeks and smile uncomfortably. "I just thought…when you said 'your place'…" I bite my lip. "I guess I pictured a studio apartment somewhere with, like, a couple mattresses and rats for roommates, not…" His brow crinkles as I motion at the living room. "Is this…is this where you're…" I clear my throat and smile awkwardly. "This is where you grew up."

He grins and chucks me on the arm. "Yeah—born and raised! Listen, I promise you, Oppa's not gonna slow you down. He keeps to himself." He juts out his chin toward the kitchen. "The rent's *really* cheap, and there's always food in the fridge…" He looks at me, his face certain. "Come on, you don't really wanna go back."

I stare around at the cozy couch and books and smell coffee

wafting in from the kitchen. I sigh and nod, keeping my nerves at bay. "No, I don't," I mutter.

Daniel nods. "Good—cuz I don't wanna drive back to midtown. Let's eat." He spins on his heels and steps into the kitchen. I sigh and follow him through the open doorway.

The kitchen is small but neat, all white and yellow linoleum. At a round table sits a thin older man dressed in a plaid bathrobe, the top buttons of a faded nightshirt visible underneath. He looks up at me from his newspaper, his eyes magnified behind large, pop-bottle glasses. He blinks and sets down his newspaper.

"Well, don't I feel underdressed," he says slowly after a minute, his voice heavily accented, nodding at my tux.

I blush, feeling like some sort of invader, but Daniel bursts out laughing. "Good one, Oppa...*sehr lustig!*" He nods back at me, moving over to the stove. "That never happens, so you should enjoy it when it does." He grabs the coffee percolator from the back burner and pulls two mugs down from a cabinet, adding, "Oppa, this is Alden. He just started working with me at the restaurant. Alden, this is my grandfather."

The old man gives a small smile and holds out his hand. "It's nice to meet you, Mr. Kirschbaum," I murmur, shaking his hand.

His brown eyes crinkle warmly. "Call me Martin, please." He motions to the other chair. "Would you care to sit down?"

I nod and take a seat, looking up as Daniel clangs a frying pan noisily against the floor. "Sorry..." He grins as he stands up, placing the pan on top of the stove. "Oppa, how long have you been up? Did you eat something yet?"

Martin shakes his head. "I heard you moving around before you left, and I just thought I'd read the news 'til you came back." He gestures with his paper. "You always get so huffy when I try to cook for myself... I didn't feel like getting a lecture."

The corner of his mouth twitches as Daniel lets out a sigh and reaches into the refrigerator. "I just remember the last time you tried to cook, you almost burned the house down," he grumbles, pulling out eggs and a carton of milk.

"That was seven years ago. Don't you think I've earned a second chance?" Martin lilts, adjusting his glasses.

Daniel shoots him a look and then turns to me. "I'll have omelettes ready in 5—that work for you?"

I start to get out of my chair, my stomach rumbling hungrily. "Can I help?"

Daniel waves me off. "I got it. Take a load off." He turns back to the stove.

I sink into my seat, Martin watching me calmly. "Your voice..." He leans in, his metal chair legs squeaking as he shifts. "You are not from here, yes?"

I nod as Daniel sets a cup of coffee down in front of me. "No, I'm not. I'm from Ireland, originally." I pick up my mug and take a sip. "Just got here a few days ago."

Martin breaks into a large grin, his smile not as bright as Daniel's, but carrying the same level of sincerity. "I knew it. There's such a musical quality to it..." He sits back and takes off his glasses, cleaning them with a napkin. "I used to teach English literature back in Berlin: Chaucer, Keats, Swift..." He purses his lips and looks over at me conspiratorially. "Lighting young minds on fire with disguised dreams of revolution—quite an extraordinary endeavor. However, our readings never carried the same...timbre that I'm sure they would if performed in their native voice—but we did the best we could with what we had." He smiles sadly. "Different times."

I grimace, not quite sure how to respond. Martin senses my discomfort and clears his throat. "But I've heard it's a beautiful country, Ireland." He raises his eyebrows. "I've always wanted to go... Is it as green as they say it is?"

I nod eagerly. "Yes, very green." I chuckle to myself, noting that everyone here has the exact same impression of my mother country. "Although it's not nearly as impressive as New York. I'm still in awe of how…big…everything is here."

Martin nods, his face serious. "It is an adjustment, no matter where you are coming from. Daunting." He stares past me, his eyes far away. "But good for fresh starts, new beginnings—either to reinvent oneself or disappear altogether." He shakes his head and smiles as Daniel places a steaming hot plate in front of him, tutting, "*Ah, ich danke Ihnen , aber Sie die Tabasco vergessen…*"

Daniel rolls his eyes and reaches for the spice rack, grabbing a small bottle of Tabasco sauce and setting it on the table. Martin grunts appreciatively and applies some to his eggs. Daniel spins back around and sets my breakfast in front of me before leaning against the counter and digging into his own food. I pick up my fork and do my best not to inhale the whole thing in one bite. It's delicious.

"So, I couldn't help notice your library." I gesture back to the living room, trying to make conversation. "Quite the collection."

Martin nods as he chews. "We had to start over when we first arrived; there was so much we couldn't bring…or had lost already." He swallows and sets his fork down. "But Erna…uh, Daniel's grandmother," he waves back at Daniel, "she was a librarian before, and she did a pretty good job going around to all of the used bookshops and finding everything." He smiles wryly and jerks his chin towards the doorway. "It's a mess right now… She would not be pleased."

I glance back at Daniel, who mouths *passed away* to me before taking another bite of egg. I nod and look at Martin, who's gone back to his paper. "Anything going on?" I ask politely.

Martin frowns and tilts his head to the side. "Slow news day. Good news day then, I suppose." He grins, pointing down to a small byline. "They discovered an x-ray star in space, ended capital punishment in Spain, the Pope canonized another saint, John Macius…" He notices when I perk up in interest at the last one.

"Do you practice? Silly question to ask an Irishman, I suppose," he adds with a laugh.

I blink. "Uh…yes. I don't get to make it to Mass every Sunday, particularly when I'm out at sea, but I try whenever I make it to port." I shrug. "Maybe that will be different now, I hope."

Martin nods, cutting slowly at his breakfast. "There is a Catholic church a few blocks down that the Haitians go to. Daniel can show you where it is."

Daniel smiles and sees this as an in. "So, Oppa." He clears his throat. "Alden's going to stay with us for a while. I figured he could bunk in with me, just until he finds a place of his own." He sets his breakfast down and wipes his hands on his jeans. "Thought it might be nice to bring some new energy into the house… What do you think?"

I tense; Daniel didn't really *ask* so much as *tell* Martin how it was going to be. I perch on the edge of my seat, waiting for the old man to blow up and throw me out, but he doesn't even look up from his eggs. "Sure, sure," he mumbles. "*Was auch immer Sie denken, ist am besten,* Daniel."

Daniel grins and claps his hands. "It's settled, then! Come on." He pats my shoulder as he moves out of the kitchen. "Lemme show you our room."

I gobble down my last bite of omelette and nod at Martin as I scramble out of my chair. "Thank you, Mr. Kirschbaum… uh, Martin," I hastily correct. "I really appreciate you letting me stay here."

He nods and holds up a hand, going back to his newspaper.

I follow Daniel through the living room and back into the front hall. "We're all the way up," he says as we start to climb the stairs. He stops on the landing at the second floor and points. "Oppa's room is right there, and the bathroom…" He waves behind him. "And then this goes up to the attic." He points to two doors right in front of us, one closed, one open, revealing another flight of wooden stairs. He bounds forward and stomps up noisily. I smile and follow, trying not to make the wood creak underfoot.

The stairs lead to a large, open space. There's the same dark wood from downstairs, with a peaked ceiling like in a storybook cottage, framing a wide porthole window. Rock 'n' roll posters paper the unfinished walls, making the room feel a bit pub-like. A mishmash of albums and stereo equipment is scattered across the rug, a set of black headphones resting on top of a record player. There's also a heavy-looking desk under the window right next to a set of wooden bunk beds, elaborate carvings decorating their planks.

I step over to it and gawk at Daniel, running my hand over the woodwork, fantastic mythological creatures roaring back at me. "This is…" I breathe. I'm unable to finish, stunned.

Daniel shrugs and walks to the closet. "Yeah…Oppa did that. I had a friend back in third grade who had bunkbeds with his brother, and I thought it was the coolest thing." He crouches down and rifles through a box of odds and ends, moving aside a shiny and clearly unused motorcycle helmet. "I told Oppa about it, and, a few weeks later, he had made that." He jerks his chin. "It's kind of corny, with all the fairytale stuff on it—but, you know, it's the thought that counts." He finds what he was looking for and straightens up—a small tin that he takes over to the desk. "Bottom bunk is all yours. Hope that's okay."

I shake my head, noticing the unmade pile of sheets and blankets up top. "It's fine. Thanks. Wow…this is just breathtaking. He's very talented." I take my hand away from the carvings.

Daniel chuckles, opening the tin. "Isn't that what all grandfathers do—build stuff?" He glances over at me.

I arch a brow. "Not where I come from," I mutter, resting against the bedpost. "You're lucky to have him."

He nods. "He seems to like you… Him talking so much is unusual. And the fact that he said anything about Germany, especially the first time you met…" He bows his neck, his fingers working nimbly at something on the desk.

"Does he still teach?" I ask, leaning in to see what he's doing.

Daniel shakes his head. "Not since they left Germany. He was a professor at a pretty big university there during the war. He doesn't like to talk about it." He offers up a freshly rolled cigarette. "Smoke?"

"Thanks." I nod and take it, Daniel tossing me a book of matches. I light up and take a long drag, savoring the rich flavor. I watch him open a small plastic bag and sprinkle something green onto a clean paper. I narrow my eyes as he rolls it and hops up on the desk, opening the window.

"What are you doing? Are we not allowed to smoke up here?" I ask, eying my cigarette hesitantly.

Daniel shakes his head and motions for the matches. I throw them back to him. "No, you're fine with that. You can smoke upstairs, downstairs… Hell, if you ask him, Oppa will roll 'em for you. He goes out to Brighton Beach once a week and buys the best tobacco from some old Russian he used to know." He lights his own cigarette and takes a puff, blowing thick smoke out the window. "He just gets a little touchy about weed. You wanna…?" He holds out the joint.

I shake my head. "No, I don't—" I stop, not wanting to come off like a total loser. "I'm good, thanks."

Daniel nods and sits on top of the desk, leaning against the wall. "Cool." Mellowing, he closes his eyes and lets out a satisfied sigh.

I take another drag and look around the room. "So, if your grandfather doesn't teach anymore, what did he do for work once he got here?" I motion to the ceiling. "This place must have cost a fortune." I blush instantly at how inappropriate that was, but Daniel looks at me and shrugs.

"I dunno. They came here in…'49?" He furrows his brow. "Pretty much as soon as they were allowed to…and I know they had a small apartment down on Mulberry Street for a while." He puffs thoughtfully. "He did some translation work for the government around that time, but…again, he keeps all that pretty close to the vest, so probably don't mention it to him." He scratches his cheek. "Then they moved here, and Omma got a job at Queens Public Library and worked there 'til she died. So I guess that's what they did for money?" He smiles sheepishly.

I look at the floor. "It's fine—none of my business, anyway. I'm just grateful he's okay with me staying."

Daniel arches a brow and takes another draw, coughing a little. "Oh yeah, he's cool. I think he knew we needed to shake things up. It's just been him and me for so long…having another person around is a breath of fresh air." He rests his arm on top of his head. "It'll be nice to have someone to talk to who isn't completely paranoid and consumed with…I dunno—regret, I guess."

I stare at him quizzically. "What do you mean? What is there to regret?" I wonder, sitting down on the rug and finding an ashtray under the bed.

Daniel chuckles darkly and stubs his joint on the window ledge. "Oho! Don't get him started! The whole neighborhood's in on it…" He jumps off the desk and saves what's left of the joint back in the tin. "Little did you know when you hopped on Wendy this morning, Irish, that you were infiltrating one of the last surviving German colonies in New York." He ruffles a hand through his hair. "Just stare down at the sidewalk and look appropriately shamefaced when you walk between Central and Myrtle Avenue, and you'll fit right in."

I shake my head. "I still don't understand. Does this have to do with—what, the war? Is your family Jewish or something?" Martin did say they lost a lot before they came here.

Daniel sighs. "No. We're not. You're, um…hanging with the losing side. Sorry." He smiles wryly.

I blink, processing what he's telling me. "Why is any of that even important? The war ended thirty years ago… You weren't even born yet."

"It's not over for the guy downstairs," he murmurs, tilting his cheek toward the door. "I don't think he'll ever move on. Even when Omma was still alive, he was always so concerned with what people thought of us—you know, 'keep your head down, don't make a spectacle.' If we're going somewhere outside the neighborhood, he'll have me talk for him so as not draw attention to his accent. It's just—weird." He clenches his jaw. "But maybe he's right… Maybe we should keep paying for what happened, even generations later. Not for me to say, I guess." He shrugs and looks over at me.

I watch him, bewildered. "Oh man—heavy stuff!" Daniel adds with a laugh, perching against the side of the desk. "I feel like I've been talkin' all morning. What's your story, Irish? Why'd you decide to come to New York?"

I frown and blow out my cheeks. "I honestly don't know. I had been working on the boat for a couple of months, down in the engine room…and I'd seen a bunch of different cities all over the world, but something about here stuck, I suppose." I snort as Daniel shakes his head at me. "Sorry…that's not much of an answer! I guess I just felt like this was a place I could make something of myself. You hear all these stories about 'if you can make it in New York, you can make it anywhere'—and I just wanted to try that." I look down at my lap. "Probably a fool's errand, really. I'll be lucky if they let me stay into the autumn."

Daniel's eyes crinkle. "You're doing pretty okay for your third day here, right?"

When I shrug, he adds, "Come on, give yourself some credit! You found work, you got a place to stay…" He motions around the room.

I nod, remembering the orders Mr. Burman gave me back at Immigration. "Yeah, maybe…"

Daniel grins. "All you're missing is the girl… You got someone back home or what? Workin' to bring her over?" He looks at me expectantly.

I feel my face grow hot. "No. No girlfriend," I mutter.

Daniel purses his lips. "I get it. I heard U.K. girls are kind of stuck up... That's why all the rockers come here!" He smiles over my head at a huge poster of the Rolling Stones on the wall. "You know, girls here are more laid back, looking to have fun..."

"Yeah—me and Mick Jagger...the exact same thing." I roll my eyes.

Daniel laughs. "What kind of girl you into? Got any preferences? I probably know someone you'd like," he singsongs.

I rub my neck uncomfortably. "You know...pretty face, nice..." I mumble. This conversation has turned excruciating.

Daniel furrows his brow. "'Pretty face' and 'nice'...? Hmm, not a lot to go on."

I sigh, exasperated. "Well, I don't have a lot of *experience* to go on, I guess." Please let the floor swallow me up now.

Daniel stares at me. "Like...ever?" he asks pointedly. "Ever ever?"

I bite down on my cheek, hard. "No." I grimace. "Not ever."

Daniel balks and straightens up. "*You're a virgin?!*" he crows, grabbing his hair. "Oh man!"

I sink further down, scowling and trying to make myself invisible. "Yell a little louder—I don't think they heard you back across the river..."

"I just can't believe it!" He slaps his thigh. "You've got the kind of look that girls line up for, don't even need to try—wow!" He shakes his head incredulously as I glare at him. "This explains so much—why you're so uptight all the time! Don't worry..." He opens the desk drawer and pulls out a small address book. "We're gonna get this worked out ASAP." He wets his finger and flips through the pages.

I cross my arms. "What is that?" I snap, twiddling my head.

He holds up his index finger, motioning for me to wait as he flips a few more pages. "Here we go…" He smiles and shows me the page. "Janice Hooks and her friend Vanessa Marling…" He nods knowingly. "They are always up for a good time, and Vanessa really digs foreign guys. We'll have your little problem fixed by midnight. What time is it?" He steps over and pulls an alarm clock from the top bunk. "Probably too early to call…"

"Just stop, please—stop!" I cry, rubbing my forehead. "I'm not interested in…" I wave at the book and look away, embarrassed. "In just having a *good time.* I want it to be…sort of, special, you know?" I turn an even deeper shade of red as Daniel looks at me curiously. "With the right girl."

There's only one girl I can think of right now. I sigh as my heart sinks a little deeper in my chest.

"So…you're looking for the holy grail," Daniel states as he crouches down in front of me, ticking off his fingers. "Pretty face, nice, *right* girl…" He ignores my glower, adding, "That's a tall order."

"Maybe not," I breathe, looking out the window. "If I hadn't been such a total idiot last night…" I put my head in my hands.

Daniel's eyes go wide, and he bats my leg with his hand. "Wait—you met someone? At the restaurant?" He leans in, hushed. "Is it Muriel?"

I shoot him a look. He is completely daft. "No! It is *not* Muriel…although she is very nice!" I practically yell.

He sits back on his haunches, confused. I sigh. "There was this girl last night, one of the customers… She came in with her family." I bite my lip. "Her name is Jillian, and she's smart and shy and a goddess with the most beautiful red hair and I have no business being completely in love with her!"

When Daniel startles at my crazed declaration, I close my eyes and take a breath. "And I'm never going to see her again, so none of that matters." I shake my head. "No phone number, no last name, nothing. *And* I spilled champagne all over her, so even if I did know how to reach her, she'd probably never want to speak to me. Ha." I'm starting to wallow in dejection. "Maybe you *should* call those girls you know—put me out of my misery."

Daniel stares at me, his face pinched. "This is like…true love—destiny!" He jumps to his feet. "No—she just happens to show up, your first night working, you have some sort of moment…" When I roll my eyes, he tuts. "Don't gimme that look! Something obviously happened between the two of you, or you wouldn't be acting this way! Come on!" I let him pull me up begrudgingly. "Kismet! A spark! You can't give up that easy, Irish—there's gotta be *something* to go on…" He paces around the room.

"I can't imagine what," I groan unhelpfully. Daniel stops to think and then snaps his fingers. "A credit card—did they pay with a credit card?" He looks at me wildly. "We could look up the receipt. It would have their last name…"

"I don't know… Muriel took care of their bill." I let out a sigh of despair. "This is hopeless."

Daniel shakes his head. "No, it's not, it's not—just think!" He tears at his hair. "You must have heard them say something over dinner—about where they're from, or what they were doing in the city…"

I wrinkle my forehead. "Her dad said he was from Jersey… So I'm guessing maybe they live there?" I offer.

Daniel hems. "New Jersey is a pretty big place… Did they say what town they were from? Probably somewhere just across the river, if they were in town for dinner. That kinda narrows it down…" He continues to dart across the rug.

I cross my arms and frown. "Columbia. Her dad said she was going to Columbia for studio art—the university…today." I smile. "They were so proud of her…"

Daniel looks up, his face bright. "That's perfect, Irish!" Daniel exclaims, grabbing my shoulders. "So that's what we'll do. We'll just go over to Columbia and find her—where are my keys?" He shoves his hands into his pockets, searching.

I stare at him disbelievingly. "I'm sorry...w-what?" I stammer, my hands starting to tremble. "You know where she is?"

Daniel finds his keys and grins. "Well, I can narrow it down to an eight-block radius!" He sticks out his tongue playfully and picks up a pair of aviator sunglasses from the desk. "Come on...I bet she's up and about by now." He gets to the door and then turns to look at me, grimacing. "But you can't go like that."

I look down at myself and groan. I'd forgotten that I was still wearing my tux from last night. "I don't have any other clothes," I mumble.

Daniel nods and moves over to the closet. "You can borrow mine—here." He tosses me a clean pair of blue jeans and a faded red t-shirt. "The jeans are gonna be long, but I think you'll be okay for the rest of it."

I look down at the clothes and blink. "I've never worn blue jeans before." Only wealthy kids had Levis back home.

Daniel shakes his head. "*Who are you?* Go change!" He waves at the door. "Bathroom's right downstairs."

I nod and bolt through the door, practically jumping down to the second floor, the downstairs door slamming behind me. I bound into the bathroom and strip off my suit, my whole skin rejoicing to be free. I do stop and take the time to hang it up over the tub, as I know I will need to get back into it later tonight for work. I clench my jaw and try not to think about the restaurant right now, instead glowing with the idea that I *might* get a second chance to see Jillian again...and maybe, if the Fates are on my side, she'll talk to me.

I exhale and look at myself in the mirror. I need to shave, and I'm probably a little smelly, but otherwise—not too bad. I quickly clean up, giving myself a moment to relish the hot water coming from the tap before getting into Daniel's clothes. The t-shirt is a little more fitted around my arms and chest than I'm used to, but it works. Daniel was right about the jeans, though: they're long...

and *tight*. I shift myself awkwardly as I try to get comfortable, but at least they're not falling down.

I turn around and gawk when I see myself. "I look like…one of *them*," I breathe to my refection, taken aback by the transformation. I don't know if it's a look that I'll want to keep forever, but it'll work in a pinch. I take a deep breath and walk out into the hallway, keeping my head down.

Lost in thought, I don't even notice when I open the wrong door. "Huh—?" I wonder, looking in. Instead of a flight of stairs going up to the attic, there is a sparsely furnished bedroom. A full-size bed with a white, knit coverlet is under the window, a wooden chest of drawers with a few framed photos on the wall opposite. Curiosity getting the best of me, I step inside and run my hand along the bedspread. It's soft and handmade. Someone took a lot of care in crafting it at some point. I move over to the dresser to get a look at the photos. There is a black and white one of a man and a woman sitting at a sidewalk café somewhere in Europe, by the looks of it. Judging by the shape of the man's eyes, I can tell it's a picture of Martin and, I presume, his wife when they were in their prime. He holds Erna's hand lightly under the table, a bottle of wine between them. He looks happy, relaxed, in stark contrast to the man Daniel described. I move onto another picture of a group of teenage girls in old cheerleader uniforms, their hair done up like they're in a Doris Day movie, with a noticeably taller blonde girl in the middle laughing and smiling. They're all pretty.

"American girls…" I murmur. I pick up the final frame from the dresser and squint. It's a color photo of the same blonde girl. She's a little older, but not by much, and holding a wiggly toddler on her lap. The matching blonde hair and brown eyes are a dead giveaway: it's Daniel as a little boy. She's smiling, but not the same as in the picture with the cheerleaders. It doesn't reach her eyes.

"What are you doing in here?"

I spin around and see Daniel watching me from the doorway.

"Oh, sorry…I picked the wrong door." I set the picture down fast as Daniel steps over to me.

He nods at the last photo and sighs. "I was a total spaz…They couldn't get me to sit still for three seconds." He chuckles and tilts his head. "Not much has changed, I guess." He straightens the frame on the dresser.

I clear my throat. "Is that…is she…?" I stop and point to the blonde girl.

Daniel nods. "Yes. My mother…Rita," he answers with a small smile.

"She's beautiful." And obviously very young when she had him. I tread carefully, sensing that this is a delicate topic.

Daniel puts his hands in his pockets. "Thanks. Don't know if I inherited her good looks," he jokes, "but I think she sometimes found it more of a curse than a blessing, you know? Made growing up…difficult, I guess." He stares at the photos with a faraway stare that I recognize personally.

I inhale. "I'm sorry. I, um…" I look down and tug at my ear. "I lost my own mother just last year—cancer. I know it can be difficult…"

Daniel comes out of his haze. "Oh, she's not dead!" he exclaims, looking at me. I cringe, embarrassed that I made the assumption and shared something so private. "She lives in Reno," he continues. "That's, um, in Nevada, near Las Vegas," He blinks at me, his eyes soft. "Jesus…your mom died, Irish?"

I cough and nod my head briskly. "Yeah…but it was a while ago. I'm fine." I exhale, trying to change the subject. "What about your dad? Is he around?"

Daniel laughs at the ceiling. "One of the great mysteries of the Universe! And I don't think it's going to be solved anytime soon…" He shrugs. "I don't miss him, whoever he is."

I envy him. Sometimes not knowing is better than living through it—something I have more experience with than I'd like.

I jerk my chin back at the photos. "Do you see her often? Does she visit?"

Daniel shakes his head. "No...but she writes. She left when I was seven, so it's been a while since I've seen her..." He trails off and gestures at the bed. "I know it seems crazy that we have this room that's not being used at all, and I'd let you stay in here... but Oppa would freak. He's the same way about that damn piano downstairs." He shrugs. "I dunno—I think there's some part of him that thinks she's coming back, even after all this time." He looks at me and smiles weakly. "You're probably thinking, 'Oh man—what have I gotten myself into with these strange people!'" he half jokes, running a hand through his hair.

I shake my head. "No. Everyone has a past." I exhale. "Sorry to butt in."

Daniel pats me on the back. "You're not... You look good." He glances down at my new clothes. "Come on, let's go find your girl." He ushers me out of the room, closing the door securely behind us.

*

The sun is bright and hot when we pull onto campus, the sprawling green quad seeming out of place next to the tall cityscape surrounding it. I look around and let out a heavy sigh, taking in the old lecture halls and coeds in shorts and sundresses, laughing and strolling casually with their arms full of books and school supplies.

I shake my head as Daniel holds the bike steady. "This is pointless—like looking for a needle in a haystack."

Daniel tuts and readjusts his back. "You are going to be whistling a different tune when this all pays off..." His eyes scan the quad behind his sunglasses. "What did you say she was majoring in?"

"Studio art," I reply glumly. "I'm guessing that means drawing, painting?"

Daniel nods. "Good a place as any to start. Let's get

directions." He leans forward over the bike and gives a little bird whistle to two girls passing by.

They turn and look at him haughtily. "Excuse me, sorry to bother you…" Daniel purrs, showing off his pearly whites. The girls stop and come back around.

He sits up, smoothing his hands on his jeans. "I'm looking for the studio art building. Would either of you know where that is?" He glances at them over the top of his sunglasses, looking totally classic.

Noticing this too, the girls step a little closer. "Prentis Hall. It's two blocks that way offa 125th," the tall brunette in the tight bellbottoms offers, pointing. Her eyes quickly scan down Daniel. "Are you a new…student here?" she asks slowly.

Daniel lets out a throaty chuckle. "My friend here is signed up to be one of those…whatdya call it? Life models? For art class… He's a good looking guy, right?" He grins and jerks his head back at me.

I blush and shove my knee into his side. "Daniel…" I hiss.

The girls smile and come a little closer. "He's cute," the other girl with the pixie cut agrees, arching a brow and batting her friend on the wrist.

The tall brunette smirks and looks at Daniel. "So what are you? His driver?" she teases, pursing her lips at Wendy.

Daniel shoots her a huge grin. I sigh and rub my forehead tiredly. It's over. He's breaking out the big guns now. "Nah, I'm actually a professor," he lies effortlessly, pushing his sunglasses up.

Both girls gawk at him, surprised. "Daniel! We do not have time for this!" I grit out through my teeth.

"Yeah right," the brunette scoffs, recovering herself and calling his bluff. "What do you teach?"

Daniel bites the inside of his cheek. "Foreign languages. Romance." He winks at her, and both girls start giggling. He nods at the brunette. "You're pretty nosy. I like that… What's your name?"

"Brigitte," she replies, pouting her lips seductively.

Daniel eases back, letting out a little moan. "Brigitte as in Bardot? The French movie star?" She grins as he takes his time checking her out. "Yeah, I can see it…"

"DANIEL!" I practically kick him off the bike. "I swear to God, if we miss her—"

He nods coolly and puts his sunglasses back on. "Hate to cut this short, girls, but we've got a thing." He revs Wendy and gives the brunette a final knee-trembling glance. "Thanks for the directions. I'll see you around the quad, *ma cherie.*"

She stares at him longingly as we zoom off, Wendy sputtering noisily.

We speed over to 125th and spy the sign for studio art. After Daniel parks in front, we both look up at the old, ivy-covered building.

"So what do we do now?" I mumble, my voice shaking.

Daniel gestures to the stairs leading up to the front doors. "You go in and do a little recon, see if you can find anyone who knows a Jillian or a hot girl with flowing red locks." He grins boyishly. "At least you picked a rare hair type."

I roll my eyes and climb off the bike. "What are you going to do? Are you coming?"

Daniel shakes his head. "I'm gonna hold it down out here—but if you see like a coffee cart or vending machine…" He scratches his chin. "Maybe grab me something?"

I sigh and nod obligingly. "Fine. On the quest for the love of my life, and then a Mars bar for you." I snort. "Naturally."

Ignoring his arched brow, I turn toward the stairs, a gasp escaping my throat. It's *her*—just exiting the building, perfect and statuesque in a pale yellow sundress as she glides down the stairs, a black art portfolio in her hand. She's walking with a skinny blonde girl, laughing and brushing her ethereal red hair back over her shoulder, the sun glinting through her curls as she moves closer.

Heaven. I hold onto Wendy for support. "Oh my God, Daniel..." I whisper.

He looks up and follows my gaze, grinning in approval. "I told you we'd find her. Just call me Sherlock Fuckin' Holmes!" He pulls his sunglasses down the bridge of his nose, giving Jillian a onceover. "I see the appeal. Little curvy for my taste, but a good rack...and kind of a sexy librarian thing going on with those glasses..."

I break away from Jillian to glare at him. He sees my eyes burning and quickly adds, "I'm just learning things about you, is all I'm saying! But beautiful hair, just like you said... Pretty face, *nice*." He jerks his chin. "You gonna stand around shooting me daggers, or are you gonna go talk to her?"

I exhale and look back at her. She's stopped at the sidewalk about a hundred feet away, still talking to that other girl. "She's with her friend. I don't know..." I mutter.

Daniel slaps his thighs, exasperated. "What are we doing here, then?! Come on—quit draggin' ass!" He waves me away. "Before she's gone again!"

I sigh and clench my jaw, spinning towards her. I bounce up on the balls of my feet and take a breath. "Jillian!" I shout, waving my hand over my head. "Jillian!" She turns to see who's calling her name and our eyes meet. I stand frozen as I watch her face change from calm to awestruck, her bright green eyes going wide.

"It's you," she gasps. Blinking, she slowly walks over. I hold my breath as she stops in front of me and hesitates, not sure where to stand.

Pulling my hand down, I smile. "Hi," I state, my mind racing to figure out what to say next.

She blushes and smiles down at the sidewalk. "Hi," she replies, coyly tucking a curl behind her ear.

I clear my throat. "I don't know if you remember me, from

the restaurant last night—uh, Chez Monique..." I fold my hands behind my back so she can't see how bad I'm shaking. "I was, um...your waiter."

She chuckles. "I remember you." She pushes her glasses up on her nose. "I...I didn't think I'd ever—after the way I behaved... I didn't think I would ever be able to show my face there again."

I shake my head. "You were fine—glorious." We both blush at that. "I wish I had gotten to talk to you more," I stumble to add.

She looks at me shyly. "You never told me your name."

"Alden," I offer quickly. "And I hope *I* was okay last night... I mean, that everything was okay with your dress..." I cringe. No need to dredge up bad memories—I should have just left that to die.

I watch her expression: she's still smiling. "It was fine. Don't worry about it." She glances around. "Do you...go to school here, too?"

"Uh...no." I check back at Daniel, who is stretched across his motorcycle like he's bloody Steve McQueen. "But I knew *you* did, and I just wanted to...see you." Shit. That might be too much. I stare at Jillian, waiting for the inevitable rejection.

But she just looks at me, her cheeks rosy. "Really?" she breathes. "You wanted to see me?"

I open my mouth to say more, but get cut off. "Jillian?" The girl she was talking to earlier comes walking over. She looks at me warily and puts a hand on her hip, the short red miniskirt she's wearing riding up her thighs. "Are you ready?"

Jillian looks between the two of us and bites her lip. "Just a second, Denise..." She smiles at me. "We were just figuring out where our classes were, for tomorrow."

I nod as Denise bats her on the arm impatiently. "I have to get back. Giorgio is picking me up at 1..."

"Oh...um, okay." Jillian nods and glances at me, her pretty face suddenly pained. "Um, I guess I have to go..."

I clench my jaw, trying to think fast. "I...I just wanted to ask if you—"

"Hey, you guys engaged yet?" Daniel yells over to us.

Jillian turns beet red, and I wince. Not another interruption!

"Who's that?" Denise glares over my shoulder.

I run a hand through my hair. "That's my friend Daniel." I wave back at him half-heartedly.

Denise arches an eyebrow. "He's got a big mouth." She smirks, checking him out. "Nice bike, Daniel!" she calls back to him.

Daniel slinks over the handlebars, bemused. "Nice legs," he answers lazily. "Wanna go for a ride?"

Denise scoffs and glances back at Jillian, but then saunters over to him, swaying her hips side to side.

I shake my head in disbelief. "I don't know how he gets away with half the stuff he says," I laugh.

Jillian smiles and gives a little shrug. "You...you wanted to ask me something?" she whispers, stepping closer.

I inhale and grin stupidly. "Wouldyougooutwithme?" I rush out before something else happens. "We um...we could go to the movies...or to dinner—anywhere you want. Just—" I smile and shake my head nervously. "You'd have to be with me, go with me. If you want. What do you think?"

Her lips part breathlessly as she watches me, her gaze turning starry-eyed. "When?" she breathes.

I draw a blank, caught off-guard. "When?" I repeat. Right now. "Uh...what about...

" I look back at Daniel, who's got Denise up on his lap, giving her an impromptu lesson in motorcycle etiquette. I think fast and try to remember what Muriel told me about the schedule at the restaurant: open every night of the week except Mondays. We're dark on Mondays.

"Tomorrow." I grin. "How about tomorrow?"

Jillian frowns and shakes her head. "I can't tomorrow... We have freshman orientation. It's mandatory." She sighs, sounding actually disappointed.

I feel an instant urge to make her happy again. "Then next

Monday," I offer. She looks up at me hopefully. "I'm sorry it can't be sooner," I explain, "but I have to work. Is…is that all right?" Before I even realize what I'm doing, I reach out and take her hand.

She doesn't pull away. "Yes," she answers eagerly. "Next Monday will be fine." She gives my fingers a squeeze, and I nearly faint.

"Thank you," I croon, shaking my head dizzily. "I will be counting the days."

Her skin turns a lovely shade of pink at that, and she takes her hand away, hiding a giggle. "Me, too," she whispers.

Somebody pinch me. I spin goofily on the sidewalk, not quite sure what I should do next. "Uh…should I come and get you here, then?" I try to pull myself together and point at the art building. "Pick you up after class?"

She shakes her head, like she's in a daze too. "Oh…um, why don't you pick me up at my apartment?" She pushes her hair back and reaches into her portfolio, taking out a pen and notepad. "I have a place over on Archer." She writes down the address and hands it to me. I stare at the paper, noting the way her As and Hs have extra long tails. I fold it and tuck it carefully into my pocket, having already memorized it.

"I'll be there; 7 'o'clock." I pat my heart and walk backwards, letting out a relieved laugh. "If I don't die of happiness first." I can't believe *that* just came out of my mouth. Jillian blushes and turns away, a smile flickering across her lips.

When I drift back over to Daniel and nod dreamily, he gives me a wink and clears his throat, tapping Denise on the hip. "Well, Denise-Denise…I gotta get Wendy here back to Never Never Land. And you have to go see Giorgio."

She frowns as he helps her off the bike. "Screw Giorgio. When can I see *you* again?" She puckers her lips, flashing more leg than is decent at any time of day. I look away bashfully, but Daniel keeps his cool.

"Astronaut training camp starts up in a week, so I'm gonna be gone for, like, three months—but if you wanna get together before that, I could probably, maybe do a thing at like…11 on Tuesday night." He sighs and shrugs. "My days are just jam-packed."

I roll my eyes, but Denise seems to buy it. She bites her lip. "Yeah, okay. Call me." Leaning in, she pulls a pen from her jacket and scrawls her number on his hand. "Or I'll have to hunt you down," she adds lowly. Grabbing him by the collar, she jerks him in for a kiss on the mouth. Letting him go, she returns to Jillian with a strut.

"Get on, quick!" Daniel rasps once her back is turned. I scuttle onto the seat as he jacks the engine.

As we pull away from the curb, though, I turn and see Jillian give me a little wave. When we turn the corner, I spin back around and let out a whoop.

"I take it she said yes to whatever you proposed," Daniel yells over the din.

I slap him joyfully on the back. "We're going out next Monday night!" I crow, keeping my eyes open for the ride this time. "Ah—I am the luckiest bastard on Earth!"

"Man, and this was just the initial ask!" He laughs. "What's gonna happen when she gives it up? Have to scrape you off the ceiling…"

He grunts as I elbow him in the ribs. "Hey—I'm driving here! And you should be thanking *me*, because that friend of hers…" He shakes his head. "Psychotic! Like, certifiable! I mean…I'd do her…but then go into witness protection or something. I took one for the team there, Irish."

I pat him kindly on the shoulder. "Thank you, Daniel. And thank you for not giving up." I look out at the city. "If it weren't for you, none of this would have happened. I mean it."

He nods, satisfied, and shifts into high gear. "That's all I ask for…a little appreciation. Now, hold on. You look like you're about to float away."

We pick up speed as we head through the tunnel, my heart singing all the way back to Queens.

CHAPTER 7
LOS ANGELES—PRESENT DAY

THROUGH THE HEAVY rain, the sea of plaid outside Benny Woo's yellow food truck grows and swells, overflowing into the student parking lot as all of Sacred Heart clambers to the truck's side to look for lunch. "Gimme four more hula burgers, Daniel, extra spicy mayo!" Benny calls over his shoulder from the order window.

Daniel nods and flips a few more patties onto the grill. "Yes, Chef!" He grins, peeking over at where I sit in the driver's seat. I smile back at him as I take another bite of my Chinese BBQ pork, then lick sauce off my lips and twist the radio dial, trying to find a station.

"Oh my God, Christa!" Benny gripes as he collects cash from Andy Monroe, handing him his food. "I swear—either pop the tape deck or just leave it! I can't take the static!"

I sigh and shake my head. "I'm trying to find something good…"

Benny groans. "My mix *is* good! Little Def Leppard, little Jon Bon—perfect for roastin' pig." He jerks his chin at Daniel. "Speakin' of which, check that tenderloin in the slow cooker."

Daniel spins around and takes the lid off the crockpot,

reaching in with his bare hand. "Almost…" He stops and tastes the sauce on his fingers. "Not bad, Woo."

Benny lets out a whoop. "Aha! The student surpasses the master!" He grins at Daniel as he does a fast chop on an onion, tossing it into the cooker, then bows humbly. "This is a very big day for me."

Daniel shakes his head. "All right, all right, that'll be enough of that…" Daniel gives a sexy half smile and steps back to the grill, mopping a little sweat off his brow with a dishtowel. I shift in my seat, butterflies going crazy in my belly; I love watching him work.

Or…maybe it's just my sandwich. Either way, I start to zone out as I watch his arms flex under his t-shirt, hot steam from the grill billowing around him. And jeans that tight should come with a warning label…

"I gotta tell you, Christa," Benny's gravelly voice pulls me from my dirty daydream. I glance up at him rolling a wad of dollar bills. "Good call on the lunchtime rush. I'm gonna start making rounds to all the local high schools." He takes a couple of twenties and hands them to me. "You're good for business."

I blush and bite my lip. "I'm glad you think so, Benny." I shake my head and toss the cash back at him. "But I can't take your money—all you do is feed me for free, and now I get to eat your stuff at school?" I grin. "Clearly you haven't had cafeteria food in a while."

He blinks in surprise, then gazes out at the crowd. "Yeah, guess so…" Grinning suddenly, he looks over at Daniel. "She's a keeper, dawg…true blue."

Daniel winces and nods, staring down at the counter. Benny takes the hint and turns back to the window. "All right, who's next?" he shouts. "We got more than enough pickled daikon to go around! Hey, pretty girl…" His voice goes syrupy as I see a familiar blonde head bob over to the truck. "Whatchuneed?"

Brit Cornell lets out her trademark apathetic sigh. "I

guess…I'll have…" We all wait with bated breath while she contemplates the menu. "The beef teriyaki. How many calories are in that?"

I scoff. "Too many to count, sweetheart," Benny answers. "You want it or not?"

I guess she decides to go for it, since Benny nods and Daniel fires up a side of beef. "I can think of a couple ways she could burn 'em off…" Benny mutters under his breath as he steps back from the window.

Daniel lets out a low whistle as Benny turns back to me. "You got some hotties at this school, Christa, straight outta *Barely Legal*…" he croons.

I wrinkle my nose. "Gross, Benny. You're, like, forty." I snicker as I toss my empty dish into the trash.

Benny chuckles, garnishing a fresh plate with carrot and radish. "Just because it's forbidden don't make the fruit any less sweet. Am I right?" He bats Daniel on the arm.

Daniel just smiles and shakes his head. "I wouldn't know, man…" He glances through the window, his face breaking into a huge grin. "Hey—Jodie!" he shouts jubilantly, reaching out and clanging his spatula against the side of the truck. "Jodie Phan, in the house!" I roll my eyes and laugh as Benny cranes his neck and grins.

"Yo…4.0!" he rasps, motioning with his hand. "Yeah…4.0 to the front of the line—make a hole! Gotta feed that big, beautiful brain. 4.0, come on down…" Watching the crowd's lack of response for a moment, Benny shakes his head. "Worse than cattle," he sighs. "Aw, Hell, Jodie…just walk around to the back."

Grinning, I open the driver's side door and move over to let Jodie climb into the truck. She exhales and shakes rain off her jacket, the ends of her straight black hair starting to frizz.

"Hey." Shivering, she presses her hands against one of the oven doors. "Oh my gosh, it feels so good in here."

I smile and cock my head back to the guys. "You hungry? A new batch of pulled pork is almost ready."

Jodie clutches her stomach like she's about to throw up. "I couldn't eat anything right now, I'm so nervous... Aren't you?!" She whacks my leg.

I furrow my brow. "About what, this afternoon?" I shake my head. "Jodie—you've gone over your presentation...like...twenty times. I've heard it, it's great. You're going to be awesome."

She tugs her hands through her hair and drops her head between her knees. "Ugh, I dunno... I feel like I should have reworked the last section of my speech." She bolts upright and grabs my wrist, frantically checking my watch. "Wait—maybe I can do it right now! We have, what, fifteen minutes left of lunch?" She twists around and pulls her backpack into her lap. "Where are my notecards...?"

I rest my hand on top of hers as she starts to unzip her bag. "JODIE! Stop!" I shout. "You do this every time, like freakin' clockwork..."

She winces up at me, then sits back and takes a breath. "I know, I have to calm down..." She blinks and rubs her jaw. "It's just that you know Mr. Trundi said both Stanford *and* UCLA were coming today. Everything has to be perfect."

I lean in, set my hands on her backpack, and stare into her eyes. "And it will be. You seriously have nothing to worry about. Can't we just focus on the fact that this is the last day before break and be happy?" I grin impishly up at her. Her hard stare softens as I cross my eyes and stick out my tongue.

"You are so weird!" she giggles, pushing me back. "All right, I get it—I need to get a grip. I would pay a million dollars to be as cool and collected as you."

I smirk and tilt my head. "Fake it 'til you make it." I raise my eyebrows as I recognize the voice at the window. "Hey, speak of the Devil..."

"Mr. Trundi!" Daniel shouts, sliding next to Benny. "You came!"

I stand up and watch Mr. Trundi tug the hood back on his coat, raindrops pattering down on his bald scalp. "Hello, Daniel!" he replies brightly, glancing up at the menu. "Yes, I did hear you and Ms. Nichols mention at afterschool study hours that there would be a food truck here today…" He looks over at Benny and takes in all his tattoos. "Something about a very accomplished chef specializing in Hawaiian cuisine."

Benny smiles smugly at Daniel. "He's a lot of things, but a liar he's not!" he chuckles, slapping the Guardian on the back.

Daniel arches a brow and leans into Benny's ear. "Mr. Trundi is one of the judges this afternoon…" he whispers.

Understanding, Benny shoots Mr. Trundi a toothy grin. "Well, then! Pick your poison, Mr. Trundi. Whatever you want, on the house!" Benny motions up at the menu.

Mr. Trundi shakes his head in surprise and readjusts the grip on his briefcase. "Oh my! That's…that's very kind of you. Thank you!" he stammers, clearly taken aback. "I suppose I'll try the aloha salad with…grilled shrimp?" He looks up at Benny. "Is that all right?"

Daniel hastily crouches down by the fridge and grabs a side of chilled shrimp. Benny gestures grandly with his arms. "Of course it is! We'll throw a pina colada in with that, too—virgin, of course." Benny holds a hand out. "Can't have your judgement impaired, molding the young minds of America—but that doesn't mean vacation can't start a little early!"

Daniel has an icy cup complete with fresh pineapple and tiki umbrella ready at Benny's side before he's even finished talking. "Ah…thank you, Daniel." Benny gives him a wink as he hands Trundi the drink.

Mr. Trundi looks positively tickled. "What service!" he blusters, taking a sip, the tips of his mustache frosted with coconut. "Delicious!"

Benny nods knowingly as he passes him his salad. "None of this would have been possible without Christa," Benny replies heavily. "She's a really, *really* good friend of ours... Keep that in mind today." He juts out his chin at Trundi as Daniel shoots me a grin. "Enjoy your lunch."

"I will!" Mr. Trundi exclaims, toddling away from the window.

Benny watches him go. "It's in the bag." He stops to light a cigarette. "Just show up, and you're good." He and Daniel both smile as Jodie and I break into a fit of giggles.

Someone else steps up to the window, clearing his throat loudly before yelling, "Ahem! Excuse me!"

I stop laughing and roll my eyes. Marcus Brady. "Hel-ll-oh!" He turns it into a three-syllable word. "Is anyone there?"

Benny sighs and turns back around. "What can I get for you?" he answers nonchalantly.

Marcus pouts and puts his hand on his hip. "I'll have a hula burger with NO MAYO," he huffs, glaring at us. "I cannot stress that enough...NO MAYO...and a side of Chi-Chi fries. Do those come with any sauce?"

"Yeah." Benny grins. "Spicy mayo."

Marcus considers, then nods. "Okay, fine. No mayo on the burger, but yes on the fries. And..." He purses his lips. "A coke. With THREE straws." Jodie covers her mouth to stop from laughing.

Benny nods, tallying up the order on his pad. "Okay...that'll be 8.75."

Marcus scoffs. "I'm not gonna pay that! You just gave Mr. Trundi his for free!" He glares back at me. "What the hell, Christa? Trying to bribe the judges? Maybe I should tell Principal Schaffer what you're up to..."

Benny narrows his eyes. "That promotion is only available to certain academic professionals. Are you an academic professional? Lemme see your credentials."

Marcus grimaces. "Thought so…" Benny tsks, looking back at me with a smirk. "You like this guy, Christa?"

I wrinkle my nose and shake my head.

Benny sighs and turns back to Marcus. "All right, I'll make you a burger, but it's gonna cost you like, 15 bucks." He settles over his notepad.

Marcus balks, his mouth hanging open. "WHAT!? You can't do that—you just said 8.75!"

Benny curls his lip thoughtfully. "Yeah—better make it 20. I tell you, the cost of meat these days…"

"This…this is discrimination!" Marcus cries, his cheeks turning red. "You're not gonna get away with this, Christa!"

"Better pay him before he hikes it up even more." I flash my eyebrows. "He made this one sophomore kid pay 30 just for saying he didn't like the color of the truck."

Marcus clenches his jaw and reaches into his back pocket. "Fine." He slaps a twenty on the counter, his eyes darting over to where Daniel is working on his lunch. "You're lucky your new boyfriend is so cute, Christa, or I would take this right to the authorities," he snipes. As Daniel hides a smile, he adds, "There better not be a drop of mayo on that! Do you even have a permit for this truck? I don't think you're allowed to smoke out here…"

Benny sighs as he tosses him the burger. "Enjoy, mahalo, get the hell outta here." He turns around and takes off his baseball cap and smooths back his hair, letting out a yawn. "Oh my God, can it be naptime yet?"

Jodie gathers up her things. "Yeah, I should get going, too… It's almost time." She looks up at me. "Are you coming?"

"In a sec." I turn back to the boys, Benny leaning against the ovens while Daniel straightens up the counter, brushing old lettuce and tomato into the trash. He stops to wipe his hands on his apron, completely in his element.

"This is awesome!" Benny grins, nudging him with his shoulder. "Gettin' the band back together, like old times—grillin' and chillin', partners in crime. When you gonna come work with me for real?"

I smile as Daniel chuckles, running a wet cloth over the stove. "Yeah," he murmurs, "I've missed this, too...but life is crazy."

I sigh and look at Jodie, grabbing my backpack from the floor. "Okay, let's go. Bye, guys!" I call to them, catching Daniel's eye. "See you in about an hour?"

He grins and nods. "Yep, front and center! I'm just gonna finish cleaning up here—" He jerks his head and looks out at the crowd. "Whoa, whoa, whoa..."

Inquisitive, Benny joins him at the window. "What? What are we lookin' at?"

Daniel smacks Benny's arm and turns back around. "That's him, that's the kid!" he hisses, crossing his arms mulishly. "The Stones hater."

I crane my neck and see Ethan Liu loitering by the truck. Benny's face hardens and he tosses his cigarette in the trash. "Okay that's it—we're closed!" he yells out into the crowd. "It is my right as a private business owner to not have to feed philistines."

A collective groan goes up from outside as he slams the steel cover down on the window.

*

"In conclusion, through careful analysis of immunocytochemical reactions in mature cell cultures, I found a strong correlation between gene sequence $infsf18$ and Atherosclerosis, commonly known as heart disease." Jodie takes a breath and looks out at the audience. "The next stage of my experiment will be focused on the research of different types of gene therapy, including—but not limited to—studying possible mutations as well as complete sequence deletion."

I grin and watch from my seat behind Jodie on the cafetorium stage, lined up with the other presenters. Her fingers tremble as she grips the side of the podium, a sheen of perspiration on her forehead from the bright lights. She's in the home stretch now.

"I hope to continue my genome studies next fall at a university with access to a full spectrophotometry lab to enable the most precise results." She smiles tightly and nods. "Thank you very much."

The small crowd breaks into applause as Jodie spins around to me and crosses back to her seat. She reaches out and clasps my hand as she sits down in the empty chair next to me.

"You rocked it!" I whisper in her ear as Principal Schaffer steps to the microphone to address the audience again.

Jodie stares at me, her eyes nervous. "You think so?" she mumbles. "I kinda stuttered when I listed the lab results…"

I shake my head. "No one noticed. They were too busy being crazy impressed."

"—And last, but not least, Christa Nichols to present her study on current-day irrigation practices." Principal Schaffer motions to me, her jaw set severely.

I bite my lip and smile, giving Jodie's fingers a final squeeze before standing up and walking over to the podium. I'm temporarily blinded by the stage lights, but I smile once my eyes adjust, spying Daniel right in the front row like he promised. A few seats down from him sit the judges: Mr. Trundi, Sister Mary Elena from Holy Name, and Professor Lang from UC Davis.

"Thank you, Principal Schaffer." I clear my throat and glance down at my notecards, then back at Daniel. He stares down at his lap intently, his palm pressed to his chin. After hours of practice, I made him swear not to watch me while I presented, lest I forget everything I was supposed to say. I know as soon as I start to speak that he'll be mouthing along. I exhale and begin.

"My project studies the effects of recycled or reclaimed water on native California plant species. As the demand for freshwater grows in the golden state, the use of reclaimed water for the irrigation of major crops seems like a smart solution to deal with our limited water supply." I tuck my hair behind my ear and reshuffle my notecards. "But the long-term effects of recycled water on California's flora are unknown; will it lead to disease or to a genetic breakdown of the plant that could cause devastation to future generations? By using a standard control group set up… "

My confidence grows as I go along, even allowing myself the occasional glance at Daniel and smirking to myself as his lips quietly work along with my speech. Everything is going perfectly until I step over to my laptop to present my PowerPoint graphs.

"Oh…um…" I look down at the screen and see that the battery is about to die. I wet my lips and look at the judges. "Excuse me, I just need to grab my power cord." I motion to my backpack next to Daniel.

Mr. Trundi nods. "No problem, Christa. Take your time."

I blush and step off the stage down to the audience.

"You're doing great," Daniel says softly as I rifle through my bag. I give him a weak smile as I search for the cord. The house lights are dim, and it's hard to find anything with all my books and papers in the way. Mr. Trundi sees me struggling and nods to the A.V. club kid in the back who is handling the lights.

"Hey, Jimmy—can you bring up the cafeteria lights for a second?" he calls. The hall instantly brightens, and I find the cord.

Relieved, I show the audience. "We have life," I joke, the crowd responding with a friendly chuckle.

Daniel's hand brushes my skirt. "Go get 'um," he whispers.

Power cord in hand, I grin and hastily make my way back to the podium, not noticing the set of long legs extended across my path. Like something out of a French farce, I stumble, falling into the audience.

"Oh, crap…" I mutter to the lap I just fell into. I can feel the heat radiating across my cheeks. "I am so sorry—" I gasp when I look up, my eyes bugging out of my head.

"No worries," a silky voice replies. It belongs to a man dressed in a charcoal gray suit, accompanied by a woman in a matching blazer and black skirt. I jerk back into the aisle, glaring at them both. While I've never seen them before, I *do* recognize the large, ragged horns coming out of their heads.

Demons. There are Demons at my school.

I shiver as the woman leans in and smiles, her perfect white teeth in sharp contrast with the empty eye sockets showing the back of her skull. "Better get back up there, Christa. They're all waiting," she purrs.

I stagger to my feet and look at Daniel, choking back a scream. He's seen them too, and he sits up in his chair looking ready to pounce, his mouth pressed into a thin line. I catch his eye and give the slightest shake of my head. Not here.

When I scramble back up onstage, I swear you could hear a pin drop behind me. With shaky hands, I plug the cord into the back of my computer, finding an outlet on the floor. Realizing that I've been holding my breath, I stand up, inhale sharply, and walk back to the microphone. I find Daniel again, and this time he's looking right at me, nodding to assure me that everything is okay. I'm having a hard time believing that right now, though.

"Sorry about that," I breathe, plastering a big fake smile on my face. Gripping the computer remote in my hand, I motion to the large screen behind Jodie and the other presenters, trying to keep the quiver out of my voice. "If you could direct your attention to the first slide…"

I no longer register what I'm saying as I continue with my presentation, my eyes darting between Daniel and the Demons every five seconds. Somehow, though, words come out of my mouth—and before I know it, I'm thanking the judges and walking back to my seat to the sound of applause.

Jodie gives me a warm pat on the shoulder. "You did it! Way to go!" she whispers. I nod and smile, sweat dripping down my back. As I stare up at the podium in a daze, only about half of what Principal Schaffer is saying makes it to my brain.

I do hear how she finishes, though. "…We invite you all to

meet the presenters here, on stage, and ask them any questions you might have. We'll have a small reception out in the main lobby to follow." Nodding, she gestures for everyone to get up.

Before Jodie and I can make it out of our chairs, Daniel bounds up on stage, forming a protective wall between us and the audience. "Hey—you girls were great!" he exclaims, a little too loudly. He lingers close to my side and taps Jodie on the elbow. "What do you say we get outta here and get some tacos? I bet we could even catch up with Benny..."

Jodie shakes her head, craning her neck to see around us. "I can't—Mr. Trundi thought he might be able to get me an introduction with Professor Jing from UCLA..." She wrings her hands nervously.

I lean into Daniel. "What are they doing *here*?" I rasp. "How do they know where I go to school?"

Daniel smiles out at the cafeteria, but I can see his eyes scanning the perimeter, finding the Demons milling around in the back. "It was only a matter of time, Christa—you had to have known this was coming." He stares back at me. "But I don't think they're here to start anything..."

I clench my jaw. "I don't care *why* they're here—I just want them gone!"

Wrapping an arm around me, he pulls me close. "Shh," he breathes into my hair, reminding me to keep my voice quiet. I close my eyes and press my nose into his shirt, his scent helping me calm down.

He exhales. "It's going to be fine, Christa—I'm not going to let them touch you—"

"Nice presentation, Christa."

Feeling Daniel bristle at the interruption, I open my eyes. I sigh, relieved, when I see Ethan Liu standing next to us. "Even if you did fall all over yourself getting back on stage," Ethan adds with a smirk.

After Daniel sniffs irritably, I give him a look and pull

away, nodding to Ethan. "Thanks, Ethan. I liked yours, too… Volcanology is really interesting." I cross my arms over my chest.

Ethan looks between Daniel and I. "Seattle doesn't even know what's coming." He grins wickedly, his eyes bright. "When Rainier decides to blow, it's gonna set off a chain reaction of natural disasters down the entire coast." He scrunches his nose. "It's going to be chaos."

As I grimace and take a step back, Daniel rolls his eyes. "Yeah…*in theory*," he scoffs. "I think that idea is more a movie script than actual science."

Ethan purses his lips. "Where do you think Hollywood gets this stuff?" he exclaims. "It's based in *reality*! And I thought the simulation I displayed today was fairly accurate…"

He turns beet red as Daniel bursts out laughing. "You have no idea what a volcano exploding is like! You were totally off-base—"

I make a face and step on his foot, shutting him up. "Oh, what do you know, Dani-el?!" Ethan spits, over enunciating his name. "I saw you on that truck today, flipping burgers! Did you even graduate from high school?"

Daniel shakes his head and steps forward with purpose. I hold him back with my palm. "Okay, that's enough." Sighing, I turn back to Ethan. "Have a great Christmas, Ethan. We'll catch up with you after break."

Ethan glares at us sullenly and sulks off.

"I really can't stand that kid," Daniel growls under his breath. "He is so lucky he's still underage…"

"We've got bigger problems than Ethan Liu!" I press my fists into his stomach, his tight abs resisting the pressure, then jerk my head over my shoulder. "What do we do now about our new friends?"

Daniel exhales. "We grab Jodie and sneak out the back." He motions behind him. "At least we've got a couple weeks off to figure out what to do next."

I nod and run my hands through my hair. "Yeah, let's go."

Turning, I find Jodie standing idly by the PowerPoint screen. She looks over at me and gives a half-hearted wave. I blow out my cheeks; she looks disappointed. "Crap...she's not happy," I mutter to Daniel, tugging him by the wrist. "Come on, I think we're gonna need ice cream."

"Hi," she sighs at us after we've approached. "Mr. Trundi just told me Professor Jing had some sort of family emergency, so he didn't even come today." She stares forlornly down at her shoes. "I'm never getting into college."

I blink and grab her arms. "Hey—don't talk like that!" I exclaim, shaking her gently. "Jodie! You're being ridiculous..."

She looks up at me, her eyes brimming with tears. "No." Her voice cracks. "I'm just one in a million smart Asian girls who is trying to get into these schools... We all get straight As, we all have tons of extracurriculars, the same 'this would mean so much to my immigrant family' essay. I was...really counting on this today to set me apart." She wipes a tear off her cheek and glances between me and Daniel. "Sorry, whatever—it doesn't matter."

I tuck her hair behind her ear. "Jodie, it's going to be fine. Really; no one has even sent out acceptance letters yet. You have plenty of time." I look back at Daniel, who nods vigorously. "Seriously, you're going to get into a bunch of amazing schools—"

"Ms. Phan?" a soft voice comes up behind Jodie. She turns around to see who's talking, and I immediately recoil. The pair of Demons from earlier are standing two feet away from us.

"Yes?" Jodie answers, wiping her nose with her sleeve before taking a step towards them. "Do I know you?"

I tense, my eyes going wide.

The female holds out her hand. "Tina Pritchert, Stanford Biochem." She tilts her chin to the guy. "This is my associate, Andrew Collins."

Jodie's face brightens, and she starts to raise her arm.

"Don't—!" I lurch forward, but Daniel wraps his arm around my waist, pulling me back.

Jodie stares at me before turning to the Demons. "Yes, nice to meet you!" she replies, shaking their hands. I let out an audible sigh of relief when nothing happens.

"We really loved your presentation." Tina Demon smiles down at Jodie. "Really cutting edge for a high school senior."

Jodie blushes. "Thank you so much," she murmurs, holding her arm shyly. "I had to go over to our local community college to run the tests, but it was so worth it."

The Demons both nod in agreement. "I heard you mention that you were hoping to continue your research at a school that has a spectrophotometry lab." Tina smiles, looking smugly back at her companion. "You know Stanford has three."

Jodie grins. "Yes, the largest in the country—you guys are my first choice!" she blurts out. I look down and notice that her knees are shaking.

The Demons laugh politely. "Well, you are certainly the type of student we are looking for." My lip curls as Tina reaches out and pats Jodie's shoulder. "Intelligent, ambitious, curious... We would love to talk more in depth if you have time."

Jodie beams. "Yes—of course! Did...did you want to set up a time for an interview?"

The Demons smirk at each other. Blood boiling, I dig my nails into Daniel's arm. "Christa..." he whispers in my ear, a low warning.

"How about right now? Is there somewhere we can get a cup of coffee—talk more privately?" the male Demon chimes in, his empty eyes flicking back to Daniel and me.

Jodie bounces on the balls of her feet. "Yes, there's a Starbucks right around the corner—"

No fucking way. I break free from Daniel's grasp. "No! You can't, Jodie!" I shout, knocking into her. She stares at me, completely caught off guard. "We have that...that *thing* that we're doing!"

Jodie's face goes from elated to mortified in three seconds.

"Christa, what are you talking about?!" she hisses, bowing her head. "We have nothing planned this afternoon…"

"Sure we do!" I exclaim, biting my lip. The Demons watch me curiously as Daniel takes a tentative step forward, staying close. "We were supposed to go to the mall…pick up that thing you wanted to get for Francine?"

Jodie flushes angrily. "We can go Christmas shopping another time," she grits out through her teeth. "It's fine…"

"No…no—we really, *really* need to go today." I glare at the Demons. "The Galleria is going to be crazy if we go later. We'll never find parking."

The male Demon's mouth twitches, amused. "Christa, please…" Jodie begs, tears springing back in her eyes.

Tina Demon clears her throat. "Another time then, Ms. Phan. Really, it's no bother." Jodie opens her mouth to say something, but the Demon just smiles and arches a brow at Daniel and I. "We can touch base after break. I hope you and your friends enjoy the holiday." She gives a small wave as they both head for the exit along with the rest of the crowd.

"Crisis averted," Daniel murmurs, relaxing his stance as the double doors swing shut behind them. "For now."

Jodie is standing frozen as she watches them walk away, though, her mouth agape. "Hey," I say, batting her on the arm. She doesn't look at me. "Jodie?"

"I…I can't believe you just did that," she whispers, her shoulders starting to rise and fall. "I can't believe you would *sabotage* me like that…"

"Whoa—sabotage?" I repeat, shocked. I was only trying to save her life. I glance at Daniel, who shrugs, bewildered. "Come on, Jodie, it was nothing like that…"

She slowly raises her head, her eyes narrowed. "It was *exactly* like that. You could tell they liked me, and you couldn't handle that, so you…you ruined everything!" She holds her backpack in a vice-like grip and glares at me icily. "I thought you were my friend."

I balk. "Of course I'm your friend! You have no idea what—*who* those people were!" I stammer, quickly correcting myself when Daniel pokes me roughly in the spine. Jodie shakes her head at the ceiling. "They're the people who determine my whole future!" she snaps, her voice shrill. "Well, *would have* determined my whole future, if you hadn't butted in. God, Christa!" She bites her lip. "You knew how important this was to me—it's not some stupid game!"

"I know that!" I exclaim. "It's not a game to me, either…"

Jodie snorts. "Yeah, okay…but when you go home today, what are you going to do?" She looks at Daniel, then back at me. "Snuggle up with a movie? Maybe make some popcorn?"

I shrug, not sure how to answer.

"You know what I'm going to be doing? *This!*" She holds up her backpack, shaking her books. "Studying, researching, working. It doesn't matter that I'm on break—this is my life!"

I sigh. "I get that, J…"

She turns away, hiding her face. "No, you don't. I…I have to go."

I try to grab her backpack as she storms away. "Jodie—" I call, looking to Daniel for help.

He sighs and blocks her path. "Hey—come on, Jodie!" He smiles his most winning Cheshire Cat grin. "Christa didn't mean to hurt your feelings… This is all a big misunderstanding."

"Just stop!" Jodie spins back around, angry tears cascading down her cheeks. "Of course you'd take her side! You're madly in love with her, and both of you are too chicken to deal with it!"

Daniel looks away, rubbing his neck as she clenches her fists. "I mean, you hang around her all day, and you don't even go to school here!" she seethes, gesturing around the cafeteria, her tone turning nasty. "Just staring at her with those sick puppy-dog eyes, waiting for her to throw you a bone—it's pathetic."

When Daniel keeps his gaze trained on the floor, I step

forward defensively, my face hardening. "Hey, don't yell at him. I'm the one you're mad at."

Jodie glares at me, her eyes red and blotchy. "'Mad' doesn't even begin to cover it!" she shouts. "You *betrayed* me, Christa...all out of some stupid sense of competition, or jealousy..." She bites the inside of her cheek. "I don't—I don't totally understand it myself."

I stare at her as I reach up and tear at my hair. "What are you talking about?!" I squeak. "You think I'm *jealous* of you?"

"Aren't you? Isn't that why...why you did what you did?" Jodie shakes her head, her face pinched. "Your life is so screwed up, with your mom and your grades and your weird friends—" She motions at Daniel. "And now you've screwed up my life, too. Thanks a lot."

Now I can feel tears starting to prickle behind *my* eyelids. "I can't believe that's what you really think of me," I mutter, looking down at my boots. "I...I don't know what to say."

Jodie wavers and opens her mouth like she has more to add, but stops herself. "I can't do this right now," she exhales. "I have to get out of here."

I watch her, speechless, as she turns and hops off the stage, walking quickly to the back of the empty cafeteria and shoving the doors open.

Shell-shocked, I look back at Daniel, who is still standing where Jodie left him with his eyes downcast. "I couldn't let her go with them, right?" I rasp.

He nods slowly. "You did what you had to," he replies, still averting his gaze.

I shake my head. "Everything is so jacked up..." I watch him stare at the floor. "Hey—are you mad at me too? Why won't you look at me?"

"I'm not mad," he answers, voice soft.

Sighing, he gives me a weak smile and steps closer. I feel my face start to crumple as he pulls me into a hug. "She hates me," I whisper into his shoulder, tears stinging my eyes.

Daniel rubs my back and rests his chin next to my cheek. "No, she doesn't... She's just upset. She'll cool off."

I shake my head. "No, she won't. And I don't blame her. She was totally right—I probably have ruined her life...just not in the way she thinks."

Daniel looks at me, still holding tight. "What does that mean?"

I frown and close my eyes. "*I'm* the reason those Demons were here today. Jodie, along with everybody else in the room, was in serious danger because of me." I shrug and rub my face.

Daniel sighs and lets go, taking a seat on one of the chairs next to the mic. "I wouldn't have let that happen, Christa. You have to trust me to do my job." He crosses his arms.

I lean against the podium. "I do trust you. This has nothing to do with that—but you saw what Mandisa did to that shopgirl, Mellie!" I motion with my arm. "They're completely ruthless, and once they have their minds stuck on something, they don't stop 'til they get what they want." I shiver and clutch my stomach, a rush of memories about to swallow me whole. "They could have hurt Jodie," I explain gravely.

Daniel sits forward. "They want to hurt *you*," he replies, his voice much calmer than his pained expression. "You have to understand that everyone you love is now a liability." When I look up and glare, he adds, "That's not to say you should stop caring about them or cut everyone out of your life—but you have to be prepared. There are only going to be more instances like this afternoon as we go forward."

I shake my head. "I don't accept that. I'm not prepared to lose anyone; I'm not going back to the Warehouse..." Flashes of my mother trapped in that awful cell blast through my brain. "And I'm definitely not about to sign my best friend up for a death sentence." I clench my jaw.

"I don't think they would have killed her." He sighs, rubbing his face tiredly. "It would be such a clear violation of the Rules... It would just be stupid to try on someone as visible as the Catalyst's best friend." He shakes his head, staring out at the cafeteria. "I just wanted us to be able to go a few days without any of this…"

"What do you mean, *visible?*" I step toward him, suddenly feeling paranoid. "Are we…are we being watched? Can they see us now? Hear us?" I scan the ceiling, like I'm looking for cameras.

Daniel reaches over and pats my arm. "Not in the traditional sense. Relax." He grimaces. "But everyone knows who you are, Christa, on *both* sides. They've been keeping tabs like we're their favorite reality TV show."

I shake my head. "How?" I breathe, trying to process this new information. Other than the run-in we had with Mandisa and now today, I haven't seen a single other Demon since Alden. And aside from Daniel and Mary Carmen, I've never met another Guardian… There was Emily, but that was before I could See.

Daniel scuffs his sneaker against a chair leg. "Well, I know you got some firsthand experience with Demon surveillance last month." He arches a brow.

My stomach drops as I remember FriendFinder and Serpentine's looming face on the TV screen in my room at the Warehouse. With just the mention of a name, you could see anyone you'd ever met, no matter where they are or what they're doing. At the time, it had been a lifesaver, granting me access to everyone that I cared about while I was trapped in Hell. Now, though, I can see what a dangerous tool it could be.

"Yeah, okay," I mumble. "But what about Heaven? Do they use FriendFinder too?"

Daniel shakes his head. "They don't have to. They have a direct line," he replies.

I look at him imploringly. "What does that mean?" Suddenly dizzy, I grab him for support.

Daniel winces and takes a breath. "Mary Carmen," he states quietly. "It's not her choice, but she's a Seraphim. They can access all her thoughts anytime they want."

I gape at him and pull back, the knot in my stomach growing. "So, she's been...*spying* on me?" I hiss, holding myself protectively.

Daniel shakes his head and sighs. "No...not her, specifically. She has no idea when they're checking or what they're looking for—she doesn't even register when they do it." He clenches his jaw. "They only communicate with her when it's absolutely necessary. It's like she's permanently Haloed to them; everyone upstairs is on the same radar, completely available to one another, with no secrets." He gazes at me.

I exhale and nod. "Seems more like a massive invasion of privacy." I shrug uncomfortably, my eyes growing wide. "Wait... can they do that to you, too? Are you...'on the radar'?" I blush, picturing a bunch of Seraphim gathered around a TV somewhere watching us have this very conversation.

Daniel chuckles darkly. "No, I haven't had the pleasure. Guardians aren't...connected. We're sort of free agents until we Ascend." He narrows his eyes, his Halo dimming. "Have to earn our stripes first."

I exhale. Even though he seems put out by this, I am very grateful that his mind is being left unmolested by sketched out groupthink.

"Well, my life just got a hundred times creepier," I sigh, walking in a slow circle around the stage.

Daniel presses his mouth into a thin line. "I'm sorry."

I snicker; he says that a lot. "Whatever... It's not you." I glance up at the dark PowerPoint screen. "Maybe Jodie was right about that, too."

Daniel cocks his head to the side. "Right about what?" he murmurs.

I smile wryly. "About me being jealous of her... Maybe there's some truth to that. Normal life is kind of at a premium for me, you know?" I stop moving and tuck my hair behind my ears.

Daniel nods. "I do know that," he whispers.

"I would give anything to have my biggest worry be if I aced finals or got into that Ivy League college I had been dreaming about." I feel my face grow hot. "To be normal and just go to school and see my friends and talk about something stupid like prom…" I look up at him and see that his eyes are sad too. I long to throw my arms around him and never stop kissing him, but I know that I can't do that, either.

"Does any of this even matter?" I mumble. Daniel furrows his brow, so I point at the podium. "Science club, school…my future?" I can barely say the last one.

Daniel's whole body tenses. "Christa…"

I shake my head and lock eyes with him, both of us glowing bright. "Be real with me, Daniel. Am I…" I take a breath. "Are we going to make it past all this? Like…alive?" I tremble, not knowing if I can handle the answer.

Daniel's face hardens. "If *I* have anything to say about it. Your life—your future is the only thing that matters to me. You're gonna make it." He straightens his back.

I don't need the absence of a coughing spell to tell me he means it. I give him a weak smile. "Let's get outta here." I rap the podium with my knuckles. "Before they lock us in and we miss Christmas."

Daniel's shoulders relax and he comes over to take my hand. "Agreed. Let's let vacation begin." He pulls me close as we walk offstage.

*

Mary Carmen meets us at the door, her cooking apron splattered in red sauce. "Ah! You two are late—I was starting to wonder if something had happened to you!"

"Sorry, we missed our usual bus…" I murmur as Daniel and I follow her inside.

She smiles over her shoulder as we move down the hall, for once not looking upset by my tardiness. "It's fine—it's just that dinner's ready!" She grins and motions to the kitchen table.

I startle: it looks beautiful, covered in a delicious Italian spread and set for three. "You cooked!" Daniel exclaims appreciatively from the doorway.

Mary Carmen bats him on the arm and beams. "Yeah—don't sound so surprised! Spaghetti and meatballs…and don't worry, I checked to make sure it all cooked through!" She ushers us to the table. "Come on, sit down before it gets cold!"

I take the seat closest to the wall, Daniel sits at the head of the table, and Mary Carmen plops down across from me and hands over a big bowl of spaghetti. "So tell me, how did it go today?" she asks as she doles salad onto her plate. I stare at her for a second, then realize that she's asking about Science Club. I take a big breath and look at Daniel. He keeps his eyes on his plate, rolling a meatball around with his fork.

I sigh. "It was good. I think the judges liked my presentation." I pick up the tongs for the pasta. "I won't know how I placed 'til after break." Knowing what I now know about her Borg mind, I have no desire to share the story of our Demon visitors at school. I'm sure that would only boost viewership. I glance back at where Daniel is intent on his dinner, slowly chewing his food. Looks like I'm not alone on that.

Mary Carmen smiles at me. "I'm sure you did great. You worked so hard!" she exclaims, taking a spoonful of sauce. "How did Jodie do?"

I try not to bristle. "She did really well, too…" I answer hesitantly. "I bet she wins the whole thing."

Mary Carmen nods, taking a bite. "That's good for her. I know she's counting on it for her college applications." She blots her mouth with a napkin, glancing between Daniel and I. "Otherwise uneventful? Everyone excited about the holiday?"

She looks at me, her expression content. Staring into her eyes, I feel a chill go down my spine, imagining the millions, possibly billions of Seraphim souls watching along with her.

"Yep, just another boring day." I grimace and clear my throat. "Please pass the garlic bread."

CHAPTER 8
NEW YORK CITY—
OCTOBER, 1975

"SO...ALL IN ALL, it sounds like it's been a good first week," Mr. Burman mumbles between bites. He sets his roast beef sandwich down on the desk and wipes his mouth with a napkin.

"Yes," I answer, my eyes locked on the uneaten sandwich in front of me. "Your friend, Chef—uh...Eddie Robbins was a godsend. Thank you for putting me in touch with him."

Mr. Burman leans back in his chair. "Sure, sure. He owed me one from a while back, and really, I'm doing him a favor sending you over. I can tell you're a hard worker...Shouldn't disappoint." He looks up at me kindly, then down at my lunch. "Don't let that go to waste. It's the best pastrami in town."

I nod and pick up the sandwich, taking a huge bite. I give him a tight smile, my mouth full of bread and sauce.

He chuckles. "So you got the job and the housing all set up..." He picks up a pencil. "You're living on Myrtle now, in Queens?" He arches a brow.

"Mm-hm." I swallow. "Yes—I have the phone number if you need to call Mr. Kirschbaum..."

Mr. Burman waves a hand. "That won't be necessary. I trust you." He scribbles something on the paper and tosses the pencil off to the side. "If you had wanted to do something…unseemly… you would've had plenty of chances in the last couple days. But you did everything I asked: found work, a place to live, showed up on time today…" He grins. "You're a model citizen, Mr. Murphy."

I blush at the compliment. "Thank you, sir. I'm trying."

"Well, keep it up," he grunts, opening up the file cabinet by his knee. "At this rate, we'll have you on the straight and narrow by the new year." He closes the drawer and sets a little blue envelope in front of me. I look at him expectantly.

"Go ahead, take it."

I pick it up and open it slowly, my face brightening as I read my name in clean, dark type. "It's a work visa."

Mr. Burman holds up his hand. "*Temporary* work visa," he corrects. "And education. You can get a job or take classes anywhere you like now." He shifts in his chair smugly. "Had to pull a few strings over at Consular Affairs with Mabel. Good ol' gal from Mississippi…usually doesn't move too quick, but can be persuaded every now and again. Anyway…" He folds his hands over his paunch. "We'll need to reassess in a couple months, but for now, you're good."

I tuck the visa into my jacket. "Thank you, Mr. Burman," I murmur. "Truly…I am so grateful for everything you've done for me." I stare down at my lap. "Just…thank you."

He tilts his head to the side, taking another bite of his sandwich. "You have got to be the most sincere kid I've ever met." He chuckles, his eyes crinkling warmly. "Seriously, you wear your heart on your sleeve. It's…endearing."

I shrug, shrinking back in my seat. "I dunno—I guess I try not to take anything for granted." I take another bite of my food as an excuse to stop talking.

Mr. Burman nods. "Well, I'm rooting for you." He finishes

off his lunch with a satisfied sigh. "What else you got goin' on? Besides working your tail off?"

I clear my throat and sit up again. "Well, I, um…" I exhale and decide to tell him. "I met this girl. Just *one* girl," I add quickly, watching his face to see his reaction. The corners of his mouth are turned up in an amused sort of expression. "She's a student at Columbia…very respectable," And beautiful. And charming. And perfect. "I'm taking her out for our first date, well…tonight." My eyes dart to the clock on his desk. I've been trying not to watch the time since I got here, but I've been counting down all week. Six more hours until I get to pick her up. Her address on Archer Street is burned into my brain. I've walked by there every night after work this last week, seeing all the lights in her apartment dark. I've been wondering what she looks like while she's sleeping…dreaming…

"She sounds lovely. Whatdya got set up?" Mr. Burman asks, bringing me back down to earth.

I blink and look at him. "Oh…uh, dinner followed by a walk around the neighborhood, maybe past the theaters or uptown." I scratch my ear. "You know, just so we can get a chance to talk, get…get to know each other better." I tuck my hands between my knees, which are knocking together nervously at the thought of tonight.

Mr. Burman grins. "You should think about a carriage ride… They pick up on 5th Avenue, and they'll take you to see all the sights. She might like that."

I nod fervently, committing the idea to memory. "Thank you, sir. That's brilliant."

He snickers. "I have my moments. We're all done here for today, Mr. Murphy." He cleans up his trash and stands. "You can set up your next couple appointments with Regina out front; let's figure on checking in every month or so, just to make sure things are still going smoothly." As I get up, he walks around the desk and pats me on the shoulder. "You keep it goin' on your end, and I'll keep up mine. We'll have this all sorted out in no time."

I smile as we walk out into the hallway. "Thank you, Mr. Burman. I will. I, um..." I shuffle my feet. "I don't want to mess this up, miss my chance."

He stops in front of another office and pulls a file off the wall. "I know, Mr. Murphy. And that's how I know you're going to succeed at whatever you put your mind to." He glances up from his papers, arching a brow. "Now quit talking to me and go have fun. You've earned it—though not *too* much fun," he quickly audits. I pause, frozen to the carpet. "But...you know...the right kind of fun with your respectable girl. Let's just keep this all very respectable, at least until we've gotten your paperwork figured out." His lip twitches.

I nod. "Yes, Mr. Burman."

He smiles and waves me off as I head out to the lobby.

I take the A train back to Queens, the quiet darkness of the subway calming my nerves for a bit as the car rocks side to side. After a full week in the city, I'm starting to get a handle on all the different lines and schedules. My mind wanders as I stare through the window into the black underground, running different scenarios of tonight: what I'll say to Jillian when I first show up at her door, how I want to hold her hand, things we can talk about at dinner. I wipe my palms on my pant leg, sweating, my heart racing again. I have got to get a grip before 7:00. I take a deep breath and close my eyes, listening to the clack of the wheels against the track. It's going to go well... It has to. This isn't just some random first date. It's destiny, just like Daniel said.

I get back to the house, race up the stairs to shower, and get dressed. I hear Martin's radio playing behind his closed bedroom door as he takes his afternoon rest. Daniel is still out from this morning, and I relish having the room all to myself as I put on the freshly dry-cleaned tux I borrowed from work, not having a suit of my own to wear for tonight. I check myself one final time in the mirror before settling down on the edge of my bunk, watching the alarm clock on the nightstand tick by at a glacial pace. Despite sitting perfectly still, I can barely catch my breath. I'm willing myself to not have an aneurism before I get to see her again. What if Jillian forgot that we were going out tonight? What if, after thinking about it for the last few days, she doesn't want to see me and just hasn't had a way of reaching me to tell me so? Is this all just buildup to some crushing letdown?

I cross my arms over my stomach and try to breathe evenly; I've never felt this way about anyone before. Sure, I'd had the occasional puppy love over girls back home…but I had never worked up the nerve to ask any of them out on a date—and *they* certainly weren't looking at me like I was anything special. Just another one of Fergel Murphy's poor sodden brats, their father the town drunk and the running punchline who would take out his nasty temper on his wife and kids. I tense and push the memories back where they belong, trying to focus on tonight.

"Everything's different," I murmur to myself. "This place is different, *she's* different…" I sigh, nodding confidently. "I'm different."

I cross over to the desk and pull a fresh cigarette and the book of matches from the top drawer. Once lit, I take a long drag and look out the window, watching the sun make its way closer to the horizon.

"Yeah, it's gonna be better than different." I smile. "It's going to be amazing."

*

I give myself plenty of time to get back to Manhattan, making it to Jillian's block a few minutes before 7 o'clock. As I turn the corner, I see her sitting on the front steps, her hair vivid in the twilight. She didn't forget. She's…waiting for me.

I quicken to a run and stop before her, out of breath. "Hi," I pant, holding my side.

Jillian looks up and smiles at me. "Hi."

She slowly rises, and I gasp, awestruck. She's wearing a stunning black dress, tight on top with cap sleeves. It shows off her fair skin and the small silver cross glinting at her collarbone before billowing out into a full skirt that stops at her knees. Her golden red curls are piled prettily on top of her head, tiny baby tendrils framing her face. She looks like a 1940s film star.

"You look...beautiful," I stammer, my words not doing her justice.

"Thank you." She blushes, motioning to my tux. "You're not so bad yourself."

I shake my head, still staring. "I didn't know they made dresses like that anymore."

Jillian laughs and does a little twirl, the fabric swirling silken around her. "They don't. I found this at a resale shop in Brooklyn. I think they said it was from 1957?" She gives a light shrug and makes her way down the steps, clutching her purse in hand. When her heel catches, though, she stumbles down two steps, letting out a little squeal as she flails to grab the railing. My eyes go wide as I rush to catch her, saving her from a grisly encounter with the sidewalk. She collides into me gently, soft and small in my arms.

"You okay?" I ask, helping her straighten up but not letting go.

Jillian nods and blushes profusely. "Yeah, I'm fine." She giggles, embarrassed, and gestures at her feet. "Sorry...I guess I'm still getting used to these shoes."

I smile and squeeze her shoulders, then squint at her face. Something's missing. "Where are your glasses?"

Jillian blushes again and holds up her purse. "I have them here. I, um...I just didn't want to wear them tonight...with this dress." She looks down at her hands and then back at me, flustered. "It's fine—I just can't see stuff far away."

I nod and take her by the arm, words rolling effortlessly off my tongue. "Well then, I'll just have to stay close." I grin as she stares back at me, her lips parted. It takes all of my willpower not to stop and kiss her right then and there.

"Come on, we don't want to be late for dinner," I breathe, not taking my eyes off of her.

She nods. "Yes… Where are we going?"

As we start to head down the street, I pull her tight to my side. "Somewhere very exclusive. They don't let just anyone into this place."

Jillian tugs at her clothes nervously. "Am I…dressed well enough?" She glances over at my tux.

I laugh. "You're perfect." More than the stars, more than the moon. "Don't worry."

She smiles and looks down at her shoes, the feel of her fingers on my arm electric as we walk. This is it—I've died and gone to Heaven.

"Chez Monique?" Jillian looks up at the dark restaurant sign, confused. "I thought you said you were closed on Mondays."

"We are." I grin, taking her hand and leading her around to the side alley. "And we're going somewhere far nicer than that."

Jillian giggles as I guide her to the fire escape over the kitchen door. "Um, Chez Monique is pretty nice—it's, like, one of the best restaurants in the city…,"

"Yes, but the place *I'm* taking you to has something Chez Monique does not." I jerk my chin at her purse. "You might want to put your glasses on for this."

A small smile creeps across her face as I pull the fire ladder down and motion for her to step up. She takes off her heels and then holds my hand for support as we climb up the five flights together. When we reach the roof, she gasps and looks around, her eyes full of wonder.

"Alden…" she breathes, shaking her head. I about burst from hearing her say my name. "This is…spectacular."

I have to agree. We've made it for sunset over all of New York, the silver and gray skyscrapers cutting through the dark reds and blues of the early October sky. But even more exciting is the small table for two set up by the edge, covered in white linen and china, a single pink rose in the center. The whole roof has been adorned with tiny twinkle lights, making it look like the stars have come down to earth just for us. I spy Daniel and Muriel over in the far corner, whispering conspiratorially over a couple of small hot plates and several bottles of wine.

Daniel glances up and smiles when he sees us. "They're here," he murmurs to Muriel. She looks up and breaks into a matching grin, both of them straight out of a toothpaste ad. She nods and pulls up one of the bottles of wine.

Jillian spins back and stares at me. "Did you do all this for… for me?" Her expression shines with surprise.

I nod and point to the skyline. "You don't get a view like this downstairs." I shrug, watching her intently. "Do…do you like it?"

She shakes her head, looking from the table to the sunset. "No one has ever done anything like this for me before." She blinks. "Thank…thank you."

I blush. "Well…thank you for coming and…wearing that dress." I look down at the ground and clear my throat. "I, um…I can't take all the credit. As you can see, I had some help from people with far more experience with this sort of thing—my friends, Daniel and Muriel." I gesture as Muriel makes her way over to us.

"Good evening to you both," she purrs, smiling between us. "Welcome to Chez Daniel." I chuckle and glance back at our chef, who is hard at work and grinning ear-to-ear. Muriel purses her lips playfully and motions Jillian forward. "Can I show you to your table?"

Jillian nods, beaming as she walks over to the edge. Muriel hangs back and gives my arm a squeeze. "She's so pretty, Alden," she whispers. "And she obviously loves it—slam dunk." She flashes her eyebrows in excitement at getting to use American slang. I grin back at her and join Jillian over at the table, helping her with her chair before I sit down.

"Thank you." She starts giggling as she realizes she's still holding her shoes. "Jeez, I am a piece of work tonight!"

I laugh with her and sit across in the other chair. "No, leave them, get comfortable—should I take mine off too?" I put my ankle over my knee.

She covers her mouth bashfully. "I just didn't want to fall again on the fire escape!" Her eyes dance. "I'm sure the last thing you wanted was a trip to the hospital for our first date."

"As long as I got to be with you, I wouldn't care," I murmur. She blushes madly.

Muriel clears her throat, standing at the side of the table. "Chef has prepared," her mouth twitches as she glances over at Daniel, "a Virginia Coast bacon-wrapped sea scallop with pumpkin and apple garnish, served with a side of roasted vegetables and brie." She nods confidently.

"It sounds delicious...and smells delicious!" Jillian steals a glance over at where Daniel is cooking away. "I still can't get over all this."

Muriel holds up a bottle of wine. "I have a lovely chardonnay here with a bit of, um...snap to it. Should go well with tonight's fall flavors." She tuts as I give her presentation a little golf clap under the table. "Would you care for some, Jillian?"

Jillian nods brightly, and Muriel pours some into her glass, leaving mine empty even though I know we haven't discussed my teetotalism. I shoot her a grateful look as she walks back over to Daniel.

Jillian does notice, though. "Are you not drinking?" she asks, watching my expression.

I sit back, trying to come up with some witty excuse, but eventually I just shake my head. "No...I, um, I just never really got a taste for the stuff," I reply with a shrug. That, and I've still got the rancid breath smell stuck in my nose from a lifetime of wrestling Dad off Mum. I frown and look up as Jillian continues to listen attentively. "It's just not really my thing, that's all." I wave at her wine. "But please! Don't let me stop you. I want you to have a good time."

She pushes her glass away and smiles. "I *am* having a good time—the best time." He green eyes flicker up at me. "I don't need it."

I lean forward. "Really, I don't mind…"

"Maybe I want you to, um—" She looks at the table and tucks a curl back with her hand. "—get a taste for…me. I wouldn't want that to get in the way." She peeks up at my shyly.

Okay.

I draw in a deep breath, wondering if I flip over the table now and just lunge at her, whether Daniel and Muriel would get the hint and clear out.

Fortunately, or unfortunately, dinner arrives before I can take action. "Here we are." Muriel smiles, setting down our meals. "Scallops with pumpkin and apple."

Jillian leans into her plate and squints before pulling her glasses out of her purse. "Beautiful," she murmurs, holding up one of the thin apple slices perched atop the pumpkin mash for me to see. It's been carved paper-thin into a perfect heart, the bright red skin holding it all together, seeds still intact.

"That's amazing!" I laugh, turning around to Daniel. "I didn't know you could do stuff like that!"

He arches a brow smugly. "I'm trying out some new techniques tonight before I show Chef. Hope you don't mind being my guinea pigs." He crosses his arms and leans against the roof ledge.

"Genius at work!" Muriel grins, batting him on the stomach. Daniel smirks, clearly very pleased with himself.

"Careful, Muriel," I joke. "I don't think he needs much help in the confidence department. Wouldn't want that head getting any bigger than it already is."

Muriel giggles and looks at Daniel, who snickers. "Hey—I am standing, like, five feet away! I can hear you! We still have dessert coming up... There's plenty of opportunity—"

"That's enough!" Muriel shushes him, laughing. "Let's give them a little privacy. We'll be downstairs if you need anything." She grins at us as they walk over to the fire escape, disappearing down the stairs.

Jillian smiles and faces me, picking up her fork demurely. "Well, so far, I know that you have really nice friends and look great in a tuxedo." She arches a brow, cutting into her scallop, "Is there anything else I should know before we go any further?"

I laugh. "Ah...I can fall asleep anywhere. My one secret talent, I guess."

She nods appreciatively. "That's an impressive skill!" she giggles. "And you're obviously from...Ireland?" She tilts her head to the side. "Just guessing from your name and accent."

I sit back and nod. "Yes...although Madame Monique, the owner," I gesture to the building, "wants me to be from England instead. She thinks it'll add an air of sophistication to the place or something." I rub the back of my neck.

Jillian shakes her head and cringes. "Like putting a silk purse in a paper bag." She takes a bite of her dinner. "That's just shameful."

We both laugh. "It doesn't matter much to me one way or another," I say with a shrug. "I'm just happy to be here and working."

She nods and looks out at the now fading sky, where night is coming on strong. The white lights hover overhead, casting a bright halo around the table. "I don't know your last name," I murmur, scooping up a bite of pumpkin. "Although I'm fine just calling you Jillian." Never has there been a more perfect name in all of the Universe.

She grins. "It's O'Connor. A good, solid Irish name." She tugs
at a loose curl. "If the hair wasn't enough of a giveaway."

I perk up. "Any relation to the Caherconlish O'Connors?" I
ask.

She shakes her head. "I don't think so... Why?"

"That's the name of the mayor back home—a pretty well-to-
do family," I reply casually.

She scoffs. "Well then, definitely not! No...my family's lived
in the same three flat in Hoboken for the last...four generations?"
She puts her hands in her lap. "We just keep stacking up like
dominos. My grandparents still live upstairs."

I smile. "That sounds nice, to have your whole family around
you."

"Ha!" she exclaims. "Yeah...I guess. I'm the oldest of seven."

She glances at me to catch my reaction. When I barely blink,
she regards me skeptically. "You don't seem shocked... People usually freak when I tell them that."

I shrug. "I have four older brothers," I explain. When her eyes
brighten, I add, "Where do you think I honed my secret talent? I
also learned how to run *really* fast..."

She laughs. "Well then, you can understand the premium put
on personal space and being alone." She sighs, closing her eyes
happily. "I have my own room now for the first time since I was a
baby. It's, ah..." She grins. "Bliss. Pure bliss! Even with Denise in
the apartment."

We both laugh, remembering her brazen roommate. "Did,
um...did Daniel ever call her?" I ask, my eyes darting toward the
fire stairs.

Jillian draws in a breath and shakes her head. "No...and she's
been on the warpath ever since!" she exclaims, scrunching her
shoulders. "As if she wasn't a caged tiger before... Your friend better watch out—wanted man!!" She breaks into a new fit of giggles.

I sigh. "Yeah, sorry about that. I haven't known Daniel that

long, but I'm getting the sense that he's not easily tied down...
He's sowing his oats, I guess."

"Mmm..." Jillian looks at her plate, taking another bite.
"What about you? Are you...easily tied down?"

I stare at her intently. "Depends who's holding the rope."

We both blush, Jillian setting her fork down with a smile teasing her lips. She clears her throat. "Do you, um...do you miss your family...in Ireland?" she asks, a polite change in subject.

"No." I grimace as her smile fades. I should at least *try* to lie to avoid anything awkward—but something about Jillian makes me unnervingly honest.

"My mother passed last year, and I wasn't really close to anyone else. Started working on different ships across the Atlantic when I was finished with all her arrangements," I answer.

Jillian's eyes soften. "I'm sorry," she whispers.

I wave my hand. "It's okay, really. She had been ill for a while, the end of a very long road..." I sigh. "So pretty much as soon as I turned twenty, I was gone. I just...needed something different."

She nods. "When's your birthday?" she asks after a minute.

"March 15th."

Jillian startles and drops her fork. "No, it's not!" she laughs.

I balk at her. "I'm pretty sure it is!" I answer with a grin.
"Hold on, lemme check my papers..."

"That's my birthday too!" she exclaims, reaching over and taking my hand. "We're birthday buddies!"

I lace our fingers together and beam back at her. "How fantastic! I've never had a...a 'birthday buddy' before!" It sounds wonderfully American.

She sits back and tuts, but doesn't pull her hand away. "Don't get too excited... Sadly, it's one of the most unlucky days of the year." She glances at me mischievously.

I crinkle my brow, baffled. "What do you mean?"

She sighs. "Julius Caesar—'Beware the Ides of March'?" She moves in like she's revealing a dark secret. "'Who is it in the press

that calls on me? I hear a tongue shriller than all the music…
Cry "Caesar!" Speak…'—Shakespeare," she finishes, blushing. "I
remember it from English class."

"You're really smart," I murmur, unable to look away from
her.

She crosses her arms sheepishly. "No, I'm not," she mumbles.
"I can sort of draw and that's pretty much it. It's the only reason I
got into Columbia. My test scores were terrible." She shrugs.

I shake my head. Something tells me that her definition of
'terrible' is very different from everyone else's.

"Anyway, March 15th is the day Brutus stabbed Caesar,
the ultimate betrayal, so…unlucky." She rests her hand back on
the table.

I don't hesitate to pick it up again. "Well, I don't feel unlucky
tonight," I whisper. "Quite the opposite." I hear her breath catch
as I lean across the table, my mouth inches from hers.

"Hey…I hope you two are ready for dessert!"

I lurch back as the sound of Daniel's voice echoes from the
fire escape. "Had to haul it up five flights of stairs, so you better
be ready…"

Daniel emerges balancing two small plates, chocolate sauce
dripping over the side. Muriel follows close behind, carrying a
bottle of champagne. "Of course," I mutter, slightly flustered.
Jillian just smiles as he sets her dessert down in front of her.

"I'm always ready for chocolate." She scrunches her shoulders
and stares at her plate, which holds a fully loaded piece of dark
forest chocolate cake. "Wow."

I wait for Daniel to set the second piece down in front of me,
but instead he hands me a fork. "This one's for me and Muriel…
You can share." He gives me a wink.

I blush as he steps over to the roof's edge and sits, letting
his legs dangle over the edge. Muriel steps over and holds up the
champagne. "Any takers?" she asks, nice and easy. I look to Jillian,
who shakes her head.

"Maybe not after what happened last time..." I tease, both of us brightening as we remember the last time we got a bottle of champagne between the two of us. "For the sake of your dress."

Jillian giggles. "I think we're good." She smiles at Muriel and pushes the cake to the center of the table. "Everything has been so wonderful. Thank you so much for everything." I feel her foot brush mine under the table and edge closer.

"Of course!" Muriel grins. "We've had so much fun helping put it all together." She glances over at Daniel, her eyes going starry. I smile to myself; Muriel can barely contain her giddiness at getting to spend so much one-on-one time with Daniel.

Jillian nods at her. "Well, you've done a fantastic job. The whole thing is just..." She sighs and looks out at the skyline, then back at me. "Magical."

I can see Muriel beaming out of the corner of my eye. "Hey— if they don't want any of that champagne, Muriel, there's more for us," Daniel calls. "Just bring the bottle."

Muriel shoots me a quick grin and skips over to him. Jillian looks at me knowingly before we both break into a fit of giggles. "Here." She gets a forkful of chocolate and hands it to me. "This looks pretty dangerous..."

I put the cake to my lips and nod. "Yes—I'd better test it for your first to make sure it's safe." I try it, the cake melting down my throat. "Mmm..." I moan. "Yep, that's the real deal."

I get a little cake on the fork and offer it to her, greeted by her pretty open mouth instead. I feed her carefully. "Yum!" she exclaims, brushing her lips with her fingers. "What a treat!" She looks at me and turns pink, smiling down at the fork. "Sorry if that was a bit...forward."

I shake my head, leaning close so that our chairs now touch. "I don't think that's possible," I whisper, almost in her ear. "There isn't anything you could do to offend me." I can smell her skin from here, soft and talcum...like baby powder. It's driving me insane.

"I don't want to find out if that's true." She grins, taking another bite of cake. "This really is the nicest date anyone has ever taken me on." She stops and looks down at her hands. "Not that I have a lot to compare it to."

"Me either," I reply honestly. "I can't take credit for the cooking or the presentation...but I *did* pick out the flowers." I motion to the pink rose at the center of the table. "I know it's not much."

"That's my favorite part!" she exclaims, leaning against my shoulder. "I've been looking at it this whole time, thinking about how I want to draw it later." She goes quiet and stares at the flower. "It has to be the most perfect rose ever—perfect petals, perfect stem..." She reaches out and brushes it gently with her finger. "And the color—just glorious. Pink has a certain...sweetness...that the other colors don't have. If given the choice, I'd always go pink."

I watch her look at the rose for another moment before giggling and putting her face in her hands. "You must think I'm nuts!" she cries, grabbing my arm. "Waxing poetic about the centerpiece! I'm sorry, Alden..."

"No, I love it," I breathe. "But I'm an easy audience, I suppose, because I could listen to you read the phonebook and be completely enthralled." She blushes wildly, and I clear my throat. "Anyway...I picked it because it made me think of you." I pull the rose from the vase and hand it to her.

Jillian stares into my eyes. "Who are you, Alden Murphy?" she whispers. "And what did I do to deserve you?"

I get lost in her gaze.

"Guys—come check out this view!" Daniel yells, standing up from the ledge and swinging around the bottle of champagne. Muriel springs up, and he wraps his other arm around her. I grin and take Jillian's hand, walking over next to them. It's a clear night, the stars dim against the bright New York lights, but majestic nonetheless. Jillian holds tight to my hand.

"Look at that." Daniel waves at the view, obviously bursting with pride for his city. Muriel smiles from the crook of his arm as he points out at the skyline, glancing over at me. "Bet they don't have *that* in Ireland."

"They do not." I nod, making him grin even more. "This is the center of the universe."

"Ha! Yes—*center of the universe!*" he mimics, getting Madame's distinct shrillness spot on. We all laugh as Daniel shakes his head. "Nah...this is it." He nods quietly to himself. "Doesn't get any better. Why anybody would ever wanna leave is beyond me."

"Who's talking about leaving?" Muriel tuts up at him, a smile teasing her lips.

Daniel shrugs. "People come and go all the time, right?" He glances at his shoes. "Maybe the hustle is just too much for them, or they think the grass is greener somewhere else." His jaw tenses. "But I don't think I could ever walk away from this, is all I'm saying. Too much excitement, too much life."

We all hum in agreement. "It *is* a big world out there," I murmur, Jillian turning to look at me. "But I don't think I could leave now, either. I'm pretty taken with this place."

Jillian smiles and snuggles into me, pulling my arm around her. I sigh contentedly and look at the four of us standing together. For the first time in my life, I feel like I'm exactly where I'm supposed to be...where I belong. Daniel's right—it doesn't get any better than this.

"We should start cleaning up," Muriel sighs after a bit, turning back to the table. "Before someone notices our lights up here."

As much as it pains me, I break away from Jillian and start clearing dishes, both Muriel and Daniel protesting behind me. "Whoa! What do you think you're doing?" Daniel chides, taking the plates away from me. "The clock hasn't struck midnight yet, Cinderella! Get outta here." He jerks his head towards the fire escape. "We got this. Go have the time of your life."

I grin and grip his arm, pulling him into a quick hug before rushing back to Jillian. "Come on," I exhale. "Onto part two..."

"There's more?" she asks, her eyes wide. "I can't even imagine…"

"Do—do you still want to be with me?" I ask, suddenly unsure of myself again. "I can take you home, if you like."

"Are you crazy?!" she exclaims. "I would ride a garbage barge all the way to Staten Island if it meant I got to spend more time with you." Her cheeks flush. "Of course I want to be with you. It's not even a question."

I smile and take her hand. "Well, now that we've got that settled…" I guide her to the stairs. "Let's go!"

*

"So, a friend of mine said there were carriage rides somewhere around here." I stop and scratch my head, looking both ways down 5th Avenue. The street is alive with restaurants and shops, crowds of people crossing quickly in front of us—the typical constant bustle. If you stopped and looked long enough, I'm sure you could spot someone of every different nationality going by…but no horses.

Jillian chuckles and holds my arm. "My, you really are committed to this whole Prince Charming thing! I have to say, though, stopping to show off your equestrian skills is bordering on insanity." She taps my nose playfully with the rose from dinner.

I glare around the intersection, exasperated. "He just said they'd be here! I hate that I dragged you all the way out here—"

Jillian looks too, her eyes stopping on an alcove behind us. "You didn't drag me anywhere. Hang on a second."

I watch her quizzically as she trots over to the building stoop and crouches down to talk to someone: a homeless man bunkered down in a cardboard box. I feel the hackles on the back of my neck go up. I'm ready to step in if he gets fresh with her, but they just have a short conversation, and then Jillian pulls something out of her purse and hands it to him. With a smile, she gets up and comes back over to me, nodding at the traffic light.

"We're in the right place—but they don't run the carriages on Mondays, only the weekends." She grins and gives a little shrug.

I sigh and nod, ten different shades of embarrassed. "What did you give him?" I jerk my chin back toward the homeless man. "I hope he didn't demand money for this information…"

Jillian laughs and takes my hand as we start walking again. "No—of course not! It's just a thing I've been doing for a while." She wrinkles her nose. "You're gonna think it's weird."

"No, I won't," I reply intensely.

She blushes and grins. "I, um…I try to keep socks in my purse, men's socks…and when I see someone…you know, down on their luck…I give them a pair. They walk so much, they need to keep their feet in good shape." She sighs. "I think it's better than spare change or whatever. I'm just trying to help a little."

Of course she's out helping the homeless. She's the most wonderful, thoughtful person that ever was. Another tick against me, another proof that this girl is way out of my league. I smile weakly and look at her. "That's not weird—it's lovely. You're a lovely person, Jillian." This makes her blush hard, and I exhale. "I'm sorry about the carriage. I've had all week to plan this out, and I wanted this night to be *amazing* for you! Not just some lazy, thrown-together hang out…"

"It *has* been amazing!" she interrupts, gawking at me. "This is the best night of my life!"

I shake my head and shove my hands in my pockets. "You deserve an amazing night…and you deserve a Prince Charming, Jillian." I look at the sidewalk. "I know we just met, but I can tell you're the real thing. You're kind, smart, talented, incredibly beautiful—"

"Stop," she protests, looking away bashfully.

I don't stop. "You're a princess, Jillian, and I'm just the frog, trying to keep up."

She turns back to me and breaks into exasperated laughter. "Oh my gosh, Alden! You have to be the sweetest…" She pauses and closes her eyes. "The sweetest guy I've ever met—and also the most delusional!" We move out of the way and press up against a bakery window as a rush of people come up from the subway behind us, Jillian giggling and grabbing my hand. "Seriously! You're the one looking like something straight out of a magazine, and you're calling *me* a princess?" she demands in my ear.

I stare at her. "You look like all the princesses in the fairytales *I* grew up with," I whisper, bravely cupping her cheek with my palm. "With that hair…and those eyes—you're positively heroic."

Jillian trembles, her body going still at my touch. I pull back, afraid that I've moved too fast. She gasps, her eyes searching mine. I watch her lower lip shiver.

"Are…are you cold?" I ask hesitantly, trying to read her face.

She shakes her head. "No! I mean…maybe a little…" She wraps her bare arms around herself.

I take off my jacket and place it around her shoulders, moving a few loose curls at her neck away from the collar. "I should have given that to you earlier. I'm sorry." I say when she's snugged warmly inside.

She smiles up at me and leans closer. "Well…" I exhale and check the street one more time. "No horse, no carriage—it's just the two of us, I guess."

Jillian laughs and laces her fingers through mine. "Perfect! Let's walk."

I gaze back at her, my heart skipping a beat. "Okay…" I murmur. "Where do you want to go?"

"Anywhere," she croons, "as long as I'm with you."

Arm in arm, we walk quietly past the clubs and theaters toward the river, occasionally stopping to look in the high-end shops, their pristine storefronts decked out in red and gold to welcome autumn. Our breath comes out in puffs of mist as the night goes on, Jillian's cheeks turning the most stunning shade of pink from the cool October air. She cuddles closer to my side to keep warm, and I've never been so happy in all my life.

We get to the Brooklyn Bridge and I stop, holding tight to her hand. "Should we cross?" I ask, wary of the heavy traffic going by.

Jillian looks around. "There's the sidewalk over there… Let's just go to the middle, and then we'll turn around. I think there's a pretty nice view of the Statue of Liberty from the west side…" She smiles and pulls her glasses from her purse, putting them back on. "No use playing coy now."

I grin and wrap my arm around her as we move over the bridge, cold whirlwinds gusting heavily and pushing us closer together still. When we make it to the lookout point, I turn and stare at how the wind whips her hair violently across her cheeks.

"Look!" she cries, pointing out at the harbor. "I think I can see her!" She grins widely, trying to show me.

I glance at the water, then back at her. "She's beautiful!" I lean in so I don't have to yell quite so loudly over the wind. "But I can't seem to tear myself away from you…"

Jillian spins and faces me, holding her breath, her pink lips shining in the street lights. Before I can stop myself, I gather her in my arms and kiss her, mashing my mouth to hers urgently. I wait for her to resist, to push me away, but she doesn't. Instead, she wraps her arms around my neck and sighs, her breath warm, before kissing me back, mirroring my fervor. In that moment, I let go, my whole world exploding into fireworks.

"Alden…" she gasps after a minute, leaning back slightly to get a look at me. I'm sure I must bear some resemblance to a wild dog right now, hungry for more. "That was…" She shakes her head and tastes her lips, searching for the right word.

I tense, going back to my old self in a flash. "I'm sorry—was… was that wrong? Or…bad?" I step away, running a hand through my hair. "I've never…done anything like that before."

Jillian blinks disbelievingly. "Was that…? *Am I your first kiss?!*" she demands.

I stare over at the street, embarrassed. "You're my first *every-thing*, Jillian—first kiss, first date…" I cross my arms. "I'm sorry I'm not more…um…I mean, I hope that wasn't completely rotten for you."

She reaches over boldly and pulls me back to her. "Stop! What am I going to have to do to prove you're enough for me?" she exclaims. She reaches up and jerks my chin down so that I meet her fierce green eyes. "I don't care if you've been with a hundred other girls or just broke out of a monastery—that was amazing! I've never felt anything like it." She stares at me imploringly. "Did…did you feel it too?"

I nod, unable to tear my eyes away. "Yes, with every fiber of my being."

Jillian straightens up at that, gripping my arms tight. "Wanna see if it was just a fluke—try again?" she wonders hopefully.

I smile and lean back in, pressing my lips to hers more gently this time and letting the intensity grow on its own. This kiss, I can tell, is leaving me forever altered; whatever came before is just a memory now, lost in black and white.

CHAPTER 9
LOS ANGELES—PRESENT DAY

*J*WAKE UP LATE, the pale winter sun peeking through the curtains and sending jagged little pieces of light flittering across the walls. I sit up and rub my face blearily before remembering that I don't have school today, since it's the first day of break. Normally, this would be cause for celebration, but after everything that happened yesterday, I'm feeling less jovial than usual. I sigh and get out of bed, grabbing my sweatshirt because the house is slightly chillier than usual.

As I walk down the hall towards the kitchen, massaging my arms to try to get them to warm up, a cool gust of air blows at me from the wide-open front door—the obvious culprit. I instantly tense and glare around the foyer, looking for invaders. Instead, I'm greeted with the familiar sound of clanging pots from the kitchen. I exhale in relief and pad around the corner see Daniel crouched down at the side of the kitchen counter.

"What's with the front door?" I grumble, slouching into a chair at the table.

My Guardian looks up at me and smiles. "Hey—you're awake!" Straightening, he shuffles around to the doorway. "Oh yeah, I forgot about that..." Bending down, he gives a thick yellow extension cord that's snaking across the floor and out the door a slap against the wood. "There's some sort of wiring problem with the porch outlet," he explains, biting his lip thoughtfully. "I can't get any power out to the lights in the garden. I'm gonna try to see if I can run this thing through the living room window…"

As he starts winding the cord up around his elbow, I yawn and pull my knees to my chest. "You're here early—where's Mary Carmen?" I wonder, looking around.

Daniel smirks. "She had to be into work by 7 this morning, so she asked me come by and make sure you stayed out of trouble."

"Oh, really?" I tuck my chin into my knees, hiding a smile, then straighten up and set my feet on the chilly tile floor. "You know Trouble is my middle name—so good luck with that."

"Ha," he snorts, tossing the coiled extension cord back on the floor. "Constant Vigilance is mine."

I shake my head—he's such a dork. "Well, Constant Vigilance, would you mind if we closed up the house for a bit? I know super-heroes aren't affected by the temperature at all, but some of us are turning into icicles here." I arch an eyebrow.

Daniel rolls his eyes and chuckles. "You *do* know you live in Southern California, right? It's like…60 degrees outside and sunny." He shakes his head as he walks into the front hall and shuts the door. "Could be so much worse!"

"So now I should be punished because I didn't choose to live in the Arctic? You know your blood thins after a while out here!" I call. When he comes back into the kitchen and grins at me, I smile and feign getting the vapors. "I wasn't made for that."

"Such a sensitive soul!" he comments with a fake swoon. Stepping back to the oven, he adds, "Well, what can I get you for breakfast—before you waste away altogether?"

I lean back against the wall and shrug, my sulky mood return-ing. "I dunno… I'm not really hungry. Maybe just some toast."

Daniel frowns. "I think you mean French toast, coming right up." He grabs the butter and eggs out of the fridge and gets to work.

I sigh and run a hand through my tangled hair. "You don't have to do that," I mutter, my attitude getting the best of me. "Always cooking for me. I can get it myself."

He looks up at me curiously. "I like cooking for you," he replies matter-of-factly as he gets the egg batter ready. "Besides, we both know you're a better eater than cook."

I feel my face redden. "I can cook!" I bark defensively. "And what does that mean, 'better eater'? Are you trying to tell me something? Think I'm getting soft, roly-poly?"

Daniel gives me a look. "Please, Christa. No, you just really enjoy a good meal. It's…satisfying to watch, for me." He keeps his eyes trained on the bowl in front of him. "You sort of purr when you like something."

I let out a squeal and cover my face with my hands. "Oh my God—don't say things like that! Some stuff, you should just keep to yourself!" I shout, not sure if I'm tickled or mortified. I choose to go with the former and slink over to him.

"You know who *is* getting fat: this fish." I point at the fish tank as I pop up on the counter. It's true: when Daphne first arrived, she had been small enough to fit inside a Christmas tree orna-ment—*had*, in fact, fit inside a Christmas tree ornament. Now, she had to be close to the size of my hand, making her five-gallon tank feel more like an efficiency apartment than the luxury fish palace that it was a few weeks ago.

Daniel bats my arm. "You shouldn't talk about D-Money that way… She's just big boned!" he stage whispers.

I glare at him. "Seriously, Daniel! She's, like, doubled in size! Do you think we're overfeeding her?" I pick up the fish food and look at the ingredients. "What's in this stuff, anyway?"

Daniel furrows his brow. "Maybe she's pregnant… Can fish get pregnant?" he asks earnestly, turning back to the stove.

I balk and slam down the fish food. "Of course fish can get pregnant—but she's all alone in there, Daniel! Unless we're in store for some sort of immaculate conception Christmas miracle thing, I don't think that's what's going on here!"

He shrugs, flipping the toast with a spatula. "Stranger things have happened."

I sigh and pull my phone from its wall charger, going through my messages. I frown: there's nothing from Jodie... I was really hoping that maybe she would have calmed down overnight, but no such luck. There *is* a text from Livie, though; I read it and huff through my nose.

Daniel glances at me over his shoulder. "What's up?" he asks, turning off the stove.

I sit back and scratch my eyebrow. "Oh...my friend Livie from Group wants to know if we want to meet her and her new boyfriend for coffee on Christmas Eve. She was asking if we're free in the afternoon." I toss the phone back on the counter and pull my hands into my sweatshirt sleeves.

Daniel nods as he transfers my breakfast onto a plate and drizzles it with maple syrup. "We should be done with dinner prep by then. Sounds fun." He cocks his head to the side, taking in my sullen expression. "What? You don't look convinced."

I watch Daniel's backside forlornly as he works at the counter. It's kind of hard to be happy for your friends and their new relationships when there's not even a chance that it's going to happen for you. Not that I'm bitter or anything. "I dunno," I grumble. "Between all the holiday crap and what happened yesterday at school..." I rub my forehead wearily. "I just don't know if I'm in the mood to witness new love...unfurling, or whatever."

Daniel spins around and sets my plate down in front of me. "Nice word of the day, 'unfurling,'" he snickers, reaching into the silverware drawer for a knife and fork. I cross my legs and pull the plate into my lap, nodding thanks as he hands me my utensils.

"But you gotta get out of this funk, Christa!" he adds, leaning back against the oven and crossing his arms. "Where's your Christmas spirit?"

"Ugh!" I exclaim, almost dropping my food. "If one more person asks me that…"

Daniel rolls his eyes. "Well, you haven't been exactly Suzy Sunshine for the last couple weeks."

I grind my teeth at him. Undeterred, he nods at my French toast, encouraging me to eat. "Which I understand!" he placates. "You have a lot going on…"

I sigh and take a bite, all sins temporarily forgiven as I savor its sweet flavor. Daniel waits for my reaction. "It's good," I grunt reluctantly, spearing another forkful.

He sighs. "It just seems like it would be a waste not to enjoy the next couple days." He pushes off of the oven with his hands. "We don't have to be anywhere or do anything…and a certain Irish-brogued Demon isn't even on the same continent." Seeing me bristle at the mention of Alden, Daniel hastily finishes, "And that's a good thing—we can relax! This might be the closest thing to a vacation that we get for a while." He steps over to me, his eyes warm. "I want you to have fun, to be happy. I want…" He exhales and runs his hands through his hair. "I want to be happy *with* you," he murmurs.

My breath catches in my throat, and I put my fork down to take his hand. "I know," I whisper, watching his face. "And you have been doing such an amazing job helping me with school and getting the house ready and just…taking care of everything." I smile at him weakly.

Daniel blushes, pleased. "Well…someone had to do the lights. Mary Carmen tried to do it herself a few years back and blew the entire neighborhood's power grid."

We both laugh, and I squeeze his hand. "Thank you, Daniel. I probably don't say that enough. And…I am happy, really." I force myself to smile brighter, trying to make that last part not look like the lie that it is.

Daniel doesn't take much convincing: he breaks into his

trademark half-moon grin. "Okay—good deal!" He pulls me into a quick hug before stepping away and grabbing a dish cloth.

I go back to my breakfast, feeling more withdrawn than I did when I first woke up.

Daniel doesn't seem to notice. "So what are we doing today?" he chirps, attacking the stovetop with the rag. "First day of break, better make it count…" He stops and blinks. "What does one *do* on Christmas break?" he wonders quizzically.

I shrug. "International travel? Get drunk and ignore your kids?" I shake my head. "Maybe have a small plastic surgery procedure done, freshen up for the New Year? I dunno, take your pick."

Daniel glares at me. "Then what do *you* do on Christmas break? You know…normally?"

I rest my head against the wall and take a breath. "Usually, I would hang out with Jodie, and we'd make a bunch of those Break-n-Bake Christmas cookies and decorate them with like…a pound of frosting each. We'd then eat them all while we binge watched whatever new TV show we were into." I smile at the memory.

Daniel's eyes brighten. "*We* could bake! I know a great recipe for a chocolate macadamia nut—lemme check our flour situation." He scurries over to one of the lower cabinets and starts rummaging around, coming back up holding a crinkled bag of flour. "Yeah, we still have enough from making the gravy last month… I just think we need to go get some chocolate chips."

He stops when he sees my face and my sagging shoulders. I try to seem excited, but probably come off looking more like a deflated balloon. "It's not the same," he mumbles, putting the flour away.

I sigh and sit up. "I'm sorry, Daniel. I know you're trying. I wish nothing had happened yesterday…that it could have been just another boring day." I tuck my hair behind my ears. "I hate that Jodie is so mad at me, and there's nothing I can do about it."

Daniel nods. "You can give her time. She *will* come around,

Christa—I know it. She loves you too much to stay angry forever." I sigh and bite my lip as he pats my leg. "But in the meantime, we should do something to keep your mind off it. Let's get outta here!" He scrunches his nose.

I can't help but smile when he looks at me like that. "Where are we gonna go?" I wonder, shaking my head.

He puts his finger to his mouth thoughtfully. "Mmm… maybe Vegas, Tahoe—somewhere with blackjack?" he jokes. "I just promised M.C. I'd have you home for dinner."

I smack him on the arm and sit up. "Maybe we could go to the mall, finish up some shopping," I offer, seeing as our other shopping trip was cut short. "Last time didn't go so well."

Daniel chuckles darkly. "We'll stay away from Melrose. Nothing too boutique-y or high end—designer labels are instant Demon bait. It'll just be you and me, hangin' with the norms at Forever 21."

I laugh and hop off the counter. "K. Lemme go change."

Daniel shakes his head. "No no no! You're perfect just as you are! No one will ever recognize you in those oversized sweatpants! We're trying to blend here, Christa!" he protests.

I roll my eyes and punch him lightly in the stomach. "Yeah, right. That's not possible for you and me."

*

The Christmas tree at the Galleria fills the main atrium with its heavy evergreen bows and stretches up to the third story, the gold angel perched atop it practically brushing the vaulted glass ceiling. With just a few days left before Christmas, the mall is packed with shoppers laden down with coats and bags, wrangling crying children as they desperately try to find that last perfect something. I exhale and take it all in as Daniel and I watch from the second-floor balcony.

"So who do you have left on your list?" Daniel asks pleasantly.

I arch back on my boot heels, gripping the security rail to

keep my balance. "I gave Mr. Trundi his present last week…" A new set of flash drives designed to look like DNA molecules. His mustache almost fell off, he was so pleased. "And I got Mom and Mary Carmen done, so just Jodie." I shrug and peek at him out of the corner of my eye. "And you."

Daniel's face lights up. "You're gonna get me something? Really?" He sounds genuinely surprised.

I shake my head and stare out at the mall. "Of course I'm going to get you something! Jeez, Daniel…" I snicker. "I just don't know what, yet. What do you get the Guardian who has everything?"

He turns and rests against the balcony railing. "I don't… need…" He blushes. "…I just thought, with everything that was going on…I don't want you to have to stress about getting me anything, seriously. Your presence is my present!" He laughs awkwardly, rubbing his neck.

I roll my eyes. "Did you get me something?" I ask bluntly. When he tilts his head and grins, I add, "Yeah…so then *I'll* be the jerk on Christmas morning. Don't worry, I'll come up with something." I sigh and squint and look down to where a crowd is gathering on the first floor. "What's going on there?"

"Looks like they're lining up for something," Daniel murmurs, watching. His eyes go wide.

"What?" I bark, instantly on red alert.

"Santa…" he gasps, grabbing my arm. "Oh man—we gotta get a picture!"

I glower back at him, panic still ringing in my ears. "Really? God, you totally freaked me out just now!"

"Christa! It's almost the big day. You have to tell Santa what you want." He starts to drag me down the escalator.

"I don't want anything." I pull my sleeve back irritably. "Except to curl up in my bed and…*ignore* everyone and everything around me until New Year's." My shoulders droop as I take in the very long line. "God, this just keeps getting worse and worse."

Daniel shakes his head at me. "You don't mean that. Come on, you were in a good mood the other night when you came home and saw the tree. What happened?"

I glare at him. "Um…Demons showed up at my school and turned my best friend against me?"

Daniel frowns and stares over my head at the crowd. "Don't let them take this away from us too, Christa," he whispers. "We've lost so much as it is… Who knows if we'll get to do this again."

Looking at his rigid back, I know that this isn't a good time to be snarky. I exhale and put my smile back on. "Hey, yeah—you're right." I bat him playfully on the arm, trying to lighten the mood.

He arches a brow, smirking. "I'm *right?* That might be a first with you. Hope your mouth didn't burn when you said that."

I grimace as we get in place at the back of the line. "No, really, I've been a major drag lately. I'm sorry." I sigh. "This is your holiday, too… I don't want to ruin it for you or anybody else." I cross my arms and stare at him.

He looks positively dumbfounded. "Well, that's very big of you," he finally replies cautiously. "What's the catch?"

I hip check him. "No catch! Jeez, give me a little credit." The crowd starts to edge forward.

"No, absolutely—I should just enjoy this moment while it lasts." He puts his hands in his pockets as we shuffle along in line. "What are you going to ask Santa for?"

I sigh. "A lobotomy."

When Daniel throws his hands up in exasperation, I add, "I'm kidding! Holy cow! I dunno…" I watch a mom and her little boy in front of us, the kid playing with a matchbox firetruck. "Maybe some new jeans or, like, movie passes…"

Daniel lulls his head back and fake snores. "Boring! You gotta do better than that, Christa."

"Oh my God—it's *my* Christmas list!" I protest. "Keep your judgements to yourself!" I can't have what I *really* want for

Christmas—I look at him longingly when his head is turned. Strictly verboten.

"Oh man—you gotta be kidding me!" Daniel grumbles a minute later, throwing his hands in the air. I crane my face to see what he's looking at and feel my mood brighten as I take in the life-size poster of Dwight Carroll detailing the autograph signing that's happening right now.

"This isn't even the right line." Daniel cringes and takes me by the arm. "This town is ridiculous—can't go twenty feet without them pushing some new celebrity at you. I think we're supposed to be on the other side…"

"No—this is perfect!" I exclaim, pulling away. "He's from *Vampires Suck*!"

Daniel rolls his eyes. "Yeah, I know. I lost an hour of my existence watching his lifeless face trying to make words the other night." He scowls, still looking for the Santa line.

I shake my head. "He's Jodie's favorite actor," I explain, breaking it down for him. "If I get her an autograph for Christmas, she'll flip…" I bite my lip. "And then maybe she'll forgive me, and we can just forget what happened." I get up on my tiptoes, trying to see the front table.

Daniel takes off his hat and runs a hand through his hair, eyeing me warily. "Fine. But only because it means so much to you… for *Jodie*."

"Yes, just Jodie," I agree, hiding my smile.

Daniel grimaces as he takes in the line, both of us now noticing that it's mostly made up of middle-aged women. "This guy is so lame…" he mutters.

I smile and bounce up and down excitedly.

We eventually make it to the front of the line, where Dwight Carroll sits posed behind a large folding table. He's wearing a black leather jacket over a fitted red sweater, his sleek brown hair gelled back in a stylish pompadour. He's flanked on either side by models in sexy green elf dresses. One of them smiles at Daniel, revealing a set of fake Vampire teeth.

Daniel shakes his head at me. "Make it quick," he grits out, stepping over to a large gingerbread house display off to the side. I shoot him a look and then glance back at Dwight Carroll, surprised by the butterflies in my belly. I usually don't go all squirmy for people on TV, but even I have to agree with Jodie this time: he's *really* cute.

Noticing my hesitation, Dwight Carroll looks up at me with stunning hazel eyes. "Don't be shy," he purrs, beckoning me with his hand and nodding at the models. "They won't bite."

I can see Daniel rolling his eyes a few feet away. I smile and tuck my hair nervously behind my ears, moving over to the table.

"Hi," Dwight Carroll adds with a grin, pulling a headshot from the stack of photos to his left. "How you doing today?" He sits back in his chair, clicking his sharpie pen.

I blush, taken aback that he's stopping to make conversation. "Um...good," I mumble, putting my hands in my coat. "How... how are you?"

His grin widens, *almost* putting Daniel's to shame. "I'm good—really good. I love getting out and meeting fans. That's sweet of you to ask." His eyes crinkle as he blatantly checks me out.

I straighten up, not wanting to give him a bad view. "I don't know—it must get kind of...boring, having to talk to a bunch of people who are obsessed with you." I quirk my head back toward the line.

Dwight Carroll chuckles. "I wouldn't call them 'obsessed'..." His mouth twitches. "Just enthusiastic. So, what are your plans for the holiday?"

Caught totally off-guard by the question, I shake my head and turn a deeper shade of pink under his stare. "Uh...sleeping in?" I stammer. Pinnacle of wit, right here. I close my eyes and try again. "Maybe a little grand larceny to mix things up…" Better.

Dwight Carroll snickers at that. "You don't seem like a troublemaker to me," he croons, looking like a 1950s bad boy. "But those are always the most dangerous—the ones you don't suspect."

Holy cow, he's good. "Whatever," I mutter, not knowing what to say next. He's really drawing this out, and I can tell people behind me are starting to get impatient. "Well," I hedge, "I don't wanna take up anymore of your time…"

"Where are all your shopping bags?" he interrupts, focusing on my empty arms. "Looks like you've still got some work to do."

I shrug and bite my lip. "You know…still trying to find that perfect something."

Dwight Carroll arches a brow and leans forward. "You're pretty when you do that with your lip." He points at my mouth. "Sexy."

I feel my legs turn to jelly. Dwight Carroll thinks I'm sexy? What is happening? I turn and glance at Daniel, who is staring back at me, pacing tempestuously. He catches my eye and flashes his wrist, mouthing *Come on, already!*

I clench my jaw and jerk my chin. He throws his hands up and stalks in a tight circle.

"So…" Dwight Carroll clears his throat.

I spin back, flustered, and give him a smile. He smiles back, his pen poised over the photo. "Who should I make this out to, Christa?" he asks lazily.

I take a breath and fidget with my jacket zipper. "Um, it's actually for my friend Jodie—J-O-D-I…" I stop and blink. "Wait—how do you know my name? I…I never said it…"

He sits back, his lips puckered. "Everyone knows your name, Christa," he replies, just loud enough for me to hear. "You're a bigger star than me—but you already knew that."

I feel a shiver go down my spine and stumble backwards, but catch myself before I make a scene. Only one person *does* notice, and he's at my side in seconds. "What's going on here?" Daniel breathes into my hair, glaring at Dwight Carroll.

I shake my head and squint. "Nothing…nothing," I murmur, gawking at the actor. He's not a Demon or an Angel; he's just… Human. "You're Smudged," I whisper.

Dwight Carroll sits back and smirks. "I am so much more than that, baby," he replies coolly.

I feel bile rise in my throat as things click into place. "Oh, gross—you're a PET!" I shout, much louder than I intended due to my disgust.

Both Daniel and Dwight duck their heads, Daniel pressing his hand to my waist. "Tone it down, Christa…" he grumbles in my ear.

I hold up my hand and nod. "I know—sorry." I sneer back at Dwight, unable to keep the revulsion out of my voice. "I just can't believe that you…" Drink Demon blood. Grovel and serve psychopathic Demon masters. I exhale. "That you…*do* the things you do." I grimace. "It's vile."

Dwight Carroll narrows his eyes before letting out a throaty laugh. "That's a bit hypocritical, don't you think, Christa?" He crosses his arms and glares at us. "We all know what happened last month at the Warehouse between the two of you and Alden." When I flinch at the sound of that name, Dwight Carroll grins and adds, "If it hadn't been for that *vileness*, you wouldn't be alive right now, nor would you have the gift of Sight. You'd still be wandering around in the dark with the rest of the Mundies." He cocks his head back to the line of eager fans, now growing very restless.

I take a breath and lean against the table. "I'm not saying this because I like you or give two shits about you one way or the other," I hiss, feeling Daniel's hand tighten at my waist. "But you should get out now while you have the chance. Before they completely screw you over." I can feel my whole body trembling.

Dwight just looks at me and smiles. "It is so sad that you feel that way, truly," he moues, his voice condescending. "You have no idea what they're really capable of, how they can change your life in so many ways—for the better." He snorts. "You think I got where I am today on looks alone? Please."

"Well, it certainly wasn't based on talent," Daniel interjects, hauling me back from the table. "Come on, Christa, let's get outta here."

"Don't forget this," Dwight Carroll sniggers, holding up the signed photo. "For your friend?"

I shoot him a dirty look, my stomach churning. "No way," I scoff. "I can find her something way better than that—like, *anything* else." I take Daniel's hand and start to walk away.

"Merry Christmas, Christa!" Dwight Carroll calls behind us. "Looking forward to seeing you again soon! You'll be at the party, right? Mandisa is still awaiting your reply."

I gasp, the mention of Herod's Feast stopping me dead in my tracks. "Christa..." Daniel clenches my fingers, his eyes concerned.

I shake my head and turn slowly back to Dwight. "I...I don't know..." The truth sort of tumbles out.

Dwight Carroll breaks into a grin, and I hear Daniel draw in a sharp breath. "Well, don't keep us waiting too long!" the actor laughs, motioning his next victim forward. "You know there's nothing they hate more than impropriety." He smiles and goes back to the woman now in front of his table.

Daniel wrenches me hard by the hips. "We're leaving—NOW," he snaps. He pulls me away from the crowds toward the front entrance, his pace brisk and no-nonsense. He only stops once we're outside the mall, his fingers clenching on my wrist.

"When we're you going to tell me you were still thinking about going to that thing?!" he shouts, his eyes darting out to the street to make sure no one is coming.

I sigh and lean against the concrete wall. "God, Daniel, it's not a big deal—"

"It's a *very* big deal!" He lets go of me to yank at his hair.

"Christa, I can't believe you would even consider..." He stops and clenches his fists, taking a step back. "I can't believe you would even consider going back to them after what happened," he breathes after a minute. "What they did to you, to your mom..."

I bristle, crossing my arms and keeping my eyes trained on the ground. "I was there—you don't need to remind me."

"Well, clearly I do because you're still thinking about that party! And I know you know it's a bad idea because you didn't say anything to me about it!" He shakes his head angrily. "Why?! Why would you put yourself in that position all over again?"

"Because I need answers!" I yell, my temper catching up with me. "I need to know what I'm supposed to do, why I'm...BLUE!" I thrust my hands in his face.

He glares back at me. I sigh. "Don't get me wrong... You and Mary Carmen have been great. And you've kept me safe and... *happy*." I bite my tongue as his eyes soften. "But I need more than that, Daniel. I can't just sit around and wait for whatever is going to happen next to just fall into my lap..." I kick the wall lightly with my boot. "I have to figure out who I am now—what it means to be the...the Catalyst." I hate to even say the word.

Daniel rubs his face wearily and leans next to me. I rest my cheek against his shoulder, smelling the leather of his jacket. Even with the cool December breeze blowing at us, he's still warm and inviting.

"Okay," he finally sighs. "Okay. We'll get you what you need." He moves off the wall and takes my hand.

I glance up at him nervously. "Where are we going?" I ask as he guides me past the parking garage and back to the bus stop.

"To get you answers." He nods, looking straight ahead. "From a *legitimate* source."

I balk. "What? Who are we—?"

He squeezes my hand. "It's not far. I think the 11 goes there."

When we make it to the bus stop, he checks the map. "Yeah, should be here any minute..." He stares at me, his face grim. "I don't even know if we're allowed to do this, but I'll do anything to keep you from going back to them. Do you understand?"

I gape at him. "*Allowed?* Daniel…"

He nods at the street, the Number 11 pulling up to the curb. "Just…think before you say anything, please?" He winces. "These are people you don't wanna step outta line with, all right? Don't talk yourself into a corner."

I shake my head, my eyes wide. "Yes…fine." We step onto the bus. "But I thought you said this was a legitimate source?"

He sniggers as we take a seat. "Well…'legitimate' and 'safe' are two different beasts." He looks out the window. "Just stay close."

I snuggle into his side as the bus drives away.

*

"This is strange…" I mutter as we pull into a new parking lot. "Not that I should expect any different by now."

The bus pulls in front of a Super Target and comes to a stop, the brakes squealing noisily. Daniel stands up and shrugs. "Always finding new ways to be inconspicuous—that's the name of the game, right?" He motions for me to follow. "Dusty bookshops and secret bat caves are so last week."

I give him a small smile as we clomp off the bus and onto the sidewalk. It's not as busy as the mall, but close—it's crowded with people who are scooting behind large red carts filled with discount toys and wrapping paper.

""What—do we hover around the home goods aisle and whisper to an ottoman?" I chuckle.

Daniel tilts his head. "Not too off-base…come on."

Instead of going through the store, we take a hard left, and he guides us back to the restrooms, pulling me into the family bathroom and locking the door behind us. I search around for something out of the ordinary, but it's just got two toilets—one big, one child-sized—a sink, and baby changing table. There's a utility closet door on the far wall marked Employees Only.

I give Daniel a look. "It's just a bathroom," I say, stating the obvious.

Daniel shakes his head and takes a seat on the adult-sized toilet. "Not so fast…" He reaches onto the wall next to him: just above the toilet paper roll is a red Emergency Assistance button and speaker. He taps it with his pointer finger.

"Can I help you?" a woman's voice chimes brightly. I blink: this is a voice I've heard before.

"Yeah, it's Daniel." He clears his throat and leans back. "I have Christa Nichols with me, and we need to speak to someone at extension 1532." He watches me out of the corner of his eye.

"Of course, Guardian," the voice replies.

I startle as the lock on the utility closet door buzzes and clicks open. "Please remove your shoes before entering, and if you are wearing any timepieces, reset them now to SPT. An Agent will be with you shortly." The speaker goes dead.

I stare dumbly as Daniel kicks off his sneakers and offers me his hand. "An Agent?" I murmur.

Daniel nods. "Yeah. You said you wanted answers—so we're going to Porticullis to meet the Gray."

CHAPTER 10
NEW YORK CITY—
NOVEMBER, 1975

"OH WOW! THAT was the coolest thing I've ever seen!" Sam exclaims as we leave the 86th Street cinema and head over to the crosswalk.

Jillian shoots me a smile as she takes her little brother by the hand. "Yeah, it *was* really cool…" she chuckles, checking the street for traffic.

Sam looks up at me, a toothy Jack-o-lantern grin spread across his face. "Do you think there really are aliens out there, Alden? Just like in *Escape to Witch Mountain*?" he asks excitedly, taking my hand as we cross the road and forming a chain between the three of us. His small fingers are already turning pink from the cold.

I crinkle my brow, considering. "I never thought much about it, Sam. I guess there could be…" I gasp in mock horror. "What if they're slime green with three heads and enormous teeth?! Or they take over the planet and force us all to eat only asparagus and turnips for the rest of our lives?!"

Sam knocks playfully into my side as we make it over to the west side of the street. "No way! That's not real… They were *people* in the movie!" He lets his sister's hand go, but holds onto mine, swinging our arms as we walk. "I totally want a harmonica, just like Tony. Then I'd have magic powers…"

He furrows his brow and looks up at Jillian. "Jilly, if I had a magic harmonica, could I blow on it and not have to clean my room anymore?" He stares at her, his baby face serious.

Jillian sighs and bends down to zip up his winter coat. "I don't know if that's how it works, buddy." She gives him a onceover, stopping at his bright red hair. "Where's your hat? Did you leave it at the theater?"

Sam shakes his head. "I put it in my pocket so I wouldn't lose it." He carefully reaches into his jacket and pulls out a blue and green knit hat, handing it to her.

Jillian crouches down and pulls it on over his ears. "That's better. How are we on time?" She glances at me as she stands.

I smile. "We have time. Do you still want to go to the park?"

She opens her mouth to answer, but Sam cuts her off. "Yes! Yes! I still wanna go to the park!" he shouts, pressing his round chin into Jillian's waist, the toggles on her navy car coat catching on his zipper. "Please, please, Jilly? It's right there!" He points behind us to Central Park.

She laughs and glances at me, her fiery hair coming to life around her in the breeze. "Do you mind? I know it's getting cold…"

I take her hand and grin. "There are ways to combat that."

She blushes and squeezes my fingers, Sam watching us hopefully. "Okay, fine!" she laughs, motioning forward with her other hand while still holding tightly to mine. "Lead the way!"

"YES!" Sam crows, thrusting his fist into the air before darting on ahead.

We both smile as we watch him run, Jillian resting her cheek on my shoulder as we slowly follow. "Sorry, he's a little excitable…" She juts her chin toward where Sam is making his way over to the sprawling lawn by the carousel. "What you would call 'high energy.'"

"He's six," I answer with a smile. "He's supposed to be high energy—running around, yelling, tearing up the neighborhood." I wrap my arm around her waist. "I like him. Almost as much as his big sister."

Jillian grins, keeping her eye on Sam as he begins to climb on top of the big black rocks. "He's a good boy, tries hard."

"Of course he is. He's related to you, isn't he?" I purr into her ear.

I watch a curl of blush creep over her collar. "I'm not always good," she murmurs coyly.

I flash my eyebrows. "I find that hard to believe." Laughing, I lead her to a park bench where we can see Sam clearly.

She sits down next to me, tucking in close. "Is that a challenge?" she giggles, taking my hand again and holding it in her lap.

"No, no!" I shake my head. "I just don't picture you as a... troublemaker."

"Really? You think you know me so well?" She smirks.

The corner of my mouth twitches. "You're trying to tell me you were a rabble-rouser in school, Ms. Valedictorian?" I chuckle. "What, did you forget to return a library book?"

She wrinkles her nose and swats me on the leg. "There may have been a nun or two in my past who had it out for me!" She runs her fingers tenderly through her hair. "I suffered the occasional harsh yank of a braid when I wasn't paying attention."

"For shame!" I exclaim, my tone dark as I lean in protectively. "I'll kill 'em, kill 'em all! It'll be a massacre—bloody nuns scattered all over the highway for inflicting harm on my dear, sweet Jillian!" I brush my free hand across her cheek, her eyes widening in delight.

She giggles, resting her chin on my palm. "What about you? What were you like in school?" she asks.

I blow out my cheeks and sit back. "I spent my fair share of time locked in a custodial cupboard." I smile, only half joking. "Definitely on the receiving end of parochial school violence." I shrug. "That's just how it was."

She grins. "I don't know if I can promise the same level of retribution...with the blood and massacring..."

I scoff and pull her close. "And I wouldn't want you to! You're too good for any of that, Jillian."

She sighs and sits up. "Now we're back to 'good'—I'm always so *good*."

I frown, watching her intently. "And whoever said being good is a bad thing? I like that you're kind, courteous, responsible..." I cheat my jaw toward Sam. "The way you jumped out of your seat on the subway this morning to let that old lady sit down before I even knew what was going on. It was nice."

Jillian glances down at our hands. "*Nice*..." she sighs. "Nice girls get the short end of the stick."

I make a face. "What does that mean?"

She shrugs. "I don't know. Muriel and I were talking about it the other day when she met me down at the MOMA. It's nice to have a friend who doesn't mind looking at art while I sit and do my homework..."

"I didn't know you two were becoming friends." I smile approvingly, liking the idea very much. "That's good. She's a nice person."

Jillian rolls her eyes. "Yes, she is...and you're proving my point!" she says, exasperated. "'*Nice* is like this...unshakeable label...that makes you invisible to...a certain type of guy that Muriel likes."

I nod, suddenly understanding. "Ah, I see..."

"Sure, nice girls are thoughtful, sweet, reliable..." She looks away. "But definitely not 'sexy.'"

The corners of my mouth turn up as I watch her sulk. "Can't you be both?" I whisper into her hair. I feel her catch her breath next to me as I lean in. "Surely the two can find a way to live in harmony... I think you carry it flawlessly."

She turns to me, biting her lip. "You're both, too. Nice...and sexy." Her bright eyes search mine as she starts to shiver again. I'm hoping it's not from the cold.

"You think I'm sexy?" I ask, surprised.

She stares at me and then bursts out laughing. "You're kidding, right?" She shakes her head incredulously. "Seriously—don't you know what you *look* like?" She motions to my hair and face.

I shrug, feeling awkward. "I'm just a regular bloke from the middle of nowhere—nothing special." If anything, I probably come off like a complete country bumpkin: undereducated, under-experienced, underclass. I check my jacket lapels to make sure they're not out of order.

Jillian rolls her eyes. "Well, maybe things are different in Ireland...but here, boys like you don't..." She exhales and smooths her coat, letting go of my hand. "They don't *look* at girls like me." She gazes down at her lap, readjusting her glasses.

I give her a small smile and reach over, tucking a loose curl back behind her ear. She trembles, the skin behind her jaw rouging up. "You're the only girl I see," I breathe. "Whether I'm awake or sleeping...in a room full of people or totally, utterly alone...I'm always looking for you. I'm never really satisfied until I have you right here." I run my finger behind her ear and down the rosy patch of skin blooming across her collarbone.

She breathes loudly. "See, that's sexy," she rasps, turning to me, her face angled just the right way for me to lean in and kiss her. "You don't need me to convince you of that." She leans in a little closer.

"Mmm, maybe I do..." I smile next to her lips.

She tuts. "You shouldn't be allowed to speak. It's criminal." She gently presses her mouth to mine, a small breath passing between us as the kiss intensifies. She sighs as I tangle my fingers in her hair, wanting to devour her whole, her taste honey-sweet. I take my time searching every part of her—her tongue, the corners of her mouth, gently tugging on her bottom lip. She exhales and moves her hand inside my coat...

"GROSS!" Sam yells from the rocks, wrinkling his nose in disapproval. We quickly separate and sit chastely on the bench, catching our breath before grinning knowingly at each other. Sam watches us and nods, going back to his game once he's sure everyone is behaving themselves again.

Jillian chuckles and snuggles up to my side. "Thank you again for taking us to the movies today. That was...*nice* of you."

We both laugh. "I'm a nice guy, or so I've been told." I arch a brow.

She shakes her head. "Really, I appreciate you putting up with me having to babysit Sam. I'm sure the last way you wanted to spend your Sunday afternoon was hanging out with a little kid."

"I'm not put out!" I exclaim. "I meant what I said—I like him. He's a great kid. Excellent taste in movies..."

As Jillian grins, I add, "I'm having fun. Even if he wasn't too keen on letting us sit next to each other in the theater—which I get!" She rolls her eyes as I hold out a hand placatingly. "He's just looking out for you, being a good brother."

"Ha!" she snorts. "Hardly! I think it's more that he wants *you* all to himself." She pats me on the arm. "He's taken quite a shine to you, Alden. The way his eyes light up whenever you come by the house, it's like you're Superman."

I look over and tilt my head at Sam, who is playing King of the Mountain and roaring at the empty park. "Aww, I don't deserve that. I just like goofing off with him, is all. And I usually bring sweets, so I'm sure that helps my case." I reach into my coat and hold out the leftover Nestle bar from the movie, offering it to her.

She smiles and shakes her head. "Maybe." She peeks at me. "Did your brothers or your parents take you to the movies when you were little? Or to the park?"

I chuckle darkly. "No one took me anywhere, Jillian."

Her head pops up, and she stares at me oddly, her eyes creased with emotion. I sit up and clear my throat, hating to see her look at me like that. "But there was an old theater the next town over, and I started going there when I was about 12 or 13." I grin at her, and she relaxes again. "I'd spend every Saturday there, just to get out of the house, watching the same movies play over and over." I laugh to myself. "You know, I'd scrape together enough pocket change during the week for one show, and then once it was over, I'd hide back behind the screen and watch it play through the rest of the day. Saw a bunch of movies that way—practically had them memorized by the end."

"Like a little mouse," Jillian murmurs, reaching up to pet my hair.

I laugh. "Or a rat! Yeah…that went on for a while, 'til one day the manager caught me in the act." I grimace.

Jillian's mouth hangs open. "Big bald guy with a huge mustache," I describe. "He blew his top, hauled me out to the front—the whole theater thought there was an ax-murderer in the place or something!" I snicker. "But he cooled off, and instead of throwing me out, he put me to work." I nod approvingly. "Restocking concessions, cleaning the theater, even taught me how to load and change the reels after a while." I look off into the distance. "The projector would break down every couple nights, so I got pretty good at fixing it. That's what got me the job in the engine room on the QE2—knowing my way around machines. That theater did a lot for me… I worked there until the day I left home."

I shrug and grin at Jillian, throwing my arm around her shoulder. "So really, one could say it was the movies that got me to you. My two favorite things in the whole world."

Looking over at her, I see that her eyes are glassy. I furrow my brow. "Jillian, what is it?" I ask, concerned.

She blinks and shakes her head. "Nothing," she replies quietly after a minute. "I just feel…very lucky to know you, to be with you." She laces her fingers through mine and smiles.

"*I'm* the lucky one," I say in surprise. "You're this beautiful, smart, talented *goddess*…who just happens to let me hang around! Really, Jillian—I'm not the special one. You are."

She blushes and bites her cheek. "I think your view of me is…severely aggrandized," she sighs, squeezing my hand. "But I'll just say thank you and hope I don't disappoint you too badly at some point."

"Not possible," I huff, shaking my head. "Even if you *did* decide to go on that nun-killing spree—or maim, kidnap, coerce…" I grin at her. "I am yours."

She draws in a breath, about to answer. "Alden! Jilly!" Sam interrupts, bolting over and flailing his arms wildly. "Can we go on the carousel? Please, please?" He motions to the merry-go-round.

Jillian frowns and looks over. "Is it even running? I thought they closed it after Labor Day…"

"Yes it's running!" Sam cries. "Please? It's just a quarter!"

Jillian sighs. "I don't know, Sam. It's getting kind of late…" She checks my wristwatch and looks up at me. "It's 3:45 now."

"I want to make sure I get you back in time for Sunday dinner," I murmur, rubbing her shoulder. "Wouldn't want your parents to be cross with me for keeping you out."

Jillian smiles wryly. "I don't think you could ever make them *cross*," she teases. "They're in love with you. Are you sure you can't come to dinner?"

I sigh. "I've got to be at Monique's for service by 6. Still have to change." I brush her cheek. "Next time."

She nods. "What about the carousel?" Sam pleads. "Please, Jilly! I'll be really good for the rest of the day! I promise!"

Jillian sighs and gathers up her handbag. "Sam, Alden has to go to work, so we have to get going…"

I watch the little boy's face fall as we stand up, then grin. "It's all right, Jillian. I think we've got time for one ride." I give Sam a wink, his smile lighting up like a Christmas tree. "Here, I've got some change…"

Jillian gives me a look. "He's fine—you don't need to spoil him, Alden. You've done enough." Her jaw tightens irritably.

I lean in and graze my nose along it, sending noticeable tremors down her neck. "Let me spoil you both…please," I croon into her ear. "Besides, I want to go too. Never been on a carousel before." The truth.

Jillian sighs and pulls back, lightly shoving me in the side. "You do not fight fair at all," she laughs, giving in. "All right, fine. *One* ride, and then we're going home," she says to Sam, settling back on the bench. "I'll wait here."

"YES!" Sam gives me a high five as we sprint over to the ride. We pay our quarter each and hop on, Sam running around clockwise to find his horse. "I want the one with the green ribbon!" he shouts, bouncing up and down.

I laugh and help him up, taking the horse next to his. I gnash my teeth playfully and look over at him. "So does this thing go super fast?" I ask in a nervous stage whisper. "Like…lightning speed?"

Sam puts his finger to his mouth, thinking hard. "It goes…a little fast," he finally answers, all business. "But hold onto the bar, and you should be okay." He jerks his chin at the gold pole in front of me.

"Okay," I pant, taking a breath. "You'll help me if I fall off, right?"

Sam nods gravely. "Don't worry, I've ridden this thing a bunch of times." He blinks. "Like, five times."

I laugh as the ride starts up, the old floor boards creaking to life as the calliope trills around us. I look out as we go round and round, spying Jillian on the park bench, a small smile playing on her lips. Faster we go, the wooden horses bobbing and weaving, Jillian turning into a blur of red and blue as we pass. Every time I look, and every time I find her, it sends me soaring, spinning dizzily off into blinding happiness.

*

I get back to the house and tromp up the stairs, feeling rushed for time. Jillian and Sam's train back to Jersey was running late, and I wasn't about to leave them waiting on the platform by themselves. I hear Daniel humming loudly as I pass the bathroom, the shower water running.

"Hey!" I give the door a quick rap before sticking my head in. "We've got less than an hour 'til we gotta be there, and traffic in the tunnel was a nightmare."

"Yeah, yeah," he calls, steam wafting over the curtain. "I got this. We're gonna be fine."

He starts whistling whatever tune he had going before. I sigh and shut the door, heading up to the attic. I quickly dress and bound back down the stairs, deftly knotting my bowtie. I roll my eyes as I pass the loo; he's out of the shower now, but he'll be at least another 15 minutes getting his hair just so. I have no idea why he puts so much effort into it—it'll just go under a do-rag the minute we get to work.

I go downstairs and see Martin sitting quietly in the living room, a big book spread across his lap. He's turning the pages slowly and carefully, taking his time to run his fingers over whatever it is he's staring at.

When he looks up and sees me standing in the archway, he smiles. "Alden," he says, his voice ticking and melodic like the inner workings of a clock. "Come here," he beckons. "I want to show you something."

My eyes crinkle in surprise. Martin is always polite, but rarely forthcoming. I cross over to him and take a seat on the couch next to his easy chair. I now see that the big book is actually a photo album, row upon row of meticulously placed black and white photographs lovingly preserved between sheets of white tissue paper. He turns the book toward me and points to a series of images.

"This is my daughter, Rita—Daniel's mother," he says with a smile. I look closely at the three pictures. They start with a young girl of about eight and progress to match the blonde teenager I saw in the photos upstairs in the mystery bedroom. Martin nods and taps the picture of the child. "This was taken the day we left Germany," he explains, turning the book to me. The little girl is wearing a dark, stiff-looking wool coat and matching cap, but her face is all smiles. You can tell she's outside by the way her hair is blowing across her face, but it's hard to say where.

I look up at Martin and grin. "She's beautiful. And very happy." I ease onto the couch cushions.

Martin murmurs in agreement and spins the album back to his lap. "Yes, she was. She was so excited to come here; both Erna and I were shocked at how well she handled the move— such a big change from anything she'd ever known." He shakes his head. "But she was ready for it. After the war, there was a flood of American culture into Berlin—books, movies, magazines— and Rita couldn't get enough of it. Every week, she would go and spend her pocket money at the pharmacy on whatever new lipstick some Hollywood starlet was wearing. She loved it."

He looks thoughtfully at the picture. "She was the one who told us we should come to New York. I had the choice between here and Washington D.C., and Rita pretty much made the call herself." He chuckles. "Once she has her mind set to something, that's that. She and Daniel have that in common."

"Yes, they do!" I laugh with him. As Martin smooths the page with his hand, I clear my throat. "Daniel said she lives in…Reno, now? Nevada?" I watch him stare down at the book. "That's pretty far from here."

Martin sits still for a moment before answering. "Yes. It's… better this way. Or so she says." He looks out the window, suddenly a million miles away. I shift in my seat, trying to think of something to say.

Martin comes out of his reverie and smiles warily at me. "The past is like a stalking tiger, waiting in the grass until you least expect it; then it pounces and holds you tight."

Looking back down, he seems to remember the album in his lap. "Here, let's have another," he says, flipping the page. "Ah, here we are." He grins, turning the book back to me and motioning to a faded group shot. "These were my students," he murmurs, pushing his glasses back up on his nose with his free hand. "In Berlin."

I blink at him before focusing on the photograph. It is indeed an old class picture taken in front of an official-looking university building. The students are arranged into two rows, the girls smiling in modest day dresses and coats lined up in front with the taller boys in the back, dressed smartly in their tweed jackets and trousers. They all look about my age. A much younger Martin stands off to the side, wearing a serious expression that doesn't carry all the way to his twinkling eyes. In his left hand, he holds a still smoking cigarette down at his side. I snicker and point to it.

Martin smiles. "The photographer was reloading, said it might be a minute... I just thought I'd take advantage of the free moment outside."

"You said you taught English literature?" I ask softly.

He glances up at me and grins. "Yes. This was my master level class." He runs a finger over their faces. "We covered all the greats: Chaucer, Shelley, Swift..." His eyes tighten. "Of course, they all had to be very familiar with English to comprehend the translations. You would have been quite impressed with their proficiency. Even the ones from the country had perfect grammar."

He stops and points to one of the young men in the back. His hair is dark like mine. "He was from a town called Karlsruhe, in Baden...which is very close to where I grew up, near the Black Forest." Martin rubs his neck. "He loved hearing my stories about running through the woods as a boy, pretending I was the hero in one of Grimm's fairytales…" He purses his lips. "He probably played similar games himself. And he loved your Irish revolutionaries!" He taps my knee. "Ernst, his name was Ernst."

"You seem like you were very close to your students." I smile tentatively. "I would have loved to have had a teacher like you. Might've stayed in school longer, I reckon!"

Martin nods. "We had small classes then, not like the big lecture halls with hundreds of students like you see now everywhere. So we could spend a lot of time working on one idea or concept together before moving to the next. It was…ideal."

"Sounds like it," I reply.

Martin pulls the album back and sighs. "But things change… as they always, inevitably do," he grunts, slumping heavily in his chair. "And in those days, change came quickly, whether you were ready or not."

He looks up at me, sorrow flashing in his eyes. "We were reading Auden the day they came and took them." He flips the book back around and points to two of the boys and one girl. "Audrey, Felix, and Thomas."

I squint at the girl; I can now make out the faint outline of a star sewn onto her jacket. I look back at Martin, whose face is somber.

"They had come for the books a week earlier, and I remember being so angry with them." His voice grows thick. "I yelled at the soldiers that they were from my own collection, that they were taking private property." He smirks. "Got whacked in the gut with the butt of a rifle for that."

I sit in stunned silence, watching him. Martin tilts his head to the side and sighs. "So I didn't notice them *looking*…then. Not only to raid my library, but to steal my students as well." He clears his throat. "When they came back, I didn't say anything, not a word. They barely said anything to me, just pointed at who they wanted and motioned for them to get up. The two boys were strong about it—'stiff upper lip,' as the English like to say." He peeks at me out of the corner of his eye. "They just picked up their things and followed the men, quiet and orderly…but Audrey cried."

Martin stops and looks out the window. "Loud, fearful sobs…begging…and all I could do was stand by and straighten my papers on the desk. Such a fool!" he hisses, biting the inside of his cheek.

I lean in, trying to come up with something to say. I have nothing.

"I couldn't…I couldn't even pay her the kindness of looking at her as they carted her away. I was so afraid, myself…" He shakes his head and looks up at me, his eyes watery. "I would give anything to go back and change at least that, to go back and…acknowledge her. A shred of dignity—it was the least she deserved." He reaches up with a frail hand and pushes his glasses up, wiping away a tear.

"I'm sorry," I finally murmur, the best I can come up with.

Martin sniffles and waves me off. "Ah! I'm the sorry one!" He laughs. "Making you sit and watch an old man cry and listen to his regrets… How mortifying for you." He closes the album and sets it off to the side.

"No…not at all. I appreciate you telling me." I sit up straight.

Martin tuts. "Well, I appreciate you listening. Thank you. It is a gift." He pats my hand.

I look down at the album quizzically. "What happened to Ernst? The boy from…" I'm not even going to try to pronounce it. "From where you were from?"

Martin exhales and folds his hands over his lap. "Ernst was furious about what happened. He was never the same after that… I suspect that maybe he and Audrey were involved, but I don't know. We didn't talk about such things." He takes a shaky breath.

"A few months later, Ernst walked into an SS bar with a line of explosives strapped under his coat. It was winter." He stares at me intently. "He didn't walk back out."

"Jesus," I mutter.

Martin nods. "You can say a lot of things about what he did and if it changed anything at all… You can call him a maniac terrorist, an anarchist, a hero…" He looks away. "But you can never call him a coward."

I just sit, my hands hanging off the couch arms. "Irish, you ready?" I hear Daniel call as he thumps down the stairs. I take a breath and clear my head, glancing back at Martin, who has his normal calm expression back in place. Daniel comes into the living room, dressed in a white t-shirt and jeans, his hair still damp.

"Yeah, I'm ready," I murmur, getting to my feet. I turn to Martin and nod. "Thank you for showing me those." I point down at the album.

Martin gives me a tight smile as he slowly settles into his chair. "Of course. Something to pass the time," he replies.

I smile at him before joining Daniel over at the front door. "What did he show you?" he asks as we step out.

"Just some old pictures…" I look back at where Martin is sitting all alone with his library before Daniel shuts the door behind us.

"Oh." Daniel shrugs and we walk around to the driveway, where Wendy is waiting for us in all her polished glory. Daniel stops in front of her and rubs his arms. "Man, you can freeze your balls off out here tonight!" He shivers and thrusts his hands into his pockets for the keys.

"Would you like my jacket, darling?" I snicker.

He laughs and whacks me on the arm. "I wouldn't want to kill your look, double-O-7…" He finds the keys and gets on the bike.

I laugh, but stay on the pavement, something from earlier bothering me. "Daniel." I cross my arms. "I think you should try talking to your grandfather." I frown and look up at him.

Daniel chortles and sits back on the bike. "About what? The obsessive card catalog system he's got going for the living room?

Or how to leave a chess game permanently unfinished?" He wrinkles his nose. "What were you two talking about?"

I sigh and step over to the motorcycle. "Never mind. Forget about it."

Daniel turns and stares at me as I swing my leg over. "You're acting really weird! What? Did he say something to you?"

I clench my jaw, suddenly feeling very protective of Martin's privacy. "No…nothing. I just think, like everyone, he gets lonely." I glance at the dark living room window and then back at Daniel. "I'm sure he would love to spend some time with you…just hanging out or whatever."

Daniel pauses, a flash of emotion crossing quickly over his face. It's gone in an instant, and he straightens up before breaking into a fit of laughter. I look at him curiously.

"Yeah…okay, Sargent Pepper! This coming from the guy who is *never* alone anymore!" He leans into me and bats his eyelashes. "How are things going with 'dear, sweet Jillian'?"

I roll my eyes and shove him forward. "Very well, thanks."

I don't feel like divulging any more than that, but I know he won't let it alone. True to prediction, he bats my leg. "Well, come on! You getting some yet?"

I know he's only asking as a friend, but his prying lately is really beginning to irritate me. I unclench my jaw and take a breath. "We're taking it slow…" I reply cautiously.

Daniel scoffs. "Seriously? What's the delay?!" I sulk back on the seat as he adds, "I mean…I get that you're both crazy Catholics, but you've been together now for over a month! You're always picking her up from class or hanging out at her place… meeting the family for dinner… Come on! Surely that's gotta win you some brownie points…"

I exhale, trying to keep my temper. "It's not like that! I *like* hanging out with her family—they're nice people. No one is keeping score. We're just doing things our own way—not that any of this is your business!" Even though he isn't bringing up any sort of new, novel idea. Of course I want her—my skin is still hot from our kiss in the park—but I'm not about to let Daniel diminish what Jillian and I have with his crass backroom talk, even if it makes me come off like a complete prude.

Daniel puts up his hands in surrender. "Take it easy, Irish! This wasn't a declaration of war—I'm just making conversation!" He pops the key into the ignition and revs Wendy to life. "Don't get your panties in a twist!"

"They're not!" I yell bullishly over the motor.

His shoulders shake as we drive off. He's laughing at me, I'm sure.

*

True to his word, Daniel finds a way to sail through the tunnel and back to Manhattan, bucking all the rules of the road as he winds and eases through the traffic. But when we get to our usual stoplight, he catches me off guard when he opts to go left instead of right.

"Hey!" I yell over Wendy. "You missed the turn! We're going the wrong—" I twist around and watch the theater district fade farther away as we head into downtown.

"I just gotta make a quick stop. It won't take long," Daniel replies. "Don't worry, we're not going to be late." He jacks the bike and sends us speeding down the wide avenue. I grimace as the high-end shops of midtown devolve into the warzone that is Times Square, lined with its ratty laundries and porno theaters lit up in harsh Xs. A couple of hookers catcall to us from the front of Circus Circus, sending me into a fresh round of scowls and cringes.

"Daniel, come on! We don't have time for whatever this is!" I punch him lightly in the back. "Francois does not look kindly on tardiness, and you know Chef will blow a gasket…"

"Relax!" Daniel shouts, shaking his head. "We're almost there—it's the next block up!" He pushes Wendy faster, and I swear we're going to skid out and spend the rest of our days as a couple of blood stains smeared across 7th Avenue. Instinctually, I ram my eyes shut and grip tight with my legs until the motorcycle jerks to a stop. I look up at an old tenement building, close to a hundred dark windows staring back at me. It looks abandoned, except for the two homeless guys holding court on the front steps.

"What is this place?" I murmur, watching Daniel swing off the bike.

He shrugs and runs a hand through his hair. "I just gotta go up for a minute… You can stay out here if you want." He motions to the sidewalk.

I sputter. "Not on your life. I'm not really in the mood to get stabbed before work." I get off of Wendy and nervously shove my hands into my jacket. "You're really okay leaving your bike down here?" I glance back at the shiny motorcycle.

Daniel nods. "Oh yeah—Jo-Jo and Tino will watch her for me." He smiles at the two men sitting on the steps, who give him a friendly wave. I exhale and tuck my chin into my collar, following him up the stairs to the main entrance.

"It's totally fine that you're coming, but… " He looks at me, his tone suddenly hushed as we step into the dirty foyer. "I've known these guys for a while, and they get a little touchy around new people, so you gotta be cool, all right?" He wets his lips as we walk up a flight of dimly lit stairs, the trademark sound of a crying baby accompanied by a blaring television set echoing from one of the apartments. "You just hang back and let me do the talking."

"Fine," I whisper, wincing as we hear a man's voice shouting in some foreign tongue on the other side of a door. I pull my tux jacket around me defensively. All of this is feeling a little too close to home for my comfort.

"It's this one here." Daniel stops in front of an apartment toward the end of the hall and gives it a quick knock, shaking out his arms like he's psyching himself up. I watch him curiously; this is the most tightly wound I've ever seen him, and that's saying a lot for the guy who blasts loud rock and roll to put himself to sleep.

The door swings open, a large, olive-skinned man hulking in the archway, dark stubble dusting his chin and upper lip. "Hey, Anatoli!" Daniel chirps brightly, his easy smile back in place. He reaches over and chucks the big man on his leather-clad arm, like they're old drinking buddies. "Haven't seen you around in a while... What's been going down?"

Anatoli glares at him and then glances over at me, his eyes beady with suspicion. "I got deported," he answers finally, his voice thick and guttural, "but I'm back now." He takes a hulking step in the doorway, blocking further entry.

"Aw, that's great, man! It's been a total drag, not having you around." Daniel grins and nudges his chin toward the apartment, leaning casually against the wall like this was where he meant to be all along. "Hey, is he busy? I can't stay too long...just checking in before work—"

"Who's your friend?" He ignores Daniel's question and looks pointedly at me. I stare down at the floor, trying to avoid eye contact, probably not aiding my case at all.

Daniel laughs. "Oh, yeah! This is my roommate, Alden Murphy... He's new in town...from the United Kingdom. You should hear his accent!" Daniel snickers, glancing back at me lazily. "It's funnier than yours, Anatoli."

I clench my jaw, feeling instantly betrayed that he gave my actual name so freely to this large, dangerous-looking thug. Anatoli narrows his eyes at me. "You ever met the Queen?" he asks this with a completely straight face.

I don't know whether to laugh or cry. "No," I mumble, shaking my head.

Anatoli glares at me for a minute before letting out a heavy sigh. "He's not in a good mood, so watch that big mouth of yours," he grunts to Daniel as he steps aside, granting us passage. "And don't stand in front of the TV—his show is on."

Daniel nods and leads me down a narrow hallway into the main room. It looks like it was a perfectly nice living room at some point with a gold sofa set and matching end tables, but the heavy haze of cigarette smoke makes it feel more akin to a harbor pub than someone's home. Sitting in the center of the couch is a long, gangly pair, a man and a woman, the man's bony arm draped around the half-dressed woman's waist, her head resting in his lap. They both stare vacantly at the TV across from them. The man is wearing a blood-red shirt and brown corduroys. He has dark hair and olive skin the same as Anatoli, but his eyes are light and half-lidded, and he sports a thick mustache. The woman is of similar coloring and wearing a faded paisley dress, the bottom hem hitched up over her hip. Her hair is lank and stringy, like it hasn't been washed in weeks. Daniel ducks and guides us past, and we settle on the opposite side of the room.

The woman is the first to glance over at us, peeking up from the man's lap. Her eyes are a crystal blue, but empty of any emotion. I look away shyly as I catch a glimpse of her small bare breasts, her dress unbuttoned all the way to her navel.

"You got my money?" I jump as the man addresses us without looking away from the screen.

"Yeah." Daniel nods and steps forward, wiping his palm across his jeans. I goggle at him: *he's scared.* Can't say I blame him. I'm also no longer worried about making it to work on time—I'm not quite sure what rabbit hole he's brought us down, but I'm bright enough to know we missed Wonderland by a couple of exits.

Daniel reaches into his jean pocket and pulls out a huge wad of cash, dropping it on the coffee table in front of the man. The woman sits up as the man leans forward to pick up the money, giving it a quick count. "You keep yours?" The man's voice lilts, carrying some sort of eastern European accent.

When Daniel nods, he adds, "Right on. Now we can talk." He tucks the money into his shirt and settles back into the couch, the woman readjusting herself next to him. "Did you have any problem moving it this week?" he asks Daniel, smiling at something funny that happened on the show.

Daniel shakes his head and takes a seat in the easy chair opposite the couch. "Nope. Everyone ate it up, just like you said. Really popular in the neighborhood... The busboys over at Rina's told me the cool down on it was better than the last batch."

The man nods. "We cut it a little differently this time, trying to take some of that edge off." His eyes flicker over to me, like he's noticing my presence for the first time. "You brought someone with you."

Daniel smiles, but it's not his usual easygoing grin. "Yeah, this is Alden. He's just along for the ride."

The man takes his time sizing me up. I shift nervously, trying to keep my composure under his stare. "He cool?" he asks finally.

Daniel chuckles, arching a brow. "Lousy taste in music, but otherwise, yeah...he's cool," he replies with a shrug. I catch myself narrowing my eyes at him. If I had known I was going to bear the brunt of his every joke, I would have opted to stay downstairs with the bike.

The man puts an arm behind his head as the woman leans in and whispers something in his ear in a language I can't understand. He chuckles and turns his attention back to the TV. "Dasha says she likes his suit." He sucks his teeth and motions to me. "Like...uhh...Lee Majors on *The Dating Game*..."

I grimace and fold my arms, pacing slowly over to the window to hopefully fade into the background. "Can't beat that," Daniel answers, smiling with them. "So...I was wondering if you had my stuff ready? Not that I'm in any rush..."

The man laughs and shakes his head. "Always—how you say—'hot to trot'? Eh?" He reaches over and pats Daniel jovially on the knee.

Daniel laughs and tilts his head. "Hustle, hustle." He raises his eyebrows. "If it's not ready, I can come back later..."

"Nah, hang on a second. Hey, Anatoli!" the man calls into the hall. We hear heavy steps as Anatoli comes over and stands before us. "Go into the bedroom and get the *obține lucrurile…*" The man waves. "Bring it back out here, *lucrurile bune.*"

"Sure, Ramos." Anatoli nods and disappears back into the corridor. A minute later, he returns with several small bags of clean, white powder, setting them gently on the coffee table. My eyes widen as I watch them all huddle over them.

"*Micșorați TV…*" Ramos mutters at the girl, batting her thigh. She gets up and saunters over to the television, a silver charm bracelet that's strapped around her ankle chiming against her long brown leg as she turns down the volume. She glances over and sees me watching her without a trace of acknowledgement in her eye; it's like staring into an empty room. I look away, rattled, and return to trying to come up with ways to get out of this moment as she slips back under Ramos's arm.

"It's pure—clean, like fresh snow…" Ramos murmurs to Daniel as he takes a little powder out of one of the bags. "Uncut, straight from the source."

I see Daniel nod appreciatively. "It's gorgeous. What's the high like?"

Ramos laughs. "Like getting sucked off by a Russian tsarina— endless." Using a straight razor that was already out, he arranges the dust into three lines. "Try it."

As I gape in silence from my corner, Daniel smiles and presses his nose down to the table, giving it a quick sniff. He sits up and rests in the chair, letting out a throaty chuckle. "Far fucking out…" he breathes, holding the bridge of his nose. "Oh man, that is sweet."

Ramos grins and does a line himself. "Right? It just came in two nights ago… I've been waiting for you to come by to give it a run." He wipes his nose with his sleeve and eases back into the couch. "That last line is for you."

"Thanks, man." Daniel takes a breath and finishes off the powder, slumping in his chair contentedly when he's through.

Ramos watches him and smiles; I notice that a few of his back teeth are missing. "So this is what I want you pushing this week," he croons, starting to divvy up the bags. "This shit's not for any old kitchen spics or the blacks up in Harlem, you dig? We can charge triple what we did for the last round, so high-end clientele only. You got some of that?" He eyeballs Daniel.

Daniel nods. "Sure, sure. I've been tapping into the college market up at Columbia…" I glare at him and bite my tongue angrily, the copper metal taste of blood swirling around my mouth.

"Very good." Ramos purses his lips, motioning to the drugs. "And I'm fine if you gotta use this stuff for pussy bait—not like you need it, *Kirschbaum*." He laughs as he stretches his mouth around Daniel's last name. "But make them pay first. Put Daddy's money to good use."

"Sure." Daniel smiles tightly as he stands up and carefully rolls the bags, storing them in his pockets.

Ramos stares at him. "I expect you back here next week with a small fortune in those pants."

Daniel laughs brightly. "You'll have that sailboat in no time, Ramos!" he jokes, the jibe falling flat when no one reacts. "Anyway…we should get outta your hair." He glances over at me and nods. I exhale. Thank God—we can finally leave.

"Hang on a sec—you're not gonna finish the episode?" Ramos points at the TV. I wince as I stare at the screen; it's some sort of sitcom, an attractive couple in dark blue jeans arguing over something in their Hollywood living room while the studio audience goes nuts.

Daniel scratches the back of his head and sits back down. "Yeah, we can stay 'til the end…" His jaw tightens as I glare daggers at him.

Having no choice, though, I settle back on the wall, my arms crossed, and try to keep my attention trained on the show. Ramos and Dasha slump back into the couch, his fingers drawing small circles on her naked thigh. The phone rings in another room. "You got that?" Ramos mutters to Anatoli. Anatoli nods and leaves the room, the only one with any sort of apparent freedom to come and go in this place. I exhale, and my foot starts tapping jittery-like against the baseboard.

Ramos notices and laughs. "Your friend's kinda jumpy," he snickers to Daniel.

I reach down and hold my leg steady as Daniel clears his throat and glares at me. "Yeah...he's sort of a nervous type, can't help himself. But he's all right." He keeps his tone light. I glower at the back of his stupid blond head.

"He keeps staring at my girl like he's never seen a pair of tits before," Ramos sniggers, looking back at me against the wall. "You wanna fuck her?"

I freeze, my mouth agape. I definitely should have stayed with the bike.

Seeing my shock, Ramos busts up laughing, Daniel quick to follow. "Sorry man, he's new around here," Daniel says with a grin, slapping Ramos on the shoulder. "Not used to how stuff goes." I sigh in relief at the break in tension.

Ramos smirks, his laughter dying down. "He could get a piece. She don't mind." He coolly takes Dasha's knee and pulls her legs open, leering up at me. Crap—I thought I was okay.

Daniel draws in a sharp breath. "He's got a pretty redhead he's sweatin' it out for anyway." He shrugs. "Waiting 'til things are more official."

This really gets Ramos going. He lets out a huge snort. "Official? What does that mean?" His forehead wrinkles. "Is she, like...underage? Or needs papers?"

"No, no..." Daniel answers, doing his best to keep everything mellow. "Like...married...right?" He glances up at me from his chair. I grind my teeth in response.

Ramos's eyes widen knowingly. "Ah...I see. So what?" He looks at me curiously. "Fuck Dasha now, and then fuck the redhead on your wedding night. What difference does it make?" She not gonna know." He shrugs at the TV. "It's just pussy."

I try to read Dasha's expression through this whole exchange, but she just stares blankly ahead like she's not even here. It gives me the creeps.

"Ramos?" Anatoli pokes his head around the corner. "Dimitri wants to talk to you. Says there's a situation down at the docks…"

"Fuck—fucking idiot," Ramos grunts, pushing himself up from the couch. He lets out a sigh and turns to Daniel, who hastily climbs out of his chair. "This is gonna take a while. You better go." He slaps Daniel a high five and pulls him into a quick hug before releasing him. "I'll see you next week, brother…with my money!" He laughs and pats Daniel on the arm, moving towards the other room.

Daniel smiles as he leaves and then turns to me, his eyes wild. "Let's go," he whispers, his tone urgent again. I nod irritably and push off the wall, stalking in front of him and out of the door, finally breathing once I get out into the hall. I refuse to look at him as we make our way down to Wendy again.

*

"Okay—say *something*, Irish," Daniel mutters as he turns off the bike's engine, now safe in the restaurant's back alley. I lock my jaw and jump off the seat, knowing that once I open my mouth, I won't be able to stop yelling at him.

"Come on! You stonewalled me the whole way over. I get it! You're pissed…" He puts his keys away and holds out his arms. "Lemme have it. Let's get this over with."

"Are you out of your mind?" I hiss, halting on the concrete stairs leading up to the service entrance.

I watch his goofy smile falter as he loiters down on the pavement. "I'm sorry I made you late. I didn't know it was gonna go that long, or that he was going to bring out the merchandise." He runs a hand through his hair. "Just tell Francois the bike broke down in the tunnel. He'll give you a break—"

"Oho!" I laugh bleakly, scuffing my dress shoes against the kitchen door. "Just what we all need—more lies!" I shake my head. "When were you going to tell me you were a...what? A—a drug dealer? Is that what you are?"

He squirms sheepishly, staring down at the ground. "I guess... if you want to put it that way. That makes it sound really bad."

"It *is* really bad, Daniel!" I shout. "I don't know how you can do it. I mean..." I stop and sigh at my own naiveté. "I get that it probably feels really good...when you're doing it...but having to deal with Ramos and the other Russians—"

"Romani, not Russian," Daniel corrects me with a smile. "He's pretty proud of that, actually."

I glare at him. "Fine! It doesn't matter." I put my fingers to my temples, trying to erase the last hour from my mind. "That had to be the most...*vile*—"

"Oh come on, it wasn't that bad!" Daniel jeers.

"—horrifying, humiliating experience!" I yell right over him. "And there you were in the thick of it, like you were home for the ruddy holidays! And you know what they're—*you're*—doing is illegal? You *do* know that if we had gotten caught just...just *being* there, they'd throw me out of the country, right?!"

He sighs and rolls his eyes. "We were never gonna get caught..." he mutters.

I startle, watching him stare down at the street. "That's not the point, Daniel! Did you stop for one second to think?"

"Hey—I said I was sorry!" he cries. "I don't know what else you want me to say." He raises his hands. "I'm sorry for *scandalizing* you, corrupting you, putting you in harm's way... I just thought you were made of tougher stuff than that."

"Don't do that!" I scowl, pointing at him. "Don't you dare turn this around on me like I'm the one with the problem—"

"Problem? What's that supposed to mean?" he barks, his tone

defensive. "I gotta tell you, this coming from the guy who is staying at my house *rent free*—" He watches me, knowing he's hit a nerve. "You might wanna think about keeping your opinions to yourself, Irish."

I inhale and grip the iron guardrail in front of me. "I just think you're better than…than *that*, Daniel. Whatever you wanna call it, it's beneath you. You know I'm right." I stare at him.

He sniffs, stepping over to his bike. "Beneath me…beneath *you*." He smirks. "That's what you mean, right? Give you a work visa and a steady paycheck, and all of a sudden you're freakin' Ward Cleaver! Jesus!" He puts his hands on his hips.

"That's not what I'm saying at all, Daniel!" I exclaim. "Just listen—"

"Yeah, listen to you… too good for this shit!" he shouts back. "What—you think cuz you've got some sweet little virgin hanging off your arm, now you're a fuckin' saint?"

I see red. "So help me, Daniel, you'll stop right there if you know what's good for you," I seethe. "You leave Jillian out of this, or I swear to God—"

He closes his eyes and takes a breath. "All right, all right, sorry… Let's just cool it here." He paces in a tight circle.

I push back from the railing and tear at my hair. "How long?" I ask after a minute, breaking the silence. Daniel looks up at me. "How long have you been…working, I guess…for him—Ramos?"

Daniel sighs. "Couple months, maybe. Before you got here."

I put my hands in my pockets. "Well, you should stop! You've got a…a really good thing going here." I motion up at the restaurant. "Especially now that Baxter is going over to 21… We all know Chef wants to promote you as his sous! This crap with Ramos could ruin it all. Why would you risk that?" I shake my head at him.

Daniel crosses his arms. "It's not that easy, leaving…"

I snort. "Never is with that lot. God…" I shake my head, staring at the kitchen door. "Why do you even bother? With Chef, and cooking…you obviously make plenty of cash with your other gig."

He blinks. "I like it. And…I'm good at it." He exhales. "Plus Oppa would start to get suspicious if I didn't, wonder where all the money's coming from…" His eyes drift back to Wendy.

"Ah…right," I reply, defeated. He stares at me as I shrug and open the door. "Well, I guess that settles it, then… And since I've been instructed to keep my opinions to myself, I'll do just that. Don't want to end up with all my stuff on the front walk." I turn to go inside.

"Hey! Alden—" Daniel calls, his hands shoved in his pockets.

"Thanks for the lift," I rasp. "And for your *endless* generosity."

I watch his face fall as the door shuts behind me.

CHAPTER 11
LOS ANGELES—PRESENT DAY

"OKAY, SO...JUST GIVE me a chance to catch up here," I sigh, rubbing my jaw and taking in the immaculate office waiting room. The walls are painted a soft gray, and classical music plays in the background. "The entrance to Porticullis is through a Super Target?!"

Daniel nods and motions for me to keep my voice down. "One of the entrances, yes," he answers quietly, pointing to my feet. "Take off your boots."

I shake my head, but crouch down and do as he says. "I guess that's smart. Keeps the Humans away, since no one wants to hang around a public restroom all day." I pull off my boots and glance over at his feet, stifling a giggle at how his left big toe is poking through his sock. "What's with the no shoes thing?"

Daniel sighs and takes a seat in one of the chairs against the wall. "Levels the playing field. Portcullis is all about neutrality, and even the flashiest Demon looks like a dork with no shoes on." He looks at my thick wool socks pulled up over my leggings. "Although they didn't account for the occasional footwear model that wanders in."

I roll my eyes and take a seat next to him, holding my boots in my lap. "This place is so…I don't know, normal." I glance over at Daniel and do a double take.

"What did you expect?" he laughs.

I balk at him, aghast. "Your wings are missing, and…and you're not glowing anymore," I finally eke out. His gold aura has disappeared without a trace. I shake my head and think to check my own hands, gasping out, "And neither am I," after I do so. I sit in stunned silence for a second, before panic starts to creep up.

"Yeah, that's Porticullis." Daniel shrugs nonchalantly. "You'll be back to your beautiful blue self when we leave. No horns, wings, red marks, or superpowers are permitted once you cross the threshold. Like I said, everyone's on equal footing here. They call it 'naked souls.'" He snickers. "Though that sounds kind of dirty."

"Oh." I exhale, and my muscles relax as I let myself stare at Daniel. He looks just like when we first met; all liquid brown eyes and warm smile. I hold back my desire to touch him and instead wish I had a mirror to see myself, suddenly yearning for my own pre-Smudged face. I snap out of it and try to focus on the here and now.

"And… we're supposed to change the time?" I furrow my brow, glancing down at my watch. Without any help from me, the hands now read 3:43, even though we have to be coming up on lunchtime. "Oh…never mind." The watch must feel right at home here.

Daniel purses his lips and grabs my wrist. "When did you start wearing a watch? Don't you just use your phone like everybody else in your generation?" he asks, inspecting the timepiece.

I tut and pull my arm away. I hate when he alludes to us having any sort of age difference, even though he doesn't look a day over 19. "I wear it every day, Daniel," I mutter, shaking my head. "Not so much for the time, but for…I dunno…good luck." And I wouldn't have found him on 3 without it. I go quiet, remembering him all weak and helpless, pinned to that wall by his wings. Up until that point, I thought he was untouchable, a whirlwind force of blond hair and blue jeans. Now, I'm not so sure. I shove the gory picture out of my mind and clear my throat, turning back to Daniel. "So what happens now?" I murmur, staring at a matching pair of closed doors on the wall opposite us.

Daniel sits forward. "Well, the other few times I've been here, we waited for an Agent to show up and take us back to talk." He follows my gaze to the doors. "If we haven't broken the rules too bad, you'll get a chance to ask your questions, and fingers crossed, they'll answer."

I rub my neck, frowning. "What do you mean, if we haven't broken the rules too bad? You said something about being *allowed* to be here on the bus… What does that all mean?"

Daniel sighs. "The living aren't allowed in Porticullis. This is where the dead are issued their passage for either the Upper or Lower Realms. Think of it as a giant bus terminal." He scratches his cheek. "With a death certificate being the usual form of currency."

"Kind of like the Haunted Mansion ride? *Don't forget your death certificate…*" I joke.

Daniel gives me a look. "Come on, don't make that face!" I protest. "Everybody loves Disneyland."

"Oh, I know!" he exclaims, tugging at his hat. "And I would have been very happy to go there today instead of this!" He motions around the waiting room.

I sigh, standing up again, feeling antsy and needing to move. Daniel watches me as I try the two doors. One stays firmly locked, but the other pops open with a quiet *click*.

I give a little start as Daniel does a double take. "What are you doing?" he hisses, jumping out of his seat. I take a step back from the open door. "You're not even supposed to be here, and now you're going around breaking things?" He hustles next to me and hastily shuts the door, his eyes growing stormy.

I clench my jaw and glare at him. "I didn't break anything—it was already open!" I brush his hand away and twist the knob again. I can feel a light breeze coming from whatever is on the other side.

"I don't understand why you're freaking out so hard right now—Porticullis is supposed to be the good guys, right? We're fine."

"No, we're not!" he grits out, slamming the door shut again more forcefully this time. "Porticullis isn't good *or* bad, they just *are!*" He lowers his voice and glares at the other door, his gaze nervous. "And they are incredibly powerful…possibly more so than anyone else in the Universe!" I shoot him a confused look as he gives me a light push back toward our chairs, his tone exasperated. "Now please, let's just wait patiently—"

"More powerful than Heaven?" I interrupt, shaking my head and refusing to sit back down. "How is that possible?"

Daniel exhales. "Porticullis was the answer to a millennia-old war—the war between Heaven and Hell." He stares at me warily as I lean against the closed door. "I don't know a lot about it, except that many souls were lost before. In attempt to keep the peace, both Heaven and Hell gave up a fair amount of power to create a middle ground where Laws could be decided, disputes could be settled…" He waves a hand around the gray room. "It's a neutral space. Switzerland."

I frown. "I guess that makes sense. I mean…Agents are made up of representatives from both sides, right?" I remember what *my* Agent told me back at the Warehouse. "So they have to work together…"

"How do you know that?" Daniel looks at me quizzically.

I blink, realizing I'd never told him about how I accidentally summoned an Agent back at the Warehouse and what happened before I rescued him. I glance down at my wrist to check my watch and startle. It's gone.

"Hey, did you steal my watch?" I slap his chest, making him jump a little. "That's not cool—"

"Uh, no," Daniel sniffs, staring at me as I turn and check the floor around us. "You take me for a more skilled pickpocket than I am—I was always better at panhandling, get a little conversation going—"

"Seriously, Daniel!" I sweep my hair back, surprised at the nerves in my voice. "I just had it! Where did it go?" I spin and stare at the closed door in front of us. "Did it fall off when I opened the door?"

Daniel laughs. "*That* seems as little far-fetched…" He sighs and glances back at our shoes, stepping over to the chairs. "Relax, you just had it—I'm sure it's here…" He lifts up my jacket to check, shaking it out. No watch.

Feeling every muscle in my body tense, I spin back to the door. "It's gotta be in there!" I reach back for the knob. "I have to check!"

"HEY!" He's back at my side in an instant, batting my hand away. "What's gotten into you? Come on—they'll be here any minute. We should sit down—"

"I need my watch!" I exclaim, pushing him off.

He gapes and puts his hand on the door, keeping it closed. "Yeah, that's not going to happen, Christa!" He gives a nervous laugh as he gently pushes me away. "You're acting nuts! It's a watch… We'll get you a new one when we get back to Target."

I shake my head violently. "No, it's special! I can't lose it."

I reach for the knob, but he beats me to it, clenching it tightly. "I can't let you do that! Are you crazy?!" he brays in my ear. I watch him twist the knob, and his face changes. "It's locked again anyway, won't open—"

I growl and shove him off, wrenching the knob with my own hand. The door pops open easily, swinging inward on its hinges with a gentle creak and revealing a darkened corridor, the cool breeze lightly ruffling my hair.

Daniel's jaw drops as I step forward, my eyes scanning around for my watch. "Christa! Get back here!" he whispers furiously from the doorway. "That's it, we're going home—"

I freeze. "We can't! They're expecting us."

"I don't care." His mouth draws into a harsh line. "You're not thinking straight right now—I don't know why that watch has got you so worked up, but you're gonna get yourself killed—"

"No, please!" I give a frustrated gasp as he shakes his head. "You promised you'd help me get answers!"

"I know! We're here, aren't we?" he snaps, waving his arm. "So forget the watch and focus on what's really important."

I bite my lip and look between him and the dark hallway. I can hear the watch tickling loudly in the back of my head, just like when I was on level 3. *This* is important…whatever is on the other side of this door. I dizzy slightly at the thought and turn back to Daniel, whose face is flushed with anger.

"Please, Daniel. I have to find it," I murmur. "This isn't the Warehouse, right? This isn't a doorway to Hell, is it?" I'm only half-joking.

Daniel bristles, but his stance softens. "Yes." He instantly starts coughing. He stops and sighs. "I have no idea, actually. Probably not."

"So how bad can it really be?" I ask desperately. When he gives me a look, I add, "Seriously! We'll just go in for one minute. And I won't get killed if you're with me… We're already breaking the Rules just *being* here, right? What's one more?" I take another step forward.

"This is insane," he groans behind me, but I hear him follow.

When the door closes on its own, though, he spins back, wrestling with the knob again, this time from the other side. "Jammed again! What is it with the doors around here?" he mutters, giving up on it and starting to walk.

I crouch down for a second to check the dark tile floor for the watch. "Guess we *have* to keep going now," I tease sweetly. Daniel doesn't return my little smile, but for some unknown reason, I felt an overwhelming sense of calm the second we were passed the threshold. "Just watch your feet. Would kind of defeat the purpose if you step on the watch and crush it with your giant toes."

"Yeah, I'll watch *your* feet," Daniel grumbles irritably in reply. "And I *really* don't like this. Just stating that for the record…"

The corridor turns a corner and brightens as we make our way into a large, open hall, both of us stopping in the vestibule and holding our breath as we take it all in. 'Grand' doesn't even begin to cover it, with its high, spiraling ceilings painted the same soft gray as the waiting room. There is no art on the large bare walls, and the floor is gray marble, cold under our socks. On either side of a large aisle are rows of matching marble pews, enough to accommodate hundreds of people, but empty now. I squint down to the front of the hall, finding the source of the breeze: a line of huge open windows, the view a sprawling starry night sky. I look up around the room curiously, trying to figure out where the light inside is coming from, but to no avail. In front of the windows sits a gigantic marble table, five high-backed, dark wood chairs behind it.

I feel a chill go up my spine and lean into Daniel. "What is this place?" I whisper.

He shakes his head. "I don't know… I've never been here before. Maybe a church?" I feel him tense next to me. "It doesn't matter—your watch isn't here. We have to go."

"Wait." I silence him with my hand and cock my ear. He stops and hears it too—ticking.

I grin. "It's there—at the front." I bolt forward, Daniel narrowly missing as he lurches to grab my arm. I bound up the stone steps to the marble alter, spying my watch on the table top in front of the center chair. I walk around and grab it, the *Thank You for Your Service* engraving on the back glinting as I secure it on my wrist where it belongs.

"Okay, you found it," Daniel calls from the aisle, making his way toward me. "This is all beyond creepy, and it's time to go…"

"*How* did you get up here?" I chuckle down at the watch face, the whole thing feeling so absurd that it's suddenly funny. I turn and look at the line of chairs, their wood soft and dark. They're the only things not made of marble in this place. From this view of the pews, it all clicks into place.

"It's not a church," I breathe. "It's a courtroom…"

I graze my hand comfortably over the arm of the center chair, sending the wood glowing and buzzing, as if a million bees just flew in from the windows. I take a step back and stare dumbly between the luminous chair and Daniel, his face ashen.

"Okay—that's enough, Christa. We have to go back, *now.*" I can hear the fear in his voice. "We don't belong here—"

"That's partly true, Guardian: *one* of you doesn't belong," a voice drawls from the entrance. We both twist around and see a tall blonde woman with a perfect hourglass figure leaning against the archway. She wears a fitted gray suit that shows off her long, tan legs and bright red lipstick, her shiny hair pulled back tight in a severe-looking bun. It matches the expression on her flawless face.

I dart around the table and back to Daniel in the aisle. "Agent?" I mutter tentatively to him.

"Yep." Daniel nods, standing at attention. I watch the corner of the woman's mouth twitch as she beckons us with a meticulously manicured finger.

"Let's not dally, children," she quips, with a hint of a British or maybe an Australian accent stretching her vowels. "I think you've done enough exploring for one day."

Daniel takes my hand, and we hustle toward her down the aisle. Her gaze is almost bored as she turns on her heel and guides us back through the corridor and out into the waiting room, our stuff still lying in a heap by the gray chairs.

With an audible sigh, she holds open the previously locked second door and ushers us into what I can only assume is her office. It has the same gray color scheme as everywhere else here, the background classical music going silent as she closes the door behind us. There is a small window in one corner of the room; I squint and rub my eyes. There's not much to see—just more black night like in the courtroom, a bright crescent moon now hanging low in it.

"Sit down." The woman clears her throat and waves us over to a pair of chairs in front of a simple black desk, her hips swinging briskly as she steps around and takes her seat behind it. I look down and notice that she's also not wearing shoes. At the ends of her crossed legs, her toes are pointed like a ballerina's.

"Now, then." She opens the single manila envelope atop the desk and scans the sheet of paper inside. "Christa Nichols, Catalyst elect." I give her a baffled look as she glances up at me, then over at Daniel. "And Daniel, her Guardian, currently serving his 40th year on the Mortal Plain... Is this correct?" She narrows her eyes at him.

"Yes," he whispers, staring straight ahead. I draw in a sharp breath and stare at Daniel. I try not to look shocked at hearing his number—I'd had no idea he'd been...*dead*...that long. I guess I shouldn't be that surprised, given his obsession with audio fidelity and all things vinyl. I'm doing the math in my head when the Agent interrupts my thoughts.

"40 years... That's a long time, Guardian." She closes the file. "And a very interesting number. I hope your...administrators... aren't growing impatient at your rate of Ascension. Would hate to set a bad example in the program they fought so hard for in the first place."

Daniel bristles. "I haven't heard any complaints," he replies curtly.

She smiles. "Risky maneuver, you two showing up here—given her current mortal status." She takes her time puckering her lips around the M in 'mortal,' her gaze burning into me. "But you *were* granted access, so obviously someone out there thinks you warrant special circumstances." She smirks and lays her hands flat on the desk. "I am but a cog in the machine, here to serve. Something I'm sure you're very familiar with." She arches a brow at Daniel.

He nods cautiously. "We're hoping you can help us with some questions that we've been having," he murmurs.

"Questions?" She giggles menacingly, her teeth sparkling white. "What could the two of you possibly be curious about? I hope it's nothing like which one of you is more dishy... I'd be a rather poor judge of that." She crinkles her nose as both Daniel and I shift uncomfortably. "Sorry, I don't mean to flirt. You know what they say about old habits."

She eases back in her seat, spinning her chair wheels playfully. I attempt to do the same, but find it very difficult to relax with this woman giving us the third degree. I'm not feeling the same warm fuzzies as I did with the last Agent I met, with his wireframe glasses and affable nature. I glare back at the woman, and the words *both sides* echo across my mind. I sit up a little taller.

"Very well." She stops spinning. "What's your question?"

Daniel glances at me and leans forward. "We, um...we wanted to ask about the Catalyst—"

"I don't want to hear from you, Guardian," the Agent snaps, pronouncing *Guardian* like it's a bad word. As Daniel shuts his mouth and sits back, she turns to me, her gaze fierce. "Let her speak first."

I gulp and try to compose a sentence in my head, before taking a breath. "Why did you call me 'Catalyst-elect'?" The words tumble out of my mouth, not the first question I had planned, but my curiosity gets the best of me.

The Agent blinks, her mouth quirked into a bemused little smile. "Because that's what you are right now. It's what we call all the Catalysts before their final choice has been made." She chuckles at my startled expression. "What? Did you think you were the first? In all of Human history?"

"There are other Catalysts?" I breathe, checking Daniel. He looks just as surprised as I do.

The Agent folds her hands in her lap. "Of course. Not living and breathing—you have the market cornered there, currently." She tilts her chin. "Only one per generation, if needed. But there have been others in the past, any time particular...conflicts...arise." She chooses her words carefully as she stares us down. "You didn't come here to ask me about your title. State your question."

I sit up nervously. "I just wanted to learn more about...my role," I state as slowly and clearly as possible. "As Catalyst...elect.

I haven't…I mean…there hasn't been a lot of guidance from either s-side about what I am supposed to be…doing." My eyes dart over to Daniel, who gives me a reassuring nod. "Like…how did I even *become* the Catalyst? Why was I…chosen, or whatever? What does that even mean? And…what's the deal with the prophecy? About me choosing light or dark?" It's not much of a choice in my mind, having already firmly decided that I'm sticking with light and all that's right and good.

The Agent props her chin up with the palm of her hand. "That's quite a lot of ground to cover." She exhales, her pretty forehead wrinkling. "You're familiar with the prophecy, of course?"

"Uh, sort of…" I know it's a major BFD. I glance over at Daniel, who shakes his head.

The Agent sits up straight and looks over us. "After losing that which she loves most, the Catalyst will come to light with death's pale horse riding her heels," she recites, watching us haughtily. "Flanked by those destined for good and evil, she will be carried from the ashes and born again to judge the Fates; and of her own accord, choose to Evict Heaven or Hell."

I squirm in my seat as she pauses, looking at me intently. "The last part is unfinished…" She takes a breath. "In the wake of war and death, through the Battle of Black versus White, the Catalyst will decide once and for all; her sacrifice—" She stops and sits back. "I'm sorry. There is no more."

I stare at my lap, my mind going a mile a minute. "Christa?" Daniel murmurs, taking my hand.

I shake my head and look at the Agent. "What do you mean, there's no more?" I mumble as my brain tries to process everything I just heard.

The Agent sighs. "That's where the previous prophet left off. It's not like this stuff is an exact science!" She snorts, spinning her wheels again. "Unfortunately, she died about a decade ago, and the new prophet has yet to be revealed. Just like Catalysts, those aren't a dime a dozen. So we're all left milling about in the same dark theater, waiting for something to happen." She shrugs, her face placid. "But I think you've got more than enough to chew on with what we do know."

I nod. "I get the first part, about losing what I love most…"

"Your dad." Daniel fills in hesitantly.

I look at him, my mouth pressed thin. "Right. And the stuff about 'death's pale horse' and being carried from the ashes—what does that mean?"

Daniel is scratching his head, looking just as lost as I am. "Thank the stars you're both so good looking," the Agent sighs. "Keep up! It's a metaphor for some sort of life-threatening moment." She groans. "We all know you've had a couple of those recently, so take your pick."

Eyes widening, I nudge Daniel. "The accident! The car accident.—that's got to be it…with Tom and Riley and you saving me…" When Daniel nods intently, I add, "But the part about being flanked by those destined for good and evil, is that about you… and Alden?"

He shakes his head, confused. "I'm not sure," he replies. "I guess that would make sense…"

The Agent gives him a look, but doesn't say anything. I purse my lips in thought. "Evict Heaven and Hell—that seems pretty self-explanatory…"

The Agent nods. "Indeed. Depending on the way the wind blows, your actions will bring about the end of either Heaven or Hell, releasing an onslaught of cosmic energy back onto the Mortal Plain." She smiles wryly as my eyes bug out of my head. "Billions and billions of souls will be displaced, to be judged by the final court here in Porticullis." She exhales and crosses her arms. "Kind of a big deal."

I clench my jaw. That *was* a courtroom we were in earlier. "So…if I evict Heaven, everyone good that's already died will come back to Earth?" I feel the wind get knocked out of me as my Dad's face flashes in my mind.

The Agent cocks her chin to the side. "Some of them…yes. But there is no way the Mortal Realm can contain that amount of energy—from either side. And to use your example, if you close Heaven, you will essentially be shutting down Paradise, leaving a bunch of pissed-off Seraphim in your wake." I squirm in my chair as she twitters her head. "But if you opt to evict Hell, it means every Demon that ever existed will now walk the Earth and invade Heaven, bringing chaos and destruction with them." She holds up her hands and grimaces. "Tricky, tricky… I'm so glad I'm not you."

I put my head in my hands, the room suddenly spinning. I feel Daniel's warm touch on my back. "Christa—are you okay?" he asks worriedly.

I close my eyes and count backwards from 10, desperately trying to put this puzzle back together again. I take a huge breath and look up at Daniel. "What do *they* want?" I exhale. "Heaven, I mean."

Daniel frowns. "They want you to close Hell." He glances at the Agent, who's grinning from ear to ear. "Even if it means the end of the Earth as we know it."

I shake my head blearily and look at the Agent. "And…the Demons? What do they…"

"They want a sure thing," she answers coolly. "If you evict Heaven, they'll be the only game in town, taking full control of the Afterlife. Pretty sweet gig. But…there are…rumblings… of some sort of movement." She watches us carefully as she continues. "A resistance—in Hell. No one's sure who's leading it, but they go against their fellow Demons and support the closing of Hell as well…releasing every soul that's ever been sent there back into GenPop, along with all your favorite dictators and homicidal maniacs. A guaranteed wild ride." She scrunches her shoulders. "Decisions, decisions!"

I wince and picture some asshat in a Freddie Krueger mask wielding a chainsaw down Rodeo Drive. But then I look back at Daniel—if that's what Heaven wants…

I sit up straight and glare at the Agent. "I choose good! There is no way…" I trail off and dig my fingernails into my thighs as her lip curls, perplexed. "I'm not ever going to go dark," I explain. "I decided that a while ago…" I pause, barraged by visions of the Green Room, Level 3, Pete. I shake it off and stare at the Agent. "You have to believe me!"

Daniel takes my hand again, but I cringe as the Agent lets out a high soprano laugh. "Oh, darling! I'm hardly the one you need to convince! Your temerity is certainly endearing, but not enough to determine the fate of the Universe." She wipes a tear away from laughing so hard, instantly reminding me of Alden. "Get a clue! It's not that clean cut, good versus evil. Gods, I don't know why I even bother…" She rolls her eyes at me. "You can't possibly grasp the magnitude of all this—what's about to happen. You're like a child toddling down to say goodnight at a cocktail party—essential, of course, but so charmingly oblivious to everything going on around her." She puts her hand to her chest to catch her breath.

I sink down in my chair. "Don't laugh at her," Daniel hisses at the Agent, staring at the floor. "And don't you dare make her feel small! She's just trying to understand—"

"Watch yourself, Guardian!" she barks, her expression turning stormy. "You're on thin ice as it is, with your emotional attachment to this particular case and gross displays of affection. Don't think *that's* gone unnoticed!" Her gaze hones onto where our fingers are clasped tightly together, then goes back up to Daniel.

He sucks in a deep breath and lets my hand drop. She grins. "Trials and tribulations are occurring on a cosmic level—but it's pretty clear what you two want, and it has nothing to do with the needs of the Universe!" She laughs cruelly and leans across the desk, whispering, "Little Blue Bunny and her Fallen Star… I'm surprised you're still playing with fire after what you *saw.*" Her eyes flick over to me maliciously.

I furrow my brow. "What's she talking about, Daniel?" I murmur.

"Nothing." He stifles a cough and glares back at the Agent stonily. "You can't talk to people that way," he mumbles, his stare still fixed on her. "It's not right."

The Agent clenches her jaw. "Your sense of entitlement is astounding," she sneers, gracefully rising from her seat. "Although that shouldn't be too surprising, given your previous record." She brushes her fingertips lightly across the file as she moves over to the window. "It's all here, public knowledge: how you grew up with everyone around you catering to your every whim. Oh, you had your fair share of disappointments just like anybody else." She smiles, picking at a spot on the dark windowpane. "But until that night, you had the whole world wrapped around your finger, the Golden Boy of Myrtle Avenue." Her eyes flash as Daniel grips the chair arms so hard I'm worried he might tear them off. "It would have all been yours for the taking, if you hadn't shot yourself in the foot...and dragged those you loved down along with you."

"Stop," Daniel grits, his stare murderous. "No more."

The Agent snickers and leans against the wall. "Of course. Who am I to add to your guilt? You've got enough of that already...even if it is a little fuzzy around the edges." She smirks roguishly.

As Daniel glares at the floor, I exhale and sit forward in my chair. "All right, I think we're done here." I look between Daniel and the Agent. "We can just leave, yeah?" Agent or no Agent, I can tell that Daniel is in pain, and I'm not going to let her hurt him any further.

"Yes. You are free to go at your leisure," she replies aloofly. "If you are satisfied with what you have learned here."

I stand and give Daniel's shoulder a squeeze. "Yes, thank you." He gets up and follows me to the door.

"Just..." I turn back and look at the Agent, who is poised next to the window like something out of a film noir, the moon providing a stunning backlight. "...one more. How will I know? When it happens, when I've finally chosen?"

The Agent breaks into a huge red grin. "Oh, you'll know. It will be painfully obvious." She chuckles. "And once it's done, there's no turning back." She arches a brow, and I peek at Daniel out of the corner of my eye warily.

"Okay. Thank you for your time," I murmur as we leave.

*

"Well, that was informative...and sort of terrifying," I grumble, staying close to Daniel's side as we navigate around the bustling holiday shoppers and out of the Super Target. His assessment had been spot on: neither good nor bad, the Agents of Portcullis just...are. I shield my eyes for a second and look at Daniel, adjusting to the blinding sunlight; he still hasn't said anything since we left. Wings back in place, his face is grim as we make our way to the bus stop. I'm not used to him giving me the silent treatment, and I shift nervously as we wait by the rain shelter.

"Daniel," I whisper. "Will you please say something?"

His eyes soften at my tone, and he looks up at me. "I, um...I just need a second." He rubs his jaw and paces in front of the stop sign.

I sigh and cross my arms in front of me, wanting to touch him, but knowing that's probably a bad idea right now. "I'm sorry," I mutter. "I should have never...you shouldn't have taken me there. I had no idea that's what it was like." I shake my head. "She was borderline cruel to you." Borderline nothing.

"But it's the truth!" He scowls and steps in front of me, his eyes wild and his Halo burning. "Everything she said...about you and the prophecy and being the Catalyst, about me..." He looks away, and it takes me a minute to pinpoint his expression. He's ashamed.

"Daniel," I breathe, placing my hand on his arm. He flinches, so I pull away hastily. "I don't know what happened *before*," I exclaim, "but I don't care! None of that stuff matters anymore, all right?"

When he continues to look at me with a pained expression, I grab his jacket and pull him toward myself, not letting him get away this time. "You and me, that's the only thing..." I exhale and stare into his eyes. "…the only thing that matters. We're a team. We have to stick together to—to fight whatever is coming. And I know we both know it's BIG…so we have to let all that other crap go and keep moving forward." I nod in determination. "I mean…I make mistakes all the time…and not just forgetting to move the laundry from the washer to the dryer before I leave for the day." I wrinkle my nose. "Like, huge, ugly mistakes that have real consequences, and not just for me…" I look at him pleadingly. "And *you* always forgive me when I mess up! Why can't you do that for yourself?"

Daniel stares down at the sidewalk, leaning into my embrace. "I don't know how you can even stand to be near me now, after what you just heard." His voice is barely above a whisper. "I…I hurt people, Christa. Good people. And I can't take it back." He won't look at me.

I take a breath and close my eyes, forcing myself to imagine the worst possible scenarios in my head— gruesome, wretched things that you only see in horror movies, with Daniel as the lead villain. As I exhale, the images fade away, and all I can see is who he really is. Good. Kind. Mine.

My eyelids flutter open, and I stare at his face. "*I* forgive you, Daniel. For whatever you did, whatever happened—I forgive you." I grasp him tightly, seeing his golden brown eyes finally peek over at me. "And I know I may not be the one who needs to do that to make this all be okay, but… it'll have to be enough for now."

Daniel stares at me, his eyes glassy, then takes my waist in his hands and hugs me close. I melt as I inhale his jacket's signature scent and feel his body relax next to mine.

He's the first to pull away. "Wow…" he sighs. He finds his hat in one of his coat pockets and tugs it onto his head. "Did anything good just come of us coming here? Did you find out what you needed?"

I nod slowly, glancing out at the parking lot. "Um, yeah, I think so. You know…it helped clear up how and I guess *why* I am the Catalyst." I shrug. There's still a lot of unknowns, but at least I have a place to start. "It's something. Beats the not knowing anything at all." I grimace. "So it was worth it. Thank you."

Daniel smiles tightly. "Good. I want you to feel...okay...about everything. You know, as okay as someone can feel in your situation." He stares at me. "You're safe, Christa. And everything is going to work out. I promise." He leans against the bus shelter, looking out toward the freeway.

I take a deep breath and follow his gaze. Even with everything that the Agent told us today, there's a nagging voice still rattling off the many unanswered questions in the back of my head. Will I choose light or dark? What will happen to me and the rest of the world when I do? And what about the prophecy? When and how will the new prophet be found? Does that even matter now that the wheels are in motion?

My breath catches as I glance back at Daniel, who is watching the horizon confidently. Yes, it does matter. I think about the last word in the unfinished script—*sacrifice*. What will I have to lose before all of this is said and done? I sigh and stare up at the sky. Now would be a great time for one of those elusive Christmas miracles.

Daniel looks at me and smiles, taking my hand. I smile back at him as if everything is going to work out, even though I'm not sure.

CHAPTER 12
NEW YORK CITY—
DECEMBER, 1975

"HEY, HEY! WATCH the doorframe!" Daniel exclaims from the front of the tree, readjusting his heavy armful of evergreen. I grunt and shift the tree's trunk, trying to push through the front door. The tree shoves back against my side.

"It's fat in the middle. Can you reach over and kind of press it down where the net is bunching? I think it's stuck." I jerk my chin to show him the snowy spot I'm talking about, knowing I'll wind up with a broken foot if I drop my end. Daniel's mouth twists as he reaches over and smashes a few of the bows with his hand.

"Okay, try it now." He glances over at me, his cheeks ruddy from the cold. I grimace and bulldoze into the behemoth with probably more force than needed. The top of the tree missiles into Daniel's gut and sends him spiraling back into the front hall, a confetti of pine needles raining down on him.

He gets up, laughing and brushing green off his sweater. "Probably a little more gusto there than necessary, Irish!" He grins, watching as I get the tree inside with a final push and slam the door behind us.

"Sorry," I exhale, shaking snowflakes out of my hair as I take off my coat. "I was starting to lose my grip on the trunk after the walk back... Just wanted to be done with it."

Daniel snorts. "Well, when you pick the biggest tree on the lot, that's what happens!" He gives the tree a light kick with his sneaker, more needles sprinkling onto the wood floor.

I roll my eyes. "Come on, I know you didn't want a scraggly one either. And it wasn't *the* biggest one there... The guy showed us that crazy blue spruce—had to be the size of a ballroom. Who do think will buy that?"

"Someone *with* a ballroom." Daniel jerks his head toward the library. "Come on, Oppa wants it set up in here..."

I nod, and we both pick up our ends again and slowly navigate around the stairwell and into the sitting room. Martin is propped up in his easy chair, surrounded by the sea of Christmas boxes that Daniel and I lugged out of the garage this morning. A warm fire crackles merrily from the fireplace, Martin having lit it for the first time this season.

"Ah, there it is!" He looks up at the tree from a set of small crystal ornaments, carefully setting them back in their tissue paper. "I found the base while you were out. Should be ready to go."

Daniel and I shuffle over to the far corner of the room, where a small metal base waits on the floor. I give Daniel a wary look. "It'll fit," he answers, reading my gaze. "I go through this every year..." With a loud grunt, he hoists up his end of the tree and disappears underneath it. Using all my strength, I hold it steady as he tinkers with the base, the sound of clanking screws and bolts accompanied by light cursing coming up through the branches. With a joyful "Aha!" he finally reemerges and motions for me to let go. I take a tentative step back, and we all stare in wonder at the giant balancing atop the tiny pedestal, defying every known law of physics.

Daniel grins and gives me a high five. "Right on! Let's get the net off!"

Martin hands him a pair of scissors, and Daniel cuts quickly, releasing the branches from the net's hold. Once he's through, we look on and admire our handiwork. "Holy moly, it's *big*," Daniel mutters, staring into the green that's taking up half the living room. I nod in agreement.

"Just push the sofa off to the side of bit. Should be fine," Martin suggests, going back to the ornaments. Daniel obliges, shoving his hip into the couch to make a small aisle between the furniture and the tree. With a huff, he flops down and puts his feet up, his legs hanging off the end.

"I'm done!" he crows. "Did my thing with the base. Now it's up to you two to decorate this guy." He snuggles down into the cushions. "I'll supervise."

"That won't get annoying at all," I snicker, moving over to Martin.

He looks up with a grin and hands me the box of crystal ornaments. "Take time with these. They withstood a long journey and the last 25 years in the garage. It would be a terrible waste to lose them now."

I nod and pad over to the tree, taking the crystals out of their paper with care and finding an appropriately high bow for each one. I step back when I'm through, Martin smiling in approval.

"Perfect," he murmurs. "Those were Erna's favorites. They were in her family for a long time—belonged to her grandmother." His eyes crinkle. "Now it's really Christmas."

"Good thing, as it *is* Christmas Eve!" Daniel chuckles. "If it doesn't happen now, we're in trouble."

"I suppose that's true," Martin laughs in agreement. He turns his attention back to me as I start in on another box. "How does your family celebrate Christmas, Alden?"

I keep my eyes trained on the tree as I hook a wooden Santa and a couple of fat reindeer onto the branches. "My mother loved Christmas…one of the happier times of the year around our house," I say after a minute, deciding it's okay to open up a little.

"We never had a tree quite like this, but it was still nice. She'd have us all making garlands out of popcorn and cranberries... newspaper folded up into little shapes." I shrug. "Looked pretty good by the time she was done with it."

"It sounds wonderful," Martin replies warmly.

I give him a tight smile. "And then we'd go to Mass... Christmas Eve and Christmas Day."

"Which you're still doing...with Jillian, right?" Daniel arches a brow. "Keeping that tradition alive."

I grin. "Yeah, but just tonight—for the midnight Mass. Back home, we'd be in Church pretty much the whole time. That's kinda what you do in Caherconlish... It's not like America, with a whole bunch of presents to open on Christmas morning." The pile under Jillian's parents' tree had been seeping into the front foyer for weeks, and now threatens to take over the kitchen.

Martin's eyes widen. "Presents—yes!" he exclaims, pulling himself out of his chair.

I shoot Daniel a look as the old man excitedly shuffles into the kitchen. "What's he up to?" I ask. Daniel shrugs and wipes his nose with the back of his hand. I tense up for a moment, taking in his chronically runny, red nose. He's our own tow-headed Rudolph, although I know it's not from some flu bug. We haven't spoken about the night at Ramos's or the alley since it happened, neither one of us wanting to bring it up. Daniel does a pretty good job of making everything seem fine and dandy, cracking jokes and going on with business as usual, but I'm not sure I'm always so convincing. I turn back to the tree and try to ignore the little warning voice in the back of my head.

"Here we are!" Martin calls from the kitchen doorway, carrying a precarious stack of presents topped by a small chocolate cake.

"Martin, what's all this?" I laugh, taking the cake away before it falls. I set it down on the coffee table and sit in his chair as he crosses over to the couch, shooing Daniel to make room.

"We have much to celebrate today!" He beams, handing me

a small package wrapped in red as he takes a seat. "That's for you, Alden. Merry Christmas."

I look down at the gift in my hands and feel my throat grow thick. "Martin," I murmur. "You…you didn't have to get me anything…"

"Don't be so humble—you are family!" He nods at the present. "But don't get too excited, it's small…"

"Thank you. It's lovely. Really." I rest the gift in my lap and smile at the gooey chocolate cake in front of us. "Is this one of your Christmas traditions, too?"

Daniel rolls his eyes and sits back as Martin breaks into a huge grin. "It's his birthday!" He pats Daniel happily on the arm.

I gape at Daniel, who's gone all bashful, rubbing the back of his neck. "You didn't say it was your birthday! Why didn't you tell me?"

Daniel sighs and crosses his arms, a wry smile stretched across his face. "It's not a big deal…" he mutters.

Martin shakes his head. "He never tells anyone! Likes to keep it close to the vest!"

I tut at Daniel. "Today's your birthday…huh!" I grin as he grimaces at me. "Christmas Eve—how very…"

"Christ-like?" he asks with a smirk.

"Hardly!" I guffaw. "I wish you would've said something! I would have gotten you something…you know, other than a Christmas present." I have the new Pink Floyd LP all wrapped up and ready for him upstairs.

Daniel wrinkles his nose. "It's fine, seriously. Your friendship is enough," he jokes, batting my knee.

I give him a look, then stare back at the cake. "Did you bake this, Martin? It looks amazing…"

"Ah, no! As has been made very apparent, I do not have the same talents in the kitchen as others in this house." He looks fondly at Daniel. "Frau Bloomenshein at the corner bakery made it, like she does for him every year." He smiles and squeezes Daniel's shoulder. "It's his favorite! Since he was a little boy…"

Daniel blushes. "Okay, okay, Oppa… Are we gonna eat this thing or what?" He stands and walks off into the kitchen. "I'll get us some plates."

Martin turns back to me, all smiles. "There had been an early blizzard that Christmas… The whole neighborhood was under three feet of snow." He settles into the couch, folding his hands. "I was out shoveling, and I could hear Rita playing as I worked." He glances over at the piano, its wooden cover firmly locked in place over the keys. "She played beautifully, with such talent. I really do believe that if she had applied herself, she could have become a concert pianist, playing Lincoln Center—but like most girls her age, she had other interests." Martin shrugs. "Anyway, she was in the middle of a piece—Liszt—and the music stopped abruptly." His eyes twinkle as he looks back at me. "She wasn't due for another three weeks, so I just thought she had gone to help Erna in the kitchen with dinner…but then Erna comes running out in her stockings yelling at me to hurry up with the walk because Rita's water had broken!" He grins at the memory and adds with a laugh, "It seems our Daniel's musical appreciation began at a very young age."

"Yes!" I chuckle along with him.

Martin smiles, rubbing his jaw. "We were able to get the car out and get to the hospital just in time. It was hard for her, being almost a child herself, and the whole labor going so quickly. Hard for me too—to watch her go through it…" He takes a breath. "But Erna kept it together, like she always does, and helped her weather it. And then he was here, and you could tell she was in love the minute she saw him."

"He seems to have that effect on *all* women," I say with a grin.

Martin nods in agreement, then stops and stares at the piano, his mind drifting off to visit some unknown place. "I'm not sure what Daniel has told you about her, but she *was* a good mother—for the time she was here," he whispers after a moment. I blink, watching him. "She would take him places, read to him, sing to him every night…*Gute Nacht meine wildes ding, ich liebe dich*…uh…'Goodnight my wild thing. I love you.'" He sighs and glances at me. "His favorite book growing up was that *Where the Wild Things Are*. He didn't care much for the little boy in the story, but he loved the monsters." He smiles sadly.

I cock my head, trying to read Martin's face as his eyes tighten. "She didn't leave because of him, you know. She—"

He stops as Daniel comes back into the room. "We are majorly backed up on dish detail. I thought you said you were gonna clean up last night, Irish…after you got back from downtown!" Plates and silverware in hand, he steers around a row of cardboard boxes and plops back down on the couch, shaking his head.

I scowl, any cozy feelings that Martin helped cure a second ago gone. "I was at Jillian's later than planned—sorry!" I grumble, slouching in my seat. "I was going to tackle it this morning, but then we got roped into the boxes…"

"You two are worse than an old married couple!" Martin laughs, cutting into the cake and doling servings onto the plates. "Let's settle this with some chocolate, eh? I was just telling Alden about the Christmas you were born—"

"Aw—come on, Oppa! He doesn't want to hear about that." Daniel's cheeks redden as he accepts a piece of cake. Martin lets out a little sigh.

"No, it's fine… I like hearing old stories about you. It makes you more Human!" I tease.

"As opposed to what?" Daniel quirks his eyebrows. "Some sort of Batman-superhero?" He laughs, flexing his arms.

I roll my eyes. "Yeah…more like a super freak—"

"I, um…I had mentioned your mother…" Martin interrupts, clearing his throat and putting down the cake knife. Reaching back to the stack of gifts, he pulls a small white envelope off the top. "She sent this for you."

Daniel goes silent as he takes the letter from his grandfather. "Annual obligatory check in," he finally mutters, shoving it into his jeans. "At least it got here on time this year."

Martin watches him, his face pinched. "Aren't you going to read it? You should open it, Daniel…"

"You think there's cash inside?" Daniel laughs harshly, Martin looking down at the couch. "Probably just a bunch of goopy hearts and flowery stuff. It's fine—I'll read it later." He gets up suddenly and smooths his jeans.

"Where are you going?" Martin wonders.

Daniel runs a hand through his hair. "I gotta get to work—it's a busy night down at Monique's." He shoots me a look, warning me to keep my mouth shut. Of course he's lying—we're closed today and tomorrow and on short staff through the New Year, most of the crew gone back to France for the holidays. Muriel and Francois left three days ago.

"But you haven't even opened your present!" Martin cries, his eyes pleading, grabbing the large package that's off to his side. "Daniel…*bitte nicht gehen*…" He moves the box onto the couch and stares at Daniel like a lost puppy.

My heart aches for him. "Come on, Daniel, it's not gonna kill you to stay and open a present or two," I mumble, putting my foot in his path. Daniel grinds his teeth and glares at me, then turns around and falls back into the couch. Martin smiles, relieved.

"All right, what do we got?" Daniel grimaces, pulling the box onto his lap.

Martin looks between the two of us and gives me a wink. "Something you definitely need…and hopefully want," he answers, watching Daniel tear off the bright green paper. "Alden helped me pick it out for you."

"You were in on this, Irish?" Daniel grins. "Box of Leprechaun gold and four leaf clovers?"

I snort. "If I had known it was your birthday…"

Daniel laughs as he opens the box. "Aw…right on!" he

exclaims, pulling a brown leather jacket from its wrappings and holding it up to himself. "Really! This is really cool—I love it!" He smooths the leather with his hand.

"For when you ride your motorcycle," Martin chimes in. "You need to be wearing more protection when you're out on that thing. Your helmet probably wouldn't be a bad idea either…"

"Let's not get crazy!" Daniel chuckles, staring down at the jacket. "I don't want people to think I'm a nerd."

"Yeah, nothing says 'nerd' like not wanting to die a horrible, grizzly death on the highway." I roll my eyes and motion to the jacket. "It is possible to be cool and safe at the same time, you know."

"For sure! Oh man…" He gets up and tries it on, zipping it up for good measure. It's a perfect fit. "This is so rockin'… I'm never taking this thing off. Thank you, Oppa." In a move I never expected, he sits back down and pulls Martin into a hug. Martin embraces him and gives him a quick kiss on the lips, patting him on the cheek. I twinge at the old world-ness of it…the closeness… something I never had with any of the men in my family. I feel my skin growing hot.

"I'm happy you like it!" Martin exclaims. "You're a good boy…19 now! Time to get serious about things!"

Daniel nods sheepishly as he leans back. "That's right, Oppa, that's right."

Martin grins at me, clearly pleased. I smile back and watch as Daniel tests out all of the pockets on the jacket, sharing a matching grin with his grandfather. Martin looks down at the small present still in my hands and nods. "Open yours, Alden," he murmurs.

"Okay…" I blush and run my fingers under the tape, taking my time so as not to rip the paper. It's a book, the cover a soft tan cloth that's faded with age, a bit of gold type on the spine.

"It's Yeats…poetry—from my own collection," Martin says,

his voice low, watching me as I turn the book over in my hands. "I've been saving it for a long time for such an occasion as this."

I shake my head and stare down at the book, almost too choked up to speak. "This is…too much, Martin. I don't know if I can accept this," I rasp, holding it out to him.

He leans over and gently pushes it back at me. "What's the big deal? It's just a book!" Daniel scoffs from the couch.

Martin keeps his eyes trained on me and nods. "Yes, you can—please," he answers softly. "That book has survived a lot, and it deserves a good home with one of its own." He smiles, knowing that I know exactly what he's talking about. I exhale and grip the book tightly.

He nods and gives a small cough. "I would ask that you do me a kindness before it makes the journey up to the attic to live amongst the rest of your belongings…" He pushes his glasses up on his nose and points at the book. "That you would consider… uh…reading one to us now." He stares at me intently.

I exhale and brush my hand over the cover. "Oppa!" Daniel jeers, sitting up. "He doesn't want to do that! Come on—this is just embarrassing—"

"SHHH—SHUSH!" Martin silences him with more vigor than I've ever seen from the old man. Daniel shuts up quick and slumps petulantly into the couch. "Let the young man read the poem!" Martin shouts. "It is his birthright!" He looks back at me beseechingly.

I take a breath; it's hard to argue with that. "Yes, of course," I answer, standing and moving over to the Christmas tree, book in hand. Martin beams as I open the text. "Any particular one you'd like?"

"No," he murmurs, sitting on the edge of his seat. "Whatever you choose will be fine."

I nod and try to keep my hands steady as I flip through the pages, suppressing the urge to dash up the stairs to my bunk and never come out again. I'm definitely not a natural-born performer. I find a poem that looks to be of suitable length and clear my throat.

"Towards Break of Day," I state, my voice wavering a little. Martin sits at rapt attention while Daniel lets out a heavy sigh. I inhale and read slowly and clearly, focused on the words.

"Was it the double of my dream
The woman that by me lay
Dreamed, or did we halve a dream
Under the first cold gleam of day?

I thought: "There is a waterfall
Upon Ben Bulben side
That all my childhood counted dear;
Were I to travel far and wide
I could not find a thing so dear.

My memories had magnified
So many times childish delight.

I would have touched it like a child
But knew my finger could but have touched
Cold stone and water.
I grew wild.
Even accusing Heaven because
It had set down among its laws:
Nothing that we love over-much
Is ponderable to our touch.

I dreamed towards break of day,
The cold blown spray in my nostril.
But she that beside me lay
Had watched in bitterer sleep
The marvelous stag of Arthur,

That lofty white stag, leap
From mountain steep to steep.

I look up from the page when I'm through and see Martin's eyes brimming with tears. Daniel follows my gaze and gives a slight start, putting his hand on his grandfather's shoulder. "Oppa," he murmurs kindly. "Are you okay?"

Martin sits frozen, staring off into space, his lower lip trembling. Daniel shoots me a worried look. "Hey, Oppa...Earth to Oppa..." He gives him a gentle shake. "I know you've got an earful to tell us about that. Irish did a pretty bang-up job—even *I* liked it." He shrugs.

Martin blinks once, and Daniel and I both let out a small sigh of relief. He's back. "Thank you, Alden," he rasps, his voice thick with emotion. "That was...the most beautiful reading. To hear it in its natural accent..." He pauses, overcome. "I can die happy now."

Daniel's eyes grow wide. "Whoa! Let's not go *there*—would put a real damper on the holidays!" he cries, putting his hands up. "I do a pretty sweet Irish accent, Oppa...if I had known it meant so much to you..."

We all laugh, grateful that he's broken the intense mood. "You and your jokes." Martin shakes his head, his smile returning. He nods at me once before motioning to Daniel. "This calls for something stronger...to warm us up! *Ja?*"

Daniel's face brightens, and he gets up. "I like the way you think, Oppa... Anything you got a taste for?"

"Hmm...I think schnapps, maybe? Three glasses?"

He glances over at me, and I wave my hand in protest. "Just two. But please, don't let me stop you." I grin, sitting back down.

Martin nods at Daniel. "Two, then... The stamperls are in the cupboard above the refrigerator."

Daniel moves toward the kitchen. "Peppermint, right? I think we still have some from last year..."

"Of course! It is Christmas, after all!" Martin laughs. "And bring a glass of milk for Alden. It's bad luck to toast with an empty hand." He pats my knee happily.

I smile and settle into my chair as Daniel returns with several small, fragile goblets, the bottle of schnapps tucked under his arm. "All right, here we go…" He carefully hands me my milk before pouring the clear liquid into the two remaining tiny glasses. He gives one to Martin and then holds his up. "To adventure…to memories…to great oration!" he toasts me with a laugh.

I roll my eyes merrily. "And family," Daniel continues, patting Martin on the back. "Both new and old! This day would mean nothing without it."

"Yes!' Martin agrees huskily, raising his glass. "We are very lucky. *Prost!*" We all clink our glasses together and drink, both Daniel and Martin letting out little grunts as they put theirs back.

"Nice!" Daniel brays, pouring another round for himself and his grandfather. "Now it's a holiday! To life!"

"Yes! Long life!" Martin crows. They laugh and toast, gulping down the fiery alcohol.

I grin and shake my head; I can see where this is going. "I hate to leave what I'm sure is going to be an amazing little party here." I ease out of my chair. "But I do have to start getting ready if I'm going to meet Jillian on time—"

"To love!" Daniel shouts, and they toast again.

I smile, gather my new book, and look warily over at the unfinished Christmas tree. "You think you two can hold it down and get that thing put together before dawn?" I shake my head at all the unopened ornament boxes.

Martin waves, his cheeks already starting to pink. "Oh, sure! No problem. A little more…more…" He taps his finger on the side of the glass as Daniel refills his drink. "We'll get right to it after this one…"

"Or four," Daniel snickers, raising his glass to me. "To you,

Irish." He smiles as he slurps down another shot, coughing a little when he's done. "Merry Christmas."

"Yes!" I laugh in agreement, moving toward the hall as the happy German chatter behind me increases in speed and volume—and though I can't understand a word of it, I know it's all good. When I glance back before I head upstairs, I see them together on the couch, Martin's arm draped over Daniel's shoulders like they're old comrades catching up after the war, the clink of glasses accentuating their raucous laughter—the way it should be.

"Merry Christmas," I whisper as I slip up the stairs.

*

The church is already dark by the time I get there, the glow of candlelight guiding my way to where Jillian is waiting in the pew. Her teeth glint brightly when she sees me, smiling as I take my place beside her. The crowd is hushed as the cantor sings the Kyrie.

"Sorry—the trains are running farther apart tonight..." I whisper in her ear as she passes me a lit candle.

She runs her fingers through mine with her free hand. "It's fine. I'm just glad you're here." She leans into me, and I kiss the top of her head, her perfume filling my nose. An immediate wave of euphoria rushes over me. I grip her hand tightly as we sing with the rest of the congregation, the sanctuary packed with parishioners dressed in their holiday finest. A little girl in front of us peeks back from her father's arms, all done up in red taffeta. She gives us a bashful smile and buries her face in her dad's shoulder, her eyes darting back once in a while to see if we're still looking. Jillian giggles and squeezes my fingers. The song comes to a close, and we sit, her evergreen satin Christmas dress brushing my hip and sending shivers down my leg. It was her mother's originally; they'd been working on alterations together since Thanksgiving.

She wears her silver cross at her neck, accompanied by the new diamond earrings I gave her yesterday, not wanting to wait for Christmas Day. It had been my first experience buying jewelry for anyone, and she had laughed sweetly at my over-exuberance. Jillian looks at me now, her cheeks shining like apples, reminiscent of some old master's painting. My pulse quickens.

"You look stunning, by the way," I murmur, running my thumb along her lap.

She bites her lip and smiles. "You, too." She keeps her voice down so as not to disturb the service. "The new jacket looks good."

"I thought the tux had earned a night off." While I've been putting away most of my paychecks, I thought it would be all right to splurge a little with the holidays. Jillian chuckles quietly at my joke and sits a little closer.

We go quiet and listen to the priest as he retells the Nativity story. And even though everyone here knows it by heart, the room sits captivated, crackling with an unseen energy. Even the little girl in front of us pays attention, something I recall being terrible at when I was that age. Jillian rests her head on my shoulder as the bells chime for Consecration, and we're no longer sitting in some church in New Jersey: there is magic here tonight.

We get up to receive Communion, the choir humming *Silent Night* from the rafters as we all shuffle to the front and then back to our seats. I let Jillian go in front of me, one hand drifting across the small of her back. As usual when I'm around her, I find that I cannot be close enough, and I'm grateful that I'm holding a live flame to keep my focus on the here and now.

We get back to our pew, and the solemn service wakes up with a chorus of bells followed by a boisterous rendition of *Joy to the World* indicating the end of Mass. The lights come up, and we all blow out our candles, everyone greeting each other with hugs and well wishes. Jillian turns to me and wraps her arms around my neck, pulling me in for a kiss. "Merry Christmas," she breathes.

I smile. "Merry Christmas." I glance around at the other pews. "Where's everybody else?"

Jillian laughs and rolls her eyes. "They went to 4 o'clock so

that Mother could get back and lock herself in her room to finish wrapping. I promise you, her light will still be on when I
get home." She looks up at me ardently. "So it's just me. Hope
that's okay."

I tighten my arms around her waist. "That's not even a real
question."

She grins and buries her nose in my collar, inhaling deeply
before reaching down to grab her coat. "Walk me home?" She
takes my hand again. "Or do you have to get the train?"

"I'd rather swim all the way back to Queens than miss a
chance to walk you home. Best Christmas gift yet." I pet the silky
fabric of her dress with my fingertips.

"Sounds chilly," she teases, arching a brow.

I sigh dramatically. "The thought of you will keep me warm!"

I pull her close as we join the line of people making their way
out of the church. The little girl in red taffeta from before is being
carried out in front of us, her eyes half closed. She gives me a
sleepy wave.

It's snowing again when we make it outside, the streetlights
glowing eerily against the ice. Both of us cling to one another, out
of habit as well as from the desire not to wipe out on the sidewalk
in our dress shoes.

"Did you have a nice afternoon with the Kirschbaums?"
Jillian asks as we cross the street. "How's the tree looking?"

"Unfinished!" I laugh, watching snowflakes land in her hair.
"And I imagine it's going to stay that way, given the temperament
of the room when I left…" She looks at me curiously, and I shrug.
"We'll just have very…natural holiday decor. Like taking a walk
through the woods." I smile.

Jillian shakes her head and looks out into the night. "Did
Daniel say anything about Muriel's present?" She grips my arm
tightly, her feet skating on the ice. "She was pretty excited when
she told me about it at lunch last week."

"No…" I raise my eyebrows. "What did she give him?"

She inhales. "A new knife." She makes a face, almost slipping. "For cooking...a really nice one. Seemed like kind of a strange gift, but she told me knives were everything to chefs. And the best chef should have the best knife..." She sighs. "I wish he would just...ugh! Ask her out already! I don't get it—she's beautiful, kind...*French*!" Jillian laughs, her facing softening. "She thinks so highly of him..."

"Undeservedly," I grumble, wrapping my arm around her waist. "I don't know what his problem is, Jillian. He's got the whole ruddy world in his pocket, and he's just looking for ways to toss it away. Needs to get his head out of his arse, if you ask me."

I stop, catching my language, and take her by the hands. "I'm sorry. I shouldn't talk like that in front of you." I exhale and look into her eyes.

She grins and shakes her head. "What? I could barely understand you. Was that even English?" she jokes.

I roll my eyes. "Let's not talk about Daniel right now. I'm in too good a mood!" She squeals as I give her a twirl, her green dress fanning out around her legs. She spins back, our hands clasped, and we do a little dance, laughing and wobbling to a stop when our heels slip on the slick pavement.

"Let's talk about how you're going to sit for me in this suit!" She smiles, stepping back to admire my new clothes. "And with those long eyelashes...the whole thing is very Edwardian. We could put you by an old-fashioned window frame..." She runs her fingers along the side of my face, watching my lip curl.

Jillian draws in a breath, her green eyes growing stormy. "Don't you dare!" she exclaims with a grin, ramming her finger into my chest. "I see you trying to work up another excuse to not let me draw your portrait! Come on—you promised!"

I sigh and scratch the back of my head. "I know, I know..."

She grabs my lapels and leans in, my mind dizzying at the proximity of her perfect mouth. "Is it...are you worried I'll make you look bad?" She looks up at me, her eyes wide. "Am I not... good enough?"

I balk. "Uh...no. Your work is stunning, and you know it. You yelled at me the other day for looking at your notebooks too long! I'd still be going through them if you hadn't found other ways to distract me..." I grin, winding my arms around her. She trembles as I brush her hair aside to find my favorite spot behind her jaw, using my lips to warm her cool skin.

She starts to melt into me, but catches herself. "Don't. Change. The subject." She punctuates each word with another jab of her finger, forcing me to sigh and pull back. "Why won't you let me draw you? Seriously?"

"Why do you want to so bad?" I chortle, glancing away at a snowy street sign. "I'm nothing exceptional—just some waiter who hangs around drooling over you all day." I snort, looking back at her.

Jillian's not amused, her mouth drawn into a thin line. "That's not true, Alden. You *are* exceptional." She steps back and crosses her arms. "And you are so much more than *some waiter*... I hate that you would even say that." She shakes her head and starts walking again.

I clench my jaw and follow. "Hey...why are you mad?" I laugh, pulling her by the arm. "And what's wrong if I *am* just 'some waiter'? There's no shame in hard work, Jillian..."

"That's not what I'm saying!" She spins on her heels and glares at me. "But that's not who you are—you're...more than that! With all your hopes and dreams, talking about maybe running your own place one day..." I twinge as she puts a hand on my arm. "What about taking those business classes at City College like we talked about—"

"That *you* talked about, my darling," I whisper. "You know my hours at Monique's don't allow... I mean, maybe someday—" I cringe as I watch her face fall. "Do we really need to go into all this tonight? It's Christmas." I stop and reach for her.

She takes a breath and runs a hand through her hair. "I know…and I'm sorry. I don't want to argue." She sighs, coming back to me again. "I just don't like it when you talk down about yourself. You're pretty special to *me*." She stares into my eyes, lacing her fingers through mine. "And beautiful… whether you see it or not." She arches a brow.

I shake my head, knowing I've lost this battle. "You *are* the artist, so I suppose you know best in that department."

That gets a little smile; I let out a relieved breath. "Hey, I'll let you draw me anytime you want, wearing anything you want." Her face brightens as I flick the hem of my jacket. "We'll do it tomorrow if you like, set up a studio in the middle of your mother's living room."

"I know you're kidding, but they would love that!" Jillian exclaims. "I'd put them to work holding lights and props…"

"Oh, jeez!" I laugh, squeezing her to my side.

She giggles, and we walk to the end of the block. We stop under a street lamp on the corner, and Jillian turns to me. "I've gotten a lot of compliments on the earrings." She grins and tucks her hair back, the bright gems glittering in her ears. "Mother freaked and seems to think they imply something *more* than a Christmas present."

"What did you say?" I smile, sweeping my palm down her arm.

"I told her they were very nice earrings, but that she should put her wedding china away for the time being. She gets so carried away…" Jillian rolls her eyes, but then stops and stares at me. "She thinks you're quite serious about…whatever it is we're doing here."

Her eyes flutter shut as my hand finds its way back up to her cheek. "Well, she can't be wrong about everything," I murmur.

The corner of Jillian's mouth twitches, and she looks at my face. "But…she helped me figure out what I want to give you for Christmas," she whispers.

I grin quizzically and waggle my foot at her. "My new loafers?" Jillian had insisted that I needed new shoes to match my suit when we were out shopping and had picked them up for me when I refused. We settled it by calling them my Christmas present from her.

She exhales and shakes her head. "No...not the shoes..." Bowing her head, she reaches to the nape of her neck and releases the clasp on her necklace, coiling the small silver chain and cross and setting them in my hand.

I take a breath and stare at it. "Jillian...I don't understand..."

"It's jewelry, too," she breathes, taking a step closer. "I'm sorry it's not very masculine." She traces over the intricate latticework on the cross, letting her finger drift slowly across the plain of my hand. "You don't have to wear it if you don't want to—but it's been in my family for generations, passed down from oldest daughter to oldest daughter. It was my grandmother's last..." She pauses and wets her lips. "We're supposed to give it away." She stares at the sidewalk.

"To whom?" I ask quietly.

She inhales. "To the boy...uh...man..." She blushes and looks at me. "To the person I fall in love with."

The earth spins, and I wish I were standing closer to the lamppost so as to have something to hold onto. It's the first time either one of us has said that word, even though I've known it to be true in my own heart since the first time I saw her. I feel my jaw hang slack as I gawk at her, probably looking like a prize fool.

Jillian watches me, her eyes hesitant. "Is...is that okay?" she asks after a minute, crossing her arms protectively.

I startle. "You...you love me," I say out loud, still not believing it. Maybe there actually is a God.

She nods. "Yes, I love you, Alden Murphy. I love you."

She eyes me expectantly after the declaration, but all I can do is stand there, completely dumbfounded. After a minute, she shakes her head and turns around. "Um…sorry…" She wipes something away from her cheek, and I see that she's crying.

I pull myself together and take her into my arms. "Why are you crying?" I ask, desperately trying to figure out what I've done wrong.

She puts her face down, not wanting to look at me. "Do…do you love me too?" she sniffles.

I frown and close my own eyes. If only I could punch myself—I'm such an idiot. I tilt her chin up. "Of course I love you, you wonderful girl!" I exclaim, swinging her around. She cries happily and throws her arms around my neck as I cover her face in kisses, making sure I catch every part of her. I save her eyelashes for last and then pull back to look at her.

She beams up at me, snowflakes melting on her cheek. "I thought maybe…maybe you didn't, and I…" She shakes her head and lets out a small, high-pitched giggle. "Why would you? I still can't believe we're even together…"

"I can't believe that you would even question how I feel about you." I stop and get my bearings. "I have been in love with you from the first time you walked into the restaurant. I knew you were mine the minute I saw you." I rest my forehead against hers. "Jillian O'Connor, I will make it my life's work, 'til the day I die and beyond, for you to never wonder again if I love you."

Her eyes go wide as I get down on one knee and take both her hands in mine. "Alden, what are you doing?" she cries, her voice shrill.

I shake my head and press my lips to her cold fingers. "Just let me do this, Jillian. I know I don't have a ring—"

"ALDEN!" she squeals, taking her hands away and windmilling her arms frantically in the air. "You cannot seriously be asking—WHOOP!!"

She loses her balance and topples backwards, the ice finally claiming one of us as its victim. "JILLIAN!" I yell as I scramble over to where she's lying on her back in the snow. When I get to her, she's laughing, her cheeks bright pink.

"You crazy Irishman!" she crows, pulling me on top of her. "Have you completely lost it?" She cradles my face in her hands.

"I have not!" I reply indignantly. "I think this is the perfect time to propose to the woman I love, but then you had to go and hash it all up by falling over like some fainting ingénue!" This really makes her crack up, and I shake my head at her. "What's the matter with you?"

She laughs even harder and pulls me in for a kiss, our lips crushing together jubilantly. When we part, she lets out a contented sigh and rests her head in the snow. "This is enough!" Jillian says, smiling up at me and holding my hand, the silver cross pressed between us.

I nod. "You're right…enough for now," I breathe into her hair. "I love you, you love me, and I think…" I turn and squint up at the moon. "It must officially be Christmas. What do you have to say about that?"

She giggles, our noses brushing. "I'm speechless, utterly speechless!"

An excited growl escapes my throat. "Only one thing to do when that happens…" I pull her to myself and kiss her, over and over, knowing that we never have to stop.

CHAPTER 13

LOS ANGELES—PRESENT DAY

FLANKED BY THOSE destined for good and evil, she will be carried from the ashes and born again to judge the Fates; and of her own accord, choose to Evict Heaven or Hell… Once the course has been decided, it will fall to the Catalyst to sacrifice—

"Christa, you're dropping your end!" Mary Carmen cries from the other side of the mattress.

I startle and readjust the heavy load, pushing the prophecy and the Agent's voice to the back of mind as Mary Carmen hastily sweeps dust bunnies off of the top of the boxspring.

"Okay…let's flip it, and then we can put it back down…"

With a grunt, we turn the top mattress and let it fall back onto the bed with a soft thump. Mary Carmen exhales and smiles at me, putting her hands on her hips. "One down! Let's go do yours now…"

My jaw drops slightly as I remember all of the contraband I'd smuggled under my bed—not exactly Seraphim-appropriate. "It's fine. I just changed my sheets this morning," I scramble to lie. "Would be a waste to strip it now, only to have to wash them all over again…"

Mary Carmen considers. "Okay, I guess it can go another week." She pulls out her hair elastic and reconfigures her bun.

Even with her hair all messy, though, she still looks like a total men's magazine model, her curves perfectly accentuated by her old cleaning t-shirt and jeans. She blinks behind her glasses. "When you Windexed, did you get the bathroom mirror as well?"

I roll my eyes. "Yes, Mary Carmen! You said to do all the glass, so I did *all* the glass." I flop down on her bed, propping myself up with my elbows. "Why do we have to do all this cleaning, anyway? It's not like we have a ton of people coming over for Christmas."

"Yes, we do! You, me, Daniel..." She counts off on her fingers. "...Benny, Ellis, and I'm sure Jodie will stop by like she did for Thanksgiving..."

I count on my own hand. "Daniel doesn't count, Benny practically lives in his truck, so I doubt he'll even notice that the curtains have been vacuumed..." I frown and glance out the window. "And I wouldn't hold your breath on Jodie."

Mary Carmen stares at me, concerned. "What's going on? You haven't been yourself the last few days—and there seems to be extra tension whenever Jodie comes up. Are you two fighting?"

I glower. "I don't want to talk about it."

Mary Carmen sighs and grabs the clean set of bedsheets from the dresser, bending down to pick up a pillow. "You know I have a lot of experience with conflict resolution." She uses her Sober Students voice as she stuffs the pillow into one of the pale blue pillowcases. I work really hard not to look totally sullen as she gives me a knowing look. "You can tell me what's going on. I promise you, I've heard it all before."

Even the one about a pair of maniacal Demons showing up at a high school science fair to cause chaos and mayhem, ultimately turning best friends against one another? Doubt it.

I clench my jaw and stare up at her. "You ready to tell me about Miguel?" I reply innocently. I know I've heard that name before. I spent the last few days snooping around the house, trying to find traces of this mystery person—to no avail.

Mary Carmen draws in a sharp breath, caught off guard. That would be a no, then. I smirk. Catalyst, 1—Seraphim, 0.

I watch her regain her composure, snapping out the crisp base sheet and shooing me off the bed. "What are your plans for the day?" she asks, her tone bright again.

I wipe the smug look off of my face and crouch down to help tuck in the corners. "I don't know... Thought I might hit up the library and catch up on some stuff before the new semester starts after break." That's a half-truth. I *do* want to go to the library to do some research, but the books I plan on checking out have nothing to do with American History or AP Bio. I'm still reeling from our trip to Porticullis, both emotionally and mentally. I have to know more about the prophecy...and while the Religion section at the Los Angeles Public Library might be a long shot, it's the only place I can think of to start.

Mary Carmen gazes at me, her mouth curled into a pleasantly surprised O. "I like the sound of that!" she exclaims, tossing her comforter back across the bed. "I have to work this afternoon, so make sure you take Daniel with you."

"K..." I give her a tight smile. Daniel and I at the library... it's not one of our usual hangouts, but it has potential. A steamy make-out session in the stacks fantasy saunters through my mind, and I clear my throat. Not in this lifetime.

"Looks good." I motion to Mary Carmen's neatly made bed as she tosses her pillows back into place. "All ready for when we come in here for dessert."

Mary Carmen laughs and chucks one of the pillows at my head. "Stop! You'll be happy we did it. It's always nice to come home to a clean house." She nods in approval at the spotless bedroom as she steps back into the hall. "Make sure you finish up in the living room before you go… I found a bunch of old Cheetos and candy under the couch cushions earlier. Can't have that!" She raps a quick rhythm on the wall before walking off.

I scowl and glare at the empty doorway. "I should have read the lease more carefully!" I call after her. "I missed the fine print under 'Rent Free' that detailed the indentured servitude!"

I hear Mary Carmen chuckling in the kitchen as I slog back out to the living room.

*

"Would you stop making that noise with your mouth?" I hiss, slamming my book shut and glaring across the table at Daniel. "It's really distracting."

"Sorry." He smiles, shifting in his chair. "I didn't even realize I was doing it."

"No kidding…" I sigh and rub my eyes irritably, glancing around the empty Religion and Occult section. The very cute college-age librarian downstairs drew a little map on the back of a bookmark before showing us up to the third floor…and then shyly asking me for my phone number when we made it to the stacks. I have to admit, I *did* like his glasses—but Daniel shut that down pretty fast with a brusque, "Thank you for your help, but we've got it from here." He was the last Human contact we've had for about three hours now.

I exhale and stare at the piles of giant tomes towering around me. If I were in a better mood, I might be up for fashioning a sweet fort out of them. I shake my head. "This is pointless. There's not going to be anything about a secret Divine prophecy in a bunch of books written by mortals…" I shove a text titled *The Soothsayer and the Second Sight*. "I wish I had Mandisa's list… There have to be a couple people on that thing who have written some books."

Daniel clenches his jaw. "We don't need that. If we search long enough, we'll find what we're looking for."

I scoff and push away the *Life After Death Digest* I'd spent way too much time on when we first arrived. "Well, we're not going to find it with these winners. Just a soapbox for crazies to sound off on."

"You should be used to that by now!" Daniel jokes. "You're like…the one sane person in the asylum, right?"

I look at him warily. "Yeah, I guess. Although I'm sure Mary Carmen would say differently."

"That *she's* the only sane person?" His eyes dance.

I shrug. "Or that I'm just as crazy as the rest of you." I exhale and check my phone. At least she hasn't been stalking me all afternoon—probably wants to give me some peace and quiet for all the studying I'm *not* doing. I wrinkle my nose at Daniel. "She would be right."

Daniel smiles, fiddling with an old card catalog drawer he brought over the last time I went hunting through the stacks. "How *is* M.C.? Did she freak about yesterday?" I give Daniel a confused look, and his eyes go wide. "Wait—you didn't tell her about us going to Porticullis?"

I shrug and look down at the floor. "It didn't really come up…"

Daniel lets out a snort. "Well—yeah! Christa…you've got to tell her. That's important stuff."

"I know," I sigh, slumping down in my seat. "I will…" He gives me a face as I crinkle my nose. "*After* Christmas! She's been kind of hyper this week. Like someone maybe overlooked an ADHD diagnosis at some point…"

Daniel laughs and throws his arm over his head lazily. "She's getting excited for Friday?"

I snort. "If you call obsessively cleaning and barking out more orders than usual, then yes, she's very excited." I move a couple of books to the floor. "She's acting like this year is different than others—like there're more guests…or that's the vibe I'm getting. She seems pretty jazzed to be seeing Ellis—"

"Oh yeah, she hasn't seen Ellis in a while." Daniel nods in agreement.

I furrow my brow. "What *do* you guys usually do for Christmas?" I ask, picturing the two of them with their heads bowed over a perfectly cooked roast and holly. A twinge of jealousy accompanies my vision, and I grimace. I know I have nothing to worry about—Daniel and Mary Carmen are so far from a couple, it's funny—but just the thought of *anyone* having time with him before me…I can't help feel envious.

Better get over that. I know from that lady Agent that he's had at least forty Christmases on Earth without me, and that's just the dead ones. He's not really mine—or not that kind of *mine,* anyway.

Daniel is reaching for my hand, and I come out of my haze, laughing. "We work!" he answers, squeezing my fingers with a grin. "Me, Mary Carmen…all Guardians. Christmas is our busiest holiday. You'd be amazed at how much trouble people get themselves into between Thanksgiving and New Year's. I think I've spent my last…" He seems to count in his head. "…twelve Christmas eves in an ER waiting room?" A conflicted expression flashes across his face before he turns back to me.

"I'm sorry," I whisper.

He sighs. "Being on Catalyst detail has allowed us a few… luxuries that we didn't have before." He stares at me, his eyes warm again. "So…if Mary Carmen seems a little worked up, it's only because she's happy—looking forward to a real Christmas." He sits back. "We all are."

I blush under his gaze. "Well… I'm glad I can give you guys a little break. I'm…I'm excited, too." I mean it. This is *my* first real Christmas in a while as well. I flash him a little smile. "Just don't ask me to sing any carols around the piano or whatever— unless you want to die a slow, painful death." I catch myself and look at him. "Or…re-die? Is that a thing?"

Daniel laughs quietly and shrugs at the table. "Maybe. But we're all in luck. Mary Carmen doesn't have a piano."

"Right," I chuckle, returning to my books and feeling completely overwhelmed as the crushing task looms in front of me. I sigh. "I should just call it. There isn't going to be anything in these books. I don't even know why I tried." I close a particularly wizened-looking text and start gathering up my stuff.

Daniel tuts and takes the book from me. "Oh, come on... You can't give up that easy!" He adds the book to the stack in front of him that he's been ordering by color. "We've only been at it for a little while. Whenever you see a research montage in a movie, they're at it, like—all night, and we haven't even ordered out for pizza yet!"

I roll my eyes playfully and sit back in my chair. "What do you mean, *we*, Kemosabe?" I snatch a dark blue book out of his hand. "Far as I can tell, you've just been sitting there all afternoon, counting holes in the ceiling!"

"What?!" Daniel squeaks, disassembling his book rainbow. "No way! I've been excellent moral support! You can't argue with that!" I huff as he holds up a handful of browning paper cards. "And I've spent a fair amount of time fixing this card catalog, thank you very much! Everything was all out of order..."

I puff out my cheeks as I flip through the blue book. "No one uses those things anymore, Daniel." My eyes dart back to his catalog drawer. "Except for scrap paper. They have everything on computers now."

"Oh." I watch him frown as he glances at a shiny new laptop that's chained to a small desk behind us. "But...they still have the same call numbers, right?" He holds up one of the cards for me to see and jerks his chin back toward the shelves.

I sigh and nod. "Yeah, I guess so..." I scratch my eyebrow. "What difference does it make?"

"So they're still useful!" he exclaims, pushing the card across the table at me. "Just because they're old and...*antiquated*, it doesn't mean they're not still relevant!" He clenches his jaw, his expression suddenly wild.

I sit up slowly and tuck my hair behind my ear before picking up the card. "I never said it was irrelevant… Where is this coming from?" I glance between him and the call number.

Daniel cringes and looks at his lap. "Nothing. I'm just trying to help, and I thought…" He waves at the drawer, then back at the computer. "I just haven't researched anything in a while, all right? I'm not exactly…comfortable…with all this new technology. It makes me feel…old."

I hold back a laugh as I look at how his perfect teenage face is rearranged in a scowl. This obviously isn't a good time to tease him. "I can show you how to use the computer if you want, Daniel," I reply quietly. "I taught my Nana how to use the Internet in like twenty minutes when I was 13." It might be good for both of us, me taking the lead on something for once.

"Oh, jeez!" He throws his hands up in the air. "NOW you're comparing me to *Nana*?!" His face goes beet red.

"SHHH!!" I motion for him to keep his voice down through my giggles. "Calm down! Seriously!" I shake my head at him. "Are we still talking about this or something else?" I wave the card at him. "I didn't realize the Dewey Decimal System was like a metaphor for your life… Does this have to do with that librarian?"

"NO!" Daniel snaps, slamming his palms down on the table and pulling all the other cards back. "I just think that the card catalog is worth a second look. You might find things there that you wouldn't know to look for on a stupid computer, or whatever." He motions over at the laptop station. "Just because there's some flashy, new, sexy device—"

"*Sexy?*"

He shoots me an exasperated look. "It doesn't mean you should overlook the more reliable, trustworthy guy! The information's still the same…" He fades off at the end as he stuffs the cards back into the drawer.

I sit back in my chair, watching his lips pucker irritably. Yeah…we're definitely not talking about the card catalog anymore.

"You know what, you're right." I smile, holding tight to the card he gave me. Daniel stops shuffling and stares at me. "It's *definitely* worth a second look. What's a search engine compared to honest, hard work?"

Daniel nods slowly. "That's all I'm saying." He shifts in his chair, glaring at me. "That's the second time you've said I'm right in the last week. It's freaking me out."

I laugh. "No, really! Come on, keep going through that thing…" I pull the other end of the drawer to the center of the table. "This is all we're going to use now. That's how much I *love* the card catalog." I bat my eyelashes at him.

Daniel sighs and sits back, massaging the bridge of his nose. "Okay, now you're taking it too far."

I snicker and read the title on the card—*Ancient Revelations and the Modern Voice: A Study of an Everyday Prophet* by David Adler, M.D., Ph.D.

I shrug. "Sounds a little dry…but the author has a bunch of letters after his name, so maybe it's kind of legit?" I glance up from the card.

"Worth a shot!" Daniel jumps from his chair and marches over to the stacks. With a grin, I get up and follow, still reveling in him getting jealous about earlier. Looks like I'm not the only one who gives into their baser emotions every now and again. I slink up to his side, casually letting my fingers brush over his as we scan the shelf for the book. I can feel his hand lingering longer than it needs to as he clears his throat.

"The A's are probably up here… I got it," he murmurs, reaching up to the top ledge. He pulls down a slim gray book and gives to me.

I sweep my hand over the simple cloth cover. "It's shorter than the others," I comment. The cover's only embellishment is a small, silver imprint of a flickering candle in the center. I open it and see the title and author listing from the call card.

Daniel shrugs. "Should be a pretty quick read, then," he offers with a smile.

I nod, beginning to flip through the pages as I move back to our table. "Yeah…" I sit down in my seat and start reading.

Daniel hovers behind in the stacks, occasionally glancing over to see if I'm still focused. "Anything?" he asks after a while, my head still bowed over the text.

I look up and blink. "I don't know… It's definitely a different format than the others." I nibble my lip in thought, flipping through the pages. "It's sort of a diary…about this girl that the writer calls 'C'…and he's following her like Jane Goodall with the gorillas."

"Like an anthropological study?" I glance at Daniel as he winks. "Big word, I know."

"Yes—just like that." I turn to the middle of the book and read a passage. "*Today, C went through her entire morning routine without interruption…bath, breakfast, dressed in her favorite blue jumper. Her first episode didn't occur until we went to buy groceries at our local shop and she had a very strong reaction to one of the new store clerks… To be honest, I didn't even notice him until C started to laugh brightly at the sight of him and then threw a temper tantrum when I took her away…*" I stare at Daniel. "It sounds like C saw something that the author couldn't."

Daniel narrows his eyes. "You think she's Smudged? That's what would make the most sense…"

I shake my head. "That was my first thought, too…but then I read a little farther." I clear my throat and go back to the page. "*Once C calmed down, I was able to take her to school, where I passed her into the care of Ms. Appleton, one of her favorite teachers. While C was playing, Ms. Appleton showed me some of C's most recent drawings…disturbing images of humanoid figures with dark, gaping empty eyes and huge ram-like horns coming out of their skulls."*

I frown and look back at Daniel. "Demons," he murmurs, sitting on the edge of the table. "She definitely has the Sight."

"But jumpers, temper tantrums…playing and drawing?" I grab the back of my neck. "She sounds young, like a little kid. Have you ever heard of a Demon Smudging a child?" The idea makes my skin crawl.

Daniel draws in a sharp breath. "I mean…*I've* never seen anything like that…but I wouldn't say it's totally out of their wheelhouse."

I mash my knuckles to my mouth as I go back to the book. "The thing is, it sounds like C's really well taken care of…and the author doesn't talk about any sort of inciting incident or C going missing for a period of time. The story begins from her first word, which was 'Papa.'" I rest my chin on my palm. "Whoever this David Adler is, he was up close and personal with her. He…he loves her." I run a hand over the page.

"Like a dad…Papa," Daniel fills in.

I nod. "Maybe. If this thing is even real at all." I sigh and close the book as Daniel stands up. "Although, the description of C's drawings are the most telling thing I've come across all day…" I flip to a chapter and hand it to Daniel. "And it looks like the whole second half of the book details these episodes where C pretty much goes catatonic and starts rambling off nutty stuff…" I point to a line for him.

"*…and light will become dark, and the darkness shall engulf us all; the earth, the Heavens, the borders between good and evil permanently altered…C, age 15,*" Daniel reads, shaking his head. "Man. Sounds sort of familiar."

"Sounds like the prophecy." I stare at him, my lips pressed thin. "Or at least something like it… And it's crazy—but not Pet crazy."

"Right," Daniel grumbles, glancing back up at me. "What do you want to do?"

I exhale and take the book from him. "I feel like we have to talk to this David Adler guy. Maybe he knows something or could give us access to C ourselves." I flip back to the copyright page and wince. "Published in 1987—crap. That doesn't help us. C's gotta be all grown up now." "Hang on." Daniel pulls the book back and goes to the last page. "Ah, here we go, 'About the Author.'" He looks up at me proudly. "'David Adler attended Cambridge University, where he earned his doctorate of medicine and then went on to study the ancient cultures of pre-Columbian Central America'...huh." He points further down the page. "'He now teaches medical anthropology at the University of California, Los Angeles'—awesome!" Daniel grabs my wrist. "UCLA—that's right here. Talk about a lucky break!"

I cross my arms over my chest. "But that was thirty years ago, Daniel. What are the odds he's still teaching—or even alive, for that matter?" He's gotta be pushing at least 70, wherever he is. "Besides, all of the universities are closed for winter break. If he even still works at UCLA, he's not going to be back for another month."

Daniel grins and takes me by the shoulders. "We find a needle in a haystack, and you're rocking a defeatist attitude?! Come on!"

He pulls me close, and I smile. "All right...fine, you eternal optimist. What do you suggest?" I mumble into his shirt.

He steps back. "Let's look him up! I think I saw a phone book down on the front desk. It should have a listing for a David Adler." He pauses and holds up a hand. "*I'll* go check. You seem to have a very profound effect on the bookish types around here." He sniffs, grabbing his jacket. "That Poindexter's head might explode if you ask him to help you out again."

"Can't have that," I tease.

Daniel bites his cheek and tugs his hat on over his ears. "You think you can stay out of trouble while I go look?" he asks. "I probably jinxed us just saying the T word out loud…"

I laugh. "I'm right behind you—just gonna put some of these away and get my stuff. Go ahead. I'll meet you downstairs."

"Okay." Daniel grins and heads toward the stairs, the small gray book in hand. I grab the other books and set them on a shelving cart, giving our table a quick onceover before getting into my own hat and coat. I swing my school bag across my back and leave the quiet third floor behind, not really looking as I catapult down the stairs. I stumble right into a pair of girls with long, dark hair coming through the front doors. I stop dead in my tracks—it's Jodie and her older sister, Francine.

Jodie is surprised too, her eyes widening as she readjusts her backpack over her shoulder. "Christa—uh…hi!" She looks around nervously, tugging at the nice navy blue skirt that I know she usually reserves for church on Sundays. I furrow my brow—she's a little overdressed for the library, but I quickly let it go. Francine looms a few paces behind her, a good five inches or so taller than Jodie and closer to my height. She's got the same blank stare that she gives me whenever I see her.

I shoot them both a tight smile. "Hey, J…Francine." I nod curtly. "Welcome back to the west coast."

"Thanks," Francine replies, her tone nasal. "World's longest flight back from Providence…and the airport was a mob scene. They lost my bag, of course. I think they'll find it by New Year's…but that's the price you pay for a good education." She's not even angry or gloating, just saying stuff and being completely socially inept, like always.

"That's great." I nod, not knowing how else to respond. I turn to Jodie, desperately wanting to make things right, to say I'm sorry for what happened at Science Club the other day. I open my mouth to apologize, but, "What are you doing here?" comes out instead.

Jodie hesitates and shifts back on her heels. "Um…

studying," she answers, shyly pulling her backpack around to her front, her eyes trained on the floor. "And I'm also…meeting some people here…for coffee."

"Oh…that's cool." I nod and keep my voice light, trying not to sound totally rejected that she didn't call to see if *I* wanted to come and work things out over a little caffeine. Of course I know I'm not Jodie's only friend; she's totally allowed to do whatever she wants and go out with whoever she pleases. Just because *I'm* home sulking about what happened doesn't mean she's going to do the same thing—not everyone is a complete masochist. It just would have been nice if she'd thought to drop me a text or something. She must be meeting the other kids from Science Club… or maybe Jenny Rodriguez. They're in Gymnastics together…

Jodie watches my face and bites her lip. "It's not like that, Christa," she mumbles, tucking her hair behind her ears. "It's not anyone from school." I blush—of course she knows what I'm thinking. That's what a decade of friendship gets you. But knowing she's not in the market for a new best friend makes me feel a little better…and a little curious. I start to ask who she *is* meeting, but Francine interrupts. I startle, having forgotten she was here in the first place.

"Have you heard back from any colleges yet, Christa?" she asks, her face resembling that of a constipated duck. "Jodie has applied to at least twenty schools, but no word yet…" I watch Jodie's eyes flash from surprise at seeing me to rage at her Alan Turing-esque sister.

"It's still early," she mutters to Francine. "And everyone's on break. I probably won't know anything until February." She seethes where she stands; I know this is a major source of contention between them.

Francine sighs heavily, still not picking up on Jodie's vibe. "Well, I heard back from Brown in October of my senior year," she states with a shrug. "Early acceptance."

Watching Jodie starting to tear up, I cut in. "No, Francine…I haven't heard from any schools," I say brightly. "Actually, I haven't even applied anywhere yet. I'm still trying to figure out my next step."

Jodie looks at me gratefully as Francine shakes her head. "You should really start making some decisions, Christa, Most schools have their freshman classes set by March." She purses her lips. "It might be too late now as it is."

Jodie rolls her eyes and takes a step towards me. "I wasn't expecting to see you here." She looks at me earnestly. "What *are* you doing here?"

"Uh…" I put my hands in my pockets and scuff my boots on the tile floor.

"Nothing! Just, um…" I quickly recall the fib I told Mary Carmen this morning and make a big show of holding up my book bag. "Studying, too…for school! You know…I wanted to get a good start for the new semester."

Jodie smiles at me weakly. "That's great. I know you'll do great… You've been working so hard…" She stops and grips the straps on her backpack. We stare at each other awkwardly, neither of us knowing what to say.

I take a deep breath and decide to bite the bullet. "Jodie, I really need to talk to you about what happened—"

"Hey! I found him—he's in Cheviot Hills, just off Pico!"

Daniel comes bounding up behind me, excited. He pauses when he sees Jodie standing before me, hastily tucking the book and a small piece of paper into his back jeans pocket. "Jodie—uh…hi!" he recovers, putting on his biggest grin. He turns to focus on Francine. "Who's this? Didn't know you had a twin!"

He laughs nervously as he motions at their differing heights. When I shake my head at him, he shuts up. Jodie just sighs. "Hi, Daniel… This is my older sister, Francine. She's home from Brown."

Francine steps forward and holds out her hand, attempting to look pleasant, but just coming off more like she has bad gas.

"Francine Phan, pre-med, Brown University. How do you do?" She gives Daniel's hand a firm shake, and he smiles wider, if that was even possible.

"Daniel, Christa's friend, and I'm good—thanks for asking!" he answers sincerely. I close my eyes and rub my forehead. They're peas in a pod...and it hurts. Jodie's pained expression mirrors mine, but when she catches my eye, we both smile.

"*Who* did you find?" Jodie asks, looking between the two of us. Daniel chortles and stares at me. I know that if he opens his mouth, he'll start coughing up ash unless he tells her about Adler.

"Just this name I needed for my Wordsworth paper," I lie. "This old English Lord guy from back in the day..."

Jodie's brow crinkles. "In Cheviot Hills?"

I grimace—crap. Why does she have to be such an attentive listener all the time?

"There's a library there—a small, private collection." I glance back at Daniel, who is working really hard not to say anything. I sigh and put on a big fake grin, selling it to the cheap seats. "Very private, and he has a bunch of first editions, rare stuff..." Jodie arches a brow, and I take a breath. "You know, anything to get a leg up with Sister Margarite. She's got it out for me."

"Right." Jodie nods, looking down at the floor again. I can't tell if she bought it or not. She shrugs and bats her sister's hand. "Well, we should let you go. It sounds like whatever you're working on is important, and I've got to get ready for my meeting..." She sighs and walks past me, Francine on her heels.

I frown at Daniel, who just shakes his head. "JODIE!" I call with a wince before she heads through to the coffee bar.

She turns slowly and looks at me, her eyes sad.

"I need to talk to you." I turn down my volume, aware that the entire first floor can probably hear our conversation. "About the other day—what happened with those..." Demons. "...scouts."

Jodie stops and turns bright red. "Now's not a good time for that," she murmurs, refusing to look at me. I tilt my head, hurt and confused. "Maybe we can talk tomorrow or after Christmas, but I can't..." She shakes her head and shrugs into her backpack.

I grimace and take a step toward her, hearing Daniel exhaling next to me. "I just want to say I'm sorry, that's all...for what I did. You were right...about everything. I *am* jealous of you." Seeing her eyes sadden, I force myself to go on. "Of your life and future...and all the great opportunities coming your way—"

"Christa, stop," she pleads quietly, her eyes darting to the doors behind me, her expression mortified.

I hold my hand up. "No, lemme finish." I take a deep breath. "That's no excuse for what I did. You're my best friend, and I only want the best for you—but you have to believe me when I tell you, those scouts from Stanford—" I hitch my thumb angrily over my shoulder. "Are—"

"Impossibly late! Apologies!" I practically jump out of my skin as a woman's voice trills behind me. Daniel lets out a growl and pivots on the spot, protectively throwing his arm across my front. I gasp as blotches of panicked red make their way across my field of vision, clouding the horns and empty eye sockets. Demons—the same two from Presentation Day, still in their polished black suits and matching smug grins.

I shake my head and quickly get a grip. "What the Hell are you doing here?!" I can't keep the snarl out of my voice. Daniel holds his defensive stance, ready to throw down in front of the library checkout desk.

"Christa!" I hear Jodie cry behind me. I jerk my head around and see her face, wide-eyed and alarmed, Francine looking slightly ruffled next to her. I huff through my nose and turn back to the Demons. The female, Tina, quirks her mouth—she obviously thinks this whole thing is hilarious. Her stupid smile only makes me madder.

I lunge forward, but Daniel is a brick wall in front of me. "Don't, Christa," he whispers over his shoulder. "Look around you."

I clench my jaw and glare out at the bustling first floor, which is suddenly crowded with families and kids. The children's section is steps away, and Story Hour must have just ended.

I glare back at the Demons. "Turn around and leave now," I hiss.

They both blink at me, before Tina throws her head back and snorts, tiny peals of laughter bouncing around the room. "And miss our engagement with Ms. Phan? Of course not!" She smiles, pointing at Jodie. "After all, *she* called *us* and set up this meeting. It would be quite rude to disappear now."

I glance between the two parties, noticing Jodie straighten up as Tina acknowledges her. It sets my teeth on edge.

"Besides," Tina simpers as she saunters over to Daniel, placing a hand on his chest. He doesn't even flinch, just stares down at her coldly. "...I don't see Boy Wonder here going all 3-2-1 Blast Off with so many from the 5 and under set present." She smiles warmly as a young mother murmurs an apology for wielding a baby carriage and toddler around us to get to the checkout station. The little boy holding her hand gives us a happy grin. "That could get *very* messy."

"I will do whatever I have to do to protect her," Daniel breathes, just loud enough for Tina and me to hear.

Tina puckers her lips seductively and arches her neck back like she's about to kiss him. "I bet you would."

"Um, Ms. Pritchert?" Jodie shuffles up behind us, her voice shaky. Tina leans back and smooths her skirt, smiling broadly. "I think there are some open tables right by the coffee bar, if you and Mr. Collins are ready..."Jodie clears her throat and gently pushes between us and Tina. Daniel allows her to move us, but his frame stays coiled and ready.

Tina beams and waves back to Collins, who walks forward. "Wonderful, Ms. Phan! Lead the way..."

Jodie smiles and waves goodbye to Francine, stepping back as the two Demons brush past us. I gasp and grip onto Daniel's arm. "We have to do something!" I rasp, almost hyperventilating from watching Jodie happily chat with Tina as they move farther and farther down the hall.

Daniel shakes his head, exasperated. "There's nothing we can do, Christa! We have to let her go."

I let out a small, wounded noise, stumbling forward. Dad, Mom, Pete...not Jodie. They don't get to take her, too. "No—never!" I yell. "JODIE!" I dash down the hall, Daniel hot on my heels. I grab Jodie's arm and spin her towards me.

All of them look shocked, but Jodie is the worst of all. "Christa—what are you doing?" she squeals, wrenching away from me.

I pant, planting myself between her and the Demons. "I can't let you go with them, Jodie. They're bad, bad people. They'll ruin you—" I watch the Demons smirking at each other as I stumble over my words.

"Christa, that makes no sense!" Jodie snaps, her face furious as her eyes start to well with tears. "I can't believe you're doing this *again*... I thought I was just being paranoid not telling you about this meeting—"

"Is something wrong, Ms. Phan?" Tina Demon croons, checking her watch. "I don't think I need to remind you, but Mr. Collins and I are very busy, and this is cutting into your time. We really want to hear about the next stage of your experiment..."

"Yes, of course," Jodie breathes, giving me one last scathing look before turning back to them. "I'm so sorry—my friend is going through a lot right now, and she hasn't been herself lately. I'm ready now—"

I clench my fists as she starts to usher them back to the coffee cart, unable to stop myself. "THEY'RE DEMONS, JODIE!" I bellow at the top of my lungs. All three of them halt in their tracks, slowly turning back to me, the Demons *not* smiling.

Seemingly acting on instinct, Daniel wraps his arm around my waist. "Okay, we gotta go..." he breathes into my ear.

I wriggle in his grasp, breaking free. "No—we have to tell her. She can't go with them!" I exclaim, spinning wildly to Jodie, her expression a mix of horror and confusion.

She stares at me, her eyes glassy with shock. "Christa…what are you doing?" she finally manages. "Have you gone crazy?"

I rush over to her and grab her hand. "Jodie, please…I know what I'm saying doesn't sound real, but you have to believe me! These *people*," I motion back to the Demons, who are still frozen in place, "are dangerous, like, for real. What you see right now is a mirage—that's not what they really look like. They're not even *alive*…and they want to hurt you. To hurt all of us."

"What?" Jodie looks like she's having a panic attack as she glances between me and the Demons. "They don't want to hurt me—they're here to talk about my acceptance to Stanford. Christa, I'm begging you!" She starts to cry for real and shakes her head at me. "Please go home right now! This whole thing is bad…really bad—"

"I know!" I shout, gripping her hand tighter. "That's why I'm not leaving you here with them!"

"NO!" She tears her hand away and pushes me off. "*You're* the bad one! Or…" She pauses and wipes her damp cheek with the palm of her hand, lowering her voice. "Or something is really wrong with you right now. You're having some sort of breakdown, and I…I don't know what to do!" She looks back at Daniel frantically.

"Come on, Christa, let's go…"

He tries to pull me away, but I fight him. "No! Not without Jodie!"

"Christa!" Jodie sobs, putting her face in her hands. "Stop this! Stop right now—"

"It seems…" Tina Demon moves forward, her face calm, but I know that she's not a fan of this spectacle because she checks to make sure the guy at the coffee cart isn't watching us. We all stop and stare at her. "…it was a mistake for Mr. Collins and I to come here today. Clearly, Ms. Phan, your friend is very disturbed." She waves at me nonchalantly as Jodie sniffles. "And the company one keeps speaks volumes about character and personal responsibility, qualities that Stanford values highly." She shakes her head at Jodie as she adjusts her jacket. "I'm afraid we can no longer consider you for admission, Ms. Phan. Good luck with your research and future endeavors. Collins." She nods at her partner briskly, and they begin to leave.

Tina stops to pat my shoulder on the way. "Bold move, Catalyst," she whispers in my ear as they whisk on by. "You fight dirty… I like that."

She gives me a wink, and then they're down the hall, leaving Daniel and I staring dumbly after them and watching them walk out through the front doors. I glance back at the checkout desk. If anyone heard my little outburst, no one seems to be upset about it now, the regular quiet bustle between the librarians and patrons resuming.

I look at Daniel and exhale. "Do you think they're gone for good?"

He gives me a short nod. "I think so. They shouldn't contact her again, at any rate…"

We both turn and stare at Jodie, who is still standing by the coffee cart. She's not crying anymore, just staring at the floor, her eyes glazed over. I sigh and step towards her. "Jodie—I'm so sorry. I promise I'll explain everything—"

She silences me with her hand, her gaze turning cold and withdrawn. "Stay…stay away from me, Christa," she murmurs, her voice low.

I startle as I take in her face, which has an expression that I've never seen from her before—a mix of anger, sadness and… fear. Oh my God—she's afraid of me. I cringe back, Alden's voice ringing in my ear, explaining why we don't tell the mortals about us… It's as much to keep us safe as them. At worst, it throws off the Balance, causing chaos and destruction on an apocalyptic scale…and at best, we end up coming off as *completely insane*. She thinks I'm crazy.

"Jodie—" I breathe, but she shakes her head and darts past me, slinging her backpack over her shoulder.

"I mean it. Don't come near me!" she calls. She says nothing to Daniel as she rushes past him and up the stairs to the second floor—to find Francine, I'm guessing.

I hold my breath for a second before letting it go with a whoosh, finding Daniel with my hands. "I can't do this," I whimper, staring at the blue on my knuckles. "Any of it. I can't—"

"She's alive, Christa," he whispers next to me. "And they won't come back for her. You saved her." He nods. "You *are* doing this…with me here to help you." He grasps my hand. I quickly brush a tear off my face and look up at him, seeing how he glows bright gold against the library walls.

I'm not crazy. He's here, I'm here. And we can't go backwards, only forwards: the one true non-negotiable in the Universe.

"Cheviot Hills?" I reply shakily.

He frowns. "Yes. Are you sure you're ready? We can go another day…"

I shake my head and take a deep breath. "No. We do it today. Let's get out of here."

*

The houses in Cheviot Hills are decked to the nines, twinkling Christmas lights and inflatable Santas guiding the way to a quaint brick house at the end of the street. Daniel checks the address on the little scrap of paper from the library and nods.

"This is it." He waves to the neat green shutters framing the windows. "Professor David Adler's house."

I draw in a sharp breath and take in the place. It looks well-maintained: it's void of holiday decor, but the grass is mowed and the landscaping is trimmed and unassuming. There's a light on behind a shade in the front window. I glance at Daniel. "Do you think he's home?" I mumble, clutching the little gray book to my chest.

Daniel shrugs. "Only one way to find out..."

He takes my hand and gently pulls me up the walk. We step onto the stoop, Daniel giving the doorbell a ring. I grip his fingers. "What if this is a mistake?" I rasp, suddenly terrified of whoever is on the other side of that door. "What if he's actually a Demon, or something else altogether—"

Daniel spins towards me, but before he has a chance to respond, the door squeaks open, bathing us in yellow light. A well-built man stands in the doorframe, the only signs of his true age the wrinkles on his face and the gray in his hair. He stares at us, all of our eyes adjusting to the changing brightness.

"Uh...hi." I break the silence as I hold tight to Daniel. "Are you...David Adler?"

"Yes," the man clips as he continues to look us over, his eyes wide.

I nod and clear my throat. "Okay." I exhale and motion with the book. "I'm Christa Nichols, and this is my friend, Daniel—"

"I know who you are," David Adler interrupts, his tone hushed. "Please, come inside."

CHAPTER 14
NEW YORK CITY—
FEBRUARY, 1976

"HOLY CRAP, CAN you two keep it down?" Denise stumbles into the kitchen, barely wearing a red lace nightie, her hair sticking up in every direction. "It's Saturday morning! No one should be allowed to speak above a whisper before noon."

Jillian glares at her from the sink, slamming a hot frying pan into the water. Steam clouds up over the faucet. "It's 10:30, Denise! Not exactly dawn, for crying out loud!" She clenches her jaw and looks back at where I'm sitting at the table. I let out a heavy sigh and cross my arms.

"I'm just sayin'…maybe you guys should spend a little more time fucking and a little less fighting. It's not healthy," Denise mumbles blearily, yawning in the doorway.

I watch Jillian's whole body tense under her beige day dress, and I push away from my coffee and the blue floral tablecloth to stand up. "It's fine—I was just leaving." I grab my tux jacket from the chair.

Jillian stares at me with desperate eyes. "You don't have to be in 'til lunch." She looks frantically at the stove clock. "We still have time… We need to talk about this—"

"I don't see the point," I grumble, eying Denise warily. She takes the hint and stomps off back to her bedroom with a huff. "We keep going round in circles on the same issue."

"Because you won't budge at all!" Jillian cries, angrily wiping her wet hands on a dish towel. I groan and look away.

"*One* class, Alden! You could do one at a time—and look!" She rushes over to the mail pile and pulls the City College spring course catalog from the top. "They have night and weekend classes for business…management, finance…all the stuff you've been talking about!" She walks over to me and pushes the booklet toward my face.

I wince and turn away. "I told you, now is not the time!" I shout, instantly regretting raising my voice at her.

Jillian frowns and crosses her arms. I take a breath. "Nights and weekends don't help me because that's when I work," I try to explain for the fifteenth time. "And now they've got me on lunch three days a week… There is no way I can fit a class in, let alone the time to study for said class or meet with other students, the professor…" I shake my head at her. "I know you know all this, Jillian—"

"So cut back!" she yells, flailing her hands. "Tell them you can't work as much—or if you feel like you can't do that, I could talk to Muriel, and *she* could talk to Francois for you—"

"Don't!" I reply darkly.

Jillian pulls back and holds her breath. "This is your future, Alden! It's important—"

"So is making money!" I moan, tearing at my hair. "How do you think we pay for dinner and the movies and going out?"

"You know I don't care about any of those things!" Jillian snaps, her fair skin turning blotchy, a tell-tale sign that she is not backing off anytime soon. "And don't you talk to me like I don't understand how money and the world works—I'm not one of Daniel's airhead one-night stands—"

"I didn't say you were!" I shout, glaring at her disbelievingly.

"And I would rather we stayed in every night with just a bus pass and a stack of library books between us, if it means you could do something that really mattered!"

"The restaurant *does* matter!"

She jumps as I slam my fist down on the counter. I close my eyes, little pops of red flashing in my peripheral vision. I take a slow breath, trying to get my temper under control.

"They count on me there, Jillian," I murmur after a moment. "Francois, Chef...the whole crew. They give me more hours because I'm doing a good job—better than anyone else in front of house. I'm head waiter now, Jillian. That means I work directly under Francois. I know that may not seem like much to you...but there is potential there!"

"I know that," she grits. "And I was so happy for you when you got promoted...but I don't think it should be at the expense of your dreams. It's not worth that."

"It's not just my dreams anymore, Jillian!" My voice cracks as we bridge onto a subject that I don't want to talk about when we're both so furious. Jillian goes still and stares at me.

I exhale. "I want to build a life for us..." I mutter. "Get married, get a house, kids...the whole thing." I scratch my head. "And I want it all with you. But none of that comes for free. Working at Monique's is changing that. I've been able to save so much..."

I watch her as she crosses her arms and leans against the stove. "Alden..." she whispers. "I hear you, I do." She sighs and looks at me. "And I'm...I'm so moved...by what you just said..." She takes a shaky breath. "But I couldn't even begin to consider any of that—"

Heat courses over my collar. "Why?" I blurt. "Because I'm not as smart as you?"

She tuts and shakes her head as I lean against the wall.

"Because I don't go to college?" I wave the catalog callously before tossing it back on the table.

"Alden—no! That's not what I'm saying at all..."

"That's why you're pushing so hard for those courses, right?" I whisper, putting my hands in my pockets. "So I'm finally good enough for you?"

"Stop it! No!" Jillian cries. "You're putting words in my mouth. It's because I'm 18, and you're just 20. We're way too young to be thinking about stuff like that—"

"It's not so young where I come from." I shrug, staring at her coldly. "Guy gets a job, gets a house, gets married. Not so complicated."

Jillian puts her face in her hands. "I feel like...like you're pressuring me." Her shoulders hunch up and down, and I feel like a bastard.

"Jillian..."

I start to take a step forward, but her head pops back up, her eyes watery. "I know I've been hounding you to go back to school, but it has nothing to do with you not being good enough or smart enough for me," she spits. "I think there is more for you beyond Chez Monique, and you're too bullheaded to see it right now. Fine." She holds up her hands. "But what I am not okay with is feeling like you're putting me in a very pretty gilded cage with this whole marriage thing. My mother got married when she was 18, had me when she was 19, and has been a housewife ever since; that's not who *I* am." She points to her chest.

"I know that," I whisper.

Jillian tucks her hair behind her ears. "Maybe I want a chance to figure out who I am before I settle down...give us both a chance to make something of ourselves." She watches me cautiously. "I mean, you and I should know better than anyone what a commitment everything you're talking about is—with marriage and kids..."

"Wha-what are you saying?" I stammer, trying to process. "Do you…do you not want to be with me anymore?"

Jillian's mouth falls open. "No, Alden! Of course I want to be with you! I'm just not ready for…"

"Ready for forever. Sure, I get it." I glower. "Girl like you, with all the opportunity in the world, could have any boy she wants… Why would you want to call it with a poor sod like me?"

Jillian clutches her stomach. "Alden, don't say that! I love you! Please—"

"I know. Just not as much as I love you." I shake my head sadly. "Some fairytale." I turn and walk toward the door.

"That's not true… Alden—wait!" She's crying in earnest now as she follows me through the living room. "Don't go!"

I can feel tears stinging my own eyes as I reach the front. "I gotta go—can't miss my shift."

I turn and see her face crumple in on itself as I shut the door behind me.

*

"There you are—I was wondering when you'd turn up!" Muriel smiles from behind the bar.

I shake my head and walk briskly to the host station. "Yeah, I took the long way today. Had to clear my head."

Muriel nods as I pick up Francois's reading glasses to look over the reservation book. "Here's the deposit for last night," she murmurs, handing me the dark blue bank bag. "Pretty good turn out for a February Friday. The early warmup is working in our favor." She watches me as I tuck it into my jacket.

"Fine. I'll run it over between services," I reply curtly, running my pointer finger down the list for this evening. Full house between 7 and 10—we'll be busy.

"Dr. Prescott and his new wife will be joining us tonight." I point, recognizing the familiar last name. "I'm sure they will be feeling very celebratory, as they have just returned from their honeymoon. We need to have plenty of Dom on hand." I take off Francois's glasses and toss them back on the podium, rubbing the bridge of my nose. "The former Mrs. Dr. Prescott will also be dining around 8; let's make sure we seat them on opposite sides of the room to avoid anything...unpleasant."

"Of course," Muriel answers, frowning. "Are you all right? You don't seem like yourself today."

I give her a tight smile. "I'm fine, just feeling a little rushed. Who do we have on the docket right now?" I sigh and face the almost empty dining room.

Muriel arches a brow and points to the one occupant sitting in the far corner. "Just your regular lunchtime date. Shouldn't give you too much trouble." She pats my shoulder and walks back to the bar, presenting me with a silver tray and an already filled brandy snifter.

I nod and look over at Mr. Callaghan, who is dressed in another impeccable suit and lost in daydreams out his usual window. "Very well... We still have the veal from last night?" I ask, positioning the tray evenly across my right palm. Muriel nods. "Good. Twenty bucks says that's what he'll go with."

"I know better than to gamble with you," she giggles, turning back to the sink to wash her hands. "Save your tricks for the new American boys coming back to work tonight." She puts on her goofiest bucktooth grin and twitters her head. "'Mr. Alden, what's the difference between a béchamel and a bouillabaisse? They look so similar'...or, um... 'Gosh, Mr. Alden—she said she was allergic to fish, but I accidentally mixed up the order and gave her the prawns—do those count?'" She bites her nail dramatically. "You'll make a killing!"

I scoff; it's impossible not to laugh at Muriel's phony American accent. I clear my throat before I give it a try myself. "'Why are there so many forks, Mr. Alden? Can't they just use the same one for everything?'" I twang. Muriel laughs, and I'm grateful for the distraction. "Please tell me I wasn't that bad when I first started."

"You were a very fast learner!" She gives me a wink.

I shake my head, gliding over to Mr. Callaghan. He looks up and smiles as I set his drink in front of him. "Am I that predictable?" he chuckles, pointing to the glass of clear amber liquid. "Got my stuff ready before I even walk through the door?"

"Good taste is never predictable, sir," I croon diplomatically. "Simply a way of life."

Mr. Callaghan chortles. "Very good, Mr. Murphy, very good." He smiles at me, menu in hand. "Well, to continue that trend, I think you already know I'll go with the veal."

The corner of my mouth twitches as I take his menu. "Of course, sir. A wise choice."

I turn to leave, but he reaches out and stops me. "If you don't mind, Murphy, there was something else I wanted to get your opinion on, if you've got a minute." He glances around the empty dining room.

I pause, staring at him curiously. "Yes, of course, sir. All the time you like."

He nods and pulls a small flat box from his breast pocket, deep violet in color. He sets it on the table and pulls off the lid, revealing a brightly colored piece of silk fabric.

"This was delivered by personal courier this morning." He holds up the material for me to see: it's a light pink, with what looks like some sort of Asian-influenced pattern. Mr. Callaghan watches me as I study it. "It's a pocket square." He motions to his own suit, where a similar bit of colored cloth is perched, matching the red in his tie. "Surely an outdated accessory, but I find that, despite its antiquity, it still has a purpose."

I nod at the pink kerchief. "It's lovely, sir…a nice addition to your collection."

"Yes." Callaghan's lip tightens as he rests it back in the box and straightens it in front of him. "Tonight, I am dining with the man who sent this to me," he adds after a minute. "I anticipate his expectation is that I'll be wearing it when I meet him."

"Oh, that sounds nice," I raise my eyebrows pleasantly, folding my hands in front of me. "Have you been friends long?"

"Yes," he rasps, staring at the pocket square. "We have known each other a very long time. But he is no friend of mine." He blinks and looks over at me as I feel my stomach drop a few floors.

"Sir...I don't think I understand—"

"What I am curious about, Mr. Murphy is...do you consider it to be a show of weakness to display this gift? If I wear this tonight," he waves at the pink pocket square, "am I kowtowing to this...acquaintance... of mine, my hands out in supplication?" He looks down the bridge of his nose, his expression thoughtful. "Or is it actually a sign of power? That I'm confident enough to accept the customs of this man's table...to know that, even though I am not on my own turf and I wear the color of my enemy, I am still my own man?" He stares at me. "What do you think, Mr. Murphy?"

I take a deep breath, my mind racing. This was not your usual 'soup of the day' kind of query. "Well..." I speak slowly, giving my brain a chance to catch up. "I think the pocket square is simply a means to an end."

Callaghan appears to be listening intently, so I continue. "It gets you through the front door. Show up without it tonight, and your, um, *acquaintance*," I use his word, "may not even see you." Or worse. I clear my throat. "But if you *do* wear it, it's a statement saying you're open to negotiation, and whether that's true or not, you make your opponent think it is. Wear the pocket square. It's just a gesture, so who cares?" I shrug. "Sometimes we need to lose the small battles in order to win the war."

Callaghan breaks into a huge grin. "Sun Tzu, Mr. Murphy! Very good." He taps the side of his nose. "You're more well-read than I had realized."

I blush. *The Art of War* happened to be one of the two books making up the ship's very small onboard library, along with a highly sought-after and worn-out copy of *Lust Prowl*. I had read the former at least ten times. I stand up a little straighter and look at Callaghan, who's still smiling at me. Good. Let him think I'm smarter than I really am; someone has to.

"I believe Sun Tzu also said, 'Appear weak when you are strong, and strong when you are weak,'" Callaghan continues

I nod, back in the moment. "Exactly. He will become over-confident and let his guard down, which will ultimately lead to his defeat. And you will continue to be your own man until you choose not to be. It's what you're carrying behind the pocket square that really counts."

He chuckles. "Figuratively *and* literally." He nods as he places the box back in his jacket. "Thank you, Murphy. Very interest-ing perspective."

I take a step back and bow my head. "Of course, sir. I am at your service." Holy Christ…I hope this isn't the last time I see this man alive.

"That *is* the reason I keep coming here—the best service in town!" Mr. Callaghan takes a sip of his brandy as he squints up at me. "You look tired, kid, like you got the weight of the world on your shoulders."

I shake my head, really not wanting to get into all of it here. "My apologies, sir. I assure you, I'm quite all right…"

"Only one thing can make a man look like that," he inter-rupts, smiling wryly over his glass. "What's her name?"

I sigh. "Jillian, sir."

"Mmm…beautiful name." He nods, setting his brandy down. "She must be pretty."

"She is…and you've seen her," I reply glumly.

Mr. Callaghan's eyes brighten. "The redhead from your first night? Get outta here!" He laughs, smoothing his napkin in his lap. "Ah, that's wonderful, Mr. Murphy—good for you." He watches me as I shift uncomfortably. "But something's up. You wear your heart on your sleeve…"

"We had a row just before I came here." I shake my head. "It doesn't matter, sir. Let me get that veal in for you—"

"Whatever happened, she's probably right." He chuckles, pointing to the tarnished gold band on his left ring finger. "Take it from me: I was happily married for 42 years. They're *always* right." He quirks his eyebrows. "She knows you're not really English?"

I feel my face redden as I tuck his menu under my arm. Seeing that, Mr. Callaghan laughs. "I can hear it in your Rs, try as you might to cover it up." His eyes crinkle. "Both my parents came over from Dublin, and it's a hard sound to forget." He shrugs. "You are your own man until you choose not to be, Mr. Murphy. Wise words."

"Yes, sir." I nod quietly. "Lunch should be out soon."

"Thank you." He smiles, going back to his window.

I exhale and walk back to the kitchen. "I'm gonna need an order of the veal with the asparagus and crab!" I call over the loud radio to Daniel.

He steps away from his dinner prep and turns down the music. "What?" he yells, holding a hand up to his ear.

I roll my eyes. "Veal! I need a plate—I've only got one guy in the dining room, so let's be quick about it!" I exclaim, straightening a stack of cups and saucers on one of the storage racks.

Daniel nods and reties his do-rag. "Oh, sure, sure..." He goes over to the walk-in and re-emerges a second later with a tray of cutlets, tossing one onto the counter. "Slow as molasses today... I gotta do potatoes for tonight and then I'm done. Maybe we could all cut out early and go catch a flick or something before service?" He arches a brow at me while he seasons the meat. "Muriel was talking about that new one with Jack Nicholson—"

"This isn't last-period gymnasium, Daniel—it's work!" I answer, my tone harsher than I intended. I close my eyes and try again. "You can't shove off whenever you feel like it."

"Hey, cool your jets—I get that!" he shouts from the grill. "And for the record, I think Sous Chef outranks Head Waiter..."

so if anyone should be barking out orders…" He exhales and shakes his head. "It just seems nuts to keep the whole place open for one person. And it's a melting, soppy mess outside—no one else is coming in 'til tonight. I thought we could go blow off some steam, you know? Not a big deal." He peeks over at me while he pulls Callaghan's lunch together.

I sigh. "Francois wouldn't like it. We're scheduled for a double, we work the double." I cross my arms and lean against the wall.

Daniel shrugs. "Fine—you're the boss." He lays a few sprigs of asparagus gently across the plate. "What's the matter with you, anyway? You look like someone just shot your dog."

I glower and turn away, absently rubbing Jillian's cross that I now always wear around my neck. "Nothing. I'm fine."

"Sure, okay…" Daniel smirks over the plate and glances up at me. "How was Jillian's this morning? She feed you?"

My jaw tenses. "Yeah. We had breakfast. Ham and eggs." He's not getting any more out of me than that.

He stares at me, a goofy grin stretched across his stupid face. "Uh-oh, trouble in paradise!" he crows, transferring the veal off the heat. "What happened, Irish? Couldn't agree on a china pattern?"

"Oh, shut up, Daniel!" I snap. "Don't stick your nose where it doesn't belong, all right?"

He startles at my outburst and almost drops his frying pan. "You're surly as shit today! What's gotten into you, huh?!" He steadies his hand again as he spoons a final bit of sauce onto the dish and leers at me. "Or maybe this is because you haven't gotten into something else…" He grimaces. "This is what happens when people try to bottle up and ignore their natural impulses."

My blood boils. "Are you looking for a couple of cracked teeth?!" I bark. "Seriously, Daniel—keep going and I'll gladly help you with that!"

He holds up his hands placatingly. "Relax, Irish! I'm just jerking your chain—Jesus!" He shakes his head.

I exhale and place my hands on my hips, pacing in front of the dining room door. "Sorry. I know I'm on edge... I've got a lot on my mind."

Daniel lets out a snort. "I can see that!" He stops working and rests his hands on the counter, staring at me. "Listen, I was just messing with you a second ago. You know I don't mean anything by it."

I wave at him. "I know, I know. It's okay." I sigh and lean back against the wall. "Jillian and I had a fight this morning...our first *real* fight." I bite the inside of my cheek. "Maybe our last... I dunno."

Daniel gives me a sympathetic look. "Aww...I'm sure that whatever it is, you two will get over it and be back to swooning all over each other in no time. It's destiny, right? Can't fight that..."

I shake my head as he goes back to Callaghan's plate. "No...I'm not so sure," I mumble, glaring at the floor. "She doesn't love me, Daniel."

He stops again and stares. "Did she *actually* say that to you? Really?"

I huff. "Maybe not in those words—but yeah. She keeps pushing me to cut back on my hours here and take these college courses...like I'm not good enough for her or something. And any time I bring up us getting married..." I pause and shake my head sadly. "She has a million different reasons why we shouldn't. I think I'm losing her."

"That's a drag." Daniel nods. "But did she specifically say 'I don't love you anymore, we're through'?"

I cringe and look away. "I don't want to talk about this anymore."

Daniel nods again and moves over to the fridge, coming back with a bowl of chilled crab meat. "I get it, Irish. And I get that you're bummed…" He gently spoons some of the crab onto the plate. "But I think we should see this moment as an opportunity."

I look at him and, despite my mood, still feel awed at seeing him handle food as delicately as he would cradle a newborn baby. When his words register, though, I furrow my brow. "Opportunity? An opportunity for what?"

He grins. "An opportunity for you to get out and meet some new people—have some new experiences!"

I stare at him suspiciously. "What kind of new people? Like Ramos?"

Daniel bristles at the drug dealer's name, but quickly rebounds. "No—like girls! Hot girls!" He tosses his spoon back into the bowl.

I grunt and cross my arms. "No. That's out of the question."

"Oh, come on!" he exclaims. "Live a little! Seriously, I hate seeing you like this." I roll my eyes sullenly as he leans forward over the counter. "You're the real deal, Irish—I mean it. You're smart, you're a nice guy…" He arches an eyebrow and jerks his chin at me. "And not like *I'm* noticing, but you've got a look they'd go nuts for, you dig? Full package!"

I wince and shrink back against the wall. "I don't care about any of that, Daniel. I can't see myself goin' round with anyone but Jillian."

He lets out an exasperated growl. "You yourself just said you think it's over! No, that's the heartsickness talking." He waves his index finger knowingly. "Best way to get over that is to get back out there. Ride the snake!" He gyrates crudely to make his point.

I scowl. "Don't you mean 'ride the horse'? Back in the saddle, or whatever?"

"No—it's snake! Jim Morrison!" He looks at me like I've got two heads. "But it doesn't matter… I'm just sayin' it would be a total waste if you sit around cryin' at home waiting for Jillian to come to her senses. We know you've got what it takes to get the 'right' girl." I frown as he continues. "But tonight, how about we

don't worry about finding the right girl, but instead go for some…
'right now' girls?" He grins at his own cliché.

I straighten up and scratch the back of my head. "I dunno,
Daniel. I don't think I'm up for that."

"You have no idea what you're up for, since you've never
tried!"

I glower; if this keeps going, my lip's gonna get stuck in a
permanent sneer. "Lemme see your hand!" he orders when I
don't reply.

I look at him quizzically and hold up my right hand. Daniel
shakes his head, still laughing. "No, no—the other one." I sigh
and hold up my left hand.

He points at my ring finger. "Yep, just as I thought: unat-
tached." I seethe and put my hands behind my back.

"Listen, I've got Chef's car tonight for the market tomorrow morning." He arches a brow mischievously. "I'm meeting
those girls I told you about a while ago—Janice and Vanessa." He
shoots me a look. "Don't do that with your face! These girls are
smokin'—Janice is a tall blonde with legs for days and Vanessa has
dark hair like you and a body like Venus…" He shrugs and smiles.
"We've all partied together before, so you can take first pick. I'm
cool either way."

"Picking over your scraps, a dream come true," I mutter.

"Your attitude is terrible, and that was incredibly crass…com-
ing out of your mouth." He holds up his hand. "But I know you're
hurting, so I'm gonna let it go." He stares at me sternly. "I'm not
asking anymore, Irish. This is a direct order: you're coming out
with us tonight, and you're gonna have fun."

I snort. "Or what? You'll beat me with cold asparagus?" I
motion to the plate.

He raises his eyebrows threateningly. "Or I'm gonna blast
Sabbath every night at bedtime for the next month. Come on,
Irish! Don't make me be an asshole!" He shakes his head.

'All right, fine!" I yell, throwing my hands up in the air.

Finally triumphant, Daniel grins and does a little jig. "You won't be disappointed." He rubs his hands together excitedly. "This is gonna be the best night of your life!"

"I seriously doubt that, but I appreciate the sentiment," I sigh, resigned to my fate. I jerk my chin over at Callaghan's lunch. "How we doing there?"

Daniel pulls a dishrag from his pocket and wipes extra sauce away from the edge of the plate. "Ready. Man, this day can't go fast enough now!" He lets out a war whoop as he goes back to his prep work.

I grimace and pick up the plate, heading back out to the dining room. I wish I felt the same enthusiasm; instead, it's like someone just started my own personal doomsday clock, ticking its way toward complete annihilation.

*

Once the final dish has been cleared and the last tab closed, I make my way around to the back alley. I changed into an extra set of clothes that I keep in the office for emergencies, so I'm now dressed in brown slacks and a navy blue pullover. Daniel hadn't given me any hints as to what we were going to be doing tonight, but the tux, at any rate, would have been over the top.

I glance down the dark alley, trying to keep my loafers out of the slush. At least the weather isn't half bad; I've been told by almost everybody that this sort of early spring is unheard of around here. Jillian is excited about seeing the tulips coming up in Central Park, already making plans for a drawing session...

Dammit. Talk about a fast way to sink an evening. I take a breath and try to clear my head of any visages of Jillian smiling in front of a brightly colored field of flowers. I have to get in the game, since the deck is already stacked well against my favor.

"Hey!" I hear Daniel shout from the road, followed by a demonstrative horn honk. I crinkle my forehead and move out of the way as he slowly steers a baby blue Thunderbird down the alley, craning his neck out the driver's side window so as not to sideswipe the large vehicle's mirrors and vintage tailfins against the alley walls. He comes to a stop and grins roguishly.

"Hey good lookin'," he teases, arching a brow. "Need a lift?"

"Jesus, Daniel!" I laugh, gaping at the car. "Chef seriously let you borrow this thing?" I hesitantly smooth my hand over the pristine white leather upholstery on the other side of the window frame.

Daniel shrugs, checking the sleeve of his brown leather jacket. "Yeah… Can't exactly lug around artisanal cheeses and sugar snap peas for a hundred on an Enfield… Poor Wendy doesn't have the trunk space for it." He peeks over his shoulder. "You should see the size of this backseat. Come on, get in."

"And he's okay with us taking it out tonight?" I walk around to the other side of the car and hop inside. "Beyond official restaurant business?"

Daniel hems and haws as he shifts into second, turning out of the alley. "We…have an understanding."

I frown. "He doesn't know. Stop! This is a bad idea—"

"Hey, relax!" Daniel shouts, glancing over at me. "No, I didn't tell him. But what am I supposed to say, huh? 'Hey Chef—cool if we use your ride tonight to go snag some hot T&A? Promise we won't mess up the interior…'? Come on, Irish!" He shakes his head. "He doesn't *wanna* know that kind of stuff—better left in the dark. I'll get her back safe and sound in the morning, filled with groceries…so no harm, no foul. Besides, we're already going, no escaping now." He gasps dramatically as he shifts into third, picking up speed as we head uptown.

"I'm being held hostage by a blond, blue-jeaned rock 'n' roller." I glower as I sink down into my seat. "Put the cat out and call my mother; I don't know if I'll make it back alive after all the sex, drugs, and chaos he'll force upon me."

Daniel grins, turning a corner. "There are worse ways to go…"

I furrow my brow curiously. "Where *are* we going anyway?"

I ask, taking in the well-manicured brownstones out my window. "This is a little high end…even for the Prince of Myrtle Avenue, don't you think?"

He rolls his eyes at me before parking in front of a large, three-story, gray brick house. "It's Janice's place—well, her parents', anyway. Check it out." I follow his gaze as he points up at the roof.

"Gargoyles," I murmur, recognizing the hunched stone figures from the churches back home. "Huh." I shrug and sit back.

Daniel whacks me on the arm. "They're totally creepy, right?!" he hisses, keeping his voice low. "I always feel like I'm being watched any time I come here…"

"That's because you are an extremely suspicious character." I wave at the sort-of stolen car. "Clearly up to no good."

Daniel snorts. "Whatever. I'm gonna go give Janice the signal…" He gets out of the car and tiptoes like a bad guy from a cartoon up the walk and through the front garden. I see him crouch down and scoop up a handful of pebbles, taking careful aim before popping them up at one of the second story windows. He dashes back over and waves for me to join him on the sidewalk.

"They heard me. Should be down any minute." He grins breathlessly.

I give a reluctant nod and lean next to him against the car door. "You got any…tips, before…?" I tuck my hands under my arms, suddenly feeling incredibly nervous.

Daniel ponders this, running a hand through his hair. "You know, just be cool. Go with the flow." He pauses and then scoffs. "I know that's tough for you…so maybe tonight you just follow my lead, all right? Everyone just wants to have a good time—no need to overthink it." He straightens up and smiles as the front door creaks open.

"Right," I sigh as two laughing girls stumble out of the house, both of them shushing each other as they lock it up. It's easy to tell who's who: Daniel's descriptions were pretty spot on. Janice is the tall blonde wearing a revealing purple silk top, reminding us all that yes, it *is* still February in New York, with a leather fringe skirt that shows off ample leg. Vanessa, her darker, shorter, curvier counterpart, wears a tight kimono print wraparound dress, her large breasts pouring out of the top. Neither of them is as pretty as Jillian.

"They're hot, right?" Daniel whispers in my ear as they giggle their way over to us. "Who do you want?"

"I don't care," I grit out, scratching the back of my neck. I am seriously starting to wonder why the hell I'm here. "You pick."

I see a flicker of what looks like anger flash across Daniel's face, but he smooths it out and replaces it with his best crooked smile. "Hey, ladies!" he calls. "So glad you could join us!"

They both let out a squeal and run the last couple feet over to him, their chunky wedge heels clacking noisily on the pavement. Janice gets to him first and throws her arms around his neck. "Oh my God, Daniel!" she shrieks, throwing her head back before planting a huge, wet kiss on his lips. "It's been like…three months! What the hell?" Janice pulls back and lets Vanessa take a turn.

"I know, I know…I'm sorry! Life's been crazy!" He laughs as Vanessa jerks his chin down to her level and sticks her tongue in his mouth. I look away, trying to decide if the nausea I'm feeling is revulsion or just nerves. "But it I'm here now!" he adds when he's free to breathe again.

"It has been…like, so lame around here without you," Vanessa sighs. I cringe at how shrill her voice is, as if she's been sucking on a helium balloon. "You are officially never allowed to leave again! We're taking you prisoner!" Both she and Janice hook arms with him, and they all bust up laughing.

When they settle down, Daniel nods over at me. "Got a present for you, Vanessa," he croons, flashing his eyebrows. "Irish, this is Vanessa."

I try to muster a smile as the brunette twists her neck around, staring in my direction. "Hello." I give a weak wave. "Nice to meet you."

Vanessa's eyes light up as she bats Daniel's stomach. "Oh my God—he really *is* Irish?!" she bleats.

"Uh-huh." Daniel grins and wraps his arms around Janice's waist, pulling her down on the hood of the car with him.

I try not to grimace as Vanessa steps over to me and puts her hand on my chest. "Oh my God—you're so muscly! Are you like…a total gym rat? This is, like, my all-time hottest fantasy, fucking an Irish guy," she whispers, arching her mouth up to mine.

I instinctually reel back, smelling booze on her breath. She doesn't seem to notice, though, and just presses up closer. "And not just some grease monkey Mick from Boston! You better promise to talk dirty the whole time… Is it true that you guys like it really rough? Oh my God, I'm practically cumming right now…"

"How come she gets the sexy new boy?" I hear Janice pout from the car.

I turn and look over at her and Daniel. "Cuz I missed you, baby," he purrs into her shoulder, shrugging.

Janice yowls and shoves him in the chest. "Bullshit! Make it sound believable!"

He tenderly pushes her hair back and whispers something in her ear. Her whole body instantly relaxes, and her lips part as she starts running her hand over his inner thigh.

Crap—I'm supposed to be following his lead. I clear my throat and look down at where Vanessa is grinding into my side. "So, um…how do you know Daniel?" Perhaps I can sway her away from her obvious amorous intentions with conversation.

Vanessa puckers her lips and runs a finger along my jaw. "He went to school with Janice's cousin in Queens. Both of them were a couple years ahead of us, and we met at a party awhile back. I'd seen him around before…always the hot fucker standing by the record player with a bunch of girls hanging off him, trying to get his attention…" She sniggers. "Good luck if there's a song on that he likes, right?"

I have to agree with her there. "Yeah, right," I laugh. "He gave me a 40-minute diatribe the other day on why the music of Led Zeppelin should be treated like the Mozart of our time."

Vanessa smiles and rolls her eyes. "Oh my God, he's *in love* with Zeppelin! It's not quite as bad as his obsession with the Rolling Stones, but close!"

We both laugh, and she scrunches her nose. I look at her and wrinkle my nose, too—maybe this won't be so bad after all.

"I got something else for you girls," Daniel interjects, grinning and reaching into his pocket to pull out a baby medicine dropper. "Free samples!"

I frown. Scratch that—this is going to be horrible.

"Oohh…yes, please!" Vanessa dances away from me and back to Daniel. He checks the dropper before handing it over to her. Daintily, she sticks it up her nose and takes a quick sniff. She hands it back to him, and he does the same for Janice before taking some himself.

"Mmm, it's tingly," Janice giggles, petting his side.

Vanessa turns back to me. "You wanna bump?" she asks, wiping her nose.

When I shake my head, Daniel shrugs, capping the bottle and putting it back in his pocket. "He's all right… Freakin' powerhouse, doesn't need it." He gives me a wink.

I sigh as Vanessa comes back over and takes my arm. "So, like, are we going dancing or what?" Janice calls over her shoulder to us.

Daniel groans, stretching out his legs. "You really wanna go try to get into a club tonight? It's the weekend—everywhere is gonna be jam-packed with people comin' over from Jersey and Staten Island. And the music is gonna be awful—that's a guarantee…"

"You do this every time!" Janice smacks him on the knee. "You said you would take us to Salvation, and you never did. You said we'd go to Flamingo when it first opened, and you bailed on that one, too..." She glares over at Vanessa. "Come on, Nessa! Back me up on this!"

"I don't care what we do," she murmurs, gazing starry-eyed at me. "Let's go park."

An earthquake of anxiety twists my stomach in knots.

"Seconded!" Daniel jumps off of the car and holds open the backseat for Janice. She stands there, looking really ticked off with her jaw clenched and her arms crossed, but then Daniel laughs and takes her by the hand, gently guiding her into the car—and she's butter again.

"Irish," he calls, tossing me the keys. "You drive."

"Uh...you know I don't have an American license," I mumble. Vanessa is pulling my arm over her shoulders, tucking into me just like Jillian likes to do. Guilt washes over me in heavy, crashing waves.

"You'll figure it out," Daniel huffs, not looking away from Janice. He slams the backseat door behind him, and it's just me and Vanessa standing on the sidewalk.

"Are you, um, gonna open my door?" she giggles, pointing to the passenger side. I pull my arm away awkwardly and let her in, taking my time closing the door and then make my way over to the driver's side. I *did* drive back in Ireland, but everything is backwards here. It's like going through a ruddy looking glass as I sit on the left side of the car and buckle my seatbelt, giving a startled jump as Vanessa leans over and traces her fingers on my knee.

"These are like...Frank Sinatra pants," she snickers, her hand creeping higher up toward my lap. "Like, if you weren't such a stud, you'd totally be an old man...or, like, a time traveler from the '50s..."

"So, where are we going?" I call brightly to the backseat, trying to make it seem casual as I brush her hand off of me. Daniel and Janice are already fully engaged, their hands twisted in each other's blond manes as they snog away. I cough loudly and smack the back of my seat with my hand.

"Oi, Daniel—where to?" I ask, a little rougher this time. Daniel clear his throat and pulls back from Janice, sticking his now lipstick-covered chin up next to my head.

"Yeah, there's a spot just a few blocks from here, by the water," he grunts. "Just go back to 6th and take it all the way down." He chuckles throatily as Janice tugs him away and they get back to it.

I exhale and put the keys in the ignition, reminding myself over and over again to drive on the *right* side of the road, picturing a variety of horrible ways I could get us all killed right now. And if my own error didn't do the job, Chef would certainly finish it if anything happened to his precious Thunderbird. My palms are slick with sweat as I carefully pull away from the curb.

"So, uhhh…" I glance back at Daniel and Janice in the rearview—yeah, they're not going to be making conversation anytime soon. I take a quick peek at Vanessa in the seat next to me and see her watching me hungrily. Her hands are now back in her own lap, slowly hiking her dress up to reveal a set of black garters holding up her stockings. I take a breath and keep my eyes on the road. "What…what do you like to do for fun?"

"You," she replies coyly. I grimace and bite my tongue. A few months ago, I would have been blown away by a girl like Vanessa coming on so strong, even though I wouldn't have known the first way to go about it…but now I'm just left with a bad taste in my mouth.

I try again. "I mean, do you like books…or any movies?" I turn onto 6th and make my way down to the river.

Vanessa shrugs. "I saw *The Devil in Miss Jones* for the first time last week." She laughs.

I smile and look over at her—finally, maybe something we can actually talk about. "Oh? I haven't heard of that one. Was it any good? Where's it playing?"

She cracks up, her laugh high and piercing. "Um…yeah—I guess! It's a fucking porno!" she crows, slapping me on the arm.

I feel my face redden and sink down in my seat. "Right," I mumble. She is not making this easy. I hear Daniel groan from the back and I have to work really hard to not vomit.

I tighten my hands on the wheel as Vanessa sits up and smooths her hair out of her face. "You're kind of uptight," she sighs. It's a statement, not a question, so I just stare out the windshield. "I don't mind," she continues, scooching closer toward me across the seat. "I just think I could help you…I dunno, relax." She walks her fingers up my arm to my neck, drawing little patterns across my jugular.

I cringe, craning away, but not really having any place to go. "I'm fine. Just wanna make sure I get the car parked in one piece."

"It's a really nice car," Vanessa agrees. I take a relieved breath as she moves her hands to caress the leather seats. "Soft."

"Uh…yeah, sure." I squint through the dark and see the river, buoys blinking red out in the water. I point to a couple of empty parking spots right next to the docks. "Is this it?" I ask.

Vanessa shakes her head apathetically. I sigh and turn to the backseat. "Daniel? Is this the sp—"

I blush and spin back around hastily: Janice is perched on top of Daniel, undoing her top. "Yeah, it's great," he calls distractedly. I can hear the smooth sound of him running his hands over her skin. "Just wherever."

"Fine." Grimacing as my voice cracks, I steer the car into one of the spaces. Relieved, I turn off the car and sit back in my seat. One crisis averted. I give Vanessa a weak smile. "Didn't crash!" I huff, only half-joking. "I don't know about you, but I was reciting 'Hail Marys' the whole ride over."

"Oh my God, you are *so* adorable," she purrs, slinking against my shoulder. "No, I was not saying Hail Marys… I was thinking something a little more…devious." She presses her lips to my neck and starts making her way down, tugging at my collar with her teeth.

I close my eyes and wince. "You don't...you don't have to do that," I mutter.

She breathes into my neck, putting her hand on my leg again. "How do you like it, baby?" she whispers, her hand moving faster up my thigh this time. "I'm up for whatever—you just say the word..."

"I—I don't know..." I wet my lips and ram my head back into the seat rest.

The breathing coming from the backseat is hot and ragged. "Do you like my tiny tits?" I hear Janice whisper in a little girl voice.

Daniel moans. "You know I love your tiny tits—lemme see them again..." he rasps.

Jesus. I open my eyes and sit forward. "Okay, I think I'm good." I try to push Vanessa away, but she just takes this as an invitation to lower her face into my lap. She puts her mouth on me through the fly in my pants and tucks her hand between my legs, her fingers creeping around like worms through warm earth. I recoil—this is so far from what I want, it's disgusting.

"Hey—STOP!" I shout, reacting with a swift shove to her side.

Vanessa shoots back in her seat, a look of disbelief on her face. "Oh my God—what's your problem?!" she sneers. "Don't fucking push me!" She leans over her seat and whacks Janice on the back. "Hey—he fuckin' hit me!"

"Wait—what?" Janice spins around, pulling her blouse closed. "Did you fuckin' hit her? What the fuck?!" She turns and smacks Daniel in the chest. "Your friend's a fuckin' lunatic!"

"Whoa, whoa, whoa—everyone just calm down." Daniel rubs his face, his cheeks flushed and ruddy. "All right, somebody tell me what happened..."

"He totally freaked out when I went for his dick!" Vanessa

cries, her hands fluttering up to her face. "I was being really sweet, and then he punches me in the stomach—what the hell?!" She shakes her head at Janice, who looks at me like I'm bloody Chairman Mao.

"You're a goddamn maniac!" she snaps, turning back to Daniel. "How could you be friends with someone like this?!"

"Hey...hold on a second!" Daniel replies, his voice rising. "There are two sides to every story—let him talk!" He nods at me. "You all right, Irish?"

I grind my teeth and stare out the windshield; the only thing I want to do right now is get out of this car. "I'm fine. I didn't mean to hurt her. I'm sorry..." I sigh and face Daniel. "I...I didn't want her touching me...like *that*. I'm just not—not comfortable with all this." I wave around the car.

The girls look at each other quizzically. "Wait...are you...are you a fag?" Vanessa sits forward, her eyes suddenly bright.

"What?" I spin and glare at her.

She breaks into a high-pitched fit of giggles. "Oh my God—you totally are! It's so obvious!" she screeches, tapping Janice on the hand. "With his clothes...and his stuck-up attitude..."

I twist back and tug at my hair. "I'm not...I'm not *gay*!"

This gets them going even harder. "Hey! Shut the hell up! He's not a fuckin' fag!" Daniel shouts defensively. "He's just a virgin!"

Their laughter rocks the Thunderbird. This whole night just skyrocketed into the next stratosphere of mortification...if that was even possible.

"All right—everybody outta the goddamn car!" Daniel shouts, arching his back irritably as he refastens his belt buckle. "I mean it—out!"

The girls gape at him. "What the fuck, Daniel?" Janice huffs as she works the buttons on her blouse and scrambles for the door. "Have you lost it, too?"

"I need a second with my friend—just give us a second!" he yells at her. She shoots him a withering glare as she angrily shoves the door open, Daniel following. Vanessa narrows her eyes at me before joining them out in the parking lot.

"This is so messed up, Daniel!" I hear Janice yell at him, her voice muffled by the car door. "Let's just call it! I wanna go home—"

"Me, too. I've never been treated like this in my whole life!" Vanessa whines. Daniel holds up his hands. "Take a breath, all right? I'm gonna get this sorted out. Just…go for a walk! Cool off…" He shakes his head at the girls and opens the passenger side door, sitting down next to me in a huff.

"Okay…you like girls, right?" he asks hurriedly, watching Janice and Vanessa stalk over to a streetlamp. "It's…it's okay if you don't, just tell me—"

"Yes! Jesus Christ! What kind of question is that?" I hiss.

Daniel turns to me, his eyes wild. "Well then, get your dick up so we can show these girls a good time!" He slaps me on the thigh.

I exhale irritably and throw myself back in my seat.

"What? I don't get it… They're pretty, they're fun, they're up for anything…"

"They're *not* Jillian!" I yell.

He groans and throws his hands up in the air.

"I'm sorry, Daniel! I can't just put my feelings on the back-burner and then go out and pretend like nothing's wrong or that I'm okay doing *that*…this…" I wave at the leather seats. "…with someone I don't even know! I'm not like that."

"But *I* am… Is that what you're saying?" He narrows his eyes.

I sigh. "No…I don't think it's the same at all. I don't think that you can even understand." I look out my window and shake my head. "I love her, Daniel. Jillian." I frown and turn back. "And I can't hide it, or put it away for a night. It's who I am now." I nod resolutely.

"But…you said she doesn't love you," he murmurs. "Why torture yourself?"

I shrug. "Because my pain is the least she deserves. Whether she loves me or not, I am hers." I sigh and open my door.

"Where are you going?" Daniel shakes his head, confused, and fumbles with his door handle.

I watch him fixedly. "Where I belong. Goodnight, Daniel." I toss him back the keys.

The girls come back over, and all three of them stare after me as I walk back toward the city. "What the hell?" I hear Vanessa huff. "I didn't even get to make out with anyone!"

There's a pause, but then Daniel lets out a hearty laugh. "Aww, I bet we can fix that," he snickers. "You girls look too hot to be scowling like that. Come on…" Vanessa squeals as he pulls her to him and starts tickling under her arms. "Yeah, that's it… Don't get pouty, Janice! I know you like to be tickled, too!"

Their boisterous laughter echoes out across the Hudson. I don't look back once.

*

"Well, well, well… Welcome back, Romeo," Denise says with a smirk when she answers the apartment door. "Oh good, you brought flowers… Cover up the smell of your bullshit."

I sigh and drop the hand holding a single pink rose to my side. "Is she here, Denise? I need to see her."

She snorts and leans in the doorframe. "Oh, she's here all right. Didn't leave the house all day—she's been inconsolable!" She motions with her hands, her jaw set. "She really lost it when you didn't show up after work or call… Finally cried herself to sleep about an hour ago."

I cringe down at the floor. "I know, I really screwed up…"

Denise laughs cruelly. "You can say that again! You know, I didn't peg you as an asshole, not like your astronaut best friend." I grimace at the mention of Daniel as she crosses her arms. "But you *do* have a penis, so fool me once, shame on me…or whatever."

"Denise, please." I run my fingers through my hair. "Let me make this right. I need to see Jillian."

She shrugs and moves aside. "Hey, I'm not her keeper. Do what you want." She glares at me. "But if I hear her get upset again, I swear to God I will call the cops so fast and tell them to come collect your sorry Irish ass... My brother works down at the 9th, so you would be in for a world of pain, you dig?" She gives me her best crazy eye. "A *world* of pain."

"Got it." I keep my eyes averted as I move past her back to Jillian's bedroom. The door is closed, and I give a soft knock before opening it.

"Jillian?" I whisper as I step into the dark room. Bright moonlight pours in through the window, illuminating the bed just beneath it.

I see her curled up under her quilt, her head rising off the pillow as I close the door behind me. "Alden?" she calls, her voice small.

I nod and pad over to the bed. "Hi," I breathe, slowly taking a seat next to her. Jillian sits up and gives a light whimper as she throws her arms around my neck. I close my eyes and press my face into her hair, home.

"I didn't know if you were coming back," she says after a minute, pulling back to look at me, her cheeks glistening with fresh tears. "I'm so sorry for what I said this morning. I shouldn't be pushing you to take those classes... You have to do what's best for you. It's not my decision—"

I shush her and take her face in my hands, wiping tears away with my thumbs. "No, *you* don't have to be sorry for anything. I'm the one who needs to apologize." I watch her brow knit as I take a breath. "You were right about everything. I'm going down to City College first thing Monday and signing up for spring quarter." Jillian's eyes widen in surprise as I add, "I want to be the man you deserve—the man I deserve to be." I pause and glance out the window, seeing tiny rivulets of water coursing down the glass from the melting icicles above.

"And I'll back off on all the marriage talk—" She opens her mouth, but I tap her chin to let me finish. "Not because I don't want to marry you—that's *all* I want, Jillian—but it's not fair for me to manipulate you if you need more time. I do believe we'll cross that bridge together at some point, but only when we're *both* ready. I understand that now."

"You have to know how much I love you, Alden," she sniffles.

I smile and kiss her forehead. "And I love you, Jillian. You are…my happiness." I bite my lip, and we stare at each other. "The thought of not being able to see you…to touch you…" I run my hand over her bare arm, grazing over the lace of her white nightgown at her shoulder. "It terrifies me. There would be nothing worse."

"I'm not going anywhere. I'm here… I'm yours," she whispers, taking my hands.

I nod and look down at the quilt. "I know. I know that. Just with everything that happened today…" I sigh and give her a weak smile, Jillian squeezing my hands. "I…I just don't want us to ever be apart again. I hated every minute of it."

"Me, too," she breathes, sitting up so we're now face to face. "Let's never fight again." She kisses me, her lips warm and eager.

I chuckle between kisses. "*That* might be a trifle optimistic, but we can give it a go." I run my arms around her waist and pull her onto my lap, her mouth becoming more urgent. I feel everything go fuzzy as my mind empties itself, and all I can think about is how soft Jillian's skin is and how I yearn to know every part of her. Her body eases into mine, and our kisses deepen.

With a light pant she pulls back, wetting her lips nervously, her eyes searching mine for a moment. She blinks and reaches down to my waist with trembling hands to pull my sweater up over my head and toss it onto the floor, exposing my undershirt.

I shake my head at her. "Jillian…" I breathe, watching her as she does the same with my undershirt, leaving me bare from the waist up.

She stares at me with doe eyes. "I just want to see you," she whispers as she brushes her hands over my arms and shoulders. "All of you."

I watch her chest rising and falling, her breath quickening. I nod and very quietly stand to undo my belt. "All right," I whisper back, letting my pants and shorts drop to the floor. With a swift kick, I'm naked, my palms turned upward as I stare at her.

She exhales and sits forward, the room so quiet I can make out the fog horns blasting out in the harbor so many miles away. Despite my current state, I've never felt more at ease in my whole life.

"You're beautiful," Jillian murmurs after a minute, coming off the bed and standing before me. She gets up on her tiptoes and kisses me, starting at my shoulder and working her way up to my mouth, our lips pressing together like two missing puzzle pieces. I pull her close and let all of me feel the warmth coming off of her through her nightgown, and it quickly becomes apparent that I want more.

I pull my face back and let my fingers flutter against her cheeks. "Can I see you?" I ask, gazing into her green eyes. "Please? If that's okay…"

Jillian takes a shaky breath and steps back. With a nod, she takes the hem of her nightgown and pulls it off, exposing her large, soft breasts. I about fall over, she's so beautiful. She balls up the nightgown and holds it shyly over her stomach, her eyes downcast at the floor.

"I'm sorry—maybe we could just lay down first under the blankets… I'm not…and you're…" She blushes, refusing to look at me.

I gently take her chin in my hands. "Jillian, you are the most…" I shake my head, unable to come up with a word that truly does her justice. "I worship you. Please, let me see all of you, too."

She closes her eyes and drops the nightgown, her hands pressed into a heart around her navel. I sink to my knees and tenderly kiss each of her fingers, feeling them melt away as I find their center, Jillian gasping and running her hand through my hair as I nuzzle her skin. I pause and look up at her, a commoner standing at the foot of a temple.

"Are you sure this is what you want?" I whisper, getting to my feet, wanting nothing more than to keep going. Her cheeks are pink, matching the revealing blush that's blooming all over her chest and body.

"Yes," she exhales, grasping at the back of my neck. "More than anything."

I scoop her up and set her down on the bed, moonlight cascading across us as I lay over her and we move together, entwined and inseparable.

*

"Don't move—I've finally got you right where I want you!" Jillian laughs. I slowly open my eyes to see warm morning sunshine and my stunning girlfriend perched over me, clad in her dark glasses and nothing else, sketchbook and pencil in hand. All of me starts to wake up at the sight of her. With a grunt, I grin and grab her thighs, enjoying the sound of her squeal as I straddle her on top of me.

"Is that what all this was? Just one big coercion to get my picture?" I snicker, propping myself up on my elbows. "If so, I like your style, Ms. O'Connor."

I lean up and give a light nip to the side of her left breast. She playfully shoves me back.

"I was gonna say, I didn't hear many complaints last night!" She pops off and nestles down in the quilts next to me. "Really,

I'm almost done with the initial sketch—I've been up for about an hour now. You sleep like the dead."

I sit up as she goes back to her drawing. "I told you, it's my secret superpower." I lazily scratch at the back of my head. "What time is it, anyway?"

"10:45... We slept in," she replies, not looking up from her sketchpad.

"Crap—I gotta get to Monique's," I groan as I shamble out of bed, the sheets twisting around me like ivy to keep me from leaving. I wish I could oblige.

"I figured. Will, um..." Jillian's cheeks grow rosy under her glasses. "Will you come back tonight?"

I smile and lean over her, kissing the top of her head. "You couldn't keep me away if you tried." I watch her smile coyly as I search around for my clothes. "I know we didn't really talk about it last night..."

"Didn't *do* much talking," she purrs, arching a brow.

I clear my throat, trying to keep the replay at bay for when I don't have to go and give the daily specials speech over and over. Fool's errand.

"What I mean is, was everything...okay?" I look over at her hesitantly and grip my shorts tightly, suddenly feeling self-conscious for the first time all night. "Did it...feel okay? For you?"

Jillian looks up, her lips parted. "It was...perfect. I mean, it hurt a little, at first..." She looks away bashfully and tucks her hair behind her ear. "But I know that's to be expected...and it was, you know, a *good* hurt." She shrugs. "And then the times after that, it was just..." She giggles and bats her forehead with her sketchpad. "Do I really need to describe it for you? I thought I was pretty clear..."

I run my tongue around the inside of my mouth and check the clock. Yeah...there's no way we could do it again before I have to be at work. "Right." I grin like an idiot and shake my head, trying to get ahold of myself. "Is it all right...that we didn't wait?"

I add quietly. When Jillian looks up at me, her face soft, I audit, "I'm...I'm okay with it if you are."

Jillian nods and takes my hand. "I am. I feel like...last night was this thing that's just been building up and building up... pretty much since the first time we saw each other." She sighs heavily. "It had just gotten to this point where it was impossible to *not* move forward. Every time I'm with you, I feel like I'm about to explode..."

I nod. "Me, too. I just want you to know that you're more to me than just..." I motion to the bed, "This. The minute you want it to be official, you just say the word—"

"Ahhh!" she laughs, clasping my hand. "I thought you said no more marriage talk! You trying to make an honest woman of me?"

I shake my head. "No, no...you don't need me to do that. You're the kindest, most virtuous person I know." I hold my hands up to placate her. "I just don't want you to ever feel...wrong... about last night." I stare at her. "Because it was the best night of my life, Jillian, truly. Nothing can ever tarnish that."

Jillian smiles down at her lap, a creeping pink blush giving her away. "So...that means we can do it again?" She bites her lip and hides under the blankets, then pokes a bare leg out the other side, teasing her toe up my hip. I grow all hot again, and I know I'm not getting out of here in one piece. I grab her ankle and give it a tug, a chorus of giggles emitting from under the covers.

"What is it about you that makes me want to go out and break every rule in the book?" I growl happily, flinging the quilt off and jumping on top of her. She gasps as I pin her arms up over her head with one hand while the other works swiftly at her inner thigh.

"I won't tell if you don't," she purrs, her eyes fluttering shut as I find her soft spot with my fingers. I massage her sweetly at first, increasing my firmness in time with her breathing.

"My lips are sealed," I moan into her neck, watching with rapt attention as her eyes grow smoky and her mouth bright red.

When I walk up to the back alley, I see Daniel outside rinsing off a bunch of old milk crates with a garden hose, a cigarette dangling off his lip. He looks up, sees me coming, and switches off the hose before bending down to start going over the crates with a scrub brush.

"Hey." I stop when I get to him and put my hands in my pockets. "I thought you were off cleaning duty now that you're Sous."

Daniel shrugs. "Still do prep and cleaning. Part of the job." He keeps his eyes down as he smashes the bristles roughly into the crates. "Nice of you to show up. Figured you would have been by bright and early to chew me out for last night."

I blink, not having any idea what he's talking about. He shoots me a look, and it all clicks: the girls, Chef's Thunderbird, another random evening of humiliation. I catch myself smiling as I look back at Daniel and see that he's really worked up about it; I love that I could care less.

"Ah." I look down and scuff my shoes against the pavement, trying to look appropriately disgruntled. "You know, yeah... That was rough, Daniel." I clear my throat as he hangs his head. "But I took a walk, wound up back at Jillian's, and I think we can just move past it all." He looks at me disbelievingly, and I give him a short nod. "You can make it up to me by letting me get a drag off that. Jillian doesn't smoke, and I could really use one."

I point to his cigarette, and he quickly hands it to me. "Sure, you got it!" he exclaims as I take a long, satisfying draw, letting the smoke fill my lungs before exhaling out a heavy blue cloud. "So you guys made up?" When I nod, he goes back to his scrubbing. "Good. That makes me feel a little better about everything. You gotta believe me, Irish, I am *really* sorry how things turned out. The more I think about it, those girls were way outta line, freaking out and calling you names... We should have just gone to a stupid disco."

"Don't worry about it." I shrug, handing him back the cigarette. "Water under the bridge. Everything work out okay with Janice and Vanessa?"

"Yeah—I took care of it. Everyone went home happy." He crouches down to get another crate, watching me quizzically as I lean against the wall. "What's with you?" he asks after a minute. "You seem, I dunno...different."

"Hm?" I arch a brow at him, playing it cool. "I don't know what you mean."

He wrinkles his nose and stands up. "Yeah...there is definitely something different about you today!" He narrows his eyes and grabs my chin. "Your shave's the same... Didn't get a haircut." He puckers his lips around the cigarette as he completes his inspection. "Same boring old clothes... I don't get it! What you are hiding, Irish?"

I chuckle. "That's none of your concern." I pop off the wall as Pedro and Juan Julio come out from the kitchen, lighting up their own smokes.

When Pedro calls over to Daniel in Spanish, he holds up his hand impatiently. "*Si, si...un minuto,*" he replies. Pedro shrugs and goes back to chattering with Juan Julio. I start to walk off, but Daniel grabs my shoulder. "Hey!" He spins me around. "Are you...are you getting some?!"

Both Juan Julio and Pedro go silent as I face Daniel. I sigh and cross my arms. "What do you think?" I ask calmly, trying to negate the question.

He stops and scratches his head. "I think I used to know the answer to that yesterday...and now I'm not so sure!"

I roll my eyes as he pulls me back to him. "Come on, Irish! Don't hold out on me..." Daniel leans in to press our heads together. "Was it some rock-'em-sock-'em-headboard-knockin'-damn-I-need-a-cigarette action?!"

He stares at me as I pluck the cigarette back from his mouth. "I told you... She doesn't smoke," I reply, taking a drag.

Daniel does a double take, and Pedro and Juan Julio lean over the railing to listen in. "Holy shit, Irish!" he warbles, chucking the milk crate down the alley. "This is big fuckin' news! How was it? Did you last long? Did she like it? What were her tits like? That girl's got an amazing rack..." When I shoot him a murderous look, he takes a step back. "And a *beautiful* face—I know how you get about that! Seriously, Irish—you gotta give me something!" he cries.

I look up at Pedro and Juan Julio, who are waiting with bated breath. Daniel follows my gaze and waves at them angrily. "Hey, get outta here! *Tengo que hablar con mi hermano!*" he shouts. Pedro sucks his teeth at him, but they both move further down the alley. Daniel looks back at me eagerly. "All right...gimme the skinny!" He bats my arm. "How do you feel?"

That, I *will* answer. "I feel...content," I answer, taking one last puff before stubbing the cigarette out with my shoe. "Like I'm exactly where I am supposed to be, at this given time in the Universe. I have a girl I love, a great job, gonna start thinking about my future... It's...amazing." I shake my head and watch Daniel's face contort. "What? Why are you looking at me like that?"

He gets control of his emotions and shrugs. "Nothing—nothing. I'm...I'm happy for you, Irish. Really." I stare at him as he picks up a new crate and starts going at it. He looks...forlorn.

"Your time will come too, Daniel." I reach down and pat his shoulder. "You'll find her. It just takes time."

"Yeah—don't hold your breath," he huffs as he turns the crate. "Maybe when I'm like fifty, I'll hook up with some young hot number, rock a May/December thing. Whatever." He gives me a weak smile. "True love—that's not something that happens every day. You're lucky."

I feel my throat grow thick. "Well...I *am* Irish!" I joke,

chucking him on the arm. "As your lot likes to point out every chance you get."

"Yeah, right!" he laughs, stacking the crates in a pile. "Maybe some of your good luck will rub off on me—who knows?"

"Nah…you don't need it." I wave him off with a grin. "Besides, luck is fleeting. Who knows, you might not want what I've got in a few months. The tide is always turning."

"That's the truth!" Daniel exclaims. "I mean…while I'll come and eat the cake at *your* wedding, I'm not ready for that long walk off a short pier, you get what I'm saying?"

I roll my eyes and turn to walk over to the service entrance. "But I'll gladly give the best man speech," he calls after me, "since I practically introduced you guys—you know, if the gig's still open."

I turn back and smile. "It might be a while…but yeah, I can't imagine anyone else. It's yours."

Daniel shrugs and quirks his eyebrows, trying to be cool—but I can tell he's pleased. "All right. I guess I'll see you later."

I nod. "Yeah…see ya."

CHAPTER 15
LOS ANGELES—PRESENT DAY

PROFESSOR ADLER'S LIVING room bears a strong resemblance to Mary Carmen's, in that the walls are lined with bookshelves crammed to capacity and the furniture has been transported from a bygone era. It lacks the warmth that permeates Mary Carmen's house, though, feeling more like an abandoned library than a home. Unsurprisingly, based on the lack of lawn decor, there isn't a Christmas tree or any decorations. Adler motions for us to take a seat on the couch next to the one lamp lighting the room as he closes the front door behind us.

"Please, can I get you something to drink?" Adler mutters in a thick Scottish accent. He watches as Daniel and I shift nervously in the foyer. "I don't have much to offer you…"

"We're fine," Daniel answers, staying close to my side. He scans Adler up and down, seeing the same thing I see, which is an unremarkable Human wearing a fraying blue button-up shirt and dress slacks, a set of wire-rim glasses perched on the end of his nose.

Daniel takes a breath and gets right to the point. "You said you know who we are… I would like you to explain that before we go any further."

I straighten up at his directness, very glad he's here with me. Adler reacts, too. "That shouldn't come as much of a surprise," he says. "Anyone with ties to the Divine World knows who the Catalyst and her Guardian are." His light eyes widen, and he holds out a hand as Daniel and I both tense. "Please! You don't need to be alarmed! I am only a scholar—a passive observer in the workings of Gods and the Fates."

He breaks into a tight smile, gesturing to the book grasped to my chest. "I would ask how you found *me*, but I see you've already done some research of your own." He holds out a hand, motioning for the small gray text. I give it to him, and he stares at the cover. "I know it was a lifetime ago, but it feels just like yesterday that she was here and we were at the beginning, trying to solve our great mystery," he whispers as he opens the book. "Like ants trying to roust the Taj Mahal…"

"*She?*" I repeat, taking a step forward as Daniel puts his hand protectively on my arm. "You mean C?"

Adler nods, glancing up at me from the pages. "I'm sure our story must seem like folly to you, in light of where you've been and what is to come." A chuckle escapes his lips as he moves into the living room and settles into an old, straight-backed chair. "But for us, it was chaos every day." He goes quiet and stares at the book in his hands.

I look at Daniel, and he sighs, giving the okay for us to sit. We move slowly over to the brown couch opposite Adler and plop down. I briefly notice that there's a weird stain on the wood floor by the lamp, like someone left an old Halloween pumpkin sitting out for too long and it rotted through. I don't spend too much time on it though, instead turning back to Adler.

"How do you know all this stuff?" I ask. "Are you—was C… Smudged?" I still hate saying the word out loud with strangers.

Adler looks up at me, his eyes sad. He shakes his head. "No. But I would have given anything to have it be that simple." He sighs and sets the book on the coffee table in front of us. "No… my daughter, 'C', as I called her in the book…was the Prophet."

I hear Daniel draw in a sharp breath next to me. My mind starts racing a mile a minute, repeating the words the Agent recited in Porticullis—flanked by those destined for good and evil…carried from the ashes, born again…sacrifice…

I gape at Adler. "What do you mean, C was the Prophet? So she was the one who said—" That I'll be the one to determine the fate of the Universe. I look between him and Daniel, confused.

Adler clears his throat and sits forward. "Well, C was *a* prophet…one in a long line since the beginning of humanity." He pauses and puts his hands on his knees. "Are you sure you wouldn't like something to eat? I will gladly tell you what I know, but it is…involved." He waves at the little book. "*That* was only the tip of the iceberg, as they say."

I look at Daniel who shrugs. I *am* feeling a little hungry, not having eaten anything since breakfast at the house. I nod at the professor. "Sure…I'd take something. Thank you."

"Wonderful. Won't be but a minute." Adler gives us a small smile and gets out of his chair to pace toward the kitchen, his steps deliberate. Once he's out of the room, I spin and face Daniel.

"Okay, what do you think?" I whisper, keeping my voice low.

Daniel stares at the doorway, his gaze intense. I can tell he's thinking. "I'm not sure," he sighs. He puts his arm over my shoulder, his face drawn. "I think this guy has information that's important, but I can't shake the feeling in my gut that's saying we should cut and run…" He nods at the front door.

I bite my lip, considering. "I just think he can help us," I breathe, fidgeting my fingers in my lap. "What if he can fill the gap between what the Agent told us and—" Mandisa's list, Herod's Feast. I don't say that part so as to avoid angering Daniel, but he knows what I'm getting at.

He clenches his jaw and takes his arm away. "Do what you gotta do. Get it out of your system," he mutters, keeping his eyes forward.

I sigh, picking up the book from the table. "I know you don't want to be here," I murmur.

Daniel lets out a laugh. "Yeah—I'd rather be pretty much anywhere else!" he scoffs. "With a few exceptions…"

I nod, staring at my lap. "I know it's not hanging around reading Christmas stories by the fire, but I just want to try to get ahead of all this." I motion with the book. "See if there's any way to rein it all in before the whole world explodes. I know you get that." I sigh. "Thank you for sticking with me. It means…everything." I lace my fingers through his.

Daniel's gaze softens, and he turns to me with a smile. "Where else would I be?"

I smile back and rest my head on his shoulder as he settles into the couch. "Don't worry about anything," he murmurs into my hair. "I'm totally ready if this professor guy suddenly starts molting and he's really some giant raunchy snake monster—I got your back."

I giggle as he nudges my side. "No more late night Mystery Science Theater for you," I tease, mashing my nose into his arm. He starts to laugh too, but stops as Adler comes back into the room, balancing a plate of snacks and a few sodas.

"I found these in the back of the fridge… Hope you're okay with root beer." He sets the cans on the coffee table along with what looks like tea sandwiches.

I nod and hungrily pick one up. "Yes—thank you!" I quirk my head back toward Daniel, giving him a look.

He rolls his eyes and grabs a soda, popping open the tab. "Thanks," he mutters, taking a slurp.

Adler sits back in his chair, watching us dig in. "My wife and I moved here from England in the early 1980s," he begins, leaning in and taking one of the sandwiches for himself. "I had just completed my doctorate and had been offered a very lucrative teaching position here with the UCLA Anthropology department. My wife, Helen, was also an anthropologist. Her focus was on aboriginal Athabaskan cultures of the north, and we spent our summers driving up and down the coast, switching off on who did research and who kept house… It was a lovely time."

I smile, trying to be pleasant. "Sounds nice."

Adler nods and takes a small bite of the bread, pushing it around the inside of his mouth before he speaks again. "Helen became pregnant during our third summer here. We were thrilled." His voice is soft, and we both lean forward to hear him better. "Everything went exactly as it was supposed to: no complications, minimal morning sickness, everyone was excited for us." He motions around the room. "We bought this house and moved in three months before Colette was born…" I feel Daniel give a slight jump next to me as Adler stops and pulls out a faded photo from his pocket.

He hands it over to me. It's a picture of a young girl, maybe six or seven, with light blonde hair and big blue eyes like a Disney princess. After looking at it for a second, I reach to give Daniel a turn, but realize that he and Adler are engaged in some sort of angry staring contest, the hairs on the back of my neck going up as Adler sets his soda down slowly. I clear my throat, getting his attention.

"Colette, C…" I murmur, setting the photo next to the book.

Adler nods. "She was perfect…an easy birth for Helen, as easy as these things can be. A little bundle of pink and smiles." Adler looks at me, leaving the uneaten part of his sandwich on his chair armrest. "We didn't know what we were doing, new parents of course, but we figured it all out…and Colette was so…well, *easy.*" He shakes his head and looks down at his hands. "Sleeping, eating, doing everything that babies do…" He stares up at me, his eyes fiery. "At first."

I furrow my brow and look around the room. There are no baby pictures—no pictures at all, no family heirlooms, no kids' art projects…no evidence that anyone other than a lonely old man lives here. I feel a chill go up my spine and search for Daniel's hand. "What…what happened?" I whisper, surprised at my own hushed tone. I find Daniel's fingers pressed into the couch cushions and squeeze tight.

Adler clears his throat and rests his shin over his knee. "Colette was two when she had her first episode," he says through a clenched jaw. "That was what we called them—'episodes'… even though that makes her sound more fit for an institution than what was really going on." He folds his hands in his lap. "She had been happy and developmentally normal up until that point—could string a few words together like 'hello Mama' or 'want milk,' but then…" He inhales.

"We were getting her ready for bed when she went rigid and fell to the bathroom floor. It was terrifying." He nods at us. "We thought she was having a seizure. I tried to put my finger in her mouth to keep her from biting her tongue, but she wouldn't… she *couldn't* open her lips. Her eyes rolled back in her head, and Helen was screaming…" Adler holds his head at the memory.

Daniel and I stare at him, neither of us moving.

"And then it all stopped." Adler pats his chair arms with a sigh. "Just as quick as it began, Colette got back up and stood in front of us, wrapped in her little duck bathrobe. Helen and I were so relieved, thinking it was over…" He laughs dryly. "Then she opened her mouth."

I hold my breath, waiting. Daniel sits forward. "What happened when she opened her mouth?" he asks.

Adler's lips press thin. "She let out a great belch, like an old man—and I…I remember laughing at the time…thinking it was funny to hear such a huge noise come out of someone so little. But then she started to wretch, like she was going to be sick…" He closes his eyes. "She opened her mouth and out came…" He draws in a sharp breath. "I couldn't really look at it, it was so bright, blinding... Helen fainted, and it fell to the floor, and I knew, deep inside...that I couldn't touch it."

My eyes train down to Adler's hand, and I can see it shaking. He sees me looking and pauses before steadying himself. "Both Colette and I just stared at it for a minute before it disappeared into nothingness. Gone before it was even there." He sits back and rubs his cheek. "I thought I was hallucinating."

I sigh and sit forward. "I get that." There have been more times than I can count in these last couple of months where I thought I was seeing stuff and should be shipped off to some sanitarium. I give Adler a reassuring nod. "Kind of comes with the territory."

Adler grimaces. "Yes. After that, Colette was herself, sweet and plucky like she hadn't just vomited up a star. Helen came to, and we put the baby to bed, like every night. We went to sleep right then and there as well, all three of us together in Colette's bed...neither of us talking about what we had seen." He smiles wryly. "I thought whatever that thing was, it was just my mind playing tricks on me, a panicked father while his child had a febrile seizure—anything to rationalize. I was a fool for trying."

I look at Daniel uneasily, and Adler chuckles. "Did...anything happen after that?" I whisper.

The professor arches a brow and points at the gray text on the table. "You've read the book... I'm sure you can figure out what came next." We both watch his face grow hard. "The prophecies began the next morning at breakfast. Helen asked Colette if she wanted another pancake, and she spouted out this long untamed chain of gibberish, followed by words I will never forget." He motions with his hands. "*Like a flickering candle, I burn; the word of the Lord lighting my soul on fire... His voice is My voice, an instrument of the Fates, to be used and discarded by destiny alone.*"

"That sounds like... *Them*," Daniel rasps. I turn and stare between him and Adler.

Adler blinks, his eyes watery. "Two years old. I could *see* my child sitting next to me...hear her, touch her hand—but in that moment, I knew she wasn't mine anymore." He stops and wipes his face, tears leaking down his cheeks.

I pull my knees up to my chest, suddenly shivering. Daniel looks forward, but I can see he's searching around the room for any record of Colette or Helen as well, his face falling when he comes up short.

I tuck my hair behind my ears. "Did Heaven...or *anyone* contact you?" I ask Adler, pursing my lips. "After the first episode? To let you know what to do, what to expect?"

I startle as Adler lets out a harsh laugh. "We had no one." He sniggers with a shake of his head. "We were left completely in the dark. We thought she had schizophrenia or some other psychotic disorder, and we spent the first several years visiting every psychiatrist and specialist, going around the world, even staying at the Mayo Clinic." He stares at us grimly. "No one had a clue about what was going on. It wasn't until we went to Honduras for my research that we came across a shaman in the rainforest who took one look at Colette and uttered the word 'prophet.'"

Adler sits back in his chair. "I thought he was completely mad, of course...and that I myself was going mad for thinking he might be onto something." He looks at me intently. "You have to understand, our day-to-day life had become waiting for these moments where Colette would enter a catatonic state before spitting out a bunch of garbled words that made no sense. She'd be fine one minute, playing with her toys, and the next, she'd be gasping for breath as her entire being was taken over by this other...*entity*." His brow wrinkles as he searches for the right words. "Not only that, but she started seeing things when we went out—"

"The grocery store," I fill in, pointing at the book. "She saw someone there—a bagger or clerk—"

Adler turns to Daniel. "Yes. We could be anywhere: the store, the park, walking down the street…and it was always one of two reactions." His hands start to tremble again, and he thrusts it under the cushion, his fingers gripping around the inside of the chair. "Happy and playful, overly familiar…or terrified." He glares at Daniel. "Screaming and throwing herself into our arms, wanting to get away. I'm sure you can figure out who was who."

Daniel runs a hand through his hair. "None of you are supposed to see that. It…it must have been very…difficult…for all of you."

Adler laughs again, cruelly. "*Difficult*—yes. And not one time did any of *you* step over and offer a hint of what to do next, or reassurance…Hell—even an acknowledgment!" He stops himself as his tone grows angry. Daniel stares at the floor, and I look at Adler sympathetically, wanting to tell him how I truly get it. We all sit in silence as Adler collects himself.

"I'm sorry… Forgive me. I've just never really had an…an opportunity like this—" He pulls his hand from the chair and motions to us. "To talk about everything."

I nod and lean in, Daniel watching my every move. "Of course. We understand." I reach out and pat his knee warmly, ignoring the low growl that escapes Daniel's throat.

If Adler hears him, he doesn't say anything, just giving me a nod. "You have to understand, we became total recluses." His voice goes soft. "Only went out for essentials, stopped seeing our friends… We never knew when Colette was going to have one of her spells—they came more frequently when she was younger, along with severe nosebleeds that were hard to explain—so it was easier to just withdraw from the world into our own little bubble." He jerks his head toward the front door.

"It's…lonely," I murmur, sitting back on the couch and seeing Daniel's face pinch out of the corner of my eye. "You're instantly separated from everyone else…everything you ever knew…" I pause, staring at Adler. "Did you ever…*see* anything? Demons or Guardians?" Did he decide to go out at some point and try to take things into his own hands?

Adler shakes his head, his gaze distant. "I tried—and was refused." He frowns and glares at his hands, which I notice are trembling. "I thought…if I could see what she saw, then maybe I'd be able to help her, to understand." He huffs and rubs his jaw. "The Demons laughed me out of the building, the few times I was able to track them down. Said I had nothing to offer them." He glares at Daniel, his eyes on fire. "I would have given my life if it would have helped—but even that was deemed worthless."

"No, don't say that," I breathe, my stomach twisting in knots.

Daniel tenses next to me, but Adler turns and looks at me knowingly. "Colette was 14 when she delivered *your* prophecy," he rasps. "It was one of her most severe episodes to date. Even after, she shook, and it took her a long time to come out of it." He stares at me. "I thought I was going to lose her…for good. You know it, yes?"

I hold my breath, the words of the prophecy filling my mind, over and over again, getting louder each time. "Yes, I know it."

I watch him give a relieved sigh as he sits back in his chair. "Good. Good… That's what I needed to know…to be sure of…" He closes his eyes and rests his head back, momentarily lost.

I give Daniel a look and then cough, rousing Adler. "What did Helen think?" I ask, my voice hushed. I feel Daniel nudge my hip with his knuckles, like I shouldn't have brought her up.

Adler blinks and clears his throat. "We eventually found a school for Colette," he continues, completely evading my question, his hand back in the chair. "A small private Catholic group that had experience with children and emotional problems… They were very kind to us, and they helped us keep a record of any outbursts she had during the day. It was nice to finally have an ally while I continued my search for answers."

I frown and look between Adler and Daniel. The way Adler keeps talking about Colette and her care and *his* search for answers is making me uneasy. Something's missing. "Where are Helen…and Colette?" I ask again quietly.

Adler's face tightens, and he glares at Daniel. "Ask your Guardian," he murmurs. "He knows better than anybody."

I startle and spin to face Daniel, whose eyes are locked on Adler, his face wild. "Daniel?" I utter, terror seizing my body. Something's wrong. "What's he talking about?"

"You knew her, didn't you?" Adler jerks his chin toward Daniel. "I saw how you reacted to her name, her picture. You saw her."

Daniel sits up, not letting go of me. "Yes, I knew her… Colette." No coughing.

I draw in a sharp breath. "Daniel, why didn't you say something?" I murmur, keeping my eyes down.

He shakes his head, still focused on Adler, but his frown softens. "It was a long time ago. And I didn't make the connection when we found that book…" He motions to it on the coffee table. "I had no idea who she was or what she'd been through. I talked to her for maybe ten minutes…" He sighs, looking away from Adler. "The circumstances weren't ideal."

Adler scoffs. "That's a…*polite*…way of putting it." I watch his wrist tense, pulling something out of the chair. I gasp as he draws a small silver pistol from under his seat. "Always a kind word with you Guardians, even if you can't offer much else."

"What do you think you're doing?!" Daniel shouts at Adler as he jumps up and shields me with his body, keeping me pinned down on the couch. "Put that thing away!"

I gawk past him at Adler and the gun, my mouth open in fear and anticipation. Adler grimaces, the gun bobbing up and down in his shaking hand. He looks at Daniel, then at me, his eyes sad.

"I'm not going to...I would never hurt..." His voice grows thick as he gives me a tight smile, turning the gun on himself.

"Please—NO!" I cry, flailing my hands. No more death. Please, no more.

Adler groans. "I've been waiting for almost twelve years... Had to be sure you knew her message...since she couldn't..." His words go garbled as he starts to hyperventilate, pressing the barrel of the gun to his chin.

"Don't do this!" Daniel commands, taking a step forward. "Come on, you don't want to die—believe *me*!" He rakes a hand through his hair. "Don't take your life for granted...your friends, your work...think about your wife—"

Adler breaks into a wide, lopsided grin. "*My wife?*" he gasps, starting to hiccup. Daniel shoots me a nervous glance. "That... that might be a challenge, as you're standing on what's left of her!" He bursts into a fit of crazed laughter like he just got hit with Joker gas. Both Daniel and I look down at his feet, his sneakers squared on the dark pumpkin stain. "But that's what happens when you make a deal you can't pay with the Devil!"

I claw at the couch, panicked, as Daniel recoils off the spot and glares at Adler, the gun still tight on his face. I can feel my own breath quickening, all of this too reminiscent of Alden and Pete and the underpass. My eyes widen, and I try to get a grip.

"Whatever happened—it's in the past now." Daniel takes a tentative step toward Adler, both his hands up in passive surrender, his eyes darting between Adler's face and the gun. "You still have a chance...time to make something better..." He stops as Adler's shoulders quake.

"We tried—we both tried so hard to get her back." His voice cracks, and I can see that he's crying. "But you can't stop Fate. No one can. Gods or monsters...all of us are helpless."

He lets out a wail, and Daniel tears the gun from his hand,

disarming it as Adler collapses in on himself, sobs wracking his body. I sit up, finally taking a breath as Daniel watches him, placing a sad hand on his back.

"I'm sorry," Daniel mutters, his own tone hushed. "More than you know." Adler goes quiet, but doesn't look up. Daniel waves the gun before shoving it into his jacket. "But I can't let you do this. You know that."

He looks over at me and motions for me to get up. I grab the book from the table and head for the door. Adler doesn't make a sound as Daniel joins me and we silently leave.

I don't feel the cold as we step outside. "Oh my God... Daniel," I gasp, clutching my stomach as we walk briskly away from the house and down the nighttime street, the Christmas lights seeming dimmer this time as we pass. "I don't even know where to begin, what to say..."

"You don't have to say anything," Daniel murmurs, stopping in front of a neighboring house. "He's a sad old man with a sad old story." His eyes dart past the animated reindeer display and up to a koi pond by the front door. He stalks over to it and pulls Adler's gun from his coat, removing the bullets before letting it fall into the water with a dull plunk. He tosses the bullets into the bushes and comes back to me, his expression terse. "I'm sorry about what happened to him, but he's still mortal, Christa... He still has time to find—happiness, or whatever." He stops and puckers his lips bitterly.

"Hey." I take his hand, pulling him back from wherever he was going with that. I wave back at the koi pond. "You saved him. You stopped him from killing himself."

Daniel looks at me sadly. "I did...for tonight, anyway."

We both go quiet as we start walking again back to the bus stop, letting the night wash over us. "So...you knew Colette," I finally say, my curiosity getting the best of me.

Daniel nods, holding tight to my hand as we make our way to a large intersection, cars speeding by. "Like I said, I only met her once over a decade ago," he calls over the traffic. "I thought she was just another mixed-up kid, hanging out with Demons…"

I startle. I hadn't heard *that* part of the story.

"But she was nice and…pretty…like, *really* pretty. I remember thinking, 'What is a girl like this doing with these guys?'"

"Wait…back up!" I stumble as we cross the road, shoving the flash of jealousy from Daniel calling another girl pretty to the backburner, my emotions returning to their normal heightened extreme. "Colette…*the prophet*, Colette," I state, trying to make sense of it all, "was hanging out with *Demons*?!" I stop and gape at him when we get to the other side of the street.

Daniel nods. "Yeah…and now I can see why." He waves back in the direction of Adler's. "She was rebelling against her destiny, after a lifetime of being subjected to the whims of the Fates."

"I'm sorry, *what*?!" I can't keep the shock out of my voice. "The *prophet* was BFFs with a bunch of Demons?! And you knew that and just left her there?!" That doesn't sound like something Daniel would do, and definitely not something *Heaven* would even allow…right?

He shakes his head. "That's the thing—she wasn't alone. She *had* a Guardian with her." He gives a small smile as the memories click into place. "Ellis. It was the first time I met her…and she wasn't her usual friendly self." He scoffs. "Typical Guardian maneuver, being all territorial."

My eyes widen. "*Ellis* was Colette's Guardian?"

Daniel nods. "Yeah… At the time, I thought it was weird that a Guardian was hanging out with those Demons, and they were all cool—everybody knew who everyone was… Ellis has always been able to talk her way into or out of anything, but now it all makes sense—she was on Prophet detail."

"That's fantastic!" I interrupt. "Ellis is coming for Christmas—we can ask her about Colette. I'm sure she knows everything! Maybe she can even introduce us—"

I lurch to a halt as Daniel stops in his tracks. "What?" I shake my head, staring at him. "What is it?"

Daniel looks at me, his mouth thin. "Colette's dead. She's gone."

I stand there, my mouth hanging open. "How—how do you know for sure?" I breathe.

Daniel winces. "She was pregnant when I met her, Christa." He sighs. "With a Demon baby."

I stare at him, letting it all sink in, remembering what Alden had said about Human women who carry Demon babies—how none of them survive the birth. I close my eyes, waves of grief crashing into me. Of course she's gone—Adler wouldn't have been so ready to go himself if she was still alive. Fathers and daughters are like that.

"Oh," is all I can come up with after a minute. We start moving again. "I'm sorry," I mumble.

Daniel nods as we close in on the bus stop. "It's okay... Just add her to the list."

Hearing the anguish in his voice, I lace my fingers through his, and we wait for the bus in silence.

CHAPTER 16
NEW YORK CITY—
APRIL, 1976

"**K**EEP LIGHT ON your feet, Pedro…*la luz en sus pies!*" Chef calls over from his milk crate, cigarette in hand. "You're dragging on your left side. He's gonna get you if you keep that up…"

Spring had arrived in New York in all its technicolor glory, trees blooming pink and white, squirrels and birds chattering happily to one another along the busy avenues. As the days had grown longer, more of the crew seemed to find their way out into the back alley, lounging on the concrete steps to smoke and enjoy the sunshine. Juan Julio and Harry, one of the American waiters, had organized an amateur bareknuckle fight league between front of house and back. It had become a daily ritual to watch our respective team members rough each other up for a couple of minutes between shifts. Daniel gives me a light nudge with his sneaker, sitting a few steps up from me. "How big's the pool on Mikey?" he asks under his breath, watching one of the larger American boys pound into Pedro.

I reach into my jacket pocket and pull out a small wad of

cash, giving it a quick count. "Up 56 dollars… You're gonna bet against one of your own?"

Daniel huffs. "No! Of course not…" He glances over at the fight. "Come on, Pedro! Get your hands up!" He claps loudly, slipping me a twenty dollar bill. "I've got ten on him. Just wanna play it safe, you know what I mean?"

I roll my eyes and pocket his money. "Sure…I'll let you sort it out in the end." I'm not invested either way, not really being a gambler myself. Chef had decided that I should be the one to handle the cash after Harry 'miscounted' last week. For taking on this great responsibility, I get to keep a 3% cut each round for myself. Guess it pays to have an honest face and be good at maths.

We all wince as Mikey wallops Pedro across the jaw, knocking him flat out. We stand and give a hearty clap to the two fighters, Juan Julio stepping over to the fallen chef and tapping him lightly on the cheek. With a shake of his head, Pedro comes to, and we all give a cheer, the boys from the front jumping over to congratulate Mikey.

I turn and give Daniel a look. "Looks like you just bought yourself a pretty nice dinner." I start counting and sorting the cash and hand him his share before the others line up for their winnings. He crinkles his nose and tucks the money into his jeans.

"Pick you up at 8, sweetheart?" he jokes.

I tsk. "I'll have to check my calendar—you know my dance card is quite full…" We laugh and get up, heading up to the service door.

"Hey—we got time for one more!" Harry calls in his twangy southern accent. "Who hasn't gone?"

The guys all look around at each other, murmuring over their bumps and bruises, debating who's more beat up. Harry looks up and points at Daniel and I. "Here we go! That's a match up we haven't seen yet!" He grins. "Has either one of you fought yet?"

I glance at Daniel and see that we're wearing identical

grimaces. "We're good—kind of the sit back and watch type," I grumble. Yeah…that's not gonna go over well.

True to my prediction, the guys all laugh, and Harry shakes his head. "Aw, come on! Head Waiter versus Sous! Main event!" He crosses his arms as the boys give a roar of approval, a couple of them already taking out their money. "You can't pussy out like that, Boss." He gives me a cavalier wink.

I sigh and look back at Daniel; it'll be really bad for morale if we don't do this. Daniel shrugs and nods warily.

With another sigh, I pull off my tux jacket and start unbuttoning my shirt, a round of applause and a couple of whistles chorusing around us as Daniel does the same. Once we're down to our undershirts, we stumble slowly down to the alley to stand on opposite sides of Harry.

"I want a good, clean fight, you understand?" Harry drawls, looking between the two of us.

I stare at Daniel, who's working to keep his face serious, but failing hard as his big, toothy grin pokes through. "What's so funny?" I ask, trying to keep my voice light.

Daniel shrugs. "Nothing, nothing…" he snickers.

I narrow my eyes, a flash of annoyance washing over me. He thinks he's got this in the bag.

"Gentlemen, do you understand?" Harry asks, a little louder. When we both nod, he turns to the crowd. "Finish up those bets! I don't wanna see any cash out while this is goin' down!" He nods at Chef, who's sitting alone and smoking away placidly. "You gettin' in on this, Chef?" Harry chuckles, tossing a couple bills himself over to Juan Julio.

Chef takes a long draw and sits back. "Nope," he replies coolly, crossing his ankle over one knee. "I'm good."

Harry looks at Daniel, then back at Chef incredulously. "You're not gonna bet on your own right-hand guy? He's got at least four inches on Mr. Alden…"

Daniel snorts, and my face grows hot. Chef shakes his head.

"I'm staying out this round. Y'all have your fun." Chef stares me down, his eyes tight as his cheeks puff in and out around his smoke. I stand up a little taller.

"All right, all right." Harry shrugs and turns back to us. "You boys shake on it."

"Don't worry...I'll go easy on you." Daniel looks at me smugly as we clasp hands, sniffing as I grip a little tighter than I think either one of us anticipated.

"Thanks," I say with a smile, letting go. "That's really big of you."

Harry takes a deliberate step back. "On my count," he hollers. "3...2...1!" With a dramatic wave, Harry moves out of the way.

I crack Daniel square in the nose before he even gets a chance to make a fist. The crowd reacts as he reels backwards, his feet tripping under him as he reaches for his face. I hold position, my knuckles level with my chin, ready for him to come back.

He pulls his hand away, his expression not so confident now, a bit of blood on his fingers. "Lucky shot, Irish," he snickers, getting his hands up. "But you're gonna have to hit a little harder if you want *me* to go down on you—I'm not your girlfriend."

I grind my teeth and swing again, missing this time as he darts out of the way, and we begin to circle. I can hear catcalls and clapping somewhere off in the distance; but I don't take my eyes off of Daniel. We go around maybe three times before Daniel takes his first shot, aiming for my chin, but whacking me in the shoulder instead. I barely feel it. I grin: he's more inexperienced than I thought, jumping around with his thumbs tucked inside his fists. Good thing for him he's not going to get many pops in.

We circle again, and I watch him, mapping out his foot pattern. I know the crowd is getting restless, the catcalls turning to jeers, but I just need one more minute to determine which way he's going to duck. I throw a soft punch just to settle it, and he does exactly what I expect him to, going down on his right side. Okay—got what I need.

I huff and feign like I'm going in for a right cross. When he takes the bait, I reverse, getting him with an uppercut hard across the jaw. He lets out a grunt and staggers back. This time, though, I don't relent. Instead, I hit him again and again, bludgeoning my fists into his face. A thick current of blood is gushing from his nose now, his lower lip swelling as he tries to circle away from me to get a break. The cheers have stopped, everyone staring on in silence. I pop Daniel again, this time in the left temple, and he stops and sways on the spot.

"Okay, Boss… I think you got him." Harry comes up behind me and puts his hand on my shoulder.

I flinch and shrug him off, panting as I wait for Daniel to go down. He doesn't.

"Come on!" I hiss, hastily wiping sweat off my own brow. "Just fall already!"

I watch him teetering on his feet, but he holds his ground, a coy smile crossing his bloody mouth. I see red and pounce.

"Hey—Mr. Alden!" Harry yells, but all I can see is Daniel cracking the back of his head on the concrete as I jump on top of him. I sit down roughly on his stomach and start wailing away, ramming my fists anywhere I can get them—his face, neck, chest. He doesn't even fight back, and this only enrages me more. I know he's still conscious because I can feel his abs spasming up and down underneath me. He's…he's *laughing at me.*

"Stop that!" I shout as I take his battered face in my trembling hands. "Stop laughing!"

This only encourages him, and he lets out a crackly chuckle, spraying little flecks of blood on my face. "Do what you gotta do, Irish." He glares gravely, showing off the popped blood vessel in his left eye. "Go ahead. I want you to."

"What?" I stare down at him, dumbfounded.

He licks blood off of his lip. "Come on—HIT ME!" His voice cracks as his breath quickens. "Hit me in the fuckin' mouth—I know you want to…"

I shake my head, my resolve wavering. Before I have a chance to react one way or another, though, a set of arms reaches around my midsection and pulls me off of him.

"Let's take a walk, Irish," I hear Chef's gravelly voice say in my ear. I blink, and the tunnel vision fades away; we're moving together across the alley, Chef's calloused hand on my back. Someone's breathing is hot and ragged, and it takes me a second before I realize it's mine. I spin and see Daniel still splayed on the ground, several of the guys circling around him.

"He'll be all right," Chef murmurs, setting me down on a milk crate a few meters away from everyone. "I already sent Pedro in to get some ice."

I shake my head dizzily and put my face in my hands. "I don't know what came over me. It's like I couldn't see straight…"

"Danny Boy bit off more than he could chew is all… Didn't know what he was up against." Chef crouches down and stares up at me. "None of them did. You really threw the card today, Irish—they all lost big. Won't make that same mistake again."

I exhale. "How did you know? I mean…not to bet. To stay out of it."

Chef chuckles. "I recognized that look in your eye the first day you showed up here. The look of someone who's had to fight every goddamn day of his life." He squints and stares down the alley, before turning back to me. "It wasn't all rainbows and emerald isles back home, was it, Irish?"

I shake my head. Chef nods and grunts knowingly. "Same old story anywhere you go. Doesn't matter if it's Chicago or Dublin—poor is poor." He gets to his feet and offers me a hand. "But you've got a chance to change all that now." He cheats his head back toward the restaurant. Everyone's up and about now, Daniel nodding as he holds an ice pack to his mouth.

Chef squints at me. "You takin' classes now, right?" I nod shakily, and he crosses his arms. "You got your work here…and

I know everyone thinks you're doing a bang-up job." He jerks his chin. "And you got your girl, yeah?"

"Yes, Chef," I mumble.

Chef keeps nodding. "Mm-hm. Seems to me like you've got a little piece of Heaven right now." He arches a brow. "My advice to you, Irish, is to leave all of *that* in the dust." He waves back to the fight corner. "Forget about all that garbage and grab whatever happiness you can and never let it go." He puts a hand on my shoulder. "And don't look back, you dig?"

I nod. "Yes sir. I understand."

"Good." He smacks me kindly on the cheek. "Now go get cleaned up; we've got a busy night ahead of us."

We head back to the service door, everyone gathering up their things. I slow as I see Daniel gingerly putting his chef's jacket back on at the stairs; I'm not sure if I'm ready to confront him after what happened.

Fortunately, Harry pops up in my path. "What a fight, Mr. Alden! I didn't know you had it in you!" he crows excitedly. "I think we should pair you with Juan Julio next. He's champ in the standings right now... I think you could knock him right outta there!"

"I think Mr. Alden's fighting career has come to a close," Chef interrupts, clearing his throat. "Consider him retired."

Harry frowns, but quickly comes back. "What about you, Chef? Maybe you and Francois next? He's got those messed up hands—it would be a blood bath!"

"You watch your mouth, boy!" Chef snaps.

Harry clams up fast, his eyes wide.

Chef clenches his jaw. "That man survived a goddamn occupation. He's French Resistance. Do you even know what the fuck that means?"

Harry shakes his head, alarmed. Chef glares at him. "No? Didn't think so! Get outta here before I make you write a goddamn history paper. Don't you have prep to do?"

Harry nods and runs off. Chef snorts, calling after him,

"That's right! Mind your business! Goddammit, these kids are gonna put me in an early grave..." Gazing down the alley, he finally smiles slightly. "All right, a ray of sunshine—Muriel's here."

I follow his eyes and see Muriel coming up on her bicycle, grinning prettily from behind the handlebars. I give Chef a pat on the arm, and he waves me away as I jog over to her. Between the bicycle and the short floral print dress she's wearing, she is the picture of spring personified.

I stop and help her off the seat, doing a double take as I notice something very different about her. "You cut your hair!" I exclaim brightly.

"Yes." She pats her new short dark bob self-consciously. "I'm still getting used to it... Got it done after lunch service on Tuesday. What do you think?" She smiles, biting her lip.

"I love it," I reply, giving a sincere nod. "Very cosmopolitan."

Muriel blushes. "Thanks." Her eyes drift over to the alley, the crowd now breaking up as everyone goes inside for the afternoon shift, then cut back to my undershirt. "What's going on?" she demands. "Were you boys fighting again?"

I sigh, rubbing the back of my neck. "Eh...maybe."

She shoots me a very disapproving look. "Why you all consider beating each other senseless to be entertainment, I will never understand."

I follow her as she shakes her head and walks her bike over to the service entrance. "Gotta stay outta trouble somehow," I mutter.

"Ha!" she laughs, her eyes lighting up. "Oh—I had something I wanted to show you." She stops and lets the bicycle rest against her hip as she reaches into her purse, pulling out a slightly rolled piece of parchment paper.

She takes a breath and hands it to me. "We had our last session today. The board looks amazing... She is so talented, I can hardly believe it! She's going to win the campaign for sure. She let me keep one of the earlier sketches."

Muriel watches as I unfurl the paper, revealing a charcoal sketch of her. I catch myself blushing a little, as it's Muriel in a way I've never seen her before: straddling a straight-backed chair, dressed in a rumpled white men's dress shirt, the buttons left undone. She has a bare leg pulled up to her chest, keeping everything covered as one hand tousles her hair, the other holding a lit cigarette seductively to her lower lip.

Of course, I recognize the hand that drew it immediately. "It's stunning." I smile, handing the drawing back to her. "Truly."

Muriel grins. "Thanks. Hope you don't mind the wardrobe choice." She lets out a little giggle. "We found one of your shirts under the bed and figured we'd put it to good use."

"It's fine!" I laugh. "As long as you both are happy." I know Jillian had been working day and night trying to come up with the perfect drawing for her Illustration and Advertising class. Winston's was coming in next week to select the winner. If this earlier sketch was any indicator, she was a shoe-in.

"I am—very happy!" Muriel scrunches her shoulders, staring at the picture. "I mean, I know it's me in the drawing, but I didn't think I really...*looked* like that." She blushes wildly and gently rolls it back up. "So...um, wanton!"

"Jillian has that effect on people." I arch a brow mischievously as she locks up her bicycle. "None of us are safe!"

"Safe from what?" Daniel calls over the service railing, peeking down at us.

Both Muriel and I glance up. He looks a lot better than he did before—his left eye is still a little rough, but with the blood all cleaned up, he's pretty much himself. He sees Muriel and smiles. "Hey—you got a haircut!"

Muriel beams as he hops down the steps. He stands in front us and grins, like I didn't just beat the pulp out of him mere minutes ago. The corner of my eye twitches.

"Yes." Muriel nods bashfully, taking a step toward him. "I've never gone this short before... Can't even pull it back."

"It's nice. You look older—you know, in a good way!" Daniel corrects himself quickly with a laugh. "Not like a little kid anymore."

I see Muriel's face light up, and I look warily back at Daniel. He can't say stuff like that to her and not follow through. He nods at the paper in her hand. "What were you showing Irish? Secret love letter?" He flashes his brows. "Say anything about me?"

I roll my eyes. Muriel considers for a moment, her fingers trembling as she holds out the drawing to him. "Actually, it's a sketch Jillian did of me…for class…" She smiles nervously as he takes it and looks it over.

We both watch as his eyes grow wider, before he breaks into a huge grin. "Wow, this is hot! Your girlfriend drew this?" He holds it up for me to see, and I nod. "She's freakier than I thought… yowzers! Seriously, Muriel!" She goes three shades of pink as he blatantly checks her out. "I didn't know you could…*do* stuff like this." He shrugs and bats me on the arm. "She's smokin', right? Total stone fox…"

I glance back at the paper, trying to be respectful. "It's a beautiful drawing of a beautiful girl." I don't really want to spend a whole lot of time looking at it—too many conflicting emotions.

Daniel scoffs and turns back to Muriel. "Don't let him fool you, Muriel. He wasn't such a gentleman a few minutes ago when he gave me a fat lip," he snickers.

Muriel glares at me. "Just got caught up in the moment," I say with a grimace.

Daniel chuckles and waves me off. "Can I keep this?" he asks Muriel, gesturing with the rolled-up drawing.

She blinks, appearing to be in shock for a second, before slowly nodding her head. Daniel grins and folds it into his pocket. "Awesome…and we should go out!" He exclaims. "You know, all of us…"

Muriel holds her breath, and I hastily wipe the surprised expression off my face. "I…don't know if that's such a good idea,"

I breathe, remembering that the last time I went out with him didn't go so well. Muriel's face grows stormy as she discreetly stomps on my foot. I cough. "I mean...I'm pretty busy with classes. I've got three this quarter, plus all my hours here... You should just take Muriel out to dinner or something."

"No, no! We should all go out—the four of us!" Daniel laughs, slapping me on the back. "You, me, and the girls." He motions to Muriel, who is now grinning from ear to ear. "There's a new club that just opened up downtown It's the middle of the week, so it shouldn't be totally mobbed. We'll go dancing... It'll be fun."

I narrow my eyes at him, looking for the catch. Muriel, however, has no such reservations. "Like a double date!" she squeals, squeezing my arm to try to get me on board. "You know Jillian will love getting dressed up! Oh please, Alden..."

I sigh and smile tightly, hating to disappoint her. "Sure...all right, Muriel. Whatever you like," I murmur.

She squeals and throws her arms around my neck, before arching up on the balls of her feet to give Daniel a swift kiss on the cheek. He blushes as she rushes up the service steps. "I'll ring Jillian and let her know... I should be able to stop by her place after work to get ready!" she calls, lugging open the heavy metal door. We both smile after her as she goes inside.

Daniel turns back to me and puts his hands in his pockets. "She seems excited!" He shrugs, his trademark goofy grin back in place.

I nod slowly. "Don't screw this up, Daniel." I keep my voice low, but he gets my meaning.

He stares at me for a minute, before bursting into a fit of laughter. "God, you're always such a downer!" he sniggers, slapping me on the back. "Can't you just lighten up and enjoy the moment? Jeez..." He shakes his head and stares at the service door. "Everyone's gonna be happy, we're all gonna have a good time, and it'll be great. What could possibly go wrong?"

*

Daniel and I rush up from the W 54th Street subway station, running late to meet the girls because the train from Queens had to make an emergency stop on the way over. Daniel runs ahead, the old suit jacket that he last wore for his high school graduation flapping behind him as motions for me to follow.

"Come on, Irish—get the lead out! It's right over here…" We turn the corner and come to a stop, seeing a long line snaking its way under a brightly lit marquee.

I glare at Daniel, then back at the line. "I thought you said it wouldn't be busy!"

Daniel shrugs as we queue up. "It's a Thursday, for God's sake! I didn't know it was gonna be this nuts…"

We check out the people in front of us—a pair of mustachioed men laughing and wearing Greek togas. I furrow my brow and search the rest of the line, feeling shy and out of place in my suit from Christmas. There are plenty of people in crazy costumes—a large yellow feathered drag queen, a couple of young blokes looking like one of the bands straight off of Daniel's wall, and countless beautiful women, all vying for the doorman's attention.

I don't see our girls, though. I frown. "They're probably already inside!" I toss my hands irritably in the air. "This is going to take all night…"

Daniel pats my shoulder. "Relax, Irish—it's too early for you to be this worked up. Come on." Looking confident, he steps out of line, me sulking behind as we go up to the doorman. "How's it hangin', man?" Daniel asks, holding his hand up for a high five.

The big guy doesn't even look at him, just hulks a bit more, craning his face over Daniel's head. I sigh and cross my arms; this is impossible.

"I know you guys are really busy tonight…" Daniel hedges, unfazed even as the doorman continues to ignore him and waves a group of gorgeous, model-esque girls forward. The one wearing a sparkly sequin dress smiles at me as they pass.

"But I think I have some product that your boss might be

interested in," Daniel finishes, clearing his throat and flipping open his jacket.

The bouncer's eyes flicker over to him, then back to the line. "Shut the hell up and beat it," he grumbles. "Get your punk ass outta here. No soliciting."

Daniel chuckles and looks down at the sidewalk. "I think you might want to reconsider that. My employer is *very* interested in doing business with your employer. Please, look again."

He holds open his jacket a second time, and the bouncer turns with a grunt and squints more closely. I frown; I have a pretty good idea what he's looking at.

Confirming my suspicions, the doorman's eyes go wide. "Are you fucking kidding me? Really?"

Daniel lets his jacket close with a grin. "Just five minutes of his time, that's all I need." He jerks his head toward the club.

The doorman exhales, then waves us on. "All right. He's in the last booth on the left. Keep it short and sweet—he doesn't like games!"

"Thank you! Thank you so much…" Daniel pulls a twenty from his pocket and presses it into the doorman's hand. He nods as we move into the busy club, me keeping my head down as I pace in front of Daniel.

"Told you not to worry, Irish!" Daniel chirps, batting me on the arm.

I spin back to him, shaking my head. "I can't believe you would play that card tonight, of all nights!" I snap, my face turning red. "It was bad enough when it was just me, but now with the girls so close by?!" I glare out at the crowded dance floor, searching for either Jillian or Muriel. "How much are you carrying right now, huh? Why was that doorman so impressed?"

I start to go for his jacket, but Daniel pulls away, gaping at me in shock. "Hey—hands off! Why are you acting like this? I got us past the line, didn't I?!" he yells over the blaring dance music.

I put my hands on my hips and glare down at the floor. Daniel sighs and drags a hand through his hair. "Now, why don't you go make yourself useful and go find them while I take care of this?" he barks with a jerk of his chin.

I stare back at him blankly, which I know makes him madder. He shakes his head and points at me. "I'm not going to let your shitty attitude tank another night for me!" His lip curls. "Go find the girls, and I'll see you in a bit. When I come back, you better be having the fuckin' time of your life."

I glare at his back as he stalks off through the dancers, wanting nothing more than to turn around and go right back home—but I'm not about to leave Jillian and Muriel alone in this place. I exhale and start walking toward the bar, my mood lifting as I spy a flash of bright red hair.

Jillian spins on a barstool, sipping something clear through a dark straw. Seeing me, she grins and stands up, waving. With a white sharkskin wrap dress hugging all the right curves, the material shimmering through the otherwise dimly lit disco, she takes my breath away. I make my way over to her and put my hand on her waist, feeling the knot that holds it all together under my fingers. The last few minutes fall away as I imagine what fun it will be untying that bow later tonight…like unwrapping a present.

A low growl escapes my throat as I lean in and kiss her bare neck. "I thought you said you were wearing red tonight." I press up close, breathing in her scent of honey and clover.

Jillian brushes the tip her nose along my jaw in greeting. "Change of plans," she purrs, taking another sip of her drink before offering it to me. "Here. It's seltzer."

I take a draw off the straw and set the glass back down on the bar. "You look amazing, of course. You know how much I like you in white." She rolls her eyes as I reach into my jacket. "But it puts a little dent in my plans…"

Jillian smiles as I peek a pretty white rose blossom out of my pocket. "I fear this will clash with your dress."

She takes the rose and twirls between in her fingers. "Always so thoughtful…"

I nod and hold out a fist to her. "Not to worry, though: I brought a spare."

She laughs delightedly as I do a little sleight-of-hand and present another rose, this one soft pink. "This should do nicely."

"Smooth move, slick! Pleased with yourself?"

I flash my eyebrows as she beams and gives me a long kiss, tucking the pink flower next to her breast. I envy it.

"Thank you. And we can still use this." She motions with the white rose.

I grin. "Oh, *we* can?" I ask playfully. Jillian shrugs, biting her lip. I crinkle my nose at her. "If I didn't know better, I'd think you were plotting something, Ms. O'Connor…"

"I'm never plotting!" She giggles, looking past me out into the crowd. "Just trying my hand at playing Cupid…"

"Well, I've still got your arrow stuck in my heart, so it shouldn't be too hard." I laugh and follow her gaze. "Where's Muriel? Did she come over with you?"

Jillian nods. "Yeah. She had to go make a call, should be back any…ah! There she is!" She grins and waves to someone moving through the dancers.

I stop and hold my breath. I hardly recognize her: her skin is all cream and roses, her dark hair sleek and cloud-like as she stops in front of us. Muriel beams at us, her hands smoothing the tight red silk dress that ends at her knees. She brushes her bare arms and looks at me expectantly. "You made it!" Her eyes dart around as she looks for the final member of our party. I put on my biggest smile and step toward her, pulling Jillian with me as I give her a light kiss on the cheek.

"Yeah. The line out front was insane… You look amazing, Muriel," I murmur, glancing around the hall. "I must be the luckiest guy here; to have not one, but *two* gorgeous girls with me."

They both laugh, and we settle next to the bar. "I can't take credit for any of it." Muriel smiles at Jillian. "It's all this girl right here—the artist!"

"Well, it helps to have such a pretty canvas to work with." Jillian moves over to her, the white rose in hand. "A final touch…" Using a bobby pin from her purse, she lovingly clips the flower behind Muriel's ear, rubbing her arm when she's through. "Now you're ready."

Muriel exhales and stares back out at the dance floor; searching. "Daniel's here, right? You came over together?"

"Yeah…he's just in the loo. Should be right back." I nod, trying to keep my face calm as I lie. Muriel gives us a tight smile and turns back to Jillian. "You're sure this is okay? Maybe we should have gone some place quieter, less crowded…"

Jillian shakes her head. "Everything is fine! You have nothing to worry about… He's gonna flip when he sees you! You're hands-down the most beautiful girl here tonight."

She glances over at me, and I shrug happily, scanning the club. "You know where my bias lies, but yes, a fair amount of guys here have been checking you out. I'm ready to fight 'em off if I have to."

Muriel relaxes and starts bobbing on the balls of her feet. "All right…yes! I can do this. It's all I've wanted since…" She pauses and runs her hand along the back of the stool. "Well…too long, probably."

"It's going to be amazing—you'll see," Jillian replies confidently. "Tonight is your night, Muriel, the night when you get your Prince Charming." She smiles at me over her shoulder, and I squeeze her hand under the bar.

Muriel sighs and stares at the dance floor. "All right…I'm just getting more and more nervous standing here—where is he?" She gets up on her tiptoes and looks toward the back. "You said he was just in the bathroom?"

I exhale and try to keep my voice even. "Yeah, but I bet there's a long line. It's so busy…"

"For the men's room?" Jillian gazes at me skeptically.

I flounder for a second, feeling a light sheen of sweat break across my forehead. "I'm going to look for him." Muriel nods resolutely and steps forward.

My eyes bug out of my head, and I hastily grasp her arm. "No bother! I'm sure he's fine..." I bumble, both Muriel and Jillian looking at me as if I'd just sprouted a second head. Defeated, I let go of Muriel and try to laugh it off. "I just don't think we want to get separated here—you never know when we'll find each other again." I give a weak chuckle.

"That's fine—we'll all go look for him." Jillian hops off her stool and grabs her purse from the bar, swinging the gold strap over her shoulder. She smiles and pats Muriel on the hand as they walk forward, turning back to me to mouth, *What's with you?* to me. I shrug and shove my hands into my pockets, keeping my eyes wide open and hoping to be the one to find Daniel first.

We weave through the dancers, making our way to the restrooms where, lo and behold, there *is* a line coming out of the men's room, a lot of the same brightly costumed individuals from outside all making out with each other. The girls giggle as I scan the line; Daniel's not one of them.

"Can you peek in and just see if he's in there?" Jillian tilts her head toward the bathroom. "Maybe he's not feeling well..."

I grimace and nod, knowing full well he's not in there. I get a couple of catcalls as I cut past the line and step inside. The one stall and urinals are all occupied, and there is a man in a fireman's hat snorting thin lines of cocaine off the sink counter. Maybe Daniel *did* make his way back here after all.

"Daniel..." I clear my throat and rap on the stall door, a boisterous "Fuck you!" coming from the other side. I grimace and walk back to the hall, feeling the usual cloud of doom and gloom gathering over my head...always thicker whenever Daniel is involved.

I give a lighthearted shrug to the girls when I come out of the toilets. "Not in there," I sigh, watching Muriel's smile fade. "He must be out looking for us. Come on." I hook arms with both of them like we're starring in a 1950s musical, desperately trying to keep everyone upbeat. We shuffle back over to the dance floor, the strobe lights pulsating as some new song with a decidedly Nordic beat comes on.

Jillian squeals and squeezes my wrist. "Oh my gosh—ABBA! I love them!" She grins over at Muriel, who's looking more and more deflated with every step. "Let's dance! I'm sure we'll see Daniel out there!"

Ever the trooper, Muriel smiles at her, and they move out onto the dance floor. With a final glance around, I join them, and I feel all of our spirits lift as the three of us spin and twirl together. I give Muriel a turn just in time to catch Jillian as she trips on her heel, laughing and stumbling into my arms.

"We have to stop meeting like this!" I joke, giving her a swift kiss.

She giggles and straightens up. "Where would be the fun in that?"

Jillian's frame suddenly goes rigid, however, as she watches Muriel's back. "Muriel?" she calls to her, taking her arm. They both stare forward, and I step over to see what they're looking at.

My stomach sinks.

A few feet away, a stunning couple is writhing their way across the dance floor. The girl is tall and black, the tips of her large afro dusted in gold, matching her short lamé dress. She's got one of her long legs hitched up on the hip of the guy she's with, tall and golden-haired.

With a grin, Daniel leans in and kisses her passionately, his arms encircling her waist; somehow they manage to keep the rhythm, bouncing along while they go at it. I jerk my head and stare at Muriel, seeing a stunned expression on her beautiful face. My heart shatters into a million pieces as she just watches them for a moment before blinking and looking down at the floor. Jillian's eyes are saucer-sized as she looks between me and Daniel and the girl. I search for something to say, but come up empty-handed.

"Muriel…" I cross over to her and put a hand on her arm. "Come on, let's get outta here—"

"No…" She clenches her jaw and shakes her head, her gaze painfully locked on the two of them again, tiny pearls of moisture springing up in the corners of her eyes. They still haven't noticed us staring. "I want to stay—"

"Maybe we should get some air." Jillian steps over to her other side, taking her arm. "And then we can come back, figure this all out with a clear head…"

"No! I want to dance!" Muriel shouts, throwing us both off of her and refusing to look away from Daniel and the girl. "That's why we're here, right?"

Jillian glares at me as Muriel clutches her stomach, a strange, garbled noise escaping her lips.

I take a deep breath and step between Muriel and Daniel, blocking her view. "Okay, sure—I'll dance with you, Muriel." My own voice cracks as I put my hand on her waist and gently pull her toward me. "Come on, you're dancing with me tonight…"

"NO!" she sobs, beating her fists into my chest. I plant my feet and take it, watching Jillian out of the corner of my eye, her face creased with worry as she covers her mouth with her hand.

Tears cascade down Muriel's cheeks as she collapses into me. "I don't want to dance with you, Alden! No!" She shoves away, shaking her head from side to side, the white rose now hanging limply by her chin. With a wince, she tears it out and chucks it on the floor. "This wasn't how…this wasn't how it was supposed to be!"

She stares at Daniel's backside and at the girl's dark arms still twisted around his neck, then lets out a final gasp before she rushes back to the front of the club.

"Muriel, wait!" Jillian cries, gnashing her teeth. "Dammit!"

I startle; Jillian rarely swears. I watch her face grow red as she paces in a tight circle, staring at me in exasperation before waving to the front. "I have to go after her, make sure she gets home okay!" She frowns, shaking her head. "This was a total disaster!"

I nod, rubbing my jaw. I'm suddenly exhausted. "I know... I'm sorry." I don't know why *I'm* apologizing, but it just sort of slips out.

Jillian huffs and sneers at Daniel, who is still in the throes of...whatever the hell he's doing. "You should go collect *your friend*," she spits, looking away in disgust.

I wince; I know she's not trying to lump me in with his bad behavior...but I'm still left feeling like a puppy that just got rapped on the nose with a newspaper. "Right..." I step over to her and put my hand on her shoulder; she shakes me off. I exhale and look down at the floor. "I'll see you later—?"

"I don't think you should come over tonight." Her eyes dart back to Daniel, burning a hole in the back of his head. Yep...I'm guilty by association.

I sigh. "Right...yeah, okay. I'll see to you tomorrow." Very cautiously, I place my hand on the small of her back and kiss her cheek before she stomps off to the front doors. I feel a twinge as I watch her glorious hips sway angrily away. Okay—if I wasn't pissed before, I am now.

Seething, I turn my attention back to Daniel and the golden girl and make my way over to them. I give Daniel a brusque tap on the shoulder, and he spins around, whooping when he sees me.

"Aw—hey! There you are!" he laughs, bringing me in for a hug. I glare into his eyes, which are bloodshot and red-rimmed. He's high as a fucking kite. The girl takes a step back and smiles as he gives me a sloppy kiss on the top of my head.

"Irish—this is Martina! Marlina...Marsheena, right?!" He bats her arm tenderly, and she laughs.

"Mandisa!" she corrects him through her giggles, offering her hand to me as she leans into his side.

Daniel smiles dopily. "Mandisa! Yes!" He drapes himself over her as he slurs at me. "Doesn't she sound like a fucking music box? What a voice!" He slaps me on the chest.

He's lucky I don't pop him in the jaw right then and there. "Lovely." I stare at them both stonily.

"You're from…Kenya…no—shit!" Daniel chortles and rubs his face as she laughs and shakes her head. "Somewhere in Africa…but Irish—" He whacks me again. "She lives like…just across the way in Cypress Hills… She's a Queens girl! Isn't that crazy?!"

He gives her a high five and pulls her back under his other arm, both of them laughing like he just said the funniest thing ever.

I nod and use as much restraint as I can muster, carefully stepping forward. "Well, I certainly hate to break this up, but we've got to get going." I glare at him. "Party's over."

He gawks at me and laughs. "Wait a second—we just got here!" he yells, bumping hips with Mandisa. "Where are the girls?"

I bite my tongue so hard I swear I draw blood. At least he not so far gone that he can't remember why we came. "The girls are gone, Daniel. They left."

He wrinkles his nose and squints toward the exit. "Are you serious? They left? Bummer!" He giggles and shrugs at Mandisa. "Guess we'll have to make our own fun…"

"Yeah, I don't think so." I draw a sharp breath and take him roughly by arm. "We're leaving too, Daniel. Time to go home."

"What are you talking about?" he snorts, trying to pull away. "It's early!"

I hold firm and nod at Mandisa. "Sorry, darling… He's got a doctor's appointment in the morning—highly contagious…"

She cringes and puts her hands up, taking two steps back.

Daniel, on the other hand, glares at me as I lead him away. "You're unbelievable!" he grits out, glancing back over his shoulder. "I could have made it with that girl—"

"I know the feeling!" I snap, crossing across the back of the club to try to avoid the crowd. "You really blew it tonight, Daniel—for everyone! You should have seen Muriel's face…"

"Muriel? You said she left!" he shouts, bucking me off.

I turn on him, my teeth bared. "After she saw you with your

tongue down that girl's throat—Jesus!" My voice is venomous. "What's wrong with you?"

"She saw me? Just now?" He stares off into space, running a hand slowly through his hair.

I snarl and grab his arm again, dragging him toward the front. "Yes, you idiot! And you...*destroyed* her! Congratulations!"

We bulldoze past the purple leather booths off to the side, groups of glamorous people staring as we go. A particularly raucous gathering of partygoers stops me in my tracks, however, gridlocking us in the aisle. I turn my head—and through my rage, I see a familiar face.

The crowd breaks in front of the last booth, only one occupant—an older man wearing an exquisitely tailored suit, a bright pocket square visible from the left breast of his suit jacket. I suck in a breath—it's Mr. Callaghan. He hasn't been into the restaurant since our tete-a-tete a couple months ago; I thought...dreaded... that he was dead.

He looks up and sees me.

For a minute, we just stare at one another, not knowing quite what to do. Finally, Callaghan raises his glass to me, toasting with what I'm sure is a fine brandy. The hackles go up on the back of my neck. Somewhere, deep inside, I know that this situation just escalated from infuriating to dangerous. I blink.

"We have to go—now," I bark to Daniel, tightening my grip on his wrist and moving swiftly to the exit.

Daniel huffs behind me. "All right...jeez! I'm coming!" He winces, wrenching his hand away. "I'll walk, warden! I'll walk..."

"Good. Now shut your mouth and move."

I nervously prod him forward, not stopping to see if Callaghan is still looking.

*

"I don't get what you're so worked up about..." Daniel sighs as he tosses his suit jacket up on his bunk. "I'm not mad about that girl...uh...Mandy...Mandika..."

I let the attic door slam behind me, briefly hoping the noise doesn't wake Martin before my anger swallows me whole again. "Mandisa! And the fact that you think this has anything to do with her speaks volumes about your level of stupidity!" I wrench my tie off and throw it on the floor.

Daniel snorts. "*You* cock-blocked *me*! If anyone should be pissed—"

"You ruined everything!" I shout, my face growing hot. Daniel stares at the floor. "Like you always do! You turned what was supposed to be a fun night into a rollercoaster ride through Hell—complete with enough cocaine to float a ruddy boat!" I kick the side of the bed with my shoe, regretting it instantly. Daniel glares at me and opens his mouth to interrupt, but I silence him with my hand.

"And I wouldn't mind it so much if it was just your own life that you were mucking up, but now you're hurting people *I* care about," I hiss, taking a step toward him. He instinctually backs up. "And I won't stand for that, Daniel. Mark my words—"

"What's the big deal? It was just one girl at a club! If they had stuck around for more than half a second, we could've had a great time—"

"You broke her heart, Daniel!" I bellow, shoving him in the chest. His eyes go wide, and I back up, trying to compose myself. "Muriel's in love with you! And if you weren't so fucking daft, you would see that." I exhale and tug at my hair. "I don't understand it. She's one of the kindest, sweetest people in the world...and certainly prettier than all the other girls you go round with!" I balk at him. "She respects you and believes in you...or at least she did before tonight—"

He clenches his jaw. "Yeah? And how do you think that all ends?" he snaps, tearing open the window before lighting up a cigarette. "Think it through, Irish! I ask her out, take her on a few dates, buy her flowers…have dinner with her and her dad…" He scoffs and chews the end of his smoke. "And then what? Buy her a ring? Get married and pop out a couple kids? Yeah, right." He shakes his head and glares out the window.

I shake my head. "You make it sound like a bad thing! I get that it's not cool…or the rock 'n' roll way…" I wave up at the posters on the wall. "But why is it such a sin to just be happy together, like we were that first night on the roof?"

He laughs coldly. "You honestly think I could make a girl like Muriel *happy*?" He laughs even harder. "That's a joke, right?" He looks over at me. "She'd be miserable… We both would." He takes another draw before tossing the rest of the cigarette out the window and popping up on the desk.

I cross my arms and lean against the bedframe, my face pinched. "That's a copout, and you know it," I whisper. "You haven't even tried. You're a coward."

"Screw you! You don't know what the hell you're talking about!" His voice breaks, and he buries his face in his hands before taking a breath and looking back at me. "Don't you get it? I'm trying to protect her!"

I glare at him quizzically.

"You're right," he snarls. "She is the sweetest, kindest person in the world…and if given the chance, I would walk all over her." He sighs and rakes a hand through his hair. "Yeah…maybe it would be okay in the beginning…and we'd be happy and in love, just like you and Jillian…" I react at the sound of her name. "But then you know things would change, and not for the better." Daniel chews his nails and looks back out the window. "I'd fuck it up…like I do with everything, just like you said."

My gaze softens, and my rage starts to ebb. "Daniel, I didn't mean…"

"No…you're right." He shrugs and sits back. "I don't deserve a girl like her. And she certainly doesn't deserve me… No one does." He gets quiet and tucks his feet under him.

I feel my hands start to quake. I've never heard him talk like this before—so defeated, so destructive. "Daniel," I reply softly after a minute. "None of that's true. You're…you're a good person."

"But not as good as you." He says this with a wary smile, no sarcasm or antagonism. I go speechless as he unfolds himself from the desk and moves over to the bed, clambering up into his bunk.

I sigh and approach him. "Hey." I poke my head through the wooden rail, trying to read his expression. "Let's sort this out—we can fix it together…"

"No, I'm tired. I just wanna sleep." He rolls over so I can't see his face. "It's all for the best, Irish. You'll see."

He pulls up his blanket, and I know we're done. With a sigh, I kill the light and kick off my shoes before settling into my own bed, the room eerily quiet tonight without Daniel's music going. I close my eyes and hear him clear his throat.

"So was Jillian totally pissed at me?" he asks, his voice muffled.

I can't help but laugh. "Oh…you were about to learn the true meaning of 'hot Irish temper.'" I chuckle, resting my arms behind my head. "She is *not* happy with you."

"Yeah?" He laughs with me, shifting in his bunk.

"Yeah…let's just say that you're getting off easy with just me, mate." I tuck my pillow under my ear. "I would tread very carefully next time you see her… I know I will."

"Yikes!" he exclaims. I grunt in agreement. "But I bet that only makes her hotter…you know…in bed."

"Shut up, Daniel."

I exhale and hunker down, hearing him laugh quietly above me as I drift off to sleep.

CHAPTER 17
LOS ANGELES—PRESENT DAY

J'M TAKING MY first sip of my morning coffee when I hear a knock at the door. Mary Carmen looks up from her newspaper, her eyes darting between me and the front hall. "You expecting someone? Daniel?" she asks in her usual cautious tone.

I rub my face tiredly. Daniel was quiet the whole way home on the bus last night, his face pensive. He mumbled something about coming by in the afternoon later today…but I doubt this is him now.

I shake my head at Mary Carmen. "No…but it could be, like…the UPS guy," I grumble, getting up from the kitchen table. "It's Christmas Eve tomorrow… Can't it just be something trivial for once instead of World War III?"

Mary Carmen scoffs and pulls a pencil from behind her ear, starting in on today's Sudoku. "We should be so lucky…" Whoever is waiting knocks again. "Okay. Shout the code word if it's bad."

I roll my eyes. "'Enchilada'—did it have to be food? Couldn't it be something cool like 'chromoplast' or 'labyrinth'?"

She doesn't look up from her puzzle. "I would never remember that! I would think you were just yelling at the TV or something."

"Whatever," I mutter as I slouch down the hall to the entry-way, straightening my sweats in an attempt to be more present-able. I open the door, my eyes widening in surprise. "Jodie!" I exclaim, as she stands in her winter coat, grinning on the front porch. She bounces on the balls of her feet and holds up a large white envelope.

"I got in!" she cries, thrusting the envelope into my hands. "Oh my God—Christa! I got in!"

Still not totally processing, I look at the upper corner of the paper, where 'Yale University' is printed in regal blue script. I shake my head—Enchilada.

"Holy cow…wow!" I try to match my expression to hers, full of excitement. "That's…this is amazing, Jodie." The envelope suddenly weighs 20 pounds in my hands. "Congratulations."

Jodie exhales as I give it back to her, nodding manically. "I know! I couldn't believe it when I got the mail this morning. It's still not real… You know, I've been checking and checking obses-sively online to see if there was a status change…and then this came…" She smiles at me, clutching the envelope to her chest. "And it was like this huge weight was lifted off me, and I can breathe again—you know?"

Her eyes search mine, and I lean into the doorframe, holding on for support as I try to figure out my own emotions. "Yeah…" I grimace, happy for her, but feeling a sense of creeping, confusing sadness as well.

I exhale and look at her, reticent. "So…you're not mad any-more—about what happened with the scouts from Stanford?" I don't say the "D" word again, but I'm thinking it, loud and hot in my head.

Jodie blinks, like she's completely forgotten about yesterday. "What—oh…no!" She sighs and shakes her head, taking a step toward me. "No…I'm not mad. If anything, I'm worried about you." Watching me draw back into the entryway, she gives me an exasperated look. "Which I think is a pretty normal reaction when your best friend starts yelling stuff about made-up storybook creatures in public!" She gives an uncomfortable laugh and looks at me.

I glance down at the porch, pulling my hands into my sweatshirt sleeves. "You think that stuff's made up? I mean…Demons?" I ask quietly, looking back at her. Maybe I should just shut up and be relieved that she's so ready to move past all this. But no, it wouldn't be a day ending in Y if I didn't smack a hornet's nest at least once.

Jodie shakes her head. "I mean…yeah—unless you're counting the personal variety." She frowns, trying to read my face. "Don't you? I never took you to be…like, a Bible thumper fundamentalist or whatever!" She laughs at the thought. "Don't get me wrong, I'm the product of thirteen years of parochial school, too—I feel pretty solid on my Catechism…and I *believe* in God…" She continues to stare me down. "But like—Demons and…what—*Angels*?" I tense and close the door behind me as she says the last word in a hushed voice. "That's starting to go a little too far out of the box for me."

"I never said anything about Angels," I interrupt, crossing my arms.

Jodie shrugs. "I know. I just thought, you know, if there are bad guys…Demons—" She twitters her finger ghoulishly. "—then there must be good guys too, right? Black and white?"

I sigh. "It's not that simple." Shut up, Christa, before you shoot yourself in the foot again.

Jodie nods and looks down at her boots. "Well, whatever." She sucks in a breath and looks back at me with a smile. "The reason I really came here today was to say I'm sorry." She bats my arm as I startle in surprise at her apology, "For what I said about you… after Science Club." She reaches for my hand. "I didn't mean what I said. I should have never said any of that stuff about your life… your situation… What do I know, anyway?" She shakes her head at the porch floor.

I cringe; she was pretty spot-on with her assessment, if I remember correctly. The truth always stings the most. "It's fine," I mumble, letting her hold my hand. "I know you didn't mean it."

Jodie smiles at me. "Friends again?" I nod, and she gives my fingers a final squeeze before letting go. "I've just been so on edge with all this stupid admissions stuff!" She gives the envelope a frustrated wave, laughing. "Now that it's finally over, I can be a person again." She pauses and watches me, so I nod and try to look...normal.

She clears her throat. "You have to know, the minute I got my acceptance, you were the first person I wanted to tell." She blushes and peeks up at me. "I haven't even told my parents yet—I just jumped in the car and drove here." Her eyes start to water. "I have to know you're okay with this—that you're happy for me."

"Of course I'm happy. It's just...*Yale.*" I take a deep breath, letting the word fall heavily off my tongue. "It's like in Connecticut...far." My heart sinks—I'm never going to see her again. We've always done everything together, ever since second grade. I feel my own eyes start to tear up.

Jodie's face falls, and she crosses her arms. "I know...but it's only a plane ride away, and I'll come back for breaks." She puts her smile back in place and gives me a nudge with her foot. "Besides, you don't even know where *you're* going yet! I know you've always had your heart set on Stanford, but you've also mentioned Northwestern...or NYU..." She nods excitedly. "How cool would that be—you'd be in New York, and we could take the train to visit each other? We'd have so much fun..."

"I'm not going to get into any of those schools, Jodie," I whisper, resigned, putting my hands in my sweat pockets.

She shakes her head, and I give her a weak smile. *Sacrifice...* the word that's been haunting me for the last few days. No, my new best-case scenario is saving the world and then living to *not* tell anyone about it. Community college would be my reward for not dying a horrible death...and I know that's stretching it.

I catch myself sighing, spaced out, then look back at Jodie, realizing we're still standing on the cold front porch. She stares at me, concerned. "Don't say that," she chides, her brow pinched. "You've been working so hard since you got back... There's still a chance. I could help you—with your applications? We could do it right now!" Jodie watches me, her gaze desperate.

I shrug with a grin. "I know...but..." I really want to get this limelight off of me. "Today is about you! Why don't you come in for a while." Jodie turns pink again as I hold open the door and motion grandly. "Mary Carmen and I were just finishing up breakfast, and I know she'll be super happy for you...and we were thinking about calling up the boys and going to a movie—you wanna come? My treat...for the new Yalie." I smile widely.

Jodie beams at me and nods. "That sounds awesome! What are we seeing?"

She steps into the threshold, and I close the door behind us. "The new *Texas Chainsaw Massacre*... I told Mary Carmen it's a political documentary about deforestation in the South."

Jodie snickers. "They don't really *have* forests in the South—do they?"

"That's the 'massacre' part," I moue.

Jodie bites her lip mischievously and pulls out her phone, sending a text. "I'm in. Just telling my parents we're going to see that Pixar movie that just came out."

"Glad to see that your Ivy League acceptance hasn't turned you totally nicey-nice," I chuckle. "Wouldn't want you to go all stuffy and goody-two-shoes now."

She arches a brow, tucking her phone away. "Yeah, Francine's got that base covered. One Anne Hathaway in the family is enough..." She stops in the doorway and looks at me, suddenly self-conscious. "Yale is...a bigger deal than Brown, right? I mean...I know they're both top-tier schools..."

I chuckle and link arms with her. "Yes, Yale is totally a bigger deal... Didn't all those Wall Street creeps who stole everybody's money go to Yale?" Jodie balks and pretends to stomp on my foot. I grin. "I'm just saying— that was some hardcore white collar crime—they practically got away with murder! They obviously learned from the best. That could be you!"

We both laugh and head into the kitchen.

*

"Hey…move over one. I wanna sit next to Jodie." I give Daniel a light shove as we shuffle down the cramped theater aisle, my hip knocking into the faded red chair cushions. Daniel rolls his eyes, holding the bucket of popcorn over his head as Jodie and I push past him.

"We can *both* sit next to Jodie…" he teases, settling into a seat. Neither one of us has brought up what happened at Adler's, a subject I think we're both happy to avoid for now. "I wouldn't mind an aisle, though, for the extra legroom… Always feel like I'm trying to squeeze into a VW Bug in these seats." His knees bob against the chair backs in front of us.

I shake my head as Jodie takes her seat between us. "This place is filling up, and you gotta save a spot for Benny—just put something over that one…and don't hog the popcorn!" I point to the last chair in the row.

Daniel sighs and hands Jodie the bucket before tossing his jacket across the empty seat. "I'm surprised to see so many people turning out for a horror movie in the middle of the day," he comments, nodding down at the growing crowd of high school kids sitting in the front rows as he stuffs his hand into the popcorn.

"Everyone's out on break…and it's a *political documentary*!" I hiss loudly as Mary Carmen comes up behind me, rifling through her giant mom purse.

"Christa…did I bring my glasses?" She furrows her brow. "Or did I leave them in the kitchen this morning?"

I sigh and reach up to the top of her head, where her spectacles are perched over her dark hair. Gently, I bring them down to her nose, and she gives me a grateful smile. "Ah! Thank you…" We both sit, and I take off my coat as she continues to go through her stuff.

She pulls out a couple of boxes of candy and hands them down to us, pressing a finger to her lips. "I know I shouldn't… but the pharmacy prices are so much better than what they charge at Concessions!" Mary Carmen's eyes widen, her voice hushed. Jodie smiles her thanks as I pass her a box of Junior Mints. "Do you think it's okay? Are we hurting their business?" She suddenly stares at the candy in our hands, her expression worried.

I snicker. "Yeah…you opting to spend $5 at Rite Aid instead of here is really going to bring down AMC's bottom line." Mary Carmen frowns, so I nudge her with my shoulder. "It's *fine*, Mary Carmen! Of all the things to stress about, bootleg movie candy is very low on the list."

"Hmm…okay." She exhales and goes back to looking intently through her purse.

I shake my head and turn back to Jodie and Daniel. "So… Jodie got into Yale," I say with a smug grin.

Jodie smiles and puts her face in her hands as Daniel taps his mouth. "I think I might have heard about that in the car on the way over…whispered in secret!" He laughs and collides into Jodie. "Kind of a big deal!"

"Yeah, I guess…" Jodie grins bashfully, clearly pleased with all the attention. "I'm still getting used to the idea."

"Does this mean you're going to start dressing like a total smarty-pants, wearing tweed jackets and plaid all the time?" I joke, my eyes crinkling. "Oh, wait…we *already* wear plaid all the time!"

"Shut up!" Jodie giggles, slapping my leg. "*That* is one thing I can't wait for—not having to wear our stupid uniforms every day! Finally getting to wear whatever I want, *do* whatever I want…" She looks between us excitedly. "So much freedom!"

"I don't know if you're ready for civilian life." I smirk. "Or if it's ready for you."

"Twenty bucks says Jodie comes back for Thanksgiving next year with a nose ring and a *My Little Pony* tattoo," Daniel chimes in.

"I will take that bet…and raise you leather bondage pants." I laugh, giving him a high five behind her shoulders.

Jodie balks. "Come on, you guys—don't make fun of me!" She laughs with us. "That's not nice…"

"You're right." I nod to pacify her. "Forget *My Little Pony*… It would totally be *Strawberry Shortcake*."

"With an eyepatch," Daniel agrees. "Cutthroat."

"Stop!" Jodie pretends to beat us up, then nods down at the doors. "Thank goodness—Benny's here."

"Over here, Woo!" Daniel calls, holding up a hand.

Benny glances up and grins when he spots us, bringing with him another enormous bucket of popcorn. With a grunt, he settles into the seat next to Daniel, his puffy black parka ballooning up around him.

"Sup, homes." He shoots him a fist bump, then nods at Jodie and me. "4.0, Christa…"

"Hey, Benny." I smile, pouring myself a handful of M&Ms from one of the illicit Rite Aid boxes.

Benny glances down the aisle at Mary Carmen, still engrossed with her purse, then smacks Daniel on the chest. "Why couldn't you get me a seat next to Mary Carmen?" he grumbles, shoveling some popcorn into his mouth. "You wanna keep me all to yourself or something?"

Daniel chuckles. "Yeah…I might need to hold your hand during the scary parts."

"Seriously, bro!" Benny frowns. "How am I supposed to work my game all the way over here? I can't even talk to her…"

Daniel rubs his forehead. "You know I love you, Benny…but she is *way* out of your league. Like, another Universe. Take my word for it."

I sigh. Welcome to the club, Benny.

Benny nods, unoffended. "I get it, Daniel—she's smoking hot...like, beer commercial hot...and I know how protective you are over all your ladies." He waves down at the three of us. "You know I wouldn't do her wrong, if given the shot."

Daniel sighs. "I know you wouldn't, Benny. You're a stand-up guy." He checks Mary Carmen. "But I don't think she's looking for a relationship right now. She's working on some 'me' time." I roll my eyes as he gives a little cough.

Benny nods. "Respect... I can wait."

Daniel shoots me a look, and I shrug. Meanwhile, Mary Carmen's lips twist into a pout. "I can't find those Halls," she mutters into the depth of her purse. "I know I just bought a new bag." She starts pulling items out and lays them in my lap: keys, wallet, phone, travel Kleenex, old transit passes, contacts case, gum... I huff as the stuff keeps coming.

"So typical—you always do this!" I complain, juggling an ancient point-and-shoot camera and a pocket sewing kit. "We're fine! Just put all this stuff back. The movie's about to start—"

"Ah! Found them!" She grins, holding up a bag of cough drops. She gives them to me and points down the row, starting to gather up the contents from my lap. I snort and chuck the bag at Daniel, who looks up in surprise.

"For your grog." I scrunch my nose, motioning around the now jam-packed theater. "Wouldn't want to disturb the other patrons."

Daniel glares at me, but pops one into his mouth and tosses them back to Mary Carmen. "Thanks, Grandma," he jokes with a grin.

Mary Carmen stops what she's doing and tuts. "What—*Grandma*?" she squeals.

Daniel laughs, taking another handful of popcorn. "Sorry, I know you prefer *abuela*..." He flashes his brows.

Mary Carmen opens her mouth to retort, but Benny cuts in. "What's a-matter with you, dawg? You don't go around calling beautiful women 'Grandma'…" He quickly takes off his baseball cap and brushes back his hair Dapper Dan style before puckering his lips at Mary Carmen. "She is obviously no one's grandma. Good afternoon, Mary Carmen." His tone is all sugar and sweet.

Mary Carmen smiles warmly back at Benny behind her glasses, oblivious to his come-on. "Hello, Benjamin… So nice to see you again! Are you getting excited for the holiday?"

"Yes, *Benjamin*," Daniel snickers into his ear. "Are you excited?"

Benny ignores him. "Excited to spend it with you," he purrs at her, jerking his chin. "Celebrating the birth of our savior *together*…"

I put my face in my palm, hiding my giggles. Mary Carmen closes her eyes and nods earnestly. "Mmm…it really is a wondrous day…meant to be shared with family." She gives my knee a pat, and the theater goes dark. "Ooh! We're starting!"

I turn forward and watch as the movie screen comes to life, a couple of car commercials going off in succession before the silence-your-phone message plays. The giddy anticipation that I get every time before the previews wells in my stomach; hands down, this is the best part of the movie-going experience for me.

I glance across Jodie to Daniel, who is also watching excitedly, chowing down handfuls of popcorn. He feels my eyes on him and turns, giving me a wink. I blush and smile back, popping some more M&Ms into my mouth as the bright green preview screen comes up. We stare, waiting for it to go away and play the first attraction—but the green remains longer than it should, frozen in place.

I glance between Daniel and Jodie, then crane my neck back to the projector window. "Is the disc stuck?" I narrow my eyes, my distrust in digital projectors only growing stronger by the minute. Call me a purist, but they should never have made the switchover from film.

Mary Carmen shakes her head next to me. "I don't know… Do you want me to go out and ask someone?"

We all turn back to the screen as it pops to black, a green circle ring of flash blindness remaining in the center of the screen. "Ah—here we go…" Mary Carmen smiles and snuggles into her seat. I blink, willing the circle to fade…but, like the preview screen before it, it seems permanently imprinted. Stuck.

"Do you see that? What the Hell…" I grumble, looking back at Daniel irritably.

He pops up on his chair, his neck craning around the dark theater. "I don't like this…" he hisses, trying to keep his voice down as the rest of the audience starts to grow restless. Jodie glances up at Daniel, and I feel Mary Carmen tense next to me.

"Is that—?" Mary Carmen narrows her eyes, staring at the screen. I look too and focus on the green circle, slowly realizing that it's not my mind playing tricks on me…but a logo—one I could never forget.

"Holy shit—Daniel—" I gasp, reaching across Jodie to bat his arm.

"I know," he replies, not taking his eyes off of it, the circle growing and coming into focus: a snake eating its own tail…the ouroboros.

"What is going on?" Jodie shakes her head in confusion. "Is this part of the trailers?"

I wet my lips and sit forward, alarmed. A series of chimes go off, and my breath stops. "No—" I utter as the screen switches suddenly from black to bright white, a large, familiar face smiling down on us. "No way—"

"Hello, and welcome to Serpentine." The head blinks, his almond eyes pleasant. Jodie and the rest of the crowd calmly settle back into their seats, while Daniel, Mary Carmen, and I stare dumbfounded.

Panic streaks through my gut. "No…it can't be!" I rasp,

wrapping my arms protectively around myself, instantly flashing back to the Warehouse.

The face opens its mouth again to speak. "Times are changing; the world is changing," Serpentine begins, his gaze penetrating. "This is evident every day in our news, on the internet, in how we live our daily lives." He smiles, more smug this time. "It's changing in ways *most* of you couldn't even begin to comprehend..."

"Daniel," I whisper urgently. "We should go—"

He looks past Jodie to me, his jaw tight, then nods. We both start to get up.

"Sit down, Christa," Serpentine says, keeping his voice even. Mary Carmen grasps my wrist, and I do as I'm told, Daniel and I shifting back into our seats. I look at Jodie, then over at Benny. They're both still watching the screen with dazed expressions, clearly not having registered that the face just said my name out loud. It's some sort of spell or mortal mind-meld, rendering pretty much everyone in this theater totally vulnerable. Terror seizes my whole body.

Serpentine gives a small nod. "As I'm sure you and your team have discovered on your quest, nothing in our world is quite what it seems... Up can be down, left can be right, good can be bad and vice-versa." He arches a brow knowingly.

I glance at Daniel, his own face a mix of panic and rage. "Yeah...what's your point?" I find myself whispering up to the screen. Serpentine gives a tight smile in response, and I bite my tongue. Yep—he can hear me. Of course he can hear me.

"You might think you understand the current state of affairs, but the lines are more blurred than you realize," Serpentine continues. "And while you have yet to choose Dark or Light, there have been many behind the scenes trying to make change happen from the inside."

I grind my teeth. "I *have* chosen...Light! I told Alden the same thing last time!" I stop, forcing myself not to go back to

Level 3 and instead look between Daniel and Mary Carmen. She returns my look and gives my fingers a squeeze.

Serpentine nods. "But your actions have yet to speak for themselves," he explains, his face placid despite the fact that he's holding an entire movie theater hostage. "And as the hour of change grows closer—"

"Ahh! What does that even mean—'*the hour of change grows closer*?!" I exclaim, making Mary Carmen jump in her seat. "Can't you people just say what you mean for once and get to the point?"

"Christa…" Mary Carmen's voice is low and nervous.

I shake my head and glare back at Serpentine. "Is this about Herod's Feast? Are you on my ass looking for an RSVP, too?" I shout up at the screen.

"Christa! How do you know about that?!" Mary Carmen sputters as Serpentine laughs. It's sort of mechanical and distorted-sounding, and it's weird to see his face move like that.

"No, Christa, this meeting is not about Herod's Feast." His teeth flash white across the screen, and I shrink down in my chair. He stops laughing and stares at me, eyes cold.

"Then what?" I mutter into my chest, not wanting to meet his gaze.

Serpentine blinks. "Please recall your recent trip to Porticullis… What information did the Agent share with you?" He stares.

Mary Carmen's head spins like she's straight out of *The Exorcist*. "Excuse me…WHAT DID HE SAY?!!" she barks in my ear, then glares at Daniel. "You took her to Porticullis? When?! *How?!*"

"Not now, Mary Carmen…" Daniel whispers. She bares her teeth and throws herself back into her chair, crossing her arms in a huff. I ignore them both as I try to remember everything from our visit with the Gray.

"She…she told us about the prophecy—what would happen if I chose Light or Dark," I start to ramble off.

"Yes. What else?" Serpentine nods.

"She asked Daniel a bunch of questions about his past—how he's been here for like, forty years…" I cringe, not wanting to hurt him by bringing that bit up again.

"It's okay," Daniel murmurs, smiling reassuringly.

Serpentine's mouth is mashed into a thin line that almost looks impatient. "After that…" he says, sounding slightly rushed and glancing off-screen for a second. "About choosing to close Heaven or Hell…?" He looks at me expectantly.

"Uh…yeah," I bite my lip in thought. "Hell wants me to choose Dark and close Heaven, making them the only game in town and displacing a bunch of Seraphim," I recite almost word for word. "And Heaven wants me to choose Light, which would close Hell…basically turning Earth into a real-life version of Arkham Asylum." I shake my head. "Both amazing choices, I'm sure you can see…but…" I sigh and look at Daniel. "Like I said… I already chose Light, so…bring on the serial killers, I guess."

Serpentine sighs. This is the most…Human…I've ever seen him. He's still looking for something. "The Agent gave you a very valuable piece of information that I need you to recall RIGHT NOW." His voice rises. "I need you to say it, Christa… If I need to help coax your memory…" His eyes hone in on Jodie, still smiling lazily up at the screen. "We have ways of helping that thought process move faster."

I feel Mary Carmen sit forward in her seat as I gasp and turn to my zoned-out best friend. I pull my knees to my chest and snarl at Serpentine. "I'M TRYING—GOD!" I tear my hands through my hair. "She told us about the prophecy, about Light and Dark, what Hell wants—" A lightbulb goes off. "Wait…not *all* of Hell wants me to close Heaven!"

I stare as Serpentine breaks into a huge grin. "YES. GO ON." His voice booms around the theater.

I take a breath and scooch up. "She mentioned a movement— a…a Resistance!" I jerk my face toward Daniel, who is nodding vigorously. "They want me to close Hell as well, going against the other Demons." I narrow my eyes at Serpentine. "Is…is that what this is? Are you part of…are *you* Resistance?" Can a computer program *be* part of a Resistance? Part of *anything*?

Serpentine's smile fades, and he pulls his face back a bit, still staying in frame. "Yes, this is a message from the Resistance, Christa, reinforcing your choice to go Light." His eyes dart across all of us, his gaze severe. "When the time comes, under all circumstances, you must choose to close the gates of Hell…even if it goes against everything you might…feel or…want…in that moment." He blinks, pursing his lips, like he's trying to figure out those sorts of emotions.

I scoff. "Uh…okay. I already said I would do that—but… thanks for the memo, I guess?" I shrug and turn to Daniel, who is now looking down at his shoes.

Serpentine clears his throat, getting my attention. "The consequences of you choosing Dark would be truly catastrophic. What is written in the stars cannot be undone by forceful hands, but only through a change in one small, simple action…"

I roll my eyes. "There you go again, talking in code."

Serpentine stops, his face pinched, his eyes flashing red for a brief second. A wave of fear comes over me as I remember the last time that happened, but the moment passes quickly, and I see he's… annoyed with me. A non-corporeal being is annoyed with me. I hide my smile behind my sleeve.

"DON'T GO TO HEROD'S FEAST." He speaks slow and loud, making the three of us jump.

I glance between Daniel and Mary Carmen, then nod up at the screen. "Yeah—all right. I got it," I mumble.

Serpentine looks down for a second, collecting himself. When he looks back up, he's his usual disassociated self. "The Resistance appreciates your time, Catalyst. Go forward and choose wisely." He nods, pressing his hand flat to the screen. A faint outline of a handprint obfuscates him for a moment before clearing again, a dull glow emitting out into the seats.

I blink, and he's gone, the screen back to normal, playing a preview for some action thriller. A dull murmur resonates from the audience, as people shake their heads and readjust their jackets and bags. Jodie turns to me, rubbing her eyes. "That was a weird trailer! But I haven't been to a horror movie in a while… When did they say it was coming out? Summer?" She giggles, putting her hands in her lap.

I look over at her and startle, almost choking on my own spit. "Oh my God—Jodie—" I stare into her eyes, which are now burning bright gold.

Daniel sees my reaction and goes pale, turning and checking Benny. I can see Benny's eyes glowing in the dark as well. "No— not you, man…" Daniel breathes.

Benny looks at Daniel and laughs. "What? I got something on my face?" He snorts and brushes popcorn off his parka. Daniel jerks back toward me with an expression of panic.

"It's all of them…" Mary Carmen murmurs, craning to scan the crowd. "Every single one of them is Haloing."

I grip my chair and spin back to where Jodie is happily munching her Junior Mints, completely unaware of what's happened. I look over at Daniel and point to my own face. "Am I…?" I ask.

He shakes his head, staring at me quizzically. "No, you're not."

I draw in a breath, not knowing if this is good or bad news. Mortals are supposed to Halo, or bare their souls, after they've witnessed a miraculous act—but whatever sent everyone else off today didn't register with me…not like before.

I stare out into the sea of firefly eyes now illuminating the theater, humbled by the sight of them. Everyone suddenly seems so fragile, breakable. I frown and check out my own metallic blue hands glowing in my lap. I don't know if it's because I'm Smudged or what, but I'm definitely different.

It's something to ask Daniel about later. Now, however, I take a deep breath and turn to Mary Carmen. "What do we do?" I whisper.

She exhales, her face concerned. "I'm not sure... We can't look after everyone—there have to be at least two hundred people here. There aren't enough Guardians in the whole state to take care of this..." Her eyes dart frantically over the audience. "They are all at risk right now. I don't know..."

Suddenly, she gasps and sticks her finger in her right ear, like she's just heard something loud and piercing. She doubles over in her seat.

"Mary Carmen!" I cry, getting everyone's attention.

"Is she okay?" Jodie asks, trying to keep her voice down as the movie begins.

Daniel crouches down and zips over to us, putting his hands on Mary Carmen's knees. "What is it?" he demands, his tone urgent. "What did They say?"

Mary Carmen draws in a sharp breath and stares at him. "There have been similar attacks all over," she rasps, her head lolling forward. "A couple more movie theaters, on TV... People are out walking around with their souls totally exposed." She closes her eyes and tries to sit up. "Hell is furious, saying it wasn't them... blaming it on Guardians—but they'll be out tonight reaping the benefits for sure. No one is even talking about the Resistance." She takes a breath. "I think Serpentine was just for us. We have to do something." She shakes her head wearily.

Daniel nods and turns to me. "We should get you home." He takes my hands, "You're not safe outside..."

"I'm *fine*!" I huff, waving at my face. "I'm not even Haloing! Let me help!"

"No, it's too dangerous." Daniel gets to his feet. "This is a direct assault on us, and we are getting you out of here. Walk now, or I *will* carry you..."

"Jeez! Fine—okay!" I hiss, gathering up my stuff.

Jodie looks at me, puzzled. "What's up?" She blinks, her eyelids shuttering her glowing eyes like venetian blinds.

I cringe as I shrug into my jacket. "Mary Carmen's not feeling well. We have to get her home," I say, thinking fast. "I'm going to drive her car. I'm sorry...I know we all came over together, so I need to take you home with us now, too."

Jodie smiles. "That's okay. I don't really mind... I just came out because I wanted to hang with you guys." She waves up at the screen. "We'll catch this when it comes out on DVD."

"Great..." I nod, relieved, and glance over at Benny. "Hey, we have to go—Mary Carmen's sick," I call to him, someone behind us shushing violently. I roll my eyes at them, and Benny cranes over, concerned.

"Is she all right? Does she need me to do anything?" He stares at Mary Carmen, who is still coming back from her rocky phone call with Heaven. I bite my lip...I don't want Benny out on the streets where some douchebag Demon can get him, either.

"Yes...chicken soup! You should come back to the house and make her some—we should have everything you'll need!" I exclaim.

Benny's face lights up. "I can do that...I've got a killer recipe that uses just a little bit of chili powder, which actually settles the stomach..."

"SHHH!!" the grumpy guy behind us hisses again.

Benny shoots him a dirty look. "Chill, bro! This isn't a funeral home!" he shouts, getting out of his seat. He looks back at us. "I'm gonna get my truck—meet you back at the house."

"Good deal." I give him a tight smile as he leaves.

Jodie is searching around my feet. "Where's my purse?" she murmurs, flipping the chair cushion up. "Is it under you?"

I look down at the floor. "Yeah...here it is." I grab her light green bag and reach out to her.

I hear Daniel gasp next to me. "CHRISTA—NO! Don't touch her—"

But he's too late.

My fingers brush Jodie's, and my head slams back, a strange sucking sensation taking over my whole being, like I'm going through a vortex or falling down a wormhole. It only lasts a minute, though, and I find my feet, gulping for air and clutching my stomach.

I'm no longer in the movie theater, but somewhere old and familiar: a bedroom, a gold-framed poster of a faded chrysanthemum on the wall, the air hot and thick with cooking smells—peanut oil and coriander… It's Jodie's grandmother's house in Santa Barbara. I recognize it from the few times I went down with her family for Lunar New Year, although this feels further back, before my time.

"What the…where…" I gasp, quickly patting myself down. Ten fingers, ten toes… I'm all here, still wearing my winter coat and jeans. Before I have a chance to catch my breath, I startle and fall against the wall.

I'm not alone; there are three young kids standing in front of a TV on the dresser, playing some old video game. I recognize the small one in the middle, her long black hair halfway down her back. I'd know her anywhere.

"Jodie?" I whisper. She's young, probably about six or seven. She's flanked by two boys with matching dark hair, both a little older than her. None of them hear me or react to my presence, a ghost from another time. This is her memory… I'm *reading* Jodie.

My knees buckle at the gravity of that thought, but I quickly pull it together and pay attention. "Get the treasure chest, Hien!" the boy on Jodie's right shouts, pointing at the TV. Hien sighs, but does as the other boy says, working the game controller like he's flying an airplane.

"I can't get it," Hien complains. "It's up too high…"

The other boy huffs, smoothing his red Old Navy t-shirt. "Then get those coins under the rock. We only have to beat fifty thousand…"

I watch Jodie squirm uncomfortably between them, her eyes trained on the screen, her fingers fidgeting at her sides. She's wearing a pink party dress. I think it's the same one she wore for her birthday later that year. I can hear women chattering down the hall from the kitchen in a language I was never able to understand, but still found the sound of comforting... Pieces of my past with Jodie, our shared past. I sigh and slouch against the wall.

"YES!" Hien yells, thrusting his hands into the air, victorious. "Sixty thousand! We win!"

"No fair!" Jodie pouts, crossing her arms. "You cheated... I saw you use that extra life before the half break."

"You're just a sore loser!" the boy in red snarks into her face. I sniff; I'm starting to find him totally annoying. "We won fair and square, and now you have to do it."

"I don't want to, Bao!" Jodie spins around, and I see her face for the first time. She's almost identical to my Jodie, with the same glasses and full lips, but a little more baby fat on her cheeks. I hold my breath; this is the same little girl that I met ten years ago. "It's gross, and Mama will be mad if my dress gets dirty."

"All you have to do is just stand there and hold it—and be quiet!" Bao sneers, glancing over at the door. "If you don't, I'm gonna tell Auntie that you broke her favorite crystal Buddha and then blamed it on the dog... She'll whip you 'til your butt falls off!" He looks over at Hien, and they both snicker.

My revulsion for both of these boys grows, and I remember them now from previous visits—Jodie's cousins. We were all older when I met them, and they would mumble perverted jokes to each other in Vietnamese whenever Jodie and I were around, not even trying to be discreet. Major losers.

Little Jodie bites her lip, worry creasing her small forehead. "It *was* the dog! Bento knocked it over with his stupid tail... I was telling the truth!" she shouts.

The boys shush her, Hien shifting nervously. "You think she's gonna believe you if *I* tell her?" Bao hisses. "She listens to everything I say. You don't stand a chance."

"Just do it, Jodie…" Hien mutters, turning back to the TV. "It won't take long, and then it'll be done."

Jodie winces, holding her arm. "No, I don't want to!" she whines, looking between Bao and the door. "Please don't tell Auntie—and don't make me…"

Bao sighs heavily. "If you're not going to do it, then I have no choice." He steps toward the door dramatically.

Jodie lets out a little shriek. "Okay, fine! Okay!" she squeals, putting her face in her hands. Bao grins and turns around, Jodie reluctantly coming to stand between them again. Hien tosses Bao the game controller, and they start another round. I narrow my eyes as they both undo their pant zippers. Jodie's shoulders slump as she raises her hands to their open flies.

Bao lets out a satisfied sigh. "Yeah, like that…and don't get mean about it!" he grunts to her as she starts to work both her hands. "If you pull it too hard, I'm gonna scream, and then everyone will know what you did…"

Rage boils in my blood as I watch Jodie hang her head in shame. I don't think I've ever hated anyone as much as I hate these boys right now—even Mandisa…Alden. This is pure, unadulterated loathing.

My vision goes cloudy, and I feel the tugging again. I suck in a breath, and I'm back in the dark movie theater, crouched on the floor between Jodie and Daniel. "Christa!" Daniel shouts next my ear.

I look up dazed into Jodie's still-Haloing face. "You never told me…" I mumble blearily, my body in one world, my mind still someplace else. "You never said anything."

Jodie furrows her brow. "Christa—what are you talking about? Are you okay?" I glance down and see her hand, palm up. I'm still holding her purse.

Slowly, I finish handing her the leather strap. Jodie nods

and continues to stare at me. "What is happening? You, Mary Carmen…" She motions over to our exhausted Seraphim, still wilting in her seat. "Was there something in the popcorn? Am I next?"

"We have to get out of here, now," Daniel breathes, helping me to my feet.

I grimace and lean on him, still reeling from being inside Jodie's head. "I know. We're going… How…how long was I gone?" I whisper into his neck when Jodie's not looking. Deja vu.

"A couple seconds—no one but me noticed," Daniel murmurs. "You don't know how to control it yet, so be careful."

"I know." I get Jodie's attention, mindful not to touch her this time. "Can you help Mary Carmen? I think she just needs a little support out to the car…"

"Of course." Jodie quickly sidles up to her, gently looping her slack arm over her shoulder.

"Daniel…" Mary Carmen rasps, her silver bangles jangling as she taps him on the back. He looks over his shoulder. "We have to call everyone—Ellis, the others… Warn them that it's starting—"

"I know. I'll take care of it," he answers, holding me steady. Mary Carmen nods and slumps into Jodie.

"Is Mary Carmen going to be okay?" I ask quietly. "I've never seen her like this…"

"She'll be fine," Daniel answers as he helps me down the stairs. "The equivalent of an air raid siren just went off in her brain. She just needs to rest."

"What's she talking about, though?" I murmur, grasping his side. "What's 'starting'?"

"The War." He looks at me gravely. "Between Good and Evil."

CHAPTER 18
NEW YORK CITY—MAY, 1976

I CAN SMELL the smoke before I even step inside the kitchen.

"Start filling those tureens with water—and get the goddamn extinguisher from the pantry!" Chef waves at Juan Julio, who goes running into the back storage room. I walk swiftly over to the sink to help Pedro lug the heavy soup tureen out of the basin, then turn to Chef. "Which one is it?" I call as Pedro and I shuffle together to the back of the kitchen.

Chef, looking more mad than alarmed, stomps through the cloud of gray smoke in front of us and waves us over to the ovens. "Who do you think? Lucy Goosey—always fuckin' trouble!" he warbles, the signature vein popping out of his forehead. I try not to choke as we stand before the accused, which is spewing spit and ash like a two-pack-a-day smoker. Without a mitt, Chef angrily wrenches the door open.

"That's hot, Chef!" I warn, but he doesn't flinch, quickly assessing the flames licking the oven walls.

"All right—put that down! Put it down!" He waves at the tureen we're holding and spins back toward the pantry. "Juan! I need that extinguisher!"

Juan Julio pokes his head around the racks. "Is expired, Chef..."

"Goddammit!" Chef roars, tearing off his cap and chucking it on the floor, his bald pate gleaming under the fluorescents. "I've got a goddamn grease fire and no fuckin' extinguisher! Jesus Mary Mother of Christ!"

His eyes dart around quickly, and he glares at the shelf above him, grabbing three boxes of baking soda. His hands fly as he rips off all of the box tops and flings them around Lucy's insides. Tossing the empty cardboard behind him, he rolls up his pant leg and starts stamping out the rest of the fire with one of his large black combat boots; Juan Julio, Pedro, and I try not to look completely terrified as we watch.

The flames eventually subside, and he pulls his foot out, a new shiny burn gleaming on his ankle. With a grunt, he waves the rest of the smoke away, crouching down by the open door.

"Well, there goes a couple hundred bucks of Beef Wellington down the drain... I know that's how I like to start my week!"

With a harsh tug, he pulls a blackened pan from the oven. The Wellington looking like something straight out of Pompeii. He throws the whole thing in the trash and goes back to Lucy. "Lemme see, motherfucker, lemme see..." He reaches in and grabs the broiler; I cringe as he lets out a yowl, the hot metal clattering as he throws it out on the kitchen floor.

"Chef—should I tell Francois we're going to be a little backed up...?"

"Mystery solved!" he crows, coming out of the oven with wild eyes. "Just as I suspected! Look at this!" He holds up his hand, which is covered in some sort of grayish goo. Juan Julio and Pedro shake their heads, going back to their stations. "Son-of-a-bitch didn't clean the goddamn oven like I told him to!" he yells. "Gonna burn the whole joint down... *Whoo—ee!*" Chef looks around maniacally. "Where is my favorite lederhosen-wearing motherfucker, huh?" He glares at me. "Where's Danny Boy at, Irish? He was supposed to be in two hours ago."

"Uh...I saw him this morning," I mutter. That's a lie—last I saw him was two days ago. I've been busy keeping my head down, studying at the library for spring quarter finals, and when I'm not there, I'm at Jillian's.

Chef narrows his eyes, but just as I think he's onto me, he waves me away. "Go tell Francois to spread the word that the Wellington is off the lunch menu... You heard it here first!" He sucks his teeth irritably. "I'll call Gino... We should be able to restock before dinner. Oh—and if you see Danny Boy before me, just tell him..." He purses his lips. "Don't tell him a god-damn thing, Irish! Just tell him I'm looking for him."

Yikes. "Yes, Chef." I turn quickly on my heels and bolt out the kitchen door.

Taking a breath, I smooth my tux before stepping over to my section, grateful that the smoky aroma stayed mostly confined to the kitchen. As I'm clearing away a few plates, I hear a low, gravelly laugh; it sends shivers down my spine.

I look up and see Mr. Callaghan back at his usual table, joking with Francois. He'd been keeping his distance these last few months, and for reasons I don't totally understand, I've been relieved about that. He hadn't been rude or malicious, only having kind words for me; one could even go so far as to say he was a friend...in a way. I suppose that the talk over the pocket square rattled me more than I realized.

Regardless, he was my responsibility right now. Francois catches my eye and nods, heading back to his spot behind the podium by the bar. Callaghan sees me and smiles. I force a return smile and move over to his side.

"Long time no see, Mr. Murphy. How you been?" He sits back in his chair, straightening his tie. Maybe he doesn't recall seeing me at that club a few weeks back...*his* club, I presume. I certainly remember him.

"Well. Thank you, sir," I reply with a curt dip of my chin. "Had a very busy spring so far, with work and classes…"

"Ah—back to school? Well done!" He chuckles and gives me a warm pat on the arm. I feel my demeanor soften, chiding myself for any weird "vibes" that I've been sensing…as Daniel would say. He was just a nice old man—who happened to own a successful nightclub and may or may not have dangerous ties to the New York underworld.

I shake my head and answer him with a grin. "Yes…just wrapping up my first quarter of business school at City College." I raise my eyebrows conversationally. "I've never studied harder in my whole life… No slouching."

"I should think not." He nods in approval. "They work you extra hard your first year—to separate the wheat from the chaff. How are your grades, if I might ask?"

"On track for straight As…" I feel my cheeks redden. "If I do all right on my exams."

Callaghan smiles down at his menu. "I'm sure you'll do fine, smart man like you." He squints and points at the list. "I think I'll go with the spring pea ravioli today, try something different. Is it any good?"

I breathe a sigh of relief, happy to not have to explain about the Wellington. "Very good, sir. I plan on tucking into a bowl myself after my shift."

He laughs. "I feel like that's the question I should have been asking along—'What are *you* eating?'"

I chuckle with him, and he hands me his menu. "Yes, sir. I'll have that right out for you."

As I turn to walk away, however, he grabs my wrist. I cringe. Oh God, not this again.

"Murphy." He takes his hand away, smoothing his napkin in his lap. "I never got a chance to say thank you for the…helpful counsel…you gave me last time I was here."

I pop the menu under my arm, surprised that he brought it

up so openly. "No need to thank me, sir... I'm just glad everything seems to have worked out."

"Indeed." He breathes through his nose, smiling tightly. "You gave me a valuable gift that day...one that I was in desperate need of." He looks up at me. "Perspective."

I tilt my head thoughtfully. "Well, I'm happy to be of help... in any way I can." I take another step away, and he holds his hand up.

"I have a gift for you. One I hope you will consider strongly." He reaches into his left breast pocket and pulls out a folded piece of paper. I stare at it quizzically as he gives it to me.

"Open it." He motions, and I do so. It's a name and phone number, written on his personal stationary.

"Who is Ferrad Adimi?" I ask, trying not to trip over the Arabic-sounding name.

Mr. Callaghan grins. "He is a friend of mine who works at the Ritz Carlton hotel." He tips his chin. "'Works' doesn't really do him justice... He pretty much runs the place, both here and across the pond." Mr. Callaghan glances up at me, his eyes twinkling. "I met him for dinner last night and mentioned that I knew a very intelligent, hardworking, ambitious young man."

My throat grows thick as he nods at me. I stare at the paper, afraid that if I look up, he might say it's all a joke. "And I told him he would be a fool not to hire you straight away, lest the competition swooped you up first." He laughs and points at the paper in my hand. "He's looking forward to your call...which I suggest you make in the next few days—Mr. Adimi is not someone you keep waiting. He's a good man, though, in both life and in business. Very honest...fair." He glances quietly out the window.

I exhale and shake my head. "Mr. Callaghan...I'm not quite sure what to say."

"Say you'll think about it. And know that this isn't some gig as a bellhop." He nods at my tux. "You would be working strictly with upper management, sitting in on their meetings, helping make important decisions..." He smiles widely. "What you were made for, Murphy." He nods at his lap. "You would have to leave your work here, of course."

"Of course..." I murmur, still in a daze. I smooth the note in my hand, not sure if any of this is really real.

Callaghan laughs and stands up. "Call him, Murphy. Do it today." He takes his hat from the rack behind him, an old-fashioned black fedora.

I startle as he puts it on top of his head. "Sir, are...are you leaving?" I take a step back to give him room. "What about your lunch?"

Mr. Callaghan gives a light shrug. "I came for what I needed: to say thank you." He pats my shoulder as he steps past me. "But I'm sure it would have been delicious."

I shake my head and watch him start to walk away, blinking. "If I do this, call your...friend, will I ever see you again, sir? Since I won't be your waiter anymore?" A sudden feeling of sadness comes over me.

Mr. Callaghan's eyes soften, seeming a paler blue since the last time I saw him. "It's probably in your best interest that we never meet again, Mr. Murphy," he murmurs, looking away. "Call Adimi... He's a good man. He'll make sure you're taken care of."

I nod, confused, before glancing back at the paper. I note the letterhead script heading at the top: *J.V.C.* His initials.

"Mr. Callaghan." I smile, holding up the note. "*John* Callaghan...but what does the 'V' stand for?"

He looks back at me warily. "John Vesper Callaghan," he replies quietly. "My mother's favorite time of day...evening vespers." He smiles and walks toward the front doors.

I watch his back as he buttons his jacket, leaving the restaurant. Francois looks over at me curiously as I exhale. I give him a shrug and tuck Adimi's phone number into my pocket, my mind swimming. Hazily, I take another table's order and move back to the kitchen feeling weightless, like I'm in a dream.

Everything seems to be back under control when I get there, Pedro and Juan Julio chopping and grilling. Chef is bent over a plate, meticulously cleaning the edge with a cloth. He sees me come in and nods. "Whatchu got, Irish?" He sets the dish he was working on under the warmer.

I come to and smile. "Two raviolis, a whitefish, and a house salad," I respond clearly.

Chef grunts and calls back to Juan Julio. "Got one filet and two ravs!" he shouts, Juan Julio stepping into action. "And I need a house, Pedro!" He looks back at me. "Everybody cool out there?"

I nod. "Yes, Chef. No one even noticed."

"Let's keep it that way," he huffs, jerking his head toward the pantry. "Make sure we let Francois know about the expired extinguisher... That's the kind of thing they bust you on during inspections."

"Of course, Ch—"

We all turn as the back service door bangs open. I see Chef's eyes flicker as Daniel walks in, out of breath, and he unzips his leather jacket.

"So nice of you to join us, Danny!" Chef calls exuberantly. He's giddy and on the warpath. I settle back on the wall to watch the show.

Daniel crosses over, running a hand through his curls. "Yeah, the tunnel was all jammed up—some sort of wreck." He clears his throat and looks over at me. "Hey, Irish."

I raise my eyebrows.

Juan Julio and Pedro keep their heads down as Chef lets out a low chuckle, fixing another plate with his dishrag. "I bet there was—must've been real nasty..." He waves over to the service station. "You need a cup of coffee or something? Take the edge off?"

I hold my breath—this is going to be amazing.

Daniel shakes his head. "No, I'm good…"

"Yeah? Oh, *good!*" With a little too much force, Chef slaps his cloth down and heads back to the ovens, motioning for Daniel to follow without looking up. Daniel sighs and slumps behind him like he's on his way to the headmaster's office, the rest of us waiting for the inevitable blow up. Covertly, I tiptoe over to the storage racks, securing myself a front-row seat.

"What the hell happened to Lucy?" Daniel asks blandly, waving at the blackened oven parts still scattered across the kitchen floor.

All smiles, Chef gives a boyish shrug. "Gosh…I dunno, Danny! Maybe some motherfuckin' elves or fairies or some shit snuck in in the middle of the night and were gettin' up to some *shenanigans!*" We all jump as he lets out a crazed laugh and kicks the discarded broiler pan clear across the room.

Daniel scowls and shoves his hands into his pockets. "You're pissed I didn't clean the oven…I get it—"

"The fuck you do!" Chef shouts, putting his finger in Daniel's face. "You think I'm just saying this stuff for my god-damn health?! Huh?!"

Daniel responds with an insolent stare. Big mistake. With a roar, Chef sweeps his hand across Lucy's supply shelf, kitchen spices exploding all over the floor. "When you gonna get it in your head that this shit is important!?" Chef grabs him roughly by the arm and drags him down to the open oven; shoving his hand in and pulling out a sticky finger full of old grease. "This is like fuckin' napalm back here! Do-you-understand-the-words-that-are-comin'-outta-my-mouth?!"

Daniel clenches his jaw and looks down at floor. "Yes! I hear you! I'm sorry," he grits out belligerently.

Chef lets him go and gets back up, rubbing the bridge of his nose. "*Sorry* doesn't cut it, boy!" He slaps his leg. "We almost burned down the whole kitchen this morning—lost a bunch of the Wellington in the process. That's money, man!" He shakes his head. "Come on! I know you're smart enough to know how much that shit stings… I was counting on you to handle this!" He waves at Lucy.

Daniel shrugs. "What do you want me to say? I shouldn't be doing these crap jobs anyway—Baxter never did any cleaning when he was Sous…"

Chef's eyes go wide. "Oh, *really*? So, lemme get this straight…" He snickers and takes a step toward Daniel. "You're too good now for the 'crap jobs' around here…now that you're my Sous? Is that right?" His voice goes up on the end. "I just want to make sure I'm hearing you clearly…in my old fuckin' age!"

I freeze and wait for Daniel's answer. Defiantly, he crosses his arms and stares back at Chef. "That's right. Make Pedro or Juan Julio do it. You hired me to cook, right?" He puckers his lips as Chef looks on in complete disbelief. "So that's what I should be doing—not bullshit housekeeping."

You could hear a bloody pin drop, both Juan Julio and Pedro letting their knives hover over their work as we all wait for Chef to respond. For a minute, his face turns beet red and balloon-like, his eyes looking like they're going to burst out of his head. Instead, he breaks into a round of applause.

Daniel falters; staring at him quizzically.

"Well, la-de-da! Roll out the red carpet—we got a fuckin' celebrity, here!" Chef exclaims, waving his arms in the air. "Somebody gimme a knife!" I duck as Pedro tosses his dangerously across the rack; like a magic trick, Chef catches it and turns it to Daniel, smiling as he offers him the handle.

"Come on, hotshot—show me what you got!" he croons, motioning for Daniel to take the knife. Hesitantly, Daniel obliges. "Blow me outta the water! Make me something I've never had before. Rock my fuckin' world!"

Daniel scoffs as Chef turns his back to him. "Oh…but the

only condition is you gotta cook it on that." He waves back to Lucy. "Try not to kill yourself."

Daniel looks down at the broken oven, and his face grows red. Quietly, he rests the knife on the counter. "You made your point," he whispers.

Chef holds a hand up to his ear, smirking. "I'm sorry...what was that?"

Daniel grinds his teeth. "You made your point!" he shouts. "You're the boss. I said I was sorry...now lemme work!"

"Yeah, I'll let you work!" Chef points down the wall. "After I can see my goddamn face in every single one of these ovens!"

"Are you serious?!" Daniel moans, tearing at his hair.

Chef gets up in his face, his voice low. "Do I look like a fuckin' comedian? Get scrubbin', boy!"

He's about to turn away, but comes back fast and roughly takes Daniel's chin in his hand. "Hey—lemme get a look at you—"

He squints as Daniel tears away from him. "God—what?! Get your hands off me!" Daniel snaps, trying to look away.

Chef grabs him again, searching Daniel's red eyes and nose. "Are you messed up?" Chef rasps.

Daniel bows his head.

"Hey—look at me when I'm talkin' to you!" Chef jerks Daniel up by the jaw. Like an angry five year old, Daniel glares at him, his nostrils flared.

"You are. You're fuckin' flying right now... Aren't you?" Chef nods slowly and lets go.

Daniel shakes out his jacket, glancing at Chef. "I'm fine. I'll clean the ovens, Chef, just like you wanted..." He sails past to the sinks, looking for a bucket and brush.

Chef doesn't move, just watches him with blank eyes as Daniel gathers up supplies. He crouches down between Chef and Lucy and sprinkles in some cleaner.

"Get outta my kitchen," Chef whispers, staring at the top of Daniel's head.

Daniel starts scrubbing, his nose pressed down to the oven door.

"I said…get outta my kitchen," Chef repeats. "You're done."

I look wildly between the two of them as Daniel tosses the brush in the bucket and balks at Chef. "Come on, Chef…" he wheedles, "You don't mean that—"

"Get outta my kitchen, and don't come back 'til you're straightened out. I'm not playin', Danny. Get the fuck out," Chef says a little louder, going back to his station. Daniel gets to his feet and snorts. "You're kidding, right?" he calls, his eyes stopping and searching all of us. Juan Julio and Pedro refuse to look at him; I shake my head sadly when he finds me.

He lets out an angry laugh and kicks the supply rack, dishes rattling. "You guys are so full of shit," he hisses, zipping up his jacket. "Whatever. This job is shit, this place is shit… You're all shit." He narrows his eyes and shoves back through the service entrance, the door slamming behind him.

I spin back and look over at Chef. His shoulders are hunched, and he looks like he's aged twenty years in the last ten minutes. There's a new plate in front of him, but his hands rest unmoving on either side of it.

Slowly, I cross over to him. "Chef…" I murmur.

"Order up, Irish," he replies briskly, not looking up from the counter. "Don't let it get cold."

I sigh and take the plates, wanting to say something, but not knowing what. I walk back out and deliver the order, then head over to Francois.

"I need to step out… Everyone's taken care of right now," I murmur, jerking my head back to the quiet dining room.

Francois glances up from the reservation book, his glasses perched on the end of his nose. "Very well. I'll keep an eye until you return." He furrows his brow. "Is everything all right?"

I smile. "Yes. I won't be but a minute."

Francois nods, and I step out into the sunshine, checking the alley as I walk down the sidewalk; Daniel's already taken off. I shake my head, feeling a quick flash of remorse at my earlier excitement to see him get in trouble. I didn't expect things to have taken such a rough turn. The feeling passes though as Callaghan's note burns a hole in my pocket.

I stop at a payphone on the corner and deposit some change. Carefully, I take out the folded paper and punch up the number, holding my breath as I wait for the dial tone. I jump when a woman's bright voice comes on the line. "Ritz Carlton, this is Linda," she answers smoothly.

I inhale. "Yes, uh...I am calling for Ferrad Adimi... I was given this number by a Mr. John Callaghan." I squeeze my eyes shut and take a breath. "My name is Alden Murphy. I, um...I can just leave a message..."

"Ah, of course, Mr. Murphy," she purrs. "Mr. Adimi is expecting your call. I'll put you through."

A little bit of music tinkles on the line as she switches over. I prop the receiver against my ear, worried that I'll drop it, my hands are sweating so bad. A moment later, someone picks up. "Hello?"

"Hello, yes...Mr. Adimi?" I reply, snapping to attention. "This is Alden Murphy..."

*

"Jillian! Jillian—you're never going to believe it!"

I burst through the apartment's front door, gasping from running up the four flights of stairs. I grin as I spy her back by the sink doing dishes, awash in the warm, pink sunset light coming in from the kitchen window. She looks up as I bolt across the living room to her. "What is it?" she murmurs, shaking her head. "Is everything okay?"

"Better than okay!" I exclaim, giving her a quick kiss on the cheek. I squeeze her in my arms and grin down at her. "I got a new job!"

She wrinkles her forehead. "What? A new job—why? What happened at the restaurant?"

"Nothing like that…" I reassure her hurriedly. "Francois already knows… I put in my two weeks…"

"What? Slow down!" Jillian takes a step back and puts her hands to her temples. "You need to start from the beginning."

"Right!" I laugh, rubbing the back of my neck. "Sorry…I've been about to burst for the last couple hours of my shift… I wanted to run over here the minute I got off the phone…"

"Alden!" she cries, exasperated.

I nod and hold my hands out. "One of my regular customers has connections at the Ritz." Her eyes go wide at the mention of the famous hotel. I bounce excitedly. "He put in a good word for me with the general manager… The guy runs the whole place as well as the properties in London and Paris! Jillian…I'm going to be his assistant, his right hand man—those were his exact words on the phone! Isn't that amazing?!"

I shake her lightly by the shoulders as she stares back at me, awestruck. She draws in a breath and looks down at the floor. "What do you think?!" I crow, trying to read her expression. "Please—say something!"

"What…what about school?" she mumbles, not looking up.

I nod and take her hands, still damp with dishwater. "Mr. Adimi loves the fact that I'm taking classes and wants the hotel to pay for the rest of my tuition." I beam. "I may have to pull back a little with my new schedule…but I'll still be on track for graduation." My smile falters as she continues to look at the floor. "What's wrong? You don't seem happy…"

"Uh…sorry…" she mutters, pulling her hands away. "It seems like a dream come true, Alden, really." She goes absently back to the sink, pulling out a handful of dripping silverware.

I cross my arms and lean next to her. "I don't understand…

I thought you'd be thrilled." I stare at her as she cleans each fork and knife carefully before setting them in the dryer. "I'll be making a lot more money, my hours are going to be lined up with your schedule… It's a fantastic opportunity!" I stop, watching her shoulders sag. "Jillian—what's wrong?"

She puts her hands on the counter and looks out the window, taking a big breath. "I'm late," she whispers, keeping her eyes averted.

I shake my head, confused. "For what? Dinner?" I shrug easily and tap out a rhythm on the oven door. "Who cares, Jilly… Let's go down to Tony's for pizza and celebrate! We'll go crazy and order every topping on the menu…"

"No, Alden…" She turns to me, her voice pained. "*I'm* late. My period…"

I quit laughing and stand still, staring at her. "You're pregnant?" I breathe, my brain coming to a full stop.

Jillian bites her lip and glares down at the sink. "I don't know why it came as such a shock," she sniffs, a single tear dropping past her glasses and into the dirty dishwater. "I mean…it's not like we've been exactly careful, and we do it almost every single night. You can't keep your hands off me."

A hot collar of shame grips around my neck, cowing and humbling me. "I'm sorry…" I rasp, wanting nothing but to hold her—but my feet stay planted, my mind desperately trying to catch up.

With a gasp, she puts her face in her hands. "I like it, too!" she groans, rubbing her eyes. "But the nuns always warned us about this, right?" She laughs bitterly and shakes her head. "Sins of the flesh have consequences—endless consequences."

"Jillian…" I brush her arm with my fingers.

She shrugs away, still not looking at me. "I, um…I talked to the doctor." Her voice is dull as she tucks a lock of red hair behind her ear. "He said he could take me Friday, get it done before the weekend." She finally looks up at me, her face drawn.

"I know it seems like a million years away, but he said it's still early... Shouldn't be that tough a procedure."

My stomach sinks with a thud. "Jillian." My throat swells around her name. "No. That's not what *we* do—"

"I don't think this is exactly the time to be righteous, do you?!" She spins toward me, her eyes brimming with hot tears. "Besides—isn't that what you want? With your new, perfect job and perfect life—"

"No—NO! That's not what I want at all!" I shout, pacing back across the kitchen. I take a breath and put my hands on my hips. "Since when did a baby become a death sentence?"

"*Don't* call it that—" she cries, putting her face back in her hands.

I rush toward her and take her wrists. "That's what it is, Jillian! *Our* baby! We can't...we can't kill it!" I shake my head wildly and pry her hands down as she glares back at me with tear-streaked cheeks. "Look me in the eye and tell me that that's what you want!" I demand. "Tell me it's what you honestly want, and I'll back you—whatever the cost—"

"Of course I don't want *that*! I never wanted that—I want you!" she wails, beating her fists into my chest. "And it *is* you... You're inside of me!" She tears her hands from me and grabs her stomach. "And I am fighting with every fiber of my being to not be stupid and fall in love with it right now...because I know it will only kill me in the end, when I can't keep it, or when you leave—" Her voice cracks, and she turns away. "But I'm failing. I'm failing so hard."

"Jillian..." I breathe, my own throat growing thick. "Why couldn't we do it? We'll just have it and be together...like we're supposed to be—"

"Are you crazy?" she cries, tearing at her hair. "What would everyone say? We're too young, we're not married..."

"I don't give a damn what anyone says!" I yell, pointing down at the floor. "And I'll go bang on every church door and wake up every priest in this goddamn city and marry you tonight, if that's what it takes!"

"Be serious!" Jillian clenches her jaw, wrapping her arms around herself. "We have to be smart about this, Alden."

"I am serious!" I roar, pounding my fist on the counter. "I love you, Jillian! And I think we could make it work...and be happy! I *am* happy!" She gives me a bewildered stare as I wave down at her stomach. "I know it's not part of whatever plan you'd worked out in your head...or it's all out of order..." I rub my temple and nod. "But I'm happy. I'm *really* happy."

Jillian bites her cheek and leans against the kitchen counter. "You're happy *now*—but what happens in nine months when it's here and things get tough?" She glares at me. "You're the youngest in your family, Alden. You have no idea how much work and time..." She sighs and crosses her arms. "I can kiss my art goodbye. And how long do you think you're really going to stick around with a screaming baby and dirty diapers?"

"I will never leave you," I whisper, staring at her intently. "Like I said from the beginning, I am yours. Even if you put me out, the way I feel about you will never change." I reach up to my collarbone and rub her silver cross between my fingers. "In this world, and the next."

I can see that Jillian is starting to waver. She exhales and starts crying again, spinning back to face the window, her hands propping her up on the sink ledge. I step silently behind her and press my lips to the nape of her neck.

"Don't..." she breathes, but doesn't pull away. "When you kiss me like that, I almost start to believe that everything could be okay."

"Everything *is* okay," I murmur, wrapping my arms softly around her waist. "It's better than okay... You're just not there yet."

"How can you know that?" She shakes her head, still looking out at the sunset, the skyline draped in deep reds and blues.

"Because whatever is happening *here*—" She lets out a little gasp as I gently rest my hand on top of her stomach. "—came from love. Not from war or disease or self-loathing…but from you and me." I nuzzle my chin into her shoulder, feeling resolute. "It's going to be the best thing that's ever happened. Everything else will work itself out…jobs, school…"

She scoffs, but takes my hands in hers, gripping tightly. "I don't…I don't want to lose myself," she says quietly. "I've just started to figure out who I am, what I want…"

I nod. "I'm not going to let that happen. I will fight for you until the day I die."

She exhales, her body melting into mine. "I wish I had your confidence. You seem so sure." She brushes her fingers up my arm.

"I'm always sure when it comes to you, Jillian," I breathe into her ear. "And don't worry—I'll be sure enough for the both of us."

CHAPTER 19

LOS ANGELES—PRESENT DAY

"*S*HE MADE IT—SHE'S home." I read Jodie's text off my phone and flop into the paisley easy chair, relieved as I look at the Christmas tree.

Daniel nods, pacing past the living room couch and into the hall. "That's good," he sighs. "One person we don't have to worry about."

I watch as he stops and stares into the front mirror, readjusting the tinsel lining the frame. "What are you thinking?" I murmur. I know that I'm just asking for trouble, but he's been unusually quiet since we got home—focused on making his phone calls, but otherwise not speaking.

He glances over, his expression unreadable. "I'm thinking…" He scoffs and shakes his head. "I'm thinking about how stupid I was for thinking these last few days could just be…*simple*. No drama—that we could have a normal Christmas." He cringes. "I'm an idiot."

"Don't say that…" I stare at him, my heart aching in my chest. "We had no idea any of this was going to go down right now." I sigh and sit up, trying to look useful. "What should I be doing? How can I help? Should we be doing something about the Resistance?" There's a looming apocalypse that was detailed in *my* prophecy, and I'm just sitting crisscross applesauce like a total loser.

Daniel glances over, his eyes sad, and quickly looks away again. "There's…nothing *to* do, Christa. Yes, Heaven has declared war against Hell…but that doesn't really mean anything—not until the order goes through in Porticullis." He shakes his head. "Mary Carmen said delegates from both sides are assembling, everyone is crazy angry about what happened…but this whole thing could take a while to sort out. Red tape, or whatever." He glares at the floor. "It *is* a big deal, but doesn't really mean anything for us right now. Just more crap on top of the crap we were already dealing with." There's a hint of disgust in his voice. "We're going to sit out the storm. This isn't our fight."

I bite my lip, staring from my own blue skin to Daniel's angry, copper-gold Halo. I'm still the Catalyst, he's still my Guardian. That consistency is slightly comforting. I furrow my brow. "What about all those people from the theater? Are they going to be okay?" I kind of don't want to know the answer.

"I don't know." Daniel exhales, still pacing tiredly across the hall. "Everyone is supposed to be at a ceasefire right now…holding until we know more, but who knows if Hell will abide—"

He stops as Benny walks into the hall, his eyes still burning Halo bright. "She fell asleep mid-noodle." He gives Daniel a pat on the arm as he finds his coat. "But her color looks like it's coming back, so whatever bug she's got is probably just a 24-hour thing." He grins proudly. "She liked my soup."

Daniel nods and puts on a matching smile. "That's great, Benny. Thank you so much for coming over and helping out with Mary Carmen—we really appreciate it."

I perk up. "Yeah—thanks, Benny. And thanks for the leftovers." Standing and crossing my arms over my chest, I shuffle across the room and stop next to Daniel. "The house smells amazing. I'm gonna go hit that soup up right now."

"No worries!" Benny laughs, zipping up his parka. "Healing

hearts, healing minds—one stomach at a time. You know the drill... I just figured you all needed it after the crazy day we had." Snorting, he slaps Daniel on the chest. "I swear, *mahaloha*, you make life exciting..."

Daniel attempts a smile, but it comes out more like a grimace. "Yeah...you know it."

If Benny registers Daniel's mood, he doesn't say anything about it, just moving on after spending a few seconds examining his friend. "You still okay to host the big day?" he wonders, glancing back toward the bedrooms. "What with Pretty Mama all laid up?"

"Yeah, we're good. Christa and I are going to tackle the shopping tomorrow morning," The cheerful tone that Daniel used to have when talking about cooking for Christmas is gone.

I pop up on the balls of my feet uneasily, scrunching my toes. Benny shrugs. "Well, lemme know if there's anything you need." He nods, opening the front door, then reaches into his pocket to pull out a pack of cigarettes and a lighter. "And I'll see you...tomorrow?" He flashes his brows at Daniel as he steps out onto the front porch.

"Yeah...tomorrow." Daniel glances between the two of us. I give a small smile—something's up.

Daniel starts to close the door behind him, but hesitates. "Hey, Benny?" he calls.

"Yeah?" Benny lights up and takes a puff of his cigarette.

"Maybe stay in tonight, all right? I heard there's some weird stuff going on around town... I know you don't wanna get caught up in any of it." Daniel keeps his face calm, but there is an edge to his voice.

Benny lets out a low whistle. "Cup of chamomile and Masterpiece Theater it is, dawg!" He shakes his head with a chuckle. "I know better than to second-guess you and your hunches." He winks at me. "Me and this cat go way back. He's saved my life twice, you know that?"

I smile weakly up at Daniel. "I believe it. He's practically Superman." I reach out to brush his hand, but he flinches away. I bite my cheek—that's not good.

Benny chuckles, then gives us a wave and heads out to his truck, calling, "See ya, space cowboys!" over his shoulder.

I sigh and step back, letting Daniel close the door. "So…are you mad at me?" I murmur, moving back into the living room.

Daniel looks at me for a minute before turning away again. "Why would you think that?" he whispers.

I roll my eyes. "Maybe because you've barely looked at me since we got home, let alone talked to me?" I give an awkward laugh.

Daniel shakes his head. "I was making calls… It's important we get the word out to the other Guardians about what happened," he replies curtly.

"I know that," I whisper. "Did…anyone pick up? Are they coming?"

"No." He leans against the hall table. "No one picked up. That's not unusual."

"Sure…" I breathe, trying to catch his eye again. "But you still didn't answer my—"

"I'm not mad at you," he interrupts brusquely.

I wait for him to cough, since that has to be a lie. When there's nothing, I exhale and pretend to mop my brow. "Whew! That's a relief, since there's a bunch of stuff I need to talk to you about." What happened at the movies, how every other mortal in the theater went all shiny-shiny and I didn't…how I was able to read Jodie's soul…

"Not now," Daniel says with a frown.

I stop and wrap my arms around myself, suddenly feeling very small. "Sure…later." I sit down tentatively on the couch, clearing my throat. "I guess you'll be heading out, too?" I stare down at my hands. "Now that everyone's gone? Mary Carmen and I are in for the night…"

"No—I'm staying here."

I look up at him hopefully, but hastily avert my gaze; he's all business tonight, starting to pace in the archway again. I take a deep breath. Happy as I am to have him stay, I don't know what to do with him when he's like this. I check my attitude and try to say what I think he wants to hear.

"You don't have to worry—I'm not going to leave, try to sneak out. Had enough action for one day, thank you very much."

When my attempt to lighten the mood falls flat, I stare at my socks. Daniel stops pacing and looks at me. "I know. I trust you," he mumbles, his face unreadable again. I watch him, waiting for him to say more. He doesn't, instead just hovering some more.

I let out an exasperated sigh and finally throw my hands in the air. "Can you stop doing that? You're like Scrooge McDuck!"

Daniel stops moving, but glares at me. "This isn't a time for jokes, Christa." He shakes his head. "All Hell has broken loose—"

"And the sky is still blue," I mutter. "Don't see why this occasion warrants special circumstances."

"Because this makes it real!" Daniel shouts, crossing into the living room. "All of it—the prophecy, the war—"

"It was *already* real," I reply calmly, blinking up at him. "We've spent the last couple days going over every line of that thing—here, at the library, word for word... We figured out which stuff had already happened, talked about what we maybe thought was coming...the stuff at Adler's..."

"Maybe I don't want it to be real!" Daniel huffs, stomping to the other side of the Christmas tree. "Did you ever think of that?! For just an afternoon—Hell, for even five minutes!" He keeps his eyes downcast.

I put my hands in my lap. "Why are you acting like this? None of this should come as a surprise to you." I shake my head.

His Halo burns like a supernova for a second as he fidgets with an ornament. "It's fine! I'm fine! I'm not acting like anything!" he snarls belligerently.

I glare at him, not knowing what to do. He never yells at me like this. "Fine... I can see you're in a mood about something, and you don't want to talk about it." I clench my jaw and get up. "I'm going to bed."

"Christa—" He exhales, running a hand through his hair and taking a step toward me. "I'm sorry."

"Don't worry about it." I refuse to look at him as I pad across the floor. "We're all super stressed... It happens. Work out whatever you need to, and we'll talk when you're ready. It's okay—"

I startle as he reaches over and grabs my hand. "Hey—no, don't go." He pulls me back to him and the Christmas tree. "I'm sorry. I'm being a jerk. You didn't do anything wrong... I've just got some stuff going on in my head."

"Yeah...me, too," I murmur, keeping my eyes on the twinkly tree lights. "I like it better when we, you know...discuss it, instead of barking at each other." I turn and gaze up at his face. His Halo is that muddy copper tone that tells me he's still not himself, but his eyes are soft, so I know he's trying.

He nods. "You're right. Come on." With a sigh, he pulls me down next to him on the couch. "You start. Tell me what you need to talk about."

I take a breath and tuck my legs underneath me. "Well, for starters...how about what happened at the movies today?" I watch as he sits back on the couch with a thud. "How come everyone else in that theater starting Haloing, and I didn't? Is it because I'm Smudged?"

"No, that shouldn't have anything to do with it," Daniel murmurs. "I've seen Pete Halo a couple times since he got the Sight... He did it the night of your accident at the Underpass." He peeks over at me, his face drawn. "I'm not sure why it didn't happen to you again. I...I don't know. I wish I did. Sorry."

I wind my fingers through his. "It's okay... I guess it's not really that big of a deal." I smile and try to shrug it off. "I think the more pressing issue is that I can now read souls...sort of?" I look at him questioningly.

Daniel nods slowly. "Yeah, that did happen..." He inches a little closer, still holding my hand. "What did you see? If...if you want to tell me..."

I look down at the couch cushions, suddenly feeling very protective of Jodie, even though I typically tell Daniel everything and I know he would keep it a secret. I scratch my cheek with my other hand. "No...sure—it was a memory from when she was a kid...at her grandmother's house...just playing with her cousins." I smile tightly. "Pretty mundane."

Daniel sighs. "That's usually what you see when you first start reading souls—everyday stuff. You know, school, hobbies, last night's dinner..." He grimaces. "But the more you do it, the better you get at sifting through the noise and finding those life-changing moments, their futures... I'm okay at it." He looks away with a grunt. "But there are those out there who are *really* good at it. You know..."

Alden—he means Alden. I wrap my arm around my knees at the memory. He picked out everything he needed to know about me in about three minutes, the bastard. I cock my head to the side, thinking about what I saw in Jodie... The whole thing felt very private. Even though I wasn't trying to, I sort of...violated her. I sigh.

"Did you...did you ever see anything in me that you weren't supposed to see?" I ask, tracing circles lightly on Daniel's leg. "When *I* was Haloing?"

He sits up and stares straight ahead, pausing before he answers. "I saw everything I was supposed to see," he whispers, stopping my hand's movement. I wait for him to say more, but he doesn't.

He also doesn't cough. Good enough.

I rest my head on his shoulder. "Well, I guess that's one upside to whatever is going on with me right now." I hold up my blue hand. "I'm not an open book anymore."

"Yeah," Daniel agrees, grasping me tightly. "But you're still vulnerable…in other ways."

I close my eyes and let myself melt into him a little more. "I like that you still think that, about me. That I'm not just some cracked-out superhuman freak with a mission, *the Catalyst*—"

"That's never who you were to me." His voice is quiet, serious. "You're so much more than all that other stuff. You're always…Christa."

From where I gaze up at him, I can see that the corners of his eyes are damp. I pull my head back and touch his cheek. "Hey—are you okay?"

Daniel quickly wipes his face, clearing his throat. "Sure… It's just something in my eye—dust." He coughs.

I can't help but smile. "All right, your turn. What's bugging you?" I nudge him with my knee, then cringe as he pulls away again. I don't want to let him withdraw back into himself this time. "Come on! We said we were going to talk about this stuff… Is it about the other Guardians? Are you worried you didn't get to talk to any of them?"

"What? Oh…no," he replies huskily. "I'm sure they'll check in soon. Mary Carmen might have better luck with that." He stares at the ceiling.

I sigh. "Are you worried about her? Her little…episode…at the movies?" I wince at the word 'episode'—it makes me think of Colette Adler and the prophecy. "Or about what she heard on FM Heaven?"

Daniel chuckles and shakes his head. "No, Mary Carmen will be fine. This always happens when she gets a big message from them. She'll sleep like a rock tonight and be fine in the morning,"

"Then what?!" I exclaim, giving him a light shove. "What's wrong? I hate seeing you like this."

He smirks. "Like what?"

I sigh and wave at the space around his head, where his aura is still more rust-colored than gold. "All...murky! And grumpy, mad," I mutter, nibbling a hang nail. "It's not like you and I have the luxury of hiding our feelings from each other... I've started figuring out your different...shades."

Daniel laughs out loud at this. "My *shades*? Like...a chameleon or something?"

I raise my eyebrows. "You're more like one of those fifty cent mood rings you can buy at the mall, but yeah. You have very specific color palettes depending on if you're happy, sad...perturbed." I poke him with my index finger.

"*Now* who's the open book?" he snickers.

I shrug knowingly and snuggle back into his side.

He sniffs and puts his arm over my shoulder, both our gazes trailing back to the Christmas lights. "I just wanted you to myself for a little while," he says quietly after a minute. "I know it's selfish...but I thought that maybe we could put everything aside and not have to worry about prophecies or Haloing or Demons, about whatever comes next...and have it just be you, me, and this tree." He waves at the latter sadly. "I don't know what I was thinking. Who am I, to want that—"

I crane my neck back to him, my lips parted. "You're everything," I answer without thinking. Feeling him staring at the top of my head, I correct my course fast. "I mean...you're my Guardian, so you shouldn't feel like you have to fight so hard. I'm right here." I give him a small smile. "Not going anywhere."

Daniel nods and closes his eyes. "I know." He grips my hand tight again before pulling away. "It's late," he whispers, standing up. "You should get some sleep. It's been a very long day." He gestures at the couch. "I'll bunk out here, keep an eye on the place."

I stand up too, crossing my arms. I want him closer than the couch. "Daniel, do you think…just for tonight—" I take a step toward him and keep my voice quiet, not wanting to hear him say no, "—do you think you could…stay with me in my bed?"

Daniel sucks in a breath and rubs the back of his neck. "I dunno, Christa… That might not be a good idea…"

"We did it before—at the Factory!" I fill in excitedly, chastising myself to hold back a little.

"That was different," he sighs.

I bite my lip. Think fast. "We'll just sleep," I placate. "That's it."

Daniel shoots me a wary look. "What about Mary Carmen?" He motions back toward her room. "You sure you wanna deal with that if she finds out?"

I glare at the doorframe. "You yourself said she'd be out for the night." I widen my eyes, knowing the sight of my baby blues makes him weak in the knees. Sure enough, a tinge of yellow gold lines his Halo. "Please? I'm still freaked out from earlier—I need you."

Daniel reaches out and holds onto the couch arm, considering. I grin to myself: he's caving, I know it.

"Okay," he finally murmurs, nodding at the floor. "Just for tonight."

"Yes…just tonight."

I smile and take his hand before he has a chance to change his mind, guiding him under the mistletoe and back to my bedroom. All of the lights are off except for the little Christmas tree on my dresser. I wave at it. "You, me, and a tree," I add with a smile. Daniel's jaw tenses, but he's turning more gold by the second, so I know that at least a part of him is pleased.

I move over to the dresser and open the top drawer, pulling out my pajamas. "I'm going to go change in the bathroom." I motion to the bed. "You can just…make yourself comfortable." My butterflies are going insane.

One look at Daniel's face, and I can tell he feels the same way. "Do you..." He clears his throat and points at the pillows. "Do you have a side that you sleep on?"

I shake my head and zip toward the door. "Take your pick. I'll be right back." After he nods, I rush down the hall to the bathroom, careful not to slam the door and wake Mary Carmen. I strip out of my jeans and shirt, skipping my old sweats and hastily changing into the cute tank top and silky shorts that I bought for myself a couple of Valentine's Days ago...unable to pass up leopard-print hearts. I rake a brush through my hair and rinse some toothpaste around my mouth before glancing at myself in the mirror. The pink fabric actually brightens the blue hue of my skin, and my dark hair looks lustrous and full draped across my shoulders. I smile at my reflection; even though I know nothing is going to happen—nothing *can* happen—at least I look hot. I arch a brow at the sexy girl staring back at me and head back to my room.

I end up stopping in the doorway, though, gasping a little. The tree lights are still on, illuminating Daniel in between my bed sheets as he looks up at the ceiling, his arms crossed behind his head. I notice his clothes piled on the floor by the side of the bed...*all* of his clothes. Feeling heat prickling on my face and chest, I stare at him dumbly.

He glances over and blinks. "I went with the right side—hope that's okay," he murmurs, his eyes spending time on me, too.

I nod, still holding my jeans and clothes from earlier in the day. "Yes...of course." I shake my head and step into the room, closing the door behind me, then throw my stuff into the closet and walk around to the other side of the bed.

Daniel sits up a little as I pull back the quilt. "I, um..." He tucks the bedclothes under his hips and gestures at his stuff on the floor. "I had to take those off. They were starting to smell." He laughs awkwardly. "I'm just using the bedspread...so if you want to get under all the blankets, you can."

I nod, blushing. "Like the puritans. Gotcha." I crawl in between the sheets.

Daniel blushes too. "We have to, Christa—or I have to go..."

I rub my neck. "Say no more—I know the rules. I won't... touch you."

He winces. "Okay, yeah. I know you...know."

I give him a weak smile. This has just crossed over from exciting to completely unbearable. Embarrassed, I pull my quilt over my shoulder and roll onto my side, away from him. "Well...goodnight, I guess," I mutter into my pillow, feeling the blankets stifle me. "Better get some shut eye." I cringe; God, I'm such a dork.

"Goodnight," he answers. Hearing him exhale as he settles back into bed, I breathe deeply; I can feel his legs through the covers, stretching onto my side of the bed and warming my sheets. I pinch my eyes closed and try to think about baseball, Ethan Liu, the last time I had the stomach flu...anything to get my mind off of this gorgeous guy next to me in this incredibly small double bed. Maybe he was right—this is a bad idea... nothing like before at the Factory. *This* is torture. I wriggle under the blankets, wrapping tighter and tighter with every maneuver, trying in vain to find a decent position.

Daniel clears his throat. "Do you need more blankets?" he whispers. "Let me know if I'm—"

"No—I'm fine!" I answer irritably. "Just trying to sleep over here... I'm super, super tired."

"Okay," he answers, his tone...disappointed? My ears perk up—maybe I'm not the only one feeling rejected here. I consider for a moment, before deciding to slowly turn back over.

We're suddenly nose-to-nose. "Hello," Daniel breathes, breaking into a grin. His eyes are wide open, watching me. My stomach does cartwheels; Goddammit, what is it about those stupid Christmas lights that make him look extra tan, his teeth extra white?

I smirk and pull my hand out from the covers, smacking his bare chest. "Hi." I smile and free my other arm. "You've got me bundled up here like I'm about to make a trek to the North Pole. I can hardly move."

"Good!" he laughs, propping up on one elbow, his eyes dancing. "Better safe than sorry!"

I snort and try to move my legs. "That's, like, your freaking mantra... Didn't know it applied to sleepovers, too."

"*Anytime* I'm with you!" Daniel purrs, wrapping his arm over my swaddling. He nestles down next to me, so close that I almost have to cross my eyes to really look at him.

It's nice...even with all the blankets. I sigh contentedly. "I'm glad you're here," I whisper. "I don't like it when we're apart."

"Me, either." He smiles crookedly next to my mouth. "It's too quiet—not enough eye rolling or sarcastic commentary."

"Hey!" I giggle. "Stop—I'm not *that* sarcastic... Not all the time!"

His own laugh is deep and throaty, giving me tingles. "No... not all the time." He grins lazily, tucking my hair back, his fingers lingering behind my ear. Thank God I'm already lying down. "And I like that you're funny." He brushes his hand down my cheek. "And that you think *I'm* funny."

"You wish." I flutter my eyelashes against his face. "Funny-looking, anyway."

"Wow—5th grade burn!" he chortles, rolling back. "That stings. Truly, Christa, you're such a bully."

"You don't know the half of it." I squirm free from my blanket cocoon and clamber on top of him, starting to play-wrestle when he grabs both my hands. "Now give me all your lunch money, or you'll be really sorry." I press down on him with my thighs.

"I'm already sorry!" he crows, gently pushing back and moving his hands to my hips. "I don't know what I was thinking—going up against a tough chick like you! Mercy! Mercy!"

I squeal girlishly as he tickles up my waist, then fall back onto my side, my feet kicking the pillows. "Tickle monster—no fair!" I chuckle, nudging him with my toes. "That's like…guerrilla warfare!" I can feel one of the straps of my tank top slipping, but I don't do anything to fix it.

"Uh-huh…" He smiles and cradles one of my feet in his palm, pressing my arch to his lips and giving it a swift kiss.

We both freeze and stare at each other. "Daniel—" I breathe.

Hastily, like he's holding a bomb, he tosses my foot away and sits up on the edge of the bed. "I'm sorry." He shakes his head at the wall. "I'm sorry…"

"It's okay!" I sit up too, gaping at his tattooed naked back, the outline of his wings shimmering against the sheets. "Everything's okay, Daniel. You didn't mean anything—we were just playing around—"

"No, I should go. That was too…" His hands are trembling as he bends down, pulling at his clothes. "Too close."

Panic flares in my gut. "Daniel, please…" I whisper urgently. "Nothing happened! We're fine. You don't have to leave—"

He refuses to look at me. "You have no idea how bad that could've been… I can't make another…*mistake*…like that again," he practically spits as he shoves his legs into his jeans.

His words cut me like a knife. "It wasn't a…a 'mistake,'" I stammer, rocking back on my heels. "We were just having fun…"

"I can't just have fun with you, Christa!" he shouts, pulling his pants on too fast for me to have a chance to see anything. "Don't you get that?! It's never that simple with us!" He jumps to his feet and glares at me, exasperated.

"Why? Because I'm the Catalyst?" I bristle, my throat growing thick. "So we have to keep it professional?"

Daniel laughs harshly and gestures at me and the messed-up bedsheets. "I would hardly call *this* professional!" His mouth twists. "But maybe we should aim for that in the future—for both our sakes." He reaches down and grabs his t-shirt.

I can feel the tears coming. "You don't mean that—I know you don't," I rasp, staring at him.

He scrunches his nose and pitches his shirt on the bed. "Jesus…" he mutters, rubbing his face, then up into his hair. "Okay…" He takes a breath. "I'm going to go sleep on the couch. We both can cool off—put this day behind us and forget this ever happened." He turns to open the door.

"No!" I cry, tears trickling down my cheeks. "I don't want to forget it happened!" A sob sneaks past my lips.

"Christa…" Daniel's tone is low with warning. "I'm leaving now."

"No, you can't!" I blurt out. "You can't leave—because I love you!"

Daniel's back goes rigid, his hand frozen over the doorknob. *"What?"*

I almost don't hear him, he's so quiet, his body as still as stone. I clutch my stomach, the tears coming at their own will. "I…I love you," I repeat, more timid this time. I take a deep breath. "I've never said that to anyone before…except for my family, and maybe Jodie…" I feel weightless, like I'm floating on air. I look to him, holding my breath. "I think…I think I'm in love with you."

I can't see his face, only his sagging shoulders, his head hanging low. "Don't…" he groans.

I scramble off the bed, tugging my shorts back into place as I step over to him. "Daniel…" I whisper, inches away. "Please look at me."

He turns like he's in slow motion, and I see his eyes, full of pain and despair. My heart sinks. "Why would you say that?" His voice cracks. "Why?"

I pull back, shaking my head. "Because it's the *truth*!" I bark. "I can't *not* say it anymore—not after everything!"

"Do you know how much that hurts me?" he whispers,

looking away again. "That *you* can say it, and I…" He stops and stares at the floor. "Did you even think?"

I gasp, crushing my knuckles against my mouth. "I would never want to hurt you, Daniel—you know that!" I sob, trying to reach out for him. "But I don't know what to do anymore! What to say—"

I gawk as he shakes his head and moves past me back to the bed, getting his shirt. "*Don't say anything!*" he hisses, wrenching the t-shirt over his head. "You've done enough!" He tears at his hair as he heads back to the door.

"No!" I let out a weak cry and pull at him, hastily brushing my tears away. "You can't treat me like I'm a criminal because I have feelings for you! And you can't act like I'm alone in this! I know you can't say it—"

Daniel draws in a breath and glares at me, his eyes wild. "Stop, Christa. Stop, now." His jaw trembles.

Resolute, I bite my tongue and stare at his face. "I love you, and I think you love me, too!"

Daniel gapes at me, his aura blinding, then reaches over and covers my mouth firmly with his palm. Both of us pant as our eyes dart to the ceiling, waiting for it to crack open and smite us where we stand. We wait for what feels like an eternity.

Nothing happens.

My tears streak onto Daniel's fingers. "Don't…say another word," he finally mouths, his gaze intense. When I nod, Daniel finally draws his hand back, his stare never leaving me.

"I'm sorry," I breathe, my knees knocking together. "I'm so sorry."

Daniel wraps his arms around my waist as my legs buckle, both of us shaking. "I'm sorry, too," he sighs into my temple, laying me back on the bed and smoothing my hair out of my face. "It's me. It's all my fault."

We stop to catch our breath, still terrified that the other shoe is going to drop and that the Gods will rain down fury. There is no noise except for our breathing and the ticking of the alarm clock on the nightstand.

I finally turn my face to Daniel, my mouth dry. "I won't say it again…ever," I whisper, my heart torn in two. "I promise."

He exhales and closes his eyes, shadows flickering across his face. "I know. It's okay… We're okay." I can't tell if he's trying to convince me or himself. He smiles weakly down at me and breathes heavily through his nose. "You were just saying how you felt—you shouldn't be punished for that." He runs his thumb across my jaw.

I blink, not wanting to cry anymore, the injustice of the whole thing smarting worse than a punch in the stomach. I draw in a ragged breath. "What about you? Are you going to be punished?" I can barely get the words out.

Daniel sighs, glancing back at the ceiling. "Not any more than I already deserve. And not because of you." He smiles again and wipes a stray tear from my cheek. "You are so beautiful…"

I gasp and shake my head. "Daniel—don't…"

"It's okay." He shrugs, pulling back. "It's just the truth. It never…never hurt anyone."

I look at him sadly and pull him down next to me, twining our arms together as exhaustion takes over. With his face pressed into my neck, I wait until I hear his breaths even out, then fall fast asleep.

CHAPTER 20
NEW YORK CITY—
JUNE, 1976

I SET DOWN the heavy grocery bag and lift the corner of the mat, the key that Jillian leaves out for me when I'm running late gleaming up from the tile floor. I wipe a little sweat from my brow—the hallway is still sweltering, even so late in the day—and go inside.

"Jillian?" I call quietly. Turning my head, I see that the living room light is on, illuminating Jillian asleep on the couch. She's already in her nightgown, her sketchbook draped over her like a boxy blanket as the fan blows from across the room, ruffling the pages gently. I smile and lock the door behind me, setting the groceries down on the coffee table.

Jillian stirs and smiles when she sees me, her glasses skewed at a funny angle on her face. "Hey," she breathes, sitting up slowly. "What time is it? I tried to wait up for you...but I'm just so drained lately."

"It's late," I murmur, moving her sketchbook to the chair and sitting down next to her. "There was an event that ran over...and with Mr. Adimi out of town, I just wanted to make sure everyone got out okay after."

"Sure." She yawns and rubs my knee, looking over to the grocery bag. "You shopped? I told you I would take care of it tomorrow. We're good for breakfast…and it's not like I've been starving…" She clears her throat and shifts on the couch. "I can barely keep anything down as it is."

I nod. "I didn't do a full stock up. I actually got to talking to this really nice older woman on the train and mentioned how you've been having trouble with morning sickness…"

Jillian's eyes widen. "Alden! We said we weren't telling anyone! It's still early and we haven't figured out our plan—"

"It was a stranger on the subway—you gotta give me something, Jilly!" I chuckle, pulling at the paper bag. "Anyway, she said oranges were good for nausea…*not* orange juice—she was very specific about that—but whole, real oranges." I turn the sack upside down, a cascade of bright oranges tumbling out. Jillian laughs as I pick one up and hold it out like Hamlet with his skull. "What do you think? Should we give it a go?"

Jillian shrugs. "Sure. What do I have to lose?"

I grin at her and step into the kitchen, peeling the orange at the sink before taking down a small plate.

"What's this?" Jillian giggles from the couch. I look over and she's holding the other item I picked up—a mini guitar that was on display in the shop along with a bunch of pineapples and suntan oil.

"Ah—I just thought that was funny. I've never seen a guitar that tiny." I walk back over and present her with the small plate of orange slices.

She laughs as we trade. "It's not a guitar—it's a ukulele, from Hawaii." She smiles, sniffing the orange hesitantly. "This smells good."

"A uku-whaty?" I pucker my lips at the strange little instrument and its strange name, having never made it around to the Pacific during my travels. When I give the strings a strum, the sound comes out sprite and twangy. I like it. "How exotic!"

Jillian laughs at me as I hold it against my side and tries a bite of the orange. "You gonna play me a song?"

I flash my eyebrows playfully and attempt to squash my fingers back and forth between an A chord and a G on the tiny frets. "Sure… Any requests?"

She snorts and tucks her feet under me. "Something original. I hate covers."

I puff out my cheeks and sit up. "Tall order, Ms. O'Connor, tall order…but all right." I grin at her. "I think I've got something."

Plucking at the strings, I start singing intentionally off-key. "Oh Jillian…Jillian…with your hair so bright and *red*…you make my heart soar. It's your chest I adore, I never want to leave the bed…"

She immediately cracks up. "Wow—okay!" she laughs.

I start to bop on the couch. "You gotta eat your oranges so our baby girl can grow up and be a ginger just like you…"

"Oh—it's a girl now?" she interrupts, grinning.

I nod and give the ukulele a thrum. "Of course it is, Jilly… Her name will be Lily…" I play a final chord. "Or maybe Rose or *June*!" I end triumphantly.

At Jillian's thunderous applause, I take a bow. "Bravo! Bravo!" she crows.

I hold up my hands. "Seriously, I think that one's gonna get national radio play…huge world tour…"

"Mmm…I wouldn't quit your day job!" she teases, scooching up and holding her tummy. "You really think it's a girl?"

I nod confidently. "Oh yeah! Don't you?"

Jillian considers, running her fingers over her middle. "I don't know… I'm kind of getting a boy vibe." She smiles up at me and shrugs. "I guess one of us will be right! I think it's sweet that you've got some names… I like Lily, and Rose…" She looks over at the dried pink rose petals in a glass bowl by the lamp from our first date. "Lily Rose, maybe? That's kind of pretty."

I grin and take her hand. "I love it." I press my nose down to her nightgown. "I love it, Lily Rose!" I call inside.

Jillian laughs and pets the back of my head. "I don't think it has ears yet…and I wouldn't get too fixated on one or the other!" She tickles my neck. "It could very well be a boy you're yelling to in there."

I sit up and sigh. "I don't think so. I'm usually right about this sort of thing."

"Oh, really?!" Jillian snorts. "I think we should be prepared for both contingencies." She arches a brow. "Any good ones?"

I frown and try to think. Every time I picture our baby, it's always sweet and pink-cheeked, swaddled in pastels. I want it to be a girl. In fact, it being a boy had never crossed my mind.

"I have no idea… What do you like?" I grunt after a minute.

Jillian smiles thoughtfully. "I like…Gerald. Sort of like Derald, my dad's name, but a little different." Seeing my grimace, she bats my arm. "What? What's that face?"

"*Gerald*?" I wrinkle my nose as if I'd just gotten a whiff of something rancid. "Gerald Murphy? That's the worst!"

She laughs and gives me a light punch on the shoulder. "No, it's not! I think it's nice and good for when he's grown up."

"Yeah, if he grows up to be a dentist or tax accountant!" I shake my head and run my tongue dryly around the inside of my mouth. "No—you're gorgeous, and I love you, Jillian, but I'm not letting you ruin a person's life like that, right from the starting gate. It's cruel and unusual."

"You're a nut!" She squeals, putting her legs in my lap. "Gerald is the name of my favorite painting instructor. He's a great guy!"

"Oh, so the truth comes out!" I tease, getting to work on massaging her toes. "Should I feel threatened by this Gerald character? Is it serious?"

"Stop!" She kicks my hand as I laugh, kissing the tops of her knees.

We sit quietly for a moment, me rubbing her, and I look over at her now empty plate. "How was it?" I ask.

She nods and snuggles down into the couch. "Good. First time I haven't felt like throwing up in weeks." She sighs, looking over at me.

I smile. "Great. We'll just keep that up." I watch her as her eyelids start to droop. The foot massage does it every time.

"Wait...I wanted to show you something." She clears her throat and sits back up. "Where's my—" Spying her sketchbook on the chair, she tugs it over, flipping through the pages. "Here. I finally finished."

She hands me the pad, and I squint at the image in the soft lamplight. It's a detailed ink drawing of me sound asleep in her bed, naked from the sheets up with my lip curling contentedly like I'm a happy housecat. I look...beautiful and otherworldly. Angelic. In her elegant handwriting at the bottom is scrawled the phrase, *My Love—1976.*

"Jillian," I breathe, not looking up from the paper. I can see her grinning out of the corner of my eye. "How did you—? This is breathtaking. Do I really look like this?" I shake my head, finally gazing up at her.

She smiles. "I tried to capture you as best I could in the moment, before you woke up." She puts a hand in her hair. "But it's how I see you—how I always see you."

My eyes tighten as I lean in, kissing her softly. "I don't deserve you."

Her lips curl next to mine. "Yes, you do! You can show me how much by helping me to bed." She groans as she pulls herself up from the couch. "Jeez...what is this going to be like in a couple months?"

I laugh and wrap my arm around her waist. "I can't wait."

She stops as we shuffle past the fan. "We should bring that with us. It's still so hot back there—we should get another fan this weekend." She rubs her shoulder tiredly.

I raise an eyebrow as I reach for the power cord. "Can't we just take Denise's? She doesn't need it anymore…"

Jillian shakes her head. "She took it back to her parents' with all her stuff last week before she left—before the heat wave." She tries to cool herself with her hand. "I can't believe she's going to be in Italy for a whole year. I kind of miss her… It's lonely around here now."

I try to hide my grin behind the fan, obviously not sharing the sentiment. "I know…and what with Muriel leaving…" I glance back at Jillian as we make our way to the bedroom. "Did you want to come with me in the morning to see her off? It's early…"

"No, I can't." Jillian sighs, stepping past me to the bed as I plug in the fan. "I have an appointment on the other side of town. We said our goodbyes today at lunch." Her shoulders droop as she flips back the bedsheets. "It was…hard. I don't know why she has to go." Her voice falls hollow at the last part as she looks at me; we both know very well why she's leaving.

I peel off my clothes and climb into bed with her. "It'll be all right," I whisper into her hair. "We're going to have more company than we know what to do with soon." I give her tummy a light squeeze under the sheets.

She giggles and rolls over. "That's the truth!" She sighs and cozies into her pillow as I come up behind her, laying my arm over hers. "I guess I'm never alone anymore, really. Should enjoy the quiet while we have it."

"Indeed!" I kiss her shoulder and reach to turn off the light. She's snoring by the time I twist back.

*

I'm already awake by the time sunrise makes its way to our window, lying quietly next to Jillian and watching her side rise and fall with each breath. I check the clock and decide to get up, giving her a soft kiss before I grab my clothes and get dressed quickly in the bathroom. I don't want to miss Muriel.

The subway car is empty except for an elderly couple who are weighed down with grocery bags and a shopping cart—on their way back from the market, I'm guessing. The lady gives me a smile as I get off at Port Authority, a rush of memories flooding back into me from when I arrived in America. I make a point to avoid the men's room where I spent my first night on land and walk hurriedly onto the bus depot.

It's a good day for travel, the sky clear and light blue with tinges of pink evaporating as the sun climbs higher. The heat is not quite as oppressive as it was yesterday, and I'm comfortable in my white polo and Dockers…a happy compromise stateside between European trousers and Daniel's Levis. I check in with the service desk and find out which gate I need to go to: the west coast buses departing from level 4. I hurry up the stairs and see the back of her short dark bob where she's standing in line, a blue suitcase waiting upright by her leg.

"Muriel!" I shout, holding up a hand.

She turns at the sound of her name and grins widely, beckoning me over. I run and pull her into a fierce hug, smelling the clove scent of her French cigarettes still lingering in her hair. She pulls back and smiles at me, tears shining in her eyes. "Alden! I'm so happy you came!" She looks behind me, then quickly scans back to my face, her smile cracking a little at the edges. "He didn't come, did he?"

I sigh and shake my head. "I'm sure he's working…or something." It's the last excuse I'll ever make for Daniel with her. "You know that shop he's at now opens early."

Daniel hadn't gone back to the restaurant, instead opting to work at the local German bakery a few blocks down from the house. Our hours were totally off, and I rarely saw him anymore, crossing paths in the attic every once in a while and high-fiving in the hall. Part of me liked it better this way.

Muriel nods. "Of course, of course…" She reaches out and squeezes my arm. "But *you're* here! I am so grateful for that."

We both glance over as the bus doors open, the driver stepping off. "Five minutes, everyone," he grunts, adjusting his belt buckle. "Then we gotta ship out."

Muriel exhales and checks her purse, pulling out her ticket. I suddenly feel rushed, like I'm not going to get a chance to tell her everything I need to say, all of this seeming very final. I clear my throat and wave over at the front of the bus, the glaring white letters across the top spelling out 'Los Angeles.' "You got some flowers for your hair?" I joke weakly. I instantly cringe at my remark, remembering the night at the club all too well and her tearing that white rose from her hair before running off.

I look at Muriel to see if she's thinking the same thing, but she just smiles at me kindly. "That's San Francisco. L.A. is a very different...vibe, I hear."

I grin. "What do they put in their hair there?"

Muriel shrugs. "Peroxide, I gather." She arches a brow and pats her short hair. "What do you think? Should I go blonde?"

I snort. "I think you're lovely just as you are, but I wouldn't want you to stick out like a sore thumb on your first day there..."

When she laughs and bites her lip, I can tell that she's willing herself not to cry. "That might be unavoidable for a French girl dressed like a secretary!" She motions down to her red blouse and navy pencil skirt. "But I'll do my best. Celine, Papa's friend, will be waiting when I arrive. She'll help me get settled." She looks at me wide-eyed. "Will you look in on him for me? Papa? Not too often...just to let me know he's doing okay?"

I nod and look down at the ground. "Do you really have to go, Muriel?" This is a dangerous question, my own throat starting to grow thick.

She sighs and takes my hand, squeezing my fingers. "It's time. Time for something new...new people, new experiences." She scrunches her nose. "But I'll never forget you—that's a promise."

I can't stop the tears now. She's blurry when I look up at her again. "I'll never forget you either. You're..." I let out a sob and a laugh in the same breath. "You were my friend when no one else was, Muriel. You've always been kind, even though you didn't have to be. I can't say that about many people."

"Alden…" she chokes out, tears streaking down her face. We embrace, and she presses her nose into my collar. "Los Angeles is not goodbye!" she hiccups, pulling back to take my face in her hands. "I'm going to see you again! I'll come back and visit, and you'll come see me… Maybe we'll make our way over to Hollywood and try to be movie stars." She twitters her head. "You think they'd take us?"

"You, maybe." I smile through my tears.

Muriel pats my cheek and nods. "You'll bring Jillian… It will be so much fun."

When she stops, I look at her. "Do…do you know?" I ask quietly.

She smooths her palms down my shoulders, fixing my shirt like she always does. "Know what?"

I shake my head. "I'm…I'm going to marry her—Jillian," I cover quickly, offering up a different truth. "I'm going to propose soon—honest."

Muriel beams, wiping her tears away with the back of her hand. "How wonderful! Write me and tell me everything!"

We both grimace as the driver steps out again. "Last call! LA or bust!" he yells jovially, taking his seat behind the wheel.

Muriel gasps and hugs me tightly, putting her mouth to my ear. "You are the most gentlemanly non-Englishman I've ever know—the best," she whispers, her tone urgent. "Jillian better hold on tight if she knows what's good for her. I love you so much!"

I cry harder as she kisses me on both cheeks. "I love you, too…" I rasp as she pulls back and picks up her suitcase, sliding it into the cargo bay.

She takes the first step up and looks back at me, her eyes

nervous. "This is going to be fine. I'm going to be…" Her hands shake as she holds onto the side of the bus for support.

"It's going to be great, Muriel. I know it," I interject, giving her a confident nod. "You're going to take California by storm."

She takes a breath and smiles at me, thankful. "And you'll visit? You promise?"

The driver turns over the engine. I let out a strangled sob. "Every chance I get!"

I hold my hand up and wave as she gets on the bus, waiting as she takes a seat by the window and presses her palm to the glass. I match my hand to hers as the bus roars to life, slowly pulling away from the curb. I run to keep up, tapping the window one more time before it drives out of the station for good.

The street is empty as I stand, watching the bus fade out over the horizon, a hazy puff of exhaust quickly becoming memory. Muriel's gone, Daniel's off doing his own thing… It feels like the end of something. And I'm just…here, alone.

I look around to the empty bus gate, the station a quiet place now. I step out of the street and back inside, for a minute letting solitude get the best of me—before I remember how Jillian said just last night that she's never alone anymore. I suppose that goes for me as well. The corners of my mouth turn up as I leave Port Authority and head back to Queens.

*

The front hall and sitting room are empty when I get to the house. It's odd to see Martin's easy chair abandoned at this time of day, his morning paper scattered in loose sheets on the floor. I'm about to call out when I hear yelling coming from upstairs…two voices.

The voices are loud and angry. I frown and dash up to the second floor, worried that someone might be in trouble. I stop on the landing and look about. The only thing out of order is Daniel's mother's open bedroom door, the shouting coming from inside.

"Wie konntest du in mein Haus bringen?! Nachdem Sie wissen, was es ihr angetan hat!" I hear Martin roar.

"Oppa...stop! Just listen to me—" Daniel is with him, his tone pleading.

I rush over to the threshold and see the two men standing by the dresser, the drawers themselves flung away and stacked lopsided on one another as they argue in fast, broken German. Daniel towers over Martin, his head cowed, hands on his blue jeans as Martin shakes a brick-sized packet of white powder up in his face, his own skin flaming red.

"Was ist das für Wahnsinn?! Explain yourself!" Martin barks, switching hastily between tongues, his whole body trembling.

Daniel clenches his jaw and takes a step back. "I told you—it's not mine!" he shouts defensively, waving at the cocaine. *"Vielleicht ist sie ließ es aus der Zeit vor... Hast du auch daran denken—!"*

Daniel doesn't get to finish whatever he's yelling, as Martin hits him hard across the face, his eyes dark and heavy. The sound of the slap brings back something deep and lost inside of me. My eyelid twitches.

"Don't," Martin hisses. *"Sprichst du nicht wagen, ihr auf diese Weise—"*

Daniel glares at him, holding his cheek in stunned silence. I lurch forward, stepping between them, panic swelling in my chest. "It's mine—it's mine!" I blurt out before I even realize what I'm saying.

Both Daniel and Martin stop and stare at me, their matching brown eyes going wide.

"I, um...I hid it in here...where I didn't think anyone would find it." I glance at Daniel, who shifts nervously.

Martin lowers the brick and gawks at me. "It's yours?" He shakes his head, disbelievingly. All of the anger drains from his body as he looks at the cocaine, then down at the floor, his voice a hushed whisper. "I was cleaning, and I noticed the drawer wasn't closing properly..." He motions weakly back to the dresser, shaking his head. "It's yours. That's...that's just not possible..."

"I'm sorry." I take a deep breath and glare over the old man's head at Daniel, his own gaze boring into me. I think fast. "I know I shouldn't have brought it here, but I didn't know what else to do. I had to put it somewhere."

Martin nods, his eyes clouding in confusion as he shuffles in a tight circle. Daniel doesn't look away as Martin slowly places the drugs on top of the dresser, a pained expression crossing his face as he glimpses the old photos of his daughter. "Did you know about this?" Martin rasps to Daniel.

Daniel stares at me for another minute, searching for the right answer, then looks away at the rug and shakes his head, his mouth pressed into a thin line. "No," he answers quietly. "I had no idea."

Martin lets out a heavy sigh and rubs the bridge of his nose. "I don't understand, Alden." He turns to me and says my name with such sadness that I can feel my heart breaking, his expression checkered with disappointment. "Why you would do this, get involved with this..." He motions back to the cocaine with a sneer. "This garbage! You could lose everything! Does your counselor know? At Immigration?"

I hold my breath, growing dizzy. Jesus—please don't call Burman, please don't call Burman... "No," I reply.

Martin nods and folds his arms. "I thought you were a good boy," he murmurs. His face is still confused, but betrayal is making its way across his features. My resolve begins to waver. "We let you into our home, made you part of our family..."

"I, um..." I try to find Daniel's eyes again, but he refuses to look at me now. I nod; I started this alone, so I have to finish it... and get out in one piece, whatever the cost. I glare back at Martin, my gaze steely. "The money was too good. I only have one chance to make a fresh start here; I wanted to give myself any advantage I could." I draw a deep breath, remembering a conversation that Daniel and I had when I first moved in. It's a long shot; but I'll try anything right now. "Surely, of all people, *you* can understand that, Martin. We all make...*compromises*...to protect ourselves and the one's we love..."

Daniel's brow knits, not putting it together, but Martin's eyes grow wide. I know I've successfully hurt him, and my insides scream in shame. He stares at me blankly, his hand gripping the bedrail next to him tight. Both Daniel and I watch him, waiting.

"Get out," Martin rasps at the floor before looking up at me.

Daniel lets out a short gasp, but I nod. "I'll get my things." I step quietly from the room, leaving them in my wake and heading up the attic stairs.

"Irish—" I hear Daniel call behind me, hot on my heels. He follows and closes the door softly, staring at me as I gather my belongings from around the room. "I didn't want to have to bring all that coke here—but Ramos has been breathing down my neck—"

I hold up a hand and he stops, watching as I find a large canvas bag at the bottom of the closet and go back to the bed. He clears his throat. "Why...why would you do that? Take the hit for me like that?"

I sigh, shoving a couple of shirts into the bag. "Better to have your grandfather hate me than you, Daniel...for both your sakes." I grab my alarm clock and some pairs of cufflinks from my bunk. "Whether he was my friend or not," I look at him pointedly, feeling immensely guilty for lying and betraying Martin, "he loves you, Daniel. Every sacrifice, every hope and dream he's ever had... it's all for you. He's a good man who wants the best for you. You should try not to throw that all away."

"I will. Thank you. I owe you, big time." Daniel's voice is soft.

I shake my head and crush everything down in the sack with my elbow. "I just hope he doesn't decide to call Burman and tell him I'm a hardened criminal." I wince. "That would earn me a one-way ticket back to Ireland...or worse."

Daniel lets out a low chuckle. "You're fine. He's not gonna rat you out…though whatever you said back there did hit him pretty hard." He narrows his eyes. "What did you mean, 'compromises'?"

I swing the bag over my shoulder and take a final look around at the large bedroom with the gorgeous wooden bunkbed. "Don't worry about it—just know that you have a very lovely home."

Daniel smiles tightly. "Thanks, I guess. Where will you go now?"

I exhale. "Jillian's. This is probably for the best anyway. I should be with her. She needs me."

Daniel blinks as I give him a pat on the arm, stepping towards the door. "I'm gonna miss you," he says with a shrug. "I know it wasn't perfect all the time, but it's been…really great having you here—always having someone to talk to, joke around with…" He grins and grabs the bunk-side rail. "I always wanted a—" He stops and shakes his head. "You know."

I sigh. "Yeah. I do." I smile back at him. "I'll see you around, Daniel."

He nods and looks out the window. "Yep. Catch you later."

*

I take the long way once I get off the train, having the day off from work and knowing that Jillian will be busy for another few hours. The sky is technicolor blue, and everyone's out in their bright summer clothes—a perfect June day. I sling my bag over my shoulder and go through the park, watching the kids clamber over the big black rocks and onto the playground, throwing their bodies around like they're invincible. Despite what just happened in Queens, I can't help but smile as I walk. It's something about the uncrushable spirit of childhood, their laughter infectious.

I meander down the path, not really looking where I'm going and enjoying the cool breeze coming through the trees. Suddenly, I find myself standing in front of the carousel. There's no question that it's alive and working today, a long line going around the side, the cries and cheers coming off it distorted as it spins around and around. I grin, thinking of when Sam and I rode it together, Jillian's hair blowing bright in the wind as she watched…my beautiful girl. Sam had been begging ever since the snow melted to come back. I decide to take a ride in his honor and step in line.

We move fairly quickly. Before I know it, I'm sitting tall on the horse with the green ribbon. Kids run to and fro through the wooden animals, squealing in delight when they find their favorites. Even though it's crowded, the horse next to me stays open as the calliope music trills, and we're off. I like it this way; I glance at the empty saddle, first picturing Sam bouncing and laughing next to me…and then a different face, a new face, one I've never seen before but would recognize in an instant. I smile and reach over to grab the other gold pole.

"Hold tight, Lily Rose," I whisper, not wanting anyone around me to hear. "I gotcha… Dad's not gonna let you fall."

I nod to myself; yeah, I'll definitely bring her here. She'll love it. Sam can come too—we'll all go together. I look out at the park and grin. Everything will be different… She'll never have to grow up the way I did, surrounded by anger and violence, having to fight for every day she spends in the world. I will see to it personally that she is happy and safe, not wanting for anything…and always knowing that she's loved. That's the easy part. I already love her so much.

The ride slows to a stop, and I find myself excited to get off, ready to rush back to my new life. I head out of the park through the west gates, wanting to stop by the market before Jillian comes home. I'll cook tonight; it won't be very good, but I'll make her put her feet up and give her a laugh while I fumble around the kitchen.

I'll revel in every moment that God has graciously given me. Somewhere along the way, He decided that I should win the lottery—and I'm not going to miss a minute.

CHAPTER 21

LOS ANGELES—PRESENT DAY

*I*T'S LATE WHEN I wake the next morning, the sun already filling the room when I open my eyes. I suck in a breath and run a hand down the bed next to me. Daniel's gone, the sheets on his side cool. I sit up and look at my clock: 10:15.

"Wow...okay—time to get up." I murmur. I tiredly massage my neck as I step out of bed and find my sweats, throwing them on right over my tank top and shorts. I'm coiling my hair into a bun when I walk into the kitchen, which is already a flurry of activity.

Daniel stands with his back to the doorway, fully dressed and prepping vegetables by the stove, the counter covered in grocery bags and food. Mary Carmen sits at her chair at the kitchen table, a cup of coffee in hand. She looks up and sees me, glasses perched on the end of her nose and her hair slightly frizzed.

"Good morning and merry Christmas Eve," she says, subdued, before going back to her papers on the table. I lean against one of the chairs, checking her pallor. She seems like herself again, rosy-cheeked and put together in a clean sweater and skirt. Whatever illness caused by her fit at the movie theater yesterday

seems to have passed in the night—but she's obviously preoccupied, and I have a feeling I know why.

"Yeah, merry Christmas Eve," I reply groggily, taking in the
papers scattered in front of her. They aren't notes or any type of
writing that I recognize; instead, they look like connect-the-dot
puzzles. I point down at them. "What's going on here? Given up
on your Sudoku?"

"What? Oh—" She glances up, haphazardly shaking her head.
"No—they're star charts, actually…from the last two weeks." She
stares at the series of pinpoints in front of her. "I've never been
one for deciphering these things, but I thought I would try, what
with everything that's going on… It might give us a little insight
on what's to come…but I'm not really sure what I'm looking at."

I glance over at Daniel. He still hasn't turned around. I frown,
rubbing my neck. "What *is* going on? With everything…" I take a
deep breath, pretenses be damned. "I know both sides are meeting
in Portcullis right now—have we heard anything about how that's
going?" Is the world about to blow up?

Daniel's back has tensed. Mary Carmen looks over at him,
then back at me. "The Delegates are still locked in chambers—
trying to decide if Heaven and Hell are really going to go to war.
There's a lot of pent-up aggression from centuries of distrust…but
the Resistance has given them a common enemy." She nods down
at the star charts. "Hell has been trying very hard to keep them a
secret, but now it seems that it's become everyone's problem—so
maybe there is a chance they can work together. I don't know."
She sighs and gives me a weak smile. "If everything can stay quiet
for a little longer, maybe some real change will finally happen. We
shall see."

"Yeah…right." I look back at Daniel, who is still hard at work.
I clear my throat and walk over to him. "Hey…you did the shopping already?" I pop up on the counter next to Daphne's tank.

Daniel peeks over his shoulder at me and nods. "I thought
you might want to sleep in," he replies nonchalantly, still not

really meeting my eyes. "Isn't that what you're supposed to do on Christmas break?"

"I guess." I shrug—it's not like anything about this Christmas break has been typical so far. Sighing, I reach for my phone where it's plugged into the wall charger. When a little reminder dings on the screen, I grimace. "Crap…I'm supposed to meet Livie and her new boyfriend later." I toss the phone back and rub my face.

Mary Carmen perks up. "Livie from Group? That's nice!" she chirps, taking a quick sip of coffee. "I'm glad you're doing things outside our meetings. She's a sweet girl."

I tap at the apps on my screen, keeping my gaze down. "Yeah, she is. But I don't know, I might cancel…" I see Daniel look up from his vegetables out of the corner of my eye.

"Why?" Mary Carmen gets up and takes her mug over to the sink, giving it a rinse, her tone suddenly severe. "I hope this isn't because you're thinking of going to Herod's Feast, Christa—"

I straighten my back and growl. "NO! I said I wouldn't go!"

Mary Carmen gives me a look, then nods, apparently appeased. I sigh. "I just don't know if I'm feeling social right now—I'm kind of in a weird mood…"

"About what happened yesterday?" Mary Carmen asks. She's now moved to the doorway. My gaze darts over to Daniel, who has frozen in place, staring at the cutting board.

Does Mary Carmen know about last night and me and him? About what almost happened in my room? "Uh…" I give her a puzzled smile.

She shakes her head. "At the movies? With the mass Haloing—what started everything?!" she exclaims, gesturing widely with her hands.

I sniff and nod enthusiastically in agreement. "Right." I check Daniel; he's gone back to chopping carrots.

Mary Carmen takes a breath. "Everything is fine. Heaven checked in this morning." She taps her temple. "There were a few isolated incidents between mortals and Demons, but nothing on a catastrophic level, thank goodness." She smiles. "Everyone has returned to normal, and it looks like it's shaping up to be a pretty quiet day, at least until we hear the verdict from Porticullis… which no one is anticipating for another few days."

"Don't jinx it," I mutter under my breath.

Mary Carmen tuts and looks at the phone in my hand. "You should see Livie. You're always talking about how you want more time out of the house and with your friends… It'll be good for you."

"Yeah…you're right," I say to cut her off before she gets the chance to ask about anything else.

Mary Carmen shoots me a suspicious glance. "Very good," she mutters. I sigh again and put on my best smile; I guess Daniel's not the only one who's used to me being argumentative.

Seemingly convinced of my sincerity, Mary Carmen cranes her head around the kitchen. "Have you seen *my* phone? I wanted to make a couple calls to the other Guardians. I know you tried last night…" She waves at Daniel. "…but I'm surprised we haven't heard from anyone yet."

"In your purse, front pocket," I answer, "next to your bed." I made sure it made it to its usual resting place when we got home yesterday.

Mary Carmen smiles. "Thank you. My charger is in there. I'll just be a few minutes." Quirking her eyebrows, she pats the door-frame and leaves the kitchen.

I watch her go, then turn to Daniel. "Hey…" I murmur shyly, not quite sure what to say.

Daniel glances over, his face placid. "Hey." He reaches into a lower cabinet for the big soup pot, sets it on the stovetop, then starts transferring the prepped vegetables from the cutting board.

I hop off the counter, my frustration from last night coming back. "You could've woken me up," I say lightly, stopping next to him. I jerk my chin toward the shopping bags. "I wanted to help."

Daniel shrugs. "Honestly, you looked very peaceful where you

were, and I thought I could just go out and get it done really fast."
He moves another handful of carrots. "No subtext, I swear." He
finally looks me in the eye.

I exhale, crossing my arms. "Okay…well, give me something
to do now." I snicker at the bags of unopened produce. "Just
not onions."

Daniel laughs. "Yeah, they're definitely not your strong suit."
He opens a drawer and pulls out a peeler. "How about we put you
on potatoes? Most important dish of the day…"

I smile and take the peeler. "I think I can handle that."

I scoot in next to him at the sink, and we both get to our
respective jobs, me washing and peeling the potatoes, then handing them off to Daniel to be sliced and diced. I glance over at him
every once in a while, admiring the swift assuredness of his hands
as he cuts the potatoes into precise little cubes.

"So…how long do you think we'll be on this stuff today?" I
ask after a bit, trying to make conversation while clearly avoiding
a few particular landmines. I hold up one of the potatoes. "Think
we can stretch it into late afternoon?"

Daniel smiles and shakes his head, his knife making neat little
chopping noises. "You really want to skip out on Livie that bad?
What's the deal?"

I sigh and stop peeling, handing over another finished spud.
"I don't know… What am I even going to talk about with her?
Reading my best friend's soul and terrorist attacks from the
Demon Resistance?" I roll my eyes. "Prophecies from a dead,
pregnant could-be schizophrenic?"

Daniel furrows his brow and readjusts his grip on the knife.
"Colette wasn't schizophrenic…"

"You get my drift!" I frown, flicking potato peels into the sink
basin. "Livie's pretty open-minded, but I think this stuff might be
pushing it, even with her."

"Talk about school—about your science project," Daniel fills
in. "What you want for Christmas!"

"I don't want anything for Christmas," I interject glumly.

Daniel groans. "Well then, I'll just return those concert tickets and cool new sunglasses I've got for you under the tree!" he exclaims, dropping his knife with a clatter.

I perk up and watch as he adds the potatoes to the pot. "You got me concert tickets?" I mumble, my curiosity piqued. "What band?"

Daniel twists back, his mouth formed into an O. "Ohh... so *maybe* now someone does want something for Christmas!" He laughs, coming back over. "I've got all sorts of surprises up my sleeve, Ms. Nichols! Maybe if you wanna stay on Santa's 'Nice' list, you might check that attitude at the door."

I snicker and start in on a new potato. "All right, all right..." I frown down at my hands. "Maybe Livie and what's-his-name... Brad...Brennan..."

"The new boyfriend?" Daniel wonders.

"Yeah. Maybe they'll just be so consumed with one another that I won't have to say anything, just sit and watch them make out." I make a face. "Just how I wanted to spend Christmas Eve..."

Daniel smiles. "That's what they make fancy coffee drinks for... Just get the one loaded up with peppermint and whipped cream and stick your nose in that, right?" He gives me a light hip check. "And you're not going to be there alone! I'm still invited to this thing, aren't I?"

I blush and grin. "Yeah, if you still *want* to come... I didn't know if..." I stop, not wanting to bring up last night. Instead, I focus on peeling the skin perfectly off the potato.

Daniel sucks in a breath. "Hey." He drops his tone to softer than it was a second ago, leaning into my hair. "Of course I still want to come. I want to—" He exhales. "I *need* to be with you, Christa. Nothing's going to change that."

I turn about six shades of red and nod, slightly shocked at his statement. "Okay...yeah." I smile, setting down the potato I was working on. "You can come have coffee with me and my friend and her new, super sexy boy-toy."

Daniel makes a face. "He's *super* sexy?"

I laugh, covering my mouth with my hand. "I don't know! That's just how Livie describes him!" I shake my head and lean back on the counter. "Which probably means he looks like one of those dudes from Florida Georgia Line, since that's the type she's into."

"Oh man—then we're all in trouble!" Daniel grins, his voice growing twangy. "My chivalrous opening doors and picking up coffee is gonna seem downright paltry compared to that sort of Southern charm!" He stops his drawl and looks at me. "You said he's from the South, right?"

"I don't know." I giggle. "*Livie's* Southern—but I don't think he is…"

"Doesn't matter." Daniel sighs, checking his reflection in the microwave door. "Now I definitely need to bring my A-game— don't wanna come across like a total bum."

"I would like to see what that looks like," I tease, reaching up and ruffling his hair. "Does it involve designer duds and a fancy ride?"

"I said 'A-game,' Christa…not a Deal with the Devil." He arches a brow knowingly. "Don't wanna be mistaken for one of the bad guys cruising around in a brand new Porsche…"

"I don't think you need to worry about that," I snort. "The bright gold Halo is a dead giveaway."

He smiles widely. "Yeah, maybe…" With a shrug, he starts sorting through the bags, pulling celery and turnips out. "I just want your friends to think I'm…I dunno, cool, I guess. That's all."

I shake my head at him. "My friends think you're very cool, Daniel. Don't worry—Jodie loves you…and maybe you haven't noticed, but everyone at school is obsessed with you—" I perk up as I see Mary Carmen walk back into the kitchen, phone in hand. "Speaking of friends, how did everyone take the news? Did Ellis say what time she was coming tomorrow?" I call to her. I'm really excited to finally meet this mystery Guardian, more so now that I know she was the last known prophet's caretaker.

Mary Carmen, however, only stares blankly down at her cell. "I couldn't find any of them," she whispers, her tone grave. She looks at Daniel. "I talked to Ellis's roommate, and he said he hasn't seen her since middle of last week. Daniel…"

My Guardian stops and turns to Mary Carmen. "I'm sure she's just on a case, M.C.… Come on, you remember what that's like," he replies lightly. "Cruising around the country, no phone service… I'm sure she'll be back soon. She said she's coming tomorrow, and it's not like her to blow anybody off—"

Mary Carmen shakes her head at the floor. "No, this is different. She's really good about checking in with Raoul…and he said she hasn't even called. I'm worried." She bites her lip and stares back at him. "Have you heard from *anyone* recently? Roger? Chi?"

Daniel sighs and runs a hand through his hair. "I mean, *no*… but it's not like we're known for being all buddy-buddy with one another. Everyone likes their space." His voice falters as his expression shifts to match Mary Carmen's worried glare.

"Where *is* everyone?" she rasps, crossing her arms. "I don't like it."

"What—what should we do?" I interject quietly, not having ever seen Mary Carmen this concerned. She's our mission control. Even when all Hell was breaking loose last month, she kept her cool.

Mary Carmen rubs the back of her neck. "I need to go down to Long Beach, see if I can start to sort this out." She looks up and smiles tightly. "I bet if I ask around, I can pick up Ellis's trail—maybe even get some information on the other Guardians. It would just be good to touch base…especially now, with everything that's happening with the Resistance and Hell trying to make the Guardians their scapegoat." She sighs and reaches over, giving Daniel's shoulder a pat. "You think you can keep things under control here here until I get back?"

Daniel grins and picks up his knife, going back to cooking prep. "You got it, M.C.—me and my sous are taking care of business." He smiles at me.

I roll my eyes and look down at his hands, noticing that they're trembling a bit. Odd.

"Okay…then I'm gonna get going." Mary Carmen nods. "I don't plan to be late, but we'll see." She gives me a little wave as she swishes out of the kitchen.

I turn back to Daniel, my face drawn. "Well, that's slightly horrifying," I breathe, settling down next to him again. He doesn't look up from the cutting board. "Missing Guardians—as if we didn't have enough to deal with already."

"No one is missing," Daniel tuts. "Before I moved to LA, I used to go months without talking to another Guardian." He jerks his head back to the door. "No, Mary Carmen and I are just getting spoiled, having everybody under one roof."

I watch his hands, his knife moving faster as he slices through the turnips, then exhale and stare at him. "Well then, maybe it's just an excuse for her to sneak off and go on a wild goose chase for some face on a milk carton." Daniel gives me a weird look, and I instantly chide myself. He still doesn't know about the little side trip that Mary Carmen and I took to Encinitas. The search for Miguel Alvarez continues…whoever that is.

I give Daniel a grin and shake it off, changing the subject. "I'm glad we're all here together. The other way sounds lonely, being out there all by yourself." I imagine Daniel living nomadically, hitching cross-country from one city to another.

He sighs and grabs another turnip. "That's how it is for most of us…especially when you first start out." He shrugs. "You have to figure out quick what you're supposed to do. It's not like you get a ton of guidance from upstairs." He points with his knife. "And then once you get going, you try to keep your distance from other Guardians. Like I said, we're pretty territorial...in a friendly way—but we're all playing the same game, and everyone's vying for the most points..."

"Huh." I grin and nudge him with my hip. "How many 'points' am I worth? Am I totally sucking up all your chances for redemption?"

Daniel scoffs, trimming away a little stem. "No, you're the jackpot—full ride." He looks at me and nods. "We play our cards right, we all win in the end."

I stop and stare at my feet. What does 'winning' really look like? "Does that mean you'll Ascend?" I whisper, not looking up at him. "And then you'll be gone?"

Daniel goes silent. I can feel his eyes on me. "Yeah, I guess so," he eventually replies, his voice hushed. "Gone...*in* Heaven..." His face flashes for a second, and I can't tell what he's thinking. He looks up at me, though, and gives a big grin. "But that's not happening any time soon, Christa. Don't worry."

"Yeah." I smile weakly at him, trying not to look totally miserable at the idea of his Ascension. I must fail, though, because he looks like I just socked him in the gut.

I don't want him to feel bad...not about what's supposed to be the best moment of his existence. "Hey—let's cheer up!" I say with forced merriment, half-heartedly smacking him on the arm. "That's what we're doing all this for, right? Jingle jingle." I bite my lip. We still have time together—precious, precious time.

"Right!" Daniel exclaims, going back to his work. "And these veggies aren't going to prep themselves—OW!" He suddenly jumps and drops the knife, sucking his thumb.

"What?" I squeak in alarm.

Daniel shakes his head and blinks down at the small puddle of bright red blood dotting the turnips on the cutting board. "Did you cut yourself?" I ask, surprised. I spin toward him, glaring at the knife. "Do you need a Band-Aid?" I immediately roll my eyes—of course he doesn't need a Band-Aid; he's probably already healed.

He's still zoned out, staring intently at the cutting board. "Not now…" he rasps instead of answering, slowly picking up the knife. "Not now—not this…"

I shake my head in confusion. "Daniel? Are…are you talking to me?"

He ignores me, instead palming another turnip in his injured hand. "Paysanne," I hear him mutter under his breath, his eyes wild on the knife. "Paysanne, paysanne… Speed, waste, uniformity—come on…" I watch his hand tremble around the turnip, the knife shaking violently.

"Daniel…" I try to keep my voice even. "Are you okay?"

"Come on, come on!" He grits his teeth and lowers the blade on the turnip. "You *know* this! Paysanne the fuckin' turnip!"

I try to put my hand on his shoulder, but he shrugs me off. "Whoa—Daniel! You're starting to freak me out!" I shout sternly. "Calm down—"

"I just need to think—I…I got this!" he yells, tossing the knife down on the board. He rams his fists against his temples, glaring at the stove. "They can't take this, too—not this!"

"Daniel—what are talking about?!" My own voice grows shrill as I finally start to panic. "What's happening?" I feel my stomach drop as I look between him and the blood on the vegetables, Mary Carmen's voice ringing in my ear. The forgetting—he's losing something, right now… "Daniel!" I reach for him, concerned.

He stops and rubs his face, his aura burning hot coal red. "I just…I need to get out," he murmurs. He's wearing a crazed expression, like the look of one of those old Hollywood starlets that's completely cracked up. "Go for a walk, clear my head…" He zips to the table and grabs his jacket.

I gape as he stomps out of the kitchen. "Wait—I'll come with you!" I yell after him, following him down the hall. "You're obviously really messed up about this, Daniel… I don't like the idea of you going out by yourself like this—"

Daniel shakes his head and wrenches open the front door. "No, you stay here—and lock the door." He turns back to me for a second. "Don't let anyone but me or Mary Carmen in." He marches out onto the porch.

"Wh—" I stammer in disbelief. "What about Livie? We're supposed to meet them—"

"I'll be back soon!" he shouts from the walk. "Lock the door!"

"Gah—okay, fine!" I yell back.

I slam the door shut and angrily bolt all the locks. In a huff, I step to the front living room window and pull back the curtain, watching Daniel dart past the gate and into the street, barreling off in some unknown direction.

"Go ahead, have your nervous breakdown without me," I grumble, pitching the drapes back in place, worry still gnawing at my gut. I stare around the empty living room, realizing that this is the first time I've really been alone since everything began. I don't find it exhilarating or freeing, just eerily quiet. Creepy.

"It's just me and the garage mice, I guess." Sighing, I wrap my arms around chest. I glance at the TV and then at the crowded bookshelves. I don't really feel like watching a movie or reading right now. Instead, I just flop down on the couch, staring up at the ceiling, consumed with thoughts of Daniel.

"This is weird," I say out loud, checking out our growing cobweb situation. I rub my face wearily. "And…I'm talking to myself again. Warehouse Part 2, anyone? Crap." I groan and grab a blanket by my feet. "Whatever… I'm gonna just take a nap, and when I wake up, Daniel will be back, and it will be time to go meet Livie," I say affirmatively. "Good plan."

Sweeping the blanket over me and tucking my head under a couch cushion, I try to push the desire to chase after Daniel out of my brain.

*

I wake a few hours later, the sun having shifted in the room. With a yawn, I sit up and glance around. The house is still dead silent. I prop up on my knees and check out the window. Mary Carmen's car isn't in the driveway, so she's still gone, and there's no sign of Daniel.

"So much for 'being back soon'…" I mumble as I get up. I check the front door; it's still locked up nice and tight. I rub life into my arms and stumble down the hall, checking the stove clock when I make it to the kitchen, seeing that it's close to 3 o'clock. My eyes widen in surprise: I slept for almost four hours.

"Jeez…I must be more stressed out than I thought," I murmur, stepping over to my phone. I check my messages, hoping there's word from Daniel—to no avail. There *is* a text from Livie, though, giving the address of a coffee shop over on Melrose. I know the one; it's not far from here. She wants to meet at 4. I could make it.

"Well, fuck," I exhale, dragging a hand through my hair as I glance around the empty kitchen. All of the shopping bags and half-cut vegetables are where we left them from earlier, rotting peels and dirty kitchen tools cluttering up the counter. I frown—that's something the Daniel I know wouldn't tolerate. 'Work clean' was something he drilled into both Mary Carmen and I whenever we were cooking. He's definitely off.

I grimace and stare down the hall toward the front door, willing him to walk through it. Crickets. Wherever everyone has gone, I am the last thing on their minds right now. I take a long look around the disorderly kitchen, but there is nothing here for me to do unless I want to don an apron and pretend to be Cinderella and clean up Daniel's mess. I snort—not in this lifetime, thank you very much. Resolute, I walk out of the kitchen and back to my room.

I toss off my sweats and put on a tight black tank top and

jeans, throwing my black leather jacket over my shoulders. I find my boots back in the living room by the Christmas tree. As I'm zipping them up, I rifle through the couple of small presents under the tree. Mary Carmen's necklace and a new sweater for my mom from me, and the rest are from Daniel, wrapped in last weekend's comic section. There are two for Mary Carmen and two for me. I smile, touching the small envelope that obviously holds the aforementioned concert tickets. The other package feels like the sunglasses. I raise my eyebrows, wishing I could open those right now... Bet they'd look killer with my outfit—but Daniel would be really bummed if I didn't wait for him. I set them gently back under the tree, then saunter over to the front door.

I take a deep breath and undo the series of deadbolts, suddenly feeling very guilty for what I'm about to do. House Rule Number 1 is that Christa doesn't go out unescorted, lest there be Demons about...but that was also followed shortly by House Rule Number 2, that Christa was never left home alone—and here we are.

"It's just coffee," I mutter, grabbing the doorknob. "I'll be back in an hour, probably before they even know I'm gone." I stop and look around the quiet living room. I know I should just park it on the couch and twiddle my thumbs until Daniel or Mary Carmen comes home. Every muscle in my body tenses at the idea, though. I can't just sit here waiting for someone to show up—I'll go crazy for sure. I nod and stick with my guns, pulling open the door and stepping out into the sunshine.

It's a short walk to Melrose, the small boutique shops busy with last-minute holiday shoppers. I hastily pass the vintage shop where Mandisa accosted Daniel and me last week, catching a glimpse of Mellie smiling as she helps a customer inside. I check the Agent's watch at my wrist; I made pretty good time heading over, so I still have 30 minutes 'til I'm supposed to meet Livie and Brennan. I find the coffee shop and stand on the front sidewalk, deciding if

I want to go in early and just wait. As I'm debating, I spy a small record store across the street and pause. I still haven't found a Christmas present for Daniel, and that looks pretty perfect. After checking for traffic, I hop across the road.

"Welcome to Headline," a guy about my age with spiky blue hair and a huge nose mutters from the front desk as I bounce through the door. He gives me a quick onceover and nods appreciatively before going back to his magazine. "Nice boots."

I smile and look down at my feet. "Oh—thanks! I um…" I glance back around the store, seeing that the walls are covered in old concert posters. "I'm not sure what I'm looking for… Is it okay if I just browse?"

"No crime in just lookin'." He smirks, obviously checking me out this time, then turns up his radio. "Lemme know if you need anything."

I blush. "Thanks."

Before Sonic the Hedgehog has a chance to say anything else, I dodge back behind a rack of used CDs and peek through the titles for a bit. They're mostly old punk records…not really Daniel's type of music. But I brighten when I make it to the back of the store and see a tall metal shelf unit filled with electrical equipment.

"Hey!" I call back to the guy in the front. "Are these record players?" I rest a hand on a dusty case.

Sonic glances up. "Yup."

"Do they work?" I arch a brow.

"Sort of."

So not helpful, Sonic. But I don't care… This is a step in the right direction. Daniel hasn't been back to his place at the Factory in weeks, as Mary Carmen is not a huge fan of me spending time there with the asbestos and crumbling infrastructure. I'm sure he misses his old player. Maybe I could get him one he could keep at the house, and we could listen to records together again. I bet he'd like that.

With a grin, I start going through the old turntables, finding one that looks like it's in halfway good repair. With a grunt, I lug the heavy box to the front. "Vinyl?" I wheeze, setting the beast on the front counter with as much care as I can muster.

Sonic points to the middle section behind me. "Deftones just put out a new best of."

I glower; he's right on the money for me, of course, but after my recent experiences of guys knowing all my deepest and darkest, I wish he would just keep his hunches to himself. "Thanks, but it's not for me." I grimace. "Christmas present."

He snickers and returns to reading.

With a sneer, I head down the vinyl aisle, casually running my fingers over the new and not-so-new albums. I come to the end of the row and stop in front of a very small section labeled 'Grumpy Geezer Rock.' I grin and flip through.

"Jackpot…" I murmur, using one of Daniel's favorite words. I try to remember the names of the bands he was looking for the other night—Ozzy Osborne, maybe? As I flip through the stack, I recognize several of the covers from Daniel's own personal collection, including Van Morrison's *Astral Weeks*. I pull it out and caress it, remembering our first night together. This is what we listened to as he told me everything about Heaven and Hell, who he was…who I was. Feels like a million years ago, now.

I sigh and tuck it under my arm. I'm definitely getting this one. Even if he already has it, it'll make him think of me…of us. And we can listen to it whenever we want. I love it.

"Now for something different," I breathe, going back to the stack. I look through and come to a fraying cover of two guys shaking hands. Even though the picture is starting to whiten with age, it's pretty clear that one man is on fire. I snigger to myself: seems very apropos for our lives. I turn the album over—Pink Floyd, *Wish You Were Here*.

"Hey," I call again to Sonic, holding up the record. "Is this good?"

Sonic squints to see what I'm talking about and shrugs. "If you like weird conceptual British rock, sure." His mouth twists. "Not exactly cutting-edge by today's standards, and pretty mixed reviews when it first came out...but still a big deal."

I take another look at the cover and nod. "Okay, I'll take it." I move back to the front desk and set it down next to the turntable, along with Van Morrison. "This one, too."

Sonic blows out his cheeks and checks my stuff. "Interesting selection. This one's pretty *romantic*." He quirks his brows as he rolls his Rs. "This for your boyfriend or something?" He sounds jealous.

"No—it's for—" I stop and shake my head. You know what? Screw it. Why not live the fantasy for a hot five seconds? No one's here to tell me different...and I don't like the way Sonic is leering at me anyway—terrible manners.

"Actually, yes, it *is* for my boyfriend," I reply indignantly, tapping the records. "He's a huge classic rock fan."

Sonic sniffs and starts tallying up my order on the cash register. "Sounds totally boring. This is the same stuff my grandpa listens to."

I frown as his eyes flicker back to me. "He's not boring!" I huff. I don't even know why I bother... Who cares what this kid thinks? But I do care, apparently. I shove my hands into my pockets. "And it's *good* music! Just because it's old doesn't mean it's irrelevant... It's timeless." I sound just like Daniel.

Sonic puts his hands up. "Hey, whatever. He's *your* boyfriend." He glances at the cash register. "Your total's $41.73. Cash or credit only—no checks."

"Fine." I shake my head and pull some cash from my wallet, tossing it on the counter. "Keep the change."

Sonic sighs. "Yeah...we really can't do that."

"Whatever!" I snap, hoisting the record player and albums into my arms. "Merry Christmas!"

"Happy holidays," he replies insolently as I stomp out the

door with all my new goodies. There's a break in the traffic, and I hastily cross the street before the light changes. Livie and Brennan should be at the coffee shop any time now, and I want to make sure we can get some seats together…preferably by a fireplace.

I'm juggling everything in one hand while trying to open the cafe door when someone knocks right into me. The records go flying, but I manage to save the turntable.

"Hey—watch it!" I cry out, readjusting my grip. I grimace once I've got ahold on the player box again, staring down at the records on the sidewalk. *Astral Weeks* slipped partially out of its sleeve. "Aw, man! Come on…" I grumble, crouching down to put it back together before the record gets scratched.

A pair of beat-up red Converse sneakers stop in front of me. "Are you okay?" a voice asks softly. "Did…did anything break?"

"No, I think it's fine," I sigh, checking the record one last time before I look up. "Thanks—" I gasp, my whole body freezing.

It's another Guardian, a boy, his Halo burning bright. I quickly get to my feet, at a loss for words. "I'm sorry," he mutters, scratching the back of his head; his hair is dyed the same color as his sneakers, a blinding firetruck red… He and Sonic should start a band. "I didn't mean to bump into you like that, make you drop all your stuff."

"Really—it's okay!" I answer breathlessly, re-stacking my gifts. I can't believe I'm finally meeting another Guardian—and in the middle of Melrose, no less. "You…you know I can *see* you, right?" I lean in and whisper. The boy shifts uncomfortably. I bite my lip. "Do you know who I am?"

He winces. "I know who you are, Christa."

The way he says my name catches me off-guard; I know everyone in the Divine world knows I'm the Catalyst, but hearing my name in his mouth sounds so…familiar. I squint at his face, trying to place him. There are aspects of his expression that feel so recognizable—but the longer I look at him, the more my vision goes blurry, and it actually starts to *hurt* to stare at him…like little neuroblasts in my brain are ordering me to look away. In fact, every fiber of my being is telling me to disregard him altogether.

"Do I know you?" I ask after a minute, my tone confused. There's something about the shape of his nose...or maybe the way his eyebrows knit together...

The boy draws in a sharp breath and peeks over my shoulder, his eyes going wide. "No time! You have to get inside!" He wrenches open the glass cafe door and practically shoves me in.

I balk, my hands still full with the turntable and records. "What—what's going on?" I exclaim. "I have to talk to you—find out—"

"I said no time!" He looks back down the street, his face pinched. "Don't come out for a while, okay? Just go meet your friend and pretend you never saw me..."

I startle. This kid knows a lot about me for someone I just met for the first time. "How do you know I'm meeting someone?" I ask hurriedly.

He shakes his head and closes the door between us, then takes off running again. I take a few steps back into the cafe and stare out the front windows, gasping in shock when, a few seconds later, I finally see what...or *who*...he's running from. Two Demons dressed in dark black suits come dashing down the sidewalk from the opposite direction. I quickly duck down next to a couch, but I can still see them through the window. They don't see me, instead pointing the same way Ginger Guardian went and following him.

I slump against the side of the couch and take a deep breath. "Little close, Nichols," I mutter, running a hand through my hair. What a stupid idea... What was I thinking, going out alone? This city is overrun with Demons, worse than rats and roaches. I should just pack up and head back to Mary Carmen's, fix myself a snack and watch *Major League* on the DVR again. Daniel is obsessed with Charlie Sheen movies and was super excited when they played it on USA for the umpteenth time. Yeah, that's what I'll do...

"Christa! What are you doing over there?" a bright Southern drawl calls over the cafe noises. I stick my face up on the couch arm and see Livie waving by the front counter. She grins at me. "Hey! I got us seats in the back…"

I stand, trying to look cool as I brush floor gunk off my jeans. Livie's eyes dart around me, puzzled. "No Cutie Pie Rockstar?" she asks.

I shake my head, thinking fast. "He—Daniel—couldn't come." I shrug. "Traffic court."

"Oh." Livie nods knowingly. "That's okay! Brennan couldn't come either…had to help out with decorating for this AMAZING Christmas party he's taking me to tonight!" She bounces giddily. "I'm so excited! You should see the dress I've got for it, all sparkly and white! Looks like a million snowflakes all sewn together…" She scrunches her shoulders as she takes my arm. "But I'm so happy I get to see you! Let's get Frappuccinos, my treat!"

"Sounds great," I murmur, checking the door behind us one more time as we walk over to the barista. There's no sign of the Demons…or Ginger Guardian. I sigh. I should have followed him—I *know* I know him…somehow…

"Do you want whipped cream?" Livie taps my arm, both she and the barista smiling at me. I nod and put on a matching grin; can't worry about missed opportunities now.

Livie pays for our drinks, then ushers me to the other side of the bar. "Oh my gosh—so what has been going on, girl?" she chirps as we wait for our order. "It was so weird not having Group this week… I actually think I *miss* Michela!"

I snicker. "You should have said that in your text… I would have worn my Twisted Plum lipstick, done my hair up in pigtails."

Livie laughs and rolls her eyes. "Absence makes the heart grow fonder, right? I'm sure she'll make up for it next time we see her, have some crazy story about how her boyfriend left her tied up and hung upside down all Christmas Day for some bondage/dominance sex act—"

"LIVIE!" I crow, batting her hand playfully. "That's pretty dark—especially for you! And what do you know about BDSM?" This from the girl who spent six years in 4-H and can name every single breed of milk cow.

She arches a brow. "I've got a dark side, Christa. It's always the one's you least suspect!" She smiles her thanks as the barista hands us our drinks. "Come on, I got us the big chairs in the corner."

I follow her over to a pair of cushy armchairs right by the fireplace. Yes—wishes do come true. "This is nice," I breathe, setting down the record player and albums, warming my cold hands, and snuggling into one of the seats. "Thanks for inviting me out."

Livie sits down opposite me. "I'm just glad you were in town! Everyone else I know is on vacation in some amazing locale—like Hawaii…or Switzerland!" She shakes her head as she takes a sip of her drink, a trace of a whipped cream mustache lingering around her mouth when she pulls her mug away. "Nobody ever goes anywhere for break back home. We all just have a nice, country Christmas!" She wipes her lips with the back of her hand. "You got anything cool happening tomorrow?"

I sigh. "Oh, nothing too big…just some friends coming over to open presents, helping out with dinner…" I cringe internally. I *hope* we're still having Christmas dinner.

Livie smiles warmly. "That sounds great! I wish we had people coming over—it's just gonna be me and my little sister, my parents…" She shrugs, then brightens. "The *real* fun is happening tonight!"

I grin, happy to put the focus on her. "Yeah…so tell me about this party—and *this* boy." I waggle my eyebrows and take a draw off my cup.

Livie sucks in a big breath, and her exhale comes out as something like a squeal. "Oh-my-God, Christa! He is the most amazing guy I have ever met!" She pops her legs up to her chest excitedly while she tugs at her hair. "So sweet, so thoughtful…*so* sexy!" She mashes her mouth into her knees to keep her voice down.

"Wow." I nod obligingly. "He sounds pretty perfect."

"He is! That dress I was telling you about—he bought it for me!" She slaps the chair arm and widens her eyes at me. "Like… straight outta *Pretty Woman*, right? I mean…who does that?"

I shrug. "Someone who's pretty serious, I guess…"

Livie leans in. "You think so, Christa? We haven't established if we're exclusive yet… I really wanna make it official." She purses her lips. "He is so fine, I'm sure there are a bunch of other girls who are trying to make a play for him."

"I don't think you need to worry about that, Livie!" I giggle, motioning to her soft blonde hair and perfect complexion. "*You're* fine, too. He's the lucky one, in my opinion."

Livie blushes. "Thanks, Christa… That's sweet of you to say." She exhales and glances at me devilishly. "It started to get really steamy last night…"

I return her grin. "Oh, did it?"

We come a little closer, Livie lowering her voice to a whisper. "You're not a virgin, right?" she asks, her eyes wide. When I shake my head, she sighs, relieved. "Okay… So I've done it like… twice…with my ex-boyfriend in Tennessee? It was really dumb, like, both times." I nod, so she continues. "But it's, like…*totally* different with Brennan." She stops and exhales. "We haven't… you know…*gone all the way*…" She laughs at her own old-fashioned declaration. "But I want to, so bad. When he touches me, it's like my whole body's on fire…and not just the little baby tingles, you know? It's something *different*. Holding hands, kissing, *more*…it doesn't matter. I am like…spellbound by this guy!" She searches my face. "Do you know what I mean?"

I smile weakly. "Sort of." I *do* know what it's like to be completely enthralled with another person…except, unlike Livie, I don't get to do anything about it. I bitterly go back to last night in my mind, feeling Daniel's breath on my skin. I could have exploded just from the sheer closeness of him, his body, his scent…my home. But we can never get close enough—not really.

"What's wrong?" Livie is watching me, her face suddenly concerned.

I quickly snap back, shaking my head. "Nothing! I just remembered I have to empty the dishwasher when I get home." Brilliant, Nichols. Keep 'em coming.

"Ugh...I know what you mean!" Livie groans empathetically. "My mom's had me loaded down with extra chores all week—shampooing the carpets, cleaning out the garage..." She takes another sip of her coffee. "Is Mary Carmen treating you like a work horse? She doesn't seem like she'd be all that bad from how she is in class..."

Livie noticed Mary Carmen and I coming and going together from Group during my second week of living with her and wasn't afraid to ask. I gave her the Cliff's Notes version of my mom being in rehab and Mary Carmen stepping in as our family social worker...leaving out the Guardian Angel subtext. Livie accepted that story without a problem.

"Yeah...you know," I answer with a shrug, "no more than usual. Just the general cleaning up for company drill." I wonder if Mary Carmen has found Ellis yet, if she's found anyone. Her unease from this morning is contagious.

Livie sighs heavily. "You are *so* lucky you get to live with her! She's so nice, and she wears the coolest clothes..."

I nod. I'll give her that: Mary Carmen usually looks pretty put together—even for a woman that's been dead for...how many decades? I have no idea. Gotta give her props for keeping it fresh while she's out saving the world.

"Yeah—she's strict...but nice. That's a good word for her," I agree, downing the rest of my drink. "But don't mess around with curfew or her old cassette tape collection—she'll cut you!"

We both laugh and snuggle back in our chairs, Livie motioning to the record player. "This a Christmas gift for someone? Or you just making a habit of lugging around old music equipment?" she teases with a smile.

I snort. "Yeah, it's my present for Daniel... He's a major audiophile." I nudge the box with my toe. "I hope he likes it. I took a gamble on the player and one of the albums. The other record, I'm pretty sure he'll be into, since he already has it, but..."

"It's special?" Livie fills in, her voice soft.

I glance at her and nod. "Yeah...really special." I feel my cheeks redden. "Says stuff we can't really say out loud, you know?"

Livie sighs dramatically and puts her face in her hands. "Oh my God—you know it!" She puts her hands down and stares at me. "What am I gonna do about Brennan, Christa? Should I ask him if he wants to be my boyfriend? Do you think that's too presumptuous?"

I bite my lip and smile. "I think you have to do whatever feels right, Livie. Follow your heart." I pull my heels under me. "I don't know if I'm the best person to be giving love advice—it's not like I've ever had anything work out, like, long term."

"But you *know* people!" Livie looks at me seriously. "You get a really good read on emotional situations. Ugh! I wish Brennan had been able to come today. Then you could tell me what you think, if he really likes me..."

"I'm sure he likes you, Livie," I murmur. This whole conversation is totally starting to depress me. I tuck my hair behind my ears and begin to gather my things. "He's spending Christmas Eve with you, bought you that fancy dress... That's not something you do with someone you don't care about." I would give my right arm to have that be my situation with Daniel—getting dressed up together, hitting the town and going off to some glamorous party...but in reality, I'll be lucky if Daniel even comes home in one piece tonight. His mental state when he left earlier was not promising.

Livie grins brightly. "Yeah, I know you're right! I need to stop freaking out and just enjoy it." Her eyes widen as I sling my purse over my shoulder. "You're leaving? We just got here!"

I exhale. Much as I love her, I have to get out of here before

I start having palpitations. Listening to her talk about her perfect relationship is harder than I realized. "I'm sorry, Livie..." I bend down and pick up the record player again. "I have to get going. I told everyone back at the house that I would help get stuff ready for the morning—big day and all."

Livie nods. "Sure! Makes sense—thanks for coming! I love any time I get with you." We both stand, and I give her a little hug. "So...you think I should say something tonight?" She blinks at me with shiny eyes. "Maybe at the party?"

I smile. "I think that's a great idea. Find some mistletoe and stand right underneath it." I feel like I have sawdust in my mouth when I say that. I know where she could find some...real close by.

Livie squeals manically. "Okay—yeah! Awesome! Thank you, Christa!" She gives me another hug, then sits down again to finish her Frappuccino.

I head for the door. It's suddenly a hundred degrees in this place.

The house is exactly the way I left it when I get back. With a sigh, I turn on one of the lamps in the living room, setting the turntable and records down by the tree. I do a lap of the place to see if anyone came home while I was gone, but no other lights turned on, and the kitchen is still a disaster zone. I pull my phone out of my purse—no messages. I rub my forehead; I really, *really* don't like this. I should have heard from someone by now—especially Daniel. Mary Carmen probably has no idea that I've been left home alone all afternoon, since I would have heard her conniption all the way from Long Beach. Something is definitely off, I just don't know what.

I take off my coat in my room and turn on more lights, before heading back to Mary Carmen's closet where she keeps all of the wrapping paper. I pick two rolls, one candy cane red and white, the other a traditional green with embossed gold wreaths running across it. I set up a little workstation in front of the Christmas tree and take my time carefully wrapping Daniel's presents. Once I'm finished, I get up and re-roll the paper, crinkling the scraps in my hand.

I glance back at the gifts. I did a pretty good wrapping job, but they're missing something, like a ribbon or bow. I frown; I didn't see any other decorations in Mary Carmen's closet... Maybe I can scrounge up something from my stuff.

I head back to my room and rifle through my dresser, unsuccessfully looking for anything that could pass as Christmas-y. I move to my nightstand and pop open the drawer...but there's nothing in there that I could stick on top of a present. I snicker to myself and shut the drawer, looking down at the floor space next to the bed.

"Eureka!" I exclaim, finding a stretchy headband in sparkly silver. I hold it up and give it a yank. "Decorative as well as functional..." Daniel would totally wear this.

As I'm getting to my feet, though, I spy a flash of red peeking out from between my mattresses. I stop and pull it gently from the crease.

It's the Herod's Feast invitation. I rest my back against the bed and scan down the embossed gold script, the last line reading *The Passion Begins at 9:30*. I sigh and glance up at the clock. They're probably just getting under way with their lame costume party and open bar. Mandisa's probably dressed up like a chandelier or something equally insane. Stupid.

I get up, drop the invitation on my bed, and cross over to the window, cat's cradling the silver headband as I stare out into the darkening night sky. There's still no sign of Daniel, which is sending waves of panic thrashing through my insides. I look back around my bedroom; this is not like him. We haven't been apart for more than a couple of hours since we first met, and usually that was under the pretense of me being with Mary Carmen...or secure in some other way. He wouldn't just leave me like this. It doesn't make sense.

"ARRGGGHH!" I give a frustrated growl that no one else hears and flop back down on the bed, crossing my arms over my chest. I let the last few days wash over me, never having felt as helpless as I do now…even while I was being held hostage in the Warehouse. At least I knew my actions were *doing* something, then; I had agreed to Alden's demands to save my mother's soul. Now I'm safe, but I typically feel more like a lost puppy wagging her tail, asking how she can help and being met with simple pats on the head…not really a part of the team or allowed to make decisions. Out of control.

I huff and drag a hand through my hair. And now the shit is really hitting the fan, with the Resistance and missing Guardians… Daniel going off the rails—and here I am, sitting with my toes tucked under my old purple comforter, waiting for something to happen. I ramble off the list in my head of all the stuff that isn't my problem, isn't my fight. Someone else will handle it—just stay safe and sound, and someone else will take care of it.

I glare at the little Christmas tree on my dresser, its twinkly lights starting to double. Of course, the missing piece that no one else *would* see is that all of this stuff is connected: it all comes back to me, the Catalyst, and this mystery choice I still have to make. And despite learning more about the prophecy, fighting off Demons, and seeing the inside of my best friend's head, I'm still no closer to finding out where, when, or what my choice is. I suck in a breath and stare at my hands. There *are*…people…out there with those answers. And I'm tired of waiting.

The bright red envelope from the fancy invite leers up at me from near my right leg on top of the blanket. I don't bother picking it up as I make my way back to the front door and shove my feet into my boots.

I know where I'm going, and I don't need the address. Been there a bunch of times already.

CHAPTER 22
NEW YORK CITY—
JULY 4, 1976

"**A**RE YOUR EGGS okay? You've barely touched them." Jillian gets up from the table, clearing her plate.

I give her a jittery smile, having been on edge since deciding that today was the day. "Yeah, they're great… I'm just not very hungry right now." I watch her as she nods, starting in on the breakfast dishes at the sink.

"Are you sick? It would be so unfair for you to catch the flu or something just as I'm finally feeling better!" she giggles over her shoulder.

I shake my head and laugh with her. "Nah, I'm fine. Just nerves, is all." I shut my mouth, willing myself not to blurt out the question right here and now—I've gone to too much trouble to set everything up for tonight to blow it due to impatience.

Jillian doesn't seem to notice, though, her attention focused on a nasty grease spot on the old frying pan. "About seeing Mr. Burman today? I thought everything was going great with him…"

I nod: it is. To my knowledge, everything that happened with Daniel and Martin last month has stayed in Queens. "Ah…

we're just gonna catch up, celebrate the 4th in style with a pastrami sandwich..."

Jillian furrows her brow and stops scrubbing. I grimace. Uh-oh...she might be on to me. "Well then, is it school? I didn't think your finance exam was until next week... You still have plenty of time to study." She frowns at the sponge in her hand, giving it a whiff and reeling back to toss the offending object into the rubbish bin. "I can quiz you if you want, make some flashcards."

I stand and stretch my arms behind my head, smiling to myself as I exhale. My excitement has nothing to do with numbers or calculations. I pat the large textbook on the table dramatically. "Yeah, that would be great. I especially liked the bright pink and yellow ones you made for your art history final...with the little illustrations..." I smirk lightheartedly. "Never seen someone put so much work into a study aid before."

She rolls her eyes and chucks a dishtowel at me. "Who's Manet?"

"A pivotal figure in the transition from realism to impressionism," I recite word-for-word.

Jillian giggles. "And why do you remember that so well?"

"Because there was a naked girl on that card—Olympia."

Jillian holds up her hands. "I rest my case!" She snickers, quirking her head toward the clean, dripping pile of dishes. "You dry."

"'Kay." I smile as I pick up a bowl and go at it with the towel.

Jillian wets another dishcloth at the tap and begins wiping down the counter, finding something caked and moldy behind the faucet. "What is this?" She wrinkles her nose and holds it up for me to see.

I grin and jut out my chin. "Birthday candle! From back in March..." I lean in lasciviously. "Remember naked baking?"

She blushes wildly and smiles, setting the candle on the counter. We had celebrated our birthday by getting Denise out of the house and taking over the kitchen to make cupcakes…which we fed to each other in bed. Best birthday ever.

"We weren't *naked*!" She pushes the nub of the candle around with her finger and glances at me slyly. "We had…aprons."

I raise my eyebrows as she reaches for the trash. "Hey! You can't throw that away!" I wave at the moldy candle. "That's a memory! And maybe we can reuse it next year—"

Jillian laughs. "Gross, Alden! We can get another candle. And besides…how much naked baking do you think is going to happen with a two-month-old? Hm?" She smirks at me.

I frown. "I *will* bake, Jillian. And I *will* be naked while I do it. It's my right!"

She shakes her head and goes back to cleaning, pausing and scrubbing every little stain and coffee spot.

I arch an eyebrow. "What's going on, Jilly? You're more thorough with your cleaning than usual…"

She sighs. "I can't help it! Every little thing around here is making me crazy!" She stops and straightens up, cradling the small bump that's started to protrude under her light blue dress. It's just big enough for the two of us to notice, and we both know the days of it staying a secret are numbered.

I grin smugly. "That's what the books call 'nesting,'" I answer like a know-it-all, "getting the home—the 'nest,' if you will—ready for baby."

"Well, well!" Jillian moues, stepping back from the counter. "Looks like you've been studying more than your finance homework!"

I shrug. "Someone around here has to know what's going on."

She gives me a playful swat with her dishtowel. "I know what's going on!" She shakes her head, picking up a few odds and ends from under the window. "I'll have you know, Mr. Smartypants, that I stopped on my way home from studio the other day to look at cribs at that baby store down on 7th." She puckers her lips. "There was a white one I really liked... I thought maybe we could break into some of my Winston's winnings to get it."

I nod. She's given me a perfect lead onto another topic that's been driving me mad with anticipation for the last couple of days. "Jillian..." I stop drying and hop up on the counter, resting the towel next to my hip. "There's something I need to talk to you about."

She immediately stops cleaning and looks at me intently. "I knew there was something," she murmurs, her tone grave. "What's wrong?"

I laugh. "Nothing! Nothing is wrong!" I take her hand reassuringly and pull her toward me. "I just don't know if we want to go out and buy a bunch of nursery furniture right now."

Jillian gapes. "Alden—I just finished my first trimester! We have to start to get serious, plan things out, tell my family..." Her eyes grow wide as she stares me down. "We can't avoid it any longer."

I break into a grin. "I know! And I don't want to avoid it!" I trace little circles on her palms with my thumbs. "I'm the one who wanted to tell everybody the minute we found out, remember?"

She purses her lips. "Then what is it? What do you need to talk about?"

I take a deep breath. "Mr. Adimi is relocating back to Europe next month. He's leaving Mr. Ericson in charge here while he begins the expansion on the Paris hotel." I watch her face. "He wants me to come with him, Jillian. To France."

I hold both of her hands as her shoulders sag. "You'd be leaving?" she asks, her voice small. "Now?"

I squeeze her fingers. "*We* would be leaving." I look deep into her eyes. "I'm not going anywhere without you."

She shakes her head, and I hold up a hand. "Now, hear me out first. I've already done a bit of research into everything." I lean her up against the counter as I continue. "All of our accommodations would be taken care of; we'd have our own apartment, right in the heart of the city, fully furnished. Anything we need would be provided." I smile at her. "Including a crib."

She bites her cheek. "Okay…"

I pop to my feet and stand up straight. "I spoke to the registrar at Columbia and asked about transfer credits." Jillian's eyebrows rise wildly. "All of your classes would carry over, and you could finish out your degree at university there. We would be there in time for you to start Fall term, and then you would take off the Spring with the baby. Just like we talked about for here…"

"You called my school?" She shakes her head disbelievingly and crosses her arms over her chest.

I hold up my hands. "Just to get some answers! Nothing is set in stone," I respond, keeping my voice even. "Mr. Adimi is also bringing nannies and tutors for his own children, and when I mentioned that we were expecting, he graciously offered their services for whenever we need them—"

"You told Mr. Adimi! ALDEN!!" Jillian's face flushes red.

I take her shoulders softly. "I had to, Jillian. It's time." I exhale. "He was excited… Said that if we decide to come, the hardest part will be getting his wife to let us hold our own baby. They love kids and are happy for us." I smile. "Please, Jillian, let's just consider this for a minute…"

"Do I even have a choice?!" she cries, her voice growing shrill.

I pat her back. "Yes, you do." I nod, and she goes quiet. "We don't have to go…if you don't want to. I'll still have my job here at the Ritz, working under Ericson. Nothing has to change, if that's what you want." This calms her, and I can see she's thinking about it now. "I know it would be hard to leave your family… your home and country." I rub her arms. "I know none of that's easy, having done it myself."

Jillian takes a breath and leans back, relaxing more as the wheels start to turn in her head. "But…this would be a really great opportunity for you…"

I smile. "And for you, too! I think they make a little art in Paris."

This makes her laugh. "Yes…yes, they do," she sighs, leaning into me again. "I've never…I've never been that far away before. My parents would freak."

I nod in agreement. "They would, but we *would* come back." I give her a squeeze. "But the expansion is spread out over a couple of years…"

Jillian gazes at the floor. "Right." She frowns in thought before looking up at me, her eyes flashing excitedly in a way that makes me think of the night of our first date. "But it *would* be an adventure…"

I grin. "Yes—very much so."

She turns back to the sink, chewing her lip. She's considering it.

I massage her lower back. "You have some time to think about it. If you want to do it, though, we would be leaving at the end of August; we would need to start making arrangements soon—lots of paperwork, the move itself…" Plus an engagement, a wedding…

Jillian nods. "Of course. Wow." She shakes her head and smiles. "You never cease to surprise me."

I come up behind her and wrap my arms around her waist, resting my palm under her bump as I angle in for a kiss. "I don't want you to get bored with me, leave me for some hip, cool artist type—Gerald…"

"Ha! That would never happen!" She turns and nuzzles into my cheek, before looking down bashfully. "You look very handsome today, by the way." She flicks my white shirt collar with her finger. "Always so classy."

I pucker my lips haughtily and rest my chin on her shoulder, pressing up tight against her. "I think I might have a few minutes before I have to leave for Burman." I groan, sliding my fingers down to her dress hem and slowly hiking it up.

She crows and spins around, shoving me back with a laugh. "Scratch what I just said! Nothing but a wolf in sheep's clothing!" She blushes as she steps over and straightens her dress. "We did that thing in the shower you like last night—can't you give me a moment's peace?"

I chuckle throatily and give her neck a final kiss. "Yes—all right! I'm sorry... It's just extra tempting now that we don't have to worry about birth control." I wave at her tummy with a smile. "The crime's already been committed."

Jillian squeals and puts her face in her hands. "Way to make me feel like a...a loose woman! If people had any idea..."

"They would die of envy," I murmur under my breath as she goes back to the dishes. The morning sunlight warms her skin, glistening in the curls piled atop her head. I could watch her like this forever.

She looks over at me and shakes her head. "You're going to be late! The traffic is going to be insane today!" She looks toward the door with a smile.

I nod. "Right." I roll up my cuffs and find my keys. "Remember, Daniel is going to pick you up for the fireworks tonight and bring you back to the rooftop, where we'll watch them together. I made him promise not to drive like a maniac." I feel my palms start to sweat; there are so many moving parts today.

Jillian nods. "I got it, I got it! I'll be ready!" She beams at me. "I wouldn't want to miss your first time seeing the 4th of July..." She scrunches her shoulders excitedly. "Which might be our last...for a while."

I grin. She's in. "I love you, Jillian," I murmur from across the room.

"I love you, too." She turns and gives me a wink. "Au revoir, mon amor."

I can't stop smiling as I close the front door behind me.

I pound down the apartment stairs and out onto the sidewalk, stopping dead in my tracks when I get a look at the street.

Cars are at a standstill, every lane jam-packed. Horn honks bounce off the buildings as people reach out from their windows, shaking fists at the unmoving traffic. Crowds of people walk past, laughing and talking loudly as they wave bright American flags, the level of excitement palpable as the energy around the city grows. I shake my head and start walking, my own nerves adding to the general chaos. I stop at a payphone before I head down to the trains, punching the numbers up with a little more zest than necessary.

"Bloomenschien's," Daniel answers on the third ring, his voice carefree and easy, even though I can hear the bustle of bakery sounds behind him.

"Daniel, it's me," I state, turning and looking back at the busy street. "I just wanted to make sure you were still good for picking up Jillian later today…"

"Yep." He readjust the phone, and the muffled voice of someone else talking to him comes through the line. "I've already told them I gotta leave by 4… Should gimme enough time to change and go get her."

I huff and let my eyes wander. "Daniel—I don't know if that's going to be enough time! The city is crazy right now—and I think it's only going to get worse as we get closer to tonight. The roads are already totally impassable—"

"Relax, Irish!" Daniel sighs. "It's like it's the Bicentennial or something… Only comes around every 200 years or so!" He laughs.

I tear at my hair. "I don't have time for your jokes today! Just…just make sure Jillian is on that roof by the time fireworks start. I don't care if *you* wind up circling the block looking for a perfect parking space or whatever…but *she* needs to be up there—got it?"

Daniel blows a raspberry. "Yeah—I got it! It's not gonna be that bad… Wendy can get through spots that other cars can't. We're gonna make it, I promise! What's the big deal, anyway? It's just some fireworks."

I take a deep breath. I haven't told him about my plan, keeping him on a need-to-know basis lest he foolishly spoil the surprise for Jillian. And I wasn't about to let anything spoil tonight. "I just want tonight to be…perfect," I grit into the receiver. "You owe me one, remember? I'm cashing in right now."

Daniel gives a low whistle. "Can't argue with that! All right… one perfect night, coming right up!" He twists away from the phone and yells something into the bakery, only coming back to say, "I gotta go. We'll see you tonight!"

"Right." I nod affirmatively. "Tonight—and DRIVE SAFELY!" I hang up the phone and walk swiftly down to the subway.

*

Mr. Burman's window air conditioner unit is broken, a fact that the large man seems very unhappy about as we both sit sweating in his small office. His broad face is pinched in a frown as he waves an angry hand behind him.

"—and you would think they'd send someone up from maintenance, but oh no! They can't be bothered!" He shakes his head and leans back in his chair, putting his feet up on the cluttered desk. "Gotta nice long list of other agencies whose units have been busted since late May… We're lost somewhere between the city comptroller and the geological survey. Good luck with that, right?" He looks over at me and chuckles, checking his watch dramatically. "Should get it working just in time for Christmas. Regina tried to run a fan in here the other day—goddamn cyclone of visas and paperwork... Still sortin' out that mess." He sighs, punching away at his computer keyboard.

"My daughter lives out in Anaheim...uh, California," he quickly clarifies for me, "and she told me it's cooler there right now than here—can you believe that?!" He shakes his head, glaring at the screen. "Don't know what I'm still doing in this stinkin' city."

I give him a light shrug and a smile. "I'm fine—really, Mr. Burman. The heat doesn't bother me."

He grunts and spins his wheels, going back to his files. "I know it doesn't, Mr. Murphy... You're not one to raise Cain about much..." He squints and holds up one of the papers. "Well, it looks like your visa for next term has cleared...and we can get you started with your citizenship classes in October." He glances up at me over his glasses. "It's a nighttime meeting once a week for the next couple years—shouldn't conflict with your work at the hotel. Going over the basics, but it's stuff you'll need to know for the test. There's still a long road in front of us."

He stops as I sit forward and clear my throat. "That's...something I actually needed to talk to you about, Mr. Burman," I murmur, suddenly nervous to be bringing it up.

He sets down his papers and watches me coolly. I take a breath and continue. "Mr. Adimi, my boss at the Ritz, has given me a chance...to go work with him in Paris. I think I'm going to take it."

Mr. Burman raises his eyebrows. I wait, expecting him to blow up after all of the favors and hard work he's put in for me, but instead he breaks into a huge grin. "That's wonderful, Mr. Murphy! Congratulations!" He reaches over the desk to shake my hand.

I accept with wide eyes, gripping his fingers tightly. "I know...I know you've really put yourself out there for me," I breathe as we both settle back into our chairs. "I am so, so thankful for everything..."

Mr. Burman waves me off. "Nothing to it, Mr. Murphy—all part of the job!" He folds his hands over his paunch. "I *am* sorry to see you go… I've enjoyed our little lunch meetings this last year. But it's good for you: when opportunity knocks, you answer the door!" He laughs and reorganizes the folders in front of him. "I'll tell you right now, though, we're gonna do this all above board this time… I'm happy to help you get your papers in order before you go."

I chuckle. "Thank you, sir. I'm hoping you'll also be able to help with Jillian's—you know, my, um, my girlfriend." I blush and go quiet as he stares at me from the other side of the desk. "Hopefully my…wife…before we go."

"Really?" He looks on pleasantly as he reaches into another cabinet. "This the same girl you've been seeing the whole time you've been here?"

I nod. "Yes, the same. I'm…" I blink and stare at him. "I'm going to propose, Mr. Burman—tonight, actually."

He smiles a toothy grin. "Well—this day is looking up, busted AC or not!" he chortles. "You gotta ring? Lemme see it!"

I shake my head. "Not yet. I'm on my way over to Brooklyn after this to go get one. I have some money…" I pull out a wad of cash and put it on the desk. Mr. Burman furrows his brow and reaches over, his fingertips brushing the bills as he gives them a quick count.

"Very nice, Mr. Murphy. I can see you've been working hard," he murmurs, smiling kindly. I nod and put my money away as he leans across the desk again, this time picking up the old Don Newcombe baseball.

"You know, I caught this at a Dodger's game in Brooklyn." He rolls it lightly in his hand. "One of Newcombe's first games with the team. I was just a kid… Waited after for almost an hour in the rain for him to come out and sign it for me. People didn't really think much about Negros playing baseball back then, so this ball wasn't worth more than the stitching holding it together.

That's changed. Hmm…" He grins and tosses it to me; I catch it, surprised. "I want you to have it, Mr. Murphy."

I stare at the baseball, then back at him. "Mr. Burman, I can't take this…"

He scrunches his nose and rests his arms behind his head. "Sure, you can! It's not doing a whole lotta good serving as an old paperweight around here…" He snorts at the office walls. "No, here's what you're gonna do. You're gonna take that baseball, and you're gonna go down and see Mortimer Argyle down on 47th." He nods heavily. "Yes…Argyle, just like the socks. He's got a big shop there with lots of pretty diamonds, all sorts of interesting stuff. They may look closed with the holiday today, but just keep knocking and someone will answer. He will be *very* interested in that baseball there." He nods at the ball in my hand. "You tell Morty that J.J. Burman sent you and you want the best offer he can make. You also tell him that if he ever wants to get a crack at any of my Robinson memorabilia, he better not try to swindle you, got it?"

"Yes, sir," I answer quietly. "Are you sure?"

Mr. Burman's eyes crinkle. "I've been sure about you since the first day you walked in with that little green passport. You're a good kid, Mr. Murphy, true blue." For a minute, it looks like he's getting a little choked up. "You go buy your girl the most beautiful ring you can find—something that says you mean business." He smiles tightly and clears his throat. "And come by next week, the two of you…and we'll get that other paperwork started."

"Yes, sir." I stand up clutching the baseball in my hand. "Thank you…and…I guess we'll see you soon!"

Burman laughs and shoos me out. "Enjoy the 4th— International Man of Mystery!" He straightens his papers. "Have a hotdog for me."

"Extra mustard!" I joke.

He tilts his head. "That *is* the American way! Good luck!"

*

A few hours later, I find myself back on the roof of Chez Monique, watching the cars jerk and stop on the roads below, craning my neck to see if I can spy Daniel and Jillian coming from uptown. No luck yet, and I reach into my pocket, nervously stroking the smooth black velvet box with the tip of my finger. I exhale and pull it out, checking the ring one more time, its bright, refracting surface making prisms from the white twinkle lights that Muriel left up from last autumn. I smile to myself and study the diamond. Mortimer Argyle had two cabinets full of engagement rings, calling the first one "with the baseball" and the one right next to it "without the baseball." We both agreed that the ring surrounded by a cluster of green emeralds from the first cabinet was the obvious winner.

"Very fitting," Argyle had joked as he rang me up. "With the emeralds, and you being from Ireland and all."

I had nodded and smiled, more excited by the fact that the gems were an exact match for Jillian's eyes... This was always supposed to be *her* ring. I can't wait to give it to her. And then she'll say yes—God, I hope she says yes—and throw her arms around my neck and kiss me like we've never kissed before, and we'll laugh... Daniel will show up complaining about the traffic, and she'll flash him her hand with the ring, and he'll give me a hug, and we'll toast, giving him the bottle when we're through... And then we'll tell everyone about Lily Rose and Paris, get married in August—something small, having the ceremony in the Church, of course, with the reception maybe here at the restaurant... We'll invite all our friends. Muriel will come back, and Jilly will wear white...

I snap the little box shut and put it back in my pocket, pacing around the rooftop for the fiftieth time to make sure everything is perfect. Lights, in order. Scattering of pink rose petals, now carpeting the concrete floor. Snacks and sparkling grape juice from the Italian market with two champagne flutes, double check…triple check. I run a hand through my hair and look out to the horizon; there are clear conditions right now, the harbor sunset just visible through the New York skyline. There'll be an amazing view of the fireworks when I get down on one knee… I put my hands on my hips as my teeth start to chatter uncontrollably. I'm ready. This is it.

I take a breath and check my watch; it's a quarter to nine. I glance back at the sky, where twilight is in full effect. The newspaper had said that they would start the fireworks at nightfall, maybe another ten, fifteen minutes. I stalk back over to the roof's edge, madly checking the road to see if I can make out Wendy scooting through. No motorcycles in sight.

"Dammit, Daniel," I hiss under my breath. "You have one job, *one job*—don't screw it up…"

I shake my head and move back to the center of the roof. The waiting is excruciating. In an effort to keep myself from going completely insane, I count my steps and walk the perimeter of the roof: 82. I sigh; counting seems to help, so I crouch by the shallow brick wall and begin on the cars down below, their taillights blinking angry and red. These are harder to keep track of as they slug by around the corner, and I find myself having to start over again, my frustration increasing as the sky grows darker. They should have been here by now.

I stand and smooth out my pants, brushing roof dust from my knees. "Come on, where are you?" I mutter, pacing like a tiger as I squint out as far as I can see. There aren't any noticeable wrecks or flashing ambulances. There just isn't enough room for all of the cars trying to squeeze onto the avenue—too many pickles in the jar. I groan and switch my focus to the sidewalks. Maybe they gave up and decided to walk. The crowds of people choking past the storefronts and theaters are worse than the streets. I try for maybe two minutes before throwing in the towel. I check my watch again: 9:15. Crap. I glance hurriedly up at the sky, waiting for it to burst into color. Nothing yet, but I bet they're lighting up the floats right now…

I hear a creak on the fire stairs, and hope wells in my chest. "Jillian?!" I call, rushing over. I look down and frown; the stairwell is dark and empty, nobody there. The creaking comes again, and I turn back to the little table where the platter of cheese and fruit sits. A big, fat rat sits with a piece of cheddar hanging out of his mouth, lounging like he's ruddy Prince Charles.

"HEY! GET OFF!" I wave my arms wildly and dart back, almost knocking the whole plate over as I swat the rat away. He escapes with a challenging glint in his eye, slinking through a hole in the wall. I give the brick an angry kick with my toe. "And stay out, you mangy son of a—"

My curses are cut short as the first firework explodes across the night sky. I gasp and stare at it, a wide arc of blue sparks turning to shimmering gold. The traffic below stops, and I can hear the oohs and ahhs of the people watching from the street. My shoulders sag, and I look back forlornly at the fire escape. She's missing it… Our perfect moment has passed.

I pull out a chair and plop down, picking up a piece of brie that I'm sure that rat already got to—but I don't care. I watch the rest of the fireworks in silence, refusing to let my eyes wander to the stairs in false hope, instead using this time to plot out all the ways that I'm going to rip Daniel limb from limb when they finally do show up. I should never have trusted him with such a crucial task; I should have scheduled a car service several hours in advance to pick Jillian up, damn the cost.

I sigh and put my face in my hands, color raining down in bright blasts overhead. No…I didn't want to call a car because it would have been suspicious. My girl was too smart and too practical for that sort of thing. And if there's ever a time to count on your so-called best friend, wouldn't it be the most important night of your life?!

I clench my jaw and prop myself up with my elbows on my

knees. I suppose, really, he didn't *know* this was the most important night of my life... He didn't *know* about the proposal. I feel the ring burning hotly in my pocket. I stand up as the Grand Finale goes off, a shower of red, white, and blue flames shooting across the night. You could surely hear New York cheering, if the booms and pops weren't so deafening. I look out at the street one last time.

They must be watching it all from Wendy somewhere... together. I screw my mouth up, feeling a flash jealousy, before remembering how irritated Jillian gets at the mere mention of Daniel. She's still raw from what happened between him and Muriel. This makes me smile; she was obliging *me* this morning, agreeing to let Daniel drive her because she wants to be with me. That's right.

"It doesn't matter where you are," I murmur down to the crowd, "because you're always on my mind."

I put my hands in my pockets, gripping the ring box tightly as the world goes quiet again, the sounds of blasting explosions done and gone, replaced by familiar city sounds. I exhale; fireworks or not, this is still going to be the biggest night of our lives. Nothing is going to change that.

At that moment, I hear steps on the fire stairs, quick and light. My heart swells, and I break into a huge grin. This is it— she's here. "Jillian!" I call again, my voice more ragged this time. I hold my breath and get up on my tip toes, about to burst with excitement.

My smile freezes in place as Daniel comes up over the edge, steadying himself with a leather-clad arm. He looks up at me, his face pale and drawn. "Alden..." he whispers, shaking his head slowly.

I smirk and hold up my hands. "It's fine, Daniel. Yes, I'm pissed you're late...but it doesn't matter. It doesn't matter." I jerk my chin back to the table. "Go get some food. Where's Jillian?"

He takes a shaky breath and puts his hands on his hips, looking down at the floor. "I...I have to tell you something..."

I wave him away and crane my neck over his shoulder, waiting to see Jillian's beautiful red mane come up over the ledge—but no such luck. I furrow my brow. "Tell me later—you *did* pick her up, right?!" I turn back to him, my eyes wide. "Is she down in the alley with Wendy?"

"Yes, I did pick her up..." he rasps, not looking at me as he rubs the back of his neck. "Just like you told me to, but..." He stares at me while I search the alley, the corners of his mouth tight. "She's not here, Alden." He bats my arm. "Stop..."

I turn my attention back to him. "Where is she, then? I don't understand..." I chuckle uneasily. Maybe she'd seen through me and learned what I was planning. I've been on edge for days—with the fireworks, the ring, the proposal. Maybe she still wasn't ready...or...didn't want it. Didn't want me. I draw in a sharp breath. "Did...did she not want to come?" I glance down at the ground. "Tell me the truth, Daniel. It's okay..."

He smiles weakly, as if the expression hurts his face. "No, she wanted to come." He straightens up and frowns. "Alden, there was an accident..."

"What?!" I bark, stepping close to him, instantly going into full crisis mode. "What do you mean, there was an accident? On the road?!" My hands tremble as I rush over to the chair and grab my jacket off its back, shoving my arms quickly inside of it. "Was it the bike?! Did you bring her your helmet like I told you to? What hospital did you take her to?" I dash over to the fire stairs, swinging my leg over the side wall.

Daniel sighs and grabs my arm, his expression pained. "She's not at the hospital, Alden..."

I shake him off violently and glare. "How is she not in hospital?! Where is she?!" My tone grows strident. "Did you take her home? And why do you keep saying my name like that...!"

I stop and watch his face, noticing that Daniel's frown is so severe, it's almost comical. I go quiet and look out at the sky. "Where's Jillian?" I blink, taking a step back. "Daniel...where is she?"

His jaw tightens as he lets out a strange, guttural noise. "Ahh..." he breathes, watching his feet. He inhales a few times before looking up at me, his eyes deep and sunken. "She's dead, Alden. Jillian's dead."

I pause for a beat, his words hanging in the air before me. It's like staring up at the clouds on a warm spring day. They're thick and capacious, like you could touch them—but when you try, your hand floats right through into nothingness.

"That is..." I stare dizzily at Daniel, my vision blurring around the edges. "That is...the *cruelest* joke you've ever played." I run my tongue around my suddenly dry mouth. "Enough."

Daniel shakes his head, tears starting to leak down his face. "It's not a joke. I'm so sorry..." His voice comes out tight and strangled. "I wish it was, God—I wish it was." He takes his head in his hands and sways where he stands. "I fucked up, Alden... I'm so sorry—I really fucked up..."

"I don't..." I slur, the rooftop spinning. I stagger back to the table, grasping the edge for support. "I don't understand..."

"Anatoli came by the bakery today." Daniel coughs, wiping his nose with the back of his hand. "Wanting to send a friendly reminder that Ramos wants his money. I, um...I owe him money." He presses his palms against the top of his head.

I nod in a daze, staring at him blearily. "For the cocaine your grandfather found. He destroyed it, I'm assuming?" I sound like I'm radioing in from the bottom of the ocean.

Daniel bites his lip and looks out at the city. "From that, yeah...and before." He nervously unzips his jacket and begins to pace. "Anyway, he said that if I didn't show up with what I owed by the end of the day, then they'd come looking for me and wouldn't be so friendly anymore."

"Did you have the money?" I ask, my eyelids drooping; I

must be having a stroke. Daniel grimaces. "I took it…from the bakery." His voice cracks. "It still wasn't enough—but it was more than I had, so I thought there was a chance I could smooth things over…" He bites his nails. "I left work and got Jillian… I knew I was running out of time, and I thought we could just stop by on the way, give them the cash and be done with it." He lets out a rough sob. "That's, uh…that's not what happened."

I cross my arms and lean against the table, blood starting to rush back to my head. "You…you took Jillian, *m-m-my Jillian*," I stutter, gripping my elbows, "to that place?" I tap my toe, the rhythm bringing adrenaline down to my legs.

Daniel puts his hands at his sides and stands still. "Yes," he whispers, his eyes watching me. "I'm so sorry, Alden. I never meant for any of this to happen, you have to believe me—"

"WHAT HAPPENED TO HER?!" I bellow, bolting upright and pitching the table over on its side, grapes and glassware shattering on the roof. "TELL ME NOW!"

"They shot her," Daniel bleats, taking a step back. I double over, the wind knocked out of me. "One…one bullet to the chest…in cold blood."

I stare down at the ground, watching the twinkling lights reflecting in the shards of broken champagne flutes. I roll back on my heels and massage my cheeks with my fingers, my face feeling like rubber. I hear a low moaning and look over at Daniel. Tears are cascading from his eyes, but no noise. I'm the one who's wailing.

"Why…" I stop and shake my head drunkenly at him. "Why are you crying?"

"Because it's awful." He breathes, taking a step toward me. "For so many reasons. She, um…" He pauses and looks at his hands. "She was saying something about a…a baby…before, when they were…and she was trying to get them off of her— bunch of fucking animals," he mutters. "Was she pregnant?"

I stare blankly at the east wall, my own hands folded in

my lap. "We're going to tell everyone soon… I thought, after tonight…" I reach into my pocket and pull out the ring, setting it up on the chair next to me, a little bit of pocket lint clinging to the velvet. I pick it off absently as Daniel lets out another tight sob.

I turn my head. I'm suddenly so tired, wanting to curl up into a ball and go to sleep forever, right here on the roof. I close my eyes.

"Alden…" Daniel simpers, crouching down next to me. "I am so sorry. I know that doesn't fix anything…but you have to know—" He puts a hand on my back.

I look at him, level with his white t-shirt. I can see now that it's speckled with tiny flecks of dried blood—Jillian's blood. I stare at his shirt long and hard. It's real—it really happened. She's gone…and my world comes crashing down—a house of cards, sinking ships, lost in the dark.

A low rumble of thunder sounds in the distance, accompanied by a bright flash of heat lightning above. A storm is coming.

I open my eyes and stand, Daniel staggering to his feet at my side. Coolly, I pat my cheeks dry and straighten my cuffs, Daniel staring at me wall-eyed as I put the ring back into my pocket and start to walk toward the fire escape.

"Alden," he calls, his face still a mess. "Irish…where are you going?"

I turn back and glare at him. "To find Jillian. I'm assuming she's still there?" My voice betrays me at the end.

Daniel balks. "Yes—she is… But I'm sure they'll deal with her, um…her body." He wipes his eyes and takes a step toward me. "But she's gone, Irish! The part you loved…and they'll kill you if you show up there and try to start something! Don't you get that?!" He shakes his head.

I shrug dully. "Fine. Let them." My life lost all meaning five minutes ago. "But she deserves to be with her family. And they deserve the chance to…" I take a breath. "…to say goodbye. It's their right." And there is no way I'm leaving her with those monsters—even if I am too late.

"No…" Daniel twists his mouth and grabs my arm, pulling me back onto the roof. "I'm not letting you walk into a dragon's den out of some half-cocked sense of duty! We've all lost enough tonight!"

He startles as I shove him backwards, hissing between my teeth. "NO—*we* haven't!" I grit out, my fists tightening.

He gawks at me, his eyes like saucers. "*I* lost everything!" I shout. "My…my—" *Love…family…future.* I can't even say the words as my heart caves in on itself a bit more.

I spin back to him and bite my tongue, drawing blood. "No, you lost nothing, Daniel…but you took everything," I spit out, my breath growing ragged. "And you can't give it back."

He frowns and puts his hands in his jacket, his cheeks gaunt. "I know you're hurting right now…and rightly so." His eyes dart up to me. "But I'm suffering, too—you have no idea what it was like to…to watch what they did—to hear her…beg—"

He gasps as I slam into him, his throat pinched under my grip as I grind him into the brick wall. "Why wasn't it *you*, huh?" I rasp, clutching at his windpipe. "Why did she pay your debt, and you're still alive?"

He wheezes between my fingers, his eyes bloodshot and raw. "Because they wouldn't get their money, then!" he hisses, beating my arm hard with his fist.

I let go with a grunt and push back, Daniel gasping for air on the cold concrete and rubbing his neck tenderly. "Did you even *try* to stop it? When they were…hurting her?" Hot tears spring up behind my eyelids, and I don't even attempt to cover them up. I stare at him; aside from the blood on his shirt, he seems to have come through completely unscathed.

Daniel looks away, ashamed. "I did what I could," he says to the floor. "You weren't there. You don't know…"

"I would have given anything to be there!" I shout, kicking

one of the chairs across the rooftop. It lands with a smash in the far corner. "I would have fought and torn at them 'til they put a bullet in me, too! JESUS!" I tear my hands through my hair and gape at him. "You didn't even try! You…you didn't even try. I will never forgive you for this, ever." I shake my head. "That's a promise. You're a goddamn coward."

Daniel shuts his eyes and rests his cheek against the wall. "I know," he whispers. "I'm sorry." He hangs his head between his knees, his shoulders shaking up and down as he cries.

I watch him, unable to conceal my utter disgust. "Don't you dare!" I snarl, wrenching him up by the arm. He blinks at me with red eyes, but he does stop his blubbering. My lip curls as I glare into his face. "Don't you dare cry now! Not after what you did… You be a man and take responsibility for your part in all this!" I nod angrily and shove him toward the center of the roof.

Daniel stares at me trembling and afraid, like a little kid caught red-handed stealing from the sweets shop. His childish face only enrages me more. "You are…" I huff, putting my hands on my hips as I pace in a tight circle. "Such…a disappointment." My eyes find his, and I watch his expression change from frightened to wounded. Good. "And I don't think 'disappointment' truly covers it," I hiss, my tone venomous. "More like…a disgrace. That's what you are, Daniel." I arch a brow and pace closer to him.

He shakes his head, keeping his eyes down. "I know… Please, I said I was sorry…" he whispers to the floor. Another roll of thunder ushers in a light patter of rain, dampening our hair and shoulders.

I stop in front of him, my eyes narrowed. "You don't deserve any of the…gifts…that fate has dropped in your lap," I murmur with a shrug. "Your family, your home, your job, Muriel…" Daniel winces as I stare at him coldly. "So spoiled. And I've just sat by and watched you piss it all away, like the total fool that you are."

I see his cheeks grow red as he nods slowly. "You're right—about everything…"

I scoff and take a step back. "But ultimately, I blame myself for tonight."

He looks up at me quizzically. I shake my head, frowning. "I do. I should never have trusted her in your care. I should have known that you're too stupid and selfish to put her…or *me*…first, even for just one night." I snicker and put my hands in my pockets. "God, even your own mother saw you for what you really are—a complete failure."

"Stop, please…" Daniel whimpers. "Don't—"

"That's why she left you, right?" I cut him off, my eyes dancing. "In search of a brighter future, without that one little niggling mistake to hold her back? No matter how many 'I love you, Mamas' or hugs and kisses…you would have only dragged her down, Daniel, like you do with everybody else."

"No, no…shut up…" He stops and holds his head up, color returning to his face in bright red patches. "I get that you're mad, but you don't know anything about that. Don't talk like you know me…"

I feel my blood boiling as I lurch over to him, grabbing him rough by the arm again. "I know everything there is to know about you," I jeer. He wrestles out of my grasp, his eyes wild, but I continue. "It's simple really… You're a slightly charming, slightly good-looking guy who, when given the chance, will take advantage of anybody and everyone and suck them dry." His face darkens as he watches me circle. "You're a leech, Daniel, a parasite who preys on the kind and the meek." I run my tongue over my teeth. "You're worse than Ramos, when you get down to it. At least he's upfront about what he really is. You're just a…a liar, a fake."

Daniel straightens up and runs his hands through his wet hair. "Okay—I think it's time we call it, Irish." He glares. "Let's just both walk away." He looks back at the fire escape, raindrops gathering on his brow. "I know you've got things to…attend to, now…"

My legs turn to jelly again at the thought of going back down into a world that no longer has Jillian in it. As long as I'm up here, as horrible as I feel, there's still a part of her that's alive, like she's just waiting for me at home by the window, smiling and humming to the baby while she works.

I clench my jaw and stare at Daniel. "No," I rasp, my voice low. "No, we're not gonna do that."

Daniel sucks in a breath and shakes his head. "Then what?! You wanna just stand out here, telling me over and over again how much I screwed up? Don't you think I know?"

"You owe me that at least, don't you think?!" I cry, slicking my hair back. "You…you ruined my life, Daniel!" I start to sob, heavy and deep.

Daniel shifts uncomfortably. "Look…I said I was sorry. I don't know what more you want from me." He grabs his neck and heads for the stairs. "I gotta go. I…I can't stay here…"

"NO!" I shout, darting over and grabbing him. "You don't get to walk away from me! Not now!"

"Yes, I do!" he yells, shaking me off as he starts to cry again, too. "Look—I'm sorry she's dead, I'm sorry your life is totally screwed up now—but I don't owe you anything else! Just let me go!"

I see red, my mouth twisting in rage. "You owe me *every-thing*!" I ram into him, knocking him over onto his side, rolling him through puddles as we grapple. He sputters and squeaks as I mash my knuckles into his face, hot blood flowing from his nose and mouth. I can feel his fists flurrying into my gut, hurried and intense, more feral than the last time we fought.

We roll again, and he lets out a howl as I sit down heavily on his stomach, pieces of broken glass under him getting crushed into his neck and jacket, one rouge shard slicing him lightly across the lip. I spy one of the broken glass stems and grab it, panting as I hold it tight in my right hand.

Daniel stops wriggling and stares at my fist, his eyes darting between me and the shard. "Okay, okay…" His face trembles as his whole body goes slack in surrender. "Okay, Irish—just slow down… I know you wanna slow down—"

I glare at him, panting. "You have no idea what I want!" I sneer, constricting my legs so tight that he's gasping for air. "You threw everything I wanted away without a single thought—so callous…" I wheeze as I tear his shirt up, exposing soft, white underbelly.

Daniel's eyes widen. "Okay—if this is how it is—this is it," he wheezes, his nose running thick with mucous and blood. "Okay."

I lower the glass, letting it dangle over him, my mind a blur of red: red fireworks, red Jillian, red blood… I press the blade to his skin. "What?" I spit crazily, staring into his eyes. "What are you saying?!"

Daniel lets out a weak moan. "You gonna kill me now, Irish?" He nods frantically, staring at me, his jaw set. "Okay…do it! DO IT!"

I startle, coming out of my daze for a minute to really look at him. The warm summer rain is coming down heavier now, washing the mess from his face. I lower the glass and shake my head, getting off of him. "This is…this is…madness," I mumble, focusing on the clear light shining from my palm. "No—I…I have to go…"

I stumble to my feet, trying to set my gaze on the way out. Behind me, Daniel lets out a low laugh. "COME ON!" he slurs, wincing as he sits up, wiping his bloody nose with the back of his hand. "I'm a fucking idiot—so DO IT!" He watches me staggering away. "I owe you, right? You said it yourself…"

I stop, staring at the shard of glass in my hand for what feels like an eternity. "No, Daniel," I finally murmur. "Just go home." I take another step toward the fire escape.

I hear him grunt and shift against the wall, laughing dryly. "Figures—you can't even avenge the first girl to ever spread for you. Who's the coward now?"

My brain shuts off as I spin around, glass still in hand, and I throw myself down; plunging the blade raggedly into his side; One...two...three times. The last time, I cut something fat and sinewy, and the amount of blood spurting from the wound is like something straight out of a cartoon.

Daniel wails and slumps down against the wall, using a burst of strength to push me away. He looks up at me, his eyes soft and questioning. "You did it... I can't believe you actually did it," he gasps, blood gurgling up his throat and spraying out of his mouth, coating his teeth and lips as well as most of my shirtfront.

The sounds he's making bring me back, and I stare at him, suddenly panicked. "Daniel! Wait—oh my God!" I shake my head at all of the blood staining his clothes and the concrete around him, as if someone had spilled red paint. "No... No-no-no! I didn't mean...oh Jesus!—NO!" I look at my hand and realize that I'm still holding the broken flute stem, now covered in Daniel's mess. I cry out and toss it away, then rip off my jacket and press it to Daniel's side, trying to stanch the bleeding.

I pull his head into my lap. "Daniel, I'm so sorry... You have to believe me..." I breathe, my words ringing familiar. He tries to answer, but instead gags, his whole body convulsing as he wretches up a stomach-full of sticky, viscous red. There's so much blood, so much...

I gape around frantically, rain catching on my eyelashes as I try to think of what to do next. I see lights on in the next building over and call out to them in vain. "HELP!" I shriek, thunder booming all around us. "HELP US! PLEASE!"

Nothing.

I look down at Daniel and smooth his wet hair out of his

eyes, watching his lips turn blue under all the blood. I shake my head and let out a raspy sob. "Daniel—can you hear me?! I'm still here, and I'm sorry! Please don't—" I grimace and hold him tight.

He wheezes like a small animal. I can feel his lungs straining to expand and contract, his heart fluttering under my arm. I close my eyes and try to think…to make sense of what's happened, or figure out what to do next…

"I have to find help!" I cry, sitting up. He turns his head weakly and gazes up at me, his eyes glassy and unfocused. "It's going to be okay! I can call for an ambulance downstairs…" Yes, a plan. Monique's is closed for the night, but I can break a window if I have to. Anything…

Just as I pull my hands away from him, his whole body spasms. "Daniel—stop!" I screech, shaking my head and crouching next to him. "What—what are you doing? —What's happening?!"

I watch in horror as his arms and legs twist and flop like fish out of water, his mouth foaming wildly as he turns over onto his belly. He's shaking so badly, I think he might come right off the ground…like some sort of great cataclysm.

I weep.

And then it stops. All of it—the rain, the crying, Daniel. The city is silent with him, his body motionless and still, suddenly smaller than I remember. For a minute, I stare fixated at the hem of his right jean leg, the denim submerged in a watery puddle of pink petals and blood. It's slowly seeping up his leg, like when you leave a paper towel in the sink… Durable, absorbent.

I blink and listen as the sounds of the cars and sirens down on the street return. I can hear my own breath coming out in quick, short pants. I stop and put my hand over my nose and mouth, trying to hear air coming in and out of him…but there's nothing. No wheezing, no breath.

I keep my hand over my mouth to stop myself from vomiting as I reach down and rest my hand on his back. "Daniel…"

I whisper, waiting for a response—a grunt, a flinch. He just lies there, totally still...and I know—I know he's gone...but I still have to look...

Sniffling, I lay down on the ground next to him, my chest pressed against the wet roof floor. His face is smashed into the concrete in an undignified way, a small rain puddle lapping at his cheek. His eyes are open, still brown, the whites tinged blue like a China doll. They send chills up my spine.

My face contorts, and I get up, grabbing his arm and rolling him back to face upward. Now he's staring at the sky, at least. Sadness overwhelms me as I look at my friend, because that's what he is...*was*...and now he's gone. He's gone, too.

I press my lips to his cold forehead and kiss him, my tears mingling with the blood and dirt that cake his face. "I'm sorry... I'm sorry, Daniel," I cry.

I sit back and let my head hang low, the gravity of my words hitting me like a giant wave. I'm sorry...because I did this. *I did this*. I snuffed out his light, made him what he is now—a cold, dead thing. I moan in anguish. Jillian's dead. Daniel's dead.

Daniel's dead because of me... I killed him. I hold my breath and put my face in my hands. I'm a murderer. People who kill people are murderers.

I stop crying and glare at Daniel, then up at the night sky; I can feel the stars watching me through the lingering clouds. They saw everything; they know what happened, what I did, who I really am. And stars have very long memories.

I scramble to my feet and dash for the fire escape, leaving Daniel alone, lying on the ground. I almost fall on the stairs, my feet moving quicker than the rest of me. *Murderer.* The word is wet and red, like the mess back on the roof. It's the one thing you're never supposed to do—take a life. It was worse than all the other sins combined, the priests and nuns used to say, the big daddy of the Seven Deadly. Thou shalt not kill. And here I was now, running down 5th Avenue with blood still slick on my hands, having committed the most horrific crime imaginable. It was all so fast, done in an instant—shorter than the time it takes to brush my teeth. One minute Daniel was alive and cracking jokes, the next he was gone…forever. No take-backs.

My head swims, but my feet, surprisingly, know where to go. People spring out of my way, taking one look and moving aside with wide eyes. A middle-aged woman with dark hair bravely grabs my arm as I walk into oncoming traffic, pulling me back roughly to the curb. "Be careful!" I hear her yell next to me, her eyes scanning down to my bloody shirt. "Hey—are you okay? Do you need help?" But I walk away before she has a chance to finish what she's saying. I turn a corner, leaving the busy road behind and head to Archer Street…to home.

I let myself in, my keys still safely in my pocket. The apartment is dark, and I don't bother to turn on any lights as I make my way back to the bedroom. I stop on the threshold, squeezing my eyes shut and make a silent wish—that maybe, when I open them again, Jillian will be sound asleep in our bed and all of this will just be one big, horrible nightmare. But the bed is empty, its corners tucked and pillows fluffed, like Jillian makes it every morning. I slump down against the doorframe, my shoes landing with a thud as they collide with the wooden floor. I exhale and look across the rug over by Jillian's nightstand. On the floor, perched on top of a pile of textbooks, sits her sketchbook.

A sad smile cracks across my face, and I crawl over to it, resting my back against the bed. I run my hand over the cover. It's not fancy or leather-bound: Jillian thinks all of that is highly unnecessary, since she goes through them so fast. It's just a standard cardboard sketchpad, the name of the art store printed across it. My tears dampen it as I flip through the first few pages. Pictures of fruit and tables and chairs, faceless life models from school, one of Sam's orange tabby-cat, Thimble. I take my time with each drawing, savoring them as I see her hand moving in my head.

She would work for hours, her brow going between furrowed and relaxed, her fingers always so steady, so sure…

I turn the page and come to a halt, recognizing the face before me. It's my portrait, the one of me sleeping after our first night together. How calm I look, safe and happy. I'm exactly where I'm supposed to be, in love with the most wonderful girl in the world…who was right next to me, warm and alive with pink on her cheeks.

I glare at the picture. I'm no longer this person captured in ink, and I hate the contented curl of his lip, the soft easiness of his sleeping eyes. I envy him… I hate him.

With a growl, I tear out the page and crumple it into a ball, chucking it angrily against the wall, almost sending the entire sketchbook with it. But it remains in my lap, though, and through my rage and tears, I see there's a new picture…one I haven't seen before.

I wipe my eyes and look, careful to take everything in. It's a pencil drawing of a small cottage in the woods with stone walls and a thatched roof, like something out of Grimms' fairytales. Old-fashioned pane windows frame the front door like a face, making it look like a home that is happy to have people living in it. Beyond, there is a garden—and even though it's all in dark pencil, you can see the life and color in the flowers: tulips, irises, roses… The tree line breaks with sunset or sunrise, the horizon soft. An almost unnoticeable figure stands out in the distance—small and blurred, but obviously a child. My throat grows thick, and I look down to read the title in Jillian's pristine script: *French Countryside Imagined, 7/4/76.*

My eyes cloud over, and I can't bear to look anymore. I throw the book away and get to my feet, staggering out into the hall and bumping haphazardly into the walls. I can't stand it: she's all over this place, her things, her clothes, her smell. Her smell… mingled with the stench of blood all over me.

I stumble into the kitchen and dry heave into the sink.

Catching a glimpse of the rotted birthday candle from this morning, I double over; all of this is too much. My hand flops as I reach into one of the lower cabinets next to me and grab an old bottle of vodka that Denise left behind when she moved out. Jillian and I joked that we'd take to it if she ever came back. No one's laughing anymore, and I wrench off the top to take a long, hard swig, the poison burning its way down my throat. I cough and sputter, drawing in a crackly breath before I do it again, forcing half the bottle down my gullet. My stomach roils in protest, and I pitch the glass away, hearing it shatter on the floor behind me as I get sick in the sink in earnest. I pull away panting when it's through, the familiar, acrid scent of the alcohol in my vomit temporarily covering the blood. I run my tongue over my lips; I taste like my father. I gag again and look back at the kitchen floor, which covered in broken glass and spilled vodka…vodka, water…water-rain-blood-puddle-roof… Murderer.

Shut up, Shut up, SHUT UP! I tear at my face and shove myself away from the sink. I have to get out of here. I have to…leave.

I shamble out of the apartment and back onto the street, heading south. The crowds from earlier have cleared, the midnight hour fast approaching. Everyone is happy and occupied either in the pubs or at home. That's all the better for me: no interruptions.

It's a long walk, but I get a second wind, my legs taking quick strides as I make my way toward the water. The wind on the bridge is just as strong as it was the first night we came here, blowing hot and humid from the July rain as I swing my legs over the guard rail and balance on the edge. I pull the ring box from my pocket and look at the bright, shining stone one last time before I pitch it out into the night. I don't hear a splash or even a break in the waves. I sigh.

"Well, this is it…" I say to no one. The bridge looms behind me, traffic speeding by, no one noticing the lone figure clinging to its side. I close my eyes and pull Jillian's cross from my collar, giving it a kiss before tucking it back next to my heart.

"I love you, Jillian. I am yours, and you are mine," I whisper. "Never forget that."

I turn my head, and she's here, red hair in the breeze, her smile wide and bright. In that moment, I see everything that was and everything that will never be. I grip the rail behind me, my toes dangling over the side and eclipsing the shadowy water below. I exhale.

"God give me wings…"

My eyes roll up to the sky, which is black like the water. You can't even tell them apart, except for the stars…which are always watching, ever watching, vigilant.

They see me take a breath and jump—a falling star, falling far. Becoming one with the black.

CHAPTER 23

LOS ANGELES—PRESENT DAY

*T*HE WORLD IS a circus.

You have your barkers, your high-flying trapeze, the freak show with bearded ladies and men swallowing burning coals for cash, the beautiful bareback rider galloping her pale, rose-covered steed through death-defying feats. You have your clowns, your daredevils, your snake charmers, and your lion tamers.

And at the heart of it all is the ring master, the man with the top hat and the wicked grin, waving his hand and beckoning you deeper into the fray…making that which seems dangerous safe as can be. Step right up.

But I knew better. I've been to the belly of the beast and made it out alive. I swore to never go back…to not be tempted by the bright lights and smiling faces, by that man in the hat with his secrets and his sweet words. I knew better. *Know* better.

*

The crowd outside of Trinity has its own pulse, a huge mass of laughing, cavorting, beautiful bodies all eager for Earpiece's attention as he keeps them at bay with his little velvet rope. Every one of them is mortal, of course, but that doesn't stop them from wanting to get into the biggest Demon party of the year, Herod's

Feast well disguised as a night of Christmas Eve debauchery for everyone without a family or a fireplace to go home to. I lose a good hour milling with the norms, waiting for my turn at the front, the bass from the club resonating down the street.

Earpiece's eyes widen when he sees me, though, and he quickly ushers me forward. "You didn't have to wait—you should have just come up!" he yells over the din, holding the rope aside for me. I look at him curiously. I know now that he's definitely Human too, but possibly Smudged and able to see my blue glow. That—or he's really good at remembering faces.

"I didn't know," I reply, checking every being that comes and goes out of the club. I see a wide variety of Humans decked out in their holiday finest, ranging from the top designers down on Rodeo to full period costumes encrusted in gold and jewels. And while I don't see a Demon among them, I *do* notice the line of paparazzi being held back on the other side of the doorframe by a couple of Trinity's hulking goons, their camera flashes going nuts as more bigshots show up.

I glance down at my jeans and tank top. I'm hopelessly under-dressed, but whatever. I zip my jacket with an affirmative hand—I didn't come here to impress anybody. I'm here for answers.

"I can go right in?" I ask Earpiece. He nods vigorously and waves me through. I hurry past, anxious to continue my search. I come to a halt as I enter the main hall, however, my breath stopping in my throat.

It's like walking onto another planet. Silver and gold tinsel hangs down willow-like from the exposed pipes, the dance lights flashing around the striking aerialists that are spinning silky webs with their scarves twenty feet off the floor. The crowd below applauds as one of the aerialists swings from her perch and soars across the club, clasping her fellow performer's hands in the nick of time.

I glance over at the bartender, who is shirtless and wearing what looks like a severed polar bear head as he pours frothy red and blue drinks into martini glasses for a packed house. All of the surfaces have been lined with crystal icicles, making the place look more like a mystical winter fairy cave than a city nightclub.

Off to my left, furthermore, part of the dance floor has been frozen over, creating a mini ice rink. Women in their high heels slip out onto it, squealing in delight as they skid and grip their date's arms for support. Everyone has a mask: gold, silver, red, black…ranging from simple, to stunning, to grotesque. If I didn't hate this place so much, I would be dazzled. I sigh and touch the wall next to me, quickly drawing my hand back, my fingers chilled. They iced the walls. I'm in a fucking igloo.

"Demons," I mutter, shaking my head. I'm about to walk to the bar when I hear a little cough behind me.

"Coat check?" a silvery voice asks. I turn and recognize a head-ful of pink hair—Cameron, one of the regular waitresses here. Her face is sweet and lovely, her flawless body draped in black silk. She holds out an orange token.

"Oh." I frown, looking between her and inside, putting my hands in my jacket pockets. "Won't I get cold? With all the ice and stuff…?"

Cameron giggles. "Not after you try one of our signature drinks—the Heat Miser! That's the red one… It'll warm you right up." Her eyes dart playfully over to the bar.

I give her a look. "Yeah, I'm good, thanks." I remember all too well what happened last time I tried one of Trinity's 'signature' drinks.

"As you like," Cameron replies, demure and without taking offense. She gestures to a table behind her that's lined with different styles of masks. "Can I offer you a disguise? I don't think we have one that will fully cover your Excellence." She flashes her eyebrows bashfully at me. "But some of these are pretty… I think the silver would best accentuate—"

"I said I'm good!" I snap. Her gaze goes to the floor, and I suddenly feel guilty for being rude to her. She's Human, for Godsakes—just doing a job.

You don't need to feel bad. She knows who she works for. She wants be just like them, remember? A nasty little voice hisses from the back of my head.

I sigh as an internal conflict ensues, then motion toward the back table. "Sure—I'll take the silver one, thanks," I grumble. Cameron brightens and gives me the half-face silver mask, tiny gold flowers embellishing the brow. I startle at the weight of it, expecting one of those flimsy plastic things you find at a party supply store—but this is real metal, molded thin and pliant. The flip side is lined with soft leather, a strong matching cord laced through to tie it in place.

"May I?"

I nod as Cameron moves behind me and helps me put it on, smoothing my hair when she's through. I shrug uncomfortably, but not because of her touch.

She comes around again, her face beaming. "There! Radiant, your Excellence." She nods, taking a step back and folding her hands.

I blink behind my mask, puzzled. "Uh…thanks, I think." I rub my neck. "Why would you call me that—'your Excellence'?" It's awkward for even me to say.

Cameron's eyes widen. "Would you prefer I called you some-thing else? I thought, since it had been Revealed…" She looks around nervously. "I'm sorry if I spoke out of turn…"

I hold up my hands. The last thing I need is for the wait staff to start freaking out on me. "No—everything's fine! You don't have to call me…anything." I exhale and squint into the dark club. "I'm looking for someone…and I don't know who." I give an exasperated sigh and watch Cameron nod slowly, like she's tak-ing everything I say very seriously. I realize, as I stare around at the icy walls, that I have no idea where to begin right now on my search for the scholars on Mandisa's list. Look for a group of nerdy people wearing glasses and whispering about me? I glance at the crowd—not many of that type hanging around right now... My eye stops on a half-dressed woman wearing what looks like red body paint, flames licking up her very trim sides to a pair of full breasts.

I frown and look back at Cameron. "Have you seen Mandisa?" I ask. Best to go straight for the source.

Cameron smiles, nodding her head enthusiastically. "Yes, of course! She's been here since noon, making sure every last detail was perfect." She waves up at an ice sculpture of what looks like a three-headed monster devouring babies by the armful. Cameron smiles up at it. "Isn't it just glorious? Mandisa designed it personally..."

I shiver, trying to hide my revulsion and force my expression to neutral. "Yeah—it's really something..." I pucker my lips and turn back to the crowd. "I'm just gonna see if I can track her down—"

"I'll take you to her."

I jump as a new voice comes from my periphery and wrench off my mask to see who's talking. It sounds like—"*TREVOR?*"

I gape, taking in the skinny redheaded kid standing before me. It's Trevor, all right: the same freckles, the same annoyed smirk... and about half a foot taller than the last time I saw him, wearing a brand new tuxedo. I stare at the young Amalgam, half-Demon, half-Human—and now clearing my height by at least two inches.

"Holy cow! You've grown like a beanpole since I last saw you!" I laugh, surprised at my own jubilance. "Wow! It's only been...a month, right? You've grown up so much!" I nod at his tux appreciatively. "You clean up nice!"

Trevor glances at my smugly, pleased at my reaction. When Cameron smiles at both of us and moves off to help a new patron, the young Amalgam leans in, reeking of aftershave. "I'm thirteen now," he says smugly. "Just had my birthday last week."

I smile as his voice cracks at the end, the obvious signs of puberty setting in. He plays it cool, though, and glares at me through narrowed eyes. "I didn't think you'd show up tonight. Everyone's been talking about you, as usual." He sounds slightly irritated at this. "Saying that you wouldn't be able to stay away. Not with what happened yesterday…" He arches a pale eyebrow at me.

I exhale, frowning. He knows about the Resistance attacks. "I wasn't planning on coming. Well, maybe…I didn't know." I shrug noncommittally. "But with everything that's going on, I thought I would just…check in, make sure everyone's behaving themselves." God, I'm pathetic.

"I bet," Trevor snorts. "I didn't realize you'd suddenly joined the Gray…but then again, you do always act like you know everything—so that's pretty perfect, actually."

"*You* know about the Gray?" I gape at him again, then catch myself. Of course Trevor knows about the Gray and Porticullis—he grew up in this world.

He's just another person who knows more than me, does more… I look at the floor self-consciously as Trevor shakes his head. "Um, yeah, duh." He sniffs, glancing behind me. "Where's your Guardian? What—did he go missing again?" My cheeks flush angrily as he breaks into a large grin. "I figured if you showed up, you'd, like, have a SWAT Team with you." He chuckles darkly. "Not like they would have stood a chance."

"No, I came alone." Trevor looks surprised at this, and I question if it was a good idea for me to give up that information. I tap my boot at the edge of the ice. "I thought it might be easier for me to get to Mandisa if I didn't have my full entourage." Is this easy, or stupid? I glance up at Trevor. "Have you seen her? I really need to talk to her."

"Yeah, she's here." He puts his hands in his pockets, probably attempting to look like a rakish 007, but actually looking like a kid playing dress-up in his dad's suit. I cringe, remembering *who*

Trevor's father is. Crossing my arms, I glare at him. "Well…are you going to take me to her or what?" I snap.

Trevor sighs and rolls his eyes, walking forward into the club and deftly maneuvering around the dancers. "Do you ever take a night off?" he calls back over his shoulder as I follow. "You're the only person I know who can turn the biggest party of the year into something boring…like parent/teacher conferences." He twists his lanky frame around to glare at me once more.

"Everyone needs a hobby," I sigh, doing my best to avoid bumping into any of the other partygoers—which is kind of tricky, as I'm cutting a straight line through a massive throng of chaos. A woman in a high-necked Victorian gown backs into me, putting a hand on my shoulder as she offers an apology. I keep walking deeper in.

"What's with all the crazy costumes? And where are all the Demons?" I bark at Trevor, doing a double take as one of the aerialists twirls down and steals a drink from the bar, the crowd cheering loudly.

Trevor balks. "Didn't you read your invitation—it's a masquerade!" He motions at my mask, still clutched in my right hand. "And what do you mean, where are all the Demons? They're everywhere!"

I come to a full stop and stare at him. "What are you talking about?" My eyes dart around the jam-packed club. I don't see any horns or empty eye sockets. "I don't see…"

Trevor groans. "It's Feast Night—HELLO! They're all Glamoured—the one night of the year they're allowed. Jeez! They've been coming in all night!" He waves back at the doors. "*Everyone* here is a Demon, except for a couple of Pets and, well… you."

I feel my skin grow cold—and not from the icy walls. I look back at the woman in the Victorian dress, her dark hair pulled into an elaborate updo on top of her head. We could almost be twins…

"They're all…Demons?" My voice is small, but Trevor still hears me, nodding irritably. I rack my brain—yes…Mandisa mentioned that at the shop on Melrose…but it's kind of hard to remember *what* she was saying while she was dangling a young shopgirl over the precipice of death. I take a deep breath. "They look so…*normal*." I try not to sound shocked, but fail.

Trevor rolls his eyes. "Yep. From sundown 'til dawn—wearing the faces they died in." He points to the bar. "You wanna drink? They'll give me whatever I want." He grins menacingly.

I shake my head, back to looking for Mandisa. "No…if I don't find Mandisa, I have to go…"

"Party pooper," Trevor teases, his lip curling. "Whatever. I'm gonna try the Snow Miser… It's supposed to make your whole body feel like an ice cube." He bats my arm as I crane my neck around the club. "I'll also ask the bartender about where Mandisa went! They *are* the eyes and ears of this place… I thought you knew how to do recon. Watch a spy movie, why don't you."

"What? Oh—thanks." I give him a small smile as he huffs away toward the bar, then sigh and turn back to the crowd. The music is growing louder, and the mood in the entire place is shifting into full-on rave mode. Everyone seems to take the cue and head out onto the dance floor, making it only harder for me to make out individual faces and tell who's who.

"AH! You came—how marvelous!"

I jump at the sound of that beautiful voice, spinning around to face Mandisa. Her tall, thin body is wrapped tightly in a bright red kente cloth, a startling contrast against the black and white and shimmering jewel tones. Trevor was right; she's completely Glamoured, not a trace of anything Demonic across her angular face…like the first time I met her in the Warehouse, before I was Smudged. She looks fantastic, of course—but that doesn't mean she's any less dangerous. She gives me a bright smile.

"Mandisa." I nod, straightening my back. "Yes…I came."

She puts a warm hand on my shoulder, and I fight the urge

to shrug her off. If she feels me flinch, she doesn't bat an eye, just leading me further into the throng. "Christa, I am so glad you're here…and perfect timing!" She gestures to the small Middle Eastern man standing next to her, his expression grave. "This is Dr. Khattab. His flight just arrived from Cairo not an hour ago!" She chuckles pleasantly.

"How do you do?" the man murmurs quietly, taking my hand and staring at me hungrily. Hesitantly, I shake his hand, noticing his fingers taking the time to brush over the blue of my wrist. I draw back, totally creeped out. My eyes dart back to Mandisa, who leans in conversationally.

"I was so concerned that Dr. Khattab wasn't going to make it… He's one of the names from my list!" My ears perk up as she puts an arm around the small man, adding, "You two will have so much to talk about—and with Professor Adler no longer attending—"

"What?" I bristle at the mention of Colette's father. "Adler?"

Mandisa nods emphatically. "Yes, that's right! The two of you were acquainted." She says this so flippantly, my stomach ties itself it knots. She knows we were at his house the other night—probably had surveillance on the place. Now, she's smirking. "Surely you must have heard…"

"Heard what?" I demand, my jaw locked.

Mandisa sighs and glances between Dr. Khattab and me. "Mmm, poor man…a rather nasty incident involving an overdose of sleeping pills." She tuts sympathetically. "At least it was quick and painless—a small solace."

My heart sinks. "He's dead?" I rasp, my hands shaking. Daniel will be devastated. *I'm* devastated.

Mandisa sighs and nods. "We will all remember him for his brilliant research and contributions to our community… And regardless!" Mandisa grins and gives Khattab a light push toward me. "*We* still have tonight, and Doctor Khattab is a world-renowned religion and mythology expert! He should be able to answer any questions you have about the prophecy…or being the Catalyst." She glances past me and waves at someone behind us. "Ah! Sabine just arrived—excuse me." She smiles at Doctor Khattab and me before sauntering off, clapping in delight and hugging a large woman decked out in head-to-toe diamonds who I can only assume is a very old friend or conspirator.

I turn back to Khattab. "I…I think I might need a minute…" I clutch my middle as nausea rocks my insides; I'm still feeling violently thrown off by the news about Adler. I turn to look for a restroom, but Khattab grabs my elbow.

"I can't believe I'm finally seeing you in the flesh." He's practically licking his chops as he eyes me up and down. "After years of study and servitude…to finally be in your presence…"

I shake out of his grasp and narrow my eyes at him, wanting nothing more than to get away. "I'm sorry—this was a mistake." I regret ever coming here, and I have no problem telling him just that. "I should have never come here tonight. This is…pointless." I nod a curt goodbye and take a step away.

He puts his hand on me again, this time holding me gently by the wrist. I glare at him. I've got a good half-foot on the tiny, compact man and easily gaze over him, noting the shiny bald spot on the back of his head. I could take him with one punch—I know I could.

Maybe he notices my glare—because he lets go of me, his manners back in check. "Why *did* you come?" he asks politely, watching me through his half-moon spectacles.

I sigh in frustration and look at him. "To find answers. About me…being the Catalyst." I drag my fingers through my hair. "About what happens next, this big choice I'm supposed to make. Daniel—uh, my Guardian—and I have been trying to figure it all out on our own—"

"Ah, yes, the Sacrifice," Khattab interrupts calmly.

That gets my attention. "I'm sorry, did you say 'Sacrifice'?" I shout, the bass from the club speakers thumping in my ears.

Khattab stares at me, the corner of his mouth twitching. "Yes… 'Once the course has been decided, it will fall to the Catalyst to sacrifice'…" he recites, his eyes searching mine.

I glare back at him. "Yes, that's the prophecy!" I cry urgently. "I know that—but what are you saying? That *Daniel* is the Sacrifice? What the hell do you mean?" I almost reach out and shake him, but control myself.

"Of course." Khattab scratches his chin like he's talking to himself. "As the earlier part of the prophecy reveals, a major theme in the Catalyst's life is that she continues to sacrifice that which she loves most… These things always have a balance—the Catalyst experiences a loss at the beginning, so there must be one of equal measure at the end—"

"You don't know that!" I shout, my breath growing ragged as people keep laughing and dancing all around us. "The prophecy isn't even finished yet! We have no clue what's coming!"

Khattab purses his lips thoughtfully. "True, but based on previous prophecies of a similar nature, we can predict what the outcome—"

"No, you can't!" I know I sound truly unhinged now, but I can't bring myself to care. "You don't know me, and you don't know Daniel—I would never do anything to hurt him!" The sheer idea of it sends me spiraling.

Khattab stands there, looking nonplussed. "But you will," he replies logically, like I just tried to tell him 2 plus 2 equals 51. "All of my research indicates—"

"Screw you, and screw your research!" I cry, stumbling backwards. "And stay away from me… I don't know who you think you are—but *this*," I wave wildly, "never happened!"

I stalk off, leaving Khattab standing alone and blinking behind his little glasses. Gasping for air, I grab my stomach and dash over to the bar, desperate to get away from Khattab and Mandisa and all of their lies.

Seeing Trevor sitting on one of the stools, I squeeze in next to him. He grimaces at me. "What's with you?" he wonders, puckering his lips as he takes a sip of his blue drink.

I grip the side of the bar, trying to steady my shaking legs. "Nothing!" I yell, probably giving myself away.

Trevor rolls his eyes and sets his glass down. "You're such a drama queen, freaking out all the time." He shakes his head. "Is relaxing not in your DNA?"

My heart feels like it's about to beat itself out of my chest. "Not now, Trevor!" I force myself to exhale. Fuck that pocket-sized doctor… Mandisa probably coached him ahead of time on what to say just to rile me up. He's probably not even a real doctor, just an expert in making shit up…

"You need a drink!" The words sound off coming out of Trevor's tween mouth. He pushes what's left of his blue cocktail in front of me. "Seriously! It makes your toes tingle…"

I bite my lip and shove the glass away, sending it skating across the icy bar. "No—I don't want a drink!" Feeling like I'm about to burst into tears, I slam the bar with my hands. "I have to go…"

Trevor's eyes flash with disappointment, his lips curling in a sneer. "What? You just got here! You can't leave now—the Passion's gonna start soon!"

I shake my head and step back onto the main floor. "I don't even know what that means…but this was a horrible idea, and I have to get home and find Daniel—"

"Christa?"

I spin at the sound of my name. The dancers part, and my knees buckle. I catch myself before I hit the deck, confronted by two very familiar faces.

"Oh my God—what are you doing here?!" Livie crows, pulling me into a hug. I can't breathe, my world going fuzzy as I slip into an honest-to-God panic attack—not able to tear my eyes away from her date.

"What are *you* doing here?" I manage to rasp into Livie's ear, willing myself not to throw up all over her beautiful white dress.

She pulls back and smiles, ushering the boy behind her forward. "The big Christmas party I told you about! Remember?" She beams and takes his hand. "Christa, this is Brennan...my *boyfriend*." She grins as she links arms with him.

Oh my God, no...I'm gonna be sick.

"Hello, Christa," he purrs, staying close to Livie's side as his brown eyes glint back at me, debonair in his pristine, black suit. Every hair on the back of my neck shoots up. I glare at his hand where it's wrapped around Livie, caressing her hip.

"Don't touch her," I snap, a grim suspicion creeping in. "Get your hands off her, Riley."

Livie looks between the two of us, confused. "I'm sorry...do you two know each other? And...why...why are you calling him Riley?" She shifts uneasily, still gripping his hand tight.

I feel my lips pull back from my gums. "Because that's his name, Livie."

Riley B. Anderson...Riley *Brennan* Anderson—a little tidbit I'd long forgotten in order to make room for more important things in my memory. It should have been an instant red flag, seeing as it's not a very common name, if I'd only been listening, paying better attention...

"Is...is that true, Brennan?" Livie turns to him, her expression suddenly uneasy.

He smiles widely and pets her arm. "Yes. Brennan is my middle name...and what I prefer to go by now in my new life." He nods at me, then smiles at Trevor, who's still standing behind me. "Amalgam."

Trevor straightens up, his face steely. "First level," he returns in greeting.

Livie continues to look confused. I shut my eyes woozily—suspicion confirmed. Riley's dead...for real. And a Demon. My ex-boyfriend is a Demon. Fuck.

"So...how do you two know each other?" Livie asks quietly,

not the happy girl she was a few moments ago, shuffling her feet under the hem of her sweeping gown.

Riley pats her cheek reassuringly. "Christa is someone from my past...so she knows me by my old name. Nothing you need to be concerned about, love, merely a coincidence. " He kisses her forehead, and she visibly calms down and melts into him.

I tense. "Know a lot more than your name," I snarl, staring him down. "Where you been, Riley? Everyone's been *real* worried." Teachers, friends...his parents. If only they knew what their quarterback star had turned into.

Riley chuckles as Livie looks back at him, worried. "Here, of course! With my new family." He motions around Trinity. "Isn't it magnificent? So glad you decided to join us tonight..."

"Just leaving, actually!" I yell. Trevor startles as I reach over and grab Livie's arm. "And you're coming with me, now. I'll take you home—"

"There we go," Trevor mutters to himself. "Was waiting for that shoe to drop—completely crazy and off her rocker..."

Livie shakes her head and tears away from me. "What—NO! What is going on? None of this makes any sense! Why are you even here, Christa?!" She stares back at me, tears glistening in her eyes. "I mean...you're my friend and all...but I thought this was *my* big thing! There's just a lot happening right now—"

I balk as Riley pulls her into a hug, shushing her against his chest. "It *is* still your big night! I'm not going to let anyone ruin that for you—I promise..." He shoots me a devious look over his shoulder, making my blood boil. I want to blurt out *"He's a Demon!"*—but I have no idea how much Livie knows, and after what happened with Jodie, I'm not going to be the one to blow up her world if I don't have to. I just need to get her out of here.

"Livie—" I risk the few steps between us and put my hand on her shoulder. She turns and looks at me with a tear-stained face, her cheeks flushed and blooming like pink tulips. I take a deep breath. "I know this is all really overwhelming and confusing..."

I glower as Riley holds back a laugh, Livie staring at me disbelievingly. "But you have to trust me right now when I say we really have to go. It's not safe for you here."

"Why?" she breathes, gaping around the fantastic hall. "It's beautiful here...and did you see all that security at the front door? They're not letting just anybody in!" She gazes at Riley like he's freaking Andrew Garfield. "And I'm here, with you...with Brennan..." She blushes and peeks dreamily back at me while he massages the exposed small of her back. "Nothing bad could ever happen when I'm with him."

"Famous last words," Trevor mumbles out of the side of his mouth.

I could smack him. "Livie, listen to me!" I exclaim, getting up in her face. "You have to get out of here—before it's too late! If you don't want to leave with me, fine—but just go!"

She giggles awkwardly and looks back at Riley, who smiles down on her. Trevor sighs apathetically. "I'm serious!" I reiterate, knowing that I sound like an old biddy who everyone thinks has lost her marbles. "I don't know what's going on here, but I have a hunch it's not good—"

"It's time." Cameron comes up behind Riley and Livie, smiling good-naturedly. She offers her hand to Livie, who grins back and quickly wipes the tears off her face.

"Okay...yes! I'm ready!" She turns back to Riley, her eyes wide. "Are...are you coming?"

Riley nods. "Of course. You go ahead and let Cameron help you get ready. I'll catch up."

Livie takes Cameron's hand and looks back at me. "Goodbye, Christa," she says resolutely. "I hope you have a nice Christmas."

"LIVIE!" I cry, watching the two girls walk away. Once they're out of sight, I turn on Riley, my face rabid. "Where is she going?! What are you going to do to her?!" I demand, punching him in the chest.

He stands there and takes it, looking bored. "Nothing she

doesn't want to do!" he snaps, his whole demeanor going from saccharine sweet to harsh and repugnant now that Livie's gone. "Mind your own business, Catalyst! This is one thing that doesn't concern you—"

"You're damn right, it concerns me!" I shout back. "She's my friend, Riley! I won't let you hurt her."

He sighs and rolls his head back as the song in the club changes over to new beat. "Let's dance! I'm getting tired just standing around here like a couple of nobodies," he drawls, his eyes boring into me. "Come on, I know how much you love dancing—usually leads into other activities that I know you're good at. Should I fake an Irish accent? That seemed to work pretty well the last time we were here."

"Get serious!" I snap, noticing Trevor take a step forward next to me.

Riley laughs. "Or maybe I need to put on a Rolling Stones t-shirt and make you a sandwich...God! You've become so predictable, Christa!" He snorts. "More than when we were together anyway, if that's even possible."

"And you've become more of an asshole, if *that* was possible!" I spit. "Guess that comes with the territory though."

Riley shrugs his big football shoulders and winks. "Dance with me, come on."

"No—I'm leaving." Even though my gut is telling me to stay and help Livie...I have to go find Daniel. Everything is just so messed up.

"She's with me, anyway," Trevor interjects, both Riley and I doing a double take. Trevor turns beet red. "You know, just for the party..."

"Okay, Half Breed!" Riley guffaws, bursting into a fit of cruel laughter. "I know Christa's pretty down for whatever, but you look a little young—even for her. Have your balls even dropped yet?"

I shoot him a dirty look, but Trevor sticks out his chin

defiantly. I can see his upper lip trembling like he's about to cry, though. Great.

"All right—that's my cue! Riley—Brennan, whatever your name is—fuck off and merry Christmas!" I pretend to tip my hat. "See you on the battlefield." I start to walk off.

"Dance with me now or she dies, Nichols," Riley breathes behind me.

I stop dead in my tracks and slowly turn to face him. He's got a stupid, shit-eating grin on his face. "Livie," he clarifies. "I'll kill her—you know I mean it."

"You…wouldn't dare," I hiss, stepping deliberately back over. "Besides the fact that I know you haven't had a chance to screw her yet…doesn't that break one of your Rules, or whatever? With the Universe?"

Riley snickers. "We have ways of working around that—*I'm* here, aren't I?" He arches a brow. I shake my head, not having any idea what he's talking about. "Come on—don't test it. One dance."

I sigh and look back at Trevor, who shrugs dejectedly. "Whatever," he grumbles, scuffing his shoes. "You're gonna do whatever you want. No one ever listens to me anyway…" I watch him storm off and through the front doors, leaving the club in a huff.

I look back at Riley. "Fine. Let's get this over with."

I stomp onto the dance floor, Riley following in my wake. We get to the center of the action and I roll my eyes, starting to shuffle my feet back and forth. Riley snickers at my expression and tries to put his hands on my waist.

"Yeah—not on your life!" I shout, shoving him away. "You said *dance*, not grope!"

"You're so uptight." He smirks, moving his feet in time with the music. He has better rhythm than I remember. "Impressive how you can make something inherently fun completely suck—"

"Well, what is this, Riley?" I snap. "Huh?! Is this some sick twisted point you're trying to prove? Still mad about the last time we were here together?"

Riley chuckles and leans into my ear. "No, I'm not mad. You screwing me over that night was actually the best thing that ever happened to me."

I glare at him, puzzled. He grabs my hand and twirls me—against my will, I might add. "If you hadn't been unfaithful to me—" he continues.

I scoff. "*Unfaithful?* That's a little strong, don't you think? It's not like we were married for 25 years or whatever." I do my best to keep dancing and avoid touching him at the same time, which is hard. I probably look like an awkward frog hopping around on the dance floor.

Riley laughs. "If you hadn't found Alden that night, none of this would have happened." He smiles sardonically.

I stop dancing and glare at him. "What do you mean?" I whisper. I know he can still hear me.

"I wouldn't have met Alden in the first place, I wouldn't have drank as much as I did…" He arches a brow and pulls me back again, our hips swaying. "I wouldn't have killed Tom—"

"Don't put that on me!" I snarl, my face growing hot. "Take responsibility for yourself and your own shitty actions!"

Riley shrugs. "And after everything was said and done, I wouldn't have met the same end I did." He grins. "I'm here because of you, Christa. I'm dead because of you."

A chill runs down my spine. I withdraw completely from him. "Shut up. That's…that's not true." It's all bluster: I have no idea what's true anymore.

Riley sighs. "Believe whatever you want, but I have no reason to lie to you—"

"That's what you all say!" I growl, looking away from his face. I glare around the room, spying Mandisa off by the bar, having a gay old time with a group of wildly dressed Demons who look like gold-spattered pirates. I narrow my eyes and turn back to

Riley. "What *are* you doing here anyway?" I sneer. Riley's looks at me curiously, so I add, "Doesn't Hell only let their smartest, most manipulative work in the Mortal Realm? You're not exactly known for your cunning and wit."

Riley smiles at the dig. "You're right. I was on my way to serving an eternity in the Lower Realms…to toil and burn, never to see the light of day again…" He sucks in a breath dramatically. "Pretty scary stuff."

"So what happened?" I grumble.

He winks. "I happened to mention in my placement interview that I knew you *intimately*." His grin grows wider. "And they sent me straight up! Nepotism's a bitch, isn't it?" He grips my hand as the music relaxes and we move into a slow dance.

"Unbelievable," I seethe, staring back into the crowd. It's getting late… I really need to get out of here, but my curiosity is getting the best of me. I glare up at him. "So is that why you picked Livie? To get close to me?"

Riley nods and taps my nose patronizingly. "Very good! I mean…it wasn't because she's, like, actually cool to be around…" He makes the crazy gesture by his temple. "Always yakking away with that annoying accent… She's got a hot body, at least, so that part wasn't so bad. Got her to shut up for a while—"

"You're disgusting," I hiss.

He grips my side harder, and we move to the music. I glare into his eyes. "You know your death still hasn't been confirmed at home, right?" I watch his face, hoping for some sort of reaction, but he just stares at me blankly. "Your friends…your parents, they're all still hoping you're coming back…that you're just off on some spirit journey because of what happened to Tom—"

This *does* elicit something inside him, his eyes flickering bright for a minute. "Well, it's not like I can exactly just show up on my front steps and tell everyone I'm home for Christmas," he replies coldly. I watch his jaw harden. "That ship has sailed, thanks to you…"

I shake my head at the guilt that's welling in my chest. No. *I didn't kill Riley*—whatever happened is on him. He made his own bed. I stop and think of my mother; dealing with Dad's death... *I didn't kill him, Christa.* I feel my eyes water.

"Why not?" I turn back to Riley. "I mean...they don't know you're a Demon. Can't you just go and make up some BS story about how you're only back for break and then you're going to stay with friends in Vegas or something?"

Cold comfort is better than none at all. I think of the few times I met Riley's parents—the quintessential proud sports mom and dad, with matching smiles and Sacred Hearts Athletics sweatshirts, making snickerdoodles for the whole team after every game. They're nice.

Riley glares at me sourly. "You can only see me because it's Feast Night. There's a whole different set of rules for the next couple hours." He stares over my head at the wall. "Sure—my parents would be thrilled, their baby boy come home—a true miracle..." His scowl turns into a wicked grin. "Until they woke up Christmas morning to a complete stranger in their kid's bed, having no idea who the Hell I am...some new face they've never seen before." He sniffs. "Sucks, right?"

I look down at my feet and nod. "Yeah... I'm sorry." That *is* terrible.

Riley makes a farting noise with his mouth. "Whatever. You can bet some of the others have fun with it!" He jerks his chin around at the growing mass of Demon partygoers. "You know... especially if they had a hot wife before—one more night of magic—the bitch thinks she's fucking a ghost or something." My face contorts as he shrugs coolly. "The whole thing just sounded kind of lame to me. After a while, everyone you know is already dead, or, like, old and ugly...so who cares?"

I gape at him, speechless. He chuckles and puts his hands on my waist again.

"Wow," I finally manage. "If there was ever a shadow of

a doubt that you *didn't* belong here...you just sealed the deal. Thank you for easing my conscience."

Riley shakes his head. "What the Hell does that mean?"

I let out a howl. "It means get your hands off of me, you fucking dirty Demon!" I cry, tearing away from him. "You're a monster!"

Eyes blazing, Riley grabs me, pulling me back. "I don't care who the Hell you are or who you think you are—no one talks to me that way!" I gasp in pain as he smashes his nose to mine, his hand hurting my back. "You're gonna learn some respect, if it's the last thing I—"

"May I cut in?"

Riley jumps back, releasing me in a flash. "Yes, of course." He puts his head down and steps away. "Whatever you like, sir."

I hold my breath and close my eyes. I don't need to turn around to know who's standing behind me—I'd recognize that voice anywhere.

"Hello, Sweet Girl," Alden drawls as I turn to face him. "You're looking well."

I clench my jaw. "Likewise." I can't think of anything else to say, my whole body trembling. He's wearing one of his standard dark suit jackets, black on black with a small pink rose tucked into the lapel. He gently tugs off a matching black mask, revealing the stunning pair of cool blue eyes that hooked me in the first place. Still as beautiful as ever...and still terrifying.

"Do you need anything, sir?" Riley simpers next to us. I feel embarrassed for him—it's so strange to see him...groveling.

Alden sighs. "Only a moment of privacy, thank you," he replies sternly. "You should be getting back to your date anyway, right? It's almost time."

"Yes, sir. Thank you." Riley shoots me a final glare before scuttling off into the dancers, making his way to the back offices.

I turn back to Alden and shake my head. "I don't think I've ever seen him move so fast," I snort. "Even on the football field."

Alden chuckles and steps toward me, putting his hand on my waist. I flinch, but I don't pull away as he sweeps me off to another song, his burnt paper scent in my nose. I'm screaming inside, but my body stays calm and easy, moving effortlessly to the music. Alden smiles at me, our faces inches from one another.

"We do have a pretty strict hierarchy in place around here... First Levels learn quickly who not to mouth off to. I also think he sees me as a bit of father figure. Odd," Alden answers, his eyes searching mine.

It's strange, seeing him like this... I'd become so accustom to the mythical horns and skeleton features. The little voice in the back of my head is wailing to run away, but *I don't want to.* The two of us are dancing like old friends when I should be scream- ing and sprinting in the opposite direction. I can understand how mortals...or *anyone* who sees this face...could be swayed into doing whatever he wants. Treacherous.

I frown. "What are you doing here? I thought you were sup- posed to be abroad."

Alden shrugs. "I decided to come back early. Spend the holi- days at home...among family and friends." He grins lasciviously.

I bristle—there's the Alden I remember. "Quite a party you've got going here," I remark coolly, glancing around the packed club, the front doors now closed to any further occupants. "Seems like you're not the only international traveler here." I point to a group of Asian tourist types decked head to toe in Louis Vuitton.

Alden looks over and snickers. "Yes, it's the event of the year. There are a few rival parties in Rio and Ibiza, but we've pretty much got the market covered for North America." He narrows his eyes at me. "I have to say, I *am* surprised to see you here tonight." He doesn't waver as I accidentally step on his toe. "Figured you and Daniel would have some big Christmas plans—"

"We do," I interject, "Big plans. Cooking a huge dinner together... Hosting a bunch of people tomorrow..." I hear the edge in my voice and know Alden notices it too, arching his brow.

"Sounds magical," he croons, gazing around the hall. "Is he here? I would love to say hello, wish him a merry Christmas."

"No!" I exclaim. Alden gives me a surprised look. I hesitate. "I mean...he's doing recon." I use Trevor's word from earlier. "He'll be back any minute." God—there is no way he's buying that. *I* don't even believe it.

Alden chuckles, readjusting his hand at my side as the music changes to a more seductive beat. "Well...I am curious to hear what he finds. Should be interesting. So many unanswered questions, right now." He does some fancy footwork, moving us further toward the offices. I look back nervously at the locked doors. All of the staff is suddenly very busy—something's about to happen.

"What's everyone so hyped up about?" I murmur, jutting my chin toward a group of workers who just appeared, hastily constructing some sort of stage at the back of the room.

Alden's lip twitches. "Didn't you read your invitation? It's almost 9:30... The Passion is about to begin."

I shake my head. "Yeah...I don't know what that is."

"An old tradition." Alden's expression grows stoic. "Don't worry—you'll be perfectly safe."

I freeze. Nothing good ever follows the words *you'll be perfectly safe*. "What about the other mortals? Are they okay, too?" I have no idea what's about to happen...but anything involving Demons and a few lone Humans can't be kosher.

I feel Alden's grip tighten, his gaze darting around the club. "Like I said, you will be protected." He clears his throat, glancing past me. "You should appreciate it tonight... Might be the last one like it, what with the Resistance making their play."

My eyes widen. "You know about the Resistance?"

Alden nods. "Of course. They've been around for decades in the Lower Realms—plotting, preparing for that one shining moment to take their cause to the Mortal World." I see his mouth turn down slightly at the corners. "It's only a matter of time 'til it all comes crumbling down..."

"They want me to close Hell," I whisper. I have no idea why I'm telling him this. It's not like I trust him, but I just can't hold back. "The Resistance. I don't know why."

"Isn't it obvious?" Alden smiles. "They're bucking against a broken system—one of extreme punitive measures that only further destroys broken souls instead of trying to heal them." His face grows cold. "Heaven preaches love and forgiveness, but for some reason, they have no problem cutting out a large part of the Human population from that equation—for what? A few mistakes?"

"Murder and rape aren't mistakes," I murmur. Alden's grip tightens around my fingers. "Abuse, lies, betrayal. Some people are truly...evil. They need to pay for what they did."

I watch his eyes soften, and he lets out a heavy sigh. "I see that your time with the good and righteous has rubbed off," he sneers. "Although, I thought they'd be teaching lessons about rehabilitation somewhere in that mix as well..." His face brightens. "Speaking of which, how *is* dear old Mum anyway? Enjoying herself down in Del Mar?"

I cringe, the passive amity we had a minute ago gone. He chuckles. "Happy, healthy, supported? It's no trouble really... Had to cut cable to make the budget all shake out, but I think it's worth it..."

"Get over yourself!" I snap, shoving away. "I didn't ask you to pay for anything, to have any part in our lives." I turn to leave, but Alden grabs my hand.

"Oh, come now—don't be like that!" he chortles, pulling me back. "We left on good terms...all things considered."

"Yeah—after you had Daniel beaten and bloodied, pinned to a wall!" I cry. "We barely made it out of there still breathing—"

Alden shakes his head. "You know I had no part in that!" he shouts incredulously. "Daniel said so himself! You might want to make sure things are straight in your own house before pointing fingers..."

"Oh, what does that mean?!" I cry, glaring at him. "Tell me!"

"It really isn't my place to say!" He wrinkles his nose. "Try asking Danny or Mary Carmen some time... Give 'em a chance to cough up a lung first, and then I bet you'll get the truth."

"Shut up," I snarl, trying to free my hand. He's got me in a vice lock. "And let go of me! You can't keep me here—there's no Deal like last time!"

With a sniff, he releases me. "Quite right. Glad to see you have a better understanding of the Rules...as we all go merrily along..." He looks toward the back of the club, where the workers are now finished assembling a large platform. "But if you leave now, you're going to miss the show—and what a tragedy that would be."

I exhale and watch as everyone starts to move instinctually to the back, the excitement in the hall growing to a fever pitch. "I don't get you people," I hiss, getting Alden's attention again. "The pageantry, the grand displays and showmanship...for what? A way to break up the monotony? Pretend your existences aren't so horrible?"

"You tell me," he replies coyly. "As you're more like us now than I'm sure you'd like to admit." He flashes his eyebrows. "What was it like the other day, not Haloing like all the other little Humans? Hm? At the theater?"

I stare at him, my spine rigid. "What do you know about that?"

He shrugs. "I know you left the Warehouse last month...*off.*" He smirks. "Maybe a little more...wrong...than before?"

I shake my head slowly. "No—shut up. You don't know what you're talking about..."

Alden chuckles. "One of the side effects of spending time on 3." He watches me as I hold my breath. "Mind you, not many mortals live to tell *that* tale—you're one of only a handful throughout all of existence." He clucks his tongue. "Just another way you're *so* cool, Christa, so different..."

"Shut up," I hiss, staring him down. "None of that's true."

Alden rolls his eyes. "Right. Tell me, though, read any good souls lately?"

"No!" I lie ferociously. "And I don't have any superpowers or whatever, so just back off!" I glance at the doors. "I'm leaving, and don't try to stop me—"

Suddenly the house lights go dark, a pleased murmur coming up from the crowd. "Hold that thought, darling," Alden purrs in my ear, stepping behind me. "The play's about to begin. Wouldn't want to be rude to the actors."

"What?" I rasp, turning to face the stage as a spotlight comes up.

The audience watches silently as the black curtain parts and out steps a girl in a white dress: Livie. The bright light washes her out, but it doesn't make her look bad...just younger. More innocent.

"No…" I shake my head and take a step forward.

Alden shushes into my hair and wraps an arm around my waist, holding me in place. "Don't do anything foolish, Christa… Let's leave the scene to the players," he sighs.

"What is she doing up there?!" I jerk my chin toward him, my teeth bared. "What's happening? Tell me now—"

Alden makes a face. "Just watch. This isn't Shakespeare… All will be made clear very soon."

I turn back to the stage, my lips trembling. Livie stands there, wide eyed and nervous, her knees knocking under her dress, the crystals glinting in the light. She takes a deep breath and acknowledges the audience with a nod, being met with thunderous applause. She breaks into a wide grin and does a little curtsey, holding her hands gingerly out at her sides.

"What?" I ask, totally baffled.

I look at Alden again, who's smiling darkly. "Our brave heroine," he whispers, keeping his eyes on Livie. "Surely you can relate—the star of our age-old passion play."

I bite my cheek. "Stop…" I watch as a hush goes over the crowd; you can hear the pipes tinkering in the walls as Livie turns her attention to stage right, her costar making its entrance.

A tiny baby deer trots onstage—unescorted, its spindly legs tripping over themselves as it cheerfully bounds over to Livie. She crouches down and holds out a cupped hand, which we can now see is filled with oats. Livie smiles princess-like as the fawn chows down, its cotton tail waggling behind it. Livie pets its neck sweetly.

"Alden," I whisper cautiously, craning my neck around the hall, looking for snipers or something equally awful—poised for someone to destroy this serene picture. "What's going on? I can't—"

"Remind me to never take you to the ballet," he scoffs, putting a finger to my lips. "Really, now—don't say a word."

I let out a low grumble as my eyes are drawn to the left side of the platform, where a man dressed in stagehand black steps quietly out from the curtain to Livie's side, setting a table and something sharp and light on top of it; Livie picks it up and displays it for the audience: a knife…or, more accurately, a dagger with an ornate handle.

I clench my fists. "What's she going to do with that?" I hiss.

Alden rests his chin on my shoulder. "The conflict in our story presents itself: our heroine must make a choice." He tilts his cheek toward Livie, looking intently between the knife and the fawn. "Does she choose mercy or self-interest? Sacrifice her own needs, or someone else's? Tricky, tricky…"

Dread seeps into me. I take a deep breath as Livie seems to contemplate these very questions in front of a crowd of hundreds. "Jesus Christ—is she going to kill that thing?!" I almost shout. Alden shushes me harshly, and I glare back at Livie, who is thrusting the blade into the air, her arm shaking in the light.

I spin around and face the complacent Demon. "No—no! She can't!" I growl, grabbing his lapels. "This isn't her! She would never hurt anyone—especially an animal!" This is the girl who, upon spotting a mouse at Sober Students a few weeks ago, caught it in a juice glass and took it out to free it in the courtyard. This is the girl who'd regaled us with tales of Joey the Bear and her other assorted fauna back in Tennessee. No way was *this* going down.

Alden shrugs. "You'd be surprised what people are capable of when presented with everything they've ever dreamed of. Ah—here we go." He nods to the left side of the curtain.

I twist back and let out a snarl as Riley joins Livie on stage, his black suit contrasting smartly against her white dress: a bride and groom standing before their five hundred most beloved friends. This is starting to feel like the most fucked up wedding of all time.

Riley helps Livie to her feet and brushes his hand lovingly across her cheek. She melts into him like no one is watching. My stomach spasms while everyone else collectively coos.

"Alden, you better start explaining, or I am going to crash this beast like Kanye, so help me—"

"You will do no such thing," Alden murmurs, shaking his head. "This is where they take us back to the old days of Herod; he already had an idea in his head... he just needed a little extra coaxing to really motivate him. Watch—"

He waves a hand, and I see that Livie is fingering the dagger again, turning slowly back to the fawn. I want to cry out, yell her name, tell her to stop, but my voice has left me as I watch her expression change from fearful to confident, her mouth pressed into a thin line as she brushes her hand over the deer's neck again, holding the knife steady.

I gasp as she suddenly grips the fawn's nape, holding it firmly as she plunges the dagger into its throat, its hooves clattering against the floor as she swiftly drags the blade through its flesh. The animal doesn't cry out; it never gets the chance, just falls to the ground, its muscles twitching as it quickly dies.

No one makes a sound—no clapping, no cheering. I suck in a breath, taking the whole scene in, my eyes focusing on the platform itself: the bolts and clamps, metal beams keeping the whole thing up. I stare back at Livie, whose hands are dripping with blood as she kneels next to the dead creature, smoothing its fur, her face drawn. I clench my jaw.

Sacrifice.

"Is that what you wanted me to see?" My friend totally compromising everything she believes in?

I turn to Alden, thinking it's over. He doesn't respond, just points back to the stage like the freakin' Ghost of Christmas Future. I look and see Livie get up, Riley pulling a handkerchief from his pocket and carefully cleaning her hands for her. He takes the dagger from her and cleans the blade as well, holding the knife in his right hand. He pulls Livie to him again, kissing her passionately. I roll my eyes.

"This is what gets you guys turned on?" I mutter.

Alden doesn't flinch. I follow his gaze back to the stage and flash from disgust to terror as Riley looks Livie in the eye and slowly hands her back the dagger. Livie keeps her gaze trained on him as she plunges the blade into her own stomach, her lips parting in a surprised gasp as she pushes the knife deeper.

"NO!" I cry out as she collapses like Scarlet O'Hara into Riley's arms, red staining her beautiful dress. Red on white, blood on bandages, time on 10… Livie trying to kill herself, Adler—both finally succeeding…

"Livie!" I shout across the silent hall. A few people turn to stare at me as I lunge forward, Alden grabbing my wrist. "Help her!"

"Keep her back!" someone shouts, and everyone crams together, making a wall between me and the stage. Alden holds me protectively as I glare wild-eyed, watching my friend bleed out.

"It's fine, Christa—just wait," Alden murmurs, pressing his lips to my ear. I shake my head dumbly, shocked and horrified.

Riley and Livie haven't seemed to notice what's happening in the audience. Like he's done it a million times before, Riley folds back the cuff on his sleeve cuts his own arm, using the same blade that Livie just stabbed herself with. Gently, he presses the wound to Livie's mouth, encouraging her to suckle. She obliges, weakly drawing in mouthful after mouthful of Demon blood. She lets out a ragged breath and sits up blinking, her eyes as wide as saucers as she takes in Riley and the crowd. Slowly, she gets to her feet, still holding Riley's hand. She's healed...and Smudged.

The audience breaks into booming applause, shouts of "Bravo!" and "Bella, bella!" echoing around me. Riley grins at Livie and pulls her into another hug, kissing her face and neck all over. The audience parts, not caring if I get through or not now, the mood celebratory as a Demon woman in a long black dress comes on stage to hand Livie a gigantic bouquet of flowers.

Hesitantly, I turn and look at Alden, his face grim. "*That*— is how you make a Pet," he comments, keeping close so I can hear him over all the noise. I grimace and look back at Livie, the dead baby fawn still at her feet and her dress soaked with blood. Unaware that she's just summed up the clusterfuck that is Demon-Human-Divine relations in a three minute charade. She's grinning and waving like she just won Miss America— it's one of the most gruesome things I've ever seen.

"I have to get out of here...now," I slur at Alden, feeling like I'm about to faint.

He nods and steadies me against him. "That's good, because in about five minutes, this whole place is going to get burnt to the ground."

I pull back and glare at him, but I see that his mouth is severe. He's not joking. "What—" I breathe, looking dazedly at the guests around us. The large Demon woman who Mandisa greeted earlier is standing right next to us, her diamonds glittering brightly as she cheers and claps. She didn't hear what Alden said—no one did.

I exhale. "You mean, all these people—"

"Demons," Alden corrects, pulling me away toward the back offices.

I shake my head. "They're all going to get killed? Burned

up?" My legs turn to jelly as I look back a final time at the happy Christmas party scene, everyone now filing up onstage to congratulate Livie and Riley. Alden hoists me up, and we keep moving.

"That's right, Sweet Girl...courtesy of your local Resistance chapter." He waggles his eyebrows playfully.

I stop dead in my tracks. "You?" I rasp, trying to wrap my head around everything. "You're part of the Resistance?" Along with Serpentine and who else?

Alden nods and clasps my hand, pulling me onward. "Took a refresher course in explosives this last week on my visit to Beirut... Had a Hell of a time getting my red and blue wires mixed up. Hope I got it right this time." He wrenches open the back fire door.

"ALDEN!" I exclaim, jerking away from him. He sighs and checks his watch, tapping his toe impatiently by the door. I wave back to the party. "We can't leave all those people in there to die! We have to say something—evacuate—" I search the wall by his head for a fire alarm, anything to get everyone's attention.

Alden narrows his eyes. "Let them burn," he whispers. "It's for the best... You'll see."

I do a double take. I've never seen him look so serious... so determined.

"You don't mean that." I shake my head. "What about everything you said about love and forgiveness earlier? Where did that all go?" I suddenly regret what I said about murderers and rapists... I'm feeling kind of hypocritical.

He sucks in a breath. "There are casualties in every revolution. We need to get the attention of *both* sides, give them a common enemy in order for change to really happen."

I look at him quizzically, feeling torn. While part of me totally agrees with what he's saying, I'm not okay with one of those casualties being my friend. "I have to go back for Livie!" I exclaim, darting away and back into the club.

"Christa—NO!"

The fire door slams as Alden chases behind me, but I bolt through the dark club, the DJ now back to work playing some holiday remix as I shove through the line of Demons and clamber up onstage, coming face to face with Livie.

"Christa?" She's still beaming and is just as surprised to see me as she was earlier. Her eyes brighten as she looks me over. "Oh my God—it's true! I can totally see you!"

"Livie—we have to get out of here NOW!" I tear her hand away from Riley. He gives me a dirty look. "The whole club is about to blow, and there is no amount of Demon blood that is going to save you from that—"

"What are you talking about?" She shakes her head happily, still staring at me. "I can't believe how...*blue* you are! Riley said—"

"CHRISTA!" I hear Alden yelling for me by the stage apron. I groan, exasperated, and hold fast to Livie's hands.

"Please...I'm begging you—come with me!" I cry. "I don't want you to die, Livie! You have to listen—"

"Already did that once tonight!" she jokes, breaking into a fit of giggles.

Riley leans over. "Get outta here, Christa. Everything was awesome before you showed up...and you're just making it suck balls, like you do with everything," he sneers.

Livie hears the malice in his voice and startles, before giving me a sympathetic look. "I'm fine, Christa, really." She puts on a big grin and pats my arm. "Go on home and I'll call you tomorrow, okay? Wish everyone a merry Christmas—"

I plant my heels into the floor and take a deep breath. "I'm not leaving without you, Livie. You have to believe me—"

"We do, and that's why I'm pulling Rank now," Alden grumbles, coming up behind me on the platform. He nods at Riley. "First Level, take your Pet out the back fire entrance and keep running 'til you can't run anymore—got it?"

Riley's face goes slack as he glances between the two of us. "Uh...um, yeah...okay," he stutters.

He takes Livie by the arm, leading her offstage, to the disappointment of the line behind us. Alden eyes me impatiently. "We really need to get out now, unless you're suddenly flame retardant!" He heads for the hall.

I nod. "Yes, okay…"

"CHRISTA!"

I spin, hearing someone yell my name from somewhere in the crowd. I hear it again. "CHRISTA!"

My eyes scan the floor, and I cry out when I spy my favorite red hat in the audience. "DANIEL!" I shout back, scrambling offstage. I make it to the floor, but lurch backward as Alden grabs me roughly by the arm.

"You can't be with him tonight! He has to stay, but you have to go!" Alden shouts, the music switching over to a loud swing version of "Jingle Bells." I spin around and glare into his cold blue eyes.

"Wait—you knew he was here?!" I yell shrilly. "Daniel?!"

Alden looks behind himself nervously and then glares back at me, exasperated. "Of course I knew he was here—he showed up about twenty minutes ago looking for you!" He starts to drag me back to the fire door. I try to tear away from him, but his grip is too strong. "Why do think I've been holding onto you so tight? He'll regenerate, Christa—you won't! Just leave him!"

"Are you kidding me?! And let him burn up?!" I shove into him hard, catching him off balance. He lets go of my arm and slips back for a second. "That's what all of this is about! Not some… stupid political movement—it was a plot!" I shake my head, furious. "You're…you're just trying to keep us apart! NO!"

"Christa—stop!" I hear Alden yell behind me as I bolt away. "You don't understand—we both saw it—when you were Haloing, from before!"

His voice disappears under the club noise, and I rush across the dance floor, clawing my way past dancers and drunks. They laugh and squawk like hungry crows amongst each other as I frantically search for him, reaching the spot where I thought I saw him.

"Daniel? Daniel!" I wail, my voice lost in the music. Tearing at my hair and out of breath, I spin around—and he's there, pulling me urgently into his arms, his hands grasping the back of my jacket.

"Christa!" he yells into my ear. I grip on tighter, never wanting to let him go again.

He wheels back and stares at me, his eyes crazed. "What are you doing here?! I thought you weren't gonna come to this thing!" I can see a bright flicker of anger amidst his relief. "I came back to the house and you were gone, and then I found the invitation on your bed—"

"I know...and I can explain—but not now!" I put my hands up. "We have to get out of here—Alden rigged the club with explosives, and it's about to pop—"

"What?!" His face twists in rage as he scans the club. "He's here?! Where?"

I moan. "Daniel! We have to get out of here, or we're gonna be toast!" I take his hand and pull him toward the back.

He's still craning his head around as we pass the bar. "That dirty, no good..." he mumbles, resisting my efforts to get us out of the hall. "He's probably been here the whole time—Mandisa was lying through her teeth the other night—I knew it! Sitting around, laughing at us..."

"None of that matters now!" I cry. "This place is gonna blow, and there's nothing we can do!" I scan again for fire alarms, but come up empty handed. Even if I were to start yelling "Fire!", I doubt anybody would listen...especially after what happened during Livie's big transformation.

Daniel shrugs. "So what? It's just a bunch of Demons."

"How can you say that?" I grit out. What is wrong with everyone tonight? "Am I the only one with any compassion around here? God—"

I get interrupted by a massive explosion going off in the far west corner. Bits of wall and shrapnel fly everywhere, silent for a second before everyone starts screaming and running chaotically. Through the smoke, I can see that there is now a giant, burning hole where the divider wall between the main hall and front foyer used to be. Before the panic has a chance to spread through the entire room, another explosion goes off in the southeast corner, flames licking up to the exposed pipes.

Daniel stares between the damage and me, his eyes growing wide. I stare back, my face pinched.

He grasps my hands. "Okay…let's get you out of here!" he exclaims, picking me up and pitching me over the corner of the bar to avoid the crazed stampede that is now taking place as everyone runs howling in circles around the club. As Daniel dashes around to the other side, I look back to the front doors and see bodies throwing themselves up against them, unable to get out. They're still locked.

"Daniel—"

I point, and he glances back, helping me off the bar. He watches grimly. "Let's try this way!" he exclaims, whisking me down the hall into a crushing mass of more people, everyone clambering against the back fire exit door. More people come up behind us, everyone pushing and shoving. Daniel puts his arms up and creates a little pocket of air around me.

"What's happening?!" I cry out over all the yelling. "This door was open a few minutes ago!"

"Not anymore!" Daniel shouts. He uses his height to look over the crowd, his back bowing as more people crash into him. "The heat from the blasts is probably sealing it shut… I can't see if anyone is getting out—there are too many—"

I let out a little squeal as my feet get pushed up by a screaming face under my boot. Daniel hoists me up by the waist, but that doesn't alleviate the fact that I'm squashing someone's nose with my heel. Bodies cover the floor, Demon or Human—it's impossible to tell tonight, but they all belong to people who are trying to get out and getting trampled in the process. I redirect my attention to the jammed door, trying not to look down.

"This isn't going to work—we're not going to be able to get out this way!" Daniel yells into my ear.

I suck in a breath, the air growing thin and hot. "What do we do?!" I cry back. "The front doors are just as bad—"

I gasp as Daniel buckles into me, a particularly large man with a wide, foaming mouth trying to smash past us, flailing his arms wildly. Without hesitation, Daniel pops his fist back and knocks him out.

"We're gonna have to make a hole!" Daniel answers, his forehead beading with sweat. "I can do that—but I need to get you outta the way—"

"Alter? You mean Alter?!" I'd seen him do it once before, back on 3. While it might be extremely helpful, it's also extremely dangerous.

Daniel nods grimly, so I make my way over to the wall on my left and start to inch backwards. "Okay—I think if I can make it to the office doorway, I can hide in the recess while you do it—"

Another deafening explosion goes off, making bells ring in my head. This one was closer, and I feel all the air get sucked out of my lungs, right before a thick helix of flame blasts down our hallway.

"CHRISTA!" I hear Daniel shout as he throws himself on top of me, plastering me to the wall. He thrusts my head into his armpit and wraps his jacket around whatever parts of me he can cover, his legs and hips blocking mine. I let out a yelp as my exposed left hand smolders, speedily drawing it to my chest and looking at it from the safety of my Daniel tent. The skin is cracked and gooey, definitely burnt, but I can still move my fingers and the nails are intact. I squeeze my eyes shut and press into Daniel, the roar of the fire so loud that I almost can't hear him screaming next to me.

Almost.

And then it's quiet again, instantly. I poke my nose out from Daniel's coat and smell cool night air. Opening my eyes, I see that the fire burnt away the entire exit door. If I squint, I can make out a light shining hopefully from the back alley. I take a deep breath and carefully peel away from the wall.

"Daniel…look—"

I stop short and gasp, looking up at his face—or what's left of it.

He blinks back at me with his good eye, the one that was pressed into the top of my head, the only familiar feature left on his now molten face. The other eye is just gone, his skin twisted in hot red swirls over the socket. His nose and ears have melted away, too. Faint indents of where the cavities should be are the only reminder that they were ever there in the first place. His hat and beautiful hair are in cinders, a little patch of red wool stuck to his forehead. He gives me what looks like a smile with what's left of his mouth, physically unable to speak.

I'm too shocked to cry. "Thank you," I whisper, putting my hand lightly on the spot on his jaw that was tucked into me. He nods and sees my injured hand, shakily running his own charred finger stumps over it. He groans.

I wince. "Oh my God—I'm fine!" I sputter, laughing and tearing up at the same time. Leave it to Daniel to be worried about me when he's half melted like a wax candle. I stare into his remaining eye. "We have to get out of here… You're going to start regenerating soon."

He nods, bends down, and picks me up in a fireman's carry with a heavy grunt. I shake my head and try to get down. "Are you nuts?! You're the one who should be carried!" I wave down his backside, where his leather jacket is shockingly still intact. He grunts in refusal and points at the floor. I suck in a breath, grimly understanding why it had been so quiet for the last few minutes.

Saying that not everyone fared as well as I did would be an understatement. Daniel gingerly steps over a carpet of unrecognizable body parts toward the exit, all of them blackened to a crisp. Squinting with his one eye, he tries to avoid stepping on anyone is particular, which is impossible, as even *I* can't tell where one person ends and the next begins. My mind is in panic mode, unable to really focus on any specific aspect, fuzzy…and probably for good reason. All I can think is that this must be what the Lower Realms look like.

"Catalyst…" A scorched arm reaches up from the mosaic. "Christa…"

I look down and find the face attached to the hand, recognizing a set of bright white teeth, her thick, full lips burned away. Mandisa.

"Catalyst…" she rasps, her fingers trembling. I count and feel woozy—she only has three.

I tuck into Daniel, trying not to look down as he shambles toward the exit and out into the night. When we finally get to the landing, he stumbles, setting me down on the concrete before collapsing against the rail. I look around, remembering this alley all too well; Alden attacked me here—my mind, my body… It's a place that's held bad memories ever since. Now, it's our salvation.

"Come on, let's get you down to the street… You can stretch out there." I tenderly put Daniel's destroyed arm around my shoulder and guide him down the steps, taking it very slow as we make our way away from the club. I help him relax against the dumpster when we get there, his chest heaving up and down.

"Just rest." Watching his face, I can already see his new nose forming. I rub his leg, trying to be comforting. "You'll be back to you soon."

"Christa!" I jerk my head around at the sound of my name coming from the stairs. Alden dashes out of the service door, or what's left of it. "I've been looking everywhere for you—" He comes to a stop in front of me, putting his hands on his knees. His face is covered in black ash—he must have been inside when the explosions went off. He didn't leave.

He sees Daniel, or what will be Daniel very soon, and his eyes widen. "Jesus—where were you two?" He stares at Daniel's deformed features.

I glare. "In the back hallway. The door was jammed. We couldn't get out." I exhale and put my head in my hands. "It doesn't matter! What you did back there—" I wave to the now dilapidated Trinity, the skeleton of the building visible on one side, smoke still rising from the front marquis. "You annihilated those people... I have no idea how many are dead—"

"The Demons will regenerate. It will take them a few days, but they'll be back," he answers hastily, still catching his breath. "You're still together." He looks down at Daniel and me.

"Yes, we are! No thanks to you..." I turn and lean into Daniel, his mouth now able to open and close, clear reddish fluid seeping out of him. "Why do you care so much if we're together or not?"

Alden keeps his eyes on Daniel, shaking his head. "It doesn't matter anymore... Doesn't matter. What's done is done." He sucks in a breath as Daniel starts convulsing next to me, spitting foam everywhere.

"It's okay, Daniel! Everything is going to be okay!" I cry, gripping his blue-jeaned leg. He sputters and coughs like a freight train. I glare at Alden, who just keeps staring at us. "What?!" I snap, shaking my head.

Alden looks intently at Daniel. "Nothing. I've just never seen him like this, not since..." His voice fades.

I lay a hand on Daniel's chest, feeling his heart hammering inside. Alden keeps staring at him blankly, sending me into a blind rage. "Don't you look at him!" I shout defensively, waving Alden away. "You don't...*deserve* to see him like this—*this* is what it means to be completely unselfish, something you could never understand." I look back at my Guardian struggling to rebuild himself, wanting nothing more than to wrap him in my arms and never let go.

"You're right," Alden nods, his voice calm. "I don't understand." He pauses and clears his throat.

I gape at him and shift uncomfortably, watching him waver back and forth. "He's very vulnerable right now," Alden finally continues, his gaze locked on Daniel's misshapen face.

I sniff, waiting for him to add to that. He just keeps staring, his mind working behind his eyes. "Yeah...well, if anyone decides to try something, they're gonna have to go through me first." I set my jaw, keeping my hand on Daniel. I can hear the thin wail of sirens in the background—on their way here, no doubt. Alden doesn't say anything, but reaches and jingles something in his pocket. At that moment, Daniel bolts upright, glaring at Alden for a second, liquid pus still leaking out of his newly healed nose and mouth. I quickly move behind him to support him with my body, giving him a soft place to lie. Daniel keens back, his eyes closing again, lost in pain.

"Why are you still here?" I bark at Alden. "Don't you have someone better to terrorize? Just leave us alone!"

Alden shakes his head, coming out of his daze. "Right...of course." He takes a step back and readjusts his jacket, then turns to walk off, but doubles back. "I, um...I think he might have dropped this." He reaches into his pocket and pulls out a small, gold pocketknife. I give him a puzzled look as he lightly tosses it to me, catching it with my good hand. I study the neatly folded blade, the metal cool on my skin.

"Where did you find this?" I ask, shaking my head.

Alden shrugs. "Oh, you know...around." He scratches the back of his head. "But it's his—I'm sure of it. I know he'll be happy to see it when he comes to."

I look at the knife again and remember a conversation that Daniel and I had a few days ago—about an important Guardian knife that he had last left with Pete. I sigh, realization sinking in. That must have been where he was all afternoon—up in Pasadena to visit Pete's old house and pick up his knife, only to drop it during all the chaos a little while ago. I grip it firmly in my palm and arch an irritable brow at Alden.

"Fine. I'll give it to him when he wakes up." I watch as he nods, pacing in a tight circle, lingering. "You can go now!" I add with a growl.

Alden stops and smiles weakly at me. "Thanks for the dance, Christa. Never a dull moment."

"Unfortunately. Now get out of here before I use this thing on you," I snap, gesturing with the knife. Alden snickers and heads out the way he came, refastening his coat before disappearing around the corner.

I turn back to Daniel and gasp, watching his hair fill back to its regular, glorious length, his face stitching itself back into place. I don't know how long I sit there staring at him, but every second is a miracle. At some point, rescue workers show up with ambulances and fire trucks, hauling stretchers back and forth through the front doors, but they never make their way around to the alley, leaving us to heal in peace. Daniel stays unconscious as his regeneration magic works, regrowing his eyelashes one by one, his face almost completely healed.

I smile and stroke the edge of his lip. "You're amazing," I breathe, not caring if he can hear me or not. I arch my head down and kiss him gently on his forehead.

His eyes flutter open. "Christa," he wheezes, his voice still raspy from the fire.

I blink back my tears and smile, holding his face in my hands. "I'm here…and we're good! All good!" I sigh and look back at the burnt-out club. "Can't say the same for Trinity, though."

Daniel takes a shaky breath and carefully sits up, resting on his new, perfect hands. "What a mess." He shakes his head at the sight. "Just…everything."

"Yeah," I breathe, remembering I'm still holding the pocketknife. "Hey." I hand it to him, electricity brushing between us at the touch. "Your knife. Would be a bummer to lose it again."

Daniel's eyes widen as he stares at the knife. "Where did you get this? I've been looking all over…"

I wrinkle my nose, confused. "Uh…isn't that where you went today? Pasadena?" Daniel stares at me in matching puzzlement, so I add, "You know, Pete's house? Checking his stuff?"

Daniel looks back at the knife, his face unreadable. "I didn't go to Pasadena today, Christa…"

I roll my eyes. "Well, whatever! It's back! It's yours, right? Alden said you would recognize it."

Daniel's back goes rigid, and he sits in silence for a minute before he answers. "Yes, it's mine." He looks at it once more, then back at me. "Can you hold onto it for a while? Like I told you…it needs to be with someone I've helped," he says, almost bashfully.

I blush, honored that he chose me…however obvious a choice that might be right now. "Yeah, sure! No biggie," I say, trying not to sound too excited as I tuck the knife into my back pocket. Sighing, I bat his knee. "So where *did* you go today? You were gone a long time."

Daniel nods and smiles sadly. "Yeah…I just had to sort some stuff out." He stares at his lap. "Nothing too cool… Well, except for one thing. I'll show you."

I smile at him expectantly as he gets to his feet and helps me up. I wince as he grasps my burnt hand, though, having forgotten that I was hurt at all. Daniel, however, remembers and snaps to attention.

"Christa! Why didn't you say something?!" He gingerly takes my bad hand and holds it up to his face, inspecting my injury. "Oh man, this could get infected! We gotta get you to a doctor!"

"Daniel—it's fine! Really…I'll just throw a bandage on it when we get home."

"No, you won't! You have no idea how bad this could be— you're still in shock, for Godsakes!" He frowns, ushering me down the alley. "You might need debriding, graphs…"

I balk at him. "What? No! I don't wanna spend my Christmas

Eve in the ER!" I catch myself as Daniel shoots me a look. "Sorry…"

"Guess you're my Lucky 13," he grumbles, almost laughing at how absurd that sounds. He sighs and smirks as we get to the end of the alley, waving at a shadow parked in front of us. "At least we'll get there in style—and before you even ask, I'm driving."

I take a look at what's waiting for us and let out a howl, throwing my arms around his neck. "Oh my God—are you serious?!" I squeal, jumping up and down. Even in the dark, I can see my reflection in the polished chrome handlebars. It's the most gorgeous motorcycle I've ever seen—Hell, the most beautiful machine I've ever seen, putting the bike in Mellie's shop to shame with its shiny matte-black paint job and decorative orange flames. I practically purr as I run my hand over the leather seat, so soft and buttery. It's baller.

"Where did you get this?" I exclaim, unable to contain my delight. I toss my leg over the side and get comfortable, leaving room for Daniel in front of me.

He smiles, the first real one I've seen from him all night. "Benny. It's a *loaner*—let's be super clear on that!" He grins wryly and takes his spot. "He has an old buddy down at Falcon Motorcycles, owed him a favor." He puts the key in the ignition and gives it a rev, the bike growling underneath us. I've never heard such a sweet sound in my life.

I wrap my arms around Daniel's waist and hold on tight, gripping his sides with my thighs. "Never been on the back of a bike before," I whisper in his ear.

He clears his throat, the patch of skin where my lips just brushed blushing bright red. "I've never had *you* on the back of a bike, either." He laughs, squeezing my leg. "A first for us both."

He smiles as we speed off into the night.

CHAPTER 24

...25...

My eyes shoot open to the feeling of someone ramming the heel of their hand between my
shoulder blades, jarring me to life as I gasp for breath. I gulp in
mouthful after mouthful of sweet, glorious air, my head pounding as the blindness subsides and my vision comes back into
focus. I can see clearly...more clearly than ever before, making
out every individual eyelash framing my periphery, dark and
lush. I blink, startling myself as the lashes rustle like pine needles against my skin. My hands grip leather.

I come to.

I'm alone, staring down at my own lap, the same beige pants
and white shirt I was wearing earlier now soft and clean. Slowly,
I turn my head; I'm sitting in a chair, a fairly comfortable chair
actually, a cream-colored cushion supporting my back. I purse
my lips, the sensation of feeling each muscle around my mouth
wrinkle overwhelming, and I decide to try to keep every movement from here on out as subtle as possible—just until I figure
out what's going on...

I'm alive—God, I'm alive. Flashes of the bridge run through
my mind, muddled, but I can remember that I jumped. I exhale
shakily... I don't know how I would have survived that—the

fall, then the water. But maybe there was some sort of Divine Intervention. Maybe what everyone at Church had been going on about for so long is true…

Relief washes over me as I carefully lift my arms and study my hands. The tendons and ligaments ache as I move, but they *are* moving. Again, I take a deep breath, quickly coughing as the air scratches around the inside of my lungs. Too much. Have to go slow. I glance around, hope welling in my chest. There *is* a God… There must be…and He saved me. I'm saved.

26.

The number rings like a bell in my head, and I almost jump out of my seat in alarm. The sound subsides and is replaced by a low, pleasant noise—music. I tilt my head and listen. Quick and cat-like, my eyes dart around to see where it's coming from. I locate a small speaker above in the ceiling that's playing classical music, some sort of violin concerto. I relax and take in the rest of the space, my bearings coming back to me slowly.

The room is small, the walls painted a soothing forest green. A maple bookshelf on the opposite wall boasts three white, lit candles that are flickering warmly next to a closed door. There are two other matching cream chairs next to my own, accompanied by a mixed-wood coffee table at my feet. I lean in and study the magazines and books resting on it, their covers glossy with pictures of beautiful people. I squint and try to read the words, but I can't make heads or tails of it, like I'm in a dream or they're written in gobbledygook. I take a breath and sit back. It's a waiting room—I'm in a waiting room.

27.

The ringing happens again, and I grab my temples, trying to steady myself. It goes away just as fast as it did before, and I shudder—but before I can completely freak out about numbers and bells going off in my head, the door next to the bookcase opens, and a young, thin Asian man smiles back at me.

"Mr. Murphy." He knows my name, and he takes a step toward me. "Can you walk?"

I gape at him for a moment, then nod, gingerly unfolding myself from the chair, my joints clicking like a marionette as I baby step across the room to him. Everything hurts, and I try to focus on anything else so as not to cry out in pain. I stare at the man's clothes, the clean, unassuming white linen making his short black hair stand out. The only adornment that he wears is a long silver chain with a ring pendant; when I get a little closer, I can see that it's a snake eating its own tail.

"We don't have much time," he murmurs as he rests a hand on my arm when I finally make it to him. "We had to jump through a bunch of hoops just to get her down, and we have possibly ten minutes before both sides realize she's here…" He holds open the door and points for me to go inside. "All we ask is that you listen."

She? Jillian? My head is pounding in agony and confusion. "Where am I?" This is the first time I've tried to speak since I woke up. My voice is raspy, and it feels like my throat is on fire.

"It doesn't matter. With any luck, you won't be here long." The man ushers me past the threshold. "She's waiting."

I suck in a breath, the anticipation overwhelming as we enter a small office. I'm quickly disappointed when it's not my beautiful redhead sitting behind the desk, but a dark-haired Latina woman who is wearing the same white linen as the man, a bright crimson streak cutting across her face. She stands as I come into the room, her eyes wide and expectant.

"Alden." Her voice is kind and foreign as she steps around the desk and helps me into one of the chairs opposite. The walls are the same dark green as in the waiting room, the furniture a dark oak with more white candles. The Asian man closes the door behind us, scanning the doorframe as he runs his palm over the wood before turning back to us, his hands folded in front.

The woman leans against the desk, smiling weakly at me.

"You're here," she breathes, reaching out and clasping my hands; hers are warm and soft. I stare at her hands in mine, so confused, when—

28. It's like a bomb going off in my brain, my eyes rolling back momentarily. The woman watches me, concerned, as I come to… The ringing was more violent this time.

"Where…where am I?" I whisper once I'm able to talk again. I shake my head and pull my hands away from hers, embarrassed to be holding onto a complete stranger for so long.

The woman looks over at the man for a second before turning back to me. "You are in my comrade's office," she replies slowly, keeping her tone even. "That part is not out of the ordinary… You were always going to come here first." She stops and stares at me, her eyes somber. "Do you remember what happened to you?"

"Mary Carmen…" the man calls from the doorway, his voice wary. "We don't have time for that—"

"Please." She holds up her hand, still polite and quiet, but determined. "He needs a chance to acclimate, to grasp what's happening…"

"Unaffordable luxuries," he tuts, shaking his head. "They will keep you both here if they find out—"

"I understand." The woman—Mary Carmen—nods at him, then turns back to me. "Alden…tell me what you remember."

"I…" I blink, the sensation too much again, and try to shift in the chair, pain spasming up to my hip. I wince and stare behind her to the desktop. It's bare, save for a single white manila envelope and a black ink pad with a heavy-looking metal stamp, molded into the shape of a circle. I squint and see that it's the same snake eating its tail as the one on the man's necklace.

"I jumped," I state evenly, looking back at Mary Carmen, who is watching me. "From the bridge, after—"

The rooftop…fireworks…rose petals…broken glass… Daniel. Murder. M for Murder. *I'm* a murderer… I can't even bring myself to say the words as I choke out a breath and look up at Mary Carmen, noticing the soft gold light that seems to be emanating from her insides. It's beautiful, the most beautiful thing I've ever seen…like a star. The stars were watching…

"Please, tell me where I am." I pull my eyes away from her and search the walls. "None of this makes any sense… How did I get h—"

29.

I cry out and hold my head, my skull about to explode with the pressure of the number. That was the worst one so far.

I glance up at Mary Carmen. "29… There's a…a c-counting, in my head," I pant as my hand flutters at my ear. "It's on the number 29… Keeps going up…"

Mary Carmen frowns and looks over at the man, who sighs and walks over to us, hovering next to my chair. "You've been dead a total of 29 minutes," he states methodically. I stop panting and gape at him. He glances between Mary Carmen and me. "It's a constant reminder of your eternity. It will eventually fade into the rest of the noise in your mind, but you will never forget that it's there. I know it's painful…right now." He keeps his face void of any emotion.

I tilt my chin and stare at Mary Carmen. "I'm—*I'm dead?*" I rasp, not comprehending the concept. I feel another flash of disappointment, confusion, dread. "But I thought, I mean…I'm alive, I'm all here…" I check my hands, the small joints in my fingers pulsating as I twitch them into motion.

"His Re-Corp has already begun… He'll be delirious in minutes." The man shakes his head impatiently at Mary Carmen. "They'll be in to pick him up for transport."

Mary Carmen leans in again, sympathy brimming in her bright eyes; the red mark gets less jarring the longer I look at her. "Yes, you are really dead. I am so sorry, Alden." She takes my hand again, and I know she means it. "I know it must be incredibly difficult for you to understand all this…but there is much we need to discuss, and we only have a little bit of time left."

"What's your number…in your head?" I don't know why I ask, but I look up at her, curious. Surely, if I'm dead, she must be too, and the man as well. And this is…the afterlife? I glance around at the candles flickering against the green walls—not exactly what I was expecting.

I look back at Mary Carmen and watch her pretty face crease with sadness. "I don't have a number," she whispers after a moment. She gives a worried look to the man, who simply stares at her and sits on the edge of the desk, keeping his back ramrod straight.

"Enough. We must move on." He looks at me. "If this were like any other normal entrance interview, we'd already be addressing your placement." He gives Mary Carmen a look, and she sighs and draws her hand away, folding her arms over her chest. He continues by pulling the folder on the desk forward, opening it and giving the papers inside a quick scan. "You were already set for work in the Mortal Realm; that works very strongly in our favor…"

I shake my head, trying to ignore the searing pain that is making its way up from the base of my spine and into my neck. "Placement? Mortal Realm?" I almost laugh at the strangeness of the words. "What does that even mean?" This is nothing like anything I could ever imagine—it's so…bureaucratic.

The man glances up from the file, his eyes severe. "It means you're avoiding the Lower Realms altogether. Highly irregular for someone who just murdered their best friend."

30. The room spins, and I grip the chair arms for support, a bit of bile making its way up my gullet accompanied by a fierce wave of nausea. I clamp my lips shut, not wanting to be sick all over myself in front of these people. "Where am I?" I ask again quietly when I can control myself.

Mary Carmen looks like she's about to cry, but the man keeps his face unreadable. Neither of them answer, and they don't need to; of course I know where I am. I'm where all killers go, in the end. To burn and to toil.

"Jillian." I wince as I sit up too fast, my voice edged with worry. "My..." Love, life, soulmate. "My Jillian. She died, too—" My breath catches, and Mary Carmen hurriedly leans in. I close my eyes and whisper. "Please tell me...where is she?"

The man sighs, and I hear him flip open the file again. I look at him as he scans down the paper. "Ms. O'Connor and Baby Girl Murphy have become one with the Stars, neither Above nor Below. That is the case for girls in her...situation."

I gape at him, horrorstruck, as he sets the file back on the desk. Mary Carmen gives my arm a gentle tap, nodding. "That is a *good* thing, Alden! That is how we say they are in Heaven—they are safe." She looks at me with wide eyes. "Above is the Mortal Realm—the Earth—and Below—" She stops herself and drops her chin slowly toward the floor. Below is here...where we are now. *Not* Heaven. I nod, understanding.

"But she's all right," I breathe as Mary Carmen gives me a tight smile. "And..." Now I'm smiling, too. "It *was* a girl. I knew it." A warmth overtakes my insides, making the blistering agony that's spread through my arms and legs disappear for a moment.

Mary Carmen gives my knees a squeeze. "Yes! How wonderful for you!" She beams at me. "Did you...have a name picked out?"

We both laugh sweetly at this. "Yes, I did... When—when can I see them?" My query is cut short as a scream gurgles out of my mouth, pain shredding through my midsection and sending me quaking and trembling to the floor.

"Alden!" Mary Carmen cries out, joining me on the floor. She looks up the man urgently. "Serpentine, help me get him back in the chair!"

The man crouches down and deftly puts a hand under my

arm, pulling me back up. I lean forward dizzily as the pain subsides and rest my forehead on the edge of the desk. "His re-corp is in full effect," I hear the man whisper to Mary Carmen. "Get him now before we lose him—"

"What's happening to me?" I slur, still staring down at the floor, little pops of color bursting in front of my eyes.

I feel a soft hand go to my back. "You are re-corporializing. Uh—" Mary Carmen searches for words. "You...your soul...is being put back into a body—for when you go up to the Mortal Realm. The other Demons will be waiting for you when you arrive in three days' time." She rubs my back slowly. "It's a painful process. I'm sorry... None of this is easy... That's why we are here, meeting now." I glance over and watch her wet her lips nervously. "We need you to help us...to end all this—"

31. I howl and throw my head back, gripping the desktop for support as another round of hammers beat into my brain.

"I...I can't make it stop!" I cry, my fingers clawing into the wood. I feel something under my hand: papers, the manila folder, all of its contents spilling across the desk. Mary Carmen and Serpentine stand back as I lift my face to eye level with the file. "What are these?" I ask blearily, squinting down at a pile of photographs, ranging in age and distress.

I hear Mary Carmen hiss behind me. "Alden, no—don't touch those!" she snaps.

But it's too late. I reach over and pull out an old black and white one, voices immediately filling my head.

"Look at the camera, boys—be still, Sean! And stop pulling at your collar, Alden!" My mother, chiding us boys to stand up straight for one of the few times she got all five of us cued up for a photograph. I look down at the fading image. We're all in hand-me-down short pants with the same light blue eyes, none of us smiling. I remember how she hadn't bought any meat at the market for weeks, saving her extra grocery money just to be able

to pay the photographer—and how Dad had given her a bloody nose that night when he found out about the extra expense.

"I don't..." I shake my head, bewildered, and look back at where Mary Carmen and Serpentine are both frozen behind me. "How can I hear them? In my head?" It's like I've been brought back there to that moment just by touching the picture.

"No more, Alden—put them down... They are not innocent!" Mary Carmen takes a step toward me, but Serpentine puts a hand out as I turn back to the stack. I stop breathing as I find a more recent one, a glimmer of red catching my eye. It's me and Jillian, the two of us together on a bench in Central Park, my hand grazing Jillian's cheek. She smiles as I lean in to kiss her. The memory comes back, hot and searing; I can feel the cold November wind on my cheek, her lips so close to mine.

"Remarkable," I rasp, not wanting to put the photo down, but I continue on the though the pile, wanting more. I flip ahead, and the images turn unfamiliar—still with Jillian and I, but of moments I can't recall. I get to one where we are clearly older, my hair starting to gray at my temples, Jillian's eyes creased beautifully at the corners. Two teenage children stand between us, a pretty girl with dark hair who looks about 17 standing with Jillian. Next to me is a tall boy with red hair, smiling wide, his arm draped lovingly over my shoulder. I run my thumb over his face, and my own voice is in my ear, tinny and distant.

"He looks just like you—completely perfect." I hear the smile on my lips, accompanied by a small, snuffling sound. A baby.

"Ha!" Jillian laughs brightly, the sheer magic of her voice making me stumble backwards. "It's so funny... Lily was like your twin—still is!" The sounds of cuddling come through. "He looks just like Sam... Should we call him that? Name him after his uncle? I think he'll like that..."

"This never happened," I mumble, turning back to Mary

Carmen and Serpentine, still grasping the family photograph in my hand. "None of it."

Mary Carmen moves over to me, biting her lip. "It's a type of torture, Alden. They're meant to hurt you."

Serpentine clears his throat. "The Fates like to include a pre-view of what your life would have been like." He nods down at the photographs scattered across the desk. "How you would have gone to Paris, found success, made a fortune, a family…a future." Serpentine folds his hands. "It's a juxtaposition of what is and what never shall be."

I feel my knees buckle again and sink back into the chair, aches creeping through my joints, the pain from earlier return-ing full force. "She's gone, isn't she?" I whisper at Mary Carmen, who is back at my side. A tear drips down my cheek. "Jillian. I'm never going to see her—either of them—again." Another truth, another wave of despair.

Mary Carmen grimaces. "I can't answer that. I'm sorry." She glances at Serpentine, who gives a light shrug.

"All the more reason for you to join our cause," he replies firmly, staring at me. I look over at him weakly, unable to do much more than turn my head at this point. "This is no ordi-nary entrance interview, Mr. Murphy. The other Demons have no idea we are approaching you like this… They think I am merely preparing you for re-corp and your transport back to the Mortal Realm, where you will join them in culling more lost souls for Hell—"

"*Demons?*" I exhale, the word making me truly afraid for the first time since I've arrived. Demons are real? Visions of forked tails and ghoulish teeth fill my mind.

Serpentine nods. "You will become familiar very soon; that is something we cannot prevent." He quirks his head toward Mary Carmen. "But you have been Marked, Mr. Murphy…by prophecy."

"Something big is coming." Mary Carmen nods at me, her

tone growing excited. "Something the Divine world has been waiting for—for centuries." She takes a deep breath. "Our system is defective. The divide between Heaven and Hell has grown too great, the punitive measures taken down Below too severe. How can one expect a broken soul to heal when we forgo forgiveness and use hate and torture to break them more?" She looks at me, her gaze imploring. "Before he died, the last prophet foretold of a Trinity, made up of a fallen star, a prizefighter from Below, and one whose soul has not yet touched the ground…" She closes her eyes before continuing. "This Trinity will cause a great change in the Universe, bringing the righteous to justice and the downtrodden to hope." She puts her hand on my arm and looks back at Serpentine. "We think that you are that prizefighter, Alden, the one from Below. You are going to change the Universe." She gives me a light squeeze, her face breaking into a smile. "Well—what do you think?"

"I…" I take a breath, my mind racing—I'm back on the roof with Daniel, plunging that glass into his side…watching him bleed out in my arms, his skin cold and clammy. Regret for my actions is mixed with pure, raging malice. How can I change the Universe when I am still so consumed with my own loss, my own vengeful hate?

32. The bell rings sharp and true, and I'm unable to focus through the pain as I lose control of all my nerves and muscles. The number fades, but the ringing remains; I realize it's not coming from inside my head, but from a speaker set into the ceiling.

"Not now," I hear Serpentine mutter, crossing behind the desk. His hand searches for something on the underside, but to no avail as the ringing continues.

Mary Carmen gawks at him. "What is that? What's happening?" She grips my arm protectively. I would reach up and take her hand, but I can't move, my body grasped by numbing paralysis. I see her searching around the room, her eyes settling as she finds the speaker in the ceiling as well.

"It's the final requiem bell, for his transformation." Serpentine shakes his head and comes back around the desk. "They want to make sure he comprehends what the Lower Realms are really like, so he'll feel...grateful for his placement. I can't stop it... We just have to let it play, try not to listen..."

My head shakes horribly, little bits of spit flecking from my mouth. Mary Carmen takes her sleeve and wipes my chin, letting her hands linger at my jaw. "It's going to be all right," she murmurs, her breath warm on my face. "Stay with us... We are here for you—"

The quiet is shattered by background noises coming in through the speaker. I mash my mouth into a thin line and listen hard...to the swish of fabric, people moving around, the occasional cough, a TV on low in the background.

"Fuck, it's a re-run. Anatoli, change the channel." I recognize the lazy, drawling voice in an instant: Ramos.

I suck in a breath, my chin and lower jaw trembling, staring at Mary Carmen as we both hear steps go across the room and the turn of a dial.

"Why's your face all screwed up like that, Kirschbaum? Ramos laughs, accompanied by the quiet flick of a lighter. "You trying to remember where you put the rest of my money?"

"I told you—I don't have it." I grimace as I hear Daniel answer, hoarse and broken. "I got you a couple grand. If you give me a little more time, I can—"

"Ohhh, you know I don't like excuses!" Ramos tuts, couch springs squeaking as he sits down. "No product, no money...*big* problems! You're lucky you brought your little friend here for me to work out some of my frustration on, or you'd be, ah, what do they say? Singing a different tune." He snorts, and Anatoli joins him, chortling under his breath.

"Please..." A light whimper sounds from further off, and I bolt up in my chair in agony. Jillian!

"N-No..." I sputter, Mary Carmen moving her hands back

to my arms to help me stay upright in the chair. Serpentine sighs and crosses his arms as we continue to listen.

I hear Daniel again, louder this time. "You guys have had your fun. Why don't you let her go—she needs a doctor. I'll stay. Just...just let her go, okay?"

My insides tear themselves apart as I hear the other men laugh, course and vile. "I might get hungry later!" Ramos chuckles, getting up again. "What if I want a midnight snack?"

I hear his shoes move across the room, padding lightly on the rug, followed by a terrified squeal from Jillian. "Please—no more!" Her voice is rough from crying. "I'll give you anything you want—just please—stop! Stop!" She cuts herself off by screaming.

Ramos shushes her. "I've seen all your insides, *fată drăguţă*," he purrs. "And unless you've got a secret roll of cash somewhere, I've already got everything I want from you." He whistles, clucking his tongue. "Where are my manners? You wanna taste, Kirschbaum?" He pauses; Daniel doesn't reply. "Maybe that will help, uh, jog your memory..."

I hear Jillian's ragged breath, hot and afraid. It's too much to bear. "Please—turn it off!" I bark at Serpentine, slurring my words. "Enough!"

He slowly shakes her head. "You know I can't." He raises his gaze to the ceiling. I bite my cheek hard, squeezing my eyes shut as the tape continues.

"No," Daniel whispers. "She's with my best friend..."

"Aww...come on!" Ramos cajoles. "He's not here. What he gonna do?" I clench my jaw as he and Anatoli laugh. "I know she's a little more messed up than when you first got here...but pretty hair, pretty titties, so sweet—wasn't she sweet, Anatoli?"

"Like warm, cherry pie," Anatoli chimes in.

I want to vomit. *33.* I barely hear it now.

Both men snicker. "Real deal, Kirschbaum... Haven't you

ever wondered what it's like for your friend," Ramos croons, "sinking into *this*...?" Jillian yelps in pain, and I flail in my seat.

"Stop—you've hurt her enough!" Daniel shouts. "You don't have to do this... Let's you and me just talk this through—"

"You're done talking!" Ramos booms. "I wanna see some action! We hear stuff about you all the time, *de la vărul lui Dimitri...Annika...*" he calls in Romani. I hear Anatoli grunt in response.

"She was losing her fucking mind," Anatoli grumbles. "Talking about some tall German kid who rocked her world, running her mouth off to the whole neighborhood about it."

"Ah, is that you?" I can hear the smile on Ramos's face as he moves back over to Daniel. "You like to fuck Romanian girls?"

"This motherfucker fucks anything wet between the legs," Anatoli jeers. "Black, Jew, Spic...he don't care."

Ramos blows out his cheeks. "Then what's the problem? Pretty little thing like our girl here... Show us how it's done, Kirschbaum!"

"Not like this—come on..." Daniel grits out through his teeth. "This is fucked up!"

"I hear German guys got small pricks," Anatoli pipes up again. "Maybe he shy about that."

"Let's take a look, shall we?" Ramos sniggers.

I hear wrestling on the couch, and someone kicks the coffee table. "Get the fuck off me!" Daniel cries out. He grunts, getting the wind knocked out of him as he gets socked in the gut one... two times.

"Stay down!" Ramos bellows, getting off the couch.

I can hear Jillian crying softly in the background. "Please don't hurt him," she begs. "It's okay, Daniel—everything is okay..."

"Stay out of this, whore!" Ramos snaps, making my blood boil. "Keep your fuckin' mouth shut, if you know what's good for you!" He turns back to Daniel, delivering another blow. Daniel moans.

"You know, my mother was fifteen when *your* people," Ramos slows, stalking around the space, "came to her village, burned all the houses, rounded up her father and her brothers with all the other men to shoot them in the town square."

"Those aren't *my* people," Daniel hisses. "I'm an American."

Ramos scoffs. "And then they put all the crying women and children in the community center, where they were gonna burn them alive, but not before those clean-cut soldiers had a little fun." He sucks his teeth. "Oh, they weren't supposed to...with the ţigani şobolan murdare...but that didn't stop them. We're all men, right?" He laughs, breathing through his nose.

"They had no problem taking turns on my mother, one after the other...and now *we* have some fun with *your* friend. See how it all comes around?" He tsks, growling at Daniel. "Look at me when I'm telling a story!" I hear him jerk Daniel's face.

"You know how she survived? She crawled through a window in the basement and ran like hell into the woods while they were setting the fire, living like a wild beast for eight days before the French found her. Hmm..." I hear him shrug. "Guess it pays to be a rat sometimes. We showed those Nazi bastards, in the end—"

He stops as Daniel snorts, his laughter growing. "What so funny, bitch?" Ramos snaps. Daniel chortles.

"That you think you did anything—like you're a goddamn war hero, when you're just some low-life drug dealer." I can see his face in my head, that same half-smile. Ramos moves toward him, his steps deliberate. He smacks Daniel across the face, the slap reverberating off the office walls.

"*My* people survived, against all odds," Ramos hisses. "And your people are forever marked, a shit-stain on our existence. My mother survived."

"I'm sorry they missed her," Daniel murmurs, wheezing.

I can hear Ramos's rage as he starts pummeling him again. "Daniel, no!" Jillian cries, the sounds of a hard beating coming through the line. "Stop! Please—STOP!"

"Enough of this shit!" Ramos bellows, out of breath. "*Obține arma mea, Anatoli!*"

Anatoli sighs and leaves the room. "No, no!" Jillian screams as Ramos drags her up.

"Hey—no! Don't touch her!" Daniel shouts. "Get your hands off her!"

"Where's my money, motherfucker?!" Ramos yells back.

I hear Anatoli's heavy steps as he returns and hands Ramos something metal and heavy. Tears spring to my eyes. "No..." I breathe, my whole body shaking.

"It's gone! It's gone! I'll get it! Don't do this—come on, man, take the gun offa her!" Daniel cries as Jillian wails in the background.

"You bet you fuckin' will!" Ramos replies, wrestling with Jillian. "With interest, shithead!"

"Please—I'm pregnant! I'm pregnant... Don't do this!" Jillian pleads, her voice strangled and weak.

Ramos laughs cruelly. "You keep sayin' that—but I don't see no baby!" he jeers. The gun shifts against skin and fabric, Jillian's sobs muffled. "It don't matter anyway... He can't pay, and someone has to—choose your friends more wisely next time."

"STOP! Please—" Daniel shouts.

Ramos spits at him. "Her blood is on your hands," he mutters, cocking the gun.

"No—No—No...!" Daniel moans as Jillian starts to hyperventilate. "Please—please!" she pants, harried. "Daniel, tell Alden I love—"

One shot, and the line goes dead, the noise and yelling replaced with loud static before it turns off altogether.

I sit and stare at the ceiling, my right arm flopping like a fish against me. "It's over," Mary Carmen says to break the silence, her voice soft as she looks nervously at the door. "It's over, Alden…"

I don't answer, but I can feel a different response making its way up. With my eyes glazed, I fall out of my chair and wretch onto the floor, mouthful after mouthful of thin, black water spewing out of me. All of me shakes as my stomach empties itself, the vomit getting on my clothes, foul-smelling and dank. It's hard to tell which part is spasming more—my insides or out.

When I'm through, I lay on the floor, feeling the cool hardwood under my cheek. It's soothing, even through the tremors. Mary Carmen kneels down next to me, pulling my head onto her lap as my shaking worsens, her fingers sifting through my hair.

"He took everything," I rasp, my eyelids fluttering. Mary Carmen's hands stop. "All of it gone—like she was never there… like *I* was never there." I give a choked little laugh. "I *deserve* to suffer…for what I did. I know that." My tone goes stoic. "But so should he. Daniel. He needs to…I…can't—" I wince and look up at Mary Carmen. "No, I can't…I *won't* forgive him." Never.

Mary Carmen sucks in a breath and rests her palms on either side of my face, tears shining in her eyes. "In time, maybe change will soften your heart. We are all on our own paths…and you have to know, at that moment when Mandisa intervened at the club, neither of you stood a chance—you or Daniel. It was a true turning point."

"Mandisa?" I narrow my eyes, confused. I have to wrack my brain for a minute to find the name. The tall black girl from the club with Daniel?

Mary Carmen nods. "A Demon, yes. Hell has been conspiring against both of you—with your destinies so strongly intertwined…" She stares at me. "You have to fight this. Do not let hate poison your soul now, not when there is still hope—"

"*Hope?*" I laugh in earnest now, my lungs shuddering. "Hope for what?"

Mary Carmen cradles me against her. "For your Ascension, Alden. Redemption." She holds me up, face to face. "If you can put aside your hurt and join us."

She grasps my hand, her bright Halo enveloping me and bathing us both in gold. My pain fades away, and I can see clearly, able to move my hand over to hers. I look into her eyes, and for the briefest moment, they are not a soft golden brown, but bright emerald green, piercing my soul like only *she* could. My beautiful girl.

"Yes," I reply, holding tight to Mary Carmen. "Yes, I will join your fight."

She exhales, wiping away tears from her face as Serpentine steps forward, lifting me back into my chair. "You will have do everything just as if this meeting never happened, still go through re-corp, still serve in the Mortal Realm, still work for Hell." He moves quickly to the desk and picks up the silver circle stamp and ink pad. "The brand is the final part of the transformation."

He pushes the stamp into the pad, but Mary Carmen stops him. "No—he will not be marked the same as the others. He is different, special." She smiles at me, nodding. "So he remembers his true purpose…" Mary Carmen places her own hand, palm down, on the pad, coating it with slick, black ink.

Serpentine stares at her quizzically, then sighs. "No one else will have such a mark. Put it somewhere discreet." He sets the pad and stamp back and moves over, unbuttoning the top three buttons on my shirt.

I look at them both hesitantly as my pain from earlier returns. "Brand? Like with fire?"

"We're out of time—do it now, Mary Carmen," Serpentine orders.

He watches the door as she presses her hand to my bare chest. I cry out as my skin melts away, the smell of burning flesh filling the room. The pain spreads like wildfire from my chest up to my face, making me go blind for a moment as the agony sears the inside of my skull. Feeling like my whole head is about to split open, I scream like an animal, feral and screeching.

After what seems like a millennium, Mary Carmen pulls away and walks quietly back to the chair behind the desk. Panting, I roll my head up and watch as Serpentine motions for her to open the top drawer. She takes out a tiny hand mirror and hands it to Serpentine.

"I will see you soon, Alden." She gives me a smile as she disappears into thin air, a bit of gold dust the only reminder that she was ever here at all.

"'Soon' being a relative term," Serpentine sighs.

I stare between the spot where Mary Carmen just was, then back at him. "Are you leaving, too?" My voice is weak and haggard.

Serpentine shakes his head. "I cannot. I will never leave this place, no matter what the outcome. Here." He holds up the mirror. I gasp, staring at the horrifying visage before me.

34.

My familiar blue eyes are gone, replaced with large, round, empty sockets, like a grotesque Halloween decoration. Two enormous, twisted horns protrude from my head, cutting through my hair, making me look like a grizzled, dead goat. Gingerly, I peel back my shirt and see a scalding red handprint burned over my heart, my skin still smoking. I yell and throw the mirror away, glaring at Serpentine.

"What—what's happened to me?" I cry, my voice harsh and raw.

Serpentine gives me a large grin and shrugs. "Welcome to the world, Greater First Level Demon Alden Murphy. Pleasure to make your acquaintance."

CHAPTER 25

LOS ANGELES—PRESENT DAY

*I*T'S THE FULL moon that lights our way down the quiet highway, the sky clear, stars visible even with the bright city sprawl. I cling tightly to Daniel with my freshly bandaged hand, letting the cold air whip through my hair as we cruise down the 101 on our hot chrome and metal steed. At first I thought I would be scared on the motorcycle, having never ridden one before—but from the second Daniel kicked it to life, we can't go fast or far enough for me. I've never felt so free.

With wide eyes and a big smile, I point at the beach, the moon a perfect double reflection on the water. We've been here before, and I have to yell in his ear over the motor to be heard. "Hey—remember?" I rest my hand on his hip, feeling the warmth under his t-shirt. "Do you wanna go down and park for a bit?"

I feel his side tighten momentarily, before he reaches over and gives me a squeeze, holding the bike steady with his other hand. "Yeah…sure. For a bit," he calls back. He takes the next exit for the Santa Monica Beach, me reveling in the fact that we're the only people for as far as I can see.

He parks the bike and peeks over his shoulder, giving me a small smile. We're back where it all started, the Malibu cliffs shadowed off in the distance, the beach a smooth wash of white glowing bright next to the dark water. The only thing missing is Benny's truck. I can't remember a more beautiful night.

"This okay?" Daniel asks, swinging off the motorcycle, the serene sound of the ocean waves taking the place of the roar of the bike. I nod as he helps me down, keeping our hands locked together even after I've got my feet on the ground.

We walk out onto the familiar sand. This is the exact same spot where we came after our first night together—with the breakfast burritos and laughing and talking, getting to know each other…where we almost had our first kiss.

I smile at him now, still holding his hand as we stroll across the beach. I jerk my chin back to the bike. "*That* was insane! Forget Mary Carmen's stinky old Civic—"

"I won't tell her you said that," Daniel interjects with a grin. "She's very proud of that car."

I roll my eyes and wave at our flame-covered ride. "I have never done anything like that before! Is that what it's like on every motorcycle?"

I feel Daniel grip my fingers. "If you mean the wind in your face, life or death, freedom at 80 miles per hour and looking cool while you do it…" We both laugh. "…then yes, that's pretty much what all motorcycles are like. This one just does it with *class*." He quirks his eyebrows and pulls me a little closer.

I smile, wrapping his arm around my shoulder. "Well, I might be addicted. You're going to have to tell Benny his friend can't have the bike back."

Daniel lets out a hearty guffaw. "We better forget the beach, then—start heading for the border. Those guys will be out for blood!"

I bat him playfully on the chest. "It was super fun… Thank you." I grin. "Best Christmas present ever."

"Thought you might think so," he murmurs, his eyes soft. "It was pretty fun for me too, taking you on your first ride."

I can feel my face starting to hurt from smiling so much, a

welcome change from the rest of the evening. We stop and take in the view, the cliffs larger than life from here. "So pretty," I murmur, resting my head against his shoulder.

"You're prettier," he mutters into my hair.

I punch him lightly in the side. "Don't tease," I sniff, but I am secretly (or not so secretly) very pleased. I nestle into the crook of his arm and sigh contentedly. My spot.

"That was crazy, seeing Alden again tonight," I whisper, immediately hating myself for bringing it up during our picturesque moment—but it's one elephant in the room that we can actually address.

I feel Daniel tense next to me. "What's crazier is that he blew up that club with all those Demons in it," he answers coldly. "I mean...I've always known he was a genius and super manipulative, but I didn't take him for a psychopath, you know?"

I scrunch my forehead in thought. "I don't know if that's what this was. He's part of the Resistance, I guess."

When Daniel stops and looks at me quizzically, I nod. "He told me. Said they're about to make their play in the Mortal Realm...whatever that means."

Daniel frowns. "Hopefully not more bombings and attacks on Humans... Don't see why they should have to pay for a war that's not even about them."

"Isn't that the cost of war, though? Tragic civilian deaths in the name of power and glory?"

Daniel doesn't answer, just staring out over my head. I sigh. "Whatever. At least Alden seemed a little cooler with you tonight. Found your knife after you dropped it and returned it... Maybe things will get better—"

"That's not what that was, Christa," Daniel says with a tight smile. "*He* had the knife. He took it from Pete, after he murdered him. You were there—you just didn't see what he took."

I startle, the memories flooding back. "Oh my God, you're right..." I gape at Daniel. "Does that mean he's had it this whole time? What about the Guardian rules? How were you able to still—"

"I helped him," Daniel whispers, "a long time ago. I told you—we have a very long past...but I think I understand now why he did what he did, became the...man, I guess, that he is now. I think I get it, after all this time." He smiles sadly at me, lost in thought.

Wherever he's gone, I can't follow. Instead, I blush. "Why are you looking at me like that?"

He sees my expression and lets out a heavy sigh. "Nothing. Can we talk about something else? I, um...I don't want to think about Alden tonight, if that's okay."

"Sure." I nod. "Anything you want."

Daniel looks out and points to the waves, which are coming in slow and easy. "Let's get a little closer to the water, okay? What do you think?"

"Yeah, sounds good." I smile, shivering a little.

Daniel notices and goes for his jacket. "You cold? You can take this if you want."

I wave in protest. "No, I'm okay—I have mine. And you need that!" I motion to the faded brown leather. "It's, like, your super-hero cape...and I can't believe it's still in one piece after tonight!"

Daniel chuckles as we mosey down to the shore. "It's been through a lot, that's for sure...almost as much as us." His eyes dart down to my wrapped-up hand. "How are you doing? Does it hurt?"

I shrug, carefully tucking it under my arm as we arrive at the water's edge, scuffing my boot toe along the surf. "It's fine. The wait at the ER was worse," I snicker.

He sighs. "Yeah... I'm sorry about that. I just wouldn't want you to go home thinking it was no big deal, then have it *turn* into a big deal." He bends down and picks up a few pebbles, skipping them into the water. "I'm sure that was not the way you wanted to spend your Christmas Eve."

"I wanted to be with you," I reply softly, lacing my fingers with his. "So…mission accomplished."

He stops and looks down at our clasped hands, then back out to the ocean. His hair flutters back in the wind. "Yeah…mission accomplished." He blinks, keeping his gaze locked on the horizon.

I watch him, worry creasing my face. I'm sure that if I had a mirror, I'd look like I've aged about a hundred years… Honestly, I'm surprised I can even stand up straight. Daniel is as beautiful as ever, though, glowing gold against the black as he stares wistfully out at the sky, one hand on his hip, the breeze flapping his jacket. He looks…sad. Like he did the other night when everything went off the rails in my room.

I swing our arms to get his attention. "I bet Mary Carmen will be back when we get home. Maybe she even brought Ellis with her." I shrug. "Maybe we can get Christmas started early."

Daniel turns to me, his eyebrows arched pleasantly. "Yeah? Did you hear from her today? Did she find her?"

I shake my head. "No… I just figured she'd been gone a while…and there must be some good news after this day. I know she'll flip when she sees us coming up on that bike…" I fade out as I lose him again, his eyes dull, focused on the moon.

I sigh and dig my heels into the sand. We just survived a massive terrorist attack; we're alive and breathing, left mostly unscathed. We should be laughing and celebrating, joking around like always. So why does it feel like we just took a turn down Melancholy Way?

Taking a breath, I sidle up and join him in staring out at the water, our shoulders brushing. "Daniel, what's going on?" I whisper, trying not to sound neurotic. "You look like you're a million miles away. Talk to me…"

"It's almost exactly the same," he murmurs under his breath. I perk up, confused, but at least he's saying something. He smiles wistfully and gestures at the moon. "But so much brighter in real life…and the sounds and smells, those can't really be predicted."

I make a face. "Daniel—what are you talking about? The last time we were here was in the daytime, remember? With Benny—"

"No." He shakes his head and looks at me. "I saw this when you were Haloing...when I read you."

I catch my breath and stare at him. "I'm sorry—what? When?" I know I haven't Haloed recently...apparently due to my time in Hell on 3. Me and Orpheus, I guess. I furrow my brow. "Back at the Factory?"

Daniel nods and looks away again, his voice going quiet. "I was so afraid right after, knowing what was coming, but not really wanting to believe it because I had just found you and all I wanted was a little more time." He smiles down at me. "I thought that if I kept us busy enough or put up a Christmas tree and decorated the house, we could pretend a little longer that this wasn't going to happen, that it wasn't real—"

I cross my arms, unable to tear my eyes away from him. "Daniel, you're really starting to scare me." I tremble, my tone severe. "*What* is about to happen? I don't understand any of this—"

"This is where I die, Christa," he answers calmly. "This beach, tonight. With you. This is where I stop being your Guardian."

"Die? What—you can't die... You're already—" I stumble backwards, feeling like someone just socked me in the gut. "Like, you're going to Ascend?" I ask breathlessly. "Is that what you mean?"

"No, I'm not Ascending," he answers sadly. I wait for him to start coughing. He doesn't.

"It's not—no—it can't be." I circle him on the sand, trying to process the idea any sort of reality without him. I can't—I won't. I suck in a sharp breath and glance out at the horizon, thinking about what Dr. Khattab said about the prophecy at the Feast: Sacrifice. Daniel is the sacrifice. No.

A cluster of thunderclouds form over beyond the cliffs, starting to drift toward the moon. "This is all from one vision you had while I was Haloing?" I exclaim. "And if you knew this was going to happen, why did we even come here?!" I wave my hands around at the beach.

"You wanted to come here," he replies quietly.

A streak of panic rushes through my gut. "Not if I knew this was where you were supposed to die—God!" I slap his stomach and shake my head, glaring at him. "No...no way. Who knows if it's really true! Or even still going to happen—destinies can change..."

"Not this," he whispers. "Remember what Adler said... You can't fight the Fates. Gods or monsters—we're all helpless."

I glare at him and suck in a breath. Bullshit. I'm neither God nor monster. "I refuse to believe that there isn't a way around this," I say firmly. "We can stop whatever is going to happen—"

"No, we can't." He doesn't take his eyes off me. "And I don't know if I want to, anymore."

I shrug angrily and put my hands on my hips. "So what, you're just giving up? You have one vision, and that's it, you're done fighting...done being with me?"

He bites the inside of his cheek. "It's not like that." He stares at me, his eyes sad. "I'm trying so hard not to be selfish, Christa, to be who *you* need me to be." He drags a hand through his hair. "But I don't know who that is anymore... The lines have gotten so blurred—"

"I need you *here*!" I shout, my voice growing shrill as I point down at the sand.

"Don't you get it? I love you! Do you hear me?!" Watching him wince and look back at the water, I take a shaky breath. "I'm sorry—I know I promised I would never say it again—"

"Why do you even want me?" Daniel rasps, staring at me incredulously. "I can't remember my last name, my birthday..." He puts his hand to his mouth for a second. "I have no idea who I was, or who I even am—"

"*I* know who you are!" I yell, taking a step toward him.

The sky rumbles off in the distance. Daniel watches me, tortured.

"You're the person who has saved me more times than I count," I hiss, grabbing his arms. "You brought me back to life. I was going nowhere fast before I met you—and you changed all that! I'm better because of you." I grip his jacket tightly. "You're a good person... You care about what happens to people—"

"No—*I only care about you!*" he snaps wildly, grabbing me by the wrists. I startle at his force. "I wish I cared! No, *you* care, Christa! You care more than anyone I've ever met—about your family, your friends—people you don't even know!" He lets go of me, his face haggard. "I don't deserve you, to be with you, not after what I did—"

He spins away, facing the water. I clench my jaw. No—I'm not letting him get off that easy. "Just tell me—" I grab his shoulder and turn him back to face me, my voice low. "What could possibly be so bad that you think you don't—"

"I can't remember!" he grits out through his teeth, taking a step back. He pauses and exhales, composing himself. "And I am so ashamed of that, Christa. You have no idea..." He speaks out to the ocean, and I almost don't hear him. "To only have this... fading image of what I did—the damage I caused..." He glances back at me, his face pinched.

My mood softens, and I take his hand. "You're not done yet," I murmur, not taking my eyes off of him.

He glares at me. I can't tell what he's thinking, but I don't care. "You're not done...*changing* yet, Daniel. You're still growing...becoming the person you're supposed to be. The person I know you are." Tears spring into my eyes. "*My* person."

He lets out a strangled sigh and wrenches me to him, burying his face in my hair. I give a euphoric breath—yes...now we're finally where we're supposed to be.

"I want to be that person—so bad, Christa!" he cries, his shoulders shaking up and down. "But I don't know how!"

I let out a little wail and mash myself into him, willing us to become one body, one soul. The wind picks up around us. "I can't let you die," I mumble into his shirt. "I won't...whatever happens next."

"It's not something you can stop." His voice cracks. "It's happening right now."

I pull back, shaking my head frantically. "Daniel, no..." I can feel myself hyperventilating as I gape at him. "Let's just go! We can run away—" I start to tug him by the hand back up the beach toward the bike.

He doesn't move. I look back at him and see tears streaking down his face. "I'm not afraid anymore, Christa," he whispers, smiling through his tears. "If it's our destiny, then it's our destiny. I've accepted it."

"Accepted wh-what?" I stammer.

Daniel runs his hands through his hair. "I don't care what they do to me, who they send—those Archs can stick me back on 3 and let me rot for all I care, because I'm not afraid, and I know the truth—"

"What? Archs put you on 3? *Archangels*?!" I cry. "Daniel— whatever is going on, we have to—"

He puts his hands on my waist. "Christa—shh, it's okay. It— *this*—was always going to happen. And I'm...I'm okay with it, just—" He looks at me and smiles his biggest Cheshire Cat grin. It makes my heart melt. "Tell me what you *really* want for Christmas, Christa. And I will give it to you—whatever you want."

"I want you." It comes out before I have a chance to stop myself. I cartoonishly clap a hand over my mouth, like I can shove the words back inside.

Daniel smiles and comes back to me. "And you can have me, all of me. I am yours. Always." He runs his hand across my cheekbone and up into my hair.

I stare at him, panic seizing me. "Daniel—don't... It's blasphemy—"

He takes a deep breath. "I love you, Christa Nichols. I have loved you from the first time I saw you, and that will never change. I love you more than anyone else, this Earth, myself. " He takes my hands. "Loving you is the most selfish and unselfish thing I could ever do. And if this is my crime…then let me burn."

"DANIEL!" I shout, but it's too late.

He leans down and presses his lips to mine, and it's over; for a perfect moment, we are one body, one mind, one heart, his cinnamon taste sweet in my mouth. I give into him completely, my soul hanging out somewhere above us. Feeling him this close, finally, is the shining bright spot of my stupid, fractured life. I link my arms through his and crash into him, urgently learning every turn in his mouth, memorizing this time, because I know—

Daniel is the one to pull back gasping, not taking his hands away from me, but wincing down at the sand.

I hold him tight, panting. "What is it?!" I exclaim, crouching down next to him. He cries out and keens his head back, still not disconnecting from me, but clearly in pain.

"It's starting," he wheezes, looking back at me. He puts my hands on his cheeks and does the same to me, gripping my jaw, then turns and looks out at the sea, where the water is now roiling. "It's okay… It was meant to be—"

"Daniel—you can't leave me!" I wail, tears blurring my vision. "I need you—I love you!"

"Ahh…I love you!" he breathes, kneeling up and pulling me into a hug, his whole body trembling. "It's gonna be okay… You have Mary Carmen—and the others—and you're so smart, you're gonna figure this all out—"

"NO!" I shake my head, kissing him again fervently. "Don't say that—I…I want more time! PLEASE!" I shout up at the sky, my cries drowned out by the fierce wind.

Daniel gets to his feet, pulling me up, then staggers away from me, doubling over. I try to go to him, but he waves for me to stay back. "I don't know how this is gonna go, but I'm not taking you with me!" he yells. "You've got too much to do…to give… You're gonna have the best life—I know it!" He tries to scramble to his feet to get to me, but falls back to the sand.

"Daniel, no!" I cry, stretching my hand to him.

He smiles at me. "I'm just glad I got to be with you, even for a little while… So lucky…" He throws his head back in a pained yowl, like his insides are being torn apart.

"DANIEL!" I just sit and watch, crying on the sand.

Piece by piece, he breaks apart, golden bits flying and fading off into the sky like flittering sparks from a bonfire. He's gone within seconds, leaving the sky calm, the wind and clouds disappearing without a trace—taking my Guardian with them. I'm alone again…just me and the moon.

I sit and stare at my jeans, letting the sound of the waves wash over me, forgetting where I am or even that I exist. I'm sure I must look completely pathetic, hunched on the sand in a little ball, not knowing which way is up or down. With every minute that goes by, I sink deeper and deeper, since it's another moment that he's gone and I can't reach him… Never again.

"Fuck you," I whisper to my lap, anger welling up inside me. I stagger to my feet and direct my rage where I really want it to go, screaming at the sky. "FUCK YOU! How dare you!" I curse the stars, shrieking until my throat is raw. "You judgmental pieces of shit! Do you have any idea what you've done?! Who you've taken?! He was mine! MINE!"

Who's the selfish one now? I kick the ground, spraying bits of sand and rock out into the surf, and glare at the moon, like I'm waiting for it to explain itself—to say anything—an apology, a rationale.

I get silence, of course; it's just the moon, after all. I may be completely destroyed, but I'm not fucking nuts.

Devastated, I leave the beach, leave the bike, leave Santa Monica, and head for home.

It has started raining again by the time I make it to the house, my clothes soaked through and my hair lank. Mary Carmen's car is in the driveway. Numbly, I wonder if she knows yet—if FM Heaven gave her a newsflash about Daniel. She's not pacing around the living room, so I assume she's asleep.

I don't make any attempt to be quiet as I come through the front door, my boots squeaking loudly on the wood floor. The tree lights are still on from earlier, a grim reminder that it's officially Christmas Day—and officially the worst day of my existence.

I shuffle into the kitchen and lean, exhausted, against the doorframe. For a brief second, hope wells in my chest as I see all of Daniel's dinner preparations still on the counter. But everything's just as we left it, except it looks like someone tidied a bit, peels thrown away, milk back in the fridge. Tears leak quietly down my face, and I don't have the energy to try to stop them. I slump down and let my emotions overwhelm me, not seeing Mary Carmen come up behind me.

"Christa, what's wrong?" she murmurs, rubbing her eyes drowsily. She's dressed in her long white nightgown, her hair mussed from sleep. She crouches down to my level and puts a hand on my arm, only causing me to break down worse.

"Christa!" Mary Carmen exclaims, her voice worried. "Please tell me, what's happened? Oh my…" She reaches up to the counter and grabs a box of tissues, bringing them down to the floor in front of me.

"I can't…" I snuffle, wiping my nose with my bandaged hand.

Mary Carmen sees my injury and gasps. "What happened? Are you hurt? Where is Daniel?!" She spins around, trying to see in the living room. "I need to know—"

"He's gone," I sob, putting my face in my hands. "Daniel's gone."

"Gone where?" Mary Carmen exclaims, pushing my wet hair

out of my face. "Christa, please—get ahold of yourself and tell me where you've been and what's happened to you! Was it Demons?"

I shake my head, crying harder.

"Christa!" She takes my shoulders and gives me a quick rattle. "I've been trying to reach you all night, but you never picked up your phone. I couldn't find Ellis or anyone else… I think there's a problem—"

"It doesn't matter," I reply hollowly. "None of it matters anymore." I pull away from her and lay my head against the cold floor.

"How can you say that? Christa—you're acting crazy!" She sits up and pats my leg. "Please…what is going on? Where is Daniel? He can give me a straight answer—"

"I told you, Mary Carmen, Daniel's gone." I can barely get the words out. "He's…not coming back."

She blinks at me, still waking up, looking confused. "What do you mean, he's not coming back? He…he left town? Now?" She shakes her head and tries to hoist me back upright.

I collapse against the wall, dead weight. "No…he's gone," I repeat blandly. "He's not mine anymore. He's—"

"You're not making any sense, Christa. Damn it, where are my glasses?" Her voice is full of panic as she stands and pats down the counter frantically. "He can't just be gone… How did this—"

"He told me he loved me, and then we kissed, and then he was gone!" I spit, kicking out at one of the kitchen chairs. Mary Carmen startles as it clatters against the wall. "And I love him too, and now we're being punished!"

That's exactly what happened, right? I'd felt chaotic and beautiful with my soulmate…and now *this*. I'll spend the rest of my life stuck in an empty hole without him. God, be merciful and make it a short sentence.

Mary Carmen goes silent. I turn and glare at her, waiting for her to go off on me—for tempting him, for being stupid—but she's got her finger in her ear, her eyes wide.

"Wait—stop… I can't hear…" Mary Carmen stumbles,

holding onto the counter for support with one hand and grabbing her temple with the other. "Ah—stop!" She winces and keels over, pressing her palms to the floor.

I gasp and scramble over to her. "Mary Carmen! What's happening?!" I practically shout in her ear.

She sucks in a breath and cries out, pinching her eyes shut.

"Shit—not you, too!" I yell, holding onto her arm.

She shakes her head and opens her eyes, staring at me. "No… no…" she breathes, scanning me desperately. "It can't be…"

"Mary Carmen!" I yell again. "What are they saying?"

"They're not saying anything." She exhales, her pupils doing crazy circles. I gape at her. "They're…they're *screaming*—" She cringes again and grabs her skull in pain, her eyes rolling back in her head.

"MARY CARMEN!" I cry, trying to get her back. She gasps, her whole frame trembling as she regains focus. "Why are they screaming? What's wrong?" I bark.

Mary Carmen puts a hand on her chest and leans back, catching her breath. "The Gates of Heaven are closing… Heaven is closing…" she pants, grabbing my shoulders. "You evicted Heaven, Christa. You've Chosen."

"What?" I draw back, alarmed. "No, I didn't! How can you say that? I didn't—"

"Look." Mary Carmen's eyelids flutter as she holds up my hand. "You're not blue anymore, Christa… Look. It's done."

I hold back a scream as I stare at my good hand, which is covered in fair ivory skin. No glow, no blue. I push up my sleeve and gawk.

I'm perfectly ordinary. Fuck.

END OF BOOK 2

EPILOGUE
WAILEA PUBLIC
HOUSING— MAY, 1980

AUNTIE MARLENE BURNT the pineapple again.

I can smell the crackly, torched fruit out in the hall, burning my nose and making my stomach growl in vain. I don't need to listen hard to hear her angry cursing coming from the inside of the apartment. She's screeching words that would make Mama stick Dial in my mouth for saying, even though she yells worse just at the jerkwads who cut us off in the crosswalk when we walk to the KTA.

I stand at the door for a second, thinking about just going back to Arlo's and eating pork and beans with him and the rest of my crew. The old hippie was always nice to us neighborhood kids—making us food, letting us borrow his tape player and Tom Petty cassettes, giving us money for cigarettes—even though he was broke as a joke. But I knew Auntie Marlene would be mad if I didn't come back for dinner…gross as it was. With a sigh, I go inside, preparing myself for Auntie's wrath.

"Where you been, Benny Woo?" she squawks before I even get a chance to shut the door, stretching the Es in 'been' like all the Maoli ladies do. I roll my eyes and step into the tiny kitchen to see her standing by the stove, smoke wafting around her as she fans her purple hibiscus apron over our destroyed dinner. She looks up at me, her leather face pinched and mad. So…business as usual.

"Nothin'…just listening to some music over at Arlo's." I shrug, tucking my hands into the waistband of my shorts. It don't matter what I say, truth or lie—she gonna bust me up the head the minute she steps away from that oven.

She stares at me for a minute before opening her mouth. "What I tell you 'bout hanging out with that old man? He a crazy motherfucker!" She eyes me wildly. "And if you think he giving you kids all that shit for free, you are mistaken, son… He gonna want something in the end."

I exhale and look up at the ceiling. "Jeez, Auntie Marlene, it ain't like that…" Arlo was cool. He just wanted someone to listen to his old stories about Jimi Hendrix at the Monterrey Pop Festival and Vietnam. Lonely…no harm in that.

She huffs, darting around the breakfast bar quick and hornet-like, and grabs a pitcher of juice she made this morning. "Well, I'll have you know, while you were out hanging with those good-for-nothings and that old man, you missed a call from your mama!" My heart sinks as she relays this news gleefully, like she gets joy from seeing me miserable. "She said she not gonna be able to call again 'til next week, lost her phone privileges—"

"For what?" I shout.

Auntie glares at my tone, but doesn't stop to scold me. "She popped off at a guard—said he was trying to start something… You know how she lies." She pulls some glasses from the dish rack.

"Did she say if she talked to the parole board?" I ask hurriedly. Mama was up for early release for good behavior, if she minded her p's and q's, as she liked to say.

Auntie Marlene scoffs in my face. "Are you kidding me? There's no way she's getting out now! Not after what she pulled… She's lucky they just took away the phone, didn't throw her in a hole! They do that, you know…"

I stare dejectedly into the living room, where Uncle Dado and Ricky are sitting on the couch, watching some news program. "Do we still get to visit next weekend?" I look at Auntie hopefully. "They didn't take that away…"

"I don't know…but I told you, I can't take you cuz I have to do Mrs. Kalani's hair on Saturday. So unless you got a fairy god-mother or a pumpkin or some shit, you not going!"

I feel my face grow hot. "That's not fair! You said you would take me and that we'd never miss a visit—you promised her—"

WHACK. Auntie comes around like she was always standing right next to me and boxes me in the ear. Quick as a flash, she's back to hovering over her Spam and burnt pineapple, leaving me swollen and wincing.

"You should be countin' your lucky stars that I even took your skinny *hapa* ass in!" she sniffs, shaking her head. "And if Nani wasn't my baby sister and all the trouble she cause, you'd both be out, shucking coconuts at the resorts. So be grateful for what you got!" She jerks her head back to the living room. "Now go tell them it's time to eat!"

I push my glasses up on my nose and stomp the fifty feet to over past the couch where Uncle Dado and Ricky are, putting myself squarely in front of the TV. Uncle Dado doesn't register and just keeps smoking his cigarette, but Ricky sits up, his face a matching pissed-off boy version of Auntie Marlene's, the faint shadow of a mustache coloring his upper lip. He's real proud of that stupid mustache, says it happened the day after he turned fif-teen, the same day he said he lost his virginity behind the 76 with the nightshift girl. He's such a liar.

"Hey! Relocate, dillweed! I'm trying to watch *the news*!" He emphasizes 'the news' like this is something he always does…like he's actually smart. He almost didn't move up to 10th grade. Mr. Jammers, the high school principal, only let him pass to keep him 'matriculating'—a.k.a., getting the hell out of there. I'm only ten, and I can do his homework for him.

I put my hand on my hip and snort. "Yeah right, Ricky. Like you ever cared about the news…"

Ricky pretends like he's gonna get up and punch me, but then just motions back to the TV. "When it's a big fuckin' deal, I do! That volcano they've been talking about on the mainland for the last couple weeks blew her fuckin' lid… Turn your butt around and look!"

"What? There are no volcanos on the mainland…" I spin to face the TV.

Sure enough, there's a headline plastered across the bottom of the screen: *Washington's Mount St. Helens Ravages Countryside.* A blonde news lady is at the scene, her face drawn and concerned as the world blows up behind her. "…and the devastation continues here in Grant County," she sighs, microphone in hand. "While most of the town has evacuated, we are still receiving reports of people left behind—the few remaining landowners who refuse to leave what they say is rightfully theirs, despite fire raining from the Heavens…" She motions to the ash-black sky before turning and gesturing to a raging river that is filled with mud and uprooted trees rushing by.

"It is the river that will ultimately lead to their demise. Without the use of rescue helicopters, aid workers cannot pass the wild torrents. This is a grim reminder that when Chicken Little says the sky is falling, it might be a good idea to listen…and get out. Amy Andrews, KTLA News, reporting from Grant County, Washington."

"Shit." Catching myself cursing, I cover my mouth before Auntie hears. I turn and face the couch, where Uncle Dado and Ricky are still dazed and watching the screen. "Do you think those people she was talking about will get out of there, Uncle Dado?" I ask.

The old man sits forward, chewing pensively at the cigarette hanging off of his lip. "Pele will have her pound of flesh when it's due," he finally answers calmly. He takes another big puff off his smoke and says nothing more.

Ricky lets out a snort and waves at the TV. "Those *haole* fucks think they know everything." He smirks. "If that was me, I would have lifted a speedboat and blasted the hell outta there—couldn't pay me to stay!" He sits back and scratches his balls through his red basketball shorts.

"Shut up—no, you wouldn't, Ricky," I mutter, turning back to the TV. It's gone to a split screen, one of the news anchors back in the studio asking Amy Andrews some questions. I don't really pay attention to what they're saying. My eye is drawn to the far corner of Amy's screen.

I wouldn't have seen them if I weren't looking, with the camera tightly focused on Amy's Barbie-like face, the volcano ash making everything behind her hazy. But yes—they're there…what looks a family of five: a mom, a dad, and three little girls, standing on a small embankment in the middle of the river, water gushing past them. The mom and girls are small with dark hair, while the dad looking like Paul Bunyan—a big dude with a beard, wearing a flannel shirt. There's another guy with them too, smaller than the dad, but still tall, wearing jeans, a leather jacket, and a girl's red hat. Yeah…it's definitely something a girl would wear. The two guys look like they're arguing while the girls just sit by watching, looking scared, the baby crying in the mom's arms.

"What?" I whisper to myself, pressing my nose up to the TV to get a better look. They're definitely yelling at each other, the skinny guy waving his arms in the air as the lumberjack guy shakes his head at the ground.

"HEY!" Auntie Marlene yells from the kitchen. "I said food was ready! I'm not gonna stand around all day—"

"Just a second!" I call, not taking my eyes off the screen.

Uncle Dado and Ricky stand up. Ricky, being the jerk that he is, flicks the power button on the remote, smiling smugly. I freak as the screen goes dark. "HEY! I was watching that!" I yell, switching it back on.

"Dinner's ready, *hapa*," Ricky teases. I glare in frustration at the screen, which is awash in green… Now I have to wait for the stupid thing to warm up again. I have to know what happens to those people…even if it's just watching them get washed away. My gut sinks a little at the thought.

The news comes back, and thank Jesus, they're still talking to Amy about rising floodwaters in Seattle. The shot is still the same, the people still up in the corner of the screen—only now, there are only three: the mom, the dad, and the little baby.

"Shit—where are the kids?!" I hiss at the screen. Did those two little girls get swept away? But then the mom starts waving her arms and jumping up and down like she's happy…*really* happy—like, relieved—as the guy in the goofy red hat *swims* up to the embankment and pulls himself out with the help of a fallen tree. He nods to the lady and the baby and hitches them up on his back, jumping back into the water and swimming them out of the shot.

"No way!" I breathe. That guy must be, like, super strong to be able to swim through all that—like the Hulk or the Thing… out of control!

After what feels like an eternity but is probably more like five minutes, the dude comes back and gets back on the embankment with the dad, who's still shaking his head, holding tight to a messed-up evergreen tree coming out of their little patch of ground. The young guy yells at him, waving his arms like a crazy person, even punching Paul Bunyan's arm and motioning for him to get on his back. The dad clearly says no.

I shake my head and push my glasses up. "No way he can carry that guy…" Paul Bunyan must be pushing 260—a total stackhouse.

"Benny Woo! NOW!" Auntie yells again. She's gonna skin me alive in a second.

"Okay—" I cringe and spin back to the TV, but I don't turn it off. Instead, I put my hand over the power dial and wait. Something's gonna happen... I have to know—

The red hat guy puts his hands on his hips and takes a breath. The dad looks away for a second, and when he turns back, the young guy slugs him square across the jaw, knocking him out. My mouth hangs open in a silent scream. That's the coolest thing I've ever seen on TV—and my best friend Georgie Tanaka has cable.

The young guy looks down at Paul Bunyan and sighs, before swinging the big man over his shoulders in a fireman's carry and jumping back in the water. He swims out of sight, and the report comes to a close. Holy shit.

"Benny Woo—if I have to come over there and tell you one more time..." Auntie Marlene's voice is murderous.

I jump to my feet, my eyes still bugging out of my head. "Coming!" I rush over to the breakfast bar to get my Spam and burnt pineapple, taking it with a heaping side of Auntie's rage.

END

SPECIAL THANKS

As always, big hugs and immense thanks are due to my wonderful family and friends: Steve and my girls, my parents, my amazing in-laws and nieces and nephew, and my extended family, which has grown to include wonderful friends across the country. It is through your encouragement and inspiration that I can sit down every day and plink out a line or two on the old laptop. Thank you to my brother, Michael Jacobson, for designing and managing my website, katiejaros.com. I'm so lucky to have you!

Thank you to my fabulous team of readers, Elizabeth Abbott, Jessica Rakus, Alyssa Martoccio, Megan Mackinnon, and Kinzie Fergueson, for all of their hard work and much-needed feedback. You guys made this book so much better!

I want to send a special thank you to America Young, who's wise words made me rethink my work and what it means to not only be a writer, but a GOOD writer. Still working on that, but I feel like I'm getting closer.

Thank you to Jocelyn Kelley from Kelley and Hall Publicity for getting the word out about *Lost Souls*...and to Nini Church and my other friends at Goodreads for taking a chance on my work. Thank you to fellow author, Robyn Bachar, for her both her inspiration and support. Thank you to Danica and Michael at Edit 24-7 and the design team at Damon Za for helping my books transform from manuscripts to polished products. Finally, thank you to Cindy over at Island Books and Gregory Rathbone and Nancy Henkel and the King County Library System for making a life-long dream of mine come true by putting *Lost Souls* on the shelf!

It's been an amazing year, and I can't wait to see what comes next—hopefully a third book! Cheers.